MW00805051

Dedicated to:

Shell: Your kindness and generosity are a constant
reminder to me of God's grace and love.

Frank, Geordie, Jye, Mark, and Simon:
Thank you for your ceaseless friendship.
Without you, this book would not exist.

Fragged Empire: Core Rule Book.

Copyright (C) 2015 by Design Ministries.
"Fragged Empire" trademarked by Wade Dyer.

Design, Layout and Production:
Wade Dyer
www.designministries.com.au

www.fraggedempire.com
contact@fraggedempire.com

ISBN: 978-0-9924979-2-7

First Edition.

Printed in China.

Betrayed by your creators, you are a genetically engineered
remnant, emerging from the ruin of genocidal war.

You and this new civilisation are on the precipice
of great opportunity and danger.

www.fraggedempire.com

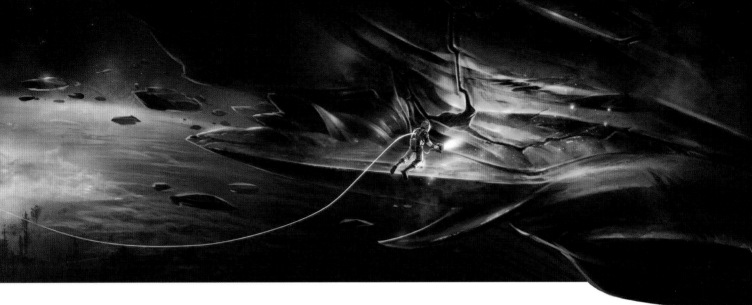

It is over 10,000 years into the future.
Earth is forgotten.

Humanity is dead.
Genetic erosion, brought on by thousands of years of apathy.

You are one of many genetically engineered descendants.
Created by the eugenicist Archons (humanity's heirs), or the vengeful monster X'ion.

A genocidal war has ravaged the known galaxy.
X'ion won, killing the Archons, destroying their empire, and then abandoning his army to vanish without a trace.
This event threw the galaxy into 100 years of brutal tribalism.

After 100 years, your people have just re-entered space.
No one knows what's out there.

Four surviving races have banded together.
Not out of a common direction, but out of necessity.
No one knows where this new society is headed.

Each race is struggling for survival.
They need each other.

What's in the Name?

Fragging

A term used to describe the assassination of a leader during wartime by their own soldiers, usually in a manner that could look like an accident (eg: dropping a fragmentation grenade at their feet), commonly during the heat of battle.

Can also describe the manipulation of the chain of command to have a subordinate deliberately killed by placing them in great mortal danger, such as sending a soldier or unit on a suicide mission.

» Did your people kill their creator?
» Were you betrayed by your creator?

Fragmentation

Denoting the process or state of breaking or being broken into smaller disconnected parts. Used to describe both physical and metaphysical breakdowns.

» Will society's broken nature be its downfall?

Frag

A popular term used for killing someone in a computer game.

Because this is a game where you kill people.

Key Setting Themes

Post-Post-Apocalyptic Setting

Exploring the state of the universe after a cataclysmic event is a popular theme in science fiction literature. It allows us to delve into the nature of civilisation, humanity, and rediscovery after we have lost all that we know.

This setting does not take place immediately after this cataclysmic event (a genocidal war), but a hundred years later. Enough time has passed for people to partially accept what has happened and start to rebuild. You are at the dawn of a new civilisation, a time of great opportunity and danger.

» What should this new society look like?

Cultural Tension

Shaped by the Great War and what it took to survive it, the races have had one hundred years to create their own distinctive cultures, formed from their experiences, core beliefs, and genetic nature.

These races have only had a few years to interact with one another: not enough time to fully understand or accept each other. Their delicate coexistence is held together more by need than choice.

» What do you live for?

Genetic Engineering

Humanity is long dead, but they managed to created their own genetically engineered successors: the Archons. The Archons repopulated their inherited empire with their own creations in an effort to create the perfect race. This pursuit not only led to a wealth of technological advancements, but also empire-wide genocidal war. Eventually, the Archons fell to their deaths at the hands of their own vengeful creations.

» What responsibility comes with the ability to make life?

Exploration

This new society is built not only on the ruins of the Archons' empire, but also on top of the ancient human empire and who knows what else.

» What is out there?

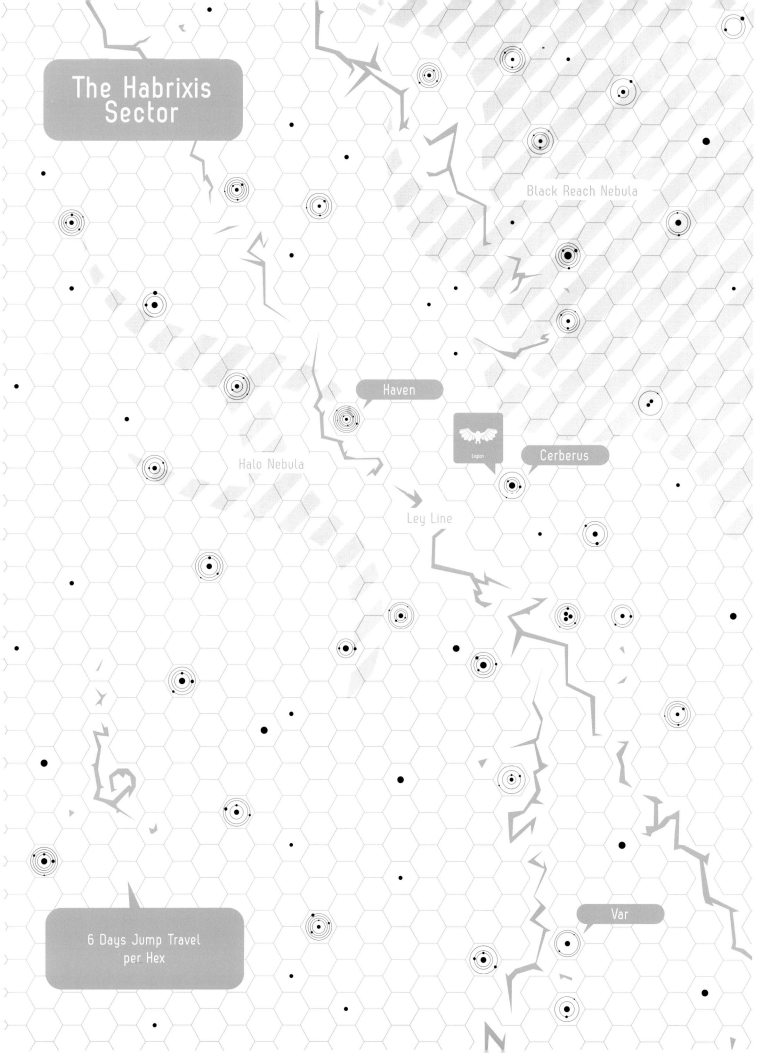

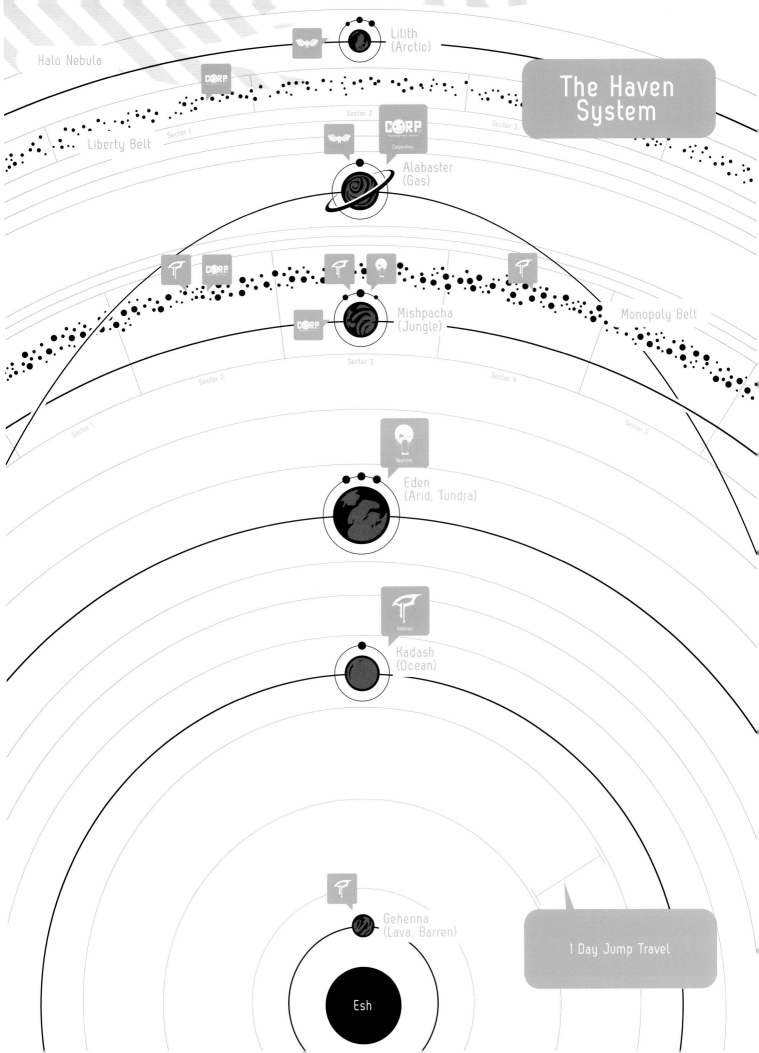

Short Story: Galatèa

They were only four hours into their voyage, and Rachel was ready to pistol-whip her boss.

One good smack in the face, it'd barely hurt him.

It would actually hurt quite a lot, and Rachel had a feeling that Theodore would take it personally.

She contented herself with screwing in a loose bolt more vigorously than was necessary, wiping beads of sweat from her forehead as she did so.

Theodore might not have been her boss in the traditional sense – more like the guy who owned the ship and made sure the occupants didn't kill each other. But he was still a typical Corporation lackey: obsessed with hierarchy, efficiency, money and a host of other Corporate concerns that Rachel didn't care for.

"Swag, status report."

Rachel glanced over her shoulder and saw the hazy blue, hologramatic head and shoulders of Theodore himself. Of course, he couldn't possibly make the trip all the way down to the engine room. Too many flashy displays needed his attention.

"Repairs 92% complete," she replied in an exaggerated monotone. "Hull stability achieved, Archon drive almost at full capacity, Gauss batteries loaded, Ley Line system…"

"Report to the bridge."

The hologram flickered and vanished, and she grinned. Technically, information overload wasn't insubordination, so it was Rachel's favourite method of irritation. It would sate her urge for a good pistol-whipping, for the moment at least.

With a sigh, the young Kaltoran tucked the spanner into her tool-belt and began the journey through the bowels of the ship to the bridge. She definitely wasn't in a hurry.

***

The Galatèa wasn't a large ship, designed as it was to be operated by a skeleton crew, but it still took Rachel a fair effort to extricate herself from the tangle of wires and machinery that formed the engine room. It was a cut 'n' shut vessel, formed from at least two different Kaltoran hulls and a Legion gunship, and stuffed full of the best spare parts the crew could… "acquire".

Still, the Galatèa's unique nature made her repairs and various patch jobs all the more interesting. It was the one part of the job that Rachel truly loved. With practiced precision, she swung herself onto the main catwalk that led to the exit. Heights and darkness never bothered her, or any Kaltoran; after all, she'd grown up in a gigantic pit city with dwellings honeycombing the deep crust of her home world. A childhood of badly lit walkways and cramped metal spaces made the engine room of the Galatèa practically roomy.

She emerged into the hallway, unbinding her long blue dreadlocks, and almost ran headlong into Maximus. The Legionnaire grabbed her by the shoulders with strong, gentle hands, thus avoiding the collision. Not that it would've hurt him, given that he was eight feet of pure simian muscle wrapped in red Tactical Armour.

"Watch out, four-ears." Maximus grunted, letting her go and stepping to the side.

"Sorry, Max," Rachel said, smirking as she walked around and punched him on the arm. "I'll try not to hurt you."

"Captain called?"

"Yeah. Probably another scolding."

She arranged her face in what she thought was an approximation of Theodore's and put on her best high-class Corp accent.

"Swagger, I think you might have set the self-destruct. If we're not dead in two minutes, I'm taking this out of your commission."

Maximus stared at her, expressionless.

"That was good," Rachel said, pointing at the Legionnaire as she turned towards the bridge. "Your impersonations are almost as good as mine."

In reality, Rachel knew Maximus was a firm believer in Legion tradition: never disrespect a commander.

Just then, as Rachel was about to round the corner, she heard Max's soft rumble.

"Captain would sound more growly."

She whirled around to see Maximus disappearing into the armoury, and stood motionless for a moment before giving a short laugh. Maybe she could mould their ship's gunner into a rebel after all.

***

Rachel had to pass the lab to get to the bridge, and she used this opportunity to check in on the group's resident Nephilim. A young woman in appearance, with grey skin and tendril-like hair, Hraks stood observing their prize, the mysterious piece of tech they'd swiped from under the noses of unscrupulous Draz raiders. No one was exactly sure what it was; it looked like a simple cube, a quarter meter wide, metallic silver with glowing purple veins in a fractal pattern and no visible controls, save for a large purple button

in the centre. Rachel had been all for pressing it, but Theodore had forbidden any action until they knew it wasn't something that would blow a hole in their ship. The artefact was suspended in an Electro-Gravity field in the centre of the lab, with Hraks intensely studying data readouts on the surrounding displays.

"How's it coming along?" Rachel said, leaning against the doorframe. She immediately cursed herself.

Too chirpy.

"Not good," Hraks replied, without shifting her eyes from the console. "The artefact does not respond to any testing or diagnosis method I currently have access to on this backwards ship."

"Aw, be nice to Galatèa. She does her best."

Rachel leant in to view the box, which saved her having to make awkward eye contact with Hraks. The two had a curious and volatile relationship; Rachel thrived on its curious nature, while Hraks thrived on its volatility. Rachel had little personal experience outside her home world's pit cities, but she had many memories, genetically passed on from her parents and grandparents. Dark memories of death and suffering, brought on by Hraks's people, the Nephilim.

Despite this, Rachel was keen to make new memories, better memories for the children she was yet to have. She wanted to build some kind of positive relationship with Hraks.

The Nephilim had no room for such focused prejudice; Nephilim were equally prejudiced against everyone, even their own kind.

Hraks was a Nephilim Emissary, grown in a lab no more than three years ago, with a head full of false memories to give context to her implanted skills; a brilliant mind that jostled for space with an aggressive thirst for knowledge. Rachel couldn't imagine what it was like to be born full-grown.

Rachel turned from inspecting the mystery box to see the Nephilim woman gazing at her with a curious expression.

"What?" Rachel asked.

"I was curious about your relationship with the ship," Hraks replied. "You spend such a great deal of time in the engine room. And you refer to it as if it were a person. As if it were alive, or… one of us."

"Some Nephilim ships are alive."

"The Galatèa is obviously not alive."

Rachel stepped back from the gravity field and folded her arms, pausing to think.

"You can still form attachments to things that aren't alive; you make it alive. With… your imagination."

"That is foolish," Hraks replied, turning back to her work.

Rachel needed to word things in a way that Hraks could accept.

"Think of it this way… by forming an attachment with something, it increases our investment in that thing…"

"Thus facilitating the lengths to which you will go to support said thing." Hraks was facing Rachel again. "That sounds like you are voluntarily choosing to believe a lie because you lack the faculties to…"

"I know the ship is not alive in the traditional sense of the word. People don't always mean exactly what they say."

"That is also foolish."

Hraks once again turned back to her work.

"Did captain not call for you?"

"Right," the girl replied, backing out the door and nearly tripping over some loose coils. "Right, yeah. I'll get on that. Good luck with the… thing."

Hraks may have replied, but the lab door slid shut before she could hear it.

***

The Kaltoran reached the door to the bridge and jogged on the spot for a few moments, just to make it seem like she'd been hurrying. Then she pressed her hand to the scanner, and the door to the bridge slid open.

By bridge standards, it wasn't all that impressive. A large transparent steel window loomed over four chairs, arranged in a rough square, none of which were used regularly. Rachel was mostly in the engine room, Hraks in the lab, Maximus in the gun-pod, and Theodore at the navigation console as he was now, cigarette in mouth, one hand in his pocket and the other tracing coordinates on the display.

Texos, Theodore's personal drone, was engaged at the pilot's station as always, its thin metal arms extending from a small circular hovering metal shell. Despite Theo's constant control over the drone, knowing that the fate of their ship lay in the cold metallic stick-fingers of a lifeless probe gave Rachel the shivers.

"Reporting for duty," she barked, standing at the bridge's midsection and breathing heavily.

"I could hear you jogging outside the door."

Rachel kept up her charade for a few more moments before rolling her eyes and leaning against the railing.

"Fine. What do you need me for?"

Theodore took a few moments to respond, engaged as he was in some kind of complex calculation. Rachel watched him for a moment, standing there in his impeccable dark suit and gold vest, cigarette hanging loosely from his mouth. His short hair was so controlled it was like he'd run over it with a toothbrush; the same could be said for his sparse stubble. Spotless, clean-cut, and utterly collected at all times; Theodore was practically the physical embodiment of the Corporation.

"I have a new assignment for you," he said, removing the cigarette from his mouth and staring straight ahead into literal space. "It's going to last for the remainder of the voyage."

"Just remember I still have repairs from our escape," Rachel replied. "I'm not even sure if we'll get them done before we dock."

"This takes priority."

"As in, higher priority than life support?"

"Ask Hraks to deal with that. I want you to work on optimising our Ley Line drive. We need more speed."

He said it so matter-of-factly, as if it were as simple as asking someone to pass the salt. Rachel bristled and folded her arms.

"Hraks is busy with the artefact and I've told you, we…"

The sensor consoles suddenly changed from green to red. Rachel wasn't well-versed in sensor displays, but she made the assumption that this was a bad thing. Red generally meant trouble. The wailing siren was also a clue.

"Unknown vessel approaching!" chirped Texos in its usual high-pitched monotone that Theodore refused to change for some reason. "Signs of aggression! Unidentified beam technology, locking on! Recommend…"

"Calm down, Texos," Theodore said, unruffled as his hands moved in a blur across the console. "Give me visual."

Rachel stepped out of the way as a slightly fuzzy hologram sprang to life in the middle of the bridge, showing a large, well-armed battleship. The Kaltoran swallowed, instantly recognizing the ancient Archon design: Mechonid.

"So they found us," the captain mused. He reached to the far right of his holographic console and held down the intercom control. "Maximus, in the very unlikely event that you aren't already inside the gun-pod, I need you in there. We have Mechonids on our tail. Hraks, if you're…"

He and Rachel were thrown off balance by a sudden tremor that ran the full length of the ship, causing the lights to flicker. With her four keen ears, Rachel traced the echo to its source, and felt her blood run cold.

"The engine room," she breathed, already sprinting through the hologram and into the main corridor. Theodore called her back, but she couldn't stop. Somehow, they'd found a way onto the ship. Those foul machines could be inside, ruining all her precious work. If they did enough damage, it could cripple the Galatèa, leaving them all stranded – or worse. She wouldn't allow that to happen.

The trip from the engine room to the bridge had taken minutes; the return journey was over in seconds. Rachel charged through the door and heard the echoes from down below. It was cannon fire. Fuelled by the unbridled rage of a girl who finds someone touching her stuff, Rachel vaulted over the catwalk and jumped from one pile of machinery to another. She descended into the bowels of the ship, wincing as the sound grew louder, until a brief somersault brought her to a walkway directly above the floor of the main engine room.

Peering over the rail, it was exactly as she'd feared: a Mechonid stood flanked by machinery, firing its gun-arm at everything in sight. White-hot rage flooded through Rachel's veins, but she forced herself to think. That thing was a vaguely humanoid hunk of metal, and she was slightly more squishy. An array of purple orbs formed the Mechonid's sensor cluster, and she decided that these were her best target.

Rachel silently drew a long dagger from her leg holster, wishing she had her gun. A flick of a switch bathed the blade's metal in a blue glow – all the better to slice rogue machines into bits. With a final glance, the young Kaltoran flung herself over the railing, dagger raised over her head and her lips parted in a silent battle cry.

This was when the plan went wrong. In the split-second before the blade made contact, Rachel identified a faint aura similar to her dagger's around the Mechonid. It was an uncommon feature, but this machine was obviously meant to be an advance guard and was therefore better protected. It had a burst shield, and it was too late to account for; her strike was already descending. The dagger deflected off the shield and flew into the mass of machines, leaving Rachel to awkwardly land clinging to the Mechonid's head.

She wasn't there for long, leaping off and landing in a crouch, just in time for the Mechonid to wheel around and let loose with a barrage of cannon fire. She leapt forward, rolled, and came up in a sprint, ducking as shells flew over her head. Scooping up her fallen dagger, Rachel dove behind the Galatèa's large dorsal landing-gear piston and pressed her back against the cold metal. The gunfire halted, replaced by the clanking of Mechonid footsteps.

She didn't have her gun. Her dagger wouldn't work against the shield. She only had seconds before the Mechonid began tearing the place apart once more. This was definitely not what she'd signed up for.

Rachel gritted her teeth and grasped the hilt of her weapon. The only option was to stall for time.

She pulled herself onto the large piston and saw the Mechonid raise its purple sensor orbs towards her. The gun-arm followed, and Rachel leapt to the next shot-blocking hunk of metal. She hopped from one piece of machinery to the next, ducking and weaving through pipes, coils, beams, and every other piece of haphazard equipment in the cluttered engine room. The Mechonid slowly turned on the spot, but she knew the room better than it did, and she gave it no chance for a clear shot.

It was as she ducked behind a mass of thick coolant coils that the firing abruptly stopped. For a moment, Rachel thought that it had run out of ammunition, and she drew her dagger in preparation. Then there was a hiss of rapidly released gas.

Oh crap.

She'd never expected it to use a missile in such close quarters. The girl emerged from her hiding place in time to see a tiny torpedo arcing towards her position. She broke into a sprint, but the explosion blasted her off her feet.

By explosion standards it was small, but this didn't occur to Rachel as her slight frame catapulted through the air, landing almost directly in the middle of the engine room floor. The wind left her lungs and she came to a stop, the world spinning.

Splayed on her back, Rachel raised her head just in time to see the barrel of a gun being pointed in her face.

So this is it.

Strangely, all she could think about was the fact that their water coils were now in flames and utterly ruined. The ship would now have cooling problems for the rest of the voyage.

The barrel lit up with a purple glow and made a sound like rushing wind, signalling the end of the girl's life.

Then there was a loud clang, followed by an electrical discharge. The Mechonid's head snapped upwards and it began to tremble. Rachel was forced to roll backwards as the robot pitched on its face and lay in a heap, devoid of power.

Theodore stood a little way off, smoke wafting from both the cigarette in his left hand and the pistol in his right. As per usual, he looked like he was posing for a photo-shoot. If he hadn't just saved her life, Rachel would've rolled her eyes.

He lowered the gun, and Rachel stood on shaky legs. She noticed that the back of the Mechonid's head was emitting an orange glow and a slight fizzling sound, and realised that Theodore had switched his pistol from his usual energy rounds to swivel rounds – using a miniature nuclear reaction to fire an irradiated bullet at ridiculous speeds, spinning fast enough to cut through most known substances.

The Corporation considered these weapons illegal, given their penchant for uranium leaks. Theodore's gun was shielded, but many an intrepid adventurer had been swindled by shady dealers into carrying shoddy nuclear handhelds.

"Where'd you get that?" Rachel panted, still catching her breath through the rippling pain down her side.

"You're welcome," he replied.

"Since when do you have a new gun?"

"You can thank me any time."

"But your people consider those things illegal. Even having a gun equipped with…"

"They're very effective against distracted targets with burst shields."

Rachel's calmer thoughts finally caught up with her adrenaline-laced ones.

"Uh… thanks," she said, feeling sheepish.

A curious expression flashed across Theodore's face; was it concern? In a moment, though, he was back to his reserved self.

"Don't mention it," he grunted, spinning his pistol in a full circle. It collapsed into a flat rectangle, which he clipped into his belt buckle. "Besides, there's a larger issue at hand."

They took the elevator to the top of the engine room and made their way to the bridge, where Hraks was already in the pilot's seat.

Rachel limped straight for the diagnostics console, while Theodore moved to his own command station. Hraks expertly avoided a hail of purple bolts as Galatèa returned a well-aimed burst of Gauss fire, striking the Mechonid ship's rear thruster and practically shearing it off.

"Status report," the captain ordered.

Rachel scanned the display and compressed the information in her head. Theodore wasn't a huge fan of frills.

"We're stable. They managed to land a hit on the hull, but the damage is minimal; shields are at 90% efficiency."

"I suggest holding on," Hraks said, vigorously jerking the controls to the left. Rachel caught a brief glimpse of a cluster of missiles careening towards them before her view-screen tipped on its side and they went into a spiral. The homing missiles collided with each other and exploded, leaving only a few on their tail. Seconds later, a storm of shells from the Galatèa's gun-pod cut down the stragglers.

Theodore, who hadn't even stumbled during the ordeal, waved his hand across the holographic display, splaying it over the front viewport.

"Hraks, offensive pattern," he said. "Give Maximus the best shot possible."

Hraks nodded and brought them around to face the Mechonid ship, which had sustained even more damage in the interim. For a moment they were stationary, then the engines roared to life, propelling them straight for the enemy vessel.

"Engines at max output," Rachel reported. "Our acceleration is stable."

The ships traded fire, and Rachel winced as the occasional shot pierced their shields.

"Maximus, aim for the fuel cells on my mark," the captain ordered. A grunt from the intercom was the only response. They were getting closer. They could now physically see the Mechonid ship – a large, cruel vessel shaped like a claw. It dwarfed the Galatèa, but this would work to their advantage, making it an easier target. They were almost at the collision point, where their ship would be smashed like a bug on a windshield.

"Bank down," Theodore barked, and Hraks sent their ship into a half-spiral that had them sailing underneath the Mechonid ship.

"Fire!"

Maximus let loose with their most powerful weapon: a Legion rail gun, modified for close range and maximum damage. The Mechonid fuel cells ripped open, the single shell carving a deep scar on the ship's underside. Rachel transferred power to the engines as Hraks punched the throttle. They blasted out from the shadow of the great ship in time to see the fuel cells go up in flames, quickly consumed by the lack of atmosphere. The Mechonid ship was dead in the void.

There was silence for a moment before Rachel realised that it was her job to speak next.

"Uh… Mechonid ship is crippled. Their auto-repairs seem to be underway, but they don't have movement. The Galatèa is stable; minor damage to landing gear, and two shield nodes are burnt out."

"That'll give them something to worry about," Theodore replied. "Maximus, report to the bridge. We…"

The entire ship shook, and Rachel was thrown out of her seat. The metal floor didn't make for a particularly soft landing.

"What was…"

The sentence remained unfinished as a purple crack ripped open in the centre of the bridge, flooding the room with light. A Mechonid tumbled out of the breach, landed on its feet, and immediately aimed its gun at the main console.

Hraks was faster. The Nephilim whipped out her spine rifle and blasted the Mechonid's head off with a well-placed burst of bone needles. It trembled and collapsed, the crack in the air already sealing. There was another moment of shocked silence.

"Hraks, get us out of here," Theodore ordered, turning back to the navigation console and punching in a destination. "Full speed. I don't know how they're getting onto the ship, but I want them gone."

Hraks dropped her rifle and gunned the engines. In seconds, the Mechonid ship was a speck in the distance, and rapidly vanishing.

"Rachel, with me," the captain continued. Rachel nodded and drew her gun as Theodore unfolded his own.

"You think there are more?"

"Almost certainly. We'll meet up with Maximus, then…"

They both halted as the corridor outside echoed with gunfire. There was the sound of grinding metal, clanking footsteps, and a lot of roaring, followed by an ominous wrenching. Theodore crossed to the door, pistol aimed forward, and reached for the button. Before he could press it, the door slid open, revealing the hulking frame of Maximus.

Rachel exhaled with relief as she saw he was unharmed. Then she noticed the two Mechonid heads dangling by wires from the Legionnaire's hands, with their bodies lying in the corridor beyond. They might have been robots, but it was somehow still a gruesome sight.

"I checked," Maximus grunted, still framed in the doorway. "They're all dead."

Theodore nodded and holstered his pistol. When Maximus said there was no more fighting to be done, there usually wasn't.

"So it's over?" Rachel breathed, sinking back into her chair. They were away, and everyone was safe. Her stupid, argumentative, dysfunctional family was safe. Her relief was palpable. Theodore

kicked the headless Mechonid body that lay in the centre of the bridge with an expression of disdain.

"It's not over until I find out how they got on my ship, and that damn artefact is sold. Hraks, take them apart." Without a backwards glance, Theo turned and left the bridge. Maximus still holding the Mechonid heads, watched him go.

"Let's just be glad there were only the four of them," Rachel said, to break the silence. "I wouldn't want to go up against an entire ship's worth."

Maximus grunted and stalked out, but not before mumbling something that sounded very much like "Speak for yourself."

Rachel glared at the back of his head, but the Legionnaire didn't notice.

***

The Mechonid husks lay piled in the lab, where Maximus had dumped them hours beforehand. Three were missing their heads, while one had a single bullet hole in its central processor.

The lab was dark, lit only by the soft purple glow of the box suspended in the Electro-Gravity field.

There was a soft hum. The sound wasn't loud enough to penetrate the walls, but it echoed around the room and seemed to multiply until it created a mechanical harmony. The purple veins of the box began to pulse erratically, as if transmitting some kind of code.

The Mechonid that still retained its head stirred. Then its purple sensor orbs flickered and slowly lit up, one by one.

15

Timeline

Golden Age — 10,000+ Years
- Electronic Technology Singularity
- Ley Lines Created
- Humanity Stops Advancing
- Genetic Erosion Tipping Point
- Archons Created
- Last Human Dies

Age of Creation — 3,000 Years
- Archons Start Genetically Engineering New Races
- Vargarti Created
- Kaltorans Created
- X'ions Created

Great X'ion War — 6 Year
- X'ions & Archons Fight, Single X'ion Escapes
- X'ion Returns with Nephilim Army
- Legion Hastily Created
- Last Archon Dies & X'ion Leaves

Years of Darkness — 100 Years
- Legion & Nephilim Lose Capacity to Continue Fighting
- Corporation Rediscover Space Travel
- Corporation Settle in Haven System
- Corporation & Nephilm Trade Alliance Formed
- Kaltorans Return to Space

Rebirth — 5 Years
- Legion & Corporation Economic Alliance Formed
- Now

Short Story: History

"History is a tricky thing. You'd think that it would be static… and it is. But like anything, it changes depending on what angle you look at it from, and the longer you look, the more nuanced it becomes." Gregory sunk back into his office chair as he settled in for a long discussion with his dear friend, Grofix.

It had been a long shift, and both friends were keen to make the most of the temporary stillness in Gregory's office to indulge their philosophical and intellectual pursuits.

"Thas iz troo." Grofix took a seat on the nearby coffee table. The fact that none of the many chairs in the room could accommodate his tail said a lot about the type of people Gregory was "supposed" to entertain. "Itz also doos not helps that wees ar trying to look buck thruw ten thousand yeargs of time and thruw manyz collapsed empirez."

Even Gregory found it hard to understand his friend's heavy accent at times. He often repeated what he had just heard, to make sure he had listened correctly — a form of "active listening" as he liked to think of it.

"Yes, we are trying to look back over a long time and through the haze of many fallen empires, the greatest of these clearly being the humans, and only the religious dare to speculate what came before them." Gregory took a cigar from his desk drawer as he keyed the word "human" into his computer's Stream Search program.

Humanity

"The problem with talking about a long-dead race, one which has shaped our universe so much, is that we can't help but reduce them down to a caricature. A soulless list of notable achievements and failures." Gregory fiddled with his unlit cigar as he thought about where to start. "While I'm sure humans were just as culturally diverse as us, how can we know for sure? Maybe they invented emotions, currency… and family."

That last point struck a painful emotional chord in Gregory's capitalistic heart.

"Weez cans specululate all night if youz want. But we dontz haz time." Empathy did not come easily to Grofix; it wasn't in his genes. But even he could emulate it, if it would make this information exchange more efficient. "Whatz is this 'soullezz' list?"

Gregory quickly regained his composure, lighting his cigar.

"We can't be exactly sure about the order of events; the Stream Search gives them as follows: reached electronic-based Technology Singularity…"

"Az whutz?"

"Um… 'A point of exponential technological progress," Gregory paraphrased, looking to his friend for a visual cue that his answer was sufficient; it appeared to be. "Leading to a singular momentous event known as The Reality Fracture, resulting in what we call Ley Lines – mappable areas of space where some scientific laws can be bent, namely the ability to travel faster than light without exponential mass increase or time dilatation – enabling humanity to spread throughout the galaxy, possibly further, and to terraform many worlds. With more resources and space than they ever needed, humanity found itself without want, and all conflict ceased."

"Hmrgh…" Having been created for conflict, Grofix found this concept difficult to believe and more challenging than any other human achievement.

"But humanity became stale. They stopped learning, advancing, travelling, or growing."

"Thass what happenz when you stop fightin for life."

"Evidently…" While Gregory's idea of healthy conflict was far less physical than his friend's, he did agree. "… Leading to their genetic erosion, and a breakdown in their biological diversity. They died in the billions to disease, famine, and birth defects, troubles they had forgotten how to fight. Out of desperation, they created the Archons…"

The Archons

"… A genetically engineered race, created to replace humanity."

Gregory paused for a moment; any thought of his creators, the Archons, brought up complex thoughts and feelings.

"They iz like your negligant parenttz and myz estranged grandparents," Grofix mused. He never quite knew how to think of the Archons. But he momentarily put these thoughts to the side; very soon Gregory would get to his creator, X'ion, and then the Great War. That is where his people came in.

"Not wanting to tread in the footprints of their creators, the Archons did not work towards rediscovering what humanity had formerly achieved. Rather, they pushed out in a different direction, most prominently in repopulating their inherited empire with their own genetically engineered creations. All in a effort to create the perfect race, to be called the X'ion."

Gregory started to seethe as he brought to mind what the Archons had done to his people. Closing down his computer screen, he shared his own raw thoughts.

"They were terrible parents. Pouring their favour out on some, like the ridiculous Kaltorans, and limiting the potential of their 'failed' offspring… like us, the Corporation!" Gregory was almost standing now, from memories of what he and his people had gone through.

"Welz you showdz themz."

"Yes… yes, we did… or more to the point, your people did." Gregory sat back down. "But before we get to that, we need to talk about your own failed parent."

Grofix's expression remained unmoved.

X'ion

"After three thousand years and hundreds of new species, the Archons thought they had finally created the perfect race, worthy of the title 'X'ion'." Gregory rotated his chair to face the large transparent Synth Steel window, giving him a fantastic view of the large gas giant 'Alabaster' that his company's space station was mining for fuel and other chemical compounds.

"Thatz iz correct," Grofix also got up to look out the window. "Butz the Archonz change their minds, they think they notz worth it… how many X'ion had been made at this pointz?"

"Twelve… they were still in the genetics lab where they had been created. Not yet given their own world." An awkward smile crossed his face as he voiced a thought: "Imagine if they had been given their own world and allowed to breed."

"Thenz I darz say we would notz be talkin here as friendz."

"True." Gregory stood up to get a better view of the planet and the space station they were on. "The X'ion did not take the Archons' removal of their title well. I imagine the fight that followed was brutal. But the X'ion did not stand a chance; the Archons flew in reinforcements and quickly killed all of the X'ion… all but one… He, she… it… does X'ion have a gender?"

"Don't knowz."

"Well 'it' stole a ship and fled out into uncharted space, the Archons giving chase for almost five years according to the local pub speculation."

"It wouldz bee back."

"Yes, but it's worth talking about the changes to Archon culture first."

Grofix turned to look directly at Gregory. This was the part of the story he had heard very little about.

"The Archons became ideologically fractured over differing perspectives on 'perfection' and the need to test their existing children. Many Archons thought they needed trials of hardship to grow and prove themselves, while other Archons pushed for all current genetic projects to be halted."

"Isnt itz strange that we carez about all zisss so muchz."

"Not strange at all; in many ways our culture and history shape us more than our genetics."

This idea was contrary to Grofix's upbringing, where the nature of one's birth defined one's entire life. But if this belief was the result of his cultural upbringing, then it only added weight to Gregory's point.

"History shapes us, especially momentous history, like war."

The Great War

"When X'ion returned, it brought a diverse army of genetically engineered warriors." Gregory looked at Grofix. "Your people, the Nephilim, as you have come to be named."

"Myz mother fought during that warz."

"Are many who fought in the war still alive?"

"Yes, manyz… at leastz a fifth of the peoplz from my city." Grofix thought for a little while. "We callz the older Nephilim 'Purebloods'. We suspectz sumz of them can livs for hundrez of yearz. Butz I am notz a Pureblood; I amz a 'Hybrid' as I comez from two different Pureblood species of parentz. Us Hybrids we is veryz diverse."

"And what about the 'Emissaries'? They are very similar to us."

"Yezz, they is new… only made in the lastz few yearz. But we arz off topic; lez get back to the war."

"Yes, well… while it was technically a war, it was closer to a slaughter. X'ion's army of Nephilim and fleets of organic spacecraft laid waste to almost every world with nuclear, biological, and ground combat. Some of the Archons in their stupidity welcomed the war, thinking that it would not only test their children but also themselves."

"Yuz, they werz tested… and found lacking. Theyz all deadz now."

"Once X'ion had killed the last Archon, it just left. Abandoning its army, your people. No one knows why."

Grofix did not know how to feel about this. He had not fought during the war and held no allegiance to his creator.

Re-Emergence

"A hundred years later and we are only now just starting to grasp what happened back then." Gregory sat back at his desk, bringing up a hologram of their solar system, the Haven system. "Our people survived, yours, the Kaltorans and the Legion. We are all now acting outside the scope of our original design."

"Tey possibly leftz uszz to learn to standz on our own?"

"I have heard thousands of ideas as to how this is all part of the 'Creator's' plan. I choose not to believe that; they were created just like us. Flawed, just like us."

Grofix paced the room thoughtfully as Gregory smoked.

"Butz wherez we at nows? Everything hangs on a thread… we have only re-emerged back into spacez a few years ago…"

"My people have been back in space for over fifty years now!" Surprised by his harsh retort, Gregory rotated his chair to face away from his friend.

Grofix loved conflict and misread this as an invitation to speak more forcefully.

"Yus, oh Corporate master!" he said sarcastically, his accent clearing up slightly as his thoughts suddenly focused. "And you don't knowz waz out there! You don't know if X'ion is coming back to finish the job! You escapez from yours wretched home world youz comes here, to this Haven system to build comfortable home for yourselves."

"Grofix I didn't…"

"Still so desperate to prove youselvezz to your dead parents. Wellz I dontz have to proovez myself, I amz Nephilim! If weez wanted, we could killz you allz. There iz more of uz and we haz tha weapons!"

"Damn it, Grof! I and everyone knows that the Nephilim are the military might in this system. But we also know that you need us!" Gregory was now standing, but still not looking at his friend… eye contact would just encourage his genetic desire for conflict. "We all need each other; we don't have a choice. No matter who was to win another war, they would be dead a few years later. You need a stable society and economy."

Steadying himself against a wall, Grofix held his words back. He knew Gregory was right, but his instincts fought against his logical mind. It screamed at him to take the position of authority, both physically and verbally. But Gregory was right; for a race that had no discernible genetic gifts, their occasional wisdom was impressive.

"We all need each other." Gregory could sense that Grofix was calming himself. "Despite the often-greedy nature of my people, we do provide spacecraft fuel and manufacturing. Your people provide science and a cost-effective labour force…"

"Hmmmm."

"… The Legion provide us with an effective military force and a passion for law enforcement." Gregory turned to look his friend in the eyes. "Damn it… we even need the Kaltorans; they provide a large amount of raw minerals and food."

"Iz not onlyz tangiblezz things thaz we oferz each other. We helpz each other find balance, to balance each other's natures."

"There is wisdom in your words my friend…"

Corporation

See pg: 198 for extensive Corporation write-up.

Rejected by their creators (the Archons) as inferior, the Corporation (formerly known as Vargarti) have grown to love the Great X'ion War because it freed them from an existence of insignificance and irrelevance. Discarding their racial identity, they are now eager to prove themselves. Not a nation in the classical sense, the Corporation is a massive corporate entity comprising millions of smaller, affiliated business enterprises – a purely capitalistic society.

Corporation Trait, pg: 340
» +2 Maximum Resources and Influence.
» Gain 1 Resource and Influence.
» +1 Wealth, Operations, and Tactical.
» –1 Fate.
» –2 Maximum Strength.
» Complication: Prejudice from Kaltorans.

Play a Corporate if you:
» Value social power.
» Value money and possessions.
» Value the individual over the group.
» Care about your appearance.
» Want to be a space merchant.
» Refuse to be defined by your genetics.

Physical Qualities
» Average Height: 1.7m.
» Average Weight: 75kg.
» Average Life Span: 80 years.
» Yellow patterned skin along neck, back, shoulders, and hairline.

Home World: Alabaster, pg: 256
Alabaster is a massive gas giant, rich in helium-3, with a single large moon and distinctive ring made of ice and rock particles, gathered as its orbit occasionally brings it close to the Monopoly asteroid belt.

The X'ion War left the Corporate home world, Varsphere, a desolate wasteland. After fifty years, the rediscovery of space travel enabled the (newly renamed) Corporates to search for a new home. Accessing Archon data banks, they were able to locate a rare gas giant in a nearby system that could be harvested for vital spacecraft fuel and other valuable chemicals. Naming the newly claimed planet "Alabaster", they quickly set about building a new home for themselves.

The Corporation has built numerous large chemical-mining space stations in close orbit to the dangerous Alabaster atmosphere. These stations undergo constant repair and expansion, using asteroid-mined materials and imported supplies. Space travel around Alabaster often frustrates pilots, who face a relentless bombardment of digital advertisement and near-constant traffic deadlock.

Corporation Culture
Largely motivated by a desire for personal success and shaped by social expectations, Corporate culture is deceptively simple to outsiders. While most Corporates are materially well provided for, nearly all present an image of greater personal success than they have actually achieved, especially around other Corporates.

No matter how impoverished, every Corporate will have at least one set of expensive-looking clothes to wear in public. The most wealthy frequently throw extravagant parties to firmly establish public knowledge of their success.

Corporates mostly live on large, crowded, and hastily constructed space stations orbiting the gas giant Alabaster, with large central chambers full of garish advertisements and shops, and surrounded by large space ports.

The Corporates are the greatest unifying force in the Haven system – with most of their manual labour and production done by Nephilim-created biological drones called "Flesh", law enforcement largely managed by the Legion, and even food and raw minerals provided for by trade with the often-troublesome Kaltorans.

Common Characteristics
Abrasive, decisive, entrepreneurial, organised, and pragmatic.

Common Male Names
Aaron, Dale, Derrick, James, Lucas, Malvin, Milo, Steve, or Theodore.

Common Female Names
Abbey, Amy, Isabel, Judy, Julie, Rita, Robyn, or Stephanie.

Common Family Names
Angelson, Bolt, Cartove, Darrison, Jefferson, or Smith.

Example Corporation Character
Theodore grew up in the early years of the Corporation's space colonisation of Haven. Both parents struggled to even meet their own basic needs, forcing Theodore to do whatever it took to survive. Theft, violence, hunger, and sickness followed his every step.

He took any job he could get, anything for a shot at a better future. Eventually, growing tired of the daily drudgery of space colonisation, he moved into security, then into arms dealing as a freelance rep for Body Count Conglomerate™ – a new and dynamic group of companies that catered to a growing demand for armaments and munitions, regardless of intent.

Having put together a diverse and eclectic team, Theodore can make connections amongst any culture and go anywhere he wants. Theodore does not know what this uncertain future holds for him and his crew, but he is eager to make the most of it, possibly one day by starting his own company.

Kaltoran

See pg: 212 for extensive Kaltoran write-up.

Born with the genetic memories of their ancestors, Kaltorans are an innately gifted and flexible race. They are eager to make a new future for themselves, though they struggle with the "genetic memories" of not only the Great X'ion War but the extreme measures taken by their ancestors to survive it.

Kaltoran Trait, pg: 340

» Reduce all Untrained Primary Skill Roll penalties by 1 (except Wealth).
» +1 Awareness, Command, and Small Arms.
» +1 Fate.
» +2 Defence vs Stealth.
» Reduce all Limited Vision and Low Light penalties by 1 Step.
» Gain Language: Kaltoran.
» –1 Wealth.
» –2 Maximum Focus.
» Unwanted Flashback: If you roll triples with any Fate re-roll, you immediately gain a Minor Psychological Condition (which may be removed with an appropriate Extended Care Healing Roll).
» Complication: Prejudice from Corporation.

Play a Kaltoran if you:

» Value friends and family above all else.
» Want to be a space rogue.
» Make spontaneous decisions.
» Like to make lots of different Skill Rolls.
» Enjoy tactile and dirty technology.
» Distrust greedy Corporates.

Physical Qualities

» Average Height: 1.65m.
» Average Weight: 70kg.
» Average Life Span: 120 years.
» Dreadlock hair.
» Four pointed ears.

Home World: Kadash, pg: 266

A holy planet of the Kaltoran people during their golden age of favour with the Archons, and terraformed into a paradise planet by the ancient humans, Kadash was once a jewel of their empire.

During the Great X'ion War, the losing Kaltorans continually fell back in a fighting retreat. Kadash was their last stand. In a final effort to survive, the Kaltorans modified ancient human terraforming equipment to vaporise much of the water on the planet's surface, wracking their world with violent storms and tidal waves.

The Kaltorans dug beneath the ocean floors and deep into the planet's crust, making new cities for themselves. These cities are complex tangles of caverns and tunnels woven around large hollow chambers, making use of extensive life support systems and airlocks to allow free access to their ancient submersible spacecraft.

Kaltoran Culture

Everything revolves around family for a Kaltoran, a core trait reinforced by the genetic memories that each Kaltoran passes down to their children.

For almost a hundred years after the Great X'ion War, the Kaltorans went to extreme measures to survive, descending into brutal tribalism and cannibalism, horrors and survival instincts that are now passed on to every Kaltoran. Overcompensating for the failures of their ancestors, Kaltorans are often overly optimistic, passionate, and eager for a clean slate and a better future.

With large families and limited living space, they have learnt to make the most of their limited resources, creating eclectic and dense subterranean cities. Kaltoran businesses are frequently run from within family homes or directly from a spacecraft's cargo hold, often selling raw minerals, fish, or weapons.

Kaltorans have a very small and focused government that only deals with major social concerns. Local laws are dictated by prominent family Elders and popular opinion. Few rules are enforced, but those that are, are often dealt with severely and quickly: all Kaltorans carry a weapon – even children and especially the elderly.

Common Characteristics

Cunning, driven, fun-loving, inquisitive, friendly, loyal, opportunistic, optimistic, and thrifty.

Common Male Names

Adam, Aaron, Cain, Daniel, Elijah, Gideon, Jacob, James, Jamie, Joseph, Jude, Lot, Matthias, or Nathan.

Common Female Names

Ana, Danielle, Debra, Elizabeth, Esther, Eva, Eve, Iva, Jayne, Joan, Mary, Rachel, Rebekkah, Sally, Sarah, Talia, or Zera.

Common Family Names

Chillax, Filch, Game, Jinx, Juked, Omni, Swagger, or Thrift.

Example Kaltoran Character

Rachel Swagger is the adopted middle child of a family of 14. Her family was always active, complicated, and fun. Her siblings were born soldiers and leaders – two traits she was not born with, though she is an amazing mechanic.

Rachel has the genetic memories of her ancestors, including her great grandfather, a master technician to an Archon lab. She inherited his ability to fix anything with an engine and his love for meeting new people. Her grandmother, who fought the Nephilim during the Great X'ion War, gave her the ability to keep a level head in combat. But she also feels her mother's fears and pain from the Dark Years: fear of losing her children to cannibals, and the pain of knowing that her children would remember the horrible things she did to survive.

The Dark Years are in the past, and Rachel is keen to make a better future. Finding work on a spacecraft was her best hope of realising this dream. Her people needed to get out there and make new memories to pass on, not to dwell on the pain of the past.

Legion

See pg: 228 for extensive Legion write-up.

A physically imposing race, hastily created by the Archons to fight their losing war against X'ion, the Legion now struggle to create a stable society and to find meaning without a war to fight. In recent times the Legion have formed a close economic relationship with the Corporation, acting as enforcers for hire.

Legion Trait, pg: 340
» +1 Resolve, Gunnery, and Heavy Arms.
» +1 Armour.
» +2 Defence vs Impair.
» Never requires 'Environmental Outfit or Equipment: Arctic'.
» Gain Language: Legion.
» Requires 'Environmental Outfit or Equipment: Temperate' outside Arctic Environments or be Suppressed each Turn.
» –1 Armour when at 0 Endurance.
» –2 Maximum Movement.

Play a Legion if you:
» Value honour, duty, respect, and skill.
» Want to be a space soldier.
» Want to be tough.
» Love big guns and heavy armour.
» Can hold a grudge.
» Distrust monsters.

Physical Qualities
» Average Height: 2.4m.
» Average Weight: 180kg.
» Average Life Span: 60 years.
» Scaled, lizard-like skin.
» Often large and muscular.

Home World: Cerberus Prime
The Legion continued to fight for decades after the Great War, employing guerrilla warfare tactics against the remaining Nephilim forces. But supplies grew thin and the Legion needed a home. They chose the Cerberus system.

With only three planets orbiting a large, unstable star, the Cerberus system was chosen as a home for its defensive attributes and because its third frozen planet was ideal for Legion physiology.

While the Legion no longer consider themselves at war, they are very insular and are suspicious of outsiders entering their territory. They will often search merchant ships and escort travellers to make sure they don't wander.

Secondary Planet: Lilith, pg: 268
The outermost planet of the Haven system, Lilith is a cold tri-mooned world that functions as a base of operations for the Legion. They use the world to facilitate their interactions with the other races and provide refuge for working Legion mercenaries.

Legion Culture
Created by the Archons to be resilient and skilled warriors, these traits have not helped to create a sustainable society during the hundred years following the Great X'ion War. Choosing to have a family or take on full-time civilian work is considered a great and noble sacrifice.

Legion culture is very rigid with many heavily enforced laws. Very protective of their homes, few outsiders are able to visit their small and heavily fortified cities. Settlements have few businesses, as food and other supplies are distributed according to need.

A lot changed for the Legion after they made contact with the other races. The attraction of living a life of action has proven a strong incentive for many Legion. Giving up their pursuit of a self-sustaining society, many now act as mercenaries and enforcers, especially for the Corporation. Old grudges have made interactions with the Nephilim difficult, but the situation is currently stable. They enjoy a natural comradeship with the Kaltorans as they share similar goals despite their contrasting natures.

Common Characteristics
Efficient, focused, honourable, loyal, organised, protective, proud, and stubborn.

Common Male Names
Ajax, Ares, Bacchus, Cronus, Hector, Janus, Mars, Theseus, Vulcan, or Zephyrus.

Common Female Names
Aglaia, Aurora, Brisa, Cassandra, Danu, Electra, Eris, Hydra, Ismini, Kynthia, Medea, or Selene.

Common Family Names
Antonius, Augustus, Aurelius, Brutus, Casca, Cinna, Crassus, Gracchus, Lepidus, Scaevola, or Vespillo.

Example Legion Character
He was born Ares Vespillo, but everyone called him Maximus. Life was very straightforward for Max – not simple… he just always knew what to do. His life had focus and clarity.

Like every Legion, he was born to be a soldier. His parents had sacrificed much to raise him and support their community through their hunting business, but things didn't need to be like that anymore. The other races could provide much of that now. The Corporation could build things, the Kaltorans could provide food, and the Legion could provide protection. The Archons had made them all with a purpose, he thought. But real life was not as straightforward as he would have liked. Maximus learnt this in his first week working as a mercenary on a Corporation merchant ship.

Their Corporate captain was constantly manipulating their clients and suppliers. Their Kaltoran mechanic was extremely fun and kind, but her emotions hung on a thread at times. Their Nephilim medic and resident scientist was the most complex. She was rude and arrogant, but she had clarity and focus about who she was, two traits that Max wished they did not share.

Nephilim

See pg: 242 for extensive Nephilim write-up.

Nephilim: A junk-word term used to describe the diverse descendants of X'ion's genetically engineered army. Created to wage war on the Archons and their creations, before being abandoned by their creator, X'ion, once the war was won.

The Nephilim have an eclectic, primal, and often violent society supported by advanced biological technology. While publicly no longer loyal to X'ion, many Nephilim pursue genetic perfection at any cost.

Nephilim Trait, pg: 340
» +1 Bio Tech, Engineering, and Exotic.
» +1 to all Spare Time Rolls.
» +1 Recover.
» Gain Language: High X'ion or Primal X'ion.
» -1 Conversation.
» -2 Culture.
» Complication: Prejudice from Kaltorans and Legion.

Play a Nephilim if you:
» Value innate ability and science over all else.
» Are motivated by intellect and instinct.
» Like to defy presumptions.
» Possibly want to look like a monster.
» Believe the end always justifies the means.
» Don't mind modifying your body and genetics.

Physical Qualities
» Average Height: 1-2.5m.
» Average Weight: 50-290kg.
» Average Life Span: 20-300 (est.) years.
» Wide range of appearances.
» Often have features of mammals, fish, and/or insects.

Home World: Eden, pg: 260
Before the Great X'ion War, Eden was the Kaltoran home world. Once covered in thriving megacities, lush forests, and great lakes, it is now a wasteland of deserts, salt plains, and ruins. Its surface is littered with giant craters, radiation, poisonous gases, and roaming monsters.

Decades after the Great War and without supplies, the Nephilim ships slowly fell into disrepair. In a desperate attempt to survive, they landed (or according to some, crashed) many of their ships onto the surface of Eden.

Over the remains of these ancient warships, the Nephilim built Necronus, a towering black metal and biological city. The weak masses live amongst the crumpled bases of its many towers, while the most powerful live at the top — a position that must be constantly maintained through force and influence as their towers continue to grow taller.

Nephilim Culture
Life is cheap in this brutal society that values both intelligence and strength. Largely shaped by perceived genetic superiority, the Nephilim split themselves into three broad categories: Purebloods, Hybrids, and Emissaries.

Purebloods are ancient Nephilim who fought in the Great War or are pure blood descendants of those that did. Often large and imposing, they are a living reminder of their people's past service to their creator, X'ion.

Hybrids are the diverse and mixed offspring of the Purebloods. Diverse in appearance and nature, Hybrids make up the bulk of the Nephilim population.

Emissaries are the newest of the Nephilim. Created only a few years ago, they are born fully grown, with a head full of knowledge and memories that are not their own. With the aim of alleviating cultural tension with the other races, they are bred with a physical form closer to those of their former enemies. However, their Nephilim form is not hidden, only softened.

Nephilim culture has very few laws and is only stabilised by the self-serving wills of its powerful leaders, who are largely unconcerned with the masses.

While the Nephilim are easily the most powerful military force in the Haven system, they know that long-term survival and prosperity depends on their forming some kind of functional relationship with the other races — a feat that is incredibly difficult given their war history, old ties to X'ion, appearance, and brutal culture.

Common Characteristics
Blunt, dismissive, focused, proud, honest, instinctual, intelligent, ruthless, and fierce.

Common Names
Beytah, Hegh, Heghta, Hraks, Huch, Jagh, Jatmey, Lonta, Mangghom, Ngabtah, Porghmey, Qeh, Qehpu, Sagh, Yempu, or Wabmey.

Example Nephilim Character
Hraks is only three years old, a child by most races' standards. But she was born fully grown, her head filled with valuable skills and fake memories, which give context to her personality and thoughts. As a Nephilim Emissary, her purpose is to mingle with the other races, a task she was built for.

Spending time in the local space port bars, she was able to pick up work as a medic for a small mercenary group. Life as a mercenary was ideal for Hraks, allowing her to gain real memories and expand her skills, especially in biological technology and combat.

Despite her constant confidence and gifts, the other races often find Hraks difficult to deal with. Her appearance is a constant reminder of darker times, and her blunt way of speaking often causes confrontations. But things would inevitably change. The races would eventually become acclimatised to each other, the past would be forgotten, and they would learn that the Nephilim know best.

Rules Introduction

Welcome to Fragged Empire

What You Need to Play

At least three six-sided dice (3d6) per player.
Character Sheet print outs (can be downloaded from the website).
Pens or pencils.
A laminated square-grid battle map.
Whiteboard markers.
Character and spacecraft miniatures.
Rulebook (print or PDF).
Two to five friends!

If You Are Familiar with Tabletop RPGs

If you are an experienced tabletop role player, you will easily pick up the Fragged Empire rules. (Though as you know, it always takes time to learn a new game system.)

To see what sets this system apart from others, we recommend you read the Traits section (pg: 33) and Acquisition section (pg: 54). Of course, taking a look at a character sheet will give you a good feel for where the simple and more intricate rules of the game are. Don't forget to check out our YouTube channel.

www.fraggedempire.com
Read this book alongside a printout of the character sheets, and watch our YouTube rules videos.

If You Are New to Tabletop RPGs

The simplest way to think of a tabletop RPG is that it is like a computer RPG, but the rules and story aren't automatically done for you (most computer RPGs started as tabletop RPGs). The story in a tabletop RPG is told by you (a single character) and a Game Master (GM), who runs the game. You are not constrained by what a program says you can do. If you can think of it, you can attempt it.

Learning to play a tabletop RPG can be a daunting task. The best way to learn is from a friend who is already familiar with RPGs or from watching a recorded game on YouTube. You may need to read through this book a few times. Best just read it once, then play a small game, then read it again and play a slightly larger game.

Glossary of Common Terms

GM = Game Master (the person who runs the game).
PC = Player character.
NPC = Non-player character.
1d6 = A six-sided die (like you get in most board games).
3d6 = Three six-sided dice.
1d3 = The result of 1d6, divided by two, and rounded up.

Key Features of the Rules

Adaptable Rules

While these rules are designed for use within the Fragged Empire setting, they are robust and flexible enough to be used for most science fiction settings with just a little creative "house ruling". One of the best ways to alter the feel of a game is to increase or decrease the characters' Resources (pg: 56) and Influence (pg: 58).

Simple 3d6 Resolution System

Most Skill Rolls are resolved with a simple 3d6 dice roll. If your roll, plus any bonuses or penalties, equals or exceeds the required amount, then you succeed.

Nonlinear Character Progression

Characters have many options available to them, with no set paths for ability or equipment progression. This allows for characters to quickly specialise or diversify and to create unique combinations of abilities and Equipment.

Low-level characters, specialised properly, can be dangerous threats to high-level characters. Even if two characters have similar Attributes, Skills, or Equipment, they can function quite differently because of their differing Traits.

Best for Long Sandbox Games

Fragged Empire can be used to play short games, but it is best when used for long sandbox-style games. In this post-apocalyptic setting, you will regularly have to make the most of what little resources you have, balancing short-term sacrifices and long-term gain.

Tactical Miniatures Combat

This ruleset includes intuitive tactical combat in which you will need to react not only to your environment (cover is your friend), but also to your opponents' actions. It also includes optional rules for miniature-free combat (pg: 96). GMs are encouraged to make combat a part of the story and to reward intelligent play. As there are no perfect, statistically balanced encounters, the players' creativity, skill, and teamwork will be the key to victory.

Optional: Game Types

Ragtag Band of Misfits
(Standard Game)

Joined together by unlikely circumstance or need, you and your oddly matched team are trying to make your way in a hostile and mysterious galaxy.

Small freelance mercenary groups and merchant ships are the lifeblood of the Haven system. They are able to quickly respond and adapt to ever-changing opportunities and dangers.

» Start at Level 1.
» Start with 3 Current Resources and Influence.
» Start with 3 Spare Time Points.
» Often involves the party owning a spacecraft.

Casual Game
(Easier Combat)

The galaxy is not quite so dangerous.

» Start at Level 1.
» Start with 3 Current Resources, Influence.
» Start with 3 Spare Time Points.
» Often involves the party owning a spacecraft.
» Each player character gains +1 Armour.
» Player character spacecraft do not gain -1 Armour at 0 Shields.
» All Small Arms, Heavy Arms, Tactical, and Exotic Weapons gain +1 Clip.

Survival
(Great for Horror Games)

Bound together out of need or desperation, you and your companions are just trying to survive to see another day.

Please note: It is recommended that you and your players have reasonable grasp of this rule system before you run a game of this type, as managing combat and Spare Time Points can be a little overwhelming.

» Start at Level 1.
» Start with 0 Current Resource and Influence.
» Start with 6 Spare Time Points.
» +4 Equipment Slots.
» -1 Fate.
» +1 Max Resources and Influence per 2 Levels (normally +1 per 1 Level).
» Gain 2 Spare Time Points per session (normally 1).
» Personal Combat Weapons with infinite Clips or Ammo cost +2 Resources.
» Weapon Clips do not refill during Downtime.
» Refilling personal Combat Clips, Ordnance Clips, rebuilding Destroyed Drone Bodies require a Spare Time Roll of 14t.
» Your character dies if any Attribute reaches -2 (normally -5).
» Optional: Food and Water must be acquired with Spare Time Rolls (see Food Supplies, pg: 137).
» Optional: Intense Damage (pg: 309).

Story Focus
(Light Combat Rules)

Physical conflict is primarily a tool for moving the story forward. While it may be prominent and an important part of your game, it does not need to take up such a large portion of your game time.

Please note: This game type discards much of the combat and equipment rules. Some knowledge of these systems is still advised.

» Start at Level 1.
» 0 Max Resources (never increased).
» Influence is only used to gain Perks and Complications, not for acquiring a spacecraft.
» Any time you would gain Resources or Influence, gain a Spare Time Point.
» Start with 3 Influence and Spare Time Points.
» Always use Optional Theatre of the Mind Combat Rules (pg: 96 and 166).

Character Overview

Making a Character

The Game Master defines your starting Level (usually Level 1).
Select your Race.
Distribute 18 Attribute Points (0-5 Points each).
Select your Trained Skills.
  6 Primary Skills (Everyday or Professional).
  2 Personal Combat Skills.
  2 Vehicle System Skills.
Select your Traits, 1 per Level.
Starting Resources, Influence and Spare Time Points = Your Level+2.
  Allot Resources and Influence.
  Spend Spare Time Points (you may automatically gain any item or service that costs 14t or less, no roll required).

Starting Level, pg: 32

See pg: 341 for a full list of available Traits.

Your character usually begins at Level 1 (with 1 Trait).

You start with Resources, Influence, and Spare Time Points equal to your Level +2. You gain 1 additional Trait, Maximum Resource, and Influence per Level.

Level 0 is a child or unskilled.
Level 1 to 4 is averagely gifted.
Level 5 to 9 is skilled.
Level 10 to 19 is amazingly gifted.
Level 20 or more is legendary.

Choosing Your Starting Traits
The Trait(s) you select at character creation should represent your character's defining nature and history. Some Traits can only be selected at character Creation (eg: Old).

Attributes, pg: 34

You have 18 points to distribute amongst six Attributes: Strength, Reflexes, Movement, Focus, Intelligence, and Perception. Each Attribute may be set from 0 to 5.

0 represents an impairment of some kind.
1 or 2 is average.
3 or 4 is impressive.
5 is amazingly gifted.

Trained Skills, pg: 38

Select 6 Primary Skills, 2 Vehicle System Skills, and 2 Personal Combat Skills to be Trained in. All other Skills are considered Untrained.

Trained Skills give a +1 bonus to your Skill Rolls.
Untrained Skills give a -2 penalty to your Skill Rolls.

Resources and Influence, pg: 54

See pg: 113 for full Equipment rules.
See pg: 141 for full Spacecraft rules.
See pg: 358 for a full list of available Equipment.

You start with Resources and Influence equal to your Level +2. Resources represent your ability to maintain weapons and equipment, while Influence represents your favour with an NPC group (or groups) and reflects your ability to maintain a spacecraft.

Allotted, Not Spent
You do not decrease your Resources or Influence when you acquire, lose, or change your equipment or spacecraft. Resources and Influence represent the quality and quantity of equipment and spacecraft the character may maintain at any one time.

Spare Time Points, pg: 64

You start with Spare Time Points equal to your Level +2 (eg: a Level 1 character starts with 3 Spare Time Points). You may keep these Spare Time Points for later, or you may spend them on any Spare Time Item with a cost of 14t or less, no roll required (each item still cost 1 Spare Time Point, no matter the roll difficulty).

Any use of Spare Time Points after character Creation uses the standard Spare Time Point rules.

Level 1 Legion, Character Creation Example
Derrick starts at Level 1. For his race he chose Legion. He wants to define himself as a leader, so he selects the Leadership Trait "Inspiration". He has 3 Resources, 3 Influence, and 3 Spare Time Points. He spends his Resources on a Shotgun (2 Resources) and a Combat Outfit (1 Resource). He saves his 3 Influence until he can combine it with his companions to buy a larger spacecraft. He spends 1 Spare Time Point on a Toolbox: this normally requires a Spare Time Roll of 14, but does not during character creation.

Making a Character

Best done alongside the GM and other players.

Start with a character idea before you start building.

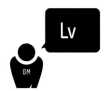

GM Sets the Starting Level
You usually start at a game at Level 1.
An average person is Level 1-4.

Select Your Race
You may select one Race.

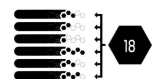

Distribute 18 Attribute Points
You have 18 points to distribute amongst 6 Attributes.
Each Attribute may be set from 0 to 5.
An average person has 1 or 2 points in each Attribute.

Select your Trained Skills
A Trained Skill grants a +1 bonus to your Skill Rolls.
An Untrained Skill has a -2 penalty to your Skill Rolls.
Select 6 Primary (Everyday or Professional), 2 Personal Combat Skills, and 2 Vehicle Systems to be Trained in.

1 Trait per Level

Select 1 Trait per Level
You may have up to 1 Trait per area: Level, Resource, Influence, Attribute, Fate, Trained Primary Skill and up to 2 Traits per Trained Vehicle System or Personal Combat Skill.
You need to meet all Requirements for any Trait you select.

Allot Resources and Influence, Spend Spare Time Points
You start with Resource, Influence and Spare Time Points each equal to your Level +2.
Resources are primarily used to acquire Weapons and Outfits.
Influence is primarily used to acquire a spacecraft.
Spare Time Points are used to acquire minor items or services, or to make Equipment Modifications.
You may start with items or Modifications that requires a Spare Time Roll of 14t or less without needing to roll. Each item costs 1 Spare Time Point.

Level

This represents your character's personal skill and experiential growth.

Gain 1 Level once every 3 game sessions.

When you gain a level:
Gain 1 new Trait (pg: 33).
Increase Maximum Resources and Influence by 1 (pg: 56 & 58).
You may Retro a single part of your character (see below).

Optional Retro

On gaining a new Level, you may change a single Trait, Trained Skill, or allotted Attribute Point (pg: 34). This is called a Retro.

You may not change a Trained Skill if you have already selected a Trait for that Skill. You must first change that Trait to one for another Skill, then you may change the first Skill (requiring 2 Retros).

If changing your Attributes would break a Traits Requirement, you lose the benefits of that Trait but keep the Disadvantages.

All Retro changes must be approved by the GM and will often require some in-game actions to justify the change.

Your First Few Game Sessions
GMs are encouraged to allow players to change their Attributes and Traits after a few sessions.

Gaining a Level Example

After playing three game sessions the Game Master grants Derrick the Legion and his companions a Level up to Level 3.

Derrick needs to choose a Trait. He likes being the up close and personal combatant so he chooses the Tactical Trait 'Second Wind'. This Trait has the "Legion" Requirement, which he meets.

Derrick's maximum potential Resources and Influence are also increased by 1. He wants a new Outfit, but he needs to increase his Current Resources through his actions in-game.

Derrick may also change (Retro) one aspect of his character. He is happy with his Trait choices, but the group has discovered that as a team they are missing the Programming Skill. Derrick decides to untrain one of his Trained Skills and become Trained in Programming. He asks the Game Master for permission to do this. The Game Master says he may untrain the chosen Skill, but he will need to perform some relevant in-game actions to justify learning the new Skill.

Next game session Derrick spends a Spare Time Point to purchase a Personal Computer and says he is also reading a data book on the subject in his spare time. The Game Master says this is reason enough for him to gain the Programming Skill mid-Session.

Traits

See pg: 341 for Traits list.

Traits are what set your character apart from others. They often define the nature of your Attributes and Skills, and can give access to unique abilities.

> **You gain 1 Trait per Level.**

You may select up to 1 Trait per area: Level, Resource, Influence, Attribute, Fate, Trained Primary Skill, and up to 2 Traits per Trained Vehicle System or Personal Combat Skill. This makes every Trait selection important, as each choice also means you are forgoing other Traits.

Requirements

Many Traits have requirements that must be met before that Trait may be selected.

Armour X-Y

Your Armour value must be "X" or higher.
Your Armour value can be no higher than "Y".
Armour vs Energy, Slow, or at 0 Endurance do not affect this.

Char Creation

This Trait can only be selected before your first game session. This Trait cannot normally be changed through Retro.

GM Approval

The GM must approve your selection of this Trait.
Normally requires an in-game action to justify its choice.

Maximum Attribute (Max X)

The listed Attribute must be equal to or lower than "X".

Minimum Attribute (Min X)

The listed Attribute must be equal to or greater than "X".

Psionic

You must be a Psionic (see right).

Robot

You must be a Robot (see right).

Secret Knowledge (Secret Kn)

You must have Secret Knowledge (from Research, pg: 68) in a field that thematically matches the Trait. This often represents your character learning this Trait.

Trait or Race

You must have the listed Trait or Race.

Traits Should Make Thematic Sense

Choose Traits that match your character's existing personality, history or skill use. Traits can also represent your character developing or changing throughout play.

GMs should feel free to require players to take in-game actions to justify their selecting a Trait (eg: require a character to spend time learning through reading or training).

Implant and Splice Traits

Electronic implants, biological implants, and genetic splicing are all commonplace in the Haven system, pushing an individual's abilities beyond what is naturally achievable through modifications and alterations of one's body or genetics.

All Implant and Splice Traits are identified with the word "Implant" or "Splice" in the Trait name.

If you wish to select an Implant or Splice Trait after you have created your character, you must undergo Medical Surgery, requiring a Surgery Roll (pg: 92). This Surgery Roll represents your Implant being installed into your body or your DNA being re-sequenced through splicing.

A Surgery Roll is also required if you change out (Retro, pg: 32) your Implant or Splice Trait for another Trait.

If the Surgery Roll fails, you may try again at a later time, but you do not lose the Trait.

You Are a Psionic

Some rare and gifted (or cursed) individuals can uniquely interact with reality and people's minds. This is connected to the Ley Lines (pg: 278) in some way and is not an ability that was invented by the Archons (pg: 187) or X'ion (pg: 193) (as far as we know).

You can secretly communicate to others using Telepathy (pg: 37), and you can use Weapons with the Weapon Type: Psionic (pg: 103).

You Are a Robot

You are a construction of mechanics and electronics. You are resistant and vulnerable to different things and have different needs.

» Rather than eating, you require power, lubricants, and components.
» Rather than sleeping, you power down for at least 6 hours a day.
» You are immune to poisons, but can get computer viruses.
» You are immune to low levels of radiation, heat, and cold.
» You do not breathe air.
» You are vulnerable to electromagnetic fields.
» You are vulnerable to Disruptor Weapons.
» Your mind can be Hacked.

Attributes

Attributes represent your character's raw physical and mental ability. Attributes are primarily used for combat (pg: 71) and fulfil the requirements of many Traits (pg: 33). Out of combat, they may change your Description Bonuses/Penalties (pg: 38) to a Skill Roll or determine whether an attempt can even be made, especially in situations using Strength.

> When creating a character you have
> 18 points to distribute amongst 6 Attributes.
>
> Each Attribute may be set from 0 to 5.

An average person has every Attribute at 2. A rating of 0 is impaired, and one of 5 is amazingly gifted.

There is no "social" Attribute. A character's social ability is purely determined by their Trained Everyday Skills (pg: 43).

Strength (Str)

Your physical power and general quality of health.

Primarily used to determine the size of Weapons and the weight of Outfits you can efficiently use. Also determines how resilient you are in combat.

Reflexes (Ref)

The speed of your physical response to your environment, along with your flexibility and general agility.

Primarily used to avoid being hit, and represents your melee proficiency.

Movement (Mov)

Your speed of movement and general physical stability.

Does not give any statistical boost to combat rolls, but is used to move around combat areas, managing distance, and moving between Cover.

Focus (Foc)

Your mental strength and ability to focus.

Primarily used for long-range combat, and determines your speed of Recovering from exhaustion and minor damage in combat.

Intelligence (Int)

Your clarity, speed of articulation, and thought.

Primarily used for determining who acts first in combat, and for analysing opponents.

Perception (Per)

Your ability to use your senses to perceive your environment.

Primarily used to determine the accuracy of range Attacks you make during combat.

Scientist, Attribute Example

Edwarck, a Nephilim bio-tech researcher, wants to maximise his ability to invent and use biological Prototype Weapons that will clear entire rooms of foes.

Str: 2 (Don't need to be too strong to do science.)
Ref: 3 (Average reflexes to avoid the odd attack.)
Mov: 2 (Don't plan on running around much.)
Foc: 4 (Good for long-range combat and making sure he does not need to get too close in a fight.)
Int: 5 (Gives access to the best Research Traits.)
Per: 2 (Large-area weapons don't need to directly hit their targets to kill them.)

Tough, Attribute Example

Derrick is an in-your-face Legion shock trooper; he needs to not only take a punch but also move in fast.

Str: 5 (Good for taking a hit and wearing heavy armour.)
Ref: 2 (Helps to avoid the odd attack.)
Mov: 3 (OK for getting into and out of trouble.)
Foc: 4 (Good for long range, but more important for making sure he can stay in the fight longer.)
Int: 1 (He won't be doing much tricky stuff in combat.)
Per: 3 (Average. He shouldn't miss too often.)

Sneaky, Attribute Example

Adam, a master Kaltoran sniper, needs to be able to hit targets at a great range and with deadly accuracy. There is little need for defence if all your enemies are dead before they know where they were attacked from.

Str: 2 (Enough to carry a solid rifle.)
Ref: 5 (Needed for stealth.)
Mov: 1 (Must be careful to not need to move after he sets up.)
Foc: 3 (OK for long range, but he will need to have the right equipment to boost his range further.)
Int: 3 (Needed to analyse each target carefully.)
Per: 4 (He won't often miss.)

Flexible, Attribute Example

Samantha needs to be ready for any situation as a Corporate smuggler. A nasty fight could break out at any time and in almost any environment.

Str: 2 (Most small arms are not heavy.)
Ref: 4 (Best way of staying alive is to not get hit.)
Mov: 3 (Solid movement to make sure she stays in the best cover.)
Foc: 3 (Can recover after taking a beating and keep targets within range.)
Int: 3 (Should be able to act before most in combat.)
Per: 3 (If she can keep herself well positioned, hitting her targets should be easy).

Fate

Fate is an ambiguous representation of your character's luck, destiny, and spiritual protection, or their control over their own future through advanced technology.

All characters start with 2 Fate, which may be changed through Traits (pg: 33).

Dice Re-Rolls
Each session, you may spend a Fate Point
to re-roll all dice in a roll. You may re-roll a re-roll.
Eg: Skill, Attack, or Spare Time Roll.

Unspent re-rolls are not accumulated between game sessions.

Re-Roll an Important Shot, Fate Example
Boris rolls 3d6 to Attack a target with Defence 14. Rolling a total of 6, he misses. He can either accept the failed roll or spend 1 Fate Point to re-roll.

He spends a Fate Point and re-rolls his 3d6 to get a total of 12. The first roll is ignored (even if it were better).

Unfortunately, he still misses. This is a really important Attack, so he decides to spend another Fate Point to re-roll again. This time he rolls a 16 and scores a Strong Hit (pg: 82), so he decides to keep this roll.

To decide what Attribute is Damaged, he rolls a single d6 and gets a a 1 (Strength). If he wished to, he may spend another Fate Point to re-roll this die roll, as long as he had the Fate to spend.

Avoiding Death

See pg: 90 for full Reduce Fate to Avoid Death rules.
See pg: 164 for full Reduce Fate to Avoid Destruction rules.

If you have at least 1 Fate Point, you can permanently reduce your Fate by 1 to miraculously avoid your character's imminent Death. If you wish to avoid your spacecraft's Destruction, all characters on your spacecraft must permanently reduce their Fate by 1.

Fate-Activated Abilities
Some Traits (pg: 33) give you access to abilities that cost a Fate Point to use.

Using an ability that costs a Fate Point is a Free Action (pg: 100) that takes no time.

Jacob was screwed, as if the ancestral Kaltoran spirits had come back and found out he was cheating on his wife.

The Draz junkie had the stubby little Protectron pistol barrel jammed against his forehead, pressing hard enough to make the corridor's metal rivets dig into Jacob's skull.

The junkie, a vacant sneer plastered across his face, wasn't at his steadiest.

"I will never come home late from a party and take a shortcut through the inner stations slums again! And, um, I'll do my meditation! Go visit my kids! And stop cheating on my…" Jacob's fevered, muttered promises were cut short by the rapid tread of heavy booted feet coming down the grimy and cluttered corridor, causing the grotty junkie to swear and shove the pistol somehow harder against his skull as he pulled the trigger.

There was a beautiful fizzling sound and a mild burst of heat against Jacob's face as the pistol's internal workings abruptly fused and warped.

A sudden blow to his head left Jacob reeling and bloodied as the filthy junkie sprinted down the corridor into the shadows, leaving him shuddering in relief.

"Oh, thank the ancestors…"

Three loud-booted Legionaries walked past, eyeing him warily, and turned into the dingy brothel Jacob had just crawled out off.

"… and thank crappy Corporate weapons."

Fate-Activated Ability, Fate Example
Sedrick has the "Void Touched" Trait. It allows him to spend 2 Fate Points to force an NPC to re-roll any roll.

An NPC Attacks Sedrick, rolling a 4, 6, and 6. Sedrick spends 2 Fate Points to force the NPC to re-roll. Sedrick's action is a Free Action and can be made at any point, even during the NPC's Turn.

The NPC rolls, a 3, 4, and 5. The NPC must use this roll, discarding the previous one. If Sedrick had 2 more Fate Points, he could spend them to force the NPC to re-roll again.

Languages

These example languages represent the range of communication that a character can access, be it vocal or written, based on gestures or something else entirely. All player characters can speak and write Corp (detailed below). Further languages can be acquired through Traits. GMs should feel free to give players access to minor languages through Research: Secret Knowledge (pg: 68).

At the height of their empire, the Archons not only genetically engineered races, but their cultural scientists also engineered social structures and accompanying languages. As a result, a number of drastically different languages were spoken across the old Archon Empire.

Cross-Language Communication
Use Culture Skill Rolls (pg: 45) or Research (pg: 68) for any cross-language communication.

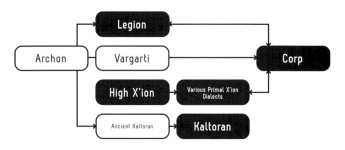

Corp

The most widely used of all languages within the Haven system, Corp is comparatively easy to learn, with short words and a limited vocabulary. It has distanced itself from its original Vargartian form by taking on a melting-pot approach to vocabulary and a simplified grammatical structure. This makes it a terrible (but often used) Corporate legal language, as even a moderately skilled lawyer can easily bend the meaning of contracts and other legal agreements written in Corp.

Many major languages within the Haven system are slowly accumulating words from and contributing words to Corp. This makes it an increasingly complicated and broadly accepted language.

All player characters have the language: Corp.

Vargartian

The language of the Corporation's original home planet has been widely out of use for over thirty years, having been largely rejected by the Corporation people as a symbol of Archon oppression and external societal control. It is still seen from time to time, and linguists with a keen eye for detail often find Vargartian words and phrases being reintroduced into Corp by savvy advertisers keen to distinguish themselves linguistically in an over-saturated Corporate market.

Archon

The language the Archons spoke during the height of their civilisation is a detail-oriented language, making it perfect for communicating technical or scientific knowledge. However, because of this, and the stigma it often has from Corporate speakers, it is not widely spoken and remains the language of the learned among the peoples of the Haven system.

Many technical manuals are written in Archon; therefore, it is an essential language for those of a scientific persuasion. The large vocabulary (of over a million distinct root-words) means that the language can elegantly communicate new and complex concepts or discoveries in any field. Archon also makes for very good poetry, especially when read aloud, owing to its melodious pronunciation.

Kaltoran

During the Great War, the Kaltorans were forced underground, where they remained for one hundred years. This spawned several unique features in their language: a touch-based component to fully express emotion, meaning, and direction, as well as severe visual communication limitations. Where Ancient Kaltoran used a full alphabet of seventy-three letters, Kaltoran uses only forty of those to spell full words. Even this limited visual format was only maintained due to the Kaltoran people's ancestral genetic memories.

The Kaltoran language is expressive, emotive and loud, often making good use of the speaker's hands in emphasis (though Kaltorans gesticulate even while speaking other languages). Kaltoran is also a useful language for explorers and archaeologists within the Haven system, as old Kaltoran ruins are very common. Although speakers of modern Kaltoran would struggle to read many of the old letters, once understood the words are still closely and obviously related.

Ancient Kaltoran

Though the "ancient" part is a slight misnomer, the Kaltorans still revere the language of their ancestors. Where modern Kaltoran is touch-oriented, loud, and emotive, Ancient Kaltoran is more harmonious, peaceful, and meditative, and it implies a deep sense of respect for places and people with most verb-forms. It is still an emotive language, and caches of engraved poetry, songs, and proverbs have been discovered across known space.

It is an extremely useful language for archaeologists to know, as many of the ruins within the Haven system are old Kaltoran cities and facilities.

Legion (and Hand Signal)

The spoken Legion language shares many similarities with Archon. Where Archon's specificity was directed towards scientific or technical descriptions, Legion has an obvious leaning towards military and tactical movements. Elaborate and verbose when needed, it is rarely poetic or figurative, favouring practicalities. It can quickly convey complex directions, especially in relation to weapons, tactics, and training.

One of the main features differentiating Legion from other Haven-system languages and dialects is that Legion features an entire sub-language, based on elaborate hand signals. Created for operational use, this short-form sign language is flexible and able to change its code structure mid-combat. This makes it almost impossible for opponents to understand what is being communicated, even if they are fluent in Legion.

High X'ion

Of all the languages in the Haven system, High X'ion, the language of the Nephilim elite and sentient Nephilim spacecraft is by far the most alien in nature. This extremely complex language makes use of a speaker's full range of available senses and entire body. Its meanings often obscured or revealed by the speaker's physical attributes, including pheromones, multiple vocal cords, posture and positioning, and many other undocumented means. Designed by the X'ion for its Nephilim army, this language was most likely made to be nearly incomprehensible to the Archons and all of their creations.

High X'ion can only be spoken by some Nephilim, though it does have a limited written form that can be understood by others.

Primal X'ion

Always crude and sharp, Primal X'ion is a junk term used for the large array of dialects the common Nephilim population speak. It has a guttural edge to it, and all of its dialects are drawn from High X'ion, although elements of Corp have begun to seep into Primal X'ion through the regular contact between the Corporation and other races.

As they change regularly, Primal X'ion dialects are chaotic and unpredictable to all except native speakers. The dialects have a wide variety of features, pronunciations, word ranges, and meanings, although amazingly the speakers of the various dialects remain able to communicate with one another due to the non-verbal, physiological aspects of Nephilim communication; these remain constant and stable.

Telepathy (Psionics)

Psionically gifted individuals are able to partially transcend all known language barriers with other psionics by directly transferring their thoughts to one another. The ability to communicate via thought to another nearby Psionic is a huge boon, but does come with limitations. A Psionic can only communicate in pictures or emotions to another Psionic within roughly fifty meters, or to a familiar Psionic mind up to approximately one kilometer away. To fully express one's self via thought, however, the Psionic must share a language with the target.

This ability is also restricted to communication between Psionics. Those without Psionic abilities "receive" nothing.

Walking the busy inner circuit of the Corporate station was a steady job, but left a lot of time for reflection.

"When we're not bored and underpaid, we are fighting and dying for the Corporates. Which does what to further the cause of our own people? Nothing! That's what!"

Decanus Augustus was used to the near-constant stream of complaint from his friend Brutus. Augustus nodded along to the flow of injustices and perceived shortcomings, adding the occasional grunt to hold up his end of the conversation.

The two turned the corridor's wide corner, its walls and ceiling filled with retail advertisements. Each had spinning, glowing, eye-catching colours and was set to headache-inducing sound-rhythms, apparently to induce enough stupidity to cause people to purchase something they didn't need from one of the multitude of crowded retail cubicles.

"... and even if it was necessary at the time, which I, for one, am not convinced about, then it should be obvious that we can easily produce a material surplus, enough to be economically viable as an independent species, instead of fighting for the Corps like they are born-again Archons..."

Without pausing or changing tone, Brutus subtly started making a secret Legion hand signal.

(We have a tail following us. 5 o'clock high, retail drone.)

"... with no respect for proper military tradition, I ask you, how..."

(Surveillance to hit where there are no patrols?) Decanus Augustus signed back.

This could be the break against the Draz Cartel they were being paid to eliminate! The scaled ridge on the back of Augustus' neck raised up as adrenaline started to be released into his system, his natural aggression responses held in check by long years of training and combat experience.

(Go to the lavatory at the next junction,) Augustus ordered. (Signal reserves helix and echo to deploy to plan gamma-3. This could be the break we need.)

"... but it sure beats a trade job..."

Skills

Skills represent a character's knowledge of and ability to interact with the universe. Characters may make Skill Rolls to determine if they succeed or fail at doing or knowing something. All Skill Rolls are made with 3d6 and modified by your Skill bonus/penalty and Description bonus/penalty. To succeed, the total of this must equal or exceed the difficulty.

Making a Skill Roll

3d6 +/- Skill +/- Description
Some Skill Rolls requires specific Tools (eg: Toolkit).

Give a Reason for Your Skill Choice

GMs may require characters to use a specific Skill, or may simply present a problem and give the players the option to use a Skill of their choice. In the latter case, the players must give reasons or justification for their Skill choices.

Skill Difficulties

Routine or Easy task: 8 or more.
Moderate task: 12 or more.
Difficult task: 16 or more.
Very Difficult task: 18 or more.

Rolls significantly above the required difficulty should produce additional positive effects (eg: completed faster than expected). Rolls significantly below should also produce negative effects (eg: activating a security alarm).

Tools and Workshops

See pg: 371 for a full list of example Tools and Workshops.

Some Skill Rolls can only be attempted if you have the right equipment (eg: to pick a mechanical lock, you will need a Mechanics Toolkit or Toolbox; you can't do it with your bare hands).

Toolkit
Eg: Wrench, bandages, or other basic tools.

Toolbox
Eg: Bank card, chemistry kit, telescope, or other practical tools.

Workshops and Dedicated Workshops
Eg: Office space, repair shop, med bay, or other work space.

Minimum Attribute Score

Some Skill Rolls, particularly for Strength-based Skills, may require a minimum Attribute score to even attempt (eg: breaking or moving an object).

Skill vs Skill

When making a Skill Roll against another player or important NPC, both characters roll, and the higher result wins.

Trained and Untrained Skills

When you create a character, select 6 Primary Skills, 2 Personal Combat Skills, and 2 Vehicle Systems to be trained in. You can always use a Skill, even if untrained; however, you must be trained in a Skill to select an associated Trait or make use of a Toolbox or Workshop.

Trained Skills grant a +1 bonus to your Skill Rolls.
Untrained Skills give a -2 penalty to your Skill Rolls.

Description Bonus or Penalty

How a character approaches a problem and how they make use of their strengths and weaknesses greatly affect the outcome of a Skill Roll, up to a +2 bonus or down to a -2 penalty.

Good Role Playing
The Description bonus should NEVER be automatically applied. This bonus is there to reward well-planned and well-described approaches to a problem.

Players should play to their strengths AND give a good description of their approach to gain the full bonus.

Attributes
If a character is playing to their Attribute strengths, then GMs should feel free to give a Description bonus (or penalty) to a Skill Roll (eg: A perceptive person finds it easier to find objects with an Awareness Skill Roll).
An Attribute should only grant a Description bonus if it is over 3. It should only grant a Description penalty if it is under 2.

Making a Skill Roll

3d6 +/- Skill +/- Description
These are for Primary Skills (mainly used outside of combat).

GM Sets the Scene and Problem
The GM describes the situation to the players, possibly suggesting a Skill choice.

Be sure to point out any major restrictions or issues (eg: they may have limited time or available tools).

Be sure to also set the mood.

Players Explain their Approach and Choose Skills
Each involved player takes a turn explaining their approach to the current situation.

The players pick Skills to use based on their approach.

Each player may select a different Skill.

Tools or Workshop
Based on a player's approach, the GM may specify if any Tools are required, such as a Toolkit, Toolbox, Workshop, or Dedicated Workshop.

GM Awards Description Bonus or Penalty
Players who put effort into describing a particularly good approach and play to their strengths should be given a +2 bonus to their Skill Roll. Playing to their weaknesses should give a -2 penalty.

Players Roll 3d6 + their Skill Bonus + Description Bonus
Each player rolls 3d6 and adds their Skill bonus (or penalty), then adds any Description bonus (or penalty).

Higher rolls are always better.

If you roll a "6" on the dice, you score a Strong Hit (pg: 42).

Strong Hits are used to make use of special abilities.

GM Describes the Outcome
After each involved player has made their Skill Roll, the GM describes the outcome of the situation, including the time taken.

High rolls of at least the difficulty should have positive results, while rolls below the difficulty may have negative results. Choice of Approach and Skill should also affect the result. For example, if two characters use different Skills and approaches to the same problem, they should get different outcomes even if their rolls are the same.

In Combat Skill Use

Primary (Everyday and Professional) Skills are usually used for out-of-combat activities. If you wish to make a Primary Skill Roll during combat, use the Prep Action (pg: 108). This will require a Combat Action (pg: 100) and let you make a Skill Roll during combat.

Some long or complicated activities may require multiple Prep Actions before they are completed.

Assisting

Players can help each other when making a Skill Roll. To Assist someone, you must make a relevant Skill Roll and get at least 10. If successful, the Assisted player gains +1 to their Skill Roll.

You may assist someone even after they've failed a roll.
Assisting a Spare Time Roll (pg: 64) costs a Spare Time Point.

A Door with and without Assistance Example

Boris has good Mechanics Skill and a Mechanics Toolbox. He tells the Game Master that he wishes to use his Mechanics Skill to unlock a door by cutting into the frame and disconnecting the hydraulics keeping it locked. The GM tells him that this is a moderately difficult task that requires a Skill Roll of at least 12 and a Mechanics Toolbox and will take at least ten minutes. The door will also be permanently unlocked unless he repairs it or rolls very well (at least a 16).

Boris rolls 3d6 and gets 8. He is Trained in this Skill, so he gains +1. He also has a Trait that grants +1 to Mechanics, and his Toolbox grants another +1 (total +3). With a total of 11, Boris has failed.

Sarah wants to assist Boris. She has a total bonus to her Mechanics Skill of −1 and needs to get a total of at least 10. Sarah rolls a 15, giving a total of 14, which is more than enough to grant Boris a +1 bonus. This brings his total to 12, so he succeeds.

Re-Attempting a Failed Roll

If you fail a Skill Roll and attempt it again within a short time, you roll at a cumulative −4 penalty.

This penalty also applies when rolling to assist, but not to Spare Time Rolls (pg: 64).

Research or Skill Roll

See pg: 68 for full Research and Secret Knowledge rules.

GMs may require a player to reach a certain amount of Research Units rather than succeed at a single Skill Roll to gain knowledge about a particularly difficult on indepth subject.

This Research can be Published or added to, as with other Research Units.

Green Nebula, Requires Research Example

The players wish to travel through a mysterious green nebula. A simple Astronomy Skill Roll informs them that their ship will be unable to travel through without severe damage.

As the players still wish to travel though the nebula, the GM requires them to gain at least 8 Units of Research on the nebula's effects on their ship. Each unit requires a Spare Time Roll of at least 12. Beau has +4 to his Astronomy Roll, requiring a roll of only 8 for each Unit. It will still take him some time to complete his Research, and he will require samples and scans of the nebula.

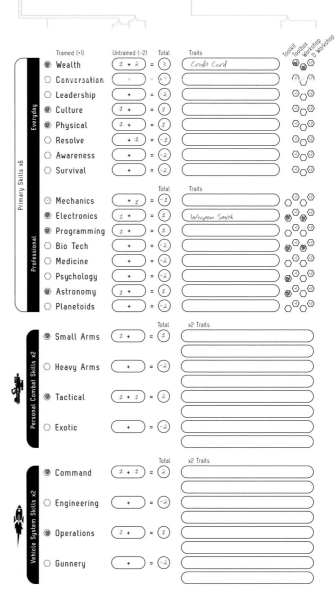

Strong Hits (Primary Skills)

Rolling a 6

When making a Skill, Vehicle System, or Attack Roll, you gain 1 Strong Hit per "6" rolled on the dice.

Each Strong Hit can be spent on a Strong Hit Option.

You may select the same Strong Hit Option multiple times, as long as you have the Strong Hits to spend.

Primary Skill Roll Strong Hit Everyone has Access to

Effort.

Combat Strong Hits Everyone has Access to

Effort, Critical Hit (pg: 88) and Critical Boost (pg: 88).

Additional Strong Hit Options

See pg: 341 for a full list of available Traits.
See pg: 358 for a full list of available Weapons.

Additional Strong Hit Options can be gained through Traits or from specific Weapons (eg: Disruptors).

Requirements

Nearly all Strong Hits have requirements to be used. The most common requirement is that you are using the correct Weapon, but you may also need to use a specific Skill.

Primary Skill (or a specific Primary Skill)

Can only be used with a Primary Skill (pg: 43) or a specific Primary Skill.

Success

Your Skill Roll must be Successful to use this Strong Hit Option.

Does not Req Success

Your Skill Roll does not have to be Successful to use this Strong Hit Option.

Not a Spare Time Roll

Cannot be used for any roll that is being used to acquire an Item or Service that costs a Spare Time Point.

Results

This is what happens if you meet all the Requirements of your desired Strong Hit Option.

Pick Thought, Conversation Strong Hit Example

Astrid's psionic abilities have grown quite strong, enabling her to pick the thoughts right from a person's mind.

Astrid strikes up a casual conversation with a local thug, hoping to find his gang's base of operations without tipping him off to the fact that she's looking for it.

Her Conversation Skill Roll results in a total of 9 (1, 2, and 6), which is not high enough to subtly gain information. But her 6 counts as a Strong Hit.

She has two Strong Hit Options she can choose to use, Effort or Pick Thought (pg: 346). She chooses to use Pick Thought, which allows her to read her Target's surface thoughts.

The GM lets her know that, while the thug speaks to her, he is not suspicious. Rather, he thinks of hanging out with friends to play computer games later that night. Astrid manages to locate an address where his friends ought to be, and she hopes that is their gang base.

Strong Hit: Effort

Pushing yourself, you reassess your situation and take advantage of a slightly different approach.

Requirements

Primary or Vehicle Skill

Can only be used with a Primary Skills (pg: 43) and Vehicle System Skill (pg: 53) Rolls.

Does not Req Success

Not a Spare Time Roll

Result: Re-Roll a Die

You may re-roll a single die (not including the die that was gave you this Strong Hit or any that have been used to cause a Strong Hit).

Name   Requirements
       (in brackets)   Result

Effort (Primary Skill, does not Req Success, not a Spare Time Roll) You may re-roll a single die from this Skill Roll.

Primary Skills

See pg: 68 for full Research rules
See pg: 370 for a full list of Tools and Workshops.

Primary Skills focus on out-of-combat tasks and are split into two categories: Everyday and Professional.

At character creation you may select any six Primary Skill to be trained in. Each Trained Skill may have a single connected Trait.

> Trained Skills grant a +1 bonus to your Skill Rolls.
> Untrained Skills grant a –2 penalty to your Skill Rolls.

Everyday Skills

These Skills are the most commonly used because they focus on your natural body, social ability, and cultural knowledge.

Wealth

Your ability to use money and barter, and your knowledge of financial values, business, and economics. Commonly used for Spare Time Rolls (pg: 64) to purchase minor items or services.

Knowledge, Ability, and Currency

Wealth is a little different from other Skills because it represents the amount of available funds your character can access, as well as their knowledge and ability.

These funds are usually Corporation Credits (pg: 274), ie: money. Your wealth might also represent other valuable items, such as precious stones or ammunition.

If you want your character to be wealthy, then you should be Trained in the Wealth Skill.

Areas of Knowledge, Ability, and Currency
» Finance (stock market, shares).
» Money (spare money to spend).
» Macroeconomics (business cycles).
» Contracts (loans, insurance, merc contracts).
» Trade (supply and demand).

Example Uses Without Tools
» Recommend an investment.
» Buy something with money.
» Know which organisations are wealthy.
» Fill out a loan application.
» Estimate the value of an item.

Example Uses with a Toolbox (Bank Card & Finance Software)
» Calculate value of investment.
» Buy something with a bank card.
» Calculate interest.
» Interpret a complex financial contract.
» Calculate the value of an item.
» Buy shares from the stock market.
» Buy something from a Data Stream.
» Calculate inflation.
» Create a legal document.
» Learn where a trade good is valued.

Example Uses with a Workshop (Office)
» Manipulate stock prices.
» Buy in bulk from a wholesaler.
» Research interstellar trade.
» Create a legal quagmire.
» Find gaps in the goods market.

Buying and Paying for Things
If you wish to purchase an item or service with money, you should make a Wealth Spare Time Roll (pg: 64).

Under 20 Credits = No Roll Required
100 Credits = 12t
500 Credits = 14t
500 Credits & Rare = 16t
1000+ Credits = 1 Resource

Wealth Spare Time Roll Example
Logan is having a friendly chat with a disgruntled Draz production worker. After a few drinks, Logan tells the GM that he wishes to pump the NPC for information on the security of the Draz factory.

The GM informs him that this will require a Conversation Skill Roll of 12. Logan rolls and gets a total of 8, far lower than what he needed.

The GM tells Logan that the NPC now knows what he is trying to do and is willing to tell Logan what he wants to know for a bribe of 500 Credits. This will require Logan to make a Wealth Spare Time Roll of at least 14 (and will cost Logan a Spare Time Point, even if he fails this roll) to see if Logan has the required funds to pay the bribe or negotiate a lower cost.

Conversation

Your knowledge of and ability to verbally communicate with NPCs in a variety of subtle ways.

Areas of Knowledge
» Diplomacy.
» Rumours.
» High Society.
» Inquiry.
» Deception (acting).

Example Uses Without Tools
» Mediate a dispute.
» Eavesdrop without being noticed.
» Be eloquent in conversation.
» Get a friendly NPC to answer a question.
» Tell a convincing lie.

Example Uses with a Toolbox (Suitcase of Clothes & Accessories)
» Run a video conference.
» Get the word on the street by wearing gang colours.
» Seduce a businessman using makeup.
» Interview using a notepad.
» Make a basic disguise.
» Interpret using a translator.
» Decipher a recorded conversation.
» Dress properly for a formal occasion.
» Create a video interview.
» Make a detailed disguise.

Example Uses with a Workshop (Event Hall)
» Host a peace conference.
» Research new social trends.
» Host a fancy party.
» Host a seminar.
» Create an alternate identity.

Example

Pulled over by a Corporation security officer for dangerous driving, Ezekiel the bounty hunter needs to talk quickly to prevent his target from getting away. The GM says this is difficult task and requires Ezekiel to make a Social Skill Roll of at least 16.

Leadership

Your ability to control and guide one or more NPCs through the force of your personality.

Areas of Knowledge
» Command.
» Interrogation.
» Oratory.
» Intimidation.
» Teamwork.

Example Uses Without Tools
» Give an order.
» Force or coerce an NPC into answering a question.
» Public speaking.
» Make a convincing threat.
» Coordinate a team.

Example Uses with a Toolbox (Rank Insignia or Interrogation Equipment)
» Requisition equipment.
» Pull rank to get answers.
» Inspire people.
» Threaten criminal proceedings.
» Create a well-coordinated plan on a map.
» Command an army.
» Torture for information.
» Give speech to a crowd.
» Intimidate a crowd.
» Organise a coordinated assault.

Example Uses with a Workshop (Conference Room)
» Host a command centre.
» Interrogation room.
» Call a press conference.
» Demonstrate military capabilities.
» Research team-combat tactics.

Example

Pirates are bombarding a Corporation colony that Mr Smith's party has been hired to defend.

In an attempt to rally the terrified civilians, Smith uses his spacecraft's loudspeakers (acting as an impromptu Leadership Toolbox) to make a rallying speech (with a +1 bonus). The GM says this is a moderately difficult task requiring a roll of a 12.

"We shall never waver! Our stand against the tide shall prevail; our loyal Child-Races are with us, and the false X'ion shall be stopped!"

– Dignified Archon speech, recorded one year into the Great War.

Culture

Your knowledge about and ability to navigate cultural customs, subgroups, laws, history, and archaeology.

Areas of Knowledge

» Customs (language).
» Governments and organisations.
» Legalese (bureaucratic and legal jargon).
» Ideologies.
» Archaeology (history).

Example Uses Without Tools

» Use an appropriate greeting.
» Know who is in authority.
» Know basics of an ideology.
» Estimate the era an object comes from.
» Identify a group by symbol or mannerisms.

Example Uses with a Toolbox (Archaeology Tools & Encyclopedia)

» Translate a phrase.
» Find out local laws.
» Understand an ideological event.
» Know of a historical event.
» Know about dangerous factions.
» Perform a ceremony.
» Understand government hierarchy.
» Look up details about an ideology.
» Remove a delicate artefact.
» Understand the workings of an organisation.

Example Uses with a Workshop (Library)

» Research traditions.
» Learn how to get a meeting with an important person.
» Break down ideological teachings.
» Research an artefact.
» Translate several pages of text.

Example

Rick wants to learn the Kaltoran Language. To do this he will have to gain 12 Units of Research (giving him the Minor Perk: Language) in the Cultural field of Kaltorans. He will also need to have access to examples of the Kaltoran Language, possibly from a tutor or by spending time amongst Kaltorans.

Physical

Your ability to endure physical hardship and utilise your strength, movement, and reflexes.

> Your character's Strength, Reflexes, and Movement Attributes may give you a +1 or +2 Description bonus (or penalty) to some rolls if you also describe your approach.

Areas of Ability
» Resilience.
» Athletics.
» Acrobatics.
» Endurance.
» Brawn.

Example Uses Without Tools
» Hold breath for a few minutes.
» One hundred push ups.
» Break your fall.
» Run for hours.
» Outwrestle an opponent.

Example Uses with a Toolbox (Climbing Gear or Sports Bag)
» Drink someone under the table.
» Climb a cliff.
» Swing over a large gap.
» Lower someone with rope.
» Hoist heavy weight with rope.
» Detox poison with water.
» Swim with flippers.
» Vault over a wall.
» Run for days with only water.
» Force something open with crowbar.

> ## Specific Environmental Equipment
> Ladders, tents, ropes, and such are not (normally) categorised as a Toolkit or Toolbox like most Tools are, as they usually have a specific function.
> These specific items can be acquired with a Spare Time Roll of 12t (see pg: 370 for a full list of available Misc Items).

Example Uses with a Workshop (Gym)
» Rehab from drugs.
» Physical retraining.
» Research martial arts.
» Hit the treadmill.
» Practice weights.

Example
Max wants to learn the Martial Arts Trait. This requires Secret Knowledge, which is gained through Research. Physical Research is ideal for learning this kind of Secret Knowledge.

Resolve

Your commitment and confidence, often motivated by a strong sense of purpose. This purpose could come from a belief in a specific cause or religion, or through mental training.

> Your character's Focus Attribute may give you a +1 or +2 Description bonus (or penalty) to some rolls if you are also descriptive in your approach.

Areas of Ability
» Bravery.
» Conviction.
» Self-reflection.
» Perseverance.
» Psionics.

Example Uses Without Tools
» Keep courage in battle.
» Resist an attempt to alter your conviction.
» Remember genetic memories.
» Push your physical or mental abilities past normal limits.
» Use a psionic power.

Example Uses with a Toolbox (Icon of Ideology or Personal Heirloom)
» Clutch your religious book for hope in a hopeless situation.
» Proselytise your ideology with passion.
» Meditate with incense.
» Resist the ideology of others.
» Channel psionic power through a focus.
» Look into the face of a horrifying creature.
» Speak with a genetic ancestor.
» Withstand extreme pain.
» Resist powerful persuasion.
» Resist a psionic power.

Example Uses with a Workshop (Sanctuary)
» Meditate on your convictions.
» Recover from mental trauma.
» Research your genetic memories.
» Retrain your mind.
» Project a psionic power.

Example
Sarah is a Kaltoran, gifted and cursed with the genetic memories of her ancestors. She wishes to draw upon these memories to learn about the Great X'ion War. The GM says that she can use Resolve to delve into her genetic memories to learn about the war from her ancestors' first-hand experiences.

Awareness

Your ability to perceive your environment through your available senses and general deductive ability. Includes your ability to hide and locate physical objects, piece together clues and identify points of interest in your environment.

> Awareness is a broad and commonly used Skill, but it has limited depth. This Skill shouldn't be used for Spare Time Rolls or Research. If a player uses Awareness to analyse a complex object or situation, they won't get many details. Instead, they'll know what Skill they should use to find the details.

> Your character's Intelligence and Perception may give you a +1 or +2 Description bonus (or penalty) to some rolls if you are also descriptive in your approach.

Areas of Ability
» Seeing.
» Hearing.
» Insight.
» Searching.
» Investigation.

Example Uses Without Tools
» Notice someone hiding.
» Overhear a conversation.
» Notice a detail.
» Look for hidden things.
» Find a clue.

Example Uses with a Toolbox (Criminology Kit)
» Take photos of people.
» Record a conversation.
» Examine a voice recording.
» Set up a hidden camera.
» Take pictures of a crime scene.
» Examine footprints.
» Bug a room with a listening device.
» Make a deduction.
» Find hidden evidence.
» Dust for fingerprints.

Example Uses with a Workshop (Forensic Lab)
» Examine evidence under microscope.
» Perform voice analysis.
» Create a wall of clues.
» Scan item for secrets.
» Conduct forensic examination.

Example
Moa is exploring a derelict Legion spacecraft and hears a strange clacking noise coming from the walls. She makes an Awareness Skill Roll to try and discern what it is. The GM tells her that the sound is mechanical in nature; something is probably broken. Moa will need to make a Mechanics Skill Roll of 12 to identify exactly what it is.

Survival

Your ability to work with and gain supplies in unconventional environments such as city slums, wild forests, barren deserts, arctic tundra, and spacecraft with limited supplies.

Areas of Knowledge
» Survival (make camp, find food/water).
» Salvaging.
» Improvising.
» Cooking.
» Tracking.

Example Uses Without Tools
» Find fresh water.
» Find a tool.
» Make a stone wrench.
» Knead dough.
» Follow footprints.

Example Uses with a Toolbox (Survival Kit)
» Start a fire in the rain.
» Lever out component with knife.
» Make a spear.
» Cook an animal on a spit.
» Track in the dark.
» Boil stagnant water.
» Disassemble a large object.
» Make Molotov cocktails.
» Cook a stew.
» Hunt game.

Example Uses with a Workshop (Kitchen)
» Make poisonous food edible.
» Ration food supply.
» Make a cake with no flour.
» Invent a new recipe.
» Cook game.

Example
Boris has set up camp deep within a forest. He wishes to gather some supplies before he moves further in. Because he has access to Cooking Equipment (Survival Toolbox), he can gather a wider range of food. If he didn't have it, he could only collect food that could be eaten raw.

Professional Skills

Mechanics

Your ability to understand, repair, and design machines: any devices with moving parts. Also covers your understanding of refined and designed materials such as alloys and synthetic polymers. Finally, it represents your structural and architectural knowledge.

Areas of Study
» Mechanical engineering (moving parts).
» Hydraulics (fluid mechanics).
» Materials science (metals, alloys, and polymers).
» Chemical engineering (reactions and processes).
» Architecture (structure and design).

Example Uses Without Tools
» Unjam a mechanical weapon system.
» Adjust flow valves correctly.
» Identify materials.
» Know how to use chemicals and reactions.
» Estimate if a support will remain standing.

Example Uses with a Toolkit (Wrench)
» Repair minor damage to a mechanical system.
» Patch hydraulic machinery.
» Detect the composition of materials.
» Detect a radiation leak.
» Build a makeshift structure.

Example Uses with a Toolbox (Toolbox)
» Repair major damage to a mechanical system.
» Replace hydraulics in a machine.
» Weld a structural joint.
» Repair major damage to a synaptronic system.
» Build a proper structure.

Example Uses with a Workshop (Repair Shop)
» Create or modify a mechanical weapon.
» Research hydraulics.
» Create an alloy or synthetic polymer.
» Build or invent a synaptronic system.
» Design a spacecraft or space station.

Example
Rachel has snuck onto the spacecraft of rival bounty hunters, hoping to disable it or slow them down.

The GM gives her two options: roll a 10 to damage their fuel intake, slowing down their launch, or roll a 16 to secretly rig their hydraulic doors to pop open after they take off. This will force them to land again in order to repair the damage, which will require some basic tools.

Electronics

Your ability to understand, repair, and design electrical devices, and your understanding of electrical signals. This skill also covers an understanding of computer hardware, cables, communication technology, and energy weapons.

Areas of Study
» Digital electronics (circuits, computer hardware).
» Electrical engineering (electricity, power cables).
» Applied physics (lasers, particle weapons).
» Telecommunication (radio, data cables).
» Optics (sensors, cameras, scopes).

Example Uses Without Tools
» Recognise a burnt circuit.
» Adjust electricity flow.
» Unjam an electronic weapon system.
» Find a good radio signal.
» Know the workings of optical devices.

Example Uses with a Toolkit (Soldering Iron & Wire Cutters)
» Make minor repairs to an electronic system.
» Patch an electrical cable.
» Configure a laser.
» Tap into a data cable.
» Attach a scope to a weapon.

Example Uses with a Toolbox (Tool Belt)
» Perform major repairs to an electronic system.
» Replace an electrical cable.
» Modify an electronic energy weapon.
» Introduce white noise to a radio frequency.
» Repair an optical device.

Example Uses with a Workshop (Technician Workshop)
» Build a computer.
» Research electricity.
» Create an electronic weapon.
» Create a communication device.
» Design ship sensors.

Example
Sarah needs to hack a computer based door lock. The GM says this can be done with a Programming Skill Roll of 14 to hack the control panel. Or, if she has some basic tools, an Electronics Skill Roll of 12 to hot wire it.

If the door is hotwired, it will be jammed open, making any hacking take a little longer. Sarah decides to hotwire the door.

Programming

Your knowledge of and ability to work with computer software and digital information, including computer locks, digital security systems, databases, firewalls, and drones.

Areas of Study
» Software engineering (programs & applications).
» Hacking (accessing protected data).
» Artificial intelligence (robotic intelligence).
» Security systems (computerised security).
» Datastream (filtering large amounts of data).

Example Uses Without Tools
» Recognise software.
» Attempt to guess a terminal password.
» Reason with an intelligent robot.
» Know the workings of security systems.
» Find something on a datastream terminal.

Example Uses with a Toolkit (Basic Terminal)
» Create a simple program.
» Hack into a computer terminal.
» Read an AI's computer code.
» Override a locked door.
» Wirelessly access a datastream with a terminal.

Example Uses with a Toolbox (Portable Computer)
» Write a computer program.
» Hack into a secure server.
» Hack into an AI.
» Override a security turret.
» Wirelessly access datastream with own terminal.

Example Uses with a Workshop (Software Lab)
» Design an operating system.
» Create a trojan virus.
» Reprogram an AI.
» Create a security system.
» Research the datastream.

Example
Lex wishes to make contact with a secretive hacker that uses many different aliases. She wishes to do this by hanging out in some little-known hacker forums. The GM says this is difficult, requiring a Programming Skill Roll of 14. She will also need access to a computer, and this task may take some time.

"Then, triangulate the signal via the nebula and done!"

"You've never hacked a thing in your life, have you?"

Bio Tech

Your ability to work with and knowledge of biological technology, genetic engineering, advanced biology, and chemistry, including implants, Bio Tech weapons, Nephilim spacecraft, and DNA.

Areas of Study
» Genetic engineering (designing life).
» Bio-weaponry (biological weapons).
» Biological systems (living technology).
» Bio-chemistry (enzymes and toxins).
» Augmentation (implants and gene splices).

Example Uses Without Tools
» Identify a genus.
» Unjam a biological weapon system.
» Configure a biological system.
» Identify strange goo.
» Recognise that a person is augmented.

Example Uses with a Toolkit (Sample Jar & Bandages)
» Take a DNA sample.
» Feed a biological weapon system.
» Bandage minor damage to a biological system.
» Take a chemical sample.
» Patch a broken implant.

Example Uses with a Toolbox (Chemistry Kit)
» Grow bacteria.
» Modify a spine launcher.
» Heal major damage to a biological system.
» Create a poison.
» Administer a gene splice.

Example Uses with a Workshop (Genetics Lab)
» Create a biological drone.
» Create a spore weapon.
» Research biological reactors.
» Research noxious substances.
» Perform implantation surgery.

Example
Simon and his team are exploring an ancient X'ion biological space warship. He is not sure if it is dead or hibernating.

The GM tells him that if he can gain access to its central nervous system or power supply, he would be able to find out. It will require a Bio Tech roll of 12, and potentially some time, to find one of these locations, then another roll of 16 with a Bio Tech Toolbox to know if it is hibernating or dead.

Medicine

Your ability to work with and knowledge of medical equipment and pharmaceuticals, as well as your ability to heal others and safely interact with the insides of living biological life forms.

> **Medicine can be used to Heal Attribute Damage (pg: 92).**

Areas of Study
» Medical care.
» Pharmacology.
» Surgery.
» Physiotherapy.
» Anatomy.

Example Uses Without Tools
» Identify a symptom.
» Recommend a medicine.
» Apply pressure to a wound.
» Relocate bone.
» Identify organ.

Example Uses with a Toolkit (Bandages, Painkillers, & Pocketbook)
» Identify a common illness from the pocketbook.
» Administer a painkiller.
» Stop bleeding by bandaging.
» Make a sling.
» Create a splint.

Example Uses with a Toolbox (First Aid Kit)
» Give medical attention.
» Administer medicine.
» Remove a bullet.
» Restrain neck movement.
» Amputate a limb.

Example Uses with a Workshop (Medical Bay)
» Give extended medical care.
» Synthesise medicine.
» Perform complex surgery.
» Conduct physical rehabilitation.
» Research anatomy.

> ## Sharing Spare Time Points
> You can share Spare Time Points (pg: 64)
> for Healing Rolls (pg: 92).

Example
Sarah has fallen sick from a common stomach virus after eating bad food from a Nephilim market.
Maximus has a Medicine Toolbox with some helpful drugs that could cure her. As they have good equipment, this First Aid Skill Roll is not difficult and only requires a 10.

Psychology

Your ability to understand the mind, such as recognizing the motivations of others, diagnosing and treating mental conditions, understanding and utilising psionic powers, and understanding biological technologies and systems which are neurological in nature, commonly called synaptronics.

Areas of Study
» Psionchology (psions and their powers).
» Psychology (psyche).
» Psychiatry (mental conditions).
» Synaptronics (biological electronics).
» Behavioural Science (behaviour of individuals).

Example Uses Without Tools
» Recognise a psionic power.
» Recognise a mental state (depression, mania, etc).
» Calm an agitated individual.
» Recognise damage to a synaptronic system.
» Gain insight into motivation and intentions.

Example Uses with a Toolkit (Synaptronic "Screwdriver")
» Detect psionic gene.
» Treat mental condition with counselling.
» Diagnose a mental condition (post-traumatic stress, bipolar disorder, etc).
» Repair minor damage to a synaptronic system.
» Detect lies during interrogation.

Example Uses with a Toolbox (Sedatives and Anti-Depressants)
» Inhibit the psionic powers of a restrained individual.
» Perform hypnotic therapy.
» Treat a mental condition with medicine.
» Repair major damage to a synaptronic system.
» Detect hidden agendas during interrogation.

Example Uses with a Workshop (Neural Analysis Lab)
» Research psionics.
» Recondition behaviour (shock therapy).
» Perform brain surgery.
» Build or invent synaptronic systems.
» Extract information during interrogation.

Example
Theodore has formed a bitter professional rivalry with another merchant who keeps getting the better of him. He wishes to figure out his rival's next move so he can counter it or cut in front of him.

The GM says this will take some time to figure out, and will require at least 2 Cultural Research Units on his rival's trade patterns. Theodore will need access to information to Research and must spend Spare Time Points.

Astronomy

Your knowledge of celestial objects, phenomena, stars, and Ley Lines. Also includes your knowledge of and ability to use astronomical equipment.

Areas of Study
» Navigation.
» Cosmology.
» Ley Lines.
» Stellar Science.
» Gravitation.

Example Uses Without Tools
» Navigate in space by following constellations.
» Understand space phenomena.
» Know about Ley Lines.
» Know star categories.
» Place a spacecraft into geostationary orbit.

Example Uses with a Toolkit (Hand Telescope)
» Estimate a location in space.
» Identify space phenomena.
» Notice Ley Line distortions.
» Identify a star's category.
» Estimate orbits.

Example Uses with a Toolbox (Telescope)
» Calculate distance from a star.
» Determine the properties of a nebula.
» Detect a Ley Line.
» Detect incoming solar flares.
» Calculate escape velocity.

Example Uses with a Workshop (Observatory)
» Perform interstellar navigation.
» Examine a black hole.
» Research Ley Lines.
» Study the composition of a star.
» Research satellites.

Example

An annoying nebula has been sucking all the energy from Sarah's spacecraft, threatening to leave the crew stranded in dead space.

Desperate to gain some insight into this phenomenon, and with no astronomical equipment available, Sarah uses her Electronics Toolbox to analyse her spacecraft's reactor. The GM says this is a difficult Astronomy Skill Roll of 16 because she does not have ideal equipment.

Planetoids

Your knowledge of planetary bodies, as well as atmospheres, flora, fauna, minerals, habitats and advanced weather effects. Also includes your knowledge of and ability to work with mining, terra forming equipment, and asteroids.

Areas of Study
» Flora and fauna (plants and animals).
» Geology (minerals and mountains).
» Meteorology (weather and climate).
» Ecosystems (habitats and forests).
» Magnets (Electro-Gravity).

Example Uses Without Tools
» Know plants and animals.
» Know types of stones.
» Predict the next few hours of weather.
» Understand ecosystems.
» Configure artificial gravity.

Example Uses with a Toolkit (Prospecting Pick)
» Take plant cuttings.
» Collect a rock sample.
» Take a rainwater sample.
» Plant a tree.
» Identify a habitat.

Example Uses with a Toolbox (Geology & Zoology Kit)
» Identify animal species.
» Examine geological properties.
» Predict tomorrow's weather.
» Create a small earth ecosystem.
» Assess ecosystem health.

Example Uses with a Workshop (Surveyor's Lab)
» Research a new animal species.
» Analyse mineral composition.
» Analyse a storm's properties.
» Research an ecosystem.
» Research Electro-Gravity weapons.

Example

Hraks has spotted a strange, orange bear-like creature. This area of the wilderness is known for violent animals, and she wants to know if she should be cautious of this particular creature. The GM says this task is moderately difficult and requires a Planetoid Skill Roll of at least 10.

Combat Skills

These skills are used in combat and split into two categories: Vehicle System Skills and Personal Combat Skills.

At character creation, you may select two Vehicle System and Personal Combat Skills to be trained in. Each Trained Skill may have two connected Traits.

Trained Skills grant a +1 bonus to any connected Weapons To Hit. Untrained Skills give a -2 penalty to any connected Weapons To Hit.

Attack & System Rolls

All Personal Combat Skills increase (or decrease if Untrained) the To Hit Roll of the respective Weapons (eg: +1 Small Arms increase all Attack Rolls with Small Arms Weapons by 1).

All Vehicle System Skills increase (or decrease) your ability to successfully pass a relevant spacecraft System Roll (eg: +1 Command increases your chance to pass a Command System Roll by 1).

Personal Combat Skills

See pg: 78 for full Attack Roll rules.

Your ability to perform different tactical actions in combat and skill at using different types of weapons.

Small Arms
Your ability to use common firearms in combat.

Small Arms Weapons:
Pistols
Submachine Guns
Rifles
Assault Rifles
Shotguns

Heavy Arms
Your ability to use common large weapons and explosives in combat. Also includes gun emplacements and spacecraft weapons used in personal Combat situations.

Heavy Arms Weapons:
Grenades
Grenade Launchers
Satchels
Cannons
Auto Cannons
Chemical Throwers

Tactical
Your ability to use common combat drones, tactical weapons, combat computers and tactical Actions in combat (including your ability to Stealth).

You can use this skill to request GM advice during combat on a limited basis. It may also be used for some large-scale combat situations, such as city sieges, where there are too many actors to play out everything in the scene.

Tactical Weapons:
Your Mind
Targeting Lasers
Tactical Computers
Turrets
Swarm Drones
Combat Drones
Assault Drones
Electro-Gravity Gauntlets
Disruptor Rifles

Tactical Actions:
Stealth

Exotic
Your ability to use uncommon weapons, personal racial powers, personally made weapons, and Melee Skill in combat.

Exotic Weapons:
Exotic includes all weapons not covered by other categories, including Melee Weapons, Prototype Weapons, and many Drones.

The resounding cracka-crack of the gauss rifle came a half second behind the dulled impacts on Brenton's Octanto™ Shielding. "Damnit!"

The red Legion forms across the narrow valley were using an awful lot of ammunition, he thought while pulling on the reload valve of his particle cannon, hearing the distinctive whoosh of the air intake. "Now, come to papa…" Nudging the business end of the cannon around the bullet-pitted rock, Brenton slowly tightened his finger on the trigger as he took aim.

An overly warm gun muzzle was placed against his head, still smoking slightly from recent fire.

"Cease fire, Corp." came the accented Legion voice.

They'd been distracting him from the scout… Damn.

Vehicle System Skills

See pg: 155 for full Spacecraft Combat rules.
See pg: 168 for full Spacecraft System Roll rules.

Your ability to use spacecraft Vehicle Systems and Weaponry in a combat situation.

Trained Skills grant a +1 bonus to any connected System Roll or Weapon To Hit.
Untrained Skills give a -2 penalty to any connected System Roll or Weapon To Hit.

Command

Your ability to pilot a spacecraft, coordinate crew, and direct fighters.

Command Weapons:
Boarding Parties
Bomber Squads
Combat Squads
Sentries

Engineering

Your ability to repair, regulate power, and recharge spacecraft shields in a combat situation.

Operations

Your ability to use spacecraft sensors and direct warheads.

Operations Weapons:
Swarm Warheads
Missiles
Rockets
Torpedoes
Mines

Gunnery

Your ability to reload, unjam, and fire spacecraft batteries.

Gunnery Weapons:
Point Defences
Blasters
Burst Batteries
Artillery

"I'm not addicted to Corporation fuel... but my ship is."

- Logan, Captain of the Astral Star.

Acquisition

Every character has access to different types of resources, whether it is money, materials, personal skill, free time, or friends. Resources, Influence, and Spare Time Points represent your access to these, and you'll use these to acquire equipment, social perks, services, and spacecraft.

Overview

Distributing Resources and Influence

Your Resources and Influence are distributed, not spent. Do not decrease your Resources or Influence when you acquire, lose, or change your equipment or spacecraft. They merely limit the total number of points you can have distributed at any one time.

The total cost of your Items can never exceed your Current Resources or Influence (see below).

Spending Spare Time Points

Unlike Resources and Influence, Spare Time Points are spent. Each time you attempt to acquire an item or service that costs a Spare Time Point, you must reduce your Spare Time Points by 1. This is not regained, even if you fail to acquire or lose the item or service.

To acquire an item or service that costs a Spare Time Point, you must make a Spare Time Roll (pg: 64).

Maximum and Current

Your Maximum Resources and Influence both equal your character's Level (pg: 32). You may never have more the 10 Spare Time Points (pg: 64) at once.

The amount of Trade Goods you can have is only limited by your Cargo space (pg: 150). There is no limit to the amount of Research Units you can have.

As your Maximum Resources and Influence go up, your Current Resources and Influence do not go up. You can only gain Resources and Influence by in-game actions (eg: Going on NPC missions, selling Trade Goods, or publishing Research).

Gaining

Resources are often gained by completing NPC missions or selling Trade Goods (pg: 66).

Influence is increased by gaining the favour and appreciation of NPCs, often through NPC missions done out of goodwill or through publishing Research (pg: 68).

Spare Time Points are gained at the start of each game session, as a reward for good role playing or as a minor reward.

Trade Goods are often purchased or looted. Research is gained in a similar way to Trade Goods.

Loot

Looting your defeated foes and stealing from your enemies is often a staple source of income for many mercenaries and explorers.

Money and Small Valuables

Characters gain a single Trade Box (pg: 66) or Spare Time Point (pg: 64) if they acquire a small amount of money or valuables.

Equipment

Characters can keep any equipment they find, but at the end of the session the total Cost of their equipment cannot exceed their Current Resources or Influence. Characters must decide what equipment they will keep.

> Any looted items may be turned into Trade Goods (pg: 66).
> A rough guide is 1 Trade Box per 4 Weight of Items.

Weapons and Outfits with Modifications
Characters may keep any Modifications on an item they loot, no additional Spare Time Rolls are required.

Items that cost a Spare Time Point
Can be freely kept, no Spare Time Roll needs to be made.

Ammunition

Found Ammunition can be used to regain a GM specified amount of Clips or Ammunition (pg: 122).

Large Amounts of Goods

Acquire an appropriate amount and type of Trade Good (pg: 66). Need to have means of moving and storing.

Large Amounts of Money

Acquire Resources. Should be particularly rare, as most large amounts of money are held in vaults, guarded banks or stored electronically.

Scientific Data

Acquire Research Units. Well documented, scientific data is rare and difficult to acquire.

Acquisition Types

Gained from In-Game Actions.
Eg: Completing a mission, looting, or selling Trade Goods.

Resources
Your ability to purchase, maintain, and cover the upkeep expenses of your Weapons and Outfit.
Often gained by completing lucrative missions, selling Trade Goods, or securing sponsorships, investments, or simply large sums of money.

Influence
Your ability to purchase, maintain, and cover the upkeep expenses of your (and possibly your group's) spacecraft. Can also represent how much respect and power you have with an NPC group.
Commonly gained by doing favours (often without payment) for a group of people, gaining access to spacecraft fuel or components.

Spare Time Points
Spent on acquiring minor objects and services, making equipment modifications and producing Trade Goods or Research.
Gained at the start of each session, for good role playing and through loot.
You cannot have more than 10 unused Spare Time Points at once.

Trade Goods
Crates of valuable goods that require storage space. Often traded up, until the owner is ready to sell to the right buyer.
Usually purchased from a merchant (Spare Time Roll) or looted from defeated foes.

Research
Your access to rare knowledge of technology or the universe.
Used to invent Technologies and improve your ability to maintain your spacecraft.
Publishing can give you fame, respect, and other perks.
Usually gained through personal studies.

Resources

See pg: 32 for full Level rules.
See pg: 66 for full Trade Goods rules.
See pg: 113 for full Equipment rules.
See pg: 358 for full Weapons list.

Resources is a broad representation of how much personal equipment your character is able to maintain. Also, personal combat scales in difficulty with your Current Resources (pg: 56).

Resources are used to acquire personal Weapons and an Outfit. The Resources requirement of an item is listed as its "Cost".

The way you acquire and maintain equipment depends on your character's skills and abilities. Resources is not necessarily just money but also the ability to maintain your own equipment.

For instance, a wealthy Corporate has more money at his disposal: if some of his equipment is damaged, he simply buys replacements or already has spares on his spacecraft. In contrast, a Kaltoran mechanic may repair his own equipment, salvaging replacement parts to make it last as long as it can. Both the Corporate and Kaltoran may have the same Current Resources.

Gaining Resources

Resources are primarily gained by doing NPC missions for payment, selling Trade Goods (pg: 66), or acquiring large amounts of cash.

You cannot increase your Current Resources beyond your Maximum Resources. Any gains above your Maximum Resources are lost.

Losing Resources

Selling or losing an item that costs Resources does not reduce your Current Resources.

Your Current Resources can only be reduced by a major event that you failed to prevent, such as losing a fight to an NPC who strips you of everything or a calculated attack on your income. Even events such as these may only reduce your Current Resources by one or two, at most.

Easy Life Bank Co. 'Making money and life easy'™

Personal Account:
000 000 000 000 009 123 . 121

"Can an ATM be condescending? It doesn't need to include all those zero's... god, now I am thinking about getting a loan. Damn I hate the Corporation! Sneaky bastards even work their magic into a simple ATM credit display".

– Rachel Swagger.

Allotting Resources

Resource points are distributed and not reduced when acquiring items that cost Resources.

At the end of each session, add up the total Resources cost of all your items. If it exceeds your Current Resources, you must pick items to keep with a total Resources cost equal to or less than your Current Resources. In this way, your character may temporarily use salvaged items, but then they must decide which items to keep and maintain and which to discard or turn into Trade Goods (see Loot rules, pg: 54; 1 Trade Box per 4 Weight).

Sharing Resources

When a player character gains Current Resources, they may be distributed between any player characters immediately. However, Current Resources may not be shared or exchanged at any later time.

Characters may share Equipment that cost Resources, but only temporarily for a session or two.

Max Resources   Lv +2 + ②= ⑧ (Merchant)

Current Res

Buying Rifle and Outfit, Resources Example

Derrick is Level 5 (Maximum Resources 7) and has 4 Current Resources. He purchases a Rifle (2 Resources) and armour (2 Resources), allotting all of his Current Resources.

If he wishes to acquire any more items that cost Resources, he must either increase his Current Resources or get rid of his Rifle or armour.

Changing Weapons, Resources Example

Brett has 7 Current Resources, 4 allotted for armour and 3 for a SMG. He wishes to change his SMG to an Assault Rifle (3 Resources). He has a few options available to him:

He could simply get rid of his SMG and buy an Assault Rifle.

If Brett managed to loot or steal an Assault Rifle (see pg: 54 for full Loot rules), he could keep his SMG until the end of the session, when it would convert into a Trade Box. The Assault Rifle he found would keep any Modifications that cost Spare Time Points (pg: 64).

Gaining Resources Example

Hraks has a Maximum Resources of 12 but only 8 Current Resources. She can gain 4 Current Resources before she hits her limit.

She has many options available to her. She could find a paying mission from an NPC, attack pirates and collect bounties, turn pirate and attack NPCs, or she could buy and sell Trade Goods (pg: 66).

She decides to try combining trading with bounty hunting. She purchases some Trade Goods and tries to find a mission hunting pirates in the same area she wishes to sell her Trade Goods.

Losing Resources Example

After a disastrous fight, Andrew and Qwarx have been captured by Draz pirates and are being held in a makeshift prison.

Eventually they manage to break their bonds and overpower the guards. But they are faced with a dilemma: All of their equipment is being held by the pirate captain. If they choose to take the safe option and leave their equipment the GM informs them they will both lose 1 Current Resource and will need to acquire new equipment. If, however, they manage to regain their equipment and overpower the pirates, they may be able to loot enough valuables to gain Current Resources.

Andrew and Qwarx choose to abandon their equipment and leave, as recovering it would just be too dangerous.

Influence

See pg: 32 for full Level rules.
See pg: 68 for full Research rules.
See pg: 142 for full Spacecraft Creation rules.

Influence is an abstract representation of a character's influence with groups of people, as well as their access to spacecraft resources such as fuel or munitions. Also, spacecraft combat scales in difficulty with your Current Influence (pg: 58).

Run on More than Just Fuel and Sweat
Spacecraft are incredibly complex and ancient machines. They require constant maintenance, fuel, and access to secure landing facilities.

This makes it almost a necessity to be sponsored by, or at the very least supported by, many more people than it takes to just crew the craft.

Influence is used to acquire and Upgrade spacecraft.
Players may combine their Influence into one pool to acquire a single large spacecraft.

Gaining Influence
Influence is primarily gained by working for NPCs without direct physical payment, publishing Research (pg: 68), or gaining spacecraft fuel, components, or parts.

Your Current Influence can never exceed your Maximum Influence.

Perks and Complications
As you gain Current Influence, you also gain Perks (pg: 60) and Complications (pg: 62) related to your in-game choices.

You'll only gain Perks and Complications at appropriate times in the story, but not before you have the required Influence.

Just thinking of his boss made him instinctively self-check his current apparel, glancing subtly at his cheaply made but expensive-looking suit, with its near-perfect OctantoTM brand tint, just like the far more expensive suit of almost the same cut and shape. Possibly made in the same factory.

It may have cost a fraction of the real thing, but the credits-to-impression ratio was quite good with other Corporates. If he'd wanted to impress Kaltorans, though, he'd best just rip holes in it and cover it in soot… Primitives…

– Theodore Bolt.

Losing Influence
Current Influence can be lost by disappointing or doing harm to NPCs who have previously given you Influence.

Perks and Complications
These are lost if your Current Influence drops below the required amount.

Allotting Influence
Current Influence can be allotted to acquire or upgrade spacecraft. As with Resources (pg: 56), Current Influence is allotted, not spent.

Sharing Influence
Current Influence can be combined to acquire a spacecraft, but it cannot be shared with others for the purpose of gaining Perks or Complications.

Max Influence   Lv +2 + (0) = (6)   (Membership)

Current Inf   ⬡⬡⬡⬡⬡⊗⬡⊗¹⁰ ⬡⬡⬡⬡⊗⬡⬡⊗²⁰ ⬡⬡⬡⬡⊗⬡⬡⊗³⁰

Perks _____ Contact: Mercenary "Nick Hathgore"_____

Complications _____

Maximum and Current Influence, Example

Geordie has 16 Maximum Influence. He has only 14 Current Influence, gained from many different jobs and some Research Publications. He may still gain an additional 2 Current Influence through further his in-game actions.

Gaining Influence, Example

A small group of mercenaries are resupplying their food supplies from a small Kaltoran logging settlement on Mishpacha when it is attacked by a horde of Feral Nephilim.

After fighting off the invaders, the local leaders thank them and try to convince the mercenaries to help them destroy the Feral tribe. However, they have very little to pay the party.

If they were to work for payment, they would only gain 4 Trade Boxes of wood. If they worked for free, though, surely the leaders would be thankful and would tell other Kaltorans, increasing the Current Influence of each player character by one.

Losing Influence, Example

Michele and her team have been doing a lot of mercenary work for the Legion High Command. Most of the group's Current Influence has come from them.

If they were to ever take any hostile action towards Legion High Command or their interests, though, they might lose some of their Current Influence.

Combining Influence, Example

Each member of Eric's group has 5 Current Influence, if they combine together, they can acquire a spacecraft that requires up to 25 Influence.

Big Ships, GM Game Style Example

James is the GM. He wants to run a Space Opera game, with the players in a big spacecraft. He lets his players know that he will be giving out lots of Influence and very little Resources. He will also be increasing each character's Maximum and Starting Influence by 5. This will make NPC spacecraft more dangerous (pg: 302).

Perks

Making friends and Publishing Research (pg: 69) grants Perks. Your choice of Perk must reflect your character's in-game actions.

You may change a Perk by using a Level up Retro (pg: 32).

Each Perk may only be selected once.

Gain a Minor Perk at Influence: 5, 10 and 20.
Gain a Moderate Perk at Influence: 15 and 25.
Gain a Major Perk at Influence: 30

Creating Perks

GMs should feel free to invent new Perks. Be careful to not make a Perk that is too close to another or imbalanced.

Research

When you achieve 12 or 16 Units of Research (pg: 68) in a single area, you may receive a Minor Perk related to that research.

Kaltoran Hero, Thematic Perk Selection Example

Rachel and her group have been working a lot with her Kaltoran Swagger family and have become quite popular with them, gaining Current Influence. Rachel has 16 Current Influence and wishes to select Perks (2 Minor and 1 Moderate) to reflect her relationship with the Swagger family.

For her first Minor Perk, she selects Minor Contact: Uncle David Swagger. Rachel and her group once saved David's mechanic business from a Draz cartel looking to extort him. In gratitude, Uncle David will always be willing to help Rachel out in any way that he can, granting +1 to any Mechanics Spare Time Rolls that Rachel might make around him.

For her second Minor Perk, Rachel chooses Language: Ancient Kaltoran. Rachel has always had faint genetic memories of her ancestral language, and with the help of her family she has managed to fine-tune this knowledge.

For her Moderate Perk, Rachel chooses Additional Income. Her family have helped her greatly, offering her spare parts, munitions, and any extra Credits that she might need.

Minor Perks

You have just started to reap some minor benefits from your new acquaintances or employment. More often than not, these are geographically localised perks.

Language

You have learnt a new language from your interactions with your newfound allies. See pg: 36 for more information on Languages.

- » Ancient Kaltoran
- » Archon
- » Corp
- » High X'ion
- » Primal X'ion
- » Kaltoran
- » Legion (and Hand Signal)
- » Vargartian

Minor Access

You have been trusted with access to a non-public space such as an apartment, warehouse, workspace, or other small facility.

- » Gain 1 Cargo space of room.
- » You must make any required Spare Time Rolls to install a Workshop into this space.
- » You may combine this with the Moderate Access Perk or the Major Access Perk, adding the available Cargo space together. Also, you may combine your Cargo space with that of other player characters.

Minor Contact

You are friends with someone who is willing to help you out. This friend is often restricted to a single geographical area, and you must travel to them if you wish to make use of their skills.

- » Pick a single Primary Skill. You gain +1 to all Spare Time Rolls with this Skill when you are with your contact.
- » This bonus may only be used once per session.

Minor Rank

You have earned your place in your organisation by proving yourself in the field. While you have very little authority to order others around, your superiors acknowledge you as someone to be respected and trusted.

- » One Companion Costs 1 less Current Resources.

"OK, the Orbital Bombardment Guidance Laser is ready, but I'm aiming by eye, so I may have to walk my shots."

- Tiro, Legion weapons inventor, scaring his allies.

Moderate Perks

You're beginning to find your place within society, and you are now respected and known by many. These benefits often travel with you and are rarely limited to a geographical area.

Additional Income

Whether by increased wages, or by careful management of, investment in, or better access to your social circle, you acquire and maintain more equipment.

» +1 Maximum Resources.

Moderate Access

You have been trusted with access to a non-public space such as a safe house, warehouse, or clinic.

» Gain 3 Cargo space of room.
» You must make any required Spare Time Rolls to install a Workshop into this space.
» You may combine this with the Minor Access Perk or the Major Access Perk, adding the available Cargo space together. Also, you may combine your Cargo space with that of other player characters.

Moderate Contact

You have earned the respect and trust of a singular gifted individual or a moderately sized group. They will reliably help you when they can and can be easily reached from many different locations.

» Pick a single Primary Skill. You gain +1 to all Spare Time Rolls with this Skill when you are with your contact.
» This bonus may only be used twice per session.

Moderate Rank (Requires Minor Rank)

By jumping through political hoops and proving yourself to your colleagues, you have officially progressed your standing and authority. You can direct your minors, but you will be expected to set an example. You will also be consulted about wider concerns. Be careful not to lose the trust of your superiors or abuse your power if you wish to progress further.

» All of your Companions gain +2 Hit.
» You must have a Minor Rank to choose this Perk.

> "You only get through this door as a friend to the people who pay me, or as a corpse. Get lost."
>
> – Embrace Family door guard on Mishpacha.

Major Perks

You are a person of political influence. You cannot shape nations but can surely influence some major areas. Often localised to a planet or wide area.

Major Access

You have a private residence on a planet, space station, or large facility.

» Gain 4 Cargo space of room with a Dedicated Workshop of your choice.
» You are not required to make a Spare Time Roll to install this Dedicated Workshop. It may be changed with a Spare Time Roll.
» You may combine this with the Minor Access Perk or the Moderate Access Perk, adding the available Cargo space together. Also, you may combine your Cargo space with that of other player characters.

Destiny

It is clear that you have an important place in the sector; you have an aura of destiny about you.

» +1 Fate

Major Contact

You are a trusted and respected colleague of a prominent leader within your sphere of influence. This gives you access to extensive inside information, and you can direct them through your relationship.

» +2 Maximum Influence.
» Gain +2 to all Spare Time and Skills Rolls when making use of your Contact.

Major Rank (Requires Moderate Rank)

After extensive commitment to duty, you are now a prominent leader within your organisation. You can direct the actions of many people, and you have near-unlimited access to your organisation's plans.

» Either all of your Companions gain +1 Body OR a single Companion gains +2 Bodies.
» You must have a Moderate Rank to choose this Perk.

Complications

See pg: 309 for full Complications rules.

As your influence grows, so too will your burdens and enemies. Choose Complications that reflect your in-game actions and story.

» May NOT be changed with a Level up Retro (pg: 32).
» May ONLY be removed or changed through in-game actions.
» A Complication may be selected multiple times.

Gain a Complication at 9, 19, and 29 Current Influence.

When a Complication would severely affect you, gain a Fate Point (pg: 35) until the end of the game session.

You can only gain 1 Fate Point each session for each of your Complications.

Nephilim Prejudice, Gain a Fate Point Example

Hrax is a Nephilim, and as such she is subject to prejudice from NPC Legion and Kaltorans. Hrax finds herself stranded and out of supplies while on a Kaltoran settlement and wishes to make a Spare Time Roll to buy supplies. The GM rules that the local Kaltorans hate the Nephilim for their past war crimes against the Kaltoran people, giving Hrax a -2 penalty on her rolls when dealing with Kaltorans.

She fails her roll by 1 and may be forced to steal supplies. As she would have passed her Spare Time Roll without the -2 penalty, the GM grants her a Fate Point because her Complication has caused her significant problems. Had she passed the roll, the GM would not have awarded her a Fate Point.

Creating New Complications

GMs can invent new Complications.

Gaining Complications Through In-Game Actions

Character can gain additional Complications from their in-game actions. However, these should be rare and should only affect one character at a time. For example, if a Hunted: Bounty would apply to multiple characters, then it should not count as a Complication; it is just part of your story.

When a character voluntarily reduces their Fate Points to avoid Death (pg: 90), this is a great time to give out a Complication (eg: Lost Limb).

Optional: Start with a Complication

All characters may start with a single Complication.

Daniel Omni laid back in the hammock strung between the reactor cooling feeds of the slow freighter Solar Savant, closing his eyes for what seemed to be the first time in days. Memories kept surfacing of the arm being torn out by that monster's teeth, leaving bloody threads of flesh dangling out the elbow. Not his arm, his grandmother's, but the remembered pain was there – and the years of living as a crippled young woman.

Below, a curtly posh voice, carrying both sophistication and a distinct whining quality, interrupted his restless doze.

"Stop slacking off! I'm paying you good Credits, Kaltoran!"

The Corp. Damnit. Daniel opened his eyes to a mere slit, peering down towards the Corp in the nifty suit and pinched face, with his sidekick: a creepy Nephilim assistant, standing silently nearby, with those familiar nightmare-inducing eyes and the teeth his grandmother always remembered.

He heaved himself out of his nook, groaning at the tired ache in his muscles as he clambered down the irregular handholds that the cooling feeds provided.

"Engine room is fine… Sir," he threw out sarcastically.

The Corporate peered around the clutter-strewn space. Seahemp washing lines with hand-beaten metal pegs, a tattered hand-woven hammock, and a jury-rigged hotplate over the heat exhaust met his critical eye.

"I distinctly remember assigning you quarters with my assistant, Kaltoran. Get your gear stowed and this slovenly mess cleaned up!"

"Damn Corps," thought Daniel. This conversation had the potential to become very difficult. But his keen diplomatic skills knew just how to defuse it.

"Reduce my pay by ten Credits a day if you…"

"… done!"

Enemy

You have made a dangerous enemy who holds lethal intent towards you. This enemy is often from within your own social circle, or might be a (possibly indirect) victim of your actions.

Your enemy is skilled and cunning, with well-defined motivations, but is not suicidal or reckless. They will often know what equipment you like to carry and your weaknesses.

» Your Enemy should be aware of all (or most) of your Traits, equipment and Attributes.
» They will most likely have Equipment and Traits that counter yours during combat.
» They may cause you trouble outside of combat.
» You only gain a Fate Point from this Complication if your Enemy reduces one of your Attributes to -0 or below.

Enemy No Longer a Threat
If your Enemy dies, or if their ability to harm you is completely nullified, then select a new Complication.

Bounty

You have a large bounty on your head, attracting the attention of more enemies. Be careful of not only underworld havens, but also of anybody whose bank balance is running a little low.

» Your GM may choose to increase the difficulty of a combat by adding a Skilled opponent (granting you a Fate Point).

Prejudice

A group of people are prejudiced against you, whether a faction, race, organisation, or other grouping. Individuals within this group may not hold this prejudice at the GM's discretion.

» -2 to all Leadership, Conversation, and Spare Time Rolls when interacting with someone who is prejudiced against you.

Reputation

Through a single prominent event or through many rumours, you've made a reputation for yourself. Unfortunately, this reputation is not a helpful one. People will make presumptions about you, often inhibiting your progress or giving unwanted attention.

More importantly, your enemies will be able to discover your location if you move in populated areas, and they can gain information on your equipment.

» NPCs are far more likely to remember you.
» Antagonistic NPCs are far more likely to discover your location when you move in populated areas.
» You may suffer -2 to Leadership, Conversation, and Spare Time Rolls when interacting with someone aware of your Reputation.

Condition

With GM permission, you may gain a Psychological Condition (pg: 73).

Spare Time Points

See pg: 38 for full Skill Roll rules.
See pg: 116 for full Modification rules.
See pg: 370 for full Misc Items and Services list.

Spare Time Points represent roughly what your character does with their spare time. This includes but is not limited to shopping for small items, haggling over Trade Goods (pg: 66), and Researching (pg: 68).

Gaining Spare Time Points

> ### Each player gains 1 Spare Time Point
> ### at the start of each game session.

Spare Time Points can also be awarded by the GM for good role playing or looting very minor valuable items (eg: loose change).

Losing Spare Time Points

Spare Time Points cannot be lost.

Spending Spare Time Points (Spare Time Roll)

> ### Cost = t
> Items, services, and Skill Rolls that list "t" after their Cost or requirement (eg: Cost: 12t) require a Spare Time Roll to acquire.
>
> ### Cost Multiple Spare Time Points
> A multiplier before a number with "t" (eg: Cost: 2x 8t) means that acquiring that item or service requires that many successful Spare Time Rolls (eg: 2 rolls of 8).

Acquiring an Item or Service that costs a Spare Time Point requires a Spare Time Roll, which is very similar to a normal Skill Roll (pg: 38). To attempt a Spare Time Roll, though, you must spend one Spare Time Point.

Describe how you are going about it and choose a relevant skill (eg: Wealth for a purchase). The GM may give you a Description bonus or penalty (up to +/- 2) based on your approach and skill choice. If you roll at least the number required (eg: an 8t item requires a total roll of at least 8), you succeed. If not, you fail to acquire that item or service.

Re-Attempting a Failed Spare Time Roll

Unlike for Skill Rolls, you do not suffer a penalty for re-attempting a Spare Time Roll. However, you must spend another Spare Time Point.

> ### Fate Point Re-Roll
> Spending a Fate Point (pg: 35) to re-roll a Spare Time Roll does not cost you an additional Spare Time Point.

Assisting a Spare Time Roll

Assisting (pg: 40) another character who is attempting a Spare Time Roll will cost you 1 Spare Time Point.

Sharing Spare Time Points

Spare Time Points may only be shared for Healing (pg: 92) and Repair (pg: 164) Rolls. Points shared in this way must be used right away.

Sharing Tools

Only one character may use a specific Toolkit or Toolbox for Spare Time Rolls per session. Multiple characters may use the same Workshop or Dedicated Workshop.

Maximum Spare Time Points

You may never have more than 10 unused Spare Time Points at any one time. Discard any additional points.

Acquiring a Flesh Rejuvenator, Spare Time Roll Example

Both Rachel and Theodore wish to acquire a Flesh Rejuvenator (pg: 139). This requires a Spare Time Roll of 14, and they each must spend a Spare Time Point.

Theodore wishes to buy his Flesh Rejuvenator. He needs to make a Wealth Spare Time Roll of 14 and find someone who will sell him one (eg: a shop).

Rachel wishes to build her Flesh Rejuvenator. This is a little more complicated as Rachel needs access to materials to make an appropriate Skill Roll.

Rachel has access to a several Trade Boxes of Bio Tech Weapons. The GM says she can salvage a few parts off these to construct her Flesh Rejuvenator by making a Medicine Spare Time Roll of 14.

Spare Time Points

Spare Time Roll • (1)

+1 Per Session
Max 10 Unused

Making a Spare Time Roll

3d6 +/- Skill +/-2 Description
To acquire an Item, Service. or Modification that costs a Spare Time Point.

Explain Desired Result and Approach
After the GM describes the situation, describe what you wish to do and your approach.

Choose a Skill Based on Approach
Your approach will determine what Skill you will roll. For example, buying an Item requires a Wealth Skill Roll, while making an Item may require an Electronics Skill Roll.

GM Awards Description Bonus or Penalty
When you put effort into describing a particularly good approach and play to your strengths, the GM may award up to a +2 bonus to your Skill Roll. If you play to your weaknesses, the GM may give you up to a -2 penalty.

Spend Spare Time Point
Reduce your Spare Time Points by one. Re-rolling a Spare Time Roll (eg. via Fate) does not cost another Spare Time Point.

Roll Dice and Add Skill Bonus or Penalty
Roll 3d6 and add your Skill bonus (or penalty), then add any Description bonus or penalty.
If you roll a "6", you score a Strong Hit (pg: 42).
Some Spare Time Rolls require more than one successful roll (eg: 2x 12t would require 2 rolls of at least 12). These cost 1 Spare Time Point for each roll. If you fail one of these rolls, you may spend 1 Spare Time Point to re-roll it.

If Successful, Gain the Item or Service
If you rolled at least the required amount, you succeed and complete the desired action.

Trade Goods

See pg: 56 for full Resources rules.
See pg: 64 for full Spare Time Point rules.
See pg: 150 for full Spacecraft Cargo rules.

Trade Goods are valuable cargo intended to be sold or traded. They are often purchased or looted (pg: 54) from defeated foes and then sold for Resources.

Trade Goods must have a defined kind (eg: Nephilim Food).

Trade Box
Trade Goods are measured in singular amounts called a Trade Box.

Acquiring Trade Goods
You must describe how you're acquiring your Trade Boxes, usually by purchasing (Wealth Spare Time Roll), looting, or salvaging (any relevant Skill Roll).

» 1 Trade Box requires a Spare Time Roll of 8.
» 4 Trade Boxes requires a Spare Time Roll of 14.

Looting or Stealing
May still require a Spare Time Roll (pg: 64).

As a rough guide, you may gain 1 Trade Box per 4 Weight of Items.

Buying from Exporter
This often grants a +1 or +2 Description bonus to your Spare Time Roll to acquire a Trade Box.

Buying from Importer
This often grants a –1 or –2 Description penalty to your Spare Time Roll to acquire a Trade Box.

Cargo, pg: 150
Storing Trade Boxes requires a certain amount of Cargo space (pg: 150), usually on your spacecraft.

If you do not have the required Cargo space, you must describe how you are storing the Trade Boxes (eg: renting Cargo space, pg: 370) or lose them.

» 1-4 Trade Boxes requires 1 unused Cargo space.
» 5-8 Trade Boxes requires 2 unused Cargo space.
» 9-12 Trade Boxes requires 3 unused Cargo space.
» 13-16 Trade Boxes requires 4 unused Cargo space.

Selling Trade Goods

Describe how you are selling your Trade Boxes, usually to a business (Wealth Spare Time Roll).

» Selling 12 Trade Boxes of the same kind grants 1 Resource.
» Selling 16 Trade Boxes of the same kind grants 2 Resources.

Selling to Importer

This often grants a +1 or +2 Description bonus to your Spare Time Roll to sell Trade Goods.

Selling to Exporter

This often grants a -1 or -2 Description penalty to your Spare Time Roll to sell Trade Goods.

Optional Trade Good Variations

These are templates that can be applied to any kind of Trade Box. You may apply multiple Variations to a single Trade Box. The same Variation cannot be applied more than once.

Variations cannot increase the Sell value of a Trade Box to more than double its original value. For example, Selling 12 Trade Boxes can never give you more than 2 Resources (1 x 2 = 2).

> **All Variations increase the Difficulty of Spare Time Rolls to acquire and Sell Trade Goods by +2.**

Dangerous

Eg: Munitions, fuel, poisonous chemicals, or wild animals.
Sells for double Resources.

If adequate precautions are not taken, this Cargo may harm you or damage your spacecraft, causing 1d6 or 2d6 Damage (reduced by Armour) to a random Attribute (roll 1d6).

Illegal

Eg: Drugs, slaves, or contraband.
Sells for double Resources.

Will result in legal complications if adequate precautions are not taken. This ranges from a short investigation (lose a Spare Time Point) to confiscation of all Trade Goods.

Valuable

Eg: Military weapons, computer hardware, or a VIP.
Requires 2 less Cargo space.

Trade Goods, Acquisition Example

Sarah has 2 spare Cargo space in her spacecraft that she wishes to fill up with Trade Goods to eventually sell. She is currently on the planet of Genenna, inside a Kaltoran mining outpost. The Kaltorans are quite keen to sell their raw ore to her, giving her a Description Bonus of +2 to acquire Trade Boxes of minerals.

Wanting to use her available space to its maximum potential, Sarah wishes to acquire 16 Trade Boxes of Valuable gems; this would normally require 4 Cargo space, but requires two less because it has the "Valuable" Variation. To gain these gems, Sarah must make 4 Spare Time Rolls of 16t. She has +2 to her Wealth Skill and a +2 Description bonus.

Each successful Spare Time Roll gives her 4 Valuable Trade Boxes of gems.

Trade Goods, Sell Example

Sarah has two different kinds of Trade Goods: 12 Boxes of Food and 16 Boxes of Gems. She is currently at the Nephilim home world of Eden. They are not particularly interested in the gems (-2 Description Penalty to sell), but would be keen to barter for the food.

To sell the 12 Trade Boxes of Food, Sarah will need to make a Spare Time Roll of 16t. She has good Wealth Skill (+2), but she knows that the Nephilim respond well to force, so she uses her Leadership Skill (+1) to demand a good price for her goods.

After Sarah does some good role playing, the GM awards her a +2 Description Bonus, for a total of +3 to her Spare Time Roll.

Trade Goods	Cargo Space:	1	2	3	4	Acquire	
Live Nephilim Food		▨	▨	☐	☐	+1 Box	8t
						+4 Boxes	14t
Raw Minerals		▨	▨	☐	☐	**Loot**	
						Weight 4	+1 Box
Kaltoran Weapons (Valuable)		▨	☐	☐	☐	**Sell**	16t
		☐	☐	☐	☐	12 Boxes	1 Res
						16 Boxes	2 Res
		☐	☐	☐	☐	**Variations**	+2t
						Dangerous	x2 Res
						Illegal	x2 Res
						Valuable	-2 Cargo

Research

See pg: 38 for full Skill Roll rules.
See pg: 58 for full Influence rules.
See pg: 64 for full Spare Time Point rules.
See pg: 38 for full Tools and Workshops rules.
See pg: 126 for full Prototype Weapon rules.

Research is the articulation and documentation of both applied and theoretical knowledge. Research serves several purposes: developing new technologies (eg: Weapons), finding new applications of existing technologies, advancing personal knowledge, and gaining Influence through Publishing your work.

> I have never had much patience for those religious types. But I have to acknowledge the similarities between their convictions and my own personal commitment to scientific advancement.
>
> In a similar way to most faiths, I am convinced that my beliefs (in Science) not only tell us what is wrong with the universe, but also offers salvation to those who take it.
>
> – Hraks, Nephilim Emissary.

As with all Spare Time Rolls, pg: 64

Players acquiring or Publishing Research must describe how they are doing so.

Research must have a defined subject (eg: Shield Technology), which defines the nature of any gained Secret Knowledge or Minor Perks.

Research Units
Research is measured in singular amounts called a Research Unit.

Acquiring Research Units
You need to describe in character how you are acquiring your Research Units, usually through studying a mysterious feature within your game (eg: a rare artefact or space phenomenon).

» 1 Research Unit requires a Spare Time Roll of 12.

Have Quality Material to Study
This often grants a +1 or +2 Description Bonus to your Spare Time Roll to acquire a Research Unit.

Have Poor Material to Study
This often grants a –1 or –2 Description Penalty to your Spare Time Roll to acquire a Research Unit.

Requires Workbench, Workshop, or Dedicated Workshop
To gain Research Units with Spare Time Rolls, you must have access to a relevant Workshop (pg: 38), usually kept on your spacecraft (pg: 150).

» 1-4 Research Units requires a Workbench.
» 5-12 Research Units requires a relevant Workshop.
» 13-16 Research Units requires a relevant Dedicated Workshop.

Found Data
Well-documented, readily understandable data useful for Research is very rare.
Found data often grants Research Units or a +1 or +2 Description Bonus to your Spare Time Roll to acquire them.

Optional Rule: Multiple Characters Involved in Research
If multiple characters are contributing to the Research on the same subject, apply the "Difficult" Research Variation to all Spare Time Rolls done to acquire these Units, and split the benefits evenly across the participating characters.

Secret Knowledge or Minor Perk
On Acquiring 12 and 16 Research Units, your character gains a GM defined Secret Knowledge or a Minor Perk (pg: 60). Your Research Subject and the nature of its acquisition will define the nature of these.

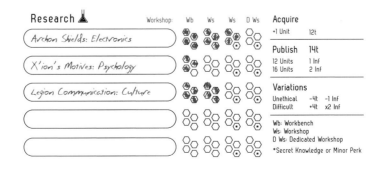

Publishing Research

When you Publish Research, describe how you are going about Publishing your Research (usually to an academic institution). This will give a group of NPCs access to your knowledge, which may shape their actions.

Research Units can only be Published once. Additional Research Units may be added to a Research subject after Publishing, granting access to Secret Knowledge or Minor Perks (pg: 60).

» Publishing 12 Research Units on a subject grants 1 Influence.
» Publishing 16 Research Units on a subject grants 2 Influence.

Publishing to an Interested Group
This often grants +1 or +2 Description bonus to your Spare Time Roll to acquire a Research Unit.

Publishing to an Uninterested Group
This often grants -1 or -2 penalty to your Spare Time Roll to acquire a Research Unit.

Optional Research Variations
These are templates that can be applied to any Research.

You may apply multiple Variations to a single Research subject. The same Variation cannot be applied more than once.

Unethical
Eg: Testing live subjects or using poor research techniques.
-4 to all Acquisition and Publish Spare Time Roll Difficulties.
Publish for -1 Influence.

Difficult
Eg: Researching Archons, X'ion, Aliens, or humans.
+4 to all Acquisition and Publish Spare Time Roll Difficulties.

Publishing this research yields double the Influence OR double the Secret Knowledge and Minor Perks given if multiple characters have contributed.

Research rather than Skill Roll
See pg: 38 for full Skills rules.

When a player wishes to gain knowledge about a particularly difficult subject, the GM may require the player to acquire some amount of Research Units rather than a single Skill Roll.

Prototype Weapons
To acquire a prototype weapon (pg: 126), this often requires Research Units of a specific amount and subject. For example, if you are required to have 12 Medical Research and you gain 16 Medical Research units in a similar area (eg: Nephilim DNA), then this fulfils that requirement.

Combat Overview

Since the Great War the universe has become a very dangerous and often violent place. Out of necessity, carrying a weapon is common practice in all known cultures.

Overview

The following is a short overview of how combat works. It may also be a good idea to have a printout of the Combat Character Sheet (download from www.fraggedempire.com) as you read these rules.

Optional: Theatre of the Mind Combat Rules, pg: 96

If you want simpler combat that doesn't require miniatures, use the Theatre of the Mind rules. No need for models or complicated Weapon Stats, just dice.

These rules are especially helpful if you have a group who is not into miniature-based combat, and they can also be used on occasion for unimportant, complicated, or large combats.

Turns and Actions, pg: 100

Once the GM decides that combat has started, time becomes carefully measured with each character taking Turns performing their Actions.

Combat is broken up into Turns and Actions. characters with the highest Intelligence often act first (see Combat Order, pg: 100). During each Turn, a character may perform 2 Actions, shown on the bottom of your Reference Character Sheet. Your 2 Actions can be in any order you want. Some Actions also enable you to Move and Attack with the one Action choice, allowing many different tactical options.

Battle Map, Miniatures, and Movement, pg: 72

To track movement in combat, it is helpful to have a large sheet of laminated paper with a square grid printed on it, along with some miniatures.
Non-permanent whiteboard markers are also useful for drawing terrain and other environmental objects.

Weapons, pg: 118

All Attacks (except for Stealth) in combat are made with a Weapon. This Weapon might be something you physically hold (eg: an Assault Rifle) or an inborn ability (eg: your Limbs).

Weapons have statistics (pg: 122) showing you how easily they hit the Target, how much Damage they deal, how often you will need to Reload, and their Weight.

As you become more experienced, you will learn how to use each Weapon to its full potential.

Most Weapons are acquired by allotting Resources (pg: 56). Innate Weapons are free.

Rolling Dice and Attacking, pg: 78

After declaring that you are Attacking, you make an Attack Roll to determine whether you hit your Target.

Normally, on an Attack Roll, you roll 3d6, add your Weapon's "Hit" Stat + your Personal Combat Skill with that Weapon, and subtract -2 for each Range Increment, beyond your first, between you and your Target.

A successful Attack Roll with a Weapon reduces the Target's Endurance (pg: 84). When a Target has no Endurance every successful attack against them causes a Critical Hit (pg: 88).

Strong Hits and Doing "Special" Stuff, pg: 82

Whenever you roll a "6" on an Attack Roll, you deal a Strong Hit. You can use a Strong Hit to cause a special effects from your Weapon, one of your Traits, or a common ability usable by anyone, such as a Critical Hit (which is used to Kill Targets).

Critical Hits and Killing Things, pg: 87

Actions with the Major Effect: Attack (pg: 107) can cause Critical Hits, used to kill Targets by Damaging their Attributes directly.

On a Critical Hit, roll 1d6 to determine a random Attribute (see pg: 88). The affected Target reduces that Attribute by your Weapon's Critical Damage minus your Target's Armour.

On each Attack, your Weapon may only cause a maximum number of Critical Hits equal to its "Rate of Fire" (RoF, pg: 122).

You die when any of your Attributes is reduced to -5. An NPC dies when any of its Attributes is reduced to 0.

Combat Is Never "Balanced"

Combats should very rarely be perfectly balanced. Players are encouraged to intelligently pick their fights, fight dirty, and be cunning. If you are able, carefully pick not only when you fight, but also who and where.

Esther was desperately lost. She could feel a thin line of warm blood trickling down her neck as she hastily moved through the warren of large life-support ducts below the Kadash pit city, stumbling through the claustrophobic black. Mossy rocks and metal plates alternated their beatings against her bruised legs.

"Those Corp bastards almost had me..." But they were the least of her troubles. Other Kaltorans were more dangerous...

or to be more precise: the tribalistic, blind Kaltorans willing to do anything to survive down here; Dark Tribes, bound to the tortures of their own genetic memories, each horrible act of survival passed onto their children.

"It's easy to doubt my reasons for coming down here, now that things have gotten tough. I just hope this pocket full of parts was worth it. There is everything down here: rare mineral deposits, ancient pre-fall ships, Archon technology, and junk..." Junk that looked

Movement

See pg: 108-111 for a full list of available Actions.
See pg: 107 for full Major Effect rules.
See pg: 104 for full Drone and Henchmen rules.

Any Action with the Major Effect: Move lets you move spaces up to a number (squares or inches, depending on your battle map) equal to your Movement Attribute (pg: 34).

Representation of Space
Each square, inch, or space represents a two-meter square.

Moving Diagonally
Does not reduce your movement.

Moving Through Characters
Allies, Friendly Henchmen, and Neutral Characters
Moving past a space occupied by an Ally, friendly Henchmen, or a Neutral character counts as Difficult Terrain (pg: 73) and costs you 2 movement.

Friendly Drones
These do not affect your movement unless stated otherwise.

Enemies
You cannot move through a space occupied by an enemy without giving a reason why or how you do so, which often requires a Skill Roll (eg: Physical Skill Roll to dodge around them).

Moving and Attacking
If an Action allows you to Move and Attack, you may only Attack before or after you Move. You may not Move partially, Attack, and then Move partially again.

Movement Example

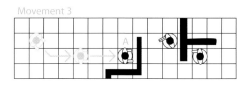

Movement 3

During combat Max (A) (Movement Attribute = 3) has two Actions each Turn. He uses both Actions to move an amount equal to his Movement Attribute.

If his Movement Attribute were Damaged (pg: 87), or gained a bonus (eg: Full Move, pg: 108, grants Move +2), this would change the amount he could have moved.

Move and Attack Example

Move then Attack

Max (A) is using the Snap Shot Action (pg: 110), which allows him to Move and Attack. For his first Action during his Turn, he moves and then Attacks. Once he makes his Attack Roll he is not able to move any more. He cannot Attack part way through his movement.

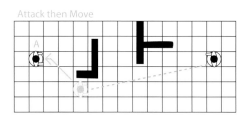

Attack then Move

For his second Action, he performs another Snap Shot Action. This time he Attacks and then Moves.

suspiciously like Archon shield tech... "By the ancestors, I hope I haven't gone to all this trouble for a fancy door stop." Her voice was swallowed up by the blackness, failing to reassure her.

Something solid rolled underfoot. "Damn it! bloody pebbles," she growled, scooping them up. Extending her arm back to throw them, she ran one between her fingers, feeling the shape... They weren't pebbles...

SHE REMEMBERED...

Grandfather Daniel... voices ahead... food... The rusted spear easily pierced his prey's neck. The spray of warm blood was intoxicating...

The fire crackled as the spit slowly rotated... He toyed with the last bones, the hunger would soon return. It always did...

Environment, Conditions & Effects

See pg: 86 for full Cover rules.
See pg: 88 for full Bleeding rules.
See pg: 109 for full Stealth rules.
See pg: 86 for full Limited Vision rules.
See pg: 125 for full Locked On rules.

Environments are external effects not caused by other characters (eg: darkness). Conditions and Effects only affect a single character (eg: blindness), and remain in effect until the GM decides it reasonable for them to be removed or a Healing Roll (eg: Surgery) or Action (eg: Escape) removes them..

Personal Combat Environment

Zero Gravity:	Moving one space costs 2 Movement. Hit −2 No Overburden Penalty.
Cover X:	Defence +X
Difficult Terrain:	Moving one space costs 2 Movement.
Open/Close Door:	Cost 2 Movement to Change.

Personal Combat Effects

Bleeding:	1 Attribute Dmg (no Armour) at the start of your Turn.
Grabbing Target:	As with Grabbed Effect but may remove as a Free Action.
Grabbed:	1 Action per Turn. May Move with Target if you have higher Str. Gain 1 Additional Action if you remove this Effect.
Limited Vision:	Targets gain Cover versus you: Light Cover (Low Light) or Heavy Cover (Blind, Pitch Black) vs You.
Locked On:	Enemies gain Hit: +Lock On vs you.
Prone:	+1 Cover Step Cost 2 Movement to Change. Moving one space costs 2 Movement while Prone.
Stealthed:	May not be Targeted while in Cover. Lost on Major Effect: Attack. Lost next Turn if 1st Action is not a successful Stealth Action.
Suppressed:	Maximum 1 Action this Turn.

Minor Interactions with Your Environment

Minor interactions include opening or closing a door, picking up an object, or passing an item to another character.

Move Major Action Effect, pg: 107

To perform minor interactions with your Environment, you must perform an Action (pg: 100) that allows you to Move. Each Minor Interaction costs 2 Movement.

Picking up an Item

Picking up an Item costs you 2 Movement, and you must have a spare hand.

If you wish to use this Weapon you must Draw (see pg: 114) it (spend Draw Weapon Actions equal to its Load Stat).

Opening a Door, Minor Interaction Example

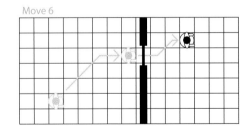

Move 6

James is in a rush, and needs to move through a door. He has a total Movement of 6 (Movement Attribute of 4 and +2 from the Full Move Action (pg: 108)).

For his first Full Move Action, he moves 5 spaces to the door, but cannot open the door because he needs 2 Movement to do so, while he only has 1 Movement remaining.

For his second Action, he does another Full Move and spends his first 2 Movement opening the door. He then spends his remaining Movement to move 4 spaces.

Difficult Terrain

Traversing difficult terrain includes moving up stairs, over rubble, into foliage, and through swamps.

> Moving to a space costs 1 Movement.
> Moving to a space of Difficult Terrain costs 2 Movement and may require a Physical Skill Roll.

Climbing

This requires a Physical Skill Roll (pg: 46) as part of your Movement Action, normally against a difficulty of 12. A better roll lets you climb faster and up more difficult surfaces.

» Ladder = No roll required.
» Small object, eg: fence = Difficulty 8
» Notched surface, eg: rocky wall = Difficulty 12
» Diverse surface, building wall = Difficulty 14
» Smooth surface, eg: glass wall = Difficulty 18 and Tools.
» Upside-down, eg: ceiling = Difficulty +4
» No free hands = Difficulty +2
» 2 free hands = Difficulty -2

If you fail this roll, you lose ALL movement this Turn. If you failed by more than 4, you fall and take automatic Endurance Damage (pg: 87), a Critical Hit (pg: 88), and go Prone (pg: 76).

» Fall 0-1m = Prone.
» Fall 2-3m = 5 End Dmg, 1 Crit Dmg, Prone.
» Fall 4-6m = 10 End Dmg, 1d6 Crit Dmg, Prone.
» Fall 7-10m = 15 End Dmg, 2d6 Crit Dmg, Prone.
» Fall 11m+ = 30 End Dmg, 2d6+6 Crit Dmg, Prone.

Swimming

This requires a Physical Skill Roll (pg: 46) each Turn you are swimming. The difficulty depends on the Weight of your Outfit and Weapons.

If you fail this roll, you lose all movement this Turn. If you failed by more than 4, you take 1 Attribute Damage to a random (1d6) Attribute, ignoring Armour (pg: 87).

» All Weapons and Outfit below Weight 2 = Difficulty 8
» All Weapons and Outfit below Weight 3 = Difficulty 10
» All Weapons and Outfit below Weight 4 = Difficulty 14
» All Weapons and Outfit below Weight 5 = Difficulty 16
» A Weapon or Outfit is Weight 6+ = Difficulty 18
» 2 free hands = Difficulty -2

Thick Foliage, Steep Inclines, Barricades, Rubbish Piles

Moving to a space with this terrain costs 2 Movement.

Dangerous Terrain

See pg: 124 for full Weapon Keyword rules.

This type of terrain includes steam vents, exposed electrical wires, security fences, and empty space. All dangerous terrain can harm your character. Most causes Automatic Damage, while some makes an Attack Roll against you.

> When a character enters Dangerous Terrain, or begins their Turn in Dangerous Terrain, the GM makes a Dangerous Terrain Attack Roll against that character.

Decompression (Automatic Hit and Critical Hit)
End Dmg 5, Crit Dmg 0
After all characters have taken their Turn, you are moved 1d3 spaces in an appropriate direction. This distance may be reduced if you are holding onto something.

EMP Field
-4 Hit, -4 End Dmg and -4 Crit Dmg to all non-Low Tech and Bio Tech Attacks made inside or through the EMP Field.

Exposed Electrical Wires (Attack Roll Required)
Hit +4, End Dmg 6, Crit Dmg 4, Energy
Splash if connected to conductive material (eg: water).

Fuel or Munitions Case (Automatic Hit and Critical Hit)
Defence 10 (Any Attack with "Energy" Keyword makes it explode).
Explode: End Dmg 5, Crit Dmg 5, Splash 1d6, Slow

Lava (Attack Roll Required)
Hit +4, End Dmg 15, Crit Dmg 8, Energy, Burn

Orbital Bombardment (Attack Roll Required)
Hit -10, End Dmg 15, Crit Dmg 6, Splash 3, Lock On +6
If you are damaged by this Attack Roll, you are knocked Prone and moved 1d6 spaces away from the centre of the Attack.

Radiation Field (Automatic Hit and Critical Hit)
End Dmg 2, Crit Dmg 3, Pen 3 min 2, Energy
-2 Hit, -2 End Dmg, and -2 Crit Dmg to all Bio Tech Attacks made inside or through the Radiation Field.

Security Fence (Automatic Hit and Critical Hit on failed Climb Roll)
End Dmg 10, Crit Dmg 3, Energy
-4 to Physical Skill Rolls to climb over.

Severe Cold or Heat
Recovery -4
-2 to Physical and Resolve Skill Rolls.

Steam Vent (Automatic Hit and Critical Hit)
Hit +4, End Dmg 10, Crit Dmg 3, Energy

Moving over Rubble, Difficult Terrain Example

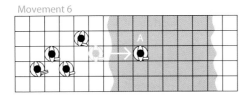

Movement 4

During combat, Bastion (A) (Movement 4) wishes to move over a pile of rubble (Difficult Terrain) to get closer to his opponents.

For his first Action he Moves, spending 3 Movement to move the three spaces up to the rubble, but cannot enter the space with rubble because it requires 2 Movement, one more than he has left.

For his second Action, he spends 2 Movement to move into the rubble. With 2 Movement remaining, he moves two more spaces, as it does not require any extra movement to move out of Difficult Terrain.

Swimming, Difficult Terrain Example

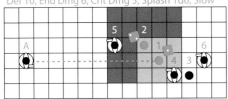

Movement 6

Ajax (A) (Movement 4) is attempting to cross a slow-flowing river to get away from a group of Nephilim mercenaries. For his first Action, he does a Full Move (Movement +2 = 6, pg: 108). Because water is Difficult Terrain, he spends the 6 Movement to move 3 spaces.

He has a Weight 4 Outfit on and is carrying a Weight 2 rifle, so he needs to pass a Physical Skill Roll with a Difficulty of 14 or he will swallow some water. He fails, unfortunately, so he takes 1 Attribute Damage (pg: 87) that cannot be reduced by Armour.

Exploding Barrel, Dangerous Terrain Example

Def 10, End Dmg 6, Crit Dmg 5, Splash 1d6, Slow

Rachel (A) Attacks a barrel full of spacecraft fuel (1), requiring an Attack Roll of at least 10 with her Flame Thrower. Because her Weapon has the "Energy" Keyword (pg: 125), the barrel explodes in a splash area of 1d6. She rolls a 1, making a second, adjacent barrel (2) explode. She rolls a 2 for the splash area of the second barrel, which does not explode the third barrel (3) as it was not Damaged.

Two of her opponents (4 and 5, not 6) take Damage from the exploding barrels (5 Endurance and Critical Damage). This may cause a Critical Hit (pg: 88) on any at or reduced to 0 Endurance. Opponent 4 does not take Damage twice.

"The Kaltoran mining stations of Gehenna have one of simplest job application processes in Haven. If you can live down here on the surface for a week while they process your application... you're in."

"Then why did they accept my application on the spot?"

"You're a cold blooded Legion... If you're strong enough, or desperate enough for a job in this fiery hell hole, then you're in."

"Yeah, I'm the second one of those two..."

Inhospitable Environment (Outside Combat)

This includes lack of food or water, and long journeys through an arctic, hot, or otherwise tough environment. Most of these environments require a Physical, Resolve, or Survival Skill Roll to avoid taking a negative Condition.

See pg: 76 for full descriptions of the below Conditions.

Journey Through Inhospitable Environment
Eg: Arctic, Jungle, Volcanic or Wasteland.

For every two days you journey, you must make a Physical, Resolve, or Survival Skill Roll of Difficulty 12.

» Failed Skill Roll = Gain Minor Condition: Worn Out.
» Failed Skill Roll by 4 = Gain Minor Condition: Exhausted.

» Barren Environment = +1 Difficulty.
» After six days = +2 Difficulty, and only make a Skill Roll once per six days.
» Limited natural resources = +2 Difficulty.
» Well planned and supplied journey = -2 Difficulty.
» Pass a Survival Roll by 2 = All Allies gain +2 to their Rolls.

Low Food and/or Water
For every two days without food and/or water, you must make a Physical or Survival Skill Roll with Difficulty 14.

» Failed Skill Roll = Gain Minor Condition: Exhausted.
» Failed Skill Roll by 4 = Gain Major Condition: Dying.

» After two days = Gain Minor Condition: Worn Out.
» After six days = +4 Difficulty.
» No food and/or water = +2 Difficulty.
» Pass a Survival Roll by 2 = All Allies gain +2 to their Rolls.

Example Conditions

Healing, pg: 92
Missing limbs, vital organ damage, stress, and many other ailments can be cured through advanced medical care, gene manipulation, and psychoanalytic techniques.

Minor Condition: Worn Out
» Eg: Minor sickness, stress, malnourishment, lack of sleep.
» -5 Endurance.
» -1 to all Spare Time Rolls.
» You may gain this Condition multiple times.
» If this Condition is removed; remove all Worn Out Conditions.

Minor Condition: Exhausted
» Eg: Sickness, radiation poisoning, major burns, minor poison.
» -10 Endurance.
» -2 Combat Order
» -1 to all Rolls.
» You may gain this Condition multiple times.
» For every third time, you gain this Condition: gain the Major Condition: Dying.

Major Condition: Dying
» Eg: Starvation, major infection, poison.
» Take 1 Damage to 1 Random (1d3) Attribute (no Armour) at the start of each day.
» This Damage cannot be Healed with a Paramedics Healing Roll.

Major Condition: Lost Limb
» Arm/Hand: -1 Hand and Gauntlet Slot.
» Leg/Foot: May only Move while Prone or while assisted.

Major Condition: Blind
» You cannot see.
» All Targets gain Heavy Limited Vision Cover (+4) versus you.

Major Condition: Deaf
» You cannot hear.
» -6 Stealth.

Major Condition: Fear
» -2 to all Rolls connected with the object of your fear. If you are trained in Resolve, this penalty decreases to -1.

Major Condition: Ignorance
» Possible examples: Lose 1 Language, become unable to use non-Low Tech Weaponry, or become unable to use computers (including Combat Computers and non-Bio Tech Drones).

Minor or Major Condition: Addiction
» You may never have more than 2 unspent Spare Time Points at once.
» -1 Wealth.

Example Effects

Prone
You are either crawling along the ground or crouched. This can help you take Cover but inhibits your Movement.

» Becoming Prone or standing from Prone costs 2 Movement Points.
» +1 Cover Step.

Limited Vision (or Low Light)
See pg: 86 for full Limited Vision Cover rules.

All of your Targets gain Light (+2) or Heavy (+4) Limited Vision Cover against all your Attack Rolls (GM discretion).

If your Targets already have Heavy Cover, then their Cover Step increases to Entrenched (+6).

Suppressed
You have been distracted during combat, possibly from panic or by physical restraint.

> The Suppressed Effect only lasts 1 Turn.
> Multiple Suppression Effects do not stack.

» You may only take 1 Action during your next Turn.

Grabbing Target
» Removed if a character succeeds at the Escape Action against you.
» Once you grab a Target, you cannot use the Weapon used to grab (usually your Limbs) to Attack a different character.
» Same rules as Grabbed Effect, but you may remove this Effect at any time as a Free Action (allowing you to perform 2 Actions during the Turn that you remove this Effect).

Grabbed
» You may only take 1 Action per Turn. The Turn in which you remove this effect, you may perform 2 Actions.
» Removed when you succeed at an Escape Action against the character grabbing you.

Stealthed
See pg: 109 for full Stealth Action rules.

Locked On
» All enemies gain a bonus to their Attack Rolls against you equal to their Weapon's "Lock On +X" (pg: 125) bonus.
» Removed at the end of combat.

Bleeding
See pg: 88 for full Bleeding rules.

Attack Roll

See pg: 86 for full Cover rules.
See pg: 87 for full Damage rules.
See pg: 108-111 for a full list of available Actions.

All Attacks (except Stealth) in combat
are done with a Weapon (pg: 118).

Attack Roll

3d6 + Wpn Hit + Skill – Range Penalties vs Trg Def
Success = Deal your End Dmg to Target's Endurance

Weapon (Hit)

Your Weapon's "Hit" Stat adds a bonus or penalty to your Attack Roll.

Personal Combat Skill

Your Personal Combat Skill (pg: 52) associated with the Weapon you are using adds a bonus or penalty to your Attack Roll.

Attacking Through a Character

When you Attack through a character to another Target, the Target gains Light Cover (+2) against your Attack.

Triples, Jammed Effect and RoF 2+

If you roll triples on your Attack Roll (eg: you roll three 4s), your Attack applies to the Target granting Cover to your intended Target, and NOT your intended Target.

If your Weapon has RoF 2+, then your Attack is applied to your intended Target AND your unintended Target (your Attack Roll total must still equal or exceed the characters Defence).

If your RoF 2+ Weapon has the Jam Keyword and your Weapon would gain the Jammed Effect. Your Attack is applied to you unintended Target and NOT to your Intended Target.

Characters Adjacent to You

When Attacking through a character adjacent to you, your Target does not gain any additional Cover.

Firing a Rifle, Attack Roll Example

Hit +4, Rng 6

Cody (A) is making an Attack Roll against his opponent (2). Cody has a +4 bonus to his Attack Roll. His opponent is 9 spaces away, which is in Cody's second Range Increment, giving a -2 penalty to Cody's Attack Roll. Cody rolls 3d6 and gets 5, 5, 1: an 11. With the bonus and penalty applied, the final result is a 13.

Range Increments (Rng)

When you Attack a Target any number of spaces away up to its Range, your Attack Roll takes no penalty. For each increment of Range beyond that, it gets a cumulative -2 penalty.

A Weapon's maximum range is its Range x10. Any Attack made beyond this distance automatically misses.

Rng 3

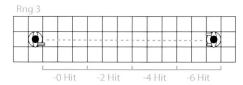

-0 Hit   -2 Hit   -4 Hit   -6 Hit

Sarah's SMG has Range 3, which she uses to Attack a Target that is 12 spaces away. This is in the fourth increment of her Weapon's range, giving a -6 penalty to her Attack Roll. If the Target were 13 spaces away, the penalty would increase to -8.

Attacking from off the Map

If appropriate, characters can be placed far away from the central Combat Area and make Attacks with long-range weapons. To do so, mark a point on the Battle Map to show where that character Attacks from and how much distance they need to add to their attacks.

Jack sets up on a distant hill and is providing covering fire for his team. The GM marks a point on the Battle Map for Jack to Attack from, and informs him that he should add 25 to all of his Ranges.

"Inheriting an empire that they did not fight to build gave no room for war in the Archon's mind. They did not have the cultural history of conflict found in their human creators or us.

When X'ion's wrath fell upon them, they needed more than their intelligence and technology. In desperation, they built us, the Legion. Having little personal experience to draw upon, they instilled in you and me the mind of a warrior, based on ancient human military traditions and customs: skill, order, and efficiency.

X'ion also had no military history to draw upon. Turning to the old gods for inspiration, he shaped his Nephilim, our ancient enemy, after the primal beast: fierce, dirty, and wild.

Now facing extinction, we are forced to adapt to a life neither of us were created for. As the Archon's culture of peace struggled with war, our violent natures threaten to kill us by resisting peace."

    – Rasmus Aer, Legion talking to his grandson.

Making an Attack Roll

3d6 +Weapon Hit +Skill –Range Penalties vs Target Defence.
All Attacks in personal Combat are done with a Weapon.

Select Your Target
Pick a Target to Attack.

Roll 3d6 and Choose to Add Rate of Fire
May roll 1 additional d6 per your Weapons RoF above 1 (eg: a Rate of Fire 3 Attack may roll up to 5d6).
1 Ammunition used per RoF used.

+Weapon Hit +Personal Combat Skill
Add your Weapon's Hit bonus and your Personal Combat Skill to your roll.

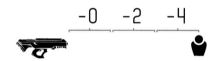

Take Penalty for Range
-2 penalty for each Range increment beyond the first.
Your Weapon's maximum range = Rng x10.

Endurance Damage
If your Attack Roll equals or exceeds your Target's Defence, they lose Endurance equal to your Weapon's Endurance Damage (End Dmg).
If your Target is at or reduced to 0 Endurance by this Attack, you deal an automatic Critical Hit (pg: 88).

Count Strong Hits
If you hit the Target, any 6s you rolled are Strong Hits (pg: 82).
Strong Hit: Critical Hit (pg: 88) is required to kill Targets.

Rate of Fire (RoF)

Some Weapons are able to spend Ammunition (pg: 122) faster than other Weapons, increasing their chance to hit, potential damage output, and ammunition depletion rate.

Before you roll any dice for your Attack Roll, you must declare how many additional d6 you will be rolling.

Spread Fire

Weapons with RoF 2 or more may Spread Fire. When you Spread Fire, you may split the dice of an Attack Roll across multiple Targets. A minimum of 1d6 must be used for the space between each target.

Attacking Multiple Targets, Spread Fire Example

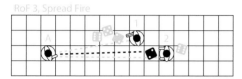

RoF 3, Spread Fire

Sarah (A) is using an SMG with Hit +3 and RoF 3. She spends 2 Ammunition, giving her a total of 5d6. She uses her Action to Attack and chooses to Spread Fire. She rolls 3d6 against the first Target (1), allots the required 1d6 for the space between, and rolls 1d6 against the second Target (2).

Her first Attack Roll has a total of 16 (6+5+2, +3 from Weapon). Her second Attack Roll has a total of 9 (6, +3 from Weapon).

Splash and RoF 2+

See pg: 127 for full Splash rules.

Weapons RoF, Not Attacks RoF

See pg: 82 for full Strong Hit rules.
See pg: 88 for full Strong Hit: Critical Hit rules.
See pg: 341 for a full list of available Traits.

For the purposes of Spread Fire, Strong Hits, and other effects affected by RoF, use your Weapon's RoF Stat, NOT the number of additional dice you roll (eg: a RoF 3 SMG may cause multiple Critical Hits, even if it only makes an Attack Roll with 3d6).

Multiple Critical Hits, RoF Example

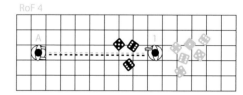

RoF 4

James (A) is dual-wielding a pair of SMGs, giving him a massive Rate of Fire of 4. James makes two Attacks against a Target (1).

For his first Attack Roll, he performs a Spray Fire, which has the Minor Effect: Hit +Extra RoF Dice. Making full use of his RoF, he spends 3 Ammunition to rolls three additional d6s. He rolls 6d6 for a massive total of 26 and 2 Strong Hits (6s). He may use both Strong Hits to cause 2 Critical Hits, as a Weapon may cause a number of Critical Hits up to its RoF. This Attack costs him 4 Ammunition.

For his second Attack Roll, he performs a Sighted Shot, which does not have the Minor Effect: Hit +Extra RoF Dice. He rolls 3d6 for a total of 17 and 2 Strong Hits. He may still use both Strong Hits to cause 2 Critical Hits: even though he couldn't add additional dice from his Weapon's RoF, its RoF is still 4. This Attack costs him 1 Ammunition.

RoF 0 or Below

You may not Attack with a Weapon that has RoF 0 or below.

Strong Hits (Combat)

See pg: 42 for Primary Skill Strong Hit rules.
See pg: 78 for full Attack Roll rules.
See pg: 88 for full Strong Hit: Critical Hit rules.
See pg: 127 for full Splash rules.

Rolling 6s

When you make a Skill, Vehicle System, or Attack Roll, any 6s you roll are Strong Hits, which you can spend on Strong Hit Options.

You may choose the same Strong Hit Options multiple times, unless otherwise stated.

Every character has access to the following Strong Hit Options: Critical Hit (pg: 88), Critical Boost (pg: 88), and Effort (pg: 42).

Additional Strong Hit Options

See pg: 341 for a full list of available Traits.
See pg: 358 for a full list of available Weapons.

Additional Strong Hit options can be gained through Traits or from specific Weapons (eg: Disruptor).

Weapon-Specific Strong Hits

Strong Hit Options listed on a Weapon can only be chosen when you assign Strong Hits from an Attack Roll made with that Weapon.

Chris's Tactical Computer gives him access to these Strong Hit Options: Target Lock, Scramble, Range Finder, and Tactical Scan. When he rolls a Strong Hit (6) with this Weapon, he can assign it to use any of these options.

Requirements

After you roll a Strong Hit, you may assign it to use any Strong Hit Option for which you meet the requirements.

Most commonly, a Strong Hit Option requires a specific Action Major Effect (eg: Attack), a Weapon Keyword (eg: Energy), or a specific Skill (eg: Conversation).

1 Use per RoF

This Strong Hit may only be used once per your Weapon's RoF (even if no additional dice are used for this Attack).

Action or Vehicle System Roll

May only be used when you are performing the listed Action or Vehicle System Roll (eg: Analyse, Stealth, Command, Engineering, Gunnery, Operations).

Attack

May only be used when your Action has Major Effect: Attack.

Crit Dmg X+

May only be used during Attacks that causes Critical Damage of X or more.

Damage

May only be used when your Action has Major Effect: Damage.

Does not Require Hit

May be used even if you do not succeed on your Attack Roll or deal Damage, at the GM's discretion.

First Range Increment

May only be used against a Target within your Weapon's first Range Increment or who is adjacent to you (if your Weapon has no Range Stat, such as most Melee Weapons).

First Range Increment or Direct Splash Hit

See pg: 127 for full Splash rules.

As with First Range Increment, but you have the additional option of causing a Direct Splash Hit even if it is outside your first Range Increment.

Hit

May only be used when you succeed on your Attack Roll.

Name   Requirements
           (in brackets)   Result

Critical Hit (Damage, Hit, 1 use per RoF, No Splash Damage) Deal your Weapons Critical Damage (–Targets Armour) to a random (roll a d6) Attribute.

Hit by X
May only be used when your Attack Roll exceeds the minimum needed to pass by X.

Locked On
May only be used when your Target is affected by a friendly Locked On Effect.

No Splash Damage
See pg: 127 for full Splash rules.

If your Weapon has the "Splash" Keyword, you must Directly Hit your Target, not just deal Damage to them from your Weapon's Splash Area (via Attacking the Ground).

Requires X Strong Hits
To use this option, you must spend X Strong Hits.

RoF X+
Your Weapon must have a Rate of Fire of X or more.

Spare Time Roll
May only be used as part of a Spare Time Roll (pg: 64).

Stealthed
You must currently be Stealthed (pg: 109).

Target Has 0 Endurance
May only be used against a Target with 0 Endurance, including ones reduced to 0 Endurance by this Attack.

Weapon Keyword
See pg: 124 for a full list of Weapon Keywords.

May only be used with a Weapon that has the listed Keyword (eg: Bio Tech, Blunt, Burn, Disruptor, Psionic).

David Faith was to be dead in a few moments.

A hail of poison spines had punched through the ship's hull. Metal shards, barbed bones, and poison globs bounced off the walls as if in slow motion. Any one of these could be the deliverer of his final breath.

Fate was toying with him as it laid bare the many tools of its will… and the fury of the Nephilim he had just quadruple-crossed.

– David Faith, conman.

Weapon Name
See pg: 358 for a full list of Weapons.

May only be used with the listed Weapon (eg: Grenade, Grenade Launcher, Mind).

Weapon Type
See pg: 102 for a full list of Weapon Types.

May only be used with a Weapon of the listed Type (eg: Combat Computer, Drone, Henchmen, Melee).

X Away from Target
May only be used against a Target at least X spaces away.

Result
The result of a Strong Hit Option only lasts until the beginning of your next Turn (pg: 100) unless stated otherwise.

Bonuses Only Last One Turn
All Strong Hit results (eg: Buffs and Effects) last until the start of your next Turn (pg: 100) unless stated otherwise.

Critical Hit and Set Alight, Multiple Strong Hit Example
Alex has just hit a Target with his Flame Thrower and rolled two Strong Hits. He spends one on a Critical Hit (pg: 88).

He cannot spend his second Strong Hit on another because it has the Requirement "1 Use per RoF" and the Flame Thrower only has RoF 1. Instead, he spends his second Strong Hit on the Strong Hit Option: "Set Alight" (pg: 354), which he gains from the Trait "Set Alight".

The tree lifted into the air, seemingly in slow motion as dirt and sludge fell to the ground in large clumps. A dozen purple eyes stared out at me. Shortly joined by two large, mud covered metal arms. Pushing upwards, the monster displayed its impressive strength and height.

Then came the noise, a high pitch digital scream as fiery purple bolts of death shot out from the darkness.

The tree fell to the ground, revealing the monster that had lain in wait for a hundred years to make this kill.

– Mechonid sighting.

Defence

See pg: 78 for full Attack Roll rules.
See pg: 115 for full Overburden rules.
See pg: 109 for full Stealth Action rules.
See pg: 111 for full Impair Action rules.
See pg: 103 for full Psionic Weapon Type rules.

When a character makes an Attack Roll against you in combat, your Defence is the number they must equal beat to succeed.

> ### Defence = 10 + Reflexes + Cover

Defence vs Impair

Your Defence vs the Impair Action.
Add your Strength to your Defence.

Defence vs Psionic

Your Defence vs Weapons with the Weapon Type; Psionic.
Add your Focus to your Defence.

Defence vs Stealth

Your Defence vs Stealth Action.

Stealth Attack Rolls are only rolled against the enemy character with the highest Defence vs Stealth, not against each Target.

> ### Defence vs Stealth = 10 + Perception + 1 per Ally (max 10)

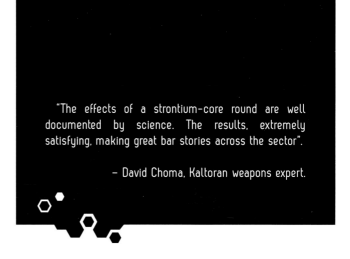

Defence While Asleep or Unconscious

While asleep or unconscious (see Blunt Keyword, pg: 124), you gain no Attribute bonus to your Defence.

Defence While Alert but Unaware of Attack

If you are alert but unaware of an incoming Attack, use your full Defence, and your opponent's Attack counts as their Surprise Round Action (pg: 101).

Armour

See pg: 88 for full Strong Hit: Critical Hit rules.

Each point of Armour reduces Attribute Damage to you by 1.

Endurance

See pg: 87 for full Endurance Damage rules.

> ### Your maximum Endurance = 10 + (Strength x5)

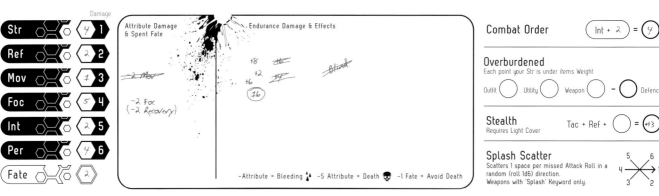

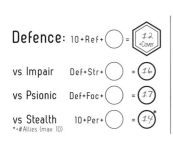

Cover

See pg: 126 for full Outfit rules.
See pg: 130 for full Utility Item rules.

Cover protects you. It not only increases your Defence Stat, making you harder to hit, and can make you immune to Critical Hits (pg: 88) while you have Endurance (pg: 87).

Cover is represented in three Steps: Light, Heavy, and Entrenched.

No Cover
If you are currently gaining no Cover, your Cover Step cannot be otherwise increased (eg: by Traits or Equipment).

Step 1) Light Cover (+2 Defence)
+2 Defence and you may perform the Stealth Action (pg: 109).

Light Cover applies whenever a non-Stealth Attack Roll is made against you.

Eg: Foliage, the edge of a round pillar, smoke, or low light.

Step 2) Heavy Cover (+4 Defence)
+4 Defence, you may perform the Stealth Action, and -2 Endurance Damage done against you by Weapons with Rate of Fire 3 (pg: 122) or more.

Heavy Cover applies whenever a non-Stealth Attack Roll is made against you.

Eg: Chest high stone wall, metal doorway, complete darkness or blindness.

Step 3) Entrenched (+6 Defence)
+6 Defence, you may perform the Stealth Action, -2 Endurance Damage done against you by Weapons with Rate of Fire 3 or more, and you are Immune to Critical Hits (pg: 88) while you have Endurance.

Entrenched Cover is only ever gained by combining multiple sources of cover. Eg: Heavy Physical Cover and Low Light OR Light Cover, equipment and a Trait.

Eg: Metal doorway and the Take Cover Action; metal doorway and Low Light Cover.

Physical Environmental Cover

This type of cover is blocking or obscuring by a physical object in the environment. Unless stated otherwise, all references to Cover refer to Physical Cover.

Shell and Splash Weapon
If a Weapon has the "Shell" Weapon Type and "Splash" Keyword, their Target's Cover value is determined from the location hit by the Attack, not the direction the Attack came from.

Front Cover
This type of cover comes only from a Utility Item or Trait, not the Environment. It grants a Cover bonus only against Attacks made within a 90 degree arc in front of your character.

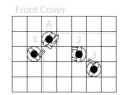 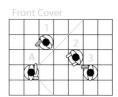

In both instances, Derrick's (A) Large Combat Shield grants him Heavy Cover against Targets 2 and 3 but not Target 1.

Front Cover can never be used to gain Stealthed (pg: 109).

Limited Vision
If your character's vision is impaired (eg: by blindness, smoke, or low light), your Target gains Limited Vision Cover. Some Traits and equipment reduce the effects of this Cover (eg: a Multispectral Visor reduces all Limited Vision Cover by one Step), and some equipment can create it (eg: Smoke Grenades).

Low Light
A specific type of Limited Vision. Anything that aids you against Limited Vision also aids you against Low Light. However, anything that aids you against Low Light (eg: a Torch) does not aid you against other types of Limited Vision (eg: smoke).

Non-Visual Senses
Vision is the primary sense that you use for locating objects and perceiving your environment. If your other senses are impaired, the GM can inhibit you (eg: If you are deafened, you would not be able to hear your team speak, but you would not gain an Attack Roll penalty).

Impairment of your non-visual senses rarely grants your Target Limited Vision Cover against you, at the GM's discretion.

Smoke Bomb, Limited Vision Example

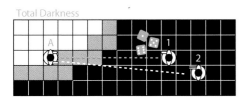

Limited Vision, Smoke Bomb

Hraks (A) and Sarah (B) are Attacking a group of enemies. The first Target (1) is hiding in smoke from a Smoke Bomb (Light Cover or +1 Cover Step). The second and third Targets (2 and 3) are hiding behind a stone wall (Heavy Cover).

Hraks (A) wants to Attack Target 1, who gains +2 Defence from the smoke (Light Cover). Target 2 would gain +6 Defence (Entrenched Cover from the stone wall and smoke). Target 3 would gain +4 Defence (Heavy Cover from the stone wall).

Sarah (B) is a Kaltoran (pg: 340), so she reduces all Limited Vision and Low Light penalties by 1 Step. This removes the Defence bonus from the smoke; for Sarah, Target 1 has no Cover, and Targets 2 and 3 have Heavy Cover.

If Sarah's Trait only reduced Low Light penalties, it would not affect this situation. Smoke doesn't reduce light, but physically impairs vision.

Total Darkness, Low Light Example

Total Darkness

Adam (A) is standing under a light during a dark night.

He makes an Attack against a Target (1) that he cannot see, so his Target gains Heavy Cover.

Adam is then Attacked by a second opponent (2) that he cannot see. Adam gains no Cover bonus against this Attack because he is in a fully illuminated area.

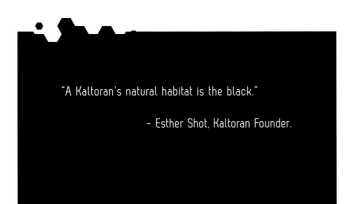

"A Kaltoran's natural habitat is the black."

– Esther Shot, Kaltoran Founder.

Damage

See pg: 78 for full Attack Roll rules.
See pg: 84 for full Defence rules.
See pg: 92 for full Healing Rolls rules.
See pg: 118 for full Weapons rules.

Attribute Damage

This is primarily caused by Strong Hit: Critical Hit (see next page). Attribute Damage can reduce your Defence (pg: 84), your Order of Combat (pg: 100), and bonuses your Actions may give you (eg: Attack Rolls and Movement).

Damaged Ligament, Attribute Damage Example

Ajax has just taken damage from a Shotgun, reducing his Reflexes Attribute by 2. This reduces his Defence (pg: 84) by 2 and and hampers any Action that would benefit from Reflexes (eg: Melee Strike).

If his Reflexes ever becomes negative, he would start Bleeding (pg: 88), his Defence would decrease further, and using Actions that benefit from his Reflex Attribute would gain a further penalty.

Endurance Damage

When you succeed at an Attack Roll (pg: 78), deal Endurance Damage to your Target equal to your Weapon's Endurance Damage.

Strength Damage and Losing Endurance

If you take Strength Attribute Damage, reduce your maximum Endurance. If this reduces your maximum below your current Endurance, reduce your Endurance to your new maximum after applying any Endurance Damage taken.

Davidson has 30 max Endurance and 25 current Endurance. He receives 3 Endurance Damage and 2 Strength Damage, reducing his max Endurance to 20 and current Endurance to 20 (not 17).

Zero Endurance

If you have 0 Endurance and receive a successful Attack Roll from an Action with the major Effect: Damage (pg: 107) you are always dealt a Critical Hit and the Critical Boost Strong Hit Option (see next page) may be applied to you.

Entrenched Cover (pg: 86) does not grant immunity to Critical Hits when you have 0 Endurance.

Recovery

You can restore Endurance by performing an Action with the Major Effect: Recovery (pg: 107).

Drones and Henchmen

All Drones and Henchmen (pg: 296) have 0 Endurance.

Strong Hit: Critical Hit

See pg: 82 for full Combat Strong Hit rules.
See pg: 78 for full Attack Roll rules.

Critical Hits are the primary method of killing or debilitating a Target. This is done by reducing their Attribute Scores.

Requirements, pg: 82

Damage
Action must have the Major Effect: Damage (pg: 107).

Hit
Succeed at your Attack Roll (pg: 78) to Hit Target.

1 use per RoF
This Strong Hit may only be used once per your Weapon's RoF (even if no additional dice are used for this Attack).

No Splash Damage
See pg: 127 for full Splash rules.

May only be applied to Targets that are Directly Hit by a Weapon with the "Splash" Keyword. Targets not Directly Hit that are within the Splash area may only take Attribute damage if their Endurance has been reduced to 0.

Result: Attribute Damage

Reduce one of your Target's Attributes, chosen randomly, by an amount equal to your Weapon's Critical Damage (pg: 122) minus the Target's Armour (pg: 84).

Random Attribute: Roll 1d6

1 = Strength	3 = Movement	5 = Intelligence
2 = Reflexes	4 = Focus	6 = Perception

Critical Hit Example

Logan has inflicted a Critical Hit (Critical Damage 3) on his Target (Armour 2). His Critical Damage is 1 (3 - 2).

He rolls a 2, so the Target reduces their Reflexes by 1, the Critical Damage.

Blunt Keyword, pg: 124
The "Blunt" Keyword means you can incapacitate a Target without killing them.

Strong Hit: Critical Boost

The Critical Boost increases the Attribute Damage you deal to a Target at or reduced to 0 Endurance.

Requirements, pg: 82

Damage
Action must have the Major Effect: Damage.

Does not Require Hit
You do not have to succeed in your Attack Roll or Deal Damage to apply the Result of this Strong Hit to your Target. GM discretion is allowed if it doesn't make sense.

Result: Attribute Damage

This Attack gains +1 Critical Damage against all damaged Targets at 0 Endurance or reduced to 0 Endurance by this Attack.

High-Armour Targets
The Critical Boost is the best way to kill Targets with high Armour once they are reduced to 0 Endurance.

Critical Boost Example

Jane Attacks a Skilled NPC with 4 Endurance. Her Attack lowers her Target's Endurance to 0, which gives her a free Critical Hit. Despite this, Jane's weapon only has a Critical Damage of 3, and her Target has 3 Armour, so her Attack will cause 0 Attribute Damage.

Fortunately, Jane rolled a Strong Hit, which she uses as a Critical Boost. This increases her Critical Damage from 3 to 4, so her Attack now causes 1 Attribute Damage.

"I applaud the Corporation for its efforts in moving people's perspective towards an economically centred ideology. However, more can be done: there are still aspects of people's lives which are considered too 'sacred' to be affected by the economic ideology.

Therefore, so that my own life is consistent I declare the following: I have no parents, only parent companies; I have no family, only co-workers; I have no children, only subsidiaries. Sacrificing the last sacred cows on the altar of free enterprise has freed me; I implore you all to likewise free your minds."

– Edward Smith, Economic Philosopher.

....

"What a selfish load of crap!"

– Sarah Thrift, Kaltoran Mother of Eight.

Strong Hit: Critical Hit

Die Roll of 6 = Strong Hit.

Requirements: Damage, 1 Use per RoF, No Splash Damage.

Result: Deal your Weapon's Critical Damage (minus Target's Armour) to a random Attribute.

Roll a "6" and Select Strong Hit: Critical Hit
Your Attack Roll (pg: 78) must succeed.
Each 6 lets you use a single Strong Hit Option.
You may cause a number of Critical Hits up to your Weapon's RoF.

Weapon's Critical Damage – Target's Armour = Attribute Damage
You can increase your Critical Damage by using a Critical Boost.

Deal Damage to a Random Attribute
Roll 1d6 to determine which Attribute you Damage.

1 = Strength	4 = Focus
2 = Reflexes	5 = Intelligence
3 = Movement	6 = Perception

Entrenched Cover + Positive Endurance = Target Immune to Critical Hits
If your Target has Entrenched Cover and Endurance above 0, they are immune to Critical Hits.

If Your Target has 0 Endurance, Gain a Free Critical Hit
If your Attack reduces your Target to or if they are at 0 Endurance: you gain a free Critical Hit against them and are able to use the Critical Boost: Strong Hit Option.

Bleeding

See pg: 73 for full Effect rules.
See pg: 92 for full Healing Rolls rules.

If any of your Attributes is reduced to below 0, you gain the Bleeding Effect.

While Bleeding, you take 1 Attribute Damage (ignoring Armour) to a Random Attribute at the start of each of your Turns.

You may only ever have 1 Bleeding Effect.

First Aid (pg: 92) removes the Bleeding Effect.

Death

See pg: 88 for full Critical Hit and Critical Boost rules.

> Player characters die if any Attribute reaches -5.
> Non-player characters die if any Attribute reaches 0.
> Drones and Henchmen die if any Attribute reaches 0.

Reduce Fate to Avoid Death

You may avoid Death by permanently reducing your Fate (pg: 35) by one. Collaborate with the GM to figure out how you miraculously avoided Death.

At the GM's discretion you may still take some Attribute Damage, and you may take Conditions or Effects (pg: 73) that are appropriate to the situation (eg: Unconscious or Lost Limb). Remove the Bleeding Effect and any others that could cause you additional Attribute Damage.

Already wounded, Theodore receives a Critical Hit from a grenade. He takes Attribute Damage to Strength, reducing it to -6. This would kill him, but he decides to cheat death by permanently reducing his Fate by 1.

The GM says the grenade instead reduces Theodore's Strength to -4 and knocks him out, giving him the Unconscious Condition.

Bleeding and Death

When an Attribute drops below 0, it causes Bleeding.
Critical Hits are the main way to kill.

Bleeding Causes Random Attribute Damage Each Turn
If any Attribute is reduced to below 0, you gain the Bleeding Effect. While Bleeding, at the beginning of each of your Turns you receive 1 Attribute Damage (ignoring Armour) to a Random Attribute (roll 1d6).

1 = Strength	4 = Focus
2 = Reflexes	5 = Intelligence
3 = Movement	6 = Perception

Bleeding Can Be Stopped with First Aid (pg: 88)
Succeed on a Medicine Skill Roll against a Difficulty of 10.
Removes Bleeding from you or someone adjacent to you.
Requires: Toolkit.
May be performed during combat.

You Die from Attribute Damage
If any Attribute is reduced to -5 or below you die.
NPCs, Drones and Henchmen die if any Attribute is reduced to 0 or below.

Avoid Death by Reducing Fate
If you would die, you may avoid Death by permanently reducing your Fate by 1. However, you may experience other consequences.

Healing Rolls

See pg: 64 for full Spare Time Point rules.
See pg: 50 for full Medicine Skill description.
See pg: 87 for full Damage rules.
See pg: 108 for full Prep Action rules.

In-Combat Healing

During combat, some minor Effects (eg: Bleeding) can be removed from yourself or an adjacent character by performing a First Aid Healing Roll of 10 or more. This can be done with any Action with the Minor Effect: Skill Roll (pg: 107).

You may also heal Endurance by using any Action with the Major Effect: Recover (pg: 108).

Out-of-Combat Healing Rolls

Attribute Damage is healed outside of combat, by making Medicine Skill Rolls on a wounded character, using one of the following three Healing Roll options:

Paramedics, 12, Requires Relevant Toolbox

Within three minutes of combat ending, you may attempt a single Paramedics Healing Roll (usually using Medicine) against a Difficulty of 12. If you succeed, you Heal a total of 3 Attribute Damage dealt during the most recent combat. This Healing may be combined or split in any way across Attributes and characters. Paramedics Rolls cannot be made on the move. After each combat, only one Paramedics Roll may be attempted per three player characters.

Extended Care, 2x 12t, Requires Relevant Toolbox

During Downtime (pg: 95), you may attempt Extended Care by making two Spare Time Rolls against a Difficulty of 12. If you succeed, you Heal 1 Attribute Damage to each of the target's Attributes and remove one Minor Condition.

Surgery, 2x 14t, Requires Relevant Workshop

During Downtime, you may attempt Surgery by making two Spare Time Rolls against a Difficulty of 14. If you succeed, you Heal 8 Attribute Damage to a single Attribute and remove one Major or Minor Condition.

The recipient of your Surgery may also gain a single free Trait Retro (pg: 32) to change any Trait to an Implant Trait.

Sharing Spare Time Points

Remember that you can share Spare Time Points (pg: 64) among characters for Healing Rolls.

Healing Rolls that don't use the Medicine Skill

Eg: Using the Wealth Skill to hire a doctor.

These often have a -2 Description Penalty.

Conditions, pg: 76

Conditions remain until they are removed by an eligible Skill Roll. Conditions are most commonly gained through intentional Actions (eg: torture), exposure to Dangerous or Hostile Environments (pg: 74), or by reducing Fate to avoid Death (pg: 90).

Other Types of Healing

Not all Healing Rolls use Medicine. Instead, use the Skill that makes the most sense.

Biological Equipment

Medicine should be used for Healing living sentient characters. Bio Tech should be used for repairing Biological Equipment.

Robots

Robots are complicated machines, so use the skill most suited to the problem, usually Mechanics, Electronics, or Programming.

The GM may describe what is wrong and might drop hints as to what you'll need to effect repairs.

Healing Psychological Conditions

Mental problems are Healed with a Psychology Skill Roll. Only use a Medicine Skill Roll if the Condition is primarily caused by a physical ailment (eg: blood clot to the brain).

Self-Healing

If you include yourself in any Healing Roll, including Paramedics, you take a -2 penalty.

Healing ✚

First Aid: Stops Bleeding   (10 +)
May be performed during Combat.
Requires: Toolkit.

Extended Care: Heal all 1   (2x 12t +)
and a Minor Condition.
Requires: Toolbox.

Paramedics: Heal any 3   (12 +2)
Req: Toolbox. Only Heals Dmg dealt this Combat.
Healing may be applied to multiple Characters.
Must be performed directly after a Combat.
Maximum of 1 Paramedics Roll per 3 Characters.

Surgery: Heal one 8   (2x 14t +)
and a Major or Minor Condition.
Requires: Workshop.
May Retro any Trait for a Implant Trait.

Healing Damage

Attribute Damage is only Healed through Healing Rolls.
Endurance Damage is completely Healed during any Downtime.

Recovery =
Focus +Bonuses

Recovery
During combat you may Heal Endurance by performing an Action with the "Recovery" Major Effect.
Heals Endurance Damage equal to your "Recovery".
Recovery = Focus + any bonuses.

12

=

Heal 3
to Damage done during previous combat.

Paramedics
Immediately after combat, you may attempt one Paramedics Roll against a Difficulty of 12. This requires an appropriate Toolbox.
If successful, Heal 3 Attribute Damage dealt during the most recent combat.
You may spread this Healing across multiple characters and Attributes.
You may only attempt 1 Paramedics Healing Roll per 3 player characters in the group.

2x 12t

=

Heal 1
to all Attributes

Extended Care
To perform Extended Care, make two Spare Time Rolls against a Difficulty of 12. This requires an appropriate Toolbox.
If successful, Heal 1 Attribute Damage to every Attribute and remove one Minor Condition.
May not be performed during combat.

2x 14t

=

Heal 8
to one Attribute

Surgery
To perform Surgery, make two Spare Time Rolls against a Difficulty of 14. This requires an appropriate Workshop.
If successful, Heal 8 Attribute Damage to a single Attribute and remove one Major or Minor Condition.
May not be performed during combat.
Recipient may gain a free Trait Retro to change any of their Traits into an Implant Trait.

Downtime

See pg: 64 for full Spare Time Point rules.
See pg: 92 for full Healing Roll rules.
See pg: 152 for full Spacecraft Perk rules.

During Downtime, you're not only out of combat, but also out of any time-critical or high-pressure situations. This time can be used to refill used Clips and Ammunition, seek medical attention, or do other activities.

Heal All Endurance

All lost Endurance is automatically Healed.

Make Spare Time Rolls, pg: 64

You may make Spare Time Rolls.

Replenishing Clips and Ammunition

If you have access to an Armoury (pg: 153) or a suitable vendor, you regain any spent Clips or Ammunition.

Replacing Lost Equipment

If you have access to an Armoury (pg: 153) or a suitable vendor, you may regain any lost Equipment.

Any replaced Equipment loses all Variations and Modifications (pg: 116) that cost Spare Time Points. An Item that cost any Spare Time Points cannot be regained without making another Spare Time Roll.

Using a Workbench, pg: 138

With access to a Workbench, you can rebuild destroyed Drones (pg: 104), repair damaged Armour, Research, and do anything else that requires a little space to work.

Resting at the Spacecraft, Downtime Example

Theodore and his group land their spacecraft into a combat zone that they have been hired to fight in.

During a later fight, they use up a lot of Ammunition, and one of them gets hit and requires Surgery. After the fight they return to their spacecraft and regain all spent Clips and Ammunition from their spacecraft's Armoury (pg: 153). Also, Theodore's companion gets the Surgery she requires in the spacecraft's Medicine Workshop (pg: 138).

After rearming and healing, they head out on foot to track down the remaining enemies who fled into the surrounding jungle and mountains.

It takes Theodore and his group a week to finish tracking them all down. During this time they can only regain spent Ammunition or Clips from what they can find, mostly from looting their enemies. They cannot perform Surgery, but they can perform Extended Care, as this only requires a Toolbox (pg: 135), not a Workshop.

Hraks had finally had enough.

Always the bottom bunk.

Having to stay in this dead metal box, with no comforting heartbeat or organic warmth, breathing this stale-smelling air, and now being treated as lesser than a bottom-feeder… by a Kaltoran!

"My turn to have top bunk, Swagger!" she declared.

Rachel rolled over, ears peaking slightly, the back pair turning a faint mottling red. "You always want top! And you just throw all your rubbish down on my bunk, from Draz cans to shed bits of skin! And now you want it BACK?!"

Hraks sighed in martyrdom. These strange people have never understood the subtlety of Nephilim culture.

"It's only a fair representation," she insisted. "It's to do with the dynamic of the microcosm within our ship and the various factors therein. The more powerful and better-made pieces of weaponry in the armoury get better positioning, in case of emergency, right?"

Rachel looked wary and cautiously ventured a "Yeeeessss…?"

Hraks paused, scratching her long tendril hair. "Then it is only fair and, if we are all being candid, logical," she continued, "that the more genetically superior of us gets pride of place. It allows us to be generous by giving the lesser member our castoffs, so we can help those of us who are less fortunate," she finished emphatically.

Rachel paused for a moment, sorting through the larger words, her lip lifting into a snarl as Hraks's full meaning became offensively clear.

"So, you want the top bunk, because… YOU HAVE BETTER BREEDING THAN ME?!"

....

"I love having my own room," Theodore mused to Max as the girls' yelling match quickly built momentum.

"The armoury also suits me well," Max added.

"I dare say that any room you laid claim to would BECOME the armoury."

Optional: Theatre of the Mind Combat

The following combat rules can be used instead of the standard combat ruleset. They require no miniatures and take less time, making them ideal for combats that don't need to be followed blow for blow, and for gamers who prefer abstract, cinematic combat over detailed, tactical forays.

Equipment
These rules do not use Equipment Stats.

Attributes
These rules only use Attributes to determine Description bonuses and for the purposes of taking Damage.

Traits and Strong Hits
These have limited use with Theatre of the Mind Combat rules.

Combat Summary
At the start of combat, the GM explains the situation. Then, in turn, each player describes what they are doing and makes a Combat Skill Roll related to their approach. The GM then describes what happens. To be victorious, one side must succeed on a number of Combat Skill Rolls equal to two times the participating PCs on that side.

Combat Skill Roll Difficulty
Easy Fight: 10 or more.
Evenly Matched: 12 or more.
Out Matched: 14 or more.
Suicidal: 16 or more.

Justify Your Skill Choice
When you act, you must justify the Skill you choose; you cannot simply use the Skill that gives you the most bonuses. The GM can dictate which Skill you must roll to match the description of your Action (eg: require a Tactical Skill Roll to hide).

Description Bonus and Penalties
If you describe your action well and play to your strengths – by making use of the environment, responding to the GM's descriptions, and so on – the GM can award you a +1 or +2 bonus to your Combat Skill Roll.

Likewise, the GM can assign a -1 or -2 penalty to you if you do not play to your strengths or are at some kind of disadvantage.

Primary Skills
You can not only use your Combat Skills, but also your Primary Skills. This often leads to creative thinking as you must still justify your Skill choice to the GM.

Successful Combat Skill Roll
On a successful roll, the GM or rolling player (with the GM's guidance) describes a positive result based on the chosen skill and stated goal.

To achieve victory, a side must succeed on two Combat Skill Rolls per involved player character on their side.

Victory
A side is victorious when they have accumulated successful Combat Skill Rolls equal to the number of participating PCs on that side multiplied by two. These successes can be rolled by the PCs in any combination.

To achieve victory, the final Combat Skill Roll must be some kind of Attack, otherwise the combat continues.

Failed Combat Skill Roll
A failed Combat Skill Roll causes 2 Attribute Damage to a player character of the GM's choice. It could be the PC who failed the roll, or the PC who put themself most at risk.

Bleeding
Characters cannot gain the Bleeding Effect (pg: 88) during Theatre of the Mind combat.

Non-Lethal Damage
If the NPCs choose to deal non-lethal damage (eg: with blunt weapons), a failed Combat Skill Roll only causes 1 Attribute Damage. If any PC has an Attribute reduced to 0 or below, they go unconscious and can no longer make Combat Skill Rolls. This does not reduce the number of successful Combat Skill Rolls required for victory.

Healing Damage
Damage is healed using the standard Healing Roll rules (pg: 92).

Retreating
Immediately before a character makes a Combat Skill Roll, they may declare that they wish to retreat. If they succeed at this Combat Skill Roll with a +2 bonus, they exit the combat. For the remainder of combat, they make no further Combat Skill Rolls and take no more Damage. This Skill Roll does not count towards the total of successful Skill Rolls required for victory, and their departure from combat does not reduce that total.

Theatre of the Mind Combat

Combat without miniatures.
Be sure to describe the fight as you roll.

GM Sets Difficulty
The GM describes the situation to the players, pointing out anything important (eg: how many enemies there are, and how they are armed), and setting the mood.

Player Explains Approach and Skill
In turn, each involved player explains their approach to the conflict, then picks a Skill to use based on their approach.

Certain Skills may require specific or suitable tools (eg: Small Arms requires a Gun).

Players who describe a particularly good or bad approach with the relevant Skill choice may gain a bonus or penalty (+2 to -2) to their Skill Roll.

Player Rolls Dice and Adds Bonuses
The player rolls 3d6 and adds their Combat Skill bonus or penalty then add, then any Description bonus or penalty given by the GM.

If you roll a "6" you score a Strong Hit (pg: 82).

GM Describes the Result
Based on the result of the roll, the approach, and the Skill, the GM describes the outcome.

(With the GM's permission and guidance, the player may describe what happens.)

Failed Roll = 2 Points of Damage to a Random Attribute (1d6)"
If the roll failed, the GM deals 2 Attribute Damage to a random Attribute: roll 1d6.

1 = Strength	4 = Focus
2 = Reflexes	5 = Intelligence
3 = Movement	6 = Perception

This Damage DOES NOT have to be applied to the character that failed the Skill Roll. It may be applied to the character who is most vulnerable.

Damage can be healed with Healing Rolls (pg: 92).

2 Successes per Character to Achieve Victory
Repeat these steps until one side accumulates successful Combat Skill Rolls equal to the number of involved PCs on that side times two.

The final successful Skill Roll must be some kind of Attack.

Option 1: Occasional Theatre of the Mind Combat

This is the most flexible option. Many (or most) of your fights will use the standard combat rules, but you may use the Theatre of the Mind Combat rules when you want to quickly complete a combat that does not need to be measured blow by blow.

Example Uses

» For when PCs have split up, and only some of them have gotten into a fight.
» For when you don't want a fight to slow down the game Session.
» For less important or lighthearted fights.

Option 2: Theatre of the Mind Only Game

This option will dramatically change the feel of the rules and will make many Traits redundant.

Example Use

» You wish to focus on spacecraft Combat, not personal Combat, so you run all personal Combat using the Theatre of the Mind rules.

Use These Rules for Theatre of the Mind Only Games

» Players may use the Traits and Combat Items listed on the next page.
» Any time a character would gain Resources (pg: 56), they receive a Spare Time Point (pg: 64) instead.
» All Weapons are purchased with Spare Time Points, not Resources (see next page).

Feral Nephilim Lair, Theatre of the Mind Example

GM: The massive Feral Nephilim beast bellows out a defiant roar as you approach its lair. The smell of rot and decay from the many half eaten carcasses scattered around the clearing fills the air.

The beast is as large as a car, with a thick brown plated hide and a horned, scarred face. Its eyes glow red and its breath fogs in the morning cold. There is no hint of intelligence in its bestial face, only violence.

Victories = 1 of 8, Combat Skill Roll Difficulty = 12

GM: Simon, you're first. What do you do?
Simon: Is there any cover around?
GM: Yes, there is a large, half-eaten carcass nearby.
Simon: Great, I draw my twin Ion Pistols and dive behind the carcass while firing.
GM: Sounds great. Give me a Small Arms Roll of at least 12, with a +1 bonus for good description since you have a high Movement Attribute.
Simon: (Rolls an 11, with +1 Description bonus and +1 Skill bonus) Awesome! I succeed!
GM: Your fast reflexes quickly get you to cover as the beast charges. Your shots catch its attention, and it goes right for you. But it stops just short, its path blocked by the decaying corpse you are hiding behind.

GM: Geordie, you're next. What do you do?
Geordie: I draw my sword and charge at the beast.
GM: You can make it, but the carcass is partially blocking your way.
Geordie: That's OK.
GM: OK, give me an Exotic Skill Roll at a –1 Description penalty.
Geordie: (Rolls an 11, with –1 Description Penalty and +2 Skill Bonus). Excellent, I succeed! Can I describe what happens?
GM: Sure, but you don't kill it.
Geordie: I charge forward, jumping over the carcass to give it a long slash down the side of its head. It bellows in rage as it slashes at me, forcing me to dive for cover as its massive claws slash my cloak.
GM: Great description. Jye, you're next.

Victories = 2 of 8, Combat Skill Roll Difficulty = 12

Jye: OK, it looks like Simon and Geordie are fairly close to it. so I'd better not use my grenades… hmm… I think I will use my Puncture Rifle.
I draw my Puncture Rifle and move around the flank, being very careful to keep plenty of distance between me and the beast. While it is uselessly trying to hit Geordie I shoot at it.
GM: Nice description, and your puncture rifle will be quite effective against such a well-armoured target. Gain a +1 Description bonus.
Jye: (Rolls a 9, with +1 Description bonus and +1 Skill bonus) Darn, I think I failed and I don't have any Fate Points left.
GM: Your shot deflects off its massive hide as it continues its relentless assault against your teammate.
Geordie, dropping your guard for just a split second and its claws lash out at your (Rolls a d6 to determine what Attribute is Damaged. Rolls a 1: Strength) torso and arm. Leaving long bloody wounds and a burning sensation in your skin. Take 2 Attribute Damage.
Geordie: Oh crap.

Victories = 3 of 8, Combat Skill Roll Difficulty = 12

GM: OK, Frank, it's your go.
Frank: Certainly I've already pulled out my flamethrower. I rush forward, giving a mighty Legion war cry as I pull the trigger, spraying it with burning death!
GM: Nice! I will give you a +1 Description bonus to your Heavy Weapons Skill Roll.
Frank: (Rolls a 8, with +1 Description bonus and +2 Skill bonus) Darn… but I spend a Fate Point to let me re-roll. (Rolls a 15) Excellent!
GM: As you charge forward with your flamethrower, your flame goes wide, but you manage to rein it in as you get close. The beast roars in rage and pain as it is covered in napalm. It turns towards you, Frank, its glowing eyes narrowing as it readies for another charge.
Simon, it is back to you. What do you do?

Traits, Theatre of the Mind Only Game

Small Arms	Requirements	Benefits
Flexible		Gain +1 to Small Arms as long as you have a combined Weapon Weight of 4 or more.
Hit and Run		If you succeed at a Retreating Personal Combat Skill Roll, it counts as a Success.
Sniper Shot		+2 for your first Personal Skill Roll made during a Combat.

Heavy Arms	Requirements	Benefits	Disadvantages
Make a Hole		Passing a Heavy Arms Combat Skill Roll gives all of your Allies a +1 bonus to their next Personal Combat Skill Roll (for this Combat).	-1, Heavy Arms.
Take Down		You may spend 1 Fate Point to make a Successful Heavy Arms Combat Skill Roll count as 2 Successes.	-2, Heavy Arms.
Unleash		+4 for your first Heavy Arms Combat Skill Roll made during a Combat.	-1, Heavy Arms.

Tactical	Requirements	Benefits	Disadvantages
Combat Leader		You may grant any Ally one free re-roll to a Combat Skill Roll. Can only be used once per Combat.	
Elusive		Your Failed Tactical Combat Skill Rolls do not result in Attribute Damage.	-1, Tactical.
Tactical Thinker		Gain +2 to future Personal Combat Skill Rolls during this Combat after failing a Personal Combat Skill Roll.	

Exotic	Requirements	Benefits	Disadvantages
Charger		+2 for your first Exotic Combat Skill Roll made during a Combat.	
Risk Taker		+1, all Personal Combat Skills	If you take Attribute Damage during a Combat encounter, you take one additional point of damage.
Technician		Once per Combat, you may make a Professional Combat Skill Roll at a +2 bonus. This action must be approved by the GM first.	

Combat Items, Theatre of the Mind Only Game

Weapon:	Weight	Description	Cost
Basic Weapon	1	Choose a Personal Combat Skill, you are now to make Combat Skill Rolls with chosen as long as you wield this weapon.	8t
Valuable Weapon	2	Same as Basic Weapon, but grants a +1 bonus to chosen Skill (does not Stack with other Weapons).	16t
Expensive Weapon	2	Same as Basic Weapon, but grants a +2 bonus to chosen Skill (does not Stack with other Weapons).	22t

Utility:	Weight	Description	Cost
Defensive Item	–	+2 to your Retreat Combat Skill Rolls.	18t
Evasive Item	–	1 use, +2 to you or an Ally's Retreat Combat Skill Roll.	14t
Med Booster	–	1 use, heal 1 additional point of Attribute Damage after a Combat.	16t
Useful Item	–	1 use, you or an Ally gains a +2 bonus to a single Combat Skill Roll.	18t

Combat Outfit, Theatre of the Mind Only Game (Max 1)

Outfit:	Weight	Description	Cost
Light Armour	–	Once per Combat you may take 1 Attribute Damage to two Attributes (2d6) rather than 2 Damage to one Attribute.	12t
Heavy Armour	–	-1 to all Personal Combat Skills, reroll first failed Combat Skill Roll made during a Combat.	18t
Stealth Armour	–	Twice per Combat you may choose to not make a Skill Roll, this does not count as a Failed Roll and you gain +2 to your next Skill Roll.	18t

Combat Turns & Actions

Overview

See pg: 102 for full Weapon Type rules.
See pg: 107 for full Action Major Effects rules.
See pg: 107 for full Action Minor Effects rules.

Combat is broken up into Turns, each representing about fifteen seconds of combat.

> Each character in combat takes a Turn.
> When you take a Turn, you may take 2 Actions.

Actions are split into three categories: Tactical, Range, and Melee. You use any Actions, even the same one, in any order.

> ### Weapon Type, pg: 102
> Each Weapon has one or more Weapon Types. These determine which Actions the wielder can perform with the Weapon.

Free Actions

Free Actions, such as Fate-activated abilities (pg: 35), may be taken at any time, even during another character's Turn.

If multiple characters wish to perform a Free Action at once, the character with the highest Combat Order acts first.

Starting Combat

Combat begins as soon as any character or the GM declares an Attack action.

Choose Standard or Theatre of the Mind Rules

At the start of each combat, the GM decides to use either the standard combat rules or the streamlined Theatre of the Mind rules (pg: 96).

Even if you would normally use the standard rules, you may wish to use the Theatre of the Mind rules for a minor combat that you don't wish to spend much time on (eg: a bar fight).

Combat Order

During combat, each character takes a Turn in Combat Order.

> Determine Combat Order by comparing
> Intelligence (+any bonuses).
> The player highest in Combat Order goes first.

If multiple characters have the same Intelligence, the character with the higher Reflexes goes first. If there is still a tie, roll a die or play a quick round of rock, paper, scissors at the start of each Turn.

Action Name ⌐ Action Major Effects ⌐ Action Minor Effects

Pick any 2 Actions Per Turn			Bonuses from the same Action do not Stack					
Tactical Actions			**Range Actions**			**Melee Actions**		
Full Move	Move	Move +2	Snap Shot	Attack Damage Move		Strike	Attack Damage Move	Hit +Ref +Extra RoF Dice Move -2
Take Cover	Move	+1 Cover Step Armour vs Slow +1 (go Prone)	Spray Fire	Attack Damage Move	Hit +Per +Extra RoF Dice Move -2	Charge	Attack Damage Move	Move +2 (Straight Line) Damage +1 (per 4 Movement)
Prep	Recover	Pick One: Draw Wpn, Reload, Un-Jam, Set Up, Pull Down, Use Stim or Skill Roll (Medical).	Sighted Shot	Attack Damage	Hit +Per Range +Foc	Block	Impair	Hit +Per +Foc On Hit: Debuff Targets next Attack: Strong Hit -1
Analyse	Attack Recover	On Hit: Boost next Attack: Crit Attribute Location +/-2	Throw	Attack Damage Move	Hit +Ref Range +Str	Impair	Damage Impair Move	Hit +Ref +Str On Hit: Pick One Debuff vs Target: Prone, Grab or Move 1
Stealth	Stealth	Vs Highest Defence On Hit: Cannot Be Targeted	Overwatch	Attack* Damage	Hit +Per *May Attack in a 180 Arc in response to any Action.	Escape	Damage Impair Move	Hit +Ref +Str On Hit: Debuff Target: Loose Grabbing Target.

Delaying Your Turn

When your Turn would begin, you may choose to delay your Turn until after another character with a lower Combat Order takes their Turn.

Once you have delayed your Turn, you may not delay it again during the same Turn. If the character you had decided to act after decides to delay their Turn, you will still act after that character.

Combat Order   (Int + 2) = (4)

Surprise Round

See pg: 108-111 for a full list of available Actions.
See pg: 104 for full Drone rules.
See pg: 296 for full Henchmen rules.

If a character or group is not expecting combat when it begins, then the Attackers gain a Surprise Round. If all characters are ready for combat when it starts, nobody gains a Surprise Round.

> ### Surprise Round
> Everyone qualifying for the Surprise Round gets a Turn in which they can perform 1 Action.

Drones, pg: 104

These may act during your Surprise Round, taking their single bonus Action, making them very effective at ambush.

Companions, pg: 105

Only gain a Surprise Round if they are expecting combat.

> "Too long have we regarded restraint a weakness."
>
> - Gri, musing on Nephilim long-term survival.

Ambush, Surprise Round Example

The GM asks Henderson to make an Awareness Skill Roll. He rolls a total of 12, which the GM says is not high enough.

Suddenly Henderson is ambushed by a mugger that he failed to notice. The mugger gains a Surprise Round against Henderson.

If Henderson had passed his Awareness Roll, then neither he nor the muffer would have gained a Surprise Round. Both would have acted in their Combat Order.

Gun Fight, Combat Overview Example

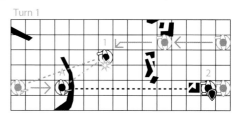

Phebe (A) is facing off against 2 opponents. They both are higher in Combat Order, so they take their Turns before she does.

Opponent 1 wishes to get as close to Phebe as possible, so he performs 2 Full Move Actions for his first Turn. Opponent 2 performs a Take Cover Action for his first Action and Attacks Phebe with a Sighted Shot for his second Action.

For Phebe's Turn, she performs a Snap Shot, moving into Cover and Attacking opponent 1. For her second Action, she performs a Sighted Shot against opponent 1.

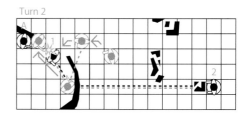

Once everyone has taken their Turn, the Round ends and the next Round begins. Opponent 1 acts first again, performing 2 Snap Shot Actions, Moving and Attacking with each Action.

Opponent 2 performs 2 Sighted Shots against Phebe. During Phebe's Turn, she performs a Snap Shot against opponent 1, enabling her to Attack and then move behind her opponent. For her second Action, she performs a Melee Strike, Attacking her Target and then moving back one space.

The fight will continue until one side (Phebe or her opponents) is either unwilling or unable to fight.

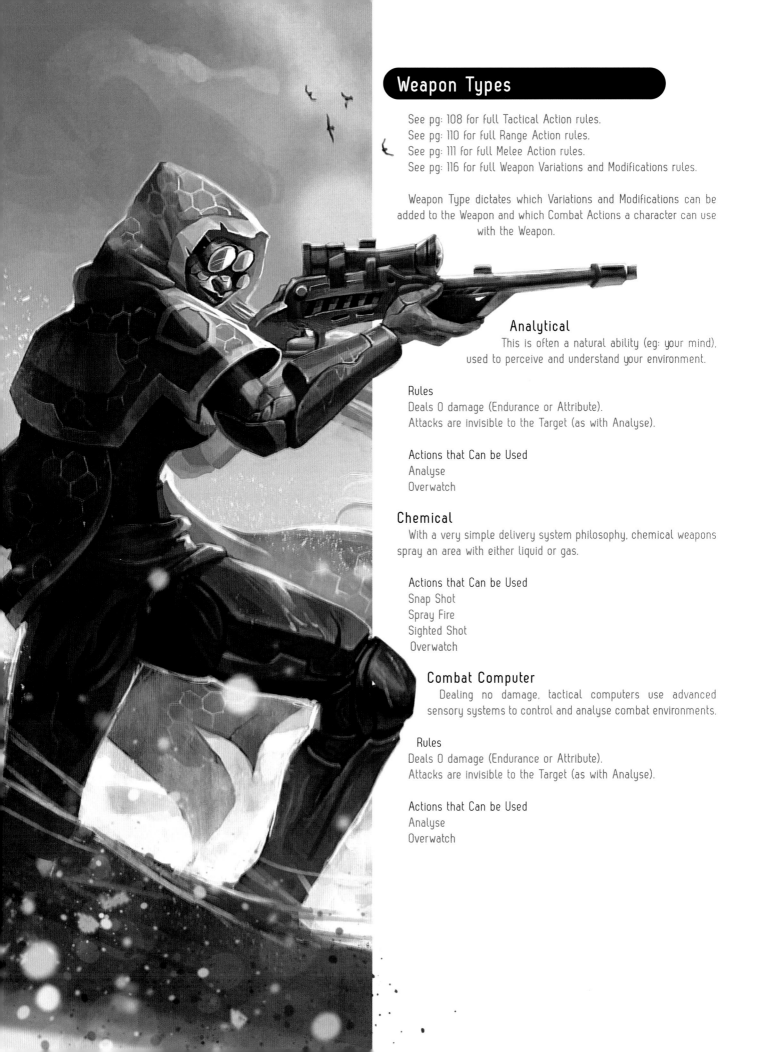

Weapon Types

See pg: 108 for full Tactical Action rules.
See pg: 110 for full Range Action rules.
See pg: 111 for full Melee Action rules.
See pg: 116 for full Weapon Variations and Modifications rules.

Weapon Type dictates which Variations and Modifications can be added to the Weapon and which Combat Actions a character can use with the Weapon.

Analytical

This is often a natural ability (eg: your mind), used to perceive and understand your environment.

Rules
Deals 0 damage (Endurance or Attribute).
Attacks are invisible to the Target (as with Analyse).

Actions that Can be Used
Analyse
Overwatch

Chemical

With a very simple delivery system philosophy, chemical weapons spray an area with either liquid or gas.

Actions that Can be Used
Snap Shot
Spray Fire
Sighted Shot
Overwatch

Combat Computer

Dealing no damage, tactical computers use advanced sensory systems to control and analyse combat environments.

Rules
Deals 0 damage (Endurance or Attribute).
Attacks are invisible to the Target (as with Analyse).

Actions that Can be Used
Analyse
Overwatch

Disruptor

Generates an (often) non-lethal electrical burst that disrupts electrical devices, nervous systems, and sensory inputs. Particularly effective versus Drones and Targets with Implants, Disruptors are a popular choice for law enforcement, slavers, and for torture due to their non-lethal nature.

Actions that Can be Used
Snap Shot
Spray Fire
Sighted Shot
Overwatch

Gun

Popular projectile delivery system due to its ease of use and production.

Rules
If the Weapon also has the "Splash" Keyword, the wielder is immune to Damage from the Weapon (eg: if you miss with an Attack and it Scatters onto you).

Actions that Can be Used
Snap Shot
Spray Fire
Sighted Shot
Overwatch

Gun or Shell

When you acquire this Weapon, choose if it has the Gun or Shell Weapon Type. Once chosen, the Weapon uses the normal rules for its Type. This choice cannot be changed.

Impairment

A flexible and useful Weapon for controlling your enemies' movement.

Actions that Can be Used
Impair
Escape

Melee

It was once thought that the closer you got to your opponent, the less important your technology became. With strength augmentation, energy blades, and nanosharpening, this idea has never been less true.

Actions that Can be Used
Strike
Charge
Block
Overwatch

Psionic

These weapons have a mysterious connection to the Ley Lines (pg: 278) and the user's mind.

Rules
Only usable by Psionic characters (pg: 33).
Attack Rolls are allways against a Target's Defence vs Psionic.

Actions that Can be Used
Psionic Weapons allways have at least one other Weapon Type. This Type determines what Actions can be used by this Weapon.

Shell

A similar design philosophy to most gun systems, but the space within its special projectiles allows for greater design variation.

Rules
If the Weapon also has the "Splash" Keyword, the Target's Cover is determined from the location hit by the Attack, not the direction of the Attack.

Actions that Can be Used
Snap Shot
Spray Fire
Sighted Shot
Overwatch

Thrown

A physical projectile, thrown using the muscle strength of the user.

Thrown Weapons only ever have the Thrown and Overwatch Actions despite any other Weapon Types (eg: Shell or Disruptor) they might have.

Actions that Can be Used
Thrown
Overwatch

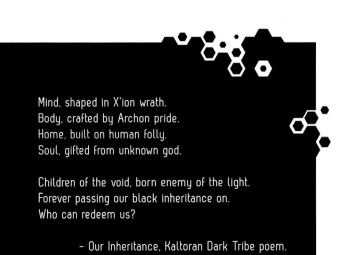

Mind, shaped in X'ion wrath.
Body, crafted by Archon pride.
Home, built on human folly.
Soul, gifted from unknown god.

Children of the void, born enemy of the light.
Forever passing our black inheritance on.
Who can redeem us?

- Our Inheritance, Kaltoran Dark Tribe poem.

Drones

Constructed devices that can be remotely controlled to fire weapons or use tools.

> **Drones have a minimum cost of 1 Resource.**

Control

Characters may have as many Drones as they can afford. During their Turn, a character may control each Drone as a Free Action (pg: 100).

Auto-Pilot
If its Controller becomes incapacitated, the Drone continues its last assigned task under the GM's control.

Always Active.
Drones do not need to be Drawn (pg: 114).

Set Up and Pull Down
Once a Drone is Set Up (pg: 126), its Controller can move independently. However, to Pull Down the drone, the Controller must be adjacent to it. Drones can take their Action during the Turn they are Set Up.

Weight, X (+Y)

A Drone always takes "X" Equipment Slots, even while Active; this represents the Controller carrying the required control systems. While carried, a Drone takes "+Y" additional Equipment Slots.

Throwing a Drone
Drones that can be Thrown (eg: Swarm Drone) deal no Damage when they are Set Up as a Throw Action (pg: 110). Once Thrown, they can take their Action on the same Turn but get no movement. All Bodies (pg: 105) in a group can be Thrown at once.

1 Action each Turn

> ### Drone Action
> On your Turn, each of your Drones may Move and Attack, Reload, Set Up, Pull Down, Analyse, Stealth, or Escape.

Surprise Round, pg: 101
All your Drones may act during your Surprise Round.

Movement, pg: 72
Drones with a movement of at least 1 can move that amount each Turn. Before or after they Attack.
They may also spend this movement on interactions with their environment (pg: 73). As required, use a Drone's Slots Stat as their Attribute (eg: Strength for moving an object).

Attack/Reload/Set Up/Pull Down
Drones may make a single Attack Roll (pg: 78), Reload (pg: 107), Set Up (pg: 126) or Pull Down (pg: 126).

> ### Attack Roll Bonus
> Add any bonuses or penalties to your Personal Combat Skill for both the Skill that matches the Drone and its Weapon. If the Drone and Weapon come from the same category, you do not gain double the Skill bonus.

RoF 2+
Drone Attacks have the Minor Effect: Hit +Extra RoF Dice (pg: 107).

Analyse (pg: 109), Stealth (pg: 109), Escape (pg: 111)
As normal, but using Drones' Slots Stat in place of the appropriate Attribute.

Destruction

Drones have 0 Endurance, pg: 87
As Drones have 0 Endurance, any hit they take causes a Critical Hit (pg: 88), making them easy to destroy.

Armour
Any Attribute Damage dealt to the Drone is reduced by this amount.

> **A Drone is destroyed if it takes 1 Attribute Damage.**

Rebuilding a Drone from a Wrecked Body
If your Drone is Destroyed, it leaves a Wrecked Body. If you can recover this, you can rebuild it during any Downtime (pg: 95) as long as you have access to a Workbench (pg: 138).

Lost Body
If you cannot recover a Drone's Wrecked Body, you lose all Spare Time Points spent on it.

Weapons

Slots
A Drone may be Equipped with Weapons with a combined Weight up to its Slot Stat.

Drawing Weapon, pg: 114
Drone Weapons are always considered Active and do not need to be Drawn.

Multiple Weapons
A Drone may have multiple Weapons, but may only Attack with one Weapon per Turn.

Defence, pg: 84

Drones have a Defence Stat that is used against all Attacks.

Defence vs Impair

Add the Drone's Slot Stat to its Defence vs Impair.

Defence vs Stealth

A Drone counts as an Ally for the purposes of determining the group's Defence vs Stealth.

Multiple Bodies

Drones can gain additional Bodies, mostly from the Drone Modification "Multiply" (pg: 365), which grants 1 additional Body per purchase.

Each Body has the same Stats, Variations, Modifications, and equipment as the original Drone.

These additional Models may move independently from the original Drone, but they may not use Attack, Escape, Reload, Analyse, or Stealth separately.

> **All Drone bodies Attack as a single Attack Roll.**

Calculating Cover and Range, Attacking

When Attacking with Drone Bodies, calculate the Target's Cover as the average of all Cover (rounded in the players' favour) calculated from the Attacking Drones (not all Drones need to Attack).

Similarly, to calculate Range, use the average Range of all Attacking Drones.

Calculating Cover and Range, Defending

Each Drone Body is Attacked and Destroyed separately. Calculate its Cover and the Range from the Attacker to the Drone Body separately from other Bodies. Do not average the Cover or the Range of all Drone Bodies.

Wrecked Additional Bodies

If you collect at least half of your Drones' Wrecked Bodies, you do not lose any spent Spare Time Points. Drone Bodies are rebuilt exactly like normal Drones.

Ammunition, pg: 122

Most Weapons have an Ammunition value equal to its RoF multiplied by some value. A Drones's RoF increases by adding additional Bodies, which also increases your Ammunition.

As Bodies are destroyed, your maximum Ammunition will be reduced. This does not reduce your current Ammunition unless it would reduce your maximum below your current Ammunition.

Drones and Cover, Multiple Bodies Example

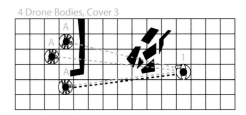

4 Drone Bodies, Cover 3

Logan has a group of Drones (A) with 3 Bodies, which count as a single Weapon. He is Attacking a Bounty Hunter (1).

Logan Attacks with all of his Drones as a single Attack Roll. Each Body beyond the first gives him +1 Rate of Fire and +1 Endurance Damage (see Drone Modification Multiply, pg: 365). Logan's Target is behind some rubble, granting Heavy Cover against two of the Drones and no Cover against one. The GM averages this to Light Cover versus the Drones' Attack.

Two of the Drones have Cover against the Bounty Hunter (1), and one has no Cover. When the Bounty Hunter Attacks, he does not average the Drones' Cover. The Bounty Hunter (1) Attacks the Drone with no Cover. Drones never have Endurance (pg: 87), so he causes an automatic Critical Hit (pg: 88) and can add a Critical Boost (pg: 88) to his Attack. If he causes any Attribute Damage (pg: 87), he destroys the Drone Body with no cover.

Companion

This is an allied sentient NPC, such as a hired mercenary or pet.

Same Rules as Drone

Companions use the same rules as Drones, except as listed below. The main difference is that they have a mind of their own.

Control

Companions have a personality and a will; they won't always do exactly what their Controller wants. If their Controller is incapacitated, they will carry on as they see fit.

They may also act under their own, GM-directed initiative.

Death

If a Companion dies, they cannot be rebuilt or resurrected. All spent Spare Time Points are lost.

Drawing Weapon, pg: 144

A Companion's Weapons are not considered always Active; they must be Drawn by the Companion.

Action Major Effects

See pg: 72 for full Movement rules.
See pg: 78 for full Attack Roll rules.
See pg: 87 for full Damage rules.

Each Action has at least 1 Major Effect. Whenever you use an Action, you gain its Major Effects.

Attack

You may make an Attack Roll (pg: 78) against a Target's Defence with a Weapon that you have Equipped (pg: 114).

Moving and Attacking

If the Action also has the Move Effect (see below), you may Move and then Attack or Attack and then Move. You may not Attack partway through your Movement.

Damage

On a successful Attack Roll, your Weapon deals its Endurance Damage (pg: 122) to your Target's Endurance.

Critical Hit and Critical Boost, pg: 88

This Action allows you to cause Critical Hits and Critical Boost Strong Hits Options against your Target.

Impair

You may make an Attack Roll against a Target's Defence vs Impair Defence Stat (pg: 84).

Move

You may move a number of spaces equal to or less than your Movement Attribute.

Recover

You may heal your Endurance by an amount equal to your Recovery Stat (pg: 93), up to your Maximum Endurance.

Stealth

See pg: 109 for full Stealth Action rules.

While in Cover (pg: 86), you may make an Attack (pg: 78) against a Target's Defence vs Stealth Stat. No Weapon required.

"So there I was: with the gun, the girl, and only thirty seconds to get the smuggled cargo of booze out before the bomb goes off! … THIS IS THE LIFE I TELL YA! THE LIFE!"

- Jonathan Swagger at the Home Brew Bar.

Action Minor Effects

See pg: 72 for full Movement rules.
See pg: 78 for full Attack Roll rules.
See pg: 81 for full Rate of Fire rules.
See pg: 84 for full Defence rules.
See pg: 73 for full Effect rules.

Minor Effects commonly give bonuses to your Attack Roll (pg: 78) and Defences (pg: 84).

No Bonus Stacking
Bonuses from multiple Actions don't stack.

Cover +X Steps

Add "X" Steps to any Cover (pg: 86) benefits you are receiving.

Defence +X

Add "X" to your Defence score until your next Turn.

Hit +X

Add "X" to your Attack Roll associated with this Action.

Hit +Extra RoF Dice

If your Weapon has Rate of Fire (RoF) of 2 or more you may spend additional Ammunition to roll additional Attack Roll dice (see pg: 81).

Move +X

Add "X" to the number of spaces you may Move with this Action.

Range +X

Add "X" to your Weapon's Range (Rng) for any Attacks made with this Action.

Boost Next Attack: X

Boost your next Attack Roll (pg: 78), taken within 1 Turn. This is fully explained under each Action with this Minor Effect (pg: 108-111).

On Hit: X

If this Attack Roll succeeds, you may do "X". Fully explained under each Action (pg: 108-111).

Pick One: X, Y, or Z

You may choose to do "X", "Y", or "Z". Each time you perform this Action, you may make a different choice. Fully explained under each Action (pg: 108-111).

Other Minor Effects

Fully explained under each Action (pg: 108-111).

Tactical Actions

See pg: 72 for full Movement rules.
See pg: 84 for full Defence Stat rules
See pg: 100 for full Turns and Actions rules.
See pg: 107 for Action Major Effect rules
See pg: 107 for Action Minor Effect rules.

Full Move

You are either running as fast as you can or spending serious effort interacting with your environment.

Major Effect
Move

Minor Effects
Move +2

Take Cover

See pg: 86 for full Cover rules.
See pg: 87 for full Damage rules.

You take Cover as you move carefully to avoid enemy Attacks, especially the slow but powerful ones.

Major Effect
Move

Minor Effects
+1 Cover Step
Increase your Cover by 1 Step. You must already have at least 1 Step of Cover.

> **Tip: Flanking and Take Cover**
> If you are relying on Environmental Cover and not Armour, be careful of flanking enemies, as you may not only lose your Cover Defence bonus, but also any immunity to Critical Hits granted by Entrenched Cover.

Armour vs Slow +1 (go Prone)
Whenever you are targeted by an Attack with the "Slow" Keyword (pg: 126), you may go Prone (pg: 76) as a Free Action (pg: 100) and gain Armour vs Slow +1 (does not Stack) until your next Turn.

Prep

See pg: 38 for full Skills rules.
See pg: 92 for full Healing rules.
See pg: 114 for full Equipment Slots rules.

You are briefly catching your breath and regaining a little focus, while possibly taking time to do a short task.

Major Effect
Recover

Minor Effects
Pick One: X

Draw Weapon (Draw Wpn)
See pg: 114 for full Make Active rules.

Makes an Equipped Weapon Active. Takes 1 Action to Draw your Weapon per its Load Stat (pg: 122).

Reload
Swaps out your Active Weapon's current Clip for a new one (pg: 122). Takes 1 Action to Reload a Weapon per its Load Stat (pg: 122).

Your Weapon may be Reload once per your Weapon's Clips Stat (pg: 122).

Un-Jam
Removes any Jammed Effects (pg: 125) from your Active Weapon. Takes 1 Action to Un-Jam a Weapon per its Load Stat (pg: 122).

Set Up, Pull Down
Activate a Weapon that requires Set Up (pg: 126), or Pull Down (pg: 126) a Weapon so you can move with it.

Use Stim
Most Stims are Load 0, so they take no time to make Active, and can be used with a single Action. If a Stim has a positive Load Stat, it must be made Active (pg: 114) before it can be used.

Skill Roll
Sometimes you need to use a Non-Personal Combat Skill during combat, most commonly Medicine for First Aid (pg: 87) to stop Bleeding (pg: 90). Often the GM will require multiple Actions to compete a task, depending on its complexity.

> **Remember, Reloading Heals You**
> Reloading is done by taking a Prep Action, which also Heals Endurance (pg: 93).

Analyse

You carefully analyse your Target to make your next Attack more accurate.

Major Effect
Attack
Recover

Minor Effects
On Hit: Boost next Attack; Crit Attribute Location +/-2
Make an Attack Roll with an Analytical Weapon (eg: Mind) or a Combat Computer Weapon versus the Target's Defence. If you succeed, your next Attack Roll against that Target gains a Boost to any Critical Hits (pg: 88) it causes: when you roll to randomly determine the damaged Attribute, you may increase or decrease the result by up to two. This Boost lasts until the end of your next Turn.

> ## Use Your Mind!
> All characters have access to the
> Tactical Weapon: Mind.
>
> You can use this to Analyse a Target if you don't
> have access to a Combat Computer.

Lining up the Shot, Analyse Example

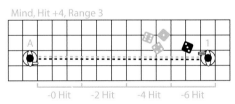

Mind, Hit +4, Range 3

-0 Hit   -2 Hit   -4 Hit   -6 Hit

Tanya (A) only has 1 Ammunition left in her Rifle and needs to kill her Target (1) by damaging the right Attribute. She spends her first Action on Analyse to improve her later Attack.

She does not have a Combat Computer Equipped, so she must use her Mind to Analyse her Target, giving her Hit +4 (Intelligence +Tactical) and Range 3 (Focus). Her Target has Defence 8, so she needs to make an Attack Roll of at least 8 (10 +4(Hit) –6(Range) = 8). She rolls an 11, which is a hit!

On her next Action, she Attacks with the Rifle Attack and causes a Critical Hit. She rolls a d6 to determine which Attribute she Damages, and gets a "3" (Movement). This isn't what she wants, so she uses the Boost given by Analyse, subtracting one to get a "2" (Reflexes).

Stealth

You attempt to hide from your enemies. Using Stealth does not require a Weapon.

Major Effect
Stealth

Minor Effects
Vs Highest Defence
Make your Attack Roll (pg: 78) against the highest of your opponents' Defence vs Stealth. If you succeed, you gain the Stealthed Effect against all opponents.

On Hit: Cannot Be Targeted
When you have the Stealthed Effect, enemies cannot make any Attack Rolls (pg: 78) against you and can also not see where you are moving and what you are doing.

Stealthed Effect
Requires Cover
You must be gaining at least Light Cover (pg: 86) to perform this Action. If you end a Turn outside Cover, the effects of this Action end.

Each Turn
Stealthed Effect is lost at the start of your next Turn if your first Action is not a successful Stealth.

Attacking
Making an Attack Roll with any visible attack, removes the Stealthed Effect from you.

Splash Attacks, pg: 127
Attack Rolls with the "Splash" Keyword can Attack a space rather than a specific Target. This means the Splash Attack can damage a Stealthed character. However, Opponents can only Attack the Ground near a Stealthed character if they have a plausible reason (GM's choice), eg: seeing someone not Stealthed disappear behind Cover before going Stealthed.

Stealth Outside Combat
Stealth has many non-combat applications, which are rolled just like Skill Rolls, except that the Difficulty is the highest of any nearby NPCs' Defence vs Stealth. (Remember, the Difficulty increases by 1 for every other NPC in the area up to +10.)

Unlike in combat, once you succeed at Stealth, you do not need to make new Stealth Rolls every Turn, just as the GM deems appropriate (eg: once per 5 minutes, or as the situation changes).

Range Actions

Snap Shot

While quickly dashing across the battlefield, you let off a quick shot with your Weapon.

Major Effects
Move
Attack

Spray Fire

You pull down the trigger and let your gun do most of the work as you keep your position flexible.

Major Effects
Attack
Damage
Move

Minor Effects
Hit +Per +Extra RoF Dice
See pg: 78 for full Attack Roll and Rate of Fire rules.

Move -2

Sighted Shot

Concentrating carefully, you minimise the consequences of attacking at long range.

Major Effect
Attack
Damage

Minor Effects
Hit +Per
Range +Foc

Throw

You throw your weapon at your opponent!

Major Effects
Attack
Damage
Move

Minor Effect
Hit +Ref
Range +Str

Overwatch

With your weapon at the ready, you wait carefully. You are either waiting to catch your target in a moment of vulnerability, or waiting to protect an area against potential attacks.

But be careful: if your target is quick enough, they might take you down before you can.

Major Effect
Attack*
Damage

Minor Effects
Hit +Per

*Special Attack Rules
Until your next Turn, if a character performs an Action in the 180-degree arc you are facing, you may make an Attack Roll as a Free Action (pg: 100). This Attack Roll is made after the triggering character's Action ends.

This Attack can only be taken against a Target within the 180-degree arc. The Attack gains no Attribute bonus (like Sighted Shot).

If multiple characters with Overwatch wish to Attack in response to the same Action, they resolve in Combat Order (pg: 100) and may choose to delay their Attack.

Overwatch, Example

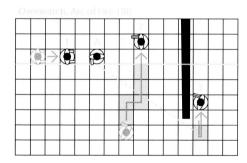

During his Turn, Simon (A) uses Overwatch.

Opponent 1 uses Move, but stays out of Simon's 180-degree arc, so Simon cannot make his Attack in response.

Opponent 2 starts within Simon's arc, but moves outside of it. Simon may Attack in response to this Action, but may not Attack opponent 2 because they are now outside Simon's 180-degree arc.

Opponent 3 starts within Simon's 180-degree arc and moves to a location still within the arc. Simon may Attack in response to this Action, and may Target opponent 3 with this Attack. If opponent 2 had performed their Action, as described before, Simon could have targeted opponent 3, either before or after their move.

Melee Actions

Strike

You move into position and strike at your target.

Major Effects
Attack
Damage
Move

Minor Effects
Hit +Ref +Extra RoF Dice
See pg: 78 for full Attack Roll and Rate of Fire rules.

Move -2

Charge

You rush at your target, putting not just your physical strength but also your momentum behind your attack.

Major Effects
Attack
Damage
Move

Minor Effects
Move +2 (straight line)
You may move up to your Movement +2, but only in a straight line.

Damage +1 (per 4 Movement)
For every four spaces you move in this Action, you gain +1 Endurance and Critical Damage for this Attack.

Block

You aim for your target's weapon, hoping to knock them off balance so they cannot get a clear shot at you or others.

Major Effect
Impair

Minor Effect
Hit +Per +Foc

On Hit: Debuff Target: next Attack Strong Hit -1.
On a successful Attack Roll against your Target's Defence vs Impair, your Target's next Attack Roll is hampered: their die range to get a Strong Hit (pg: 82) is reduced by one. If they would require a "6", rolling a Strong Hit becomes impossible. This penalty lasts until your next Turn.

Impair

Grappling with your target, trying to limit their mobility and gain the advantage through your physical strength and agility.

Major Effects
Damage
Impair
Move

Minor Effects
Hit +Ref +Str

On Hit: Pick One Debuff Trg: X
If you succeed in an Attack Roll against a Target's Defences vs Impair: you may apply one of the following Effects onto them:

Prone
Target becomes Prone (pg: 76).

Grabbed
You gain the Grabbing Target Effect (pg: 76), and your Target gains the Grabbed Effect (pg: 76).

Move 1.
Force your Target to move one space in a direction of your choice.

Escape

Using your physical strength and agility, you attempt to wrestle free from an opponent who is grabbing you.

Major Effects
Damage
Impair
Move

Minor Effect
Hit +Ref +Str

On Hit: Debuff Target: Lose Grabbing Target.
If you succeed on an Attack Roll against a Target's Defence vs Impair, your Target loses any "Grabbing Target" Effect they may have on you or another character. Also remove the corresponding "Grabbed" Effect against you or another character.

The Target of Escape may be outside your Weapon's Range (eg: using your Limbs against a Grav Gauntlet) who is Grabbing you. However, in this case you deal no Damage to the Target.

Use Your Limbs!
All characters have access to Exotic Weapon: Limb.
You can use this to Block or Escape if you don't have access to another Impair Weapon.

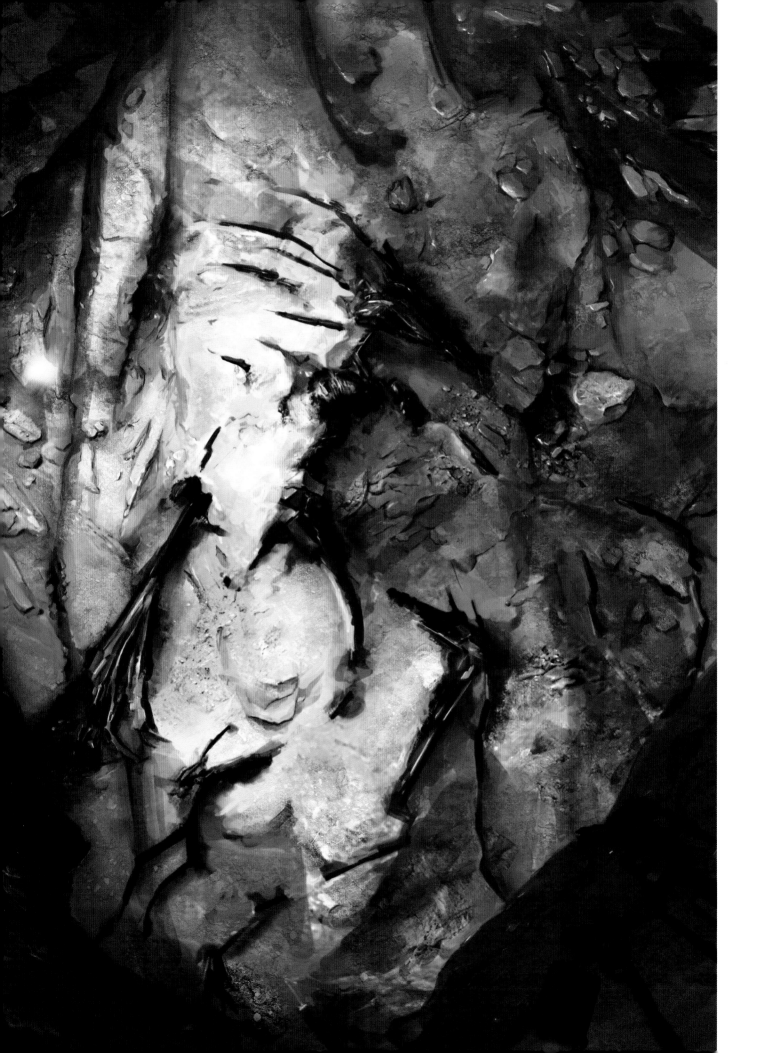

Equipment

See pg: 56 for full Resources rules.
See pg: 64 for full Spare Time Points rules.
See pg: 358 for a full list of available Weapons.
See pg: 366 for a full list of available Outfits.
See pg: 370 for a full list of available Misc Items and Services.

Overview

Weapons, pg: 118

Ranging from highly sophisticated Great X'ion War rail guns to biologically engineered spine launchers, Weapons take a great range of forms.

However, not all Weapons are lethal. Targeting lasers, your Mind, and police Disruptors also count as Weapons. Any Action (pg: 100) that requires an Attack Roll (pg: 78) requires a Weapon, whether you purchased it or were born with it.

Outfit (Armour), pg: 126

There are two general approaches to defence in combat: don't get hit, or be able to take a hit. Whether lithe stealth Tactical Armour or an Stealth Mech Suit, picking the right armour for your style of combat will be key to your survival.

You may only have one Outfit.

Utility Items, pg: 130

There is more to defence than personal ability and thick armour. A myriad of technological wonders and utility items exist to give you an edge in combat, ranging from mobile force-field cover generators to medical systems to advanced optic systems.

You may only have one Utility Item.

Misc Items and Services, pg: 136

These items or services are often one-time purchases that don't fill common, everyday requirements. They're not things like food or accommodation, more like pharmaceuticals and rentals.

All Miscellaneous Items and Services require you to spend Spare Time Points (pg: 64).

Equipment Slots, pg: 114

This is the amount of equipment that you can carry at once. Slots are taken up by Weapons and Misc Items.

Your Slots is mainly defined by your Outfit, but it's often increased by Strength Traits or Utility Items.

Overburdened, pg: 115

If your Activated (pg: 114) equipment (Outfits, Utility Items, and Weapons) has a Weight greater than your Strength, then your Defence decreases by one for each point of difference.

Stats

Each piece of equipment has various Stats that show its strengths and weaknesses.

Cost

Personal equipment costs either Resources (pg: 56) and/or Spare Time Points (pg: 64).

Equipment that costs Resources has expensive ongoing costs, such as refilling Ammunition and Clips and performing general maintenance. Equipment that costs a Spare Time Point has no costs other than the initial, small expenditure to purchase it or the time needed to construct it.

Keyword and Notes

These are your equipment's special rules. Many Traits or Strong Hits only work if you are using a Weapon with a specific Keyword.

Variations, pg: 116

These are templates that can be applied to a Weapon or Outfit. Often quite defining with many Stat modifications and Keywords.

A Weapon Type (pg: 102) dictates what Variations it can have. You may only take one Variation from each category.

Changing an item's Variation means you've sold or discarded the item and bought a new one. This removes all Modifications that cost Spare Time Points (pg: 64).

Modifications, pg: 116

These are similar to Variations, except that you can take any number of Modifications.

Modifications often only require a Spare Time Point (pg: 64), and the changes to your Weapon are often quite minor. If you lose or sell your Weapon, you lose any Spare Time Points spent on Modifications.

Equipment Slots

See pg: 118 for full Weapons rules.
See pg: 100 for full Action rules.
See pg: 126 for full Outfit rules.

Equipped Items

These are items that you're carrying in your backpack, pockets, and belts, but not your hands.

Outfit and Utility Equipment Slots

Your Outfit and Utility Item define your available Equipment Slots.

> ### Weight and Equipment Slots
> Each Item takes Slots equal to its Weight.
> Outfit and Utility Items take up no Slots.
> Two Items with the "Small" Keyword take up 1 Slot.
> You may only have two Gauntlet (pg: 125) Items
> Equipped at once.

Stored Items

These are items that you own but are not carrying. They are most commonly left back on your spacecraft and do not take up any Slots. This equipment cannot be Activated.

Drawing and Making an Item Active

See pg: 107 for full Draw Minor Effect rules.
See pg: 108 for full Prep Action rules.

Before it can be used, some equipment must be moved from your storage (eg: your backpack or belt) into your Hands. This is done by Drawing the item and making it "Active". Outfits and Utility Items do not need to be Drawn and are always considered Active.

Load Stat and Drawing.

Items with a Load Stat must be Drawn before they can be used. Drawing an Item requires you to spend a number of "Draw" Minor Effects (pg: 107) equal to the Item's Load Stat. These Minor Effects do not have to be accumulated consecutively or in the same Turn.
Items with no Load Stat take no time to make Active.

Putting an Item Away

Same as Drawing, but makes the Item not Active, and frees up your hands for other items.

Dropping an Item

See pg: 73 for full Minor Interaction rules.

This is a Free Action (pg: 100), but it cannot be done during other characters' Turns. Dropped items are left on the ground and can be picked up by any adjacent character as a Minor Interaction (pg: 73).

2 Hands

A Weight 1 Item requires one free hand to make Active.
A Weight 2 Item requires two free hands to make Active.
Utility Items list if they require hands.
Gauntlets do not use hands and do not need to be Drawn.

Weight 2+ Items may be held in one hand, but they may not be used. This allows you to Activate a second one-handed Item while carrying a two-handed Weapon, eg: drawing and using a Grenade while holding an Assault Rifle.

Drawing a Weapon Outside of Combat

Characters may Draw their Weapon at any time, especially if they are expecting a fight. This may save valuable time once a fight beings.

If a character Draws a Weapon, NPCs react appropriately, taking defensive precautions themselves, calling for help, or becoming hostile, whether socially or physically.

Quick Change, Drawing and Dropping Weapon Example

VoGrag has 2 different Weapons. A 2 handed (Weight 2, Load 2) Rifle, 2 handed (Weight 3, Load 1) Shotgun and a few 1 handed (Weight 1, Load 1) Grenade.

During his first Turn of combat, VoGrag spends 2 Recovery Actions (Load 2) to Draw (make Active) his Rifle.

A couple of Turns later, he wishes to throw a Grenade, so he spends 1 Action to Draw his Grenade and then 1 Action to Throw it. While doing this, he does not need to put his Rifle away: he can hold it in one hand, but cannot use it until he Throws the Grenade.

After he runs out of Ammunition, rather than Reloading he drops his Rifle as a Free Action and spends 1 Action (Load 1) to Draw his Shotgun. Any time during the combat, any character adjacent to the Rifle can pick it up as a Minor Interaction (costing 2 Movement).

Equipment Slots
Weapons & Misc Items, 1 slot per Weight

Outfit + Utility Item + (*1*) = (9)

			Gauntlet 1) *Electro-Grav 6*	Gauntlet 2) *-*
1) *Rifle, Wgt 2*	2) *-*	3) *Flesh Rejuvenator*	4) *Grenade*	5) *Flash Light*
6) *Medicine Toolbox, Wgt 2*	7) *-*	8)	9)	10)
11)	12)	13)	14)	15) *Implant HUD, Wgt 0*

"I was wondering, Sir…"

Oh damnit, the Musclehead was speaking again. Behind the desk, Sergeant Buford was dressed immaculately in his pressed CorpSec Incorporated Security uniform, despite the oppressive heat of this new Corporate jungle colony.

"Why is it we only post bounties on the Ammobeasts? Why not take a few deputies or send us Legion to hunt them critters down?" The Musclehead was red-armoured, as suited a Legion deputy, his helmet dangling awkwardly from one hand, occasionally tapping against his sidearm's hip holster.

Buford winced, imagining the Moron and his friends taking a hoverloader, some guns, and a couple cases of the local moonshine Draz out to the jungle after dark. The Moron was rigid with the anticipation that this conversation would lead to him hunting the "'critters," as he referred to them… This conversation would require a little show and tell.

Swivelling in his chair, Buford thrust out the stump of his leg. "I've been here two years, boy. The first year, I often went hunting with the Legionnaires during the day. Drinks, a few guns, and my friend Vibius. Not many large beasts out during the day."

He paused, making sure his slow-witted audience was listening. No danger there: the Moron was almost drooling as he stared in slack-jawed fascination at Buford's stump. "Shortly after my promotion to Night Security Coordinator, I rounded up some friends and broke into the armoury using my new codes to bring out the big guns."

"Why am I the one stuck with these oversized idiots?" Buford thought as a hungry grin broke out across the Moron's large scaled face.

"We passed the outer fence and stepped on the accelerator. We liked to hunt by the lake, lots of open ground, you know? But not three minutes had passed when something snatched Vibby from the driving console." Watching the Moron's face as he listened to this, you could almost hear the holowafers sparking.

"But how did you get back?" he asked, about thirty seconds after even Buford had expected him to. Buford sighed…

"The damned beast let me live." The shocked look on the Moron's face was almost the exact same as his supervisor's during his initial debriefing. "It chewed off my leg. One huge grasper holding me down and the other gripping me. Then, as I was pissin' out blood and screaming for my life, it lifted me up by the stump till I was danglin' in front of its ugly maw. When it spoke, I could taste my blood on its rancid breath. " Here he paused, the memory giving him chills. Imitating the grating consonants and shortened vowels of the creature that still haunted him with nightmares, he spoke softly.

"I claym wylds. Muntun to thuird ruck streem. Myn. Myn alun. Yuh gut owt, tull othur weak herd mumbers." Breathing heavily, the sergeant wiped his brow.

"Then, slung over its massive bristly shoulder it carried me like I weighed nothing… and it was silent. Nothing rustled; it didn't step on anything that cracked, nothing, though I was probably delirious with pain. Then it tossed me through the perimeter shock-fence." The Moron was agape with… bloodlust? Amazement? Disbelief?… Idiocy?

"Now, that's the first reason we only post bounties: so we don't get killed. But the second reason?" Here Buford took a drink, hand only slightly shaking. "I filed the bounties under the Tourism section's budget, not ours."

Overburdened

If you don't have enough Strength, a heavy Outfit can slow you down, and a bulky Weapon can be hard to wield effectively.

If the Weight of an Active (pg: 114) Outfit, Utility Item, or Weapon is greater than your Strength, reduce your Defence by the difference.

Overburdened

Each point your Str is under items Weight

Outfit Utility Weapon − Defence

Large Gun, Overburdened Example

Sedrick has Strength 2 and is carrying around a large Rocket Launcher (Weight 4). Whenever he Draws this Weapon (making it Active), he becomes Overburdened, reducing his Defence by 2.

If he were to also have Weight 3 Armour, his Defence would be reduced by a total of 3.

Variations

See pg: 102 for full Weapon Type rules.
See pg: 118 for full Weapons rules.
See pg: 126 for full Outfit rules.
See pg: 124 for full Weapon Keyword rules.
See pg: 358 for a full list of available Weapons.
See pg: 366 for a full list of available Outfits.

These are templates that can be applied to a Weapon or Outfit. Often quite defining with many Stat modifications and Keywords.

Weapon Type

A Weapon Type (pg: 102) dictates what Variations it can have. You may only take one Variation from each category.

Changing Variation

Represents you discarding (or selling) your item and acquiring a new one. All Spare Time Points (pg: 64) are lost and Modifications (pg: 116) are removed.

Looting Weapons, pg: 54

If you keep a found Weapon, you must keep any Variations and Modifications attached to it.

Available Variations

Gun Variations. May Select 1, Gun Only.
Shell Variations. May Select 1, Shell Only.
Chemical Variations. May Select 1, Chemical Only.
Gun Size Variations. May Select 1, Not Drone or Melee.
Drone Variations. May Select 1, Drone or Drone Only.
Melee Variations. May Select 1, Melee Only.
Melee Shape Variations. May Select 1, Not Thrown, Melee Only.
Outfit Variations. May Select 1, Outfit Only.

Research Gun Variations

May Select any 1, Prototype and Gun Only, May not Select Gun Variations.

These are alternative to "Gun Variations" that can be applied to any "Gun" Weapon Type with the "Prototype" Keyword. If one of these Variations is chosen, then no Gun Variation can be taken. All of these Variations require access to Secret Knowledge (pg: 68) before they can be chosen.

GMs are encouraged to let players invent new Variations for this category, usually by requiring Research. Variation Stats are set by the GM with careful attention given to balance (pg: 294).

Weapons with the Weapon Type "Gun" and Keyword "Prototype" must have one of each of the following Variations before they can be used.

» Gun Variation OR a Research Gun Variation.
» Barrel Variations.
» Targeting Variations.
» Loader Variations.

Modifications

See pg: 64 for full Spare Time Roll rules.

These are similar to Variations, except that you can take any number of Modifications.

Changing Modifications

Modifications may be removed at any time during Downtime (pg: 95).

Available Modifications

Weapon Modifications, May Select any Amount, Not Melee.
Melee Modifications, May Select any Amount, Melee Only.
Drone & Companion Modifications, May Select any Amount, Drones and Companions Only.
Outfit Modifications, May Select any Amount, Outfit Only.

The Perfect Gun, Creating a Rifle Example

Kirk wants to create the perfect Rifle. First he selects the Variations he wants to use, but he may only select one of each type. He chooses the Gun Variation: Rail and does not select a Gun Size Variation.

He may then choose any number of Weapon Modifications. He chooses the following: Flash Light Attachment, Laser Sight, Personalised, and Telescopic Lens. Each of these requires him to pass a Spare Time Roll.

Preference Change, Changing Weapon Example

Frank has a Shotgun with the Ion Variation and several Modifications that required him to make Spare Time Rolls. Recently he has been fighting a lot of opponents with lots of Armour, and he's found his Shotgun not very effective. He wishes to allot his Resources to a new Weapon, a Rifle.

Unfortunately, his Ion Shotgun's Variation and Modifications are lost and do not transfer to his new Rifle.

"Your favourite weapon should have a name. Not to put fear into your enemies, but rather a name that shows your love, care, and investment into your instrument.

This one right here, the 14mm Gauss Rifle with the custom grip, extended barrel, and black-light laser sight is named Nyx, after my wife.

A high-calibre, precise, and incredibly dangerous machine that has killed dozens of Feral Nephilim… just like my Gauss Rifle."

– Hephaestus, Legion family man.

Creating Weapons and Outfits

Weapons and Outfits have Limited Variation Options.
Most Modifications Require a Spare Time Roll (pg: 64).

Select Your Weapon or Outfit
You must have access to your desired Equipment (eg: shopping
   or looting).
The total Resource Cost of your Equipment cannot exceed your
   Current Resources.
You may only have one Outfit.

Choose Variation(s)
Most Equipment can only have one Variation.
Variations are chosen when you acquire your item.
Variations cannot be changed after they are selected.
Most Variations modify your Equipment's Stats and add Keywords
   and notes.

Add Modifications
You may choose any amount of Modifications.
Most Modifications require a Spare Time Roll (pg: 64).
Modifications alter your Weapon's Stats and add Keywords.

Weapons

See pg: 71 for full Combat Overview rules.
See pg: 100 for full Turns and Actions rules.
See pg: 358 for a full list of available Weapons.

These Weapons are built using standard rules. They are intended to give examples of how to make Weapons and to show some of the better-known Weapons from the Fragged Empire setting.

Protectron™, Pistol

The butt of a thousand Kaltoran jokes and pride of the Corporation, the humble Protectron™ is a masterpiece of cost efficiency and marketing. Its popularity is not found in its firepower but in its negligible upkeep cost and its lack of dependency on ammunition.

Weapons	Hit (+Skill)	End Dmg	Crit Dmg	Range	Clips	Ammo	Load	RoF	Weight	Type & Variations	Cost
Protectron	+1	2	2	4	Inf	6	1	1	1	Gun, Particle	0

Small, Jam (1-5), Energy, Does not Work in Void

Little Friend, SMG

This Kaltoran submachine gun is one of the main competitors to Corporate arms dealing in the Haven system. The Swagger family offers this robust, reliable design, with a light, compact frame and respectable rate of fire. The next time someone threatens you or your family, just introduce them to your Little Friend(s).

Weapons	Hit (+Skill)	End Dmg	Crit Dmg	Range	Clips	Ammo	Load	RoF	Weight	Type & Variations	Cost
Little Friend	+1	4	3	4	3	9	1	3	1	Gun, Self-Propelled	2

Low Tech, Works in Liquid

Apollo Gauss Rifle

The Legion's mainstay in tactical weaponry, the Apollo Gauss Rifle offers reliability and a century of prestigious service history. It packs the firepower and rate of fire necessary to take down almost any Nephilim beast, and rips up other lightly armoured targets with ease.

Weapons	Hit (+Skill)	End Dmg	Crit Dmg	Range	Clips	Ammo	Load	RoF	Weight	Type & Variations	Cost
Apollo Rifle		3	4	5	2	8	2	2*	2	Gun, Gauss	3

Jam (1-3), *Strong Hit (5-6) with all RoF 1 Attack Rolls

Bilegrub Launcher, Shotgun

Feared and respected by all who value their safety, this extremely dangerous weapon boasts a small, high-reflex brain and organic optical lens, intuitively adjusting its flammable Bilegrub rounds for maximum dispersion radius.

Weapons	Hit (+Skill)	End Dmg	Crit Dmg	Range	Clips	Ammo	Load	RoF	Weight	Type & Variations	Cost
Bilegrub Launcher	+2	6	2	2*	5	2	1	2	3	Shell, Chemical, Dispersion, Napalm	2

Splash 1, *Strong Hit (5-6) vs Targets within first Range Increment.

Low Tech, Burn, Does not Work in Void

Shroud Grenade

A specialised Kaltoran utility weapon, the Shroud Grenade explodes in a cloud of thick black Shroud smoke, hampering the vision of opponents while offering cover to you and your allies. All this is no risk to any Kaltoran, whose enhanced senses completely compensate for the darkness while other races flail about.

Weapons	Hit (+Skill)	End Dmg	Crit Dmg	Range	Clips	Ammo	Load	RoF	Weight	Type & Variations	Cost
Shroud Grenade	-2	-	-	2 (+Siv)	3	1	1	1	1	Shell, Thrown, Smoke	0

Splash 3, Creates an Area of Limited Vision (Light Cover (+2)) for 3 minutes, Does not Work in Void

Small, Slow, Low Tech

Artemis Assault Cannon

A standard-issue Legion heavy weapon dating back to the founding of the Legion, inspired by ancient human schematics. The rotating triple-barrel projects magnetically loaded high-powered Gauss ammunition at a huge rate of fire, unleashing obliteration upon single or multiple targets with ease.

Weapons	Hit (+Skill)	End Dmg	Crit Dmg	Range	Clips	Ammo	Load	RoF	Weight	Type & Variations	Cost
Artemis Assault Cannon	-4	6*	4	2*	3	25	2	5(+4d6)	4	Gun, Gauss	5, 14+

Jam (1-3)

*Optional: (Set Up 1, Pull Down 1, +2 Rng and +2 End Dmg)

Hostile Takeover™, Cannon

The latest in Body Count Conglomerate™ ground-to-ship and anti-armour weaponry. Capable of piercing all known forms of body armour and all but the most durable ship hulls, this is a big, powerful gun that shows you mean serious business.

Weapons	Hit (+Skill)	End Dmg	Crit Dmg	Range	Clips	Ammo	Load	RoF	Weight	Type & Variations	Cost
Hostile Takeover™	-2	5	4	5	Inf	2	2	1	4	Gun, Particle	5, 14+

Splash 1, Maximum Range = Rng x20 (normally Rng x10), When fired at a spacecraft use; Hit +2, Shield Dmg 2, Crit 2 and Rng 2

Energy, Jam (1-5), Does not Work in Void, Slow

Black Maw, Chemical Thrower

The embodiment of anti-personnel horror, this weapon is nicknamed the "Black Maw" for its gaping black mouth that spews thick, black antimonic acid. Melts flesh, armour, and cover alike.

Weapons	Hit (+Skill)	End Dmg	Crit Dmg	Range	Clips	Ammo	Load	RoF	Weight	Type & Variations	Cost
Black Maw	-1	4	5	2	3	9	2	3*	3	Chemical, Antimonic Acid	4

All Targets have -1 Cover Steps, *If you perform a Spread Five with this Weapon: gain +1d6 to each Attack Roll

Burn, Slow, Jam (1-5), Low Tech

TX i82™, Swarm Drone

This small hover drone is fitted for combat and is a Body Count Conglomerate™ best-seller. Comes with retractable Protectron™ pistol mounts and a microphone and speaker system, allowing for voice commands as well as interactive financial analysis. Also features a built-in cup holder.

Weapons	Hit (+Skill)	End Dmg	Crit Dmg	Range	Clips	Ammo	Load	RoF	Weight	Type & Variations	Cost
TX i82™ (Swarm Drone)	+1	1	2	3	Inf	6	1	1	1(+0)	Drone (with Particle Pistol)	2

DEF 18, Armour 3, Mov 6, Slots 2, Bodies 1, Lock on +4, May be set as thrown action (Rng = STR), Robot

Gun (Small, Jam (1-5), Energy, Does not Work in Void)

Tac Com, Tactical Computer

The Standard Legionnaire Tactical Computer, or Tac Comp, is an incredibly robust design. Using advanced targeting systems, it gives a swift and precise analysis of combat environments, as well as enemy strengths and vulnerabilities.

Weapons	Hit (+Skill)	End Dmg	Crit Dmg	Range	Clips	Ammo	Load	RoF	Weight	Type & Variations	Cost
Tac Com	+Int	–	–	Foc	Inf	10	2	1	1	Combat Computer	2

Lock On +2, Strong Hit (5-6)

Strong Hit: **Target Lock** (Analyse, Hit) Target is Locked On.

Strong Hit: **Weak Spot** (Analyse, Hit, Locked On) Until your next Turn, Boost all Attacks against Target: Endurance Damage +1.

Strong Hit: **Plot Trajectory** (Analyse, Hit, Locked On) Until your next Turn, Boost all Attacks against Target: Range +1.

Strong Hit: **Tactical Scan** (Analyse, Hit, Locked On) Until your next Turn, Debuff Target: -1 Cover Step (minimum Light Cover).

Shock Jock, Disruptor Rifle

Often underestimated due to its non-lethal and homemade nature, the Shock Jock is capable of disorienting and concussing even the most heavily armoured target into compliance, all while draining their energy systems. A popular weapon with law enforcement, bounty hunters, slavers, and Kaltorans for family corporal punishment.

Weapons	Hit (+Skill)	End Dmg	Crit Dmg	Range	Clips	Ammo	Load	RoF	Weight	Type & Variations	Cost
Shock Jock	-2	5	2*	3	3	4	1	1	2	Disruptor	3

Lock On +6, Jam (1-5), Energy, Blunt, *+2 Crit vs Robots.

Strong Hit: **Disrupt** (Attack, Hit) Debuff Targets Active Non Low Tech, Non Bio Tech Weapons: Lose Ammunition equal to RoF

Nephilim Toadie, Assistant

These small, humanoid insectoids make efficient and attentive assistants who would be happy to die for their master. Requiring minimal clothing, food, and cleaning, they not only thrive under harsh servitude, but appear to require it. These traits are quite possibly woven directly into their DNA.

Weapons	Hit (+Skill)	End Dmg	Crit Dmg	Range	Clips	Ammo	Load	RoF	Weight	Type & Variations	Cost
Todie	+3	2	2	4	Inf	6	1	1	1(+6)	Companion (with Particle Pistol)	1, 8+

Defence 16, Armour 2, Move 4, Slots 2, Bodies 1, May make Skill Rolls via Toadie

Gun (Small, Jam (1-5), Energy, Does not Work in Void)

Strong Hit: **Helpful** (Attack, Does not Req Hit) A single Ally gains Hit +2 on their next Attack (must be taken within 1 Turn).

Kaltoran Jagged Spear, Balanced Weapon

A popular weapon during the Kaltoran Dark Years. Made with a wide array of composites and alloys, this flexible archaic weapon is not to be dismissed when in the hands of a capable fighter.

Weapons	Hit (+Skill)	End Dmg	Crit Dmg	Range	Clips	Ammo	Load	RoF	Weight	Type & Variations	Cost
Jagged Spear	+1	4	4	2*	–	–	2	1	2**	Melee, Composite, Long	1, 12t

+2 Hit with Overwatch

*Max range 2, **Only ever requires 1 Hand

Combat Flesh

Despite being rather slow and docile, these Nephilim-made biological robots are incredibly tough, as they have no critical organs, and come armed with rudimentary weaponry. A potent and disposable weapon.

Weapons	Hit (+Skill)	End Dmg	Crit Dmg	Range	Clips	Ammo	Load	RoF	Weight	Type & Variations	Cost
Combat Flesh	+2	3	2	4	4	15	0	3 (+2d6)	1 (+8)	Drone (With Spine Pistol)	3

DEF 8, Armour 4, Mov 2, Slots 2, Bodies 1, Bio Tech

Gun (Small, Bio-Tech)

Legion Hound

Untrained, these wild creatures require pens made of military-grade hull plating. However, when properly trained by expert Legion instructors, these bulky carnivores require no leash, walking docilely by their master's side. All it takes is a simple hand gesture to turn them back into slavering attack beasts, ready to deliver bloody canine rage.

Weapons	Hit (+Skill)	End Dmg	Crit Dmg	Range	Clips	Ammo	Load	RoF	Weight	Type & Variations	Cost
Legion Hound	+2	4	3	–	–	–	–	1	2 (+12)	Companion, Melee	1, 10t

Defence: 16, Armour: 3, Movement: 12, Slots: 0, Bodies: 1

No Variations or Modifications,

Spacecraft Guidance Laser™, Orbital Bombardment Array

Not technically a weapon or even in production, this high-powered targeting laser was originally designed to guide spacecraft landing trajectories from the ground. As soon as it was discovered that it could be used to precisely aim spacecraft weapon systems, its schematics were promptly stolen by a dozen groups. Not recommended for indoor use.

Weapons	Hit (+Skill)	End Dmg	Crit Dmg	Range	Clips	Ammo	Load	RoF	Weight	Type & Variations	Cost
Guidance Laser	-18	9	9	9	4	2	2	1	4	Gun	3*

Lock On +10, Splash 4, Prototype, Slow, Set Up 2.

No Interior Use, Damage delayed 1D6 Turns, x2 Max Range, *Requires: Secret Knowledge (Planetoids: Atmosphere)

Weapon Stats

Hit Bonus (Hit)

Gives a bonus or penalty to your Attack Rolls (pg: 78).

Endurance Damage (End Dmg)

How much pain and stress the Weapon causes. Each successful Attack Roll (pg: 78) deals this much Endurance Damage (pg: 122) to the Target.

> ## Major Effect: Damage
> Any Action with the Major Effect: Damage (pg: 107) deals your Weapon's Endurance Damage to your Target on a successful Attack Roll.

Critical Damage (Crit Dmg), pg: 88

How effective your Weapon is at penetrating your Target's Armour and killing (pg: 90) them.

A Weapon with Critical Damage 0 or below cannot deal Attribute Damage.

Range Increment (Range)

Your Weapon's effectiveness over long distances (pg: 78).

The Maximum Range of a weapon is its Range x10.

A Weapon with Range 0 or below cannot be used to Attack, unless you use an Action to increase its Range above 0.

Clips

The number of spare Clips you have available, which you can use to regain Ammunition. Clips are usually restored at Downtime (pg: 95) or by looting (pg: 54).

A Weapon with Clips 0 or below cannot be Reloaded once they have used all their Ammunition, and only refresh their Ammunition during Downtime.

Ammunition

Each Attack reduces the Weapon's Ammunition by 1 per RoF used (pg: 81). You may only Attack if you have Ammunition available.

A Weapon's Ammunition depends on its RoF (eg: For a Weapon with Ammunition: RoF x2 and RoF: 2, its Ammunition is 4).

A Weapon with Ammunition 0 or below cannot be used to Attack.

Load Time (Load)

The number of Draw Actions required to make your Weapon Active (pg: 114).

It is also the number of Un-Jam Actions required to remove the "Jam" Effect (pg: 125) from the Weapon.

Finally, it is the number of Reload Actions required to replenish the Weapon's Ammunition with a Clip.

Eg: Sarah's Rifle has Load 2. Mid fight she needs to Reload her Weapon after her Ammunition reaches 0. This will take her 2 Actions. She can spend an entire Turn (2 Actions) to Reload or she can spend 1 Action this Turn and the 2nd Action next Turn.

A Weapon with Load 0 or below can be Drawn, Un-Jammed, and Reloaded as a Free Action (pg: 100).

Rate of Fire (RoF)

Weapons with a higher Rate of Fire can use additional Ammunition to roll additional dice on an Attack Roll (pg: 78) and cause additional Strong Hits (pg: 82).

> ## Adding Attack Roll Dice
> Additional dice for RoF 2+ Weapons can only be gained from Actions with the "Hit +Extra RoF Dice" Minor Effect (pg: 107).

A Weapon with RoF 0 or below cannot make Attacks.

Natural Weapons ✊	Hit (+Skill)	End Dmg	Crit Dmg	Range	Clips	Ammo	Load	RoF	Weight	Type & Variations	Cost
Mind	+Int+Tactical	-	-	Focus	-	Infinite	0	1	0	Analytical	Auto

Natural, No Variations or Modifications

	Hit (+Skill)	End Dmg	Crit Dmg	Range	Clips	Ammo	Load	RoF	Weight	Type & Variations	Cost
Limbs	+Exotic	Str -1	Str -1	-	-	Infinite	0	2 (+1d6)	0	Melee, Impairment	Auto

Natural, Small, Blunt, No Variations or Modifications

Weapons 🔫	Hit (+Skill)	End Dmg	Crit Dmg	Range	Clips	Ammo	Load	RoF	Weight	Type & Variations	Cost
Little Friend (SMG)	+1	4	3	4	3	9	1	3	1	Gun, Self-Propelled	2

Low Tech, Works in Liquid

Used Ammunition ⬡⬡⬡⬡⬡⬡⬡   ⬡⬡⬡⬡⬡⬡⬡   ⬡⬡⬡⬡⬡⬡⬡ Used Clips ⬡⬡⬡⬡⬡⬡⬡

Weight (Wgt)

The Strength required to optimally use this Weapon. If you have lower Strength than a Weapon's Weight, you become Overburdened (pg: 115).

The Weapon Weight also dictates how many Equipment Slots it takes to Equip and Activate it (pg: 114).

A Weapon with 0 Slots or below requires 0 Slots to Equip and Activate.

Type, pg: 102 and Variations, pg: 116

A Weapon's Type dictates what Actions can be used with it (pg: 118) and what Variation templates can be chosen for it.

Cost

The amount of Resources (pg: 56) and number of successful Spare Time Rolls (pg: 64) required to acquire and keep the Weapon.

Keywords, pg: 124

Various Traits (pg: 33), Strong Hit Options (pg: 82), and Modifications (pg: 116) only apply to Weapons with a specific Keyword.

Notes

Use this space to write the Weapon's Keywords (pg: 124), Traits (pg: 33), and other special abilities.

Natural Weapons

All characters have access to these two Natural Weapons.

Mind
Primarily used to Analyse Targets.

Limbs
Primarily used to grapple with and Attack Targets in Melee.

"–" Stat
This means the item does not normally use this Stat. Variations, Modifications and Trait bonuses (+/–) do not increase or reduce this Stat.

Set Stat Value
If a Variation, Modification, or Trait inserts a Set value (Eg: "2" not "+2" or "–2") in this Stat, then the "–" is replaced with the set value.

This Set value also replaces ANY existing (non "–") value.

Weapon Keywords

Arc of Fire X

Has no effect without the "Set Up" Keyword.

Arc of Fire and Set Up

When you start to Set Up a Weapon (pg: 126), choose a facing direction. Attacks with the Set Up Weapon may only be made against Targets within an arc of X degrees from the Weapon's facing.

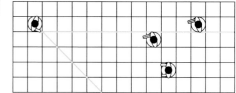

Arc of Fire 45

Derrick has Set Up his Sniper Rifle on a Tripod (with Arc of Fire 45). He can see three Targets, but only two are in his Arc of Fire. If he wishes to fire at the third, he will have to Pull Down his Tripod to remove the "Arc of Fire" Keyword.

Attribute 1d3+X

When this Weapon deals Attribute Damage because of a Critical Hit (pg: 88), determine the random Attribute Damaged by rolling 1d3. If using a d6, 1-2 = 1; 3-4 = 2; 5-6 = 3.

Bio Tech (Biological Technology)

A required Keyword for some Strong Hit Options and Traits.

Blunt

If this Weapon deals Attribute Damage that would reduce one of the Target's Attributes to 0 or below, you may knock the Target unconscious for a duration of the GM's choice. If you Hit an unsuspecting character with a Blunt Weapon during a Surprise Round (pg: 101), you may knock them unconscious at the GM's discretion.

A First Aid Healing Roll (pg: 92) may be used to revive an unconscious character. A successful Paramedics Healing Roll (pg: 92) Heals all Attribute Damage dealt by a Blunt Weapon.

Burn

A required Keyword for some Strong Hit Options and Traits.

Cost Spare Time Point Xt

Acquiring this Weapon costs the listed Resources (pg: 56) and requires a Spare Time Roll (pg: 64) with a Difficulty of "X".

Looted Items with this Keyword do not require a Spare Time Roll to keep.

Electro-Gravity

A required Keyword for some Strong Hit Options and Traits.

Energy

Your Weapon can ignite flammable Environmental objects.
A required Keyword for some Strong Hit Options and Traits.

For One Session Only

This Modification remains in effect until the end of the session. If this Modification is acquired towards the end of a session, it may be kept until the end of the next session with GM permission.

For One Session Only and Optional

May be used for any single session (not just the one it was acquired during).

Gauntlet

You may only ever have two items with this Keyword Equipped at once. They require 1 Equipment Slot (pg: 114) for each point of Weight above 1 (a Weight 1 Gauntlet requires no Slots).

Items with this Keyword do not need to be Drawn (pg: 114) to be made Active, take five minutes to Equip, and do not require Hands to use.

Jam (X-Y)

If you make an Attack Roll (pg: 78) with this Weapon and get triples equal to, or between "X" and "Y" (eg: you roll three 2s) that are not Strong Hits, this Weapon gains the Jammed Effect.

When a Weapon has multiple "Jam" Keywords (eg: from a Weapon and a Variation), select the lowest "X" and highest "Y".

Jammed Effect

» This Attack deals 0 Damage, but still consumes Ammunition.
» This Attack causes no Strong Hits.
» This Weapon cannot be used to Attack until you perform a number of Actions with the Un-Jam Minor Effect (see Prep Action, pg: 108) equal to the Weapon's Load Stat.

Jam (+/-Z)

Reduce or increase "Y" by "Z".

James has a Weapon with Jam (1-4) and a Trait that gives this Weapon Jam (-1). This results in the Weapon having Jam (1-3).

Henchmen, pg: 296

Weapons wielded by Henchmen cannot gain the Jammed Effect.

Lock On +X

When a Target of this Weapon is affected by a friendly Locked On Effect (pg: 76), gain a +"X" bonus to your Attack Roll.

Some Strong Hit Options and Traits require a Target to have the Locked On Effect on them for you to gain additional bonuses.

Derrick uses his Targeting Laser with the Analyse Action. He rolls a single Strong Hit and uses it to Strong Hit: Target Lock. This applies the Locked On Effect to his Target.

Derrick has an SMG (Lock On +2) and a choice of two Targets. One Target has the Locked On Effect, and the other doesn't. He chooses the Target with Locked On, so he gains +2 to his Attack Roll with the SMG.

Lose X

Removes the "X" Keyword from this Weapon.

Low Tech

This Weapon is resistant to Disruptor Strong Hits.

Modification Rolls +/-X

All Spare Time Rolls (pg: 64) made to attach a Modification to this Weapon gain a bonus or penalty of +/-"X".

Natural

Natural weapons, such as fists, cannot be Disarmed and do not need to be Drawn.

No Variation or Modifications

This Weapon cannot have a Variation or Modification. Common for Natural Weapons.

Optional

You may choose whether to use this Weapon Modification on each Attack you make with the Weapon it is attached to.

If the Modification has a penalty attached to it, this only applies if the Weapon Modification was used and lasts until the start of your next Turn.

Weight

If an Optional Modification increases the Weight of its Weapon, it always increases the Weight, not just when used.

Only X

This Weapon can only be used by characters with a specific qualification "X" (eg: a specific Race or Trait).

Pen X min Y (Penetration)

When this Weapon does Damage to a Target (ie: Critical Hit, pg: 88), reduce the Target's Armour by "X" to a minimum of "Y" vs your Damage.

When a Weapon has multiple "Pen" Keywords (eg: from a Variation and a Trait), select the highest "X" and lowest "Y".

Jason fires his Puncture Rifle (Pen 1 min 3) at a Target (Armour 4). The shot reduces the Target's Armour by 1, to a minimum of 3, reducing the Target's Armour to 3.

Prototype

See pg: 68 for full Research rules.
See pg: 116 for full Variation rules.
See pg: 116 for full Modification rules.
See pg: 363 for a full list of available Prototype Variations.

From the homemade rifle to the mad scientist's experimental death ray, a Prototype Weapon is not something you can get off the production line. Though time-intensive to construct, they often prove very powerful, especially in their creator's hands.

Prototypes have their own Variations (Research Gun Variations, pg: 363). Accessing these requires Research. GMs are encouraged to work with players to carefully create new Weapon Variations. These are often hard to balance, so players should be forgiving and allow the GM to tweak the Variation, even after it has entered use.

Steps to Creating a Prototype Gun:
» Acquire a Prototype Weapon from the Exotic Weapons list.
» Add a Gun Variation OR a Research Gun Variation.
» Add 1 Barrel Prototype Gun Variation.
» Add 1 Targeting Prototype Gun Variation.
» Add 1 Loader Prototype Gun Variation

Requires X

This Variation or Modification cannot be selected unless the Weapon has "X" (eg: a specific Keyword).

Robot

This Drone counts as a Robot (pg: 33).

Set Up X, Pull Down Y

See pg: 107 for full Action Minor Effects rules.
See pg: 108 for full Prep Action rules.

This Weapon requires "X" Set Up Actions before it may be used. If you Move before finishing these Actions, the Set Up Actions must be restarted.

After setting up or using a weapon with the "Pull Down" Keyword you may not move with that Weapon until you perform "Y" Pull Down Actions.

Turret, Set Up and Pull Down Example

Peterson's Turret (Set Up 2 and Pull Down 1, Move 0) will take him 2 Set Up (Recovery) Actions to set up before it can Attack. These Actions can be taken during two different Turns and don't have to be right after each other. His Turret can Attack the same Turn that he finishes setting it up.

When Peterson is ready to move it to another location, he must spend 1 Pull Down (Recovery) Action to place it in his backpack. He can then move around with his Turret, but must spend another 2 Set Up Actions before it can Attack again.

> "This metal and wire is nothing but the scaffolding to the monument we are constructing that is our flesh and blood."
>
> — Xalcan, Nephilim genetic engineer.

Slow

Weapon counts as Slow.

Small

Weight 1 or 0 items only.
Two Small items use only 1 Equipment Slot (pg: 114).

Splash X

Described in detail on the next page.

Stealth +/- X

While you have this Weapon Equipped, gain a +/-"X" bonus or penalty to all Stealth Rolls (pg: 109).

Strong Hit (X-Y)

See pg: 82 for full Strong Hit rules.

This Weapon causes Strong Hits on dice rolls of "X" to "Y".

Normally, a Weapon causes Strong Hits on rolls of "6". Derrick's Rifle has Strong Hit (5-6), so it causes Strong Hits on rolls of "5" to "6".

Strong Hit +Z

Reduce the minimum dice roll needed for your Weapon to cause Strong Hits by "Z".

Derrick has two Weapons: his Rifle, with Strong Hit (5-6), and his Pistol. If both Weapons gained Strong Hit +1, then the Rifle would cause Strong Hits on rolls of "4", "5", or "6", and his Pistol would cause Strong Hits on rolls of "5" or "6".

Strong Hit -W

Increase the minimum dice roll needed for your Weapon to cause Strong Hits by "W". May remove the ability to score Strong Hits.

Works in Liquid

This Weapon may be fired while it or your Target is submerged in liquid. Also, liquid does not provide Cover to your Target.

> Weapons do not normally work when submerged in liquids. Being submerged in liquid normally grants Heavy Cover.

Splash X

This Weapon deals its Endurance Damage (pg: 122) to all characters within "X" spaces of the Target.

When declaring an Attack with a Splash Weapon, you have two options: Directly Attack a Target or Attack the Ground.

Option 1: Directly Attack a Target

Make an Attack Roll vs your Target's Defence, as normal.

In addition to the Attacked Target, all characters within "X" spaces of the Target suffer Endurance Damage (no additional Attack Rolls required). However, characters other than the Target CANNOT suffer Critical Hits unless they have 0 Endurance or were reduced to 0 Endurance by this Attack.

Option 2: Attack the Ground

Specify a space to Attack rather than a Target. The Defence of the space is 10.

All characters within "X" spaces of the attacked space may take Endurance Damage. However, they CANNOT suffer Critical Hits unless they have 0 Endurance or were reduced to 0 Endurance by this Attack.

Shell and Splash Weapon

If a Weapon has the "Shell" Weapon Type and "Splash" Keyword, their Target's Cover value is determined from the location hit by the Attack, not the direction the Attack came from.

Failing an Attack Roll

When you fail on a Splash Attack Roll, the attack Scatters by a number of spaces equal to the degree of failure in a random direction (GM discretion allowed, usually by rolling a d6).

Example 1d6 Random Direction:

Gun/Melee and Splash Weapon

If you have a Weapon with the "Gun" or "Melee" Weapon Type and the "Splash" Keyword, you cannot damage yourself with this Weapon (eg: if your Attack Scatters onto yourself).

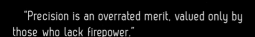

"Precision is an overrated merit, valued only by those who lack firepower."

- Nicholas Price, CEO of Tick Tock Co.

Direct Hit and Attack the Ground, Splash Example

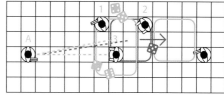

Splash 1, Direct Hit & Attack the Ground

Zeqwardos (A) is making two Attacks with her Shotgun (Splash 1).

For her first Attack, she Directly Attacks a Target (1), rolling a Hit. This does Endurance Damage to both her Target (1) and the adjacent Target (2). She also rolled a 6, giving a Strong Hit. She may apply a Critical Hit to the Target (1) that she Directly Hit, but not the adjacent opponent (2).

For her second Attack, she Attacks the Ground beneath an opponent (3). She rolls and gets a result of 11, which beats the Space's Defence of 10, giving a Hit. This causes Endurance Damage to the opponent (3). She also rolled a Strong Hit, but she cannot use it to cause a Critical Hit against the opponent (3) because their Endurance is still positive.

Spread Fire, RoF 2+, Splash X

If you Spread Fire (pg: 81) with a Rate of Fire 2+ Attack, calculate all locations hit (including dice used on spaces between Targets). All Targets within "X" spaces of locations you hit take Endurance Damage. Damage is not combined if Targets are within "X" of two or more locations that are hit.

Splash 1 & RoF 3

Sarah (A) has a Shotgun (End Dmg 3, Splash 1, RoF 3). She Attacks (Hit +2) the Ground (Defence 10) and Spreads Fire over three spaces. Her first and third Attack Rolls hit, but her second Attack Roll misses by 3, causing it to Scatter in a random direction by three spaces. Causing 3 Endurance Damage to Targets 1 and 3.

Splash X and/or Splash +/-Y

If your Weapon already has the Splash X Keyword, and a Weapon Variation or Modification (pg: 116) grants it Splash +Y, add "Y" to " X".

If your Weapon does not have the " Splash X" Keyword, and a Weapon Variation or Modification grants it Splash +Y, then your Weapon gains Splash +Y.

Outfits

See pg: 71 for full Combat Overview rules.
See pg: 84 for full Defence rules.
See pg: 87 for full Damage rules.
See pg: 114 for full Equipment Slots rules.
See pg: 366 for a full list of available Outfits.

These Outfits are built using standard rules. They are intended to give an example of how to make an Outfit and to show some of the better known Armours from the Fragged Empire setting.

You may may have 1 Outfit.
Outfits do not need to be Activated to use.
Outfits do not take up Equipment Slots.

Legion Assault Armour, Tactical Armour

Designed to withstand the best and worst of Xion's abominations, this flexible yet heavily reinforced armour gives the wearer almost unmatched protection against energy weapons. It is usually adorned with regimental designs, personal symbols, and kill markings. High-density hull-grade metals are often complemented by embellishments of trinkets, fur, and horns.

Outfit	Armour	Defence	Endurance	Cover	Frt Cover	Slots	Weight	Variation	Cost
Legion Assault Armour	2	+	+	+		10	3	Tungsten Carbide	2

Armour vs Energy +1

Octanto™ Business Suit, Clothing

This elegantly cut business suit carries a subtle statement of luxury and refinement to anywhere its esteemed owner could desire. Built with the latest Octanto™ technology, it emits a tightly focused burst shield, powered by our patented Nick-Hyd energy accumulator, to protect its most affluent wearers in those times when a stout Legionnaire cannot.

Outfit	Armour	Defence	Endurance	Cover	Frt Cover	Slots	Weight	Variation	Cost
Octanto™ Business Suit	0	+	+ 10	+		8	0	Shield Notes	1, 14+

+1 Conversation, Shield, -1 Armour when at 0 Endurance

Parasitic Regen Suit, Retractable

A design dating back to the Great X'ion War, these Nephilim-bred parasites form a near-unbreakable bond with their host. They survive by extracting vital nutrients from their host's bloodstream and fatty tissue. They work hard to protect their food source by covering the host in a sturdy carapace and boosting their regenerative abilities.

Outfit	Armour	Defence	Endurance	Cover	Frt Cover	Slots	Weight	Variation	Cost
Parasitic Bio-Suit	2	+	-5	+		8	0	Parasitic	2

+1 Conversation, Not obvious that you are wearing Armour, Set Up 1, Pull Down 1, Bio Tech, Removal of this Outfit requires a successful Surgery Healing Roll

Mk II Stalker Suit, Combat Suit

This suit is favoured by Legion scouts, Corporate assassins, and those who prefer a chunk of cover between themselves and gunfire. The Stalker series provides moderate protection and produces an optical haze around the wearer, blurring them against nearby objects to increase the advantage the cover provides.

Outfit	Armour	Defence	Endurance	Cover	Frt Cover	Slots	Weight	Variation	Cost
Mk II Stalker Suit	1	+	+	+ *		8	1	Haze Mesh	2

*Cover grants you +2 additional Defence.

Breaker Combat Vest, Combat Suit

When a Kaltoran is looking for a lightweight body armour solution that favours not being hit over absorbing impact, they choose this option. Salvaged armour combined with a signal distortion field makes this vest deceptively effective, especially when an agile user takes cover.

Outfit	Armour	Defence	Endurance	Cover	Frt Cover	Slots	Weight	Variation	Cost
Scram Suit	1	+	+	+		6	1	Scram Suit	1

Shield, Remove any Locked On Effect on you at the start of your Turn

Tech Assist Armour, Combat Suit

Engineers, hackers, and combat medics are just a small cross-section of the skilled amateurs and professionals who have need for both protection and utility equipment. Custom-made armour such as this boasts a wide array of built-in tools for almost any use, including drills, knives, wire splicers, and an integrated computer. A favourite of both legitimate and not-so-legitimate specialists.

Outfit	Armour	Defence	Endurance	Cover	Frt Cover	Slots	Weight	Variation	Cost
Tech Assist Armour	1	+	+	+		6	2	Technical Outfit	2, 14↑

Counts as a Toolbox (+1) for all Trained Professional Skills

Mk XII Stealth Suit, Combat Suit

Rumours claim that these incredibly sophisticated Archon-designed suits originated in ancient human technologies. Legion units in the X'ion War were occasionally equipped with them, allowing near-perfect invisibility. But they are not common, given their high upkeep cost and mediocre physical protection.

Outfit	Armour	Defence	Endurance	Cover	Frt Cover	Slots	Weight	Variation	Cost
Mk XII Stealth Suit	0	+ 1	+	+ 1		8	0	Stealth Suit	5, 14↑

Shield, *You always have Light Cover (+2) or +1 Cover Step

Strong Hit: Invisible Strike (Attack, Does not Require Hit) At the end of your Turn make a Free Stealth Action.

Outfit Stats

Armour

When you take a Critical Hit (pg: 88), reduce the Attribute Damage you take by your Armour.

Defence

Increases your Defence Stat (pg: 84), making you harder to hit.

Endurance

Increases your Endurance Stat (pg: 87).

Cover, pg: 86

Increases or decreases your Cover Steps. However, you must be in Environmental Cover to gain this bonus.

Front Cover (Frt Cover)

Grants you Front Cover (pg: 86).

Equipped Equipment Slots (Slots), pg: 114

Defines the amount of Equipment you can carry.

Weight

The Strength required to optimally use this Outfit. If you have lower Strength than a Outfits's Weight, you become Overburdened (pg: 115).

Outfits take up 0 Equipment Slots.
Outfits take up 0 Hands.
Outfits do not need to be Activated (pg: 114).

Variations, pg: 116

Use this space to list any Outfit Variations that you have applied to this Outfit.

Cost

The amount of Resources (pg: 56) or Spare Time Points (pg: 64) you need to spend to acquire and keep this Outfit.

Keywords, pg: 134

Various Traits (pg: 33), Strong Hit Options (pg: 82), Variations (pg: 116), and Modifications (pg: 116) may only apply to Outfits with a specific Keyword.

Modifications, pg: 116

These are templates that are applied to your Outfit.

BAM! BAM! BAM!

"Why the hell isn't it going down?"

"It's a mech suit covered in 30mm of military grade Tungsten Carbine... and your Corporate pop gun is a glorified kids toy."

Notes

Use this space to write down Outfit Keywords (pg: 134), Trait Benefits (pg: 33), and other notes.

"–" Stat
This means the item does not normally use this Stat. Variations, Modifications and Trait bonuses (+/–) do not increase or reduce this Stat.

Set Stat Value
If a Variation, Modification, or Trait inserts a Set value (Eg: "2" not "+2" or "-2") in this Stat, then the "–" is replaced with the set value.

This Set value also replaces ANY existing (non "–") value.

Utility Items

See pg: 114 for full Equipment Slots rules.
See pg: 368 for a full list of available Utility Items.

You may only have 1 Utility Item.
Utility Items do not need to be Activated to use.
Utility Items do not take up Equipment Slots.

Utility Items' Stats function exactly like Outfits.

Outfit	Armour	Defence	Endurance	Cover	Frt Cover	Slots	Weight	Variation	Cost
Combat Suit	1	+	+	+		8	1	Tungsten Carbine	2

Armour Vs Energy +1

Utility Item	Armour	Defence	Endurance	Cover	Frt Cover	Slots	Weight	Variation	Cost
Guards	+	+	+	+			2		141

Gauntlet, Defence Vs Impair +2

Phantom Cloak, Adjustable Camo Net

An offshoot of the Legion Ghost Cloak, this versatile cloak makes use of charge-sensitive pigments that can alter their hue to match a dozen pre-set patterns, blending the user into their surroundings. While not as advanced as many other stealth technologies, it is far cheaper and may give you the edge you need.

Utility Item	Armour	Defence	Endurance	Cover	Frt Cover	Slots	Weight	Variation	Cost
Adjustable Camo Net	+	+	+	+		+	0		10↑

Stealth +2

Ammunition Pack

Tired of running out of ammo? Fired six shots, and that was three clips? Need to take down just one more hostile to be safe to loot and drink? Know what you need? More ammo! An extra clip for every relevant weapon you carry, and maybe an extra stashed on the side, just to make the bad guys suffer.

Utility Item	Armour	Defence	Endurance	Cover	Frt Cover	Slots	Weight	Variation	Cost
Ammunition Pack	+	+	+	+		+ 2	3		1

All of your Weapons gain +1 Clip. You may spend 1 Fate Point at any time to grant you or an adjacent Ally +1 Clip.

Defender, Burst Shield

An incredibly powerful tool in the right hands, the Defender takes the primitive concept of a physical handheld shield and pushes it to new levels. This wrist-mounted force-field generator projects a small forward barrier that wraps around the user to create a nearly impenetrable cocoon.

Utility Item	Armour	Defence	Endurance	Cover	Frt Cover	Slots	Weight	Variation	Cost
Burst Shield	+	+	+	+	Light (+2)	+	0		1

Shield, Gauntlet, Take Cover Action grants you Immunity to Critical Hits while you have Endurance and are Gaining a Cover bonus

Drone Pro™, Drone Control Module

Numerous control, diagnostic, and maintenance programs are encoded into this portable drone-control computer. Specialised cleaning, repair, and upkeep sockets are built in, reducing maintenance needs for a single, low-cost drone.

Utility Item	Armour	Defence	Endurance	Cover	Frt Cover	Slots	Weight	Variation	Cost
Drone Control Module	+	+	+	+		+	2		12↑

If you Control 1 Drone with 1 Body; that Drone costs -1 Resource

Hunk of Metal, Large Combat Shield

This simple shield is often constructed of cut-off hull metal, spare armour pieces, or, less commonly, vacuum-moulded Synth Steel. Once strapped to your arm, this heavy yet mobile barrier can save lives and even provide enough cover to protect nearby allies.

Utility Item	Armour	Defence	Endurance	Cover	Frt Cover	Slots	Weight	Variation	Cost
Large Combat Shield	+	+	+	+	Heavy (+4)	-2	4		12t

Gauntlet, you may not Move and Attack with a 2 Handed Weapon (Weight 2+) in the same Turn, -1 RoF with Limbs, grants Heavy Cover (+4) to adjacent characters that are behind you

Legion Ghost Cloak

Ancient human electro-engineering provided the answer to this Archon-designed scouting apparel. Used by Legion advanced scouts and sniper teams for generations, it has recently become popular on the black market for its ability to blur the position of a stationary user and as a cheaper alternative to the far more expensive full-body stealth suits.

Utility Item	Armour	Defence	Endurance	Cover	Frt Cover	Slots	Weight	Variation	Cost
Legion Ghost Cloak	+	+	+	+1 Step*		+	1		1

Shield, Stealth +2, *Gain Light Cover (+2) or +1 Cover Step if you do not move for your Turn (you may Stealth)

Asclepius Spray, Med Spray

Almost a must-have for any combat trauma medic. The Legion's Asclepius Spray offers quick and precise injection, sterilisation, liquid suturing, and burn treatment. Recent models even utilise Nephilim Flesh Rejuvenation techniques and technologies. The best in compact paramedical equipment.

Utility Item	Armour	Defence	Endurance	Cover	Frt Cover	Slots	Weight	Variation	Cost
Med Spray	+	+	+	+		+	1		1

Gauntlet, Paramedics Heals an additional 1 (normally just 3) Point of Attributes Damage.

Portable Shieldwall™, Mobile Cover Field

Light, quick to set up, and offering significant protection against ranged fire over a moderate area, the handy Portable Shieldwall™ is based on the same technology as the wrist-worn Defender Burst Shield. Though it is too bulky to carry while active, its shielding radius is large enough that an ally can also take cover within.

Utility Item	Armour	Defence	Endurance	Cover	Frt Cover	Slots	Weight	Variation	Cost
Mobile Cover Field	+	+	+	+		+	0		2

Shield, Set Up 1*, Pull Down 1, *Creates Heavy Cover (+4) in two connecting adjacent spaces

A7 Archangel's Eye, Multispectral Visor

This advanced optical headset is worn by elite combat units and special operations forces. A suite of sensors scan the battlefield through various spectra — visual, infrared, electromagnetic, ultraviolet, and more. The A-7's sophisticated software analyses this data to instantly highlight targets of interest, environmental notes, and mission data.

Utility Item	Armour	Defence	Endurance	Cover	Frt Cover	Slots	Weight	Variation	Cost
A7 Archangel's Eye	+	+	+	+		+	0		1

Reduce all of your Target's Limited Vision and Low Light Cover by 1 Step, Defence vs Stealth +2

Octanto™ Discreet, Shield Emitter

Based on popular Node Shield technology, the Discreet is widely sold across the Haven system by the popular Corporation high-end fashion company Octanto™. Strapped to the user's wrist, the Discreet extends a charged particle shield over its wearer and a nearby ally, making it a favoured purchase of elite bodyguards and high-priced security contractors.

Utility Item	Armour	Defence	Endurance	Cover	Frt Cover	Slots	Weight	Variation	Cost
Shield Emitter	+	+	+	+		-2	2		3

Gauntlet, Shield, Take Cover Action grants You or an Ally within 5: Heavy Cover (+4) or +1 Cover Step until your next Turn

Plug 3762A, Stabiliser

Implants can cause significant problems if inactive during trauma or extreme stress. This Nephilim-made wrist-mounted accessory carefully regulates and maintains the power flow and functionality of all electronic, mechanical, and biological implants.

Utility Item	Armour	Defence	Endurance	Cover	Frt Cover	Slots	Weight	Variation	Cost
Stabiliser	+ *	+	+	+		+	0		1

Gauntlet, *Reduce penalties to your Armour while at 0 Endurance by 2 (to a minimum of -1)

The Connect, Tactical Headset

This basic tactical interface includes short-range communications, a targeting system, and a heads-up display. It is as useful in combat environments as in intraship and office communications. A near must-have for cooperative efforts in any situation.

Utility Item	Armour	Defence	Endurance	Cover	Frt Cover	Slots	Weight	Variation	Cost
Tactical Headset	+	+ 1	+	+		+	0		14↑

Short Range Comms, all of your Weapons gain Lock On +1

Outfit and Utility Item Keywords

Bio Tech
This Outfit or Utility Item counts as Bio Tech.

Communications (Short/Long)
The wielder can communicate using audio and video with other characters wielding an item with the "Communications" Keyword.

Short-range communication works to 100km, further if a network is available. Long-range communication works to 400km and often further. Short-range communications cannot normally reach orbiting spacecraft from the ground.

Cost Spare Time Point Xt
This item costs the listed amount of Resources (pg: 56) and requires a Spare Time Roll (pg: 64) of at least "X". This does not apply if the item was looted.

Environmental Gear (X)
Allows the wearer to function in the listed environment. It may not reduce all penalties of the environment (GM discretion), but removes all immediate threats of death. Can also provide limited protection in environments similar to the listed environment.

Arctic
Full-body suit, fitted with special protections against the most common arctic threats, such as cold and wind.
Comes equipped with snow shoes, fog-free visor, and walking staff.

Mountains
Climbing gear and durable clothing, suitable for travelling over difficult rocky terrain.
Comes equipped with climbing boots, grappling hooks, security lines, camping gear, and a thick jacket.

Space
Full suit, fitted with protections against common threats in a space environment, including cold, radiation, and decompression. Filled with a single day's worth of oxygen.
Comes equipped with magnetic boots, winch cable, and very limited mobility thrusters.

Flight
Enables the user to ignore most movement limitations, dangerous terrain, and climbing obstacles.
Move as per normal Movement rules (pg: 72), but ignore all Difficult Terrain and some Hazardous Terrain (GM discretion).

Gauntlet
You may only ever use two items at once with this Keyword.
Outfit and Utility Items require 0 Equipment Slots to be Equipped. Gauntlets take 5 minutes to Equip, but do not require any Hands to use.

Moving past the credit-check desk, she is gorgeous, exotic, with star-shaped tattoos around her clear blue cybernetic eyes, seemingly framing them just for him.

The music starts… A gentleman always invites the lady: "Hello and welcome to the Body Count Conglomerate: Armour Division. Your number-one choice for both quality and low costs! I'm Salesperson Smith; how may I help you this evening?"

"I need protection. At least 8/9ths laser diffraction, heat absorption, in some kind of hardened reflexive mesh." Her low, aggressive voice made him certain. The music was starting off nice and slow, building in tempo… Now for the dance's first steps.

"Certainly, we have the usual designs, both bulky Legion plates and the less rigid Kaltoran and Corporation designs, but I have a feeling you would be more interested in our newest stock… Right this way, if you please."

He leads her across the dance floor, past the various display armour. Legion "bulkers" on the left, and more lithe, formfitting armour on the right. Pulling aside the "Employees Only" curtain, he motions her through.

"Just over here." He waves a hand towards a nondescript light grey skin-tight mesh suit with only a faint diagonal pattern along the contours. "This piece, the Uberweave 3000, just arrived."

"Is this some sort of a joke?" Her growl was somehow lower than before and full of angry passion. It almost made him smile. Even her hand tightening around the butt of her pistol confirmed he still had it.

"Not at all, my dear. If you will permit me to demonstrate some of the fantastic features of the Uberweave…" His dance partner cocked her head beautifully, then nodded. Her beautiful eyes narrowed suspiciously, slightly scrunching up her eye tattoos.

His voice droned on as she glanced around at the "employee area". Bit too richly done up for a real one, she concluded. Much more likely to be part of this creep's sales technique… I wonder where I could get decent drink in this pathetic heap of a station… Suddenly her ears pricked up to the sound of music…

"… So in effect you would be wearing real diamonds, woven over your skin, protecting you from your foes and impressing your comrades."

"So… I'd be covered in real diamonds?" she said, trying to sound bored as her excitement grew.

"Of course." He interjected smoothly.

Oh, he had the right moves… He was the master of the dance floor. "If you look closely, you can see that they are arranged to fit…"

Even with all the right dance moves, a genetically engineered lady was still in it for the diamonds.

Modification Rolls +/-X

All Spare Time Rolls (pg: 116) made to acquire a Weapon Modification for this Weapon gain the listed bonus or penalty.

Set Up X, Pull Down Y

See pg: 108 for full Prep Action rules.

This item may only be used after performing "X" Actions with the Minor Effect: Set Up. If you Move during before completing all these Actions, all the Set Up Actions must be done again.

After setting up or using an item with the "Pull Down" Keyword, you may not move with that item until you perform "Y" Actions with the Minor Effect: Pull Down. If you Move before completing all these Actions, all these Pull Down actions must be done again.

Utility Items

You may move away from this item after setting it up. However, you must return to the same or an adjacent square to pull it down.

Shield

This Outfit or Utility Item uses an energy field to generate a specific effect (eg: a holographic field makes the user invisible) or makes the user resistant to damage.

Some Traits (eg: Shield Breaker) deal additional Effects against characters with a Shield item.

Misc Items and Services

See pg: 64 for full Spare Time rules.
See pg: 370 for the Misc Items and Services list.

Access

Sometimes you'll need access to facilities that you don't own. Usually rented (Wealth Skill Spare Time Roll).

Workshop, 10t

Space in either a local's personal shed or shared business space (eg: Mechanics Workshop).
Gain access to this Workshop for 1 session.

Dedicated Workshop, 16t

An entire workshop, often used by a dedicated business.
Gain access to this Dedicated Workshop for 1 session.

Storage Space (4 Cargo space), 10t

Either a storage shed, work space, or a long-term docked spacecraft. Usually used to store your Trade Goods.
Gain access to 4 Cargo space for up to 3 sessions.

Enforcer Backup, 14t

You have gained the aid of 1d3 combat-ready men or women, often police, local mercenaries, or thugs. They help you out because of a common interest: you might be paying them, or they might be enforcing the law, for example. Don't abuse their aid, though, because they won't go on a suicide mission or do everything you ask.

Long Distance Spacecraft Travel, 14t

Public transport, for if you don't have access to your own spacecraft, or are arranging travel for another. Passenger transportation is a widespread and common service to almost all people.

Transports up to 5 characters for 6 days of travel (pg: 151).

Healing

Performed by yourself or another, medical practice is a serious undertaking. It often requires specialised tools and a measure of skill.

Extended Care, 2x 12t

When a patient has many symptoms and minor problems, it can be quite crippling. Extended care includes changing bandages, administering helpful pharmaceuticals, and keeping an eye on how the patient is doing.

Requires an appropriate Toolbox and heals 1 point of Attribute Damage to each Attribute and removes a Minor Condition (eg: poison or infection).

Surgery, 2x 14t

A direct, invasive, and focused approach to healing traumatic damage or curing the worst conditions. Surgery requires a place to operate, correct tools (Workshop), patience, and talent.
Can heal up to 8 Damage to a single Attribute and remove a Major Condition (eg: terminal virus or severed limb).

Also, the recipient of your Surgery Healing Roll may gain a single free Trait Retro (pg: 32) to change any Trait to a Implant Trait.

Spacecraft Repair, pg: 164

When a spacecraft breaks, it is costly both in resources and time. If you are skilled and have the right tools, it is best to fix it yourself, but you can always pay another to do it for you.

Maintenance, 2x 10t

Any spacecraft that sees battle will need maintenance and care. Requires a Toolbox and heals 1 Attribute Damage from every Attribute or remove a Minor Condition (eg: virus or extensive rust damage).

Rebuild, 2x 14t

Repairing major damage often requires pulling apart and rebuilding an entire system to properly repair the damage.

Requiring a Workshop, rebuilding heals up to 8 Attribute Damage to a single Attribute and removes a Major Condition (eg: destroyed wing, contaminated fuel line, destroyed computer system, or mutinous crew).

Change Out, 14t

Every now and again you will want to change your spacecraft's load-out, such as changing a weapon system, refining its layout, or adding new crew.

Requires a Workshop and lets you change 1 Attribute point (reducing one and increasing another), Weapon system, or Trait.

"I love Kaltoran ships. They take the concept of multiple redundancies to whole new level. Just the other day I rebuilt the engine coolant system and ended up with enough spare parts to fix the landing gear."

- James Thrift, chief engineer of the Aqua Sun.

Flash Light, 1 Slot, 8t

A small, simple, but effective light source. Held in one hand, it illuminates dark areas, but also illuminates you to some degree, making your presence known to others.

Requires 1 Action to Draw, requires 1 free hand (pg: 114), and can be used with a Free Action. Reduces all Low Light (pg: 86) penalties over a square area with a 3-space radius and all Attacks against you.

2 Flares, 1 Slot, 8t

Easily obtainable, flares completely illuminate a specific area.

Requires 1 Action to Draw, requires 1 free hand (pg: 114), and can be Thrown (pg: 110) at Range increments of 3 (pg: 78). Reduces Low Light penalties by 2 Steps in Splash 4 and by 1 Step in Splash 8.

Specific Environmental Equipment, 2 Slots, 12t

This equipment allows you to function in a specific hostile environment. It might include climbing gear, a tent, or cooking equipment.

Survival Rations, Weight 1, 8t

Frozen food cubes, dried meat, and plenty of water; these are the staples of military and survival rations. A must for long journeys away from civilisation. They're easy to acquire, but don't go far if you are not properly trained.

Food and Water for 2 days, or for 7 if you are Trained in Survival.

Pallet of Supplies, Cargo 1, 8t

A pallet of food, water, fuel, and other non-combat supplies. Particularly useful for long exploration or combat missions away from settled areas.

The pallet can give a spacecraft +6 Resupply, or it can be broken up into 'Food Supplies' (see below).

Food Supplies, Weight 4, 10t

A week's worth of food and water takes up a surprisingly large amount of room, but it's easy to come by in a settled area or by hunting and gathering, if you have the right wilderness training.

Food and Water for 7 days, or for 14 days if you are Trained in Survival.

Head Set, Weight 1, 12t

An incredibly useful multipurpose item, almost a must-have for all. It works at short range (100km, further if network is available), and can handle both audio and video. Also comes with a heads up display for controlling drones and other remote devices.

Satellite Backpack, Weight 3, 14t

Enables you to communicate over long distances (400+km). Particularly useful for communicating with spacecraft when you can't access a public satellite system, though the backpack's bulk is often off-putting.

Translator, Weight 1, 18t

A rare technological wonder, the translator can interpret all common languages, both text and speech, though it is no perfect substitute to personally knowing a language.

While using the Translator, you suffer -2 to all Social, Leadership, and Culture Skill Rolls dealing with the translated Language.

Non-Combat Drone, (Weight 1 (+0)), 14t

See pg: 104 for full rules on Drones.

This is a simple drone, used for menial tasks as it cannot engage in combat. May be Bio Tech.

Has Defence 8, Armour 2, Movement 4, Weight 1 (+0), and Slots 0.

GPS Mapping Computer, Weight 1, 12t

A useful device for keeping track of Allies. Usually comes with maps of the local area. Most urban areas will have free maps available for download to this device.

Toolkit, Weight 1, 6t

Small tools helpful for when you use Professional Skills. Many uses of Skills require that you have a Toolkit (eg: opening a metal panel requires a screwdriver of some kind).

Multi Tool, Weight 1, 12t

Counts as a Toolkit (see above) for 4 Skills and only takes up 1 Equipment Slot. Select these Skills when you acquire the Multi Tool.

Toolbox, Weight 2, 16t

If you take a Skill seriously, you will want an appropriate Toolbox. A Toolbox can be used in place of a Toolkit.

A Toolbox grants +1 to one Trained Primary Skill; this bonus does not stack with other items.

Omni Tool, Weight 1, 20t

The title "Omni Tool" is used to describe a number of highly advanced and varied Archon or X'ion multi-use work tools. Able to produce a tool for almost any need, they come in a wide range of styles. Some Archon Omni Tools use advanced holographic technology, while X'ion Omni Tools may be a living shape-shifting creature.

A Omni Tool counts as a Toolbox for all Trained Professional Skills.

Workbench, Cargo 0, 10t

Low tech and extremely useful, the trusty workbench is usually little more than a flat surface with basic mounted work tools.

Workshop, Cargo 1, 14t

A cleared work space with tools is a requirement for many serious endeavours of skill.

Choose 1 Trained Primary Skill the Workshop will apply to. Workshop also counts as a Workbench.

Dedicated Workshop, Cargo 4, 16t

A serious and spacious place to work, a Dedicated Workshop is used for the most advanced research and development projects.

When you install it, choose 1 Trained Primary Skill. The Dedicated Workshop counts as a Workshop for the selected Skill and grants +2 to it, and it counts as a Workbench for all other Primary Skills.

Advanced Medical Supplies, Weight 1, 12t

A carefully selected pack of expensive pharmaceuticals, powerful mutagens, and rare tools. This kit can make a big difference to almost any applied medical endeavour.

Grants +4 to one Medicine Healing Roll; if multiple are required for a single purpose, it grants +4 to all those Spare Time Rolls. This is a one-use item.

Flesh Rejuvenator, Weight 0, 14t

Widely used by the Nephilim during the Great X'ion War, this green mutagenic fluid is a must-have for critical medical emergencies. By reading the DNA of its recipient, the fluid expands over a wide area to replace damaged, infected, or destroyed body parts, even going so far as to replace broken bones and missing flesh.

When you make a successful Paramedics Healing Roll, you may use the Flesh Rejuvenator to Heal +2 Attribute Damage. This is a Small, one-use item.

Stim Cocktail, Weight 0, 8t

A cheap cocktail of drugs and stimulants. This common cocktail can give you a much-needed boost, but it tends to lock up your muscles for a short time.

On use, Heals 10 Endurance Damage, but prevents you from Moving on your next Turn. This is a Small, one-use item.

Clear Shot, Weight 0, 12t

When you need a boost for an important attack you can't afford to miss, this Stim clears the mind of distractions and helps you focus. Just try to ignore the burning side effects.

On use, take 5 Endurance Damage and Boost your next Attack with +4 Hit. This Attack must be made within five minutes to gain the Boost. Does not Stack with other Clear Shot Stims. This is a Small, one-use item.

Psi Stim, Weight 0, 14t

A strange and dangerous Stim that opens a psionic door in your mind, allowing you to bend reality ever so slightly to your will. That door swings both ways, though, letting something or someone have a little nibble at your sanity.

On use, take 1 Focus Damage (not reduced by Armour) and Boost your next Attack with +1 Strong Hit. This Attack must be made before the end of your next Turn. This is a Small, one-use item.

Everyone knows Draz is bad for you, but it's an immensely popular and well-marketed energy and alcoholic drink. Many can't resist the promising lure of longer days with no need for sleep.

Popular with both high-flying businessmen and club-crawling rave junkies, Draz offers it all with no warning labels… apart from the back alleys littered with desperate addicts looking for their next hit.

These poor souls are the lucky ones. Pity and fear the ones who can keep getting more…

....

"All walks of life are addicted to Draz. The busy to its sleepless nights, the violent to its power, and the merchants to its sales figures."

– Well-known truism.

Pack of Draz, Weight 2, 14t

Can't afford to sleep? This powerful drink substitutes your body's natural rest cycle with a cocktail of unlisted chemicals. On use, removes your need to sleep for one night and gives you 1 Spare Time Point (pg: 64). This is a one-use item.

Street Draz, Weight 0, 12t

Concentrated Draz syrup, from which popular Draz drinks are made, diluted and mixed with a few extra ingredients.

On use, gain +2 Armour for 3 Turns, including the Turn on which it was used. At the end of the third Turn, take 1 Attribute Damage to a random Attribute (roll 1d3). This Attribute Damage is not reduced by Armour and cannot be Healed with a Paramedics Healing Roll. This is a Small, one-use item.

Pure Draz, Weight 0, 18t

Pure, lab-refined Draz. Not only is it hard to acquire or make, it is also often lethal.

On use, gain +2 Armour until the end of the combat. When the combat ends, take 2 Attribute Damage to a random Attribute (roll 1d3). This Attribute Damage is not reduced by Armour and cannot be Healed with a Paramedics Healing Roll. This is a Small, one-use item.

Spacecraft Overview

See pg: 58 for full Influence rules.

All non-Corporation spacecraft are ancient pre-War relics of a more advanced time that make use of advanced Ley Line Jump Technologies few can even begin to comprehend. Their value transcends all currency.

It is extremely rare for a crew to maintain an entire spacecraft by themselves. Steady access to fuel, munitions, supplies, and landing platforms requires friends who are willing to support your endeavours because your goals further their own interests.

Overview

Creating a Spacecraft, pg: 142

Spacecraft are created much like characters (pg: 30), spacecraft have Attributes, Traits, and some Stats. They do not have Levels, Fate, Outfits, or Utility Items.

Cost Influence

Spacecraft are acquired by allotting Influence Points (pg: 58). Multiple characters can contribute Influence Points to the same spacecraft. These Influence Points can also be spent on Weapons and Traits for the spacecraft.

Build, pg: 144

Just as each character has a Race, each spacecraft has a Build, which defines the nature of its creation, who built it, and how it was built.

Traits, pg: 144

Spacecraft may have one Trait for each of its Attributes and its Size Stat. Each Trait increases the cost of the spacecraft by 5 Influence.

Attributes, pg: 147

A spacecraft begins with 18 Attribute Points to distribute amongst 6 Attributes: Hull, Engines, Crew, Power, CPU, and Sensors. Each of these Attributes can be from 0 to 5.

Size, pg: 148

A spacecraft's Size plays a large role in determining its manoeuvrability, firepower, and cargo space. All spacecraft start at Size 3.

Weapons Slots, pg: 145

A spacecraft may be equipped with one Weapon per Weapon Slot. A spacecraft begins with Weapon Slots equal to its Size.

Cargo, pg: 150

Your spacecraft's size determines how much room it has for you to install Workshops or to store Trade Goods.

Combat, pg: 155

Spacecraft Combat is quite different from Personal Combat. In Spacecraft Combat, you and your Allies may each take control of a different Vehicle System of your spacecraft.

Velocity, pg: 158

Once you set the velocity of your spacecraft, it will continue to move at that speed until you change it.

System Rolls, pg: 168

A spacecraft has four Systems: Command, Engineering, Operations, and Gunnery. Each Turn you may attempt a single System Roll.

Scale and Relative Size, pg: 148

All spacecraft Stats and Weapons are defined relative to other spacecraft. The size and crew of an "average" spacecraft are defined by the GM at the start of your game. Are the player characters the only crew, or does each ship have hundreds?

Combat Scale, pg: 156

Some Spacecraft Combat will take place over relatively small areas, while others will be fought over huge ones.

All spacecraft Weapons and sensors are calibrated to track and fight those who are travelling at speeds comparable to their craft's own. This makes spacecraft invisible and blind to all those who are travelling at far different velocities.

Spacecraft Creation

Spacecraft are created like characters (see pg: 30). Read the Character Creation rules before you read this section. Also, read this section alongside a Spacecraft Character Sheet.

Find a Suitable Spacecraft

Before you can customise or build your spacecraft, you will need to locate one through your in-game actions. Your spacecraft will often come with a history of its own, possibly with a name, along with allocated Attributes, Weapons, and a Build. When the players find a craft, GMs are encouraged to allow then to shift around some Attribute Points.

Unable to Pay the Required Influence

If players cannot pay the required Influence, their spacecraft's Weapons and Traits decrease at the end of the session until they can pay the Influence cost. This represents the spacecraft falling into disrepair.

Attribute Points, pg: 147

When creating a spacecraft, distribute 18 points amongst 6 Attributes: Hull, Engines, Crew, Power, CPU, and Sensors. Each Attribute may be set from 0 to 5.

0 is a lack of a system.   3 is average.
1 or 2 is below average.   4 or 5 is amazingly powerful.

Choose Traits, pg: 144

Your spacecraft may have 1 Trait per Attribute and Size. Each Trait increases the Influence cost of your spacecraft by 5.

Calculated Stats

Your spacecraft has a few calculated Stats that are used in and out of combat.

Cargo = (Size x4) +Hull -10   Defence = 12 -Size +Engines
Weapon Slots = Size   Armour = 3
Resupply = Size x2   Shields = 10 + (Power xSize)

Defensive Stats

These are calculated just like a character's Defence Stats but without Overburden or Cover rules and using Shields instead of Endurance.

Weapons, pg: 145

Your spacecraft may have as many Weapons as it has Weapon Slots. To mount a Weapon, it cannot have a Mount value higher than the spacecraft's Hull.

Spacecraft Perks, pg: 152

Gains 1 Optional Spacecraft Perk per Size. Some Spacecraft Perks are automatically acquired for spacecraft of a certain Size.

Creating a Spacecraft

Influence Cost = Traits (5 Influence Each) +Weapons +10
Best completed alongside the GM and other players.

Find a Spacecraft
You will need to locate a spacecraft through your in-game actions.
This spacecraft may come with a pre-chosen Build, along with Traits, Weapons, and allotted Attribute Points.

Add Up Available Influence
Multiple characters can combine Influence to acquire one or more spacecraft.
If your spacecraft's Influence cost is higher than your total Influence, it will lose Weapons and Traits until the party can pay its Influence cost.

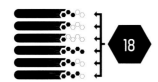

Distribute 18 Attribute Points
Distribute 18 points amongst Hull, Engines, Crew, Power, CPU, and Sensors.
Each Attribute may be set from 0 to 5.
An average spacecraft has 3 points in each Attribute.

Choose Traits
Each Trait costs 5 Influence points.
You may select 1 Trait for each Attribute, along with 1 Size Trait.

Calculated Stats
Cargo = (Size x4) +Hull –10   Defence = 12 –Size +Engines
Weapon Slots = Size   Armour = 3
Resupply = Size x2   Shields = 10 + (Power xSize)

Choose Weapons
You may have 1 Weapon per Weapon Slot (normally equal to your Size).
Each Weapon's Mount Stat must be equal to or lower than your Hull Attribute. If your Hull Attribute is ever reduced (eg: through Damage) below a Weapon's Mount Stat, it ceases to function.

Choose Spacecraft Perks
Your spacecraft may have Optional Spacecraft Perks equal to its Size.
Your spacecraft automatically gains any Automatic Spacecraft Perks that it meets the Size requirement for.

Influence Cost

See pg: 58 for full Influence rules.

A spacecraft is often too large and expensive for just its crew to maintain and supply. You will need to have the support of a wider circle of friends and allies to supply you with the fuel, munitions, parts, and landing platforms that your spacecraft will need.

One Big Craft or Many Small

Your group can pool together all their Influence to acquire one expensive spacecraft or multiple spacecraft.

At a high Level (and high Influence), you and your group are likely to acquire multiple spacecraft or a very large spacecraft with multiple Sections (see: Extra Section Build, pg: 372).

> ### Influence Cost of a Spacecraft
> = Traits (5 Influence Each) + Weapons Cost +10
>
> This cost may be paid by combining Influence from multiple characters.

Shared Effort, Pooling Influence Example

Mr Creelman and his team wish to pool their Influence to acquire a large spacecraft known as the Shadow Jakkal.

Mr Creelman has 9 Current Influence, and his four teammates have 8 each, for a total of 41 (9+8+8+8+8). The spacecraft will cost 34 Influence, leaving them 7 Influence. They spend 5 on another spacecraft Trait and hold onto the remaining 2 until they gain enough to add another Weapon or Trait.

Fighter Squadron, Spacecraft Influence Cost Example

Chris and his elite fighter squad, The Imaginers, wish to acquire a small spacecraft for each of their five members. Each member has 6 Current Influence and has taken the My Baby Influence Trait, which reduces the Influence Cost of a spacecraft of Size 2 or below that only they have paid Influence for by 10).

Each member may spend their Influence on their spacecraft as they see fit. Some spend it on better Weapons, while others give their spacecraft a Trait.

Build

See pg: 372 for a full list of available Vehicle System Builds.

Just as every character has a Race, every spacecraft has a Build. This reflects the nature of the spacecraft's construction, such as which race built it.

All spacecraft must choose a Build.

Traits

See pg: 356 for a full list of available Vehicle System Traits.
See pg: 373 for a full list of available Spacecraft Traits.

Just like character Traits, spacecraft Traits are what set your spacecraft apart from others. They often define the nature of your spacecraft's Attributes and its Size.

> ### Each spacecraft Trait costs 5 Influence.

You may select 1 Trait per Attribute (Hull, Engines, Crew, Power, CPU and Sensors), as well as 1 Trait for Size. This makes choosing each Trait important, as you'll be ignoring all the others.

Requirements

Many Traits have requirements that must be met before selecting them.

GM Approval

Selecting this Trait requires the GM's approval.
Normally requires an in-game action to justify its choice.

Maximum Attribute (Max X)

The listed Attribute can be no higher than "X".

Minimum Attribute (Max X)

The listed Attribute must be "X" or higher.

Secret Knowledge (Secret Kn)

You must have Secret Knowledge (from Research, pg: 68) in a field that thematically matches the Trait. This often represents your character learning how to install this Trait.

Size X-Y

Your Size value must be "X" or higher.
Your Size value can be no higher than "Y".

Trait or Build

You must have a prerequisite Trait or Build.

Traits Should Make Thematic Sense

Choose Traits that match the nature of your spacecraft. GMs can require players to take in-game actions to justify their selection of a Trait (eg: finding the right equipment or person to install the changes to their spacecraft).

Weapons

See pg: 116 for full Variation and Modification rules.
See pg: 145 for full Spacecraft Weapon rules.
See pg: 377 for a full list of Spacecraft Weapons.

The universe is a dangerous place, with pirates, Mechonids, and a myriad of other unimaginable threats. Your spacecraft will need Weapons, not only to defend itself, but also to attack those who would cause you harm… or who have what you want.

Shield Damage (Shield Dmg)

Functions just like End Dmg (pg: 122) but against spacecraft Shields.

Weapon Slots

Your craft may have as many Weapons as it has Weapon Slots.

Weapon Costs

Weapons that don't cost Spare Time Points cost Influence.

Weapon Variations & Modifications

As with personal equipment, spacecraft Weapons may have Variations and Modifications.

Repair Roll: Change Out

See pg: 64 for full Spare Time rules.
See pg: 164 for full Repair Roll rules.

Unlike characters, spacecraft do not gain Retros (pg: 32) to change their Attributes or Traits, and they cannot simply change their Weapons for new ones. If you wish to change an Attribute, Trait, or Weapon on your spacecraft, you must make a Change Out Spare Time Roll of 14t and have access to a relevant Workshop.

If changing an Attribute would break a Trait Requirement, you lose the benefits of that Trait but keep the Disadvantages.

All changes must be approved by the GM and will often require some in-game actions to justify the change.

New Spacecraft

If you wish to get a new spacecraft, you must make a Change Out Spare Time Roll to regain your spent Influence.

Destroyed Spacecraft

GMs are encouraged to reduce characters' Current Influence if they lose their spacecraft.

Attributes

Attributes represent your spacecraft's ability and nature relative to other craft. Attributes are primarily used for System Rolls in combat (pg: 168) and to give access to Traits (pg: 144).

> When creating a spacecraft, distribute 18 points amongst the 6 Attributes.
>
> Each Attribute may be set from 0 to 5.

An average spacecraft has 3 in every Attribute: while 0 represents the absence of a system (eg: a space station that does not move may have 0 Engines), 5 is amazingly powerful.

Many Traits (pg: 144) can only be selected if the craft meets certain Attribute requirements.

Hull

The general bulk of your spacecraft.
Primarily used to determine the craft's Cargo space and the quality of Weapons it can use.

Engines (Eng)

The rate at which your spacecraft can accelerate or decelerate.
Primarily used to adjust your Velocity and increase your Defence.

Crew

The quality and quantity of your spacecraft's crew and/or general accessibility of your spacecraft.
Primarily used for Boarding Party Attack Rolls, Repair Rolls and Launching Ordnance.

> ### Just the PCs or with NPC Crew
> Your spacecraft does not have to have NPC Crew.
> A high Crew Attribute may represent the usability of your craft.

Power (Pow)

The power output of your spacecraft.
Primarily used to determine the craft's Shield strength and its ability to boost other Systems.

Processor (CPU)

The processing power of your spacecraft's central computer or brain.
Primarily used to determine your System Roll order and ability to Lock Onto Targets.

Sensors (Sen)

Your ability to scan your environment.
Primarily used to determine the long-range accuracy of your spacecraft's gun Batteries.

Blockade Runner, Attribute Example

The Rip Tide is one of the fastest smuggling ships in the Haven system. It needs to be able to bypass the toughest military blockades.

Hull: 4 (Good-sized cargo hold.)
Eng: 4 (Great for hitting hard and changing velocity.)
Cre: 2 (Don't need a huge crew if you don't hang around.)
Pow: 3 (Good for keeping those shields up.)
CPU: 4 (Great for jumping as soon as possible.)
Sen: 1 (Terrible gun range. Ordnance will be a good option.)
Size: 3 (Average size but big enough for some cargo space.)

Gun Ship, Attribute Example

The Hade's crew want to hunt down pirates. Their spacecraft needs to be tough and powerful if it's going to survive..

Hull: 5 (Great for making sure your guns don't go down.)
Eng: 2 (Enough to manage your velocity, but no fancy moves.)
Cre: 2 (Enough for the odd patch job.)
Pow: 3 (Good enough to keep those shields up.)
CPU: 2 (Enough to keep your targets locked on.)
Sen: 4 (Great for long-range attacks.)
Size: 4 (You're a big ship, with lots of guns.)

Explorer, Attribute Example

The Mystery is a deep-space exploration vessel. It needs to be flexible: big enough to store supplies for a long journey, nimble enough to avoid danger. It also needs sensors powerful enough that it can keep its distance as needed.

Hull: 2 (Just enough for some weapons, but nothing fancy.)
Eng: 2 (Enough to manage your velocity.)
Cre: 4 (Repairs are important if you don't know when you'll dock next.)
Pow: 2 (Your shields will go down quickly if you're not careful.)
CPU: 4 (Enough to give you the edge in most combat.)
Sen: 4 (You're fantastic at keeping your distance if needed.)
Size: 3 (Average size, big enough to store supplies.)

Fighter, Attribute Example

The Sabre is a small and nimble fighter, built to provide combat escort and support for larger spacecraft.

Hull: 2 (Your guns are not that big.)
Eng: 5 (Fantastic velocity control makes you incredibly hard to hit when combined with your small size.)
Cre: 1 (You're just a one-man fighter.)
Pow: 4 (Your shields can't take much of a hit, but they'll come back quickly.)
CPU: 4 (Maintaining your edge in combat is vital to your survival.)
Sen: 2 (You will be using your manoeuvrability, not your range.)
Size: 1 (Small and nimble.)

It was an unusual ship. Most people saw the docking tentacles, the heat dissipation fins, the sensory pods, or the cargo sphincter with the elaborate mechanical crane recessed into the surrounding carapace and thought "Ugh!" But Kr'tumbra watched with parental pride and awe through the lightly tinted hull glass as the gigantic dreadnought rotated silently and gracefully, slim tentacles trailing as though in water to align itself with the Corporate cargo transfer bay, then firmly attach itself with an elaborate, artistic knotwork, allowing crew to disembark. His bio-lab birthed baby had completed her first patrol and eaten her first pirates. A resounding success on both counts.

A tear rolled down one smiling cheek.

- Kr'tumbra and his ship.

Size

See pg: 150 for full Cargo space rules.
See pg: 145 for full Weapons rules.
See pg: 151 for full Non-Combat Travel and Resupply rules.
See pg: 78 for full Attack Roll rules.
See pg: 168 for full System Roll rules.
See pg: 152 for full Spacecraft Perk rules.

Your spacecraft's Size Stat is its size relative to other craft.

Spacecraft by default are Size 3. This can be increased or decreased through Traits (pg: 144), particularly Size Traits.

Cargo = (Size x4) +Hull -10
Weapon Slots = Size
Resupply = Size x2
Defence = 12 -Size +Engines
Defence vs Boarding = 10 +Size +Crew
Manoeuvre System Roll Difficulty = Size x4
Number of Spacecraft Perks = Size

A larger spacecraft has more Cargo space,
Weapons, and Shields.

However, a larger craft also has lower Defence
and is harder to manoeuvre.

Optional Rule: Change Size Scale

On the next page, you'll see a size comparison of spacecraft within the Fragged Empire setting. However, GMs can surely change the size scale of spacecraft within your game.

The Size of an average spacecraft is always 3.

Changing the Size scale will not change the Stats of the spacecraft in your game, but it will substantially change the feel.

Huge Spacecraft, Change Size Scale Example
Samantha, the GM, wants to run a game styled as a grand space opera, featuring massive spacecraft with hundreds of crew and dozens of escort fighter squads. She informs her players that an average spacecraft of Size 3 in her game will be 200m long and have a few hundred crew. Every time a spacecraft takes Attribute Damage, several crew will likely have died. Most fighters will be manned by a living pilot, not remotely controlled, and each warhead body represents a group of warheads.

None of this affects the statistics or rules of her game, but it will significantly change the style of game.

Small Spacecraft, Change Size Scale Example
Frank, the GM, wants to run a game set at the dawn of the Rebirth, just as the Kaltorans are re-entering space and meeting the other races for the first time. These early spacecraft are quite small and rudimentary in nature. He says that an average spacecraft of Size 3 in his game will only be 18m long.

He also says that all out-of-combat Travel Time in space is tripled, but the Resupply value of each spacecraft is increased by 4. This is a minor change to the rules that will help give the game a feel of survival and space pioneering.

"Why don't we construct massive spacecraft haulers?" Peter's investors often asked this question; their ignorance was understandable. Bigger ships and smaller crew would result in bigger profit margins.

"The answer is unfortunately fairly simple. Big ships are far too slow for this turbulent, dangerous, and fast-changing economy. We need to be flexible and quick."

- Peter Sams, Star Co Inc.

Default Size Comparison

An average spacecraft is always Size 3.
An average spacecraft may have a different length in your game.

Size 1
Heavy or long-range fighter.
Commonly crewed by a single pilot.
Average length: 12m.

Size 2
Heavy bomber or scout.
Commonly manned by two to three crew.
Average length: 22m.

Size 3
The most common spacecraft size.
Commonly manned by four to five crew.
Average Length: 34m.

Size 4
Heavy combat gunship or small freighter.
Commonly manned by five commanders and five support crew.
Average Length: 50m.

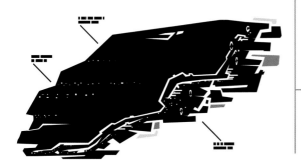

Size 5
Battleship or large freighter.
Commonly manned by six commanders and two dozen support crew.
Average Length: 80m.

Ordnance (Fighters and Warheads)
Short-range manned fighter or drone.
Launched from a larger vessel.
Commonly remote-guided.

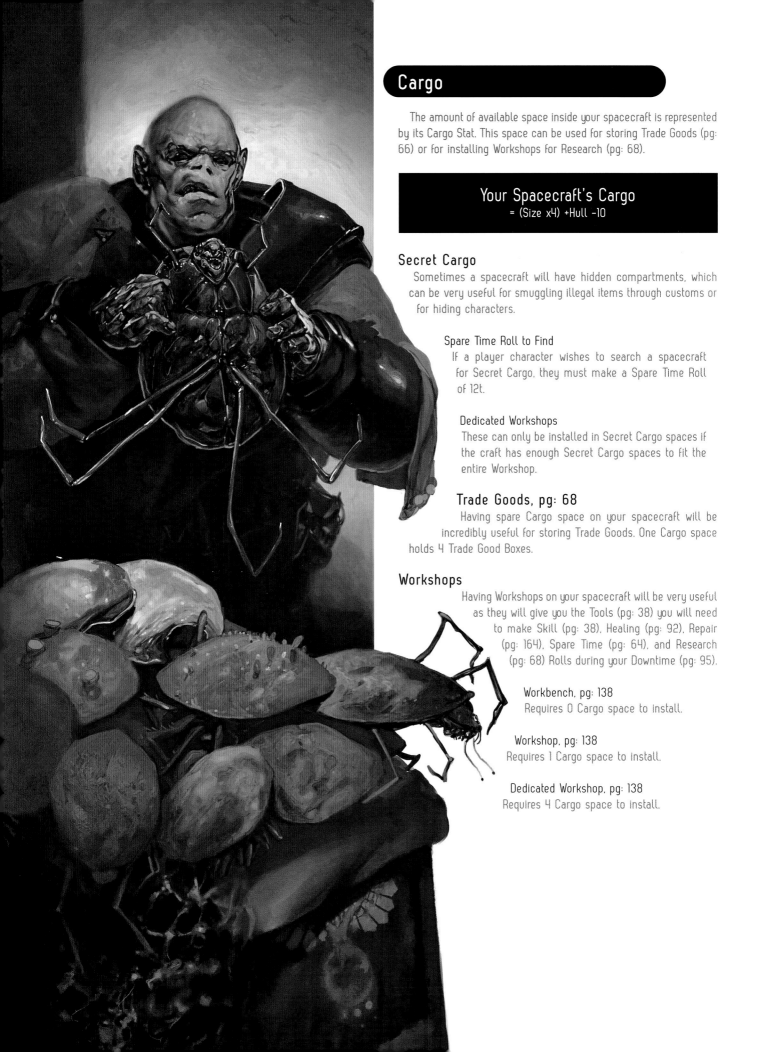

Cargo

The amount of available space inside your spacecraft is represented by its Cargo Stat. This space can be used for storing Trade Goods (pg: 66) or for installing Workshops for Research (pg: 68).

Your Spacecraft's Cargo
= (Size x4) +Hull -10

Secret Cargo

Sometimes a spacecraft will have hidden compartments, which can be very useful for smuggling illegal items through customs or for hiding characters.

Spare Time Roll to Find

If a player character wishes to search a spacecraft for Secret Cargo, they must make a Spare Time Roll of 12t.

Dedicated Workshops

These can only be installed in Secret Cargo spaces if the craft has enough Secret Cargo spaces to fit the entire Workshop.

Trade Goods, pg: 68

Having spare Cargo space on your spacecraft will be incredibly useful for storing Trade Goods. One Cargo space holds 4 Trade Good Boxes.

Workshops

Having Workshops on your spacecraft will be very useful as they will give you the Tools (pg: 38) you will need to make Skill (pg: 38), Healing (pg: 92), Repair (pg: 164), Spare Time (pg: 64), and Research (pg: 68) Rolls during your Downtime (pg: 95).

Workbench, pg: 138

Requires 0 Cargo space to install.

Workshop, pg: 138

Requires 1 Cargo space to install.

Dedicated Workshop, pg: 138

Requires 4 Cargo space to install.

Non-Combat Travel

See pg: 8 for Sector and System maps.
See pg: 278 for a Ley Line setting guide.
See pg: 288 for a Reactors and Propulsion setting guide.

Space is big... really big. But that's OK, we have Jump Drives... never mind the fact that no one really knows how they work.

Note to GM
The days spent travelling between locations is a great time to let your players use their Workshops and spend Spare Time Points.

System Travel
Travelling between planets and locations within a system of planets around a central sun will usually require days of Jump Travel.

Travelling between the blue lines marked on the System Map requires 1 day of Jump Travel. These lines are often parallel to the Sun.

Leaving a System
If you wish to leave a system, you will need to travel to the outside edge of the map first.

Sector Travel
Travelling between star systems and nebula usually requires weeks of Jump Travel if you are not moving along a Ley Line.

Travelling from one blue hex on the Sector Map requires 6 days of Jump Travel. When travelling along a Ley Line, these hexes are much larger, allowing for faster travel.

Interrupting Jump Travel
Jump Travel can be interrupted for many reasons, whether through ancient SOS beacons, pirate interdiction devices, astral phenomena, or system failures.

Partial Line/Hex
Travelling partway along a hex or line takes less time than travelling its whole length. For example, travelling from the middle of a Sector Hex requires 3 days rather than 6.

Resupply

See pg: 160 for full Spacecraft Condition rules.

This is the number of days a spacecraft can spend in space before it falls into disrepair. Anytime that you land your spacecraft in a friendly city, your Resupply refills.

Your Spacecraft's Resupply
= Size x2

Pallet of Supplies, pg: 137
A Pallet, acquired through a Spare Time Roll, extends your spacecraft's Resupply by 6 at the cost of 1 Cargo space.

Foraging for Supplies
Player characters are encourage to be creative in their approach to regaining their Resupply. GMs should give players a chance to forage their local area for what they need. During the Great X'ion War many spacecraft where shot down and remain un-salvaged. There are also numerous hidden caches waiting for their creators to return.

Running out of supplies is a great opportunity for a story. It is simply not possible to always bring the supplies you will need for a long journey into uncharted space.

Low Resupply
For each day of Jump Travel beyond your Resupply, the GM applies a negative Condition to the party or spacecraft that reflects the situation. The most common effects of low Resupply are Low Fuel and/or Low Food/Water.

Minor Condition: Low Fuel
» You can make one more Jump (including Combat Jump). If this does not take you to a safe location where you can refuel, the craft gains the Major Condition: Out of Fuel, pg: 162 (may not Jump, x10 travel time outside of combat).

Minor Condition: Low Munitions
» Your Fighters have Hit -4.
» You may only Launch your Warheads one more time.
» All of your Batteries have 1 Clip.

Minor Condition: Disrepair
» -2 to all System Rolls.

Low Food/Water
See pg: 75 for full Low Food and/or Water rules.

Gabriel Tempson stalked from one end of the terminal and diagram-studded laboratory to the other. Back and forth, muttering and occasionally smacking a technical dossier, notebook, or old food container to the floor in frustration. "It makes no damn sense!" he screamed at the cluttered lab, stained walls showing just how destitute his "theory-heavy" research had made him.

"Okay, from the start, Gabe," he muttered.

"When the right Ley Energies are directed at a small enough point in local space-time, we get an energy flicker, and if we then follow that up with a micro-burst of neutron radiation, we get an opening of a temporary portal, allowing directed post-lightspeed travel within a shielded bubble, without any time dilation, exponential mass increase… or anything else that makes sense."

Here he paused, looking towards one of the terminals to check his notes. "Now, wait… What if the flicker we get is more of a signal? And something else is opening the Ley Line anomaly? Some kind of human-tech machine! Ha! Of course! It's all so obvious!"

"Okay, so I'll need to check all this… If we start modulating the frequency of these energies… and alternating the durations we could… Yes!"

Vicious joy infusing his expression, he swaggered across the lab to the single locked drawer and punched a code into the electronic lock.

With a slight hiss and thunk the drawer shot out to full extension, revealing his one remaining asset of any value: a Corporate Credit card.

Aboard the ship Radiant Freedom, a monitor beeped. "Hey! Looks like we might have a job! Check it! Deep space research and exploration… nice"

- Beginning of a partially debunked Ley Lines theory.

Spacecraft Perks

See pg: 309 for full Complication GM rules.

As spacecraft become larger, they often gain non-essential but important functions. While these minor features do little to improve the overall combat ability of the spacecraft, they are often incredibly useful to their crew.

Gain Optional Spacecraft Perks equal to your spacecraft's Size. Gain ALL Automatic Perks that your spacecraft's Size meets.

Size Requirements
Most Perks have a minimum or maximum Size requirement.

Creating Perks
GMs can invent new Perks. Be careful to not make a Perk that is too close to another or imbalanced.

Different Size Scale, pg: 148
When using the optional Change Size Scale rule, you will need to reduce or increase the Size Requirements of most Perks to fit the feel of your game.

For example, if you increase the physical size of the average Size 3 spacecraft to hundreds of meters, it makes sense that a spacecraft of this size would have several Large Rooms, and a Size 2 (or even 1) spacecraft might even have several Large Rooms.

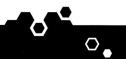

"That's right, sir, we do…. Yes, indeed, we sell those. What credit bracket would you be offering, sir? … I understand that, sir. But I'm afraid 'culture clash' does not give a line of credit according to company policy. That's why… No, sir, we can't accept an 'I owe you' for that. However, if you… I'm sorry, sir, but threats require me to end this conversation."

The low-paid Corp with the threadbare suit sat in the dim metallic office, staring at the wall. "Bloody Kaltorans, third one today." he muttered. Then a small ping rang from the unadorned small cube in front of him.

"Hello, and welcome to the CorpSafe Complaints line. How may I be of assistance to you today?"

Optional Perks

These minor features of your spacecraft may be overlooked by the casual observer, but they can be incredibly useful.

+5 Shields (Size 1-2, not NPC)

This carefully calibrated shield system makes your spacecraft surprisingly hard to destroy.

+1 Cargo

A little extra thought has been put into your spacecraft's construction, giving it some more room.

+2 Resupply

The commonly used life support, fuel, and munitions systems on your spacecraft are of higher quality than normal, letting you travel just a little bit further than others.

Deep Space SOS Beacon

Your spacecraft is equipped with several small but valuable distress beacons. They are only to be used in the most dire of circumstances, where the risks of remaining unnoticed outweigh the risks of attracting the attention of unfavourable or hostile ships. The beacons will alert all nearby spacecraft (even those mid-Jump) to your distress with a pre-recorded message.

Those of an unscrupulous and cunning nature frequently use such systems to attract unsuspecting ships into their trap.

Escape Pods (Size 3-5)

Despite hoping such measures will never be needed, your crew will be slightly put at ease by knowing that their spacecraft comes equipped with short-range escape pods.

If you spacecraft is Destroyed, all player characters may take a escape pod to avoid Death.

Shuttle (Size 4-5)

Your spacecraft comes equipped with a small (less than Size 1) space-worthy Shuttle, able to ferry a small crew to and from a planetary surface.

Brig (Size 3-5)

Your spacecraft has a dedicated jail area with multiple cells, made from metal bars or force fields with a dedicated backup power supply.

Armoury

A fully stocked Armoury allows your crew to regain all used Clips and Ammunition during their Downtime.

Additional Rooms (Size 3-5)

Your spacecraft has several more rooms than one of its size normally would.

"Why does our new ship smell like an old Legion and have no comms or kitchen?"

– Graeme Toffindell, Corporate.

Automatic Perks

Nearly all spacecraft come equipped with certain systems and features that make them suitable for space travel. As spacecraft become larger, they often have more functions so they can accommodate their larger crew.

Ejection Seats (Size 1-2)

If your spacecraft is Destroyed, all player characters will be safely ejected and avoid Death as long as they have an Outfit suitable for the void of space.

Comm System

Your spacecraft is equipped with a Radio (pg: 274), allowing it to contact others with a Comm System.

Life Support

Your spacecraft is equipped with air filtration, artificial gravity, waste disposal, temperature control, and myriad other systems to allow life inside the safety of its hull.

Jump Drive

Your spacecraft is capable of opening a Jump Portal (pg: 288), allowing it to travel at extraordinary speeds outside of combat.

Docking Clamp (Size 2-5)

Your spacecraft is able to dock with other spacecraft.

Airlock (Size 2-5)

Your spacecraft has air-cycling chambers that allow its crew to exit and enter from hostile environments such as the void of space without harming the craft's integrity.

Corridors (Size 3-5)

Your spacecraft is large enough to feature open chambers and corridors through which its crew can walk.

Small Rooms (3-5)

Your spacecraft has several small rooms that can be used for a wide variety of purposes (eg: bedrooms).

Large Rooms (5)

Your spacecraft has several very large rooms inside its considerable bulk.

Spacecraft Combat

During the Great War, most spacecraft were either constructed for or retrofitted for heavy combat use. Though the Haven system is no longer in a state of open war, the widespread use of these well-armed vessels has cultivated an expectation that all spacecraft are to be armed.

Overview

The following is a short overview of how spacecraft Combat works. We suggest printing out the Spacecraft Character Sheet (download from www.fraggedempire.com) to have as you read over these rules.

Just Like Personal Combat
Spacecraft Combat uses many of the same mechanics as Personal Combat (pg: 71). It is assumed that you are familiar with these rules before reading this chapter.

Combat Scale, pg: 156
While the scale of a Combat Area does play a part in personal Combat, it plays a much larger thematic role in spacecraft Combat.

Spacecraft have sensors and weapons calibrated to detect and interact with craft and objects moving at a similar speed to their own ship's.

Spacecraft travelling much faster or slower than your spacecraft will be invisible to your sensors. Likewise, the faster your spacecraft travels, the less information your sensors will give you on stellar objects (eg: planets) and phenomena.

In practice, the GM can play with scale to make combat have the desired feel (eg: a planet could take up a single space on your Battle Map, or it could take up 12 spaces).

Turns and System Rolls, pg: 168
Just like personal Combat, spacecraft Combat is broken up into Turns. On each Turn, a craft gets System Rolls, equivalent to Actions.

But unlike personal Combat, characters do not perform two Actions. Instead, they may each attempt one System Roll. System Rolls are broken up into four categories: Command, Engineering, Operations, and Gunnery. Most System Rolls may only be successfully used once per Turn.

Battle Map, Miniatures
As with personal Combat, a laminated square Battle Map will be very useful for running spacecraft Combat.

Velocity, pg: 158
Spacecraft manage their movement quite differently from characters. At the start of its Command System Roll Phase, a spacecraft moves in the direction it is facing by the number of spaces equal to its Velocity.

Command System Rolls are used to increase or decrease your spacecraft's Velocity.

Weapons, pg: 145
Spacecraft Attack with Weapons, which come in three main types: Fighters, Warheads, and Batteries.

Fighters and Warheads work similarly to Drones (pg: 104), while Batteries work similarly to Guns (pg: 102).

Rolling Dice and Attacking, pg: 78
This works just like personal Combat, except that there is no Cover, and you may always add any additional dice for RoF 2+ Attacks.

Strong Hits, pg: 82
This works just like personal Combat.

Critical Hits and Destroying Things, pg: 164
This works just like personal Combat. Spacecraft have Shields, rather than Endurance, but they function the same.

Your spacecraft is Destroyed when any of your Attributes are reduced to -5.

NPC spacecraft are Destroyed when any of their Attributes are reduced to 0.

Fights Are Never "Balanced"
Just as with personal Combat, spacecraft Combat is very rarely perfectly balanced. Players are encouraged to intelligently pick their fights, fight dirty, and be cunning. If you are able, carefully pick not only when you fight, but also who and where.

Combat Scale

See pg: 158 for full Spacecraft Velocity rules.

While the scale of a combat does play a role in Personal Combat, it plays a much larger thematic role in Spacecraft Combat as spacecraft can only engage in combat with other spacecraft that are travelling at a comparable Velocity to them.

If a spacecraft is travelling much faster or slower than you, you might be able to detect them outside combat with a Sensors Skill Roll, but you usually cannot engage them with your Weapons.

Determining Combat Scale

At the start of Spacecraft Combat, the GM determines the scale of your fight. If you are travelling between planets, you are likely travelling at high Velocity, increasing your combat scale. If you are orbiting a planet or exploring an asteroid field, your Velocity is likely low, decreasing your combat scale.

For any spacecraft to engage one another in a combat, the two must match in combat scale.

All Thematic Feel

Changing your combat scale does not affect the mechanics of combat. However, it greatly alters the feel of combat, as it defines the nature of your environment.

Alone in a Crowded Sky

Because spacecraft must have comparable Velocity before they can engage in combat, a spacecraft can feel alone in a crowded area of space.

Eg: You are fighting around a busy trade hub, but it may take some time for other spacecraft to speed up or slow down enough to be able to join in your combat.

Small Combat Scale, Low Velocity

When combat takes place over a very small area of space, an entire side of your Battle Map might be a planet, or your entire Battle Map could be the inside of a large space station or a mountain range inside a planet's atmosphere.

Large Combat Scale, High Velocity

When combat takes place over a very large area of space, entire planets might only take up part of a single square on your Battle Map.

Changing Combat Scale

Rather than making a Combat Jump System Roll (pg: 175), you may leave combat by changing your combat scale, leaving your Opponents at a different scale.

If you do this, your GM may have your Opponents follow you once they meet the Velocity requirements. Please be patient with your GM as they redraw your Battle Map to match your new combat scale.

Increasing Combat Scale

Your spacecraft must remain at Velocity 6 for 5 Turns.
At the start of your sixth Turn, you may choose to leave the Combat Area by increasing your combat scale.

Decreasing Combat Scale

Your spacecraft must remain at Velocity 1 for 5 Turns.
At the start of your sixth Turn, you may choose to leave the Combat Area by decreasing your combat scale.

Combat Jump, pg: 175

As with moving off the edge of your Combat Area (Battle Map), changing your combat scale increases the number of required successful Combat Jump System Rolls by 2.

Outside Combat

Outside combat, the GM should require a Skill Roll (eg: Astronomy, Planetoids, or Operations) for a craft to detect and analyse other spacecraft, objects, or astronomical phenomena. For a detailed analysis, a spacecraft must have low Velocity, leaving it at Small combat scale if combat does start.

"The Archons be damned! Why can't they design a targeting system that doesn't require us to match our target's velocity!" Alexis hated computers but loved combat. This made his career choice to be a space pirate all the more odd. "… I know, I know. Relativistic particle displacement sensors… bla, bla, bla. It's all crap. If we can see them on our sensors, we should be able to shoot them!"

Alexis gripped his command chair as his crew burned their forward thrusters. The ship shook violently as their forward motion fruitlessly fought to stay in control.

Beep, beep, beep.

"Captain. Velocity reduced, and weapon systems have once again locked on."

"Well blast them to X'ion before we lose them again!"

Example Combat Scales

This example shows four battles going on around the planet Eden.
While in combat, none of these spacecraft can sense or Target any spacecraft at a different combat scale.

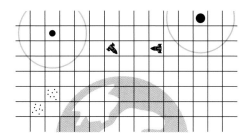

Small Combat Scale
The planet may not affect the mechanics of combat.
Moons count as Objects.
Mark the Gravity Fields of the moons.
Space debris count as Dust Clouds.

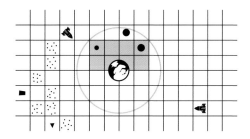

Average Combat Scale
Planet counts as an Object.
Mark the Gravity Field of the planet.
Moons count as Objects.
Moderate and large Asteroids count as Objects.

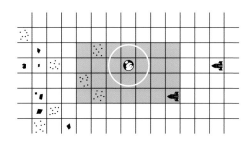

Large Combat Scale
Planet counts as an Object.
Mark the Gravity Field of the planet.
Asteroids count as Objects.
Clusters of moderate Asteroids count as Dust Clouds.
Large Asteroids count as Objects.

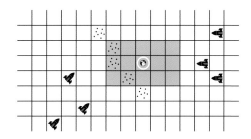

Massive Combat Scale
Planet counts as an Object.
You may mark the Gravity Field of the planet.
Small Asteroids count as Dust Clouds.
Large Asteroid fields count as Dust Clouds.

Velocity

See pg: 174 for full Command System Roll rules.

A spacecraft moves depending on its Velocity, which is changed through Command System Rolls.

> **Your Velocity can never exceed 6 or drop below 1.**

> ## Tracking Velocity
> To track your Velocity, keep a d6 next to your spacecraft miniature on your Battle Map.

Command System Rolls, pg: 174
This is the main way to alter your spacecraft's Velocity and to Turn it.

> ## Think Ahead
> Forward thinking is key to managing your spacecraft's movement.
>
> Changing your spacecraft's Velocity or facing does not affect its movement until its next Turn.

Order of Action
The spacecraft with the highest Velocity (or Size, if equal) takes their Command System Roll Phase first. This is often a disadvantage because other spacecraft can change their Velocity and facing in response to you.

Move Before Rolling
At the start of your spacecraft's Turn, move it forward a number of spaces equal to its Velocity. Do this before making any System Rolls.

Altering Your Velocity
When you alter your spacecraft's Velocity, do not move the spacecraft. Just change the value on the d6 next to the spacecraft.

When rotating the facing of your spacecraft, you must do so in increments of 45°. Changing your facing is commonly done as part of a Command System Roll. Facing cannot be changed before or partway through a spacecraft's movement.

Ordnance
Do not use Velocity rules to dictate the movement of Ordnance.

Collision
Space is big, and unintentional collisions in open space are rare. Your spacecraft can go through spaces with spacecraft or Objects. However, doing so may cause consequences to you.

Environment, pg: 160
Some parts of the Environment (eg: Objects) may apply effects to your spacecraft if you pass through them or end movement in the same space.

Spacecraft
If your spacecraft ends its movement in the same space as another spacecraft, they immediately move to an adjacent space of their choice.

Ally Spacecraft
If you end your movement in the same space as an Ally spacecraft, the GM immediately moves the Ally spacecraft into an adjacent space.

Ordnance
Resolve as if it were a spacecraft.

However, your Ordnance may not voluntarily end its movement in the same space as a spacecraft, Ordnance, or Environmental Object.

Friendly Ordnance
Resolve as if it were an Ally spacecraft.

Leaving Combat Area
Anytime your spacecraft leaves the edge of the Battle Map – whether by altering your combat scale (pg: 156), making a Combat Jump System Roll (pg: 175), or by simply flying off the edge of the map – you leave the Combat Area. If your Opponent follows you, the GM may need to redraw the Battle Map.

If you perform a Combat Jump, your opponent should rarely be able to follow you.

Turning
See pg: 173 for full Turning rules.

"In many ways the modern space merchant has much in common with the brutal Legion Nomads or the vicious Kaltoran Dark Tribesmen, living on the edge as they fight over limited resources."

– Klarhkrakar, Nephilim Biomass Merchant.

Velocity

A spacecraft always moves at the beginning of its Turn.
A high Engine Attribute allows you to quickly change your Velocity.

Track Velocity
At the start of combat, place a d6 next to each spacecraft miniature. These will be used to track each spacecraft's Velocity.
Spacecraft cannot have Velocity lower than 1 or higher than 6.

Set Velocity
At the start of combat, each spacecraft sets its starting Velocity (1-6). The aggressor (who started the fight) sets their Velocity last.
If desired, the GM can set the Velocity of any or all spacecraft.

Then
Make any Command
System Rolls

Move at the Start of your Command System Roll Phase
The spacecraft with the highest Velocity (or Size, if equal) takes its Turn first. The others follow in the same order.
At the beginning of its Turn, move a spacecraft forward a number of spaces equal to its Velocity.

Altering Velocity and Facing
To alter your spacecraft's Velocity, use Command System Rolls.
Other effects may change Velocity.
You may also change your spacecraft's facing by using Command System Rolls.

Spacecraft Collisions
If your spacecraft ends its movement in the same space as another spacecraft, the other craft immediately moves to an adjacent space of their choice.

Welcome to CorpSafe, Valued* Employee!

Management wishes to congratulate you on passing the extensive background and aptitude tests, and to remind you of articles 9 through 27 of the Employee Contractual Obligations clause, particular the in-house by-laws and punishments concerning Unlicensed Trading, Unlicensed Information Brokering, and the bi-weekly mandatory physiology and anti-espionage scan and physical.

Duties will include but are not limited to; securing CorpSafe premises, personnel, data, and assets; possible acquisition of said premises, personnel, data, and assets; stripping and disposal of biological and mechanical assets found and acquired or slain during the course of your duties. Offered bribes from competitors and otherwise are to be accepted and logged with payroll, and the offending party is to be detained for questioning. For more details on duties and procedures, please contact Personnel Resources on CorpSafe Comms channel 23.

*Employee #252a3g has a current estimated worth of 9,057 credits per annum with 3rd tier security and equivalent information clearance for the contractual period.

Environment, Conditions & Effects

See pg: 156 for full Combat Scale rules.
See pg: 158 for full Velocity and Collision rules.

Space is massive, with a huge range of environments. Some are barren and empty, while others are cluttered and exotic. This list of example Environments is only a small taste of what is out there.

Your Combat Scale will GREATLY affect the nature of your Environment.

Atmosphere (Tiny Combat Scale Only)

Most spacecraft are not designed to function effectively inside a planet's atmosphere. They are heavy, lack an aerodynamic shape, and often propel themselves forward with pure force. Engaging in combat inside a planet's atmosphere can be incredibly dangerous for an ill-equipped spacecraft.

Atmosphere with Mountains (Objects)

» At the end of its Turn, spacecraft receive 1 Engine Attribute Damage (not reduced by Armour).
» At the end of each third Turn, this Damage increases by 1 for the remainder of combat.
» All Weapons suffer -2 Hit and -2 Range.

Dust Cloud

A field of small rocks, ice, or debris can be moderately hazardous to navigate, especially at high speed.

Dust Cloud

» If your spacecraft starts its Turn in a Dust Cloud, or if it enters one, it takes Damage equal to its Velocity. If the spacecraft has or is reduced to 0 Shields, it also receives a Critical Hit (pg: 164).
» You receive -2 to all Attack Rolls made while within or through a Dust Cloud (penalty stacks for each space of Dust Cloud).

Fighters
These may not move through a Dust Cloud.

Warheads
These may not Attack Targets within a Dust Cloud or move through a Dust Cloud.

Tiny Combat Scale
Any time a spacecraft takes Attribute Damage, they may leave behind a small cloud of debris.

Small Combat Scale
A space station waste disposal port may periodically expel a cloud of waste.

Massive Combat Scale
Your spacecraft is travelling so fast that much of an asteroid belt is little more than a small blip on your sensors.

Gravity Field

Most commonly caused by a large planetary body, these fields may prove quite advantageous to a skilled pilot. They offer another way to change your spacecraft's facing and increase its Velocity.

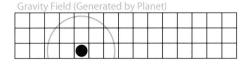

Gravity Field (Generated by Planet)

» On entering, your spacecraft gains +2 Velocity.
» On entering, or at any time within the field (even part way through your Movement) you may make a free 45° Rotation towards the source (usually a Object) of the Gravity Field.

Field Size

Gravity Fields are usually at least 3x3 spaces. If a field is a single space, it should also include an Object in that space and allow the spacecraft to change its facing in any direction.

Overlapping Gravity Fields

If a spacecraft enters a space where Gravity Fields overlap, it may choose for any number of the overlapping fields to affect the ship.

Small Combat Scale

The Combat Area is dominated by a central planet with a Gravity Field that extends across half the Battle Map.

Large Combat Scale

A planet and its two orbiting moons make for some interesting manoeuvring opportunities.

Massive Combat Scale

Your spacecraft is only affected in any significant way by large planetary bodies.

Nebula

It would be an insurmountable task to categorise the wide array of astral phenomena within the galaxy. Their effects and sizes vary hugely; some are common, such as clouds of helium or ionised gas, while others' nature are a mystery.

Nebula

» On entering, remove all Locked On Effects (pg: 125) on your spacecraft or which you have applied to other spacecraft.
» May have additional, GM-defined effects.

"And then we turned towards the planet, and held on as we slingshotted around till we were clear. Bit nasty before that, though."

– Nif'tan, Nephilim Hybrid and trade captain.

Object

Often large, these physical objects will need to be carefully navigated to avoid a collision.

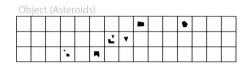

Object (Asteroids)

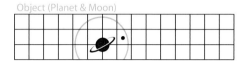

Object (Planet & Moon)

» On entering: reduce your spacecraft's Velocity by 2. If your resulting Velocity is above 2 your spacecraft takes 1 Attribute Damage to a random (1d6) Attribute (no Armour).
» You receive -2 to all Attack Rolls made while within or through a Object (penalty stacks for each different Object).

Destroying an Object

Some smaller Objects (and portions of larger ones) can be destroyed by Attacking them.

Most Objects have 8 Defence and 3 Armour. If they receive 1 Attribute Damage, most will be partially or completely Destroyed. This may leave a Dust Cloud in the same space.

Fighters and Warheads

May not move through Objects.

Tiny Combat Scale

There are lots of things to crash into as you fly around the inside of large space station.

Small Combat Scale

Each individual asteroid needs to be avoided.

Massive Combat Scale

At this speed, only planets needs to be carefully avoided.

Other Spacecraft and Ordnance

See pg: 158 for full Collision rules.

"They got onboard! Captain, what do we do?"

"Shoot them, you stupid idiots! … and don't puncture the hull!"

Example Conditions

Make Repairs, pg: 164
Missing parts, vital system damage, rust, viruses, and other problems can be repaired through many different construction and resupply methods.

Minor Condition: Low Fuel
» You only have the fuel to make one Jump. If this does not take you to a safe location where you can refuel, you gain the Major Condition: Out of Fuel.

Major Condition: Out of Fuel
» May not Jump.
» Outside combat, your travel time increases by x10.

Minor Condition: Low Munitions
» Your Fighters have Hit –4.
» You may only Launch your Warheads one more time.
» All of your Batteries have 1 Clip.

Minor Condition: Disrepair
» –2 to all System Rolls.

Minor Condition: Damaged Communications
» You may not use your spacecraft Radio.
» –1 Sensors.

Minor or Major Condition: Virus
» –1 Power, CPU, or Sensors.
» May have secret, GM–defined effects.
» You may gain this Condition multiple times.

Major Condition: Damaged Engines
» You may only Turn once per Turn.

Major Condition: Damaged Reactor
» –10 Shields.
» –1 to all System Rolls.

Major Condition: Decompressed Room
» –2 Cargo space.
» One or more rooms onboard may only be accessed by characters able to enter a Void.
» You may gain this Condition multiple times.

Example Effects
Boarded
While engaged in a spacecraft fight, you are boarded by enemy troops!

> See pg: 180 for full
> Boarding Party Weapon rules.

» Your spacecraft may gain this Effect up to five times at once.
» At the start of your opponent's Command System Roll Phase, they may make 1 Boarding Party Attack against you as a Free Action.
» If this Boarding Party Attack fails, remove 1 Boarded Effect from your spacecraft.

Locked On
Functions just like Locked On in personal Combat (pg: 125).

» All enemies gain a bonus to their Attack Rolls against you equal to their Weapon's "Lock On +X" bonus.
» Removed at the end of combat.

On Fire
See pg: 164 for full On Fire rules.

Function similarly to Bleeding (pg: 88).

Attack Rolls

See pg: 78 for full Attack Roll rules.
See pg: 168 for full Spacecraft System Roll rules.
See pg: 145 for full Spacecraft Weapon rules.

Attack Rolls and Range in spacecraft Combat work just like in personal Combat. A Weapon's Type determines what System Roll Action is used to Attack with that Weapon.

Fighters use Command System Rolls (pg: 174).
Warheads use Operations System Rolls (pg: 176).
Batteries use Gunnery System Rolls (pg: 177).

"Our societies are the offspring of two horrible parents: genocidal war and a hundred years of desperation. This generation will never overcome such powerful influences. But maybe the next can be born of two slightly better parents: tolerance and prosperity. And maybe their children can finally be good parents."

– Achilles, Legion father.

Damage

See pg: 87 for full Damage rules.

Spacecraft receive Damage like characters do, except that spacecraft have Shields in place of Endurance.

Armour
By default, spacecraft have 3 Armour.

No Cover
There is no Cover (pg: 86) in spacecraft Combat, but some Environments (pg: 160) reduce spacecrafts' To Hit chance.

Strong Hit: Critical Hit & Boost

See pg: 88 for full Strong Hit: Critical Hit & Boost rules.

Critical Hits and Critical Boosts work just like they do in Personal Combat.

Destruction

If your spacecraft has an Attribute reduced to -5 or below, it is Destroyed and all characters on board are killed. An NPC spacecraft is Destroyed if it has an Attribute reduced to 0 or below.

Reducing Fate to Avoid Destruction
If your spacecraft would be Destroyed, you may avoid this if all PCs on board permanently reduce their Fate (pg: 35) by one point each. The GM should come up with some suitable way for you to have miraculously avoided Destruction.

You may still take Attribute Damage (usually reducing an Attribute to 0). You should also lose 'On Fire' or any other Effect on your spacecraft that could cause additional Attribute Damage. The GM should feel free to apply any Effects (pg: 160) or Conditions (pg: 160) they think are thematically reasonable (eg: Lost Wing).

Spacecraft Perks, pg: 152
Some spacecraft Perks (eg: escape pods) may help characters avoid Death during if the spacecraft is Destroyed.

On Fire

The On Fire Effect works just like the Bleeding Effect (pg: 88) for characters, but applies to spacecraft.

Damage Control System Roll, pg: 175
This System Roll removes any On Fire Effects from your spacecraft.

Repair Rolls

See pg: 38 for full Skill Roll rules.
See pg: 64 for full Spare Time Point rules.
See pg: 160 for full Spacecraft Condition rules.
See pg: 95 for full Downtime rules.

In-Combat Repair
In combat, Shields are Repaired by performing a System Roll with the Minor Effect: Regen Shields (eg: Damage Control).

Unlike in personal Combat, Attribute Damage to a spacecraft may be Repaired during combat with a Patch Job System Roll (pg: 175).

Out-of-Combat Repair Rolls
Spacecraft Attribute Damage may be repaired outside combat by making a Mechanics, Electronics, or possibly Bio Tech Skill Roll, using one of three Repair Roll options:

Change Out, 14t, Requires Relevant Workshop
See pg: 145 for full Repair Roll: Change Out rules.

Quick Fix, 12, Requires Relevant Workshop
Immediately after combat, you may make one Quick Fix Repair Roll against a Difficulty of 12. If you succeed, you Repair 2 Attribute Damage dealt to your spacecraft during the most recent combat. This Repair may be combined or split across the spacecraft's Attributes as desired. Each character can only make one Quick Fix Roll, and the number of Quick Fix Rolls made after one combat cannot exceed the number of relevant Workshops on the craft.

Maintenance, 12t, Requires Relevant Toolbox
During Downtime, you may make a Maintenance Spare Time Roll against a Difficulty of 12. If you succeed, you Repair 1 Attribute Damage and remove one Minor Condition from the spacecraft.

Rebuild, 2x 14t, Requires Relevant Workshop
During Downtime, you may make two Rebuild Spare Time Rolls, both against a Difficulty of 14. If you succeed, you Repair 8 Attribute Damage to one Attribute and remove one Major Condition from the spacecraft.

Sharing Spare Time Points
Remember that you can share Spare Time Points (pg: 64) for Repair Rolls

Healing a Non-Mechanical Spacecraft
Not all Repair Rolls are made with the Mechanics or Electronics Skills. Instead, use the Skill that makes the most sense. For example, if you are attempting to repair a Nephilim spacecraft, you may use the Bio Tech Skill.

Damage & Repair Rolls

Critical Hits are the main way to Destroy spacecraft.
Attribute Damage may be repaired through Repair Rolls or through the Patch Job System Roll.

Destroying Spacecraft
If an Attribute is reduced to –5 or below, your spacecraft is Destroyed. NPCs and Ordnance are Destroyed if any Attribute is reduced to 0 or below.

If your spacecraft would be Destroyed, you can avoid this if all characters on board permanently reduce their Fate by 1. Other negative effects may result.

On Fire
If any Attribute of your spacecraft is reduced to below 0, your spacecraft gains the On Fire Effect.

While On Fire, at the beginning of each of its Turns, your spacecraft takes 1 Attribute Damage (not reduced by Armour) to a Random Attribute (roll 1d6).

A Damage Control System Roll (pg: 175) removes On Fire.

Damage Control

Regen =
Power +Bonuses

The Damage Control System Roll Heals Shield Damage equal to your "Regen".

Regen = Focus + any bonuses.

1/ ☐
12
= **Heal 2**
to Damage done during previous combat.

Quick Fix
Immediately after combat, you may make one Quick Fix Roll against a Difficulty of 12. Requires a relevant Workshop.

On success, Repairs 2 Attribute Damage to the spacecraft taken during the most recent combat.

This Repair Roll may only be rolled once per available Workshop.

12t
= **Heal 1**
to any Attribute

Maintenance
Performing Maintenance requires a Spare Time Roll against a Difficulty of 12. Requires a relevant Toolbox.

On success, Repairs 1 Attribute Damage and removes one Minor Condition from the spacecraft.

May not be performed during combat.

2x 14t
= **Heal 8**
to one Attribute

Rebuild
Performing a Rebuild requires two Spare Time Rolls against a Difficulty of 14. Requires a relevant Workshop.

Repairs 8 Attribute Damage from one Attribute and removes one Major Condition from the spacecraft.

May not be performed during combat.

Optional: Theatre of the Mind Combat

See pg: 96 for full Theatre of the Mind Combat rules.

These rules work like the Theatre of the Mind rules for personal Combat, except that the characters use the rules for Vehicle System Skills rather than Personal Combat Skills where applicable, and where otherwise noted.

Retreat

Unlike Theatre of the Mind for personal Combat, in spacecraft Combat a single character may not be able to retreat by themselves if they're on a spacecraft with other characters.

Retreating from a spacecraft Combat often involves your spacecraft Jumping through a portal (Engineering) or out-manoeuvring (Command) your opponents.

» To Retreat from combat, half of the characters on board the spacecraft (rounded up) must succeed on a Vehicle Skill Roll.
» This roll does not receive the +2 bonus (as normal for personal Combat).
» When the required successes have been rolled, all characters on board the spacecraft are removed from combat.

Spacecraft Size Variation

For games using only Theatre of the Mind Combat, the players must select a spacecraft Size Variation. This will determine their spacecraft's Cargo space and the amount of Weapons it can have.

Optional: No Spacecraft Combat

Not all campaigns and games need to have your PCs in a spacecraft with Weapons. In these games, use the Theatre of the Mind Combat Only game rules, but only require one successful Vehicle Skill Roll per player, rather than two.

"Boarders are neutralised, Captain," Eloise barked into the bridge as she held her still-bleeding side.

"Acknowledged. Set the crew to shield and engine repair." replied the heavyset captain, never taking his eyes from the screens. Another shattering crunch amidships caused the lights and monitors to go out, plunging the ship into darkness as the enemy cruiser punched through their flickering shields.

"We've been hit in the reactor, sir. We're uh… dead in the void, sir." came her voice from the darkness.

Traits, Theatre of the Mind Only Game

Command	Requirements	Benefits	Disadvantages
Master Pilot		Gain +1 to Command as long as your spacecraft is Size 2 or less.	
Team Player		Grant a free spacecraft Combat Skill reroll to an Ally, once per Combat.	
Evasive		Your Failed Command Combat Skill Rolls do not result in Attribute Damage.	−1, Command

Engineering	Requirements	Benefits	Disadvantages
Just Fixed That		Gain +2 to future spacecraft Combat Skill Rolls during this Combat after failing a Combat Skill Roll.	
Find Weakness		Gain +1 to future spacecraft Combat Skill Rolls during this Combat after failing a Combat Skill Roll.	
Overload		+1, all Personal Combat Skills	Receive 1 additional Attribute Damage during each spacecraft Combat.

Operations	Requirements	Benefits	Disadvantages
Quick Lock		+1 for your first spacecraft Combat Skill Roll made during a Combat.	
Perfect Shot		You may spend 1 Fate Point to make a Successful Heavy Arms Combat Skill Roll count as 2 Successes.	−2, Operations
Check Data		Once per spacecraft Combat you may gain a free reroll.	

Gunnery	Requirements	Benefits	Disadvantages
Gun Crazy		+4 for your first Gunnery Combat Skill Roll made during a Combat.	−1, Gunnery
Cover Shot		Passing a Gunnery Combat Skill Roll gives all of your Allies a +1 bonus to their next Combat Skill (for this Combat).	−1, Gunnery
Shred Shields		+2 for your first spacecraft Combat Skill Roll made during a Combat.	

Combat Items, Theatre of the Mind Only Game

Weapon:	Description	Cost
Basic Battery	Able to make Combat Skill Roll attacks with the Battery Skill.	8t
Valuable Battery	Same as Basic Battery, grants +1 to Battery (does not Stack with other Batteries).	16t
Expensive Battery	Same as Basic Battery, grants +2 to Battery (does not Stack with other Batteries).	22t
Defensive Weapons	+1 to all spacecraft Retreat Combat Skill Rolls.	18t
Fighters	Once per Combat you may make a free Command Skill attack.	14t
	Once per Combat you may sacrifice your Fighters (losing any spent Spare Time Points) to avoid Attribute Damage.	
Warheads	2 uses, able to make Operations Skill Roll attack at +2.	12t

Spacecraft Size Variation, Theatre of the Mind Only Game (Must Select 1)

Weapon:	Available Cargo	Available Weapons	Description	Cost
Size 1	–	1	Your spacecraft is Size 1.	–
Size 2	1	2	Your spacecraft is Size 2.	–
Size 3	4	3	Your spacecraft is Size 3.	4x 10t
Size 4	8	4	Your spacecraft is Size 4.	4x 14t
Size 5	12	5	Your spacecraft is Size 5.	4x 16t

Turns & System Rolls

Overview

See pg: 155 for full Spacecraft Combat rules.
See pg: 145 for full Spacecraft Weapon rules.

Similarities to Personal Combat

Before you read these rules, please become familiar with the rules for personal Combat, specifically Turns and Actions (pg: 100).

Two System Roll Phases, pg: 170

Each Turn is split up into two Phases.
The first Phase consists of Command System Rolls,
the second Phase consists of Secondary System Rolls.

Each spacecraft does its first Phase, then each does its second.
Each character may attempt 1 System Roll per Turn.

In turn, all spacecraft resolve their Command System Roll Phase. Then, in turn, all spacecraft resolve their Secondary System Roll Phase, which includes Engineering, Operations, and Gunnery Rolls.

Making System Rolls, pg: 170

Each character may attempt 1 System Roll per Turn.
Each System Roll may only succeed once per Turn.

Skill Rolls

Unlike a Personal Combat Action, a System Roll requires a successful Vehicle System Skill Roll (pg: 38) of the appropriate type before it can be used.

Weapon Types

Each Weapon type uses a different Vehicle System to determine the bonus to its Attack Roll. These Skills also determine which Actions can be used with that Weapon.

Fighters, pg: 180 = Command, pg: 174
Warheads, pg: 181 = Operations, pg: 176
Batteries, pg: 181 = Gunnery, pg: 177

Multiple Characters on Spacecraft

Most spacecraft will have multiple PCs on them. While it is their spacecraft's Turn, the PCs may attempt System Rolls in any order they wish.

Starting Combat

See pg: 147 for full Spacecraft Attribute rules.
See pg: 158 for full Velocity rules.
See pg: 156 for full Combat Scale rules.

The GM decides when combat has started, usually once the first Attack is declared.

Select Standard or Theatre of the Mind

The GM decides whether to use the Standard Combat Rules or the faster Theatre of the Mind rules (pg: 166).

Even if you normally use the Standard Rules, you may wish to use the Theatre of the Mind rules for minor combats that you don't wish to spend much game time on (eg: evading security turrets).

Set Combat Scale

The GM sets the combat scale (pg: 156).

Set Starting Velocity

The players set the Velocity of their spacecraft, and the GM sets the Velocity of NPC spacecraft.

System Roll Order

Determining System Roll Order is similar to personal Combat Order (pg: 101). In turn, each spacecraft resolves one Phase.

Command System Roll Phase
Highest Velocity (or Size, if equal) first.

Secondary System Roll Phase
Highest CPU (or Sensors, if equal) first.

Surprise Round

Very similar to characters, a spacecraft may gain a Surprise Round if they start a fight with a spacecraft whose crew are not ready.

Gain One Free Command System Roll Phase

If you gain a Surprise Round, your spacecraft gains one free Command System Roll Phase.

At the start of this Phase, your spacecraft moves as normal. All opponent spacecraft move at the end of this Phase. Your opponents CANNOT make any System Rolls during the Surprise Round.

Spacecraft Turn

See pg: 53 for full Vehicle System Skill rules.
See pg: 168 for full System Roll rules.

Two System Roll Phases

Each Turn is split up into two Phases.
The first Phase consists of Command System Rolls,
the second Phase consists of Secondary System Rolls.

Each spacecraft does its first Phase, then each does its second.
Each character may attempt 1 System Roll per Turn.

In turn, all spacecraft resolve their Command System Roll Phase. Then, in turn, all spacecraft resolve their Secondary System Roll Phase, which includes Engineering, Operations, and Gunnery Rolls.

Characters

Each PC on a spacecraft may attempt 1 System Roll per Turn.

NPC Crew

They cannot make System Rolls unless the spacecraft has purchased a Trait (pg: 144) that allows for additional System Rolls (eg: Crew Trait: Officer).

NPC Opponent Spacecraft, pg: 302

Each Turn, the NPC spacecraft in combat may make a total number of System Rolls equal to the PCs present at the start of the combat, spread amongst the NPC craft as the GM wants.

System Roll Major Effects

Unlike Personal Combat Actions, all System Roll Effects (Minor and Major) are listed under its Roll Effects.

"Hard left! I mean port!" came the yell from up the cramped rickety stairway to the formerly Corporate half of the bridge. Weld seams and jury-rigged pipework creaked and groaned while the ship's massive engines fought against its mass and slung them hard to the side: away, presumably, from some sort of anti-ship fire.

"Okay, now a hard right. While going down, keep the speed up!" came the yell from the self-proclaimed captain. The secondary bridge – full of old Archon-designed controls, roughly relabelled with little pictures and short Legion phrases – creaked as the Legion pilot forced the awkward control sticks around.

"Okay, and full burn in five, four…"

The pilot pushed down on his dual foot controls, increasing their thrust. He winced as something crashed and scraped against the ship's hull on the starboard side as their secondary manoeuvring thrusters flashed to life.

Ordnance

Ordnance function very similarly to Drones (pg: 104) and do not require a Action or System Roll to control.

Fighters (pg: 180) may move and Attack during your Command System Roll Phase, and Warheads (pg: 181) may move and Attack during your Secondary System Roll Phase.

System Roll Name ———— Required Skill Roll ———— System Roll Effects

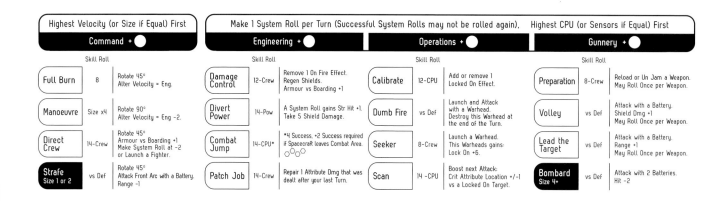

Highest Velocity (or Size if Equal) First			Make 1 System Roll per Turn (Successful System Rolls may not be rolled again),						Highest CPU (or Sensors if Equal) First		
Command + ●			**Engineering +** ●			**Operations +** ●			**Gunnery +** ●		
	Skill Roll			Skill Roll			Skill Roll			Skill Roll	
Full Burn	8	Rotate 45° Alter Velocity = Eng.	Damage Control	12-Crew	Remove 1 On Fire Effect. Regen Shields. Armour vs Boarding +1	Calibrate	12-CPU	Add or remove 1 Locked On Effect.	Preparation	8-Crew	Reload or Un Jam a Weapon. May Roll Once per Weapon.
Manoeuvre	Size x4	Rotate 90° Alter Velocity = Eng -2.	Divert Power	14-Pow	A System Roll gains Str Hit +1. Take 5 Shield Damage.	Dumb Fire	vs Def	Launch and Attack with a Warhead. Destroy this Warhead at the end of the Turn.	Volley	vs Def	Attack with a Battery. Shield Dmg +1 May Roll Once per Weapon.
Direct Crew	14-Crew	Rotate 45° Armour vs Boarding +1 Make System Roll at -2 or Launch a Fighter.	Combat Jump	14-CPU*	*4 Success, +2 Success required if Spacecraft leaves Combat Area. ○○○	Seeker	8-Crew	Launch a Warhead. This Warheads gains: Lock On +6.	Lead the Target	vs Def	Attack with a Battery. Range +1 May Roll Once per Weapon.
Strafe Size 1 or 2	vs Def	Rotate 45° Attack Front Arc with a Battery. Range -1	Patch Job	14-Crew	Repair 1 Attribute Dmg that was dealt after your last Turn.	Scan	14 -CPU	Boost next Attack: Crit Attribute Location +/-1 vs a Locked On Target.	Bombard Size 4+	vs Def	Attack with 2 Batteries. Hit -2

Spacecraft Combat Turn

Each spacecraft Turn is split into two Phases.

All spacecraft complete their Command Phase, then all spacecraft complete their Secondary Phase.

Command System Roll Phase
The spacecraft with the highest Velocity (or Size, if equal) does its Command System Roll Phase first.

Move Forward by Velocity
Before any Command System Rolls, the spacecraft moves forward a number of spaces equal to its Velocity.

Fighters
May move and Attack at any time during their spacecraft's Command System Roll Phase after the spacecraft has moved.

Command System Rolls

Each Spacecraft Takes Its Command System Roll Phase
Each other spacecraft (in descending Velocity (or Size if equal) score) takes its Command System Roll Phase before ANY spacecraft moves onto its Secondary System Roll Phase.

Secondary System Roll Phase
The spacecraft with the highest CPU (or Sensors, if equal) does its Secondary System Roll Phase first.

Warheads
May move and Attack at any time during your spacecraft's Secondary System Roll Phase

Engineering, Operations and Gunnery System Rolls
May attempt in any order.

Remaining Spacecraft Resolve Phase
Each other spacecraft in descending CPU (or Sensors, if equal) order does its Secondary System Roll Phase.
Once all spacecraft have completed this Phase, a new Turn begins.

Unlike a Personal Combat Action, a System Roll requires a successful Vehicle System Skill Roll before it can be used.

1 System Roll Attempt per Turn

Each character may attempt 1 System Roll per Turn.

Each System Roll may only succeed once per Turn, unless otherwise stated.

vs Defence (Attack Roll)

These System Rolls require an Attack Roll. These rolls function just like standard Attack Rolls (pg: 162) with a Weapon vs a Target's Defence.

Weapons that fail an Attack Roll cannot be re-used with a different System Roll.

Weapon Type

Each Weapon Type uses a different Vehicle System to determine the bonus to its Attack Roll.

Fighters, pg: 180 = Command, pg: 174
Warheads, pg: 181 = Operations, pg: 176
Batteries, pg: 181 = Gunnery, pg: 177

Firing a Battery

System Rolls with the Effect: May Roll Once per Weapon, may be successfully rolled multiple times, but each Weapon may only be used once per Turn.

On a spacecraft with 2 Batteries, the "Volley" Gunnery System Roll may be rolled twice per Turn, once per Battery.

Failed System Roll

If you fail a System Roll, no System Roll Effects are applied and your character may not make any further System Rolls.

Weapon

A failed Attack Roll still uses Ammunition.

Strong Hit: Effort, pg: 42

This Strong Hit Option may be used with any Vehicle System Roll, including Attack Rolls.

System Roll Effects

When you succeed on a System Roll, your spaceship gains the Effects listed by the System Roll. If you fail, it gains no Effects.

Alter Velocity = X

You may increase or decrease your current Velocity by up to "X".

Armour vs Boarding +X

Increase your Armour vs Boarding by "X" until your next Turn.

Attack with a Weapon

You may Attack with a single Weapon that has not made an Attack Roll this Turn. If your Attack Roll succeeds, then your Weapon deals its Shield Damage (pg: 145) to your Target.

Critical Hit and Critical Boost, pg: 88
These System Rolls can cause Critical Hits and Critical Boosts against your Target.

Hit +X

Add "X" to any Attack Rolls associated with this Action.

Launch Ordnance

You may place a single Ordnance Body in a space, which may be a number of spaces away equal to the Ordnance's Movement (eg: a Movement 3 Warhead may be placed up to three spaces from your spacecraft).

Front or Side Arc, pg: 178
Ordnance Bodies may be placed within the Front or Side Arcs of your spacecraft during the Turn they are Launched.

May Not Move or Attack This Turn
Ordnance may not (normally) Move or Attack during the Turn they are Launched. They may Move and Attack on future Turns.

» Fighters may Move and Attack during your Command System Roll Phase.
» Warheads may Move and Attack during your Second System Phase.

Fighter, pg: 180
Fighter Bodies may be Launched ALL at once (eg: a Fighter Weapon with four Bodies may Launch all four Bodies at once).

If a friendly Fighter passes through the same space as your spacecraft, it may return to your hangar to be Launched again later.

Warhead, pg: 181
Warhead Bodies must only be Launched one at a time.

May Roll Once per Weapon

This System Roll may be used multiple times per Turn, but each time must be with a different Weapon.

Range +X

Add "X" to your Weapon's Range (Rng) on any Attacks made with this Action.

Regen Shields

You may Repair Damage to your Shields equal to your Regen (pg: 165).

Reload or Un-Jam a Weapon

You may Reload or Un-Jam a single Weapon.

Reload
Swap out a Weapon's current Clip for a new one (pg: 122). Reloading requires successful System Rolls equal to the Load Stat of the Weapon (pg: 122).

Un-Jam
Removes any Jammed Effects (pg: 125) from your Active Weapon. Un-Jamming requires System Rolls equal to the Load Stat of the Weapon (pg: 122).

Remove an Effect

If this System Roll is successful, remove a specified Effect from your spacecraft. This is fully explained under each System Roll (pg: 168).

Shield Dmg +X

Add "X" Shield Damage to any Attack Roll associated with this System Roll.

Rotate X

You may Rotate your spacecraft by "X" 45 degree increments. If you choose to Rotate, you must Rotate the full amount.

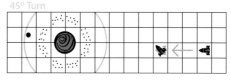

45° Turn

90° Turn

Gravity Field, pg: 161
Allows your spacecraft to Rotate part way through its movement.

45° Gravity Field Turn

Command System Roll

See pg: 158 for full Velocity rules.
See pg: 180 for full Fighter Weapon rules.

> Before you make any Command System Rolls, move your spacecraft forward a number of spaces equal to its Velocity.

Full Burn

Most spacecraft use a fly-by-wire system to translate simple guidance and throttle commands into a complex array of thruster bursts.

System Roll: 8
System Roll Effects
  Rotate 45°
  Alter Velocity = Eng

Manoeuvre

Smaller craft are able to perform incredibly tight turns, allowing them to not only change their facing but also their trajectory.

System Roll: Size x4
  You must pass a System Roll equal to the Size of your spacecraft x4 (eg: Size 3 requires a Command System Roll of at least 12).

System Roll Effects
  Rotate 90°
  Alter Velocity = Eng -2

Direct Crew

A well-trained crew can work in synchrony with each other to perform multiple tasks and gain an edge on their opponents.

System Roll: 14 - Crew
System Roll Effects
  Rotate 45°
  Armour vs Boarding +1

Make System Roll at -2 or Launch Fighters
You may immediately make a System Roll at -2 from the Secondary System Roll Phase. This does not count as that character's single System Roll per Turn, but may count as that System Roll's successful System Roll for the Turn. This may be attempted before or after you have Turned.

If you do not make an additional System Roll, you may Launch (pg: 173) all Fighter Bodies from a single Fighter Weapon.

Strafe

Smaller craft often have the same person piloting and firing, letting them rotate and change the facing of their weapons.

Size 1 or 2 Spacecraft Only
System Roll: vs Defence
System Roll Effects
  Rotate 45°

Attack Front Arc with a Battery
You may Attack a Target within the Front Arc (pg: 178) of your spacecraft with a Battery Weapon. You may attempt this Attack before or after you Turn.

Range -1

Turning and Shooting, Direct Crew Example

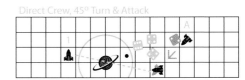

Direct Crew, 45° Turn & Attack

The spacecraft "Star Surfer" (A) and the pirate ship "Black Death" (1) have been locked in a brutal fight for some time. The one who scores the next good hit on the other is likely to win.

The Star Surfer (A) has a lower CPU than the Black Death (1), allowing the Black Death to attack first during the Secondary System Roll Phase. In a desperate gamble, the Star Surfer performs a Direct Crew System Roll, so they can swiftly Turn and Attack the Black Death during their Command System Roll.

After moving forward two spaces (their Velocity), the Star Surfer (A) passes the Command System Roll required to perform Direct Crew. Doing this, they Turn (change their facing) by 45 degrees, bringing their opponent into the Front Arc of their Batteries.

They now may make a free System Roll from any System at -2 or Launch Fighters. They choose to Attack with their Batteries, using the Gunnery System Roll of Lead the Target.

The character that made the Command System Roll now makes the Attack Roll. They have a total penalty of -1 to their roll (+2 Skill bonus, +3 Weapon To Hit, -2 Range penalty, -2 for shooting through a planetary Object, and -2 from the Direct Crew System Roll), and they need to hit a Defence of 12. They roll a 14, for a total of 13. It's a hit!

> Using multiple Command System Rolls in the same Turn is a great way to sharply Rotate your spacecraft.

Engineering System Roll

See pg: 164 for full Spacecraft Repair rules.

Damage Control

Managing blast doors, putting out fires, and regulating the power flow and calibrations of a spacecraft's shields can be a full-time job.

System Roll: 12 - Crew
System Roll Effects
Remove 1 On Fire Effect
Regen Shields
Armour vs Boarding +1

Divert Power

Knowing when to divert power to specific Systems can be key to giving you that extra boost right when and where you need it.

System Roll: 14 - Power
System Roll Effects
A System Roll gains Str Hit +1
Reduce the minimum die roll needed to cause a Strong Hit by one with with the next System Roll attempted this Turn.

Sam and Eve each attempt a System Roll. Derrick's Battery will cause Strong Hits with die rolls of 5 and 6. Eve's Engineering System will cause Strong Hits with rolls of 6. If both gain Strong Hit +1, then Sam will cause Strong Hits on rolls of 4, 5, and 6, and Eve will cause Strong Hits on rolls of 5 and 6.

Take 5 Shield Damage
Your spacecraft takes 5 Shield Damage.

> If you do not have at least 5 Shields, you may choose to take 1 Attribute Damage (not reduced by Armour) to a random (1d3+3) Attribute.

Patch Job

Repairing a damaged system right away can be key to preventing the damage from spreading.

System Roll: 14-Crew
System Roll Effects
Repair 1 Attribute Dmg that was dealt after your last Turn
You may Repair 1 Attribute Damage dealt after your last Turn, including Damage dealt during this Turn (eg: from the On Fire Effect).

Combat Jump

See pg: 288 for full Jump Travel setting guide.

"Just hold 'em off for a few more seconds, the Jump Drive just needs to power up... Just a few more... One more... Go! Go! Go! Let's get out of here!"

System Roll: 14 - CPU*
System Roll Effects
*4 Success
If you make four successful Combat Jump System Rolls, your spacecraft leaves the Combat Area by entering Jump Space through a portal. This immediately ends combat.

> Most of the time, spacecraft Combat ends with one side retreating into Jump Space.

+2 Success required if Spacecraft leaves Combat Area
If your spacecraft leaves the Combat Area by changing the combat scale (pg: 156) or by leaving the Battle Map, then you must make 2 additional Combat Jump System Rolls to enter Jump Space. This penalty may stack multiple times.

> Players are discouraged from leaving their Battle Map as doing so will require the GM to redraw the Battle Map, slowing down the game.

Get out of Here!, Combat Jump Example

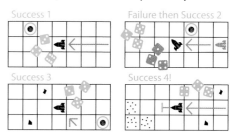

The "Aion" is in a fight that it cannot win. To escape it will need to make four successful Combat Jump System Rolls. Each roll has a Difficulty of 12 (14 - its CPU of 2), and the group's main Operations character has a +1 bonus to his Operations System Roll.

For his first attempt, the Op rolls 13, a success. The group must wait for their next Turn before they can make another roll. During their second Turn, the Op rolls a 7; this is a failure, but a second character may attempt a Combat Jump System Roll. She rolls a 13, their second success. During their third Turn, the Op rolls an 11, their third success.

During their forth Turn, the Op rolls a 13, their fourth success. They may immediately leave this combat as they jump through a portal.

Operations System Roll

See pg: 178 for full Arc rules.
See pg: 181 for full Warhead rules.

Calibrate

Spacecraft weaponry (and especially Warheads) use complex targeting systems to track their targets. By carefully managing these systems, you can improve your accuracy by filtering out irrelevant data and isolating the enemy's energy signatures.

Alternatively, you can hamper an opponent's sensors by projecting false data towards them.

System Roll: 12 – CPU
System Roll Effects

Add or remove 1 Locked On Effect
You may remove a Locked On Effect from your spacecraft or an allied spacecraft, or you may apply a Locked On Effect to any other spacecraft.

Dumb Fire

Without waiting for a clear lock onto your nearby target, you can simply aim your ordnance towards them and fire. Your warhead travels in a straight line and will not alter its path; if it misses, it will harmlessly float off into space.

System Roll: vs Defence
System Roll Effects

Launch and Attack with a Warhead
You may Launch a Warhead and Attack with it this Turn. You may not move this Warhead beyond its Launch distance, and it may only be placed within the standard Launch Arc (Front or Side).

Destroy this Warhead at the end of the Turn
This Warhead Body is destroyed at the end of this Turn, even if it did not hit another spacecraft.

Seeker

Once a Warhead has been launched into space, it will take a short moment to calibrate its sensors before it relentlessly tracks down its target. It will only stop once it has been destroyed, it hits its target, or it runs out of fuel.

System Roll: 8 – Crew
System Roll Effects

Launch a Warhead

Lock On +6
This Warhead gains the Keyword: Lock On +6.

Scan

By carefully scanning your opponent, you can target specific systems to destroy.

System Roll: 14 – CPU
System Roll Effects

Boost next Attack: Crit Attribute Location +/-1 vs Locked On Target
This functions similarly to the Analyse Action (pg: 108).

If you succeed against a Locked On Target, you next Attack Roll against that Target gains a Boost to any Critical Hits (pg: 164) it causes; when you roll to randomly determine the damaged Attribute, you may increase or decrease the result by one.

Torpedo & Missile, Seeker Example

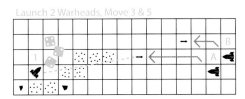

Launch 2 Warheads, Move 3 & 5

The "Free Enterprise" (A) and "Money Bags" (B) are fighting against the "The Beast" (1) near a large Dust Cloud. During its Secondary System Roll Phase, the Free Enterprise and Money Bags each launches Warheads using the Seeker System Roll: a Torpedo (Move 3) and a Missile (Move 5). Both must be placed within the Side or Front Arcs of the Launching spacecraft, and they may only be placed within the Move of their respective Weapon. Neither Warhead may make any Attacks during the Turn they are Launched.

During The Beast's Secondary System Roll, they Attack the Missile. They need to roll a 17 to hit the 14 Defence of the Missile (+2 from Gunnery Training, +3 from Weapon, and –8 for shooting through four spaces of the Dust Cloud). They only roll a 8, a miss.

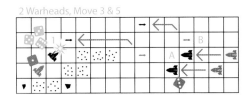

2 Warheads, Move 3 & 5

During the second Turn of the Free Enterprise (A) and Money Bags (B), each of their Warheads may move spaces equal to its Move. The Torpedo moves forward three spaces, while the Missile moves forward five spaces, making it adjacent to The Beast (1).

Because the Missile is a Melee Weapon, it may Attack any adjacent Target. It Attacks The Beast with a roll of a 14, which hits The Beast.

Any time a Warhead hits a Target, its Body is Destroyed. The Missile is removed from the Battle Map, as it will make no more Attacks.

Gunnery System Roll

See pg: 178 for full Arc rules.
See pg: 181 for full Battery rules.

Preparation

Spacecraft weaponry are often large, hulking machines of destruction, with equally large ammunition and heat sinks.

System Roll: 8 – Crew
System Roll Effects
    Reload or Un-Jam a Weapon
    May Roll Once per Weapon

Volley

By carefully planning when to fire, you coordinate your weapon systems to hit in unison, causing maximum damage to your target.

System Roll: vs Defence
System Roll Effects
    Attack with a Battery
    Shield Dmg +1
    May Roll Once per Weapon

Lead the Target

By carefully projecting the destination of your target, you improve the effective range of your weaponry.

System Roll: vs Defence
System Roll Effects
    Attack with a Battery
    Range +1
    May Roll Once per Weapon

Bombard

Large spacecraft often link weapon systems together, usually by having crew members work in trained unison or by using carefully calibrated software and hardware.

Size 4 or 5 Spacecraft Only
System Roll: vs Defence
System Roll Effects
    Attack with 2 Batteries
    These Attacks must be made with 2 different Weapons, and they may Attack two different Targets.

    Hit -2

"Reduce speed! They should go straight past us, so we can line up our jump without getting shot."

"Roger that, Cap."

"Hold it people, only a few more seconds."

"Alright, Ley-Line drive is charged in three, two, one… Jump!"

"A fine getaway chaps, this cargo should give us a good profit."

"Captain! A weird reading off to port, they seem to have…"

- Last log of the lost Star Treader 317-J.

Long Shot, Lead the Target Example

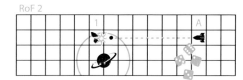

The "Mr Red" (A) has a Battery (Rof 2, Rng 3) and is seven spaces from its Target (1), giving it -4 to its Attack Roll, along with -2 for Attacking through an Object, the moon. To increase their chances, they use the Lead the Target Battery System Roll, increasing their Weapons Rng to 4.

They roll 16 for a total of 12, which is a hit. They also roll a Strong Hit, which they use to cause a Critical Hit. They used RoF 2, so their Attack uses 2 Ammunition. They may not Attack with the same Weapon again this Turn.

Fire all Guns!, Bombard Example

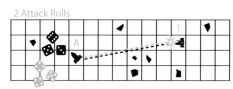

The "Big Madam" (A) is a large spacecraft (Size 4) and its Gunnery character wishes to Attack a Target (1) with two Weapons while using only a single System Roll. He uses the Bombard System Roll to make two separate Attack Rolls.

This counts as that character's successful System Roll use for the Turn, and neither of these Weapons may make an Attack Roll until next Turn.

Spacecraft Weapons

Overview

Spacecraft Weapons function similarly to personal Combat Weapons (pg: 113). Spacecraft have no Outfits or Utility Items.

Weapon Slots

A spacecraft may a number of Weapons equal to its Weapon Slot Stat (pg: 145).

Mount, Not Weight

Weapons have a Mount Stat and no Weight Stat.

For a Weapon to function, its spacecraft must have a Hull Attribute equal to or greater than its Mount Stat.

If the spacecraft's Hull is reduced below this required amount, the Weapon may not be used.

Cannot Be Overburdened

Spacecraft have no Overburdened rules.

Drawing and Activating Weapons

Spacecraft Weapons are always Active and are never Drawn.

Weapon Cost

Spacecraft Weapons cost Influence, not Resources.

Weapon Type

The Effects of a System Roll define what Weapon Type can be used with that System Roll. Each Weapon Type uses a different Vehicle System to determine the bonus to its Attack Roll.

Fighters, pg: 180 = Command, pg: 174
Warheads, pg: 181 = Operations, pg: 176
Batteries, pg: 181 = Gunnery, pg: 177

Ordnance Work Like Drones

Ordnance Weapons function very similarly to Drones (pg: 104), except that they need to be Launched (pg: 173).

Ordnance are split up into two categories: Fighters and Warheads. Fighter Bodies Attack as a single group, while Warhead Bodies Attack individually.

Firing Arc

Weapons may only Attack other spacecraft within their Front or Side Arc (see right).

Front, Side, and Rear Arcs

Batteries

Batteries may only make Attack Rolls against Targets within their Front or Side Arcs.

Ordnance

Ordnance may only be Launched (pg: 173) into a space within their spacecraft's Front or Side Arcs, but in future Turns they may Move and Attack any Target, unhindered by their spacecraft's Arcs.

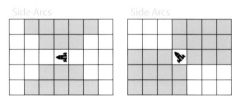

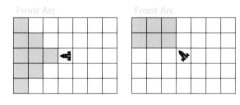

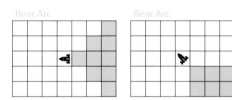

Sensor pulses monitored the incoming missile, its propulsion emitting enough heat for it to be tracked.

Crew members of the Spender Prize galaxy-corvette fired upon the incoming threat as it accelerated. Flak batteries converged fire, obliterating the incoming ordnance.

Fighters

See pg: 104 for full Drone rules.
See pg: 174 for full Command System Roll rules.

Fighters gain a bonus to their Attack Roll from their controller's Command Vehicle System Skill and may act at any time during their spacecraft's Command System Roll Phase.

Fighters need to be Launched
See pg: 173 for full Launch Ordnance rules.

Function Like Drones

Fighters, once Launched, function just like a group of Drones. They have a single Move and Attack as a group. They do not use the Velocity rules for spacecraft movement.

No Additional Weapon Cost

Unlike many Drones, Fighters do not need to be Equipped with a Weapon and do not have Slots.

Replacing Bodies

Destroyed Fighter Bodies are replaced when it makes sense (eg: when you have access to replacements in a city).

Piloting a Fighter

Some Fighters allow a PC to Pilot them (see Manned Fighters, pg: 378).

Docking

If a friendly Fighter passes through the same space as your spacecraft, they may fly back into their hangar, Docking them so they are ready to be Launched again later.

Attack Wing, Fighter Example

4 Fighter Bodies

The "Fenris" (A) is being attacked by a group of Fighters (1). As with Drones, all four Fighter Bodies make a single Attack Roll (usually gaining +1 RoF per Body).

The distance to their Target and any penalties from their Environment are averaged.

Boarding Party

See pg: 160 for full Spacecraft Effect rules.
See pg: 174 for full Command System Roll rules.

Innate Weapon

Similar to how all characters have a Limb Natural weapon, all spacecraft have an Innate Weapon, the Boarding Party, which a spacecraft can use to Attack another spacecraft to which they have applied the Boarded Effect.

Boarding Party gains a bonus to its Attack Roll from their controller's Command Vehicle System Skill, and they attack during their spacecraft's Command System Roll Phase.

Boarded Effect, pg: 162

» Your spacecraft may gain this Effect up to five times at once.
» At the start of your opponent's Command System Roll Phase, they may make 1 Boarding Party Attack against you as a Free Action.
» If this Boarding Party Attack fails, remove 1 Boarded Effect from your spacecraft.

Armour vs Boarded

Your spacecraft's Armour vs a Boarding Party Attack is 0 by default. In this case, your spacecraft is treated as having no Shields. As a result, the Boarding Party may use Critical Boosts against you.

Spacecraft vs Spacecraft

There are no standard rules for two spacecraft connecting to each other during combat and having their crews fight it out. Not to say that it should not be done, only that we encourage the players to connect to another spacecraft outside of spacecraft combat in a way that the GM thinks is reasonable.

For example, you have just reduced a NPC spacecraft Attribute to 0, and the GM says that the spacecraft has not been Destroyed but has been crippled. You then make a Command Vehicle System Skill Roll to pilot your spacecraft up alongside it to dock.

Boarding combats like this should use the personal Combat Rules (pg: 71), not the Boarded Effect.

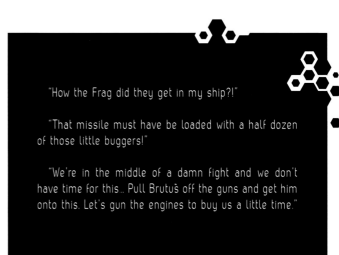

"How the Frag did they get in my ship?!"

"That missile must have be loaded with a half dozen of those little buggers!"

"We're in the middle of a damn fight and we don't have time for this... Pull Brutus off the guns and get him onto this. Let's gun the engines to buy us a little time."

Warheads

See pg: 104 for full Drone rules.
See pg: 176 for full Operations System Roll rules.

Warheads gain bonus to their Attack Roll from their controller's Operations Vehicle System Skill, and they may act at any time during their spacecraft's Secondary System Roll Phase.

Warheads Must Be Launched One at a Time
See pg: 173 for full Launch Ordnance rules.

Function Like Drones
Warheads once Launched, function just like a group of Drones. Each Body has a single Move and Attack. They do not use the Velocity rules for spacecraft movement.

Individual Bodies
Unlike Drones, Warheads Bodies do not Attack as a group. Each Warhead Body makes its own Attack Roll.

No Additional Weapon Cost
Unlike many Drones, Warheads do not need to be Equipped with an additional Weapon.

Melee
Warheads may only make an Attack Roll against an adjacent Target.

Destroyed After a Hit
If a Warhead succeeds on an Attack Roll, it explodes, Destroying its Body. A failed Attack Roll does not Destroy it.

Replacing Bodies
Destroyed Warhead Bodies are replaced when it makes sense (eg: when you have access to replacements in a city).

Battery

See pg: 177 for full Gunnery System Roll rules.

Batteries gain a bonus to their Attack Roll from their user's Gunnery Vehicle System Skill.

Function Like Guns
Batteries function just like the Weapon Type: Gun.

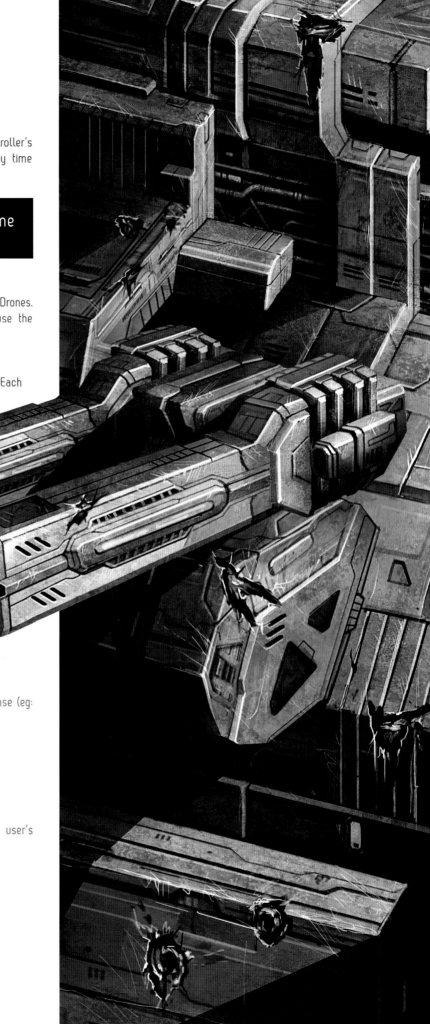

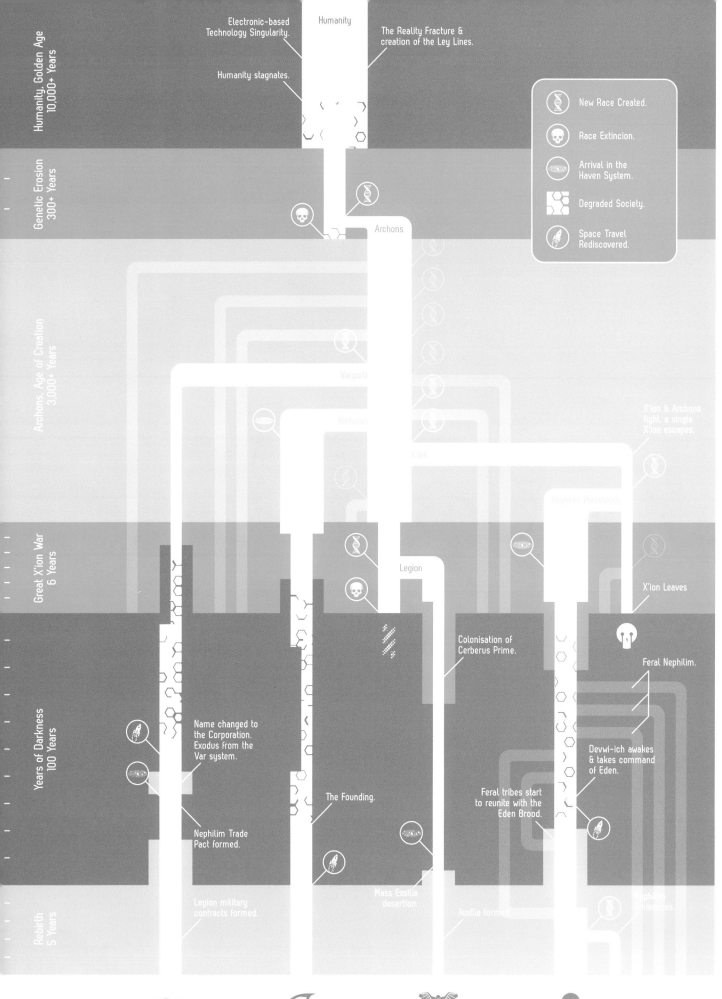

Humanity

Electronic-based Technology Singularity.

The Reality Fracture & creation of the Ley Lines.

Humanity stagnates.

Humanity, Golden Age 10,000+ Years

Genetic Erosion 300+ Years

New Race Created.

Race Extincion.

Arrival in the Haven System.

Degraded Society.

Space Travel Rediscovered.

Archons

Archons. Age of Creation 3,000+ Years

Vargarti

Natrum

X'ion

X'ion & Archons fight, a single X'ion escapes.

Nephilim Pureblonds

Great X'ion War 6 Years

Legion

X'ion Leaves

Colonisation of Cerberus Prime.

Feral Nephilim.

Years of Darkness 100 Years

Name changed to the Corporation. Exodus from the Var system.

Devwi-ich awakes & takes command of Eden.

Nephilim Trade Pact formed.

The Founding.

Feral tribes start to reunite with the Eden Brood.

Rebirth 5 Years

Legion military contracts formed.

Mass Exsilia desertion.

Auxilia formed.

Nephilim

Setting Guide

See pg: 8-9 for Sector and System Map.
See pg: 16 for Short Story: History.

This section explores the Fragged Empire setting, including planets, races, technologies, and more. The goal of this section is not to replace your creativity, but to fuel it.

Overview

The Four Core Themes
See pg: 7 for full Key Theme introductions.

» A post-post-apocalyptic setting.
» Cultural tension.
» Genetic engineering.
» Exploration.

Humanity Is Dead
It is over 10,000 years into the future, and humanity has been dead for a long time, caused by thousands of years of apathy, leading to genetic erosion. Humanity may have disappeared, but not before they changed the known galaxy forever by creating the Ley Lines, which allowed faster-than-light travel, the terraforming of millions of planets, and the creation of the Archons.

Archons
Created to replace humanity and to inherit an empire they did not build, the Archons sought to tread a different path than their human creators. While humanity primarily advanced through electronics, the Archons sought to advance through genetic engineering, as proven by their creation of thousands of races in their pursuit to create a perfect race.

X'ion
Originally thought to be the perfect race, the X'ion were praised and loved above all else. But before they were even able to leave the lab that they were created in, their Archon creators removed the title of perfection from them. No one knows how the fighting started, but ensuing combat claimed all of the X'ions' lives, except for one–who escaped far out into uncharted space.

Great War
Two hundred years after its departure, the lone X'ion returned to the Archon Empire, leading a massive army of its own creation, the Nephilim.

This Great War between the Archons, their creations and the X'ion, and its creations, lasted only six years. Once the last Archon had been killed, the X'ion left, abandoning the Nephilim.

Current Situation
Now a hundred years after the Great War, you and your people have only just re-emerged into space, making contact with the other surviving races in the Haven system.

Playable Races
There are four playable races. They have banded together not out of a common direction, but out of necessity.

» Corporation
» Kaltoran
» Legion
» Nephilim

Haven system
The Fragged Empire setting is primarily focused on the Haven system and its inhabiting races. Much of the map outside of the Haven system is left bare and unmarked; it is up to you to decide what's out there.

Threats
There are many threats to the survival of the four races in the Haven system – including the Mechonids, the return of X'ion, and economic collapse – but none are more threatening than political breakdown. If the four races do not work together, then all will fall.

Make This Setting Your Own!
Seek to make this setting your own.
Feel free to change anything.

Many questions have intentionally been left unanswered.

Many locations on the map have intentionally been left unlabelled.

Short Story: Humanity

Mryks's eyes slid open as the embryonic walls rapidly deteriorated, turning the membrane which separated her from the world transparent. Mryks pressed through the thin membranous wall, feeling it cling tenaciously to her skin as if it wanted her to stay inside where it was safe.

Tearing free, Mryks choked as air flooded into her lungs for the first time. Spilling unceremoniously onto the floor, she coughed up the syrupy oxygenating fluid from her lungs. She felt cold and her body ached from its very first use of her muscles. Mryks's eyes drifted upward to the gargantuan figure standing over her.

"Birth is painful. You will find life to be similar." Despite his massive bestial frame, the giant Nephilim's voice was smooth and calming.

"Creator…" Mryks choked, looking the Pureblood in the eyes.

"Clean yourself and get dressed. We can talk afterward." The Pureblood turned and walked to a console.

Mryks knew, instinctively, that there would be no more discussion until she had done as he'd instructed. She also knew the console her creator was inspecting was the one that had monitored her throughout the creation process. Mryks struggled to her feet and on shaking legs made her way to the shower.

Acclimatising to living came easily to Mryks. In very little time she cleaned the last of the fluids from her body and dressed herself in the clothing set aside for her. Mryks knew the world around her. She knew the ship through which she walked was called Zyprion and was a cruiser-class laboratory bioship. Mryks knew every element that went into the ship's design and construction. She also knew about herself. Mryks was an Emissary. She was made to interact with the other species. She was also aware that they would likely hate her for a war she had no part in.

It was not long before Mryks found Jughbah. He was seated at a table with two cups of Necronus tea. Across from her creator was an open chair, which she slid into. Jughbah smiled a fang-filled smile as he inspected his handiwork.

"Are you finding life pleasing?" Jughbah asked analytically.

"I have no comparison. I know so many things, but have no experience. This hour is all I know." Mryks reached for her tea.

"Life is all any of us knows. You, my creation, have the advantage of being born with all the knowledge that I could give you. You exist to be better." He folded his reptilian hands on the table.

"Be better than what? Better than you?" She lifted her gaze from her tea to once more meet her creator's eyes.

"All of us; better than everything." His reply daunted her.

"A momentous event that shapes our culture to this day, humanity created millions of long hairline fractures in reality. Bending the scientific laws that govern space and time, this resulted in what we call "Ley Lines". We still don't really know what they are. Many suspect their effects go far beyond just powering Jump drives."

"Yea, I've heard the rumours. Power-crazed psionics and a gateway for transdimensional monsters to move through."

"Well, I don't know about monsters," Leah replied, "but psionics are real, that's for sure."

- Leah and Zeus, musings on the Reality Fracture.

"The perfect Nephilim." She mused, more to herself than him.

"Don't compare yourself to the Nephilim. They have forgotten their purpose. Their improvements are for personal gain. They have been infected by the Corporates, or perhaps they were flawed to begin with. They focus on archaic notions of pride. They advance themselves for power. That can't be our purpose. The goal is advancement itself. We are no more like the rest of our species than we are like the humans." Jughbah's tone was acidic.

"The humans?" Mryks knew the word but struggled for a definition.

"You were not created with knowledge of humanity because there is little to be imparted. Conjecture, theories, and myth are all that remain of them." Jughbah could see the curiosity on his pupil's face.

"Humanity were the beings who created the Archons" he continued.

"Then they would be our great-grand sires?" Mryks interrupted.

"Forget such familial notions. I do not call you daughter, nor should you call me father. We are equals, as I believe we are the equals of the Archons and humans. In any case, there is little left of humanity in us. However, their legacy lingers on throughout the universe."

"In what manner does it persist?" Mryks leaned forward steepling her fingers.

"The next time, or first time in your case, you step on a planet, take note that it was terraformed. The humans did the vast majority of terraforming throughout the galaxy." Jughbah was pleased by his creation's interest in garnering knowledge.

"Without evidence, can we not hypothesise that it was another race?" Mryks leaned back in her chair.

"It is possible, but all species have been taught that it was the humans. There are so few things we can all agree upon. For our purposes, assume that humanity did terraform many of the worlds on which we live. From that we can surmise that they exhibited atmospheric tolerances very similar to our own."

"Yes, but these suppositions go without stating," Mryks added. "One can also hypothesise that they were vast and technologically advanced. A species would have to be to terraform so many worlds."

"Indeed. Many researchers also attribute their electronic based technological singularity to their decline. They would have experienced unprecedented growth. However, very rarely is any species ready for such rapid advance. Much like the Archons, their advances spiralled out of their control entirely." Jughbah sipped at the now-cooled tea.

"Resulting in the Reality Fracture. How did it happen?" Mryks connected the strands of information inside her mind.

"No one is certain, and there are so many contradicting theories that I would not bother speculating on the matter. We know that it happened. We know that the very fabric of reality was rent. The most important outcome was the creation of the Ley Lines. These lines emit an energy that is referred to as Ley Energy – uninspired name, I know. This energy allows our spacecraft to jump: to open portals that allow us to exceed the speed of light. This makes them very interesting indeed."

"I am aware of the Ley Lines and their uses, but you already know that. I want to know about the humans. There has to be more than you are telling me." Mryks gave a dry smile to her creator.

"I still think it is such a strange way for humanity to die… Genetic erosion… The degradation of the genome through the lack of biodiversity… Such an old and foreseeable problem."

"Well, I suppose they stopped having sex… well, at least not enough of it… My people, the Legion, are at risk of the same problem."

"We Kaltorans don't have that problem… quite the opposite at times." They both smiled. "Lack of sex! Destroyer of empires!"

"It couldn't be just that. If their society hadn't degraded through apathy, they might've survived."

– Leah and Zeus, musings on the Fall of humanity.

"There is – much more, in fact. Truthfully, and it pains me to say this, I do not know very much. X'ion did not see them as important enough to teach us. I know implicitly that we are nothing like them."

"How do you know that?" Mryks demanded a bit more forcefully than she'd intended. Realising her mistake, she bit her lip and lowered her gaze.

Jughbah ignored her outburst and sipped calmly at his tea. He could see the frustration building as Mryks's face tensed. In that moment the ancient scientist was proud. Mryks thirsted forknowledge as she was designed to do. This one would do far better than the last. Perhaps he had finally created an equal. He continued calmly.

"I know it because they are not here. They reached their peak and grew complacent. They created the Archons to inherit their universe as if they'd intended to fade into obscurity. We would never do such a thing. They stopped reaching for more. Inaction is often worse than poor action, and I can only guess this was the case. Perhaps they exhausted themselves. Perhaps reaching their singularity made them think there was nothing more to achieve. In any case, they ceased to matter when they ceased to advance. Worse still, they failed to better themselves on a genetic level."

"Meaning?" Mryks looked puzzled.

"Other species breed. That is how they expand and focus on specific traits important to the species – or, in the Kaltorans' case, doom their race to inevitable starvation and madness. They do not create life in the sense that I have created you. They form pairs of male and female parts in order to distill specific traits and add longevity to their species."

"Oh." Mryks was now more confused.

"It is nothing you have to worry about. The important thing to remember is that humanity stopped coupling, or at least stopped gaining anything new from their couplings. Their genes, like their empire, became complacent and began to erode. Of course this is all based on what little data could be collected, and I am positive many of the holes in the information have been filled in with legend. Dismiss the humans from your thoughts. We have greater things to achieve and cannot be distracted by myths and legends about an irrelevant people."

"We have to become better." Mryks understood.

"Yes. We have to advance ourselves so that no future species can dismiss our existence so easily." Jughbah grinned and rose to his full imposing height.

"Advance ourselves beyond humanity," Mryks added with a smile, not really wanting to let the matter go.

Short Story: Archons

Lucas hated storms.

He hated it even more when people seemed to enjoy them. Having grown up on a tiny dump of an island, upon which a storm meant they had to huddle inside underground bunkers while poisonous mists swirled up above, he'd grown to appreciate fair weather.

Even now, hunkered down as they were inside an ancient Archon genetics lab, watching the hail and thunder through reinforced windows, Lucas felt an old instinct to don his breathing mask.

"You're twitching again," grunted Jagh, engaged as he had been for the last two days, attempting to reactivate one of the many computer consoles that littered the lab.

"You might relish the thought of being stuck in a decrepit old genetics lab," Lucas shot back, "but if it's all the same, I'll keep waiting for fairer weather."

The Nephilim made a rumbling noise in his throat and returned to his attempts at repair. Lucas turned his eyes back to the windows.

The lab was roomy, but the dusty floors and ancient skeletons didn't do much for the décor. Add in the empty gene tanks, long-dead computer terminals, and scattered robotic Mechonid parts, and it all added up to somewhere you wouldn't want to spend any length of time. They currently stood in a circular room that stretched upwards to a domed ceiling. Twin terminals stood before row upon row of man-sized tanks, all bathed in semi-darkness. Most of the rooms in the ancient laboratory were more or less the same – consoles, benches, and dead Archons – but they'd chosen the tank room due to the light coming in from the windows. It was a sparse, cold light that flickered and danced with the hailstones, casting shifting shadows over the debris. More than once, Lucas had caught one of the derelict Mechonids moving out of the corner of his eye, only to discover that it was a trick of the light.

Their rations were stable, as was their light source: right now, it was the boredom that threatened to finish them off. Or rather, finish Lucas off: Jagh had been happily labouring over the terminals for the entire time they'd been there.

Lucas had long stopped flinching whenever a particularly large piece of hail smacked into the window. If they'd been outside, the hail would probably have crushed in their skulls by now.

"Eos, weather report," he said, and his small pod-like drone hovered to the window, scanning the sky.

"Forecast," Eos reported in a cool female voice. "Storm will pass in approximately twenty-six hours and fourteen minutes. Afterwards, expect clear skies with the chance of a shower in the evening. Your weather for the weekend…"

Lucas stopped listening.

Still over a day to go.

They'd salvaged everything they could from the lab: a few power cells, barely functioning terminals, and a whole lot of ancient data that only Jagh would understand. It wasn't the greatest haul of Lucas's career, and now he was stuck with only the Nephilim for company.

The two of them couldn't have been more different. Lucas was dressed in his impeccable green Corporate suit, tie straightened to the millimeter, white, greying hair neatly combed to one side. Meanwhile, Jagh stood a foot taller, grey-skinned, hunched over and dressed in shabby garments that hung loose over his hulking, monstrous form. He was one of the original Nephilim, a Pureblood, over one hundred years old, with impressive muscles and brains. Purebloods were feared, and for good reason.

"Still a day to go," Jagh said, looking up from his task. "Is there still nothing new to salvage?"

"The Archons didn't leave much behind when they decided to do the universe a favour and die out," the Corp replied. "True Archon tech is rare. So anything you could do…"

"You hate them." Jagh paused from his labours underneath the console.

Lucas turned to see the Nephilim scientist looking straight at him, having laid his tools to one side. If Jagh was actually engaging in conversation, their boredom had reached critical levels. They hadn't liked each other when the mission began, and the days of awkward conversation had done nothing for their friendship.

"Yes, I do."

"Why?"

"Because they were terrible parents."

Jagh frowned, and Lucas realised that he'd probably have to explain further. It wasn't like they had anything else to do.

"How much do you know about the Archons?" he asked, finally taking his eyes off the window.

"They created you," Jagh replied. "Corporation, Kaltoran, Legion, hundreds of others. I have killed a few Archons… not a particularly impressive race."

"And?"

"They were an overly proud, arrogant race that deserved to fall."

"Finally, we agree on something."

"Even though they created you?"

"Like I said," Lucas growled. "Terrible parents."

Jagh paused, got to his feet, walked over to one of the consoles, and pressed a few keys. The ancient, nearly drained power system flared to life, projecting hologram security footage. The room was filled with hazy figures, scientists, with monotone skin colours: black, white, or grey. Their features were perfect, their bodies broad and strong. Their clothing… ornate, especially for scientists.

Just looking at them made Lucas's fingers twitch. Jagh's gaze moved from the incorporeal figures to the man's face, amusement in his eyes.

Even as they watched, the peaceful research scene dissolved into bickering. A female Archon gestured towards the data terminal, her lips voicing soundless words. Another scientist replied, exasperation written on his face. Within seconds, it looked like the entire room had taken sides. Lucas resisted the urge to roll his eyes. Those were the Archons he'd grown up knowing. All the stories of splits and factions in their society were true, probably caused by petty arguments such as this one.

Another tap of the console and the images faded.

"Were they your first Archons?" Jagh asked.

"They were," Lucas replied, with an edge to his tone. "Not that I ever actually wanted to meet one."

"Oh, my mistake."

Lucas shot Jagh a glare, which was countered by a look of feigned innocence.

"At least they looked strong," Jagh said as he returned to his work on the console. "Unlike you squishy Corporates."

"Perhaps. If my race were expert genetic engineers, I'd have given myself a few abilities beyond perfect hair and big muscles, but… the Archons weren't an imaginative bunch."

"It was the humans who created them. They were the genetically unimaginative bunch." Jagha was now back under the console. "The Archons were quite imaginative."

Humans. They were a race which Lucas thought of as his true parents. Legend had it that they were explorers, electronic experts, rulers of an empire that may have spanned the galaxy, and at one stage… capitalists… corporates. Eventually they faced extinction and created the Archons as their perfect successors, gave very literal birth to them, and allowed themselves to die out. Every Corporation child knew the stories, but there was little known of humans beyond this.

"Come to think of it," Jagh said, his voice muffled by the console, "How much did your people teach you about the Archons?"

"Just that they were the perfect race that inherited an empire and vast amounts of technology. They squandered both. They didn't explore much or make use of much human technology. They carved out a small empire and played god with their genetic experiments. Trying to create the perfect race."

Even the concept still seemed idiotic to him, the same as it had when he'd learned Archon history as a boy.

"Hmm," Jagh replied. "Interesting. My people just learned how to kill them… efficiently and painfully."

"What a fascinating education you must have received from X'ion."

"The best," Jagh said with a hoarse laugh. "But I'm fascinated with your concept of them as bad parents. I do not think of my creator, X'ion, as a parent."

"The Corporation was deemed to be a failure by the Archons. Meanwhile, their other creations – Kaltorans – were showered with love, resources, entire planets… they played favourites with their children."

Lucas paused, gritting his sharp teeth. For a few moments, all that could be heard was the raging storm and the dull thud of hail striking the thick glass.

Lucas wasn't an emotional man. But he could not forget the memories of the poisonous wastelands his people had grown up on, a forsaken island, tossed to them like scraps from the Archons' table. The Kaltorans were given everything, yet the Vargarti – as his people were originally known – were made the unwanted wards on another race's planet.

These injustices had not been forgotten by the Corporation, even long after they'd fled that world and made a new future for themselves. If a real-life Archon had walked through the door "efficiently and painfully" didn't sound like such a bad option.

He was broken out of this line of thought by soft chuckling. Striding over to the console, Lucas gave the metal surface a sharp kick, and Jagh's smirking face appeared on the other side.

"Something funny?"

"I find it amusing," Jagh said in between snorts of laughter. "You grew up with all these issues. My race was the one who removed the problem. I think that our peoples should be great friends."

This set Lucas off again, and Jagh slid back underneath the console, leaving Lucas to scowl at thin air.

"Well, we get along with your people better than the Kaltorans or the Legion ever will."

"I heard…" said the Nephilim, his voice muffled once again, "The Archons never stopped in their foolish grasp at perfection. Hundreds of races, flora, and fauna all came from their labs, like this one. Previously terraformed human planets were repopulated with new life. And that was when things went wrong, as they inevitably would."

Lucas wasn't in the mood to endure more taunting. He resumed his place at the window and tried to ignore Jagh's words.

"There was a race – X'ions. Their name meant 'pinnacle of creation'. Twelve were made. They'd finally made the perfect child that they could love and praise at the expense of all others."

"I know all this," Lucas hissed. "Do you think the Corporation are ignorant?"

"You don't want me to answer that. But you do know the reason for the war, yes?"

"Disagreements over perfection," Lucas said. "The Archons started to argue with each other over what 'perfection' really was – through perfect genetics, or brought about by trial. Like the arrogant fools they were, they concluded that the X'ions could never be perfect by their standards. That didn't sit well with their new, briefly favourite children. The X'ions fought back."

"Probably," the Nephilim grunted. There was a shower of sparks, and the consoles lit up for a brief second. "Imagine, a race of arrogant fools who thought they could make everything prim and perfect."

Lucas swallowed a scathing reply.

"And then the Archons fell into more pointless arguments that tore their society apart. They were so busy debating that they stopped creating new races, which I suppose was the only plus."

"And then," Jagh said, "The war."

"The war."

As if to highlight the statement, there was a terrific clap of thunder outside the window. Neither of them flinched, but it was enough to halt the conversation.

Lucas leaned against the console, staring at the dusty, debris-strewn floor as the silence awakened the rest of the lessons he'd learned as a child. Undoubtedly the stories were skewed by Corporation propaganda, but it still held some truth.

In the midst of the Archon divide, X'ion returned. No one knew how, but in the 200 years that had passed he'd created a genetically engineered army to take revenge against its creators. The Archons called this army 'Nephilim,' and they were unstoppable. With organic warships and countless troop variants, the Nephilim swarmed the Archon systems.

The fragile empire was instantly thrown into chaos. Nephilim moved from world to world, scorching everything they could find and slaughtering billions. In their infinite wisdom, the Archons had neglected to give their creations any real way to defend themselves. Betrayal ran rampant. Archons defected and tried to join X'ion. They were killed. Races offered up Archons to quench X'ion's wrath. They were still obliterated by the Nephilim.

Lucas may not have been alive at the time, but one thing was clear from the records: the initial stage of the war was no war at all. It was pure slaughter. Jagh had been there… Lucas wondered if his role had been as a scientist.

"I hear some even welcomed the war, as a test for themselves and their creations."

"Pardon?"

"The Archons."

Lucas turned to the Nephilim, a deep-seated frustration lending an edge to his voice.

"That's a pleasant lie," he said, his voice low. "But it's not how I heard it."

"Don't presume you know everything," Jagh growled back. "I fought in the war. I saw the slaughter, and the betrayal. Your people weren't even in the war, if I remember correctly."

"It wasn't our war."

"It was everyone's war."

"You're an idiot to think that's true."

"You don't have the right to talk down to me," Jagh snarled, striking the console with the side of his fist. Amazingly, this actually worked. The terminals lit up with a soft blue glow, and their argument was momentarily forgotten.

"Marvellous," Jagh breathed. "Their records are all here. With just a bit more power…"

He tapped a few keys, and the lights in the room flickered on, one by one. They stood in the centre of rows of tanks, many of which were cracked and drained. Murky liquid still floated in a few of them. The walkways extended to a high, domed ceiling, Archon skeletons strewn all the way up. Lucas stood in the centre of the space and took in the sight while Jagh laboured at the console, loading data onto his personal computer.

"Incredible work, as usual," Jagh commented. "The data seems to suggest this lab was used to produce Legion. A durable race by design, repurposed for war. The Archons have done an impressive job; just look at this DNA splicing…"

"You might call it impressive," Lucas muttered.

"They were worthy scientists."

"Before they scienced themselves to death."

"Oh, come now, let's not belittle the marvellous work of the Nephilim."

"If you call mass murder marvellous."

Jagh bristled and halted his work. Lucas turned as he felt a glare directed at the back of his head.

"You would dare to speak as if you were there. The Nephilim were at war."

"The Nephilim were the race that stomped from one planet to the next, leaving behind billions of innocent corpses. The Archons were forced to take a race in development and turn them into soldiers to defend themselves."

"The Legion were a worthy opponent, but there were too few to stop us."

"And you would know."

"You mock my people," the Nephilim growled, baring his teeth. "Even knowing I am both your physical and intellectual superior."

For a minute, the two of them simply stared each other down. Lucas' fingers inched towards the collapsible pistol at his belt. Then with a low rumble in his throat, Jagh raised his portable computer and began to type. With a barely audible snort, Lucas went to inspect the nearest tank.

"You think yourselves the most advanced of all the races," the Nephilim said, derision in his voice. "You shower your favour over those you deem worthy of your love… the wealthy and powerful. In your pride, you seek to rule over all. Perhaps your Corporation… is not as far from the Archons as you think."

"We're creating a better future," Lucas replied in a matching tone. "Play your games, scientist. Find new ways to kill. You'll see that we're right in the end."

He looked deep into the murky liquid inside the tank and thought of the genetic mush that could have been life. Channelling all his frustration into a solid kick, he sent a stray Mechonid head bouncing off the wall and ricocheting into a metal console. The clang echoed throughout the empty space.

"Please," Jagh said, through gritted teeth. "This operation is delicate."

"What are you doing, anyway? Isn't the data enough?"

"I'm trying to reroute power through nonessential systems. The basic generators are depleted, but if I can steal some power from other sectors… ah, here we go. The security systems have a fair supply. Strange."

Lucas glanced around at the skeletons.

"Strange indeed."

"If I can just power them up for a moment…"

The effect was instantaneous. The scattered remnants of the Mechonids around the room began to twitch, light up, and attempt to pull themselves up. Lucas had already drawn his pistol when the lights faded, power transferring to the main consoles. The Mechonids were still once again.

"Nervous?" Jagh said with a hint of amusement.

"You wouldn't be so cheerful if one of them came to life and shot your head off."

Jagh tutted.

"Wastrels of human technology, activated through desperation. Like a child behind the controls of a nuclear reactor. It was bound to end badly."

"Mechonids…"

"Well, they were the worst. But who knows what else? They tried to stop their inevitable deaths by pressing a load of buttons and hoping for the best."

One of the Mechonids twitched again. Lucas was overcome with the urge to pull out his pistol and blow its head to tiny pieces. Amongst stories of the horrors of the war, he'd heard that the machines eventually turned on their creators before becoming the scourge they were today.

X'ion's army on one side, murderous machines on the other. No wonder the war only lasted six short years. Now their creations were left to fend for themselves.

"Gargh!" Jagh exclaimed as the lights went dead and they were

plunged back into semi-darkness. "Fail-safes programmed in to stop power leeching. Looks like holograms are all we're getting for now."

His tone carried an air of finality, and Lucas got the impression that the old Nephilim scientist was taking the failure personally. He'd probably sulk for hours.

All the talk of Archons had left a sour taste in Lucas's mouth. The Corporation were all about looking to the future; there was no point in pondering has-beens. They were to learn from the mistakes of their flawed parents and move on.

Jagh had already resumed tapping away at his personal computer, so Lucas was left to his own devices for however long they had to wait. Overcome by sudden curiosity, Lucas activated the hologram footage again and watched as the room filled with scientists, the creators of so many races. One of them passed straight through Lucas, engaged in machinations lost to time.

They seemed so perfect, with their muscular forms and flawless features. They were given more than any other race has, and fell so far in their self-indulgent pursuit of perfection. As if anyone even knows what perfection is.

Lucas looked into the face of the nearest Archon and felt a cold indifference. Up close, the mighty creators and inheritors of the greatest empire in history were just another created race, bound by their own failings. At that moment, the archaic generators finally failed and plunged the room into semi-darkness once more.

Somehow, Lucas found himself next to the window, gazing out at the storm. Perhaps there was a certain beauty in chaos. The Archons sought to create perfect equilibrium, and the end result was even more strife. The very system of planets they now inhabited was forged by the chaos of war, the same war that had compelled the Corporation to escape to the stars and develop into the society they were today.

Perhaps, Lucas mused, as he watched an arc of lightning illuminate the sky, storms can result in unexpected hope.

Short Story: X'ion

It was a hastily made and flawless plan.

It had very little chance of success and was only flawless because there wasn't time to point out the flaws, but this was generally what happened when Jamie was forced to be in charge.

Originally there had been five of them on the mission. Their tyrannical captain, a hulking Legionnaire named Janus, had taken the lead as they forged a path through the rocky desert crags. He was a tough-as-nails mercenary leader, but that hadn't stopped a Feral Nephilim from taking his head off in the first hour of the trek. Janus would be mourned by no one, but their sparse crew was now down to four, and their target had proven himself to be far more dangerous than they'd been told.

Now they lay concealed amongst rocky cliffs that surrounded a bone-covered clearing, their Nephilim target hidden in a nearby shallow den. Nightfall was soon, so as the first officer Jamie had been forced to come up with a strategy. It was a terrible strategy, and the whole team knew it.

Jamie could almost feel their judging eyes through the dust clouds. The young Kaltoran gritted his teeth and raised his pistol into the air as his team readied themselves.

Here goes everything.

He fired, and an energy bolt shot into the sky. As expected, the Nephilim emerged from his den and came face-to-face with one of his own kind. However, the two couldn't be more different.

Zayk was of the newest breed of Nephilim, the ones that looked mostly what people considered to be normal, not counting the grey skin and hair tendrils. Males of this class were rare, though no less effort had been put into their creation: Zayk's features were chiselled in such a way that only a Nephilim genetic lab could achieve; his body was lean and strong.

Meanwhile, the feral creature that had killed their captain was a massive, hunched-over beast with thick armoured limbs, monstrous blood-stained jaws, and large black thoughtless eyes… a mindless animal.

There was no thought given to a family reunion. Zayk opened fire with his twin SMGs, which he wielded with uncanny poise. On all fours, their target leapt back inside the hut. So far, so good. There was the sound of falling rocks and dirt as the Nephilim burst out the back of his den, only to be met by Danu.

The female Legionnaire let loose with her high-powered Gauss Rifle, forcing the feral creature up the small cliff face. It managed to reach a low plateau just as a sniper round buried itself into a rock

only inches away from its head. Isobel lay on a large boulder across the clearing at the same level, but even the distance didn't muffle her cursing at having missed the shot. In the time it took her to reload, the feral beast had pulled itself over the cliff and vanished.

The four of them met at the den's entrance, where Danu immediately verbally unloaded on Isobel.

"One shot," she hissed. "You couldn't do that much?"

"Did you notice the dust it was kicking up?" Isobel shot back. Somehow, the rough hike and lying on a rock for over an hour hadn't left a single mark on her black, expensive Corporate jumpsuit. She stood with her long rifle resting on her shoulder, her face a mask of indifference.

"Our parts of the plan were completed to perfection," Danu continued.

"Which was a miracle in itself," Jamie muttered. Everyone turned to look at him, and he remembered that he was supposed to be the leader. He blinked a few times, then cleared his throat.

"Um, right," said the Kaltoran, "So that plan didn't work. Fine, whatever. So… any more ideas?"

"No more plans," Danu growled. She punctuated this statement by cocking her rifle as loudly as possible, a completely unnecessary gesture. "We split into teams, find the beast, and take its head."

"You mean, the same plan that got Janus killed?" Isobel pointed out.

"I mean what has served us up until now. It cannot hide forever."

"It knows this desert, Legionnaire. Didn't you grow up in a frozen wasteland?"

"You know what I think?" Jamie exclaimed with a forced grin. "I think we should split into two teams. Regular radio contact, back to the ship by nightfall, don't take risks, don't lose your heads, be nice to each other, Isobel with Zayk, Danu with me, okay?"

He wheeled around and started walking, hoping that Danu would follow. She did, though she continued to snarl as they began to wind their way through the crags. It was going to be a long afternoon.

***

Every few minutes, Isobel would glance over her shoulder just to check that Zayk was still there. The Nephilim made practically no noise with his footfalls, and if he was actually breathing he did so quietly. There was also the fact that he wasn't bad to look at… for a Nephilim.

"Y'know…" she began, using her long rifle to swat at the growing number of annoying bugs, "I don't think I've ever heard you talk voluntarily."

Zayk was silent for a moment.

"Is that so?"

"Uh-huh. Surely you have something to say."

"Why would I?"

"I dunno. I've met a few Nephilim, and they're always so curious about everything."

"I… observe."

"Yeah, I noticed. So how old are you, anyway?"

Isobel glanced back and noted with amusement that Zayk seemed to be taken aback by the question.

"I, uh…" he said, "By your biological standards, you mean?"

"Nope. Exactly how long you've been alive."

"In that case… I'm nearly two years old."

"Whoa there, old-timer," Isobel replied with a short laugh. "Don't croak on me."

"I will try not to."

This might have been an attempt at humour, or he could have been completely serious. It was impossible to tell.

They came to a ruin-covered ridge, over which flowed an impressive waterfall of sand. The sunlight glinted off the rising cloud of dust, creating an unexpected panorama that was impossible not to admire.

"It's a shame," Isobel commented as they stopped to take in the view. "All of this mess is because of the war."

"How so?"

The Corporation woman gestured all around her.

"The ruins, the toxic desert… and then there are the monsters."

Zayk flinched at the final word, so briefly it would have been impossible to tell if Isobel hadn't been looking for it. They started walking along the cliff face, keeping their eyes focused on the ruins.

"Sorry," said the woman, not meaning it. "I know it's one of your own that we're hunting."

"It is a mindless beast, no different from hunting any other wild game" Zayk said. "My people have much to answer for."

"Hmm. What do you think of how your race came to be?"

"That is a… broad question."

Zayk was spared from answering for the moment. A dozen fist-sized rocks rolling down a nearby ledge instantly set them both on edge. Backed up against the cliff face as they were, manoeuvring would be difficult. Both readied their weapons and backed off a few paces. For a few moments the only sound was the subtle drone of the wind. Then the rocks shifted once again and out popped a furry puffball with disproportionately large eyes and tiny talons, upon which it stumbled in constant danger of toppling over.

The creature was around the size of Isobel's fist. Both of them relaxed, exhaling at the same time.

"Case in point," Isobel commented as they watched the tiny creature scurry back into the rocks. "Just one of the Archon's great achievements that proved how much of their time they wasted."

"You would speak of your creators in such a way?"

"In a heartbeat. Don't tell me you have lingering affection for X'ion? After he abandoned your people?"

Something remarkably like anger flashed across Zayk's face before he holstered his weapons and resumed trudging up the ridge.

"Darkness is coming," he grunted over his shoulder. "We should hurry."

Isobel stood still for a moment before rolling her eyes and moving to follow.

***

Moving in the opposite direction, Jamie was attempting to dish out a reprimand in the same manner as Janus. It wasn't going well.

"I'm just saying," he said, trailing behind the Legionnaire as she pushed her way through a narrow canyon. "We have to work together. Don't get so caught up in arguments. Let them bounce off."

"The arguments are insignificant," Danu replied. Jamie nodded in appreciation before realising that he didn't have the slightest clue what she meant.

"Uh, what?"

"The Corporation woman merely lacks professionalism. What has

The cultured surroundings of the Corporate Gentlemen's Club didn't bother the scruffy Mikhael Jinx, and neither did the snooty stares from high-class escorts, nor those that'd hired them.

"You know what X'ion's problem was?" he remarked to nobody in particular, adjusting his worn jacket as he leaned back. "The same problem as you Corps have with the fraggin' Archons."

Here he paused to resume chugging what was left in the gold-embossed bottle. "Good stuff, this crap." he muttered before continuing his tirade. "My sister said it best: Parent issues. You Corps, X'ion, the lot of you have serious parent issues." Glares from across the open clubroom followed his movements as several bulky Legion bouncers made their way across the room to him.

"Course, X'ion had overwhelming power on his side, while you lot have some pretty outfits." He took another swig in the silence that followed. "'Of course, I'm sure that'll work out for you all." he said with a smirk as he was dragged to his feet, the empty golden bottle dropping to the thick carpet with a thud as he and his unwanted opinions were escorted out.

me on edge is the Nephilim."

"Zayk? He seems… harmless. A nice guy, even."

Danu stopped in her tracks. Naturally, this meant that Jamie walked right into her back. It was rather like smacking into a stone pillar.

"How can you say that," Danu asked in a low growl, "when you remember… everything?"

Massaging the bridge of his nose, Jamie reflected on her meaning. It was true; his Kaltoran genetic memories stretched back to the war. They got a little bit fuzzy as time went on, and sometimes they became tangled with memories of his life here and now, but they were always there.

All it took was a moment of thought, and he could remember many things his ancestors had seen and felt, from the time their race was created by the Archons, the war and the horrors that followed.

He remembered when the "perfect" race had been brought into the world, named "X'ion" or "pinnacle of creation". As a favoured race, the Kaltorans had rejoiced along with the Archons. Though only twelve X'ions were ever made, some of Jamie's Kaltoran ancestors had been eager to meet their newest brothers and sisters (or just

siblings – no one really knew much about the X'ion's physiology, including their gender).

Secluded in their space laboratory, the Archons had given more love and praise to their new creations than they'd even showered on the Kaltorans. Delusions of perfection, however, couldn't last.

"You can see the war in your mind," Danu said as she began to walk, "how the Archons tried to remove the X'ion title, which led to them fighting back. Then a few hundred years later… war."

"Well, yeah," Jamie admitted, keeping a close eye on his personal rock-plow in case she decided to stop again. His nose still ached. "But water under the bridge, y'know?"

"I do not."

"Hmm. Okay, maybe it'd be better if the Archons hadn't tried to blow up their own creations out of fear, or if they'd been a little more diligent in not allowing one of the X'ions to escape out into uncharted space. But what happened, happened."

"What happened," Danu replied, her tone venomous, "was slaughter by an army of Nephilim, with their creation; X'ion at the helm."

Jamie didn't have an answer to that, which plunged the conversation back into silence.

***

Isobel stood perched on top of an ancient Kaltoran temple, which was neither as fun nor as interesting as it had sounded. The structure had long since lost any defining features, crumbling into a hulking pile of rocks with barely enough room inside for a shelter. The Feral Nephilim had been there, that much they knew.

"Case in point, once again," she called down to Zayk, who was surveying the crags and dunes. "This place was full of sentient life, the Kaltoran capital, before your Nephilim buddies came through and killed everyone."

"Are you… trying to goad me?" Zayk replied, not turning.

"Well, maybe."

In a few deft leaps, Isobel landed gracefully and dusted herself off.

"I'd just like an opinion. X'ion: good guy or bad guy?"

"That is impossible to answer," Zayk replied. "By whose standards do you measure good and evil?"

"But you must have an opinion. Or don't they teach you about those when they force-fed knowledge into your brain?"

"I don't…"

"Or perhaps," Isobel said, glancing over her shoulder as she moved towards more stone ruins, "You're all just ashamed of what X'ion did. Y'know, when it returned with an army of you lot and laid waste to everything the Archons had created. Blood, gore, entire species wiped out… it's not like you have a rich and varied history."

"Perhaps not."

"Why do you think X'ion just up and left when the war ended?"

"I do not know."

"Seems a lot like it just abandoned you like childhood toys once it had its revenge on the Archons."

"Enough!" Zayk roared, stopping dead in his tracks. The word echoed throughout the ruins and canyons, Isobel's eyes narrowed.

"Finally," she said, unconcerned. "Some emotion."

They resumed walking, keeping their distance from each other, listening for the tiniest sound.

"This is all I know," Zayk said after a few minutes. His tone suggested that he wouldn't appreciate being interrupted. "X'ion is a mystery even to us. Justice is a concept my people place little value on. But the Archons' eventual deaths were inevitable."

"Oh, absolutely," Isobel said. "I mean, they couldn't even agree on their own concept of perfection, or pretty much anything. The number of splits in their society…"

"They had no concept of war, and were unprepared," Zayk continued. "They were tested by their own creation… and failed."

Isobel waited for a few moments to see if he would keep talking, then brushed her hair over her shoulder with a smile.

"Interesting," she said, deftly stepping over a tree stump. "I do enjoy our chats."

Zayk was about to respond when a blurred grey shape blasted out from the shadows, its claws levelled at both of their heads.

***

Jamie and Danu had encountered nothing but more ruins and a few scattered bones that might have been Feral Nephilim snacks at some point. The silence was overpowering, and Jamie was about to attempt another bad conversation-starter when his companion spoke up.

"Do you remember everything? From the war?"

"Um…"

From his surviving ancestors' perspective, sure. He didn't think about it much, but sometimes, on the coldest nights, the genetic memories would leap unbidden to his mind. Visions of living biotech ships descending from the sky, filled with Nephilim soldiers who came to kill. All of them were different, thousands of genetic variants bred for different functions, but had a singular purpose. The Kaltorans quickly learned to fear them.

He remembered the Archons, hunted throughout the galaxy, some of whom had taken refuge with their created children. It hadn't saved them from X'ion's wrath.

"I remember," Jamie said, swallowing. "Mostly."

"What was it like?"

"Excuse me?"

"Real war. Tell me."

Of course. The Legion had been bred to be the Archons' soldiers in the war against X'ion. Since the conflict only lasted six years, their entire race now struggled to find purpose without the Great War. A war that no living Legion had fought in.

"Well," Jamie began, kicking aside a rock in his path, "the Kaltorans weren't exactly on the front lines. That was your people's job. But I remember a lot of fear. Since the Archons had no history of warfare, they turned to human traditions of order, discipline, and skill. That's why your people are the way they are. Whereas X'ion…"

He paused, feeling a memory come rushing back. A few of his ancestors had joined the fight. They'd seen how X'ion's troops functioned: primal, instinctual, cunning, and ferocious.

"The Nephilim were different," he concluded. "They fought like animals, while the Legion were regimented. Battles were complex and… horrific."

"Indeed," Danu said. "X'ion was ruthless, but tales are also told of its creativity. It was a thinking foe, as the Archons were, but so very different."

"Pretty much. And then there were the spies."

Danu flinched as if she'd heard a taboo word.

"What spies?"

"No one knows for sure, but we are pretty sure a war of espionage began many years before any actual physical conflict began."

Danu was quiet for a moment, before growling "Tales of X'ion's prowess in battle have been overstated, if it relied on such tactics."

Once again, there was no reply to this. The two of them trudged on, scanning the ground for tracks and listening for any suspicious sounds. Their concentration was suddenly broken by a burst of gunfire from the south."

"Target engaged," Isobel called breathlessly over the radio. "It's heading for the central temple, the place where we've stashed…"

"The ship," Jamie choked. Danu was already sprinting, with the young Kaltoran trailing behind. That beast could do some serious damage if they weren't careful.

Up ahead, Jamie saw Danu sink into a crouch as she entered the clearing. He assumed she was preparing for combat until he smacked face-first into the cloaked wing of their spacecraft. For the second time in as many hours, his nose felt like it was protesting being a part of his face.

"Ow," he grunted, trying and failing to make the word sound commanding. "Ow, ow, ow, ouch…"

He stumbled forward, ducking underneath the wing, and saw that Isobel and Zayk had the temple entrance surrounded. Zayk bore a gash on his forehead, and Isobel's armour was scratched up, but they otherwise seemed unharmed.

"It's in the temple, nowhere near the ship," Isobel reported as Jamie approached. "We've confirmed that this is the only exit, so… what happened to your face?"

"Nevermind," Jamie replied, striding to the front of the group so they couldn't see his less-than-heroic wound. "Alright, same plan as last time. I'll give the signal; Isobel will be positioned in the crevice over there; Zayk, you can force it onto the roof; Danu will cover the flank; I'll give covering fire where needed…"

"Or," Danu said, "We could just toss in a couple of grenades?"

She held up two, clenched in her fist.

"Oh," Jamie said, blinking a few times. "Uh, yes. That works too."

They blockaded the temple entrance, weapons at the ready. Danu pulled the pins and tossed the explosives into the darkness. It might have been a simple beast, but it came bounding out before the force of the blast threw it forward, and it rolled to a halt right in front of Zayk. It raised its head, and for a moment the two members of the same race simply stared at each other.

Then the feral beast snarled and rolled onto its hind legs, but it was mowed down by the full force of Zayk's SMGs. The gunshots echoed throughout the ruins, then all was still. With an unreadable expression, the young Nephilim holstered his weapons, and the others did the same.

"Nice work," Isobel commented as she strode to meet him. "For a moment there I didn't think you'd finish it."

"In many cultural ways, we have more in common with the Archons than any of their own creations. The irony of this is not lost on me, as we have now become what we were created to destroy. We in effect, are the new Archons…

I wonder if in our effort to never be replaced, our children will also one day kill us."

– Zeqwarkos, the World Eater

"Why does it matter?" Zayk murmured, before turning towards the ship. "The job is done."

"Good work by everyone, I reckon," Jamie said, talking mostly to Danu. The Legionnaire narrowed her eyes as she surveyed Zayk ascending into the ship, before shrugging and following suit.

"Hmph."

Then she was gone, leaving Jamie standing alone in the clearing. He leant over the Feral Nephilim's body, cutting off one of its head tendrils as proof of their kill.

"Command certainly was a tough burden," he said to himself as he rubbed his nose and turned towards the ship.

"Arg… the Xi…" Jamie jumped back from the beast in fright, readying his pistol as it spoke. "The X'ion, the pale master, shall come again…"

With an eerie exhalation, the beast breathed its last breath as Jamie realised he and his children would forever remember this moment.

Playable Races

The Haven system is home to four primary races: the Corporation, the Kaltorans, the Legion, and the Nephilim. The player characters of your game may be any one of these four races.

This section will help you to create a character that fits into the wider setting.

Lost Races

The Archons created thousands of races, and there are sure to be many other X'ion-created Nephilim out in the galaxy. GMs should feel free to insert additional races, especially if their game is set outside the Haven system.

CORP.

"~~Building~~ *Taking* Your Future"

Corporation

Common Name: Corp
Former Racial Name: Vargarti

Creator: Archons
Average Height: 1.7m
Average Weight: 75kg
Average Life Span: 80 years

Home Planet: Alabaster
Former Home Planet: Varsphere
Total Population: 8.9 million
Yearly Population Growth Rate: -12%

Years Since Re-emergence into Space: 53 years

Common Characteristics

Abrasive, decisive, entrepreneurial, organised, and pragmatic.

Distinctive Physical Features

Yellow patterned skin along neck, back, shoulders, and hairline.

Corporation Trait, pg: 340

» +2 Maximum Resources and Influence.
» Gain 1 Resource and Influence.
» +1 Wealth, Operations, and Tactical.
» Gain Language: Corporation.
» -1 Fate.
» -2 Maximum Strength.
» Racial Prejudice from Kaltorans.

Preferred Combat Equipment

Ion and Particle Weaponry.
Combat Computer.
Drones.
Clothing or Combat Suit.

Corporation History

During the Age of Creation, the Archons created the Vargarti but deemed them a failure. Rejected by their creators, they were forced to live on a single island on a planet controlled by another race. Not allowed to travel and with strict birth control, the Vargarti were never given the opportunity to stand on their own.

During the Great War, X'ion brought destruction and death to all children of the Archons, including the Vargarti on their home world of Varsphere. They were spared the worst, however, since X'ion's genetically engineered viruses were designed to target the planet's primary race, not the Vargarti. Even so, at the end of the Great War, Varsphere was a monster-covered wasteland, millions had died, and they had lost much of their technology.

For the Vargarti, the Years of Darkness were a chance to reimagine themselves and discard the inferior status given to them by the Archons. This reimagining began when a small group of Vargarti warlords uncovered a ruin of an ancient city from the Golden Age of Humanity and learned of an ideology called capitalism. Embracing this ideology as a means to forge their own path, these warlords united the Vargarti tribes under a new identity: the Corporation. This became a purely capitalistic society, where each person succeeded or failed based on their own ability.

As the dust from this social upheaval settled, the Corporation took to the stars. Abandoning their home world, they embarked on a great exodus to the system called Haven, where they colonised a massive gas giant with space stations. This time of space colonisation was extremely difficult, and millions died. The newly formed Corporation would have failed if not for the Nephilim. In a never to be repeated gift of generosity, the Nephilim housed the Corporation in their mighty warships and provided food, supplies, and workers.

Over the years that followed, the Corporation explored the Haven system, drawing attention from the yet-to-emerge Kaltorans, the nearby Legion, and the dormant Mechonids. The Corporation had inadvertently woken the Haven system up.

Corporation Culture

Before they were known as the Corporation, the Vargarti were rejected by their Archon creators as inferior. Because of this rejection, the Corporation has a strong sense of self-determination and refuse to be a product of their genes. For the Corporation, the Great X'ion War was a fresh start, freeing them from insignificance and irrelevance, giving them an opportunity to prove themselves. Therefore, each Corporate thrives or fails on their own merits, and judges others based on the same.

The Corporation is not a nation; rather, it is an enormous cartel made up of millions of smaller companies. It is a purely capitalistic society – entrepreneurial, competitive, acquisitive, and greedy. The philosophy of competition in the Corporation stems from the Board of Management's policies: Corporation subsidiaries are to compete with one another as if independent, so that the more profitable companies succeed and the less profitable ones fail. However, when dealing with outside races, the policy is to act like a cartel, fixing prices and forming monopolies to ensure the best price for the Corporation.

Largely motivated by the desire for personal success and shaped by social expectations, Corporate culture is deceptively simple to outsiders. While most are materially well provided for, nearly all Corporates present an image of greater personal success than they have actually achieved. This is especially true when interacting with other Corporates; you are judged on your personal achievements and in many cases hired and fired on that same basis. No matter how impoverished, every Corporate has at least one set of expensive-looking clothes to wear in public. The wealthiest frequently throw extravagant parties to firmly establish public knowledge of their success.

Corporates mostly live on large, crowded, and hastily constructed space stations orbiting the gas giant Alabaster, with large central chambers full of garish advertisements, shops, and towering buildings, surrounded by large space ports. Others live in crowded moon and asteroid outposts within the Haven system. Wherever they make their homes, you can be sure that there is an important source of income close by.

The Corporates are the greatest unifying force in the Haven system, with most of their manual labour and production done by Nephilimcreated biological drones called Flesh, law enforcement largely managed by the Legion, and even trading with the often troublesome Kaltorans for food and raw minerals. If not for the Corporation, the races would still be in the Years of Darkness, a fact Corporates don't mind mentioning when it's convenient or helpful.

Creating a Corporate Character

Agent

The Corporation are not all stock traders and financiers; they also employ agents who specialise in corporate espionage to facilitate hostile takeovers and other forms of enforcement. Excelling at covert operations and overcoming security systems, these agents can quickly respond to negotiations gone bad or fight from the shadows.

Recommended Skills
» Physical
» Awareness
» Programming
» Small Arms

Recommended Traits
» Wealth: Black Market
» Physical: Thief
» Small Arms: Crack Shot

Business

Experts on trade, businesswomen and men use their knowledge and skills to expand the resources available to them and their companions. Skilled negotiators, they often act as the public face for their group, conducting themselves with a decorum that mercenaries often lack. In combat, they lead their drones and lackeys from the rear and provide tactical data to their team.

Recommended Skills
» Wealth
» Conversation
» Leadership
» Tactical

Recommended Traits
» Intelligence: Educated
» Wealth: Barter
» Conversation: Charming
» Tactical: Hug Cover

Professional

There are some jobs for which Flesh and mechanical drones are not capable enough; these are done by corporate professionals. These highly skilled individuals often specialise in single field, such as medical care, scientific knowledge, or Flesh coordination.

Recommended Skills
» Any Professional Skills
» Tactical

Recommended Traits
» Level: Thinker
» Mechanics: Aerospace
» Programming: Data Searcher
» Medicine: Clinical Medicine

Agent   Business   Professional

Government and Law

Government: Plutocratic Oligarchy.
Leadership: Board of Management.

Board of Management

A political scientist would define the Corporation as a plutocratic oligarchy, which is to say a government run by a small number of the wealthiest people. In the Corporation, this oligarchy is represented by a group known as the Board of Management. The way in which the Board is chosen is fairly simple: each new year, all companies must report their earnings. The CEOs of the ten wealthiest companies become the Board of Management. The Board of Management is responsible for conducting diplomacy between races and deciding on any regulatory laws.

The Board of Management was originally an alliance of ten warlords that emerged victorious from the wars of the Dark Age before the enlightenment of capitalism and the space colonisation of Haven. These warlords uncovered information about the economic systems which allowed the humans of the past to rule the galaxy. It followed that to be successful they should do their best to recreate these economic systems.

Despite its many fluctuations, board membership has fallen into a predictable pattern over the last thirty years. Membership of the lower seats changes constantly as companies fall as quickly as they rise. Middle and upper seats are fairly stable, with large companies such as the Body Count Conglomerate™, Octanto™, and Stream™ firmly holding onto their places.

While the companies that make up the Board are well known, many CEOs who serve on the Board choose to keep their identities secret by acting through complex proxy networks or by simple absence. It is quite likely that multiple board seats are held by the same person. Some members of the board may not even be racially Corporate, and some may be the original founding warlords, indefinitely extending their lives through advanced Nephilim bio-tech.

Corporate Regulatory Law

At the inception of the Board of Management, it was decided that agreement between private individuals would suffice for law and order. However, when the Corporation came into contact with the other races, the social order began to break down, since there was no way to stop coups by Legion mercenaries or to battle Kaltoran piracy and other larger threats. To combat these problems, the Board of Management decided that a formalised system of regulations would be necessary; they created article 924c, better known as Corporate Regulatory Law.

These laws apply only within the confines of Corporate space, property, or claimed territory. There is nothing considered a crime, as such, only breaches in regulation, which are enforced with fines. Any breach, from murder to shoplifting, can be paid as a fine; if unable to pay, the offender is sentenced to forced indentured labour until they have worked enough to pay off the debt. The fine is determined not by the ethics of the crime, but by the economic cost of the crime. For example, killing a Kaltoran shopper who was going to spend an estimated 100cr and whose death has no other negative consequences is worth a 100cr fine. Killing a prominent CEO and causing a stock value loss of 25% could be worth millions. A person can take out life insurance on their own life to inflate the consequence of causing their death.

These fines are often left unpaid by non-Corporates. Unpaid fines are doubled in value and applied as "dead or alive" bounties. Legion mercenaries and Corporate security contractors enforce these bounties, receiving a 50% commission, while the remaining 50% is paid to the victim of the breach (minus expenses).

Breaking Corporate Law

When a character breaks a law in Corporate space, they should be fined.

Minor crimes require a Wealth Spare Time Roll. If this is not paid by the end of the next session, then it increases in cost to a Resource Point.

Major crimes cost Resources. If this is not paid by the end of the next session, the offender gains the Complication: Bounty.

Minor Crime, Examples
» Minor property damage, e.g: broken window or graffiti.
» Minor medical expenses, e.g: flesh wounds or small energy weapon burns.
» Shoplifting cheap items, e.g: stealing things that cost a Spare Time Roll or nothing.
» Inconveniencing business, e.g: "putting off" customers or murdering a Kaltoran patron.

Major Crime, Examples
» Stealing Credits or property.
» Stopping business, e.g: causing a shop to close due to damage.
» Causing loss of profit, e.g: unnecessary waste of Corporation resources or murdering a Legion or Nephilim employee.

Variable Crime, Examples
» Murder of Corporate member (depending on victim's life insurance).
» Causing a share price drop (depending on the value of the loss).

Relationship with Other Races

The Corporation is the greatest unifying social force within the Haven system. This is not for any idealistic reasons, but due to the Corporation's very nature and its constant thirst for economic growth and stability.

In their eagerness to cross most cultural boundaries, Corporate society has have very little racism. They have a talent for social cohesion and a passion for order, risk mitigation, and economic growth. As a result, they have established many cross-racial systems, such as the Data Stream (pg: 274), currency (Credits, pg: 274), and many economic infrastructures.

Nephilim Trade Pact

During their early years of space colonisation, the Corporation lost millions of lives in their efforts to establish space stations around Alabaster. They would have failed if not for the Nephilim. Showing unprecedented generosity, the Nephilim housed, fed, and sheltered millions of colonists in their ancient living warships as the space stations were being built.

Over the years, the hierarchy of both races have solidified their working relationship in the form of a trade pact. The Nephilim provide cheap labour, primarily in the form of biological drones called Flesh, while the Corporation provide near-unlimited fuel to the Nephilim.

Legion Military Contract

Both desiring order and structure and having complimentary skills sets, the Corporation and Legion have a natural synergy despite their glairing cultural differences. Most Corporates abhor personal physical risk, while the Legion relish it. Most Legion hate the monotony of economics and production, while Corporates thrive on it.

The eagerness of young Legionnaires to fight for a living has given the Corporation a lot of power over them. With no formal, overarching agreement, the Corporation hire Legion enforcers on short-term contracts or commission. Legion soldiers are a familiar sight on most Corporate space stations, facilities, and spacecraft.

The Kaltoran Problem

According to most Corporate citizens, the Kaltorans are a misguided, reckless, and frustrating race. They refuse to sign nearly any agreements with the Corporation, and if they ever do, they are more than happy to just disregard them as they see fit. They also have an utter disregard for the importance of money, preferring to barter for physical goods and services.

Despite this constant friction, the Corporation makes some effort to maintain a working relationship with the Kaltorans, motivated by their need to trade with the Kaltorans for raw materials such as food and minerals.

Economy

Exports: Fuel, Small Goods, and Transportation Services.
Imports: Enforcement Services (Legion), Exotic Goods, Unskilled Labour (Nephilim), Food and Water (Kaltoran).

Credit Chips and Banking

The economy of the Corporation is vast and complex, with the majority of calculations done behind the scene by stock market supercomputers.

Each bank of the Corporation may issue its own currency, created by making loans. This has proved helpful: if a prominent bank goes bankrupt, it only collapses the part of the economy tied to its brand of currency rather than all of it. Credit Chips (cr), used for nearly all smaller transactions, are not technically currency but rather an indicator to which all currencies are compared. The value of Credit Chips is fixed to the value of energy, which is the main commodity of the Corporation in the form of fuel. There is always demand for energy, and thus there is always demand for Credit Chips.

Because of the complexity of background transactions, Credit Chips are not simple minted coins. Each chip is a tiny computer that constantly buys and sells shares to maintain a stable value. Only a tiny fraction of the total economy is tracked on physical Credit Chips; the vast majority exists in stocks and on computers as numbers. For that reason, bank cards are used for most transactions.

Flesh Drone Workers

With the Corporation populations' dislike of manual labour and limited physical potential, almost all manual labour is done by machines or biological drones, known as Flesh. These near-mindless workers are bio-engineered by the Nephilim and provided to the Corporation as part of the Nephilim Trade Pact. Flesh drones can be found doing all types of manual labour: mining, farming, and manufacturing being the main three. On rare occasion they have also been used as an extremely rudimentary fighting force, but the Legion is generally preferred for this role.

Hydrogen Fuel

One of the main sources of fuel in the galaxy is hydrogen, harvested from the gas giant Alabaster. A flexible fuel, it can be used in volatile combustion engines or sophisticated fusion reactors. The Corporation are meticulous and vigilant not only to maintain their near-monopoly on fuel production within the Haven system, but also to maintain its high value, not allowing the market to be flooded with surplus resources.

Synth Steel

Living in underground cities for over one hundred years has given the Kaltorans a surplus of ability and equipment for mining. Their stubborn refusal to sign any trade agreements with the Corporation has pushed the Corporation to develop Synthetic Steel, or Synth Steel for short.

Although a pain to repair, this strong carbon polymer is an abundant resource, primarily used in buildings, small goods, and spacecraft.

Merchant Ships

Making use of Synth Steel and their vast production network, the Corporation produce a wide range of transport spacecraft.

Medium-sized merchant ships are by far the most efficient form of transportation within the turbulent Haven system. Large spacecraft are just too much of a liability, not flexible enough to avoid trouble and too expensive to take risks with.

Science and Technology

Scientific and technological developments within the Corporation are primarily handled by R&D departments of large companies. To Corporates, there is no purpose to science unless it yields a sellable product, leading them to focus on engineering and applied science rather than theoretical or pure research. Most of the time, profiting from scientific endeavours requires cutting corners. This is done most often in two ways: outsourcing to unethical Nephilim researchers and reverse engineering pre-War technologies.

Nephilim Partnership

A sizeable portion of the Nephilim Trade Pact is their ongoing research partnership. The Corporation regularly commission the Nephilim to conduct scientific research on their behalf. Not only are the Nephilim very good at it, but they also underestimate the value of Corporation Credits.

Exploration

Many research companies within the Corporation specialise in exploring the ruins of Haven, primarily motivated to find technology they can reverse engineer and sell. These ruins include Kaltoran ruins, Archon facilities, and ancient Nephilim warships. These missions are often successful, so freelance ships and chartered crew are hired on a regular basis.

"See that decoratively blackened patch? Synth Steel, so you know it's all quality."
– Corporate Ship Sales, with a straight face.

"See that cook-n-skewer? It can also be used for food prep, so it's not just a weapon"
– Kaltoran 'back of the ship' sales.

Genetics

Created by the Archons

The Vargarti (now known as the Corporation) were rejected by their creators, the Archons, as inferior – a failed creation. With only a few thousand made, they were not given a planet of their own but relegated to the care of another race.

Given a small island to occupy, constrained in their travels, and with enforced birth control, the Vargarti were never given the opportunity to progress as a culture… not until the X'ion War freed them.

Their rejection has been a defining feature for the Vargarti. Eventually, they rejected their racial identity and embraced a social system in which any individual can succeed or fail based on their own merits.

Overlooked by X'ion

During the Great War, X'ion's forces bombarded the Vargarti home world, Varsphere, with an array of genetically engineered viruses. These viruses were designed to target the primary population of the planet, overlooking the Vargarti, as they only occupied a miniscule part of the planet.

No Genetic Gifts

Unlike the other races, the Corporation have no discernable genetic gifts to set them apart. This has become a source of cultural pride for the Corporates, who owe their affluence and success to their personal ability and willpower, not to genetic gifts.

If their hard cultural upbringing was to thank for the Corporates' admirable social abilities and management skills, then this creates many concerns for the next generation of Corporates, who currently enjoy some measure of affluence and comfort.

Despite a lack of scientific evidence, many claim that the Corporation's social cohesion is the result of hardwired genetic traits, potentially an unforeseen and overlooked result of the Archon's genetic engineering. The Corporation vehemently opposes this position; though such a theory does not attribute their success to the Archons, it does diminish their pride in their own ability and success.

The Free Enterprise emerged from Ley Line jump space, its bulk taking time to extricate from the luminescent space bubble. Far below, the gas giant Alabaster burned with a constant golden hue. Its reflection in the Free Enterprise's chrome finish would've been impressive, if anyone had been watching from outside.

Grayson Lampwick watched from the captain's chair as the landing lights of the orbital city Alabaster 1 came into view. With a motion he ordered their navigator to bring them down. One barely noticeable tilt later and they were hurtling towards the docking bay.

They'd been gone for seven weeks. After a quick stop on Eden, they'd picked up cargo from Gehenna, then been stranded in space for a week by a broken Jump Drive. Finally they were heading home.

Grayson allowed himself a tiny sigh as the familiar towers of Alabaster 1 drew closer. His apartment was buried within, impossible to see from outside the station, but very much there and waiting.

"Take us down," he said, addressing their Legion helmsman whose name he'd yet to learn. "I need to step off the bridge to make a call."

Grayson rose from his chair and left the bridge, tracing the all-too-familiar path to his quarters. The part about the call had been a lie, but he felt no shame. In reality, he simply needed to check his appearance. It was a peculiar part of Corporation culture that was all but actual law: tend to one's appearance always, always look like you are successful. Grayson had allowed himself to slip during their time away, but it was time to return.

The floor-length mirror in his quarters was waiting. Grayson studied his features, noting changes as he went. The stubble would have to vanish. He'd grown accustomed to wearing his shirt loose. His jet-black hair, neatly slicked to the left, was mostly fine. In fact, to a casual non-Corp observer his appearance would be pristine. However, Grayson had spent most of his thirty-one years on several Alabaster stations, where outward perfection was simply a minimum standard.

He picked up his razor, then paused and activated the wall speaker. A Kaltoran tune he'd heard on Gehenna played over the speakers, entitled "Kadash Memories". He'd heard the song playing over the speakers in the docking bay, and had secretly had the file transferred to his quarters. The Kaltoran music industry was an odd scene, but at least they had a music scene. The general opinion back home on music and art was that it was great to have, but there was no money in it.

Half an hour later, perfectly groomed and garbed in his best Octanto™ grey suit with matching overcoat and golden tie, he emerged to find that they were finishing the docking process. A glance out of the front view-screen confirmed that his personal assistant was waiting for him on the docking platform.

Grayson smiled and instinctively adjusted his tie as he prepared to re-enter society.

***

Having been born on Alabaster Six, Grayson was from birth at a financial and social disadvantage. Six was mostly inhabited by low-income workers, who were themselves outnumbered by the Flesh: Nephilim-made biological drones, created to do most of the manual labour. Though inferior to robotic drones, they were far cheaper.

No truly successful person came from Alabaster 6, and few ever visited. It was an industrial station, where work equalled sweat, while the executives on Alabaster 1 sipped their refined beverages as sleek ships with every modern comfort available whizzed by them on all sides.

Nevertheless, Grayson was wearing a tie and waistcoat before he could walk. His parents were part of the very first colonists, those who built these space stations. His father laid the steelwork for over three dozen landing platforms on station 6.

Before he was even born, his parents had signed Grayson into a "secure future" work programme, otherwise known as indentured servitude. That title may have been a little dramatic, but it was a beneficial arrangement. The Corporation had paid for all of Grayson's upbringing, and in exchange he'd completed a ten-year construction apprenticeship to pay back his debt. He was only twelve when the work began.

To a member of another race, Grayson's upbringing would've seemed like a happy one, even luxurious. However, Grayson was born with a fierce desire to better himself, to transcend his limits.

By the age of twenty-two, Grayson Lampwick had been handpicked as an apprentice at a robotics firm. He was the first child of his family to set foot outside their home station. Two years later he had reached the level of executive, in charge of his own division. By the time he was twenty-six, he'd replaced a manager twenty years his senior as head of external affairs.

For Grayson, this was the ultimate goal. He'd not only managed to claw his way up from the lower echelons of society, but now he would be in command of his own ship, liaising with trade outposts on far flung worlds. He'd risen so far that even Alabaster couldn't hold him.

***

The first thing Grayson saw upon disembarking was the fixed smile of Miriam Hedgely, his personal secretary and stand-in while he was off-world on business.

She used to do his job, and while she was technically in charge while he was away, he still held complete control over the division. Grayson wasn't a vindictive man, but Miriam Hedgely was exactly the type of person he resented: born to a wealthy family, privileged in every way, convinced that she had some kind of birthright. The only reason she'd taken the job in the first place was to bide her time while she thought of the best way to stab her boss in the back.

So far, Grayson had merely found her attempts to be amusing distractions. She stood with her hands crossed in front of her, wearing a sleek green jacket and skirt. Grayson noted with some satisfaction that she'd gained a few pounds.

"Welcome back, Mr Lampwick." Miriam said, narrowing her eyes as if the words brought her pain.

"Thank you, Miriam," he replied. He didn't make eye contact; he knew the lack of gesture would rub her the wrong way. "I trust you ran things smoothly while I was away?"

His secretary chose to interpret this as a statement, and didn't reply. Meanwhile, Grayson pulled out his terminal and checked the schedule that had been automatically uploaded to his headset as soon as he'd arrived.

The terminals appeared to be merely sleek tubes of metal, as this was all they needed to be. A touch of a button on the top projected an hologram, which could be navigated using only one's eye movements. The previous model had been clunky squares, controlled by unreliable finger movements, leading some to return to screen technology. Grayson had pre-ordered his own terminal to his personal specifications.

When someone grows up poor and finds they're fabulously wealthy later in life, they tend to make impulse purchases.

14:30 – Executive Debrief.
15:30 – Final Cargo Check.
16:15 – Investor Meeting.
17:30 – Off-World Report Due.

Ten seconds in, and his schedule was already full. Grayson noted with displeasure that the report was due at the end of the day, despite the entire day being filled with meetings. He'd almost grown to enjoy the slower pace of space travel... and yet, Corporates were by nature a hard-working people. If his day wasn't full, Grayson would have found a way to fill it.

His office was exactly as he'd left it: spotless marble floors, Klargen-skin rug, holo-artwork that shimmered slightly as it displayed a roaming view of Mishpacha's island-spotted ocean. The view from his office faced the docking bay, which in Alabaster was practically a panorama. Grayson sank into his expensive chair with as much obvious satisfaction as possible, enjoying Miriam's reaction in his peripheral vision.

Silent, lightly armoured figures crept down the richly appointed hall, following a small, hovering sensor-studded drone, pointing their Disruptor rifles and Ion pistols into each ornate nook as they passed.

"Contact, thirty measures ahead. Sensor drone detects security system and combat drones. Possible target behind desk."

Dark-visored heads perked slightly as their focus and reflexes sharpened. Hand signals bought four of the six to the front, while a pair covered the hall they had just moved down.

"Holt and Smythe, Disruptor the left cabinet. Don't miss or the combat drones will be the least of our worries. Thatchen, you're with me; take the drones down."

The door was quickly kicked open as a Disruptor burst melted its unshielded electronic lock.

The large balding man behind the desk moved for his alarm button, pressing it down a half second too late to call his Legion security force, as Holt sprayed the computer nexus behind the cabinet. The combat drones fell to the quiet thrum of Thatchen's Ion pistol, leaving the four soldiers alone with a very scared man in a incredibly nice Octanto™ suit.

"Now then, Mr Executive," the leader said, pulling off his helmet, revealing a young, attractive Corp male. His pleasant smile contrasted with his Ion pistol, making his polite words a threat. "We should have a chat about… compassion, specifically: what will happen to you if you try to use familial threats against union members."

"So, developments," he said, laying his terminal on the desk.

"Most recently," Miriam replied, standing in front of the desk, "we've received word from Theodore Bolt."

Grayson laughed as she mentioned the name.

"And how is our most unconventional of contractors?"

"Apparently their mission was a success, despite minor setbacks. Mechonids were involved."

"Of course they were," Grayson said, studying Theodore's message. "That ragtag crew of his couldn't go for a quiet drink in the Electric District without bringing down the sky on their heads."

"Indeed."

Grayson studied the news from the last few weeks without a great deal of interest. New Ley Line drive developments on Alabaster 3. A feature article recommended to him by a colleague, detailing the benefits of Legion bodyguards. News of the recovery of the Draz industry.

The world was too big to worry about anything other than his own division. In his personal inbox, Grayson noticed a blinking message from his family. He would reply to them later, after the meetings.

"Alright," he said, sighing as he leant back in his chair. "Send the first client in."

Miriam nodded and turned to go.

"Oh, and Miriam?"

She turned.

"I'd really love a cup of tea."

She bristled, then nodded again and left. With the last few free seconds he had left in the day, Grayson leant back and smiled. Who ever said the life of an executive was no fun?

***

"The life of an executive is no fun," Grayson thought as he stumbled back into his apartment many hours later. It'd only been a half day, but the meetings had been relentless. He'd then stayed behind to catch up on his reports before grabbing the last shuttle of the night back to his apartment.

It was a less familiar setting than his office, and far less so than the chrome-lined hallways of the Free Enterprise, but it was still home.

"Welcome back, sir!"

Atomos, Grayson's personal cleaning bot, rose from its cradle in the entrance hall and hovered to meet its master. Once again it was the latest model, despite the fact that its owner's apartment was so scarcely used that it barely needed cleaning.

Grayson grunted a greeting and stepped around the exuberant metal orb and into the lounge. The window overlooked the Electric District; he would often spend entire evenings simply gazing down at the plethora of activity, imagining himself to be one of those free souls who nightly engaged in such revelry. Of course, he would be responding to work-related messages the whole time.

"The place should be squeaky clean," Atomos chirped, swinging from side to side. "Just this morning I gave the cooker a good do-over. And you've never even used it, so you can bet it came up looking great."

"Any messages?" Grayson asked, sinking onto his couch.

"Fourteen, mostly from your mother. I assured her that you were off-world, but she kept calling anyway."

"And the others?"

"From your father, telling you to call your mother. Did I mention how many times I've washed the external windows? I know you love to look at them."

"Through them, Atomos. But thanks."

"No problem!"

The drone returned to its cradle, and the man heaved a sigh of relief.

bleep

It was a terminal message.

Recommendation required on the Bio-Brace advertisement campaign. Seed all stations?

Grayson started to type a response, but while he was doing so three new messages appeared. He leant back in his chair and turned his gaze upwards, beyond the bright lights below and towards the hazy corona of the gas giant shining throughout the darkened skyscrapers.

One building stood out, mostly because it towered above the rest and appeared to be made from pure silver, lined with golden streaks.

The Executive Headquarters.

From his seat, the building looked so small that Grayson could have reached out with one hand and picked it up like a toy rocket. Not that he'd ever played with rockets as a boy – unlike the rest of the latest generation of Lampwicks, Grayson had spent his childhood buried in third-hand robotics manuals – but it was an amusing thought.

The colossal structure stood as a shining example of Corporation triumph, how they'd cast off their mantle of inferiority and taken to the stars to craft a new future for the entire system. They hadn't needed any genetic gifts, only hard work and an appreciation of the power of currency.

More importantly, the Executive Headquarters was where the almighty Board of Management made decisions that shaped the future of the cosmos. Grayson smiled as he slipped into his usual momentary fantasy, which simply involved him holding a business card: Grayson V. Lampwick, BM.

Not a holo-card either. It would be real paper, with real ink. Those two letters would mean everything, especially to a former resident of Alabaster 6.

Grayson was jolted out of this reverie by a blinking message on his terminal, highlighted in red. He opened it and scanned the contents before deleting all traces of it from the system. With a final, wistful glance at the carefree masses down below, Grayson donned his overcoat and headed up to the roof.

***

The man who greeted him on the deserted upper platform had short black hair, an equally dark trench-coat, and chillingly blank eyes the colour of charcoal. Nevertheless, the man bore the vaguest hint of a smile.

"Mr Lampwick," said Terrence Lightworth, not bothering to remove his hands from his pockets. He stood on the edge of the building, not at all bothered by the sheer drop.

"Terrence," Grayson replied. He made sure the door to the landing platform was securely shut before advancing, stopping a few feet away. "I didn't request your services."

"That doesn't mean you don't need them," the dark-haired man replied. "Welcome back, by the way. Have you called your family?"

Grayson remained silent, but bristled at the thought of this man being anywhere near his private life. He knew Terrence well enough by now to let the man get to his point.

"Proteon Electrics," Terrence went on, still wearing his miniscule smile. "They're dangerously close to developing Bio-Brace technology. In fact, they copied your patents."

"I have lawyers who can deal with that."

Terrence's smile vanished, though it made little difference to his persona.

"And they'll bog you down in a legal quagmire from which no one will escape unscathed," he replied. "Or perhaps you'd like me to take care of the problem. For a fee."

For what seemed like the longest time, Grayson stood motionless. Every time, he promised himself that, from that moment on, he would play it straight. And yet the world of Corporate business was cutthroat, with Terrence's ilk easy to come by for those endowed with proper funds. The Bio-Brace was a revolution that could send Grayson straight to the list of candidates for the Board of Management. The fact that Terrence even knew about it spoke volumes of his expertise.

He swallowed, hating himself for this one weakness.

"Are you still hanging around with your explosive friend?" Grayson asked. Terrence shrugged.

"If you need that kind of job…"

"No. Killing is too far."

"Suit yourself. I work better alone."

They stared each other down, Grayson unwilling to make the next move and Terrence seemingly unbothered by the silence.

"I'll be in touch," the executive said, finally. A flicker of annoyance crossed Terrence's face, but he merely inclined his head.

"Until then."

Hands shaking, Grayson turned on his heel and took the express elevator back to his quarters. He dismissed Atomos with a wave, slammed the door behind him, and ran a hand through his hair.

He hadn't said yes. This could still be solved through other means. He was good enough at his job to speed production, after which… it may already be too late.

"Atomos, Nerve."

The drone delivered a glass of the liquid into his hand, and Grayson sank back into the sofa, gazing at his reflection in the liquid. A handsome face stared back at him, a face that had aged quickly over his tenure as an executive. He'd started out so early, fresh-faced and with a burning passion in his eyes. Every boss he'd worked under had noticed it, until there was practically no other option but promotion.

Even in the hazy reflection of the glass, Grayson could see the change. The fire had died down to cinders, albeit still burning warm enough for him to throw himself into his job and achieve constant success.

He'd regained some of that passion while travelling off-world. It was almost unavoidable, traversing new worlds and facing new challenges, that the old passions would be awakened. For those brief few weeks, Grayson had felt like himself again. Not some Corporate drone, but a young man with eyes full of determination.

With a smile, the man drained the glass of Nerve and slammed it down on the coffee table.

No more shortcuts. Grayson V. Lampwick, future Board Member, didn't take the easy road. He tore along the straight path and did things his own way, possibly while tossing high-powered grenades at the incompetent masses who chose the easy road.

Grayson had never been good at metaphors. He was, however, a businessman. Taking his terminal in hand, he opened a channel to Miriam's personal quarters.

"Sir, it's past midnight," came the icy reply. Grayson ignored her, too eager to voice his idea.

"Miriam, I want you to call our Nephilim lab and have them shut down the Bio-Brace operation."

"You mean our most viable project?"

"That's the one. However, leak a few of our designs onto the Data Stream. Date them as early as possible."

"And what, exactly, will fill the gaping hole in our operations?" Grayson flipped to Theodore's message, where pictures of their mysterious prize were displayed alongside a rundown of everything that had happened on their mission.

"It won't matter," he replied, his face illuminated in a purple glow. "I know robotics technology when I see it. And I do believe we may

"Alright Audrid, you need to get those clothes off and go see Thomas in costumes." Audrid groaned as the well-groomed gargoyle of a set manager continued. "You need to be back in fifteen, or you'll run the shoot late again."

This was delivered to her slim retreating figure, as she hurried through the narrow Synth Steel corridors backstage in search of Thomas, the studio's costume designer.

"So what's the change?" Audrid asked jogging into the cramped room of floor-to-bulkhead clothing racks and flung off her top, her toned and genetically altered body barely getting a glance as Thomas snatched a mock-camouflage outfit off the racks.

"Get these on, quickly!" he said, scurrying past into the props room. She sighed, pulling the new clothing on, her frizzy red hair contrasting boldly against her elegantly mottled shoulders and neck.

"Didn't we just settle into the Octanto contract?" she called, pulling on a low-cut military-esque blazer.

"Body Count outbid them about three hours ago, and we haven't even gotten a memo yet! Take this!" He bustled out holding a realistically large weapon prop, the type only a Legion could carry without looking out of place.

"OK, fine… but keep my old costume ready in case Octanto makes a counter bid."

The court speaks to our online Stream audience "We now return to the thrilling pay-per-view court!" Above the judge's bench hangs a flashing neon sign, which reads "Protectron™ Pistol". A billboard for Draz Soda clings to the podium. The judge speaks. "Mr Collins, you have pleaded guilty of costing CorpSafe millions of Credits in life insurance and stock. Mr Collins, what assurance have you for the court that these liabilities will be paid?"

Collins's lawyer stands and while looking directly at the camera says, "Mr Friendly of Criminal Liabilities Firm (We protect your caper), for the defendant." He then turns to the judge. "Your honour, I refer you to exhibit D-1, a contract signed by both my client and the Body Count Conglomerate for the assassination of the CorpSafe CEO. In clause 112, the Conglomerate clearly indemnifies my client against any financial liabilities directly resulting from the homicide."

The Judge responds "Is a representative of Body Count here today?"

"Yes, your honour. Peters of CorpLaw (Biggest, and Best!), stand for The Body Count Conglomerate."

As the newcomer takes the floor, the animated Draz billboard flashes "Only 1.99cr". The CorpLaw lawyer speaks. "Your honour, had Collins fully upheld his end of the contract, we wouldn't be having this conversation. Clause 233a of that same contract required that Mr Collins not be caught. By his negligence, not only has he left his contract unfulfilled by being captured, but he has also cost the reputation of Body Count by having his contract made public knowledge through this hearing. Your honour, we submit that the indemnity clause no longer applies and that the defendant is personally liable for both CorpSafe's life expenses and for real and punitive damages to my client."

His lawyer cautions him, but Collins speaks in his own defence. "Your honour, I have provided a copy of my credentials to you. In addition to my record I will take you and the court step by step through my successful assassination. This will be corroborated by a video recording taken from my own camera. You will see from this footage and my statement that I have upheld clause 233a, making every reasonable effort to remain uncaught, therefore maintaining Body Count's liability."

The judge declares, "Very well. The court will review this new evidence to determine whether the liability rests with the defendant or Body Count..." The judge smiles at the camera "... after this short ad break."

have stumbled upon the find of the decade."

He ended the terminal message and opened a new one, keying in the recipients as his parents. It was too late to call, but he had all night to write and tell them everything he'd been up to. For once, business could wait.

***

Just a few hours later, Grayson stood in his almost-top-floor office and watched the sun rise over Alabaster. It was such a tiny pinprick of light at first, small enough to grasp in one fist and crush with ease. Then it crested the luminescent planet's sphere, and rays of light scattered throughout the jumbled skyscrapers of Alabaster 1. Ships whizzed back and forth far below, advertisements screamed for attention from every building, but Grayson could only focus on the sun.

He turned when the glow was too bright and returned to his desk, where his explanation for shutting down the Bio-Brace project was already prepared.

Let his rivals have their fun with stolen ideas. Once the news of obvious fraud was leaked, their stocks would drop like a stone. Meanwhile, Grayson's division would be the first to properly dissect Mechonid technology. That was a prize no one could imitate.

The clock struck eight, and Grayson sighed as he anticipated his first meeting of the day in half an hour. He cast a wistful glance out the window at the departing spacecraft, and found himself longing for open space. Nevertheless, there was work to be done here.

Before settling down to finish his report, Grayson hesitated, then opened his terminal. His song list was short, but only one caught his attention. His finger hovered over the play button. Did top-class executives on Alabaster 1 listen to music while they worked?

Grayson thought for a moment, then shrugged and pressed the button. He smiled as the soulful tunes of Kadash Memories wafted from the speaker.

Let the snobs on Alabaster 1 toil in silence. After all, Grayson Lampwick was working-class scum from Alabaster 6; he would work however he darn well pleased.

Kaltoran

Creator: Archons
Average Height: 1.65m
Average Weight: 70kg
Average Life Span: 120 years

Home Planet: Kadash
Former Home Planet: Eden
Total Population: 8.2 million + 2.6 million Dark Tribe (estimated)
Yearly Population Growth Rate: +19%

Years Since Re-emergence into Space: 5 years

Distinctive Physical Features

Dreadlock hair.
Four pointed ears.

Kaltoran Trait, pg: 340

» Reduce all Untrained Primary Skill Roll penalties by 1 (except Wealth).
» +1 Awareness, Command, and Small Arms.
» +1 Fate.
» +2 Defence vs Stealth.
» Reduce all Limited Vision and Low Light penalties by 1 Step.
» Gain Language: Kaltoran.
» -1 Wealth.
» -2 Maximum Focus.
» Unwanted Flashback: If you roll triples with any Fate re-roll, you immediately gain a Minor Psychological Condition (which may be removed with an appropriate Extended Care Healing Roll).
» Complication: Prejudice from Corporation.

Preferred Combat Equipment

Self-propelled and irradiated weaponry.
Smoke and dummy shells.
Electro-Grav equipment.
Combat suit or tactical armour.

Kaltoran History

The Kaltorans were favoured by their Archon creators and, for this, were especially hated by the X'ion. The genocide of the Kaltorans during the Great X'ion War was monstrous; it has been said that the Kaltorans suffered most in the war. In the end, their home world, Eden, was turned from a beautiful, fertile planet into a poisoned wasteland. The few Kaltorans who survived fled to to Kadash, where they descended to the bottom of the ocean and built undersea settlements. Huddled in the deep and the dark, the survivors planned to never return to the stars.

Life on Kadash was short, dark, and brutal. Huddled in their overcrowded cities and gripped by fear, the refugees savagely fought over what few resources they had. Isolating themselves into small groups, known as Dark Tribes, the Kaltorans spent generations out of the light and gradually lost their eyesight. Often the desperation was so palpable that cannibalism and slavery became commonplace. These nightmarish times lasted for seventy long years before any semblance of hope emerged; however, the deep psychological scars from these times are sustained through the curse of their genetic memories.

The return to a better life began with a new generation of Kaltorans who were tired of living in constant fear. Restarting an ancient nuclear reactor, these Kaltorans seized its power for hydroponics and lights, and they restored their eyesight and the eyesight of their children through biological and electronic implants. This rebuilding of society became known as the Founding, and those Kaltorans as the Founders. However, not all Kaltorans were ready for a new world, and many Dark Tribes remained in the tunnels below.

The Founders were much bolder than their parents, but they still feared that the Nephilim lay in wait above their planet. When they began to hear the Corporate ship transmissions, it was clear the Great War was long over. Millions of young, pioneering Kaltorans were quick to return to space in a effort to make a better life for themselves and to give their children better memories.

Government and Law

Government: Tribal Federation.
Leadership: Elders.

Elders

The Kaltorans have no centralized government and are instead organised around large family groupings. Each family is led by a senior member, often referred to as the Elder. A group of Elders from the most prominent families meet on a regular basis to discuss political matters for the betterment of their city or settlement. These meetings, simply called Gatherings, are more like informal dinners with talking points than they are a government. Each family in a Gathering is a free and independent entity but is accountable to the whole through reputation rather than law.

Each family has their own method for choosing their Elder. Most families choose the oldest capable leader, whereas some Elders are appointed by the previous one. Each Elder seeks the consensus of the family, and the power of their leadership is a reflection of their reputation as a good leader.

Reputation

Much of what gives an individual or a family higher status than another is their reputation. Kaltorans who are trustworthy, just, strong, bold, and kind are likely to enjoy greater status, as are those who have a record of good and adventurous deeds. However, Kaltorans seen as callous, greedy, or selfish are not well liked and often disowned by their families. The genetic memories which Kaltorans experience reinforce this status; children remember the deeds of their parents, both good and bad.

Enforcement and Provision

The Kaltorans do not have a true legal system; instead, each Kaltoran has a personal responsibility to care for those in need and enforce justice as they see fit. This justice is not formally codified or explained; it is up to the conscience of the individual. As a result, most Kaltorans overlook minor misdemeanours and deal out very harsh punishments to serious crimes.

Other races who visit Kaltoran settlements sometimes find that the lack of clear legal distinctions lead to a variety of difficulties. However, there is some accountability when families disagree over the fairness of a situation: the Elders of both families will meet and come to an arrangement. In the interest of peace, this often leads to Elders punishing their own family members for dealing out justice too harshly.

Minor Crime, Examples
» Theft for survival – No punishment.
» Theft for greed – Beating and/or the victim takes some of the perpetrator's possessions.

Major Crime, Examples
» Murder – Death.
» Rape – Public beating and then death.

Creating a Kaltoran Character

Founder

Of all the Kaltorans, the Founders are the most industrious: they built the present Kaltoran civilisation from the ashes of the past. While they are fond of tradition and find change hard, they understand that it is necessary and inevitable. Many Founders leave their homes in order to make a better life for their families, often working as merchants or explorers.

Recommended Skills
» Leadership
» Culture
» Mechanics

Recommended Traits
» Culture: Jack of all Trades
» Mechanics: Tweak
» Exotic: Lucky Edge

Pioneer

These Kaltorans tend to be young, adventurous, and fun-loving. They are often reckless thrill-seekers, keen to prove themselves to their families and to make new memories for their future children. Eager to make their mark on the Haven system, they take their sense of personal justice with them and often get themselves into trouble when the laws of the other races (especially the Corporation) do not serve their idea of the common good.

Recommended Skills
» Physical
» Awareness
» Electronics

Recommended Traits
» Physical: Reaction Training
» Electronics: Weapon Smith
» Small Arms: Dirty Fighter

Dark Tribes

Dark and brooding, many among the Dark Tribes are as paranoid as they are dangerous. Those who leave the familiar darkness of their homes are often exiles or seeking to settle a score with the Nephilim. These blind (and often cannibalistic) warriors are infamous throughout Haven, despite their rarity.

Recommended Skills
» Physical
» Resolve
» Survival

Recommended Traits
» Perception: 6th Sense
» Survival: Self-Reliant
» Tactical: Swift Shadow

Founder   Pioneer   Dark Tribe

Kaltoran Culture

Family

Family is the most important part of Kaltoran society. Family got them through their dark history, making it central to their lives. Family comes before anything else: Kaltorans live and work for their families and if necessary die and kill for their families. New family ties are created through marriage and adoption, and both of which are important and celebrated with large ceremonies. Each family is a subculture in its own right; each family has its own traditions and values, which new members are expected to follow. Though family members are expected to follow their family's traditions, families do not generally try to force their own traditions on others, and thus Kaltoran families can have extremely varied traditions.

It is common for multiple generations of Kaltorans to live in the same house. Since a single couple with six or more children is not uncommon, houses are often large and packed. A typical Kaltoran house might include two grandparents, six or more parents, and over a dozen children.

Gender

Gender distinction is important in Kaltoran society. Women and men are considered equal in their value to the family, but many families have distinct gender roles, especially in more traditional families. The Dark Tribes have strict gender roles: men provide food, women keep the home and raise children, but both fight. The Founders are less strict, only applying their expectations to married couples. The Pioneers have similar distinctions, with most women preferring to raise children, while the men often prefer to be the providers, but this is not always true.

Both men and women can be the family Elder. However, some families prefer a particular style of leader, leading them to favour one gender over the other.

Ancestors

The Kaltorans practice a religion of praying to ancestors for guidance. This is more than an unfounded superstition for them, as they have access to the genetic memory of their ancestors. A Kaltoran might meditate on a problem or question and pray to their ancestors for help, often finding the answer to their question deep in their ancestral memories. Because these prayers for knowledge are answered, the Kaltorans give reverence to the ancestors as thanks. Families often have busts or sculptures of especially revered ancestors on altars in their homes.

Feuds

Because families are distinct units and no central government exists, feuds between families are common. Some families have grudges that go back a hundred years, and their genetic memories guarantee that any slight will not be forgotten. Since the Founding, many families have turned murderous feuds into competitive rivalries. One such rivalry exists between the prominent Swagger and Jinx families, who regularly compete over influence and glory.

"Well, we don't have no reason for your kind to be around here, y'see. We don't take kindly to intrusions by monsters, even polite ones."

– Derek Shiv, Dark Tribe Elder dispensing local "justice" by hanging a Nephilim merchant.

Always Armed

Nearly all Kaltorans carry a weapon at all times, partly because there is a lack of any official law enforcement and partly because of their violent past. Weapons are carried like a badge of honour, and many weapons are family heirlooms. It is common for a Kaltoran to get their first (low-powered) gun at age eight.

Dark Tribes

The Dark Tribes live in a culture of fear, afraid of the X'ion and his Nephilim army who haunt their genetic memories. They even fear other Kaltorans, Dark Tribe or not, holding to their hundred-year memories of darkness and terror. Dark Tribe Kaltorans do not trust anyone outside their own family, and conflicts between tribes are common. Dark Tribespeople remain blind even though the technology exists to fix their eyes, mostly because they would have to trust others to get their eyesight fixed. The Dark Tribes are thought to be dwindling, as they are reluctant to have children, and even when they do they often send the children above to be adopted by Kaltorans not imprisoned by fear.

Founders

The Founders were the first Kaltorans to leave the darkness and try and create a better life for themselves. They are proud of this legacy and are often skilled and industrious. Despite making great cultural strides, they prefer to cooperate only with other Kaltorans, avoiding the other races and keeping to their own cities. The Founders are cautiously hopeful and slowly work towards a better future for all Kaltorans.

Pioneers

The newest major subculture of Kaltorans, Pioneers are keen for a new life away from their homes, a blank slate to write upon. The Pioneers work hard to rediscover old Kaltoran facilities, to settle both old worlds and new, and to explore the depths of space. Pioneers are more likely to trust outsiders, as they hope to replace their dark memories with new ones. Almost all Kaltorans who have returned to space are Pioneers, and because of this the other races sometimes see the Pioneers as representative of the whole of Kaltoran culture.

Relationship with Other Races

The pioneering Kaltorans want a clean slate in the galaxy, so they desire to get along with the other races. However, their enthusiasm for becoming friends has some challenging obstacles.

Corporation Culture Clash

The culture of the Kaltoran people is on the whole incompatible with the Corporation. While the Kaltorans value personal favours, good deeds, and mutual respect, the Corporation values credits and is happy to break any agreement not solidified in a contract — and Kaltorans don't sign contracts. The Corporation often lay claim to ancient facilities or areas of space, but the Kaltorans will then move in, taking what they want. Corps consider this stealing, but the Kaltorans do not if there are no Corporates living there.

Nephilim Memories

Although the Kaltorans have excellent intentions of forgiving the Nephilim for their past actions, their genetic memories make this difficult. Each Kaltoran has memories of the atrocities committed against them by the Nephilim during the Great War, and it is difficult to relate to a being who looks like those who destroyed your world and your family. It is not uncommon for a Kaltoran to experience flashbacks and post-traumatic stress when encountering Nephilim for the first time, which makes any peaceful contact awkward at best and sometimes simply impossible.

Legion Kindred Spirits

The Kaltorans get along well with the Legion. Outsiders may find this surprising, considering that the Legion prefer order and the Kaltorans may appear to thrive in anarchy. However, they both value practicality, loyalty, respect, and family.

Even when the Legion come to odds with the Kaltorans, usually because of a Corp mercenary contract, the Kaltorans are inclined to blame the Corporation rather than the mercenaries. The Legion and Kaltorans also have an unspoken barter agreement, where the Kaltorans trade salvaged Legion equipment from the Great War for mercenary services or munitions.

Another Broken Creation

The Kaltorans are in many ways a broken race; their gift of genetic memory has become a curse due to their violent past. As such, they sympathise with other broken Archon races, one of which being the Mechonids. Where other races kill Mechonids without thought the Kaltorans wish to understand them. But this curiosity won't stop them from killing a Mechonid if it puts them or their family in danger.

Economy

Exports: Food (Corporation) and Raw Minerals.
Imports: Fuel (Corporation) and Munitions (Legion).

Barter Economy

The Kaltoran economy is based on reciprocity rather than money. Items are traded directly for other items or for promises and favours. There is a general understanding that the exact value of the trade is unimportant; all that matters is that both parties in the trade feel that they have not been cheated.

International trade is primarily done through barter, which makes trading with the Corporation especially difficult as credits are not seen to have much value.

Bazaars

Kaltorans tend to conduct their trade at open markets of stalls with posted goods for barter and goods accepted in trade. In this way buyers can go stall to stall to find a barter match. If no single vendor has the desired item, a complex chain of trades will eventually result in the needed trade. Food and munitions are generally accepted for trade; however, the amount needed to barter for a highly valued item would be considerable and inconvenient to transport.

Favours and Promises

Sometimes an item is traded not for another item but for a favour or a promise that an item will eventually be produced. These promises and favours are not formal or official, but Kaltoran merchants often keep ledgers to track everyone who owes favours and promises.

Mining

The Kaltorans are talented and experienced miners, and they have made mining a cornerstone of their economy. Their settlements and cities tend to be vast excavations, which has allowed them to develop this unique expertise. Because they founded their cities on Kadash underground, there has always been significant amount of mining equipment available to them.

Conflict with the Corporation

Kaltorans and the Corporation commonly find themselves at odds in regards to mining within the Haven system. While the Kaltorans have an abundance of skills and equipment, they do not share the Corporation's passion for profit and business. The Corporation is keen to gain access to Kaltoran equipment and skills, but most Kaltorans find the Corporation's financial ambitions misguided at best.

Science and Technology

The Kaltorans have a gift for using salvaged technologies, and they don't often make things from scratch. However, deep within the memories of their ancestors lie the secrets to how these technologies work. They cannot access this knowledge consciously, but they can make use of it without realising it, jury-rigging it to make it work without the ability to explain how. One such technology is nuclear reactors, popular among Kaltorans because of the abundance of underground uranium on Kadash.

Cut 'n' Shut Ships

A popular method of spacecraft "design" in Kaltoran culture is called cut 'n' shut. In this method, two or sometimes more junk spacecraft are cut apart and re-joined to create a working nuclear-powered ship. Cut 'n' shut ships make up the vast majority of Kaltoran spacecraft, and salvage is one of the most important tools to Kaltorans.

Electro-Gravity

One powerful technology not lost to the Kaltorans is Electro-Gravity. It is used to create artificial gravity, but also for weaponry and to hold back the sea in certain Kaltoran settlements and spacecraft.

City Domes

Every Kaltoran city on Kadash is covered by a protective dome. These domes are often used to hold back the ocean, but some protect from orbital bombardment and conceal the city with camouflage. Some domes are simply reinforced steel, while others are made from Electro-Gravity fields or stealth technologies.

The machine clicked, whirled, belched steam, and groaned as it awoke. Hydraulics pumped and gears turned, gases whistled as they escaped, and a loud clunk came from deep within its bowels.

"What a mechanical marvel this is, what is it doing?"

"Nothing yet." Amos replied, "It's still booting up."

- Amos Jinx, turning on the lights.

Genetics

Favoured Children

The Archons, who made the Kaltorans, considered them an exceptional success, and found the genetic memories a unique triumph in genetic engineering. They favoured the Kaltoran race and showered them in affection, giving them the valuable Haven system along with many other solar systems to rule.

Genetic Memories

The Kaltorans were given the mixed gift of genetic memories by their Archon creators. At conception, Kaltoran child has a mind seeded with memories from both parents, grandparents, great grandparents, and perhaps even older ancestors. For each generation back a memory is, the harder it is to retain. These often-foggy memories are slowly gained as the Kaltoran goes through puberty.

This trait is a mixed blessing. The Kaltorans benefit from the skills and knowledge of their ancestors, but they are also cursed by terrible and haunting memories of their troubled history.

Note to GM

Kaltoran genetic memories can be a great way to start, progress, or develop a story or character.

Feel free to give your Kaltoran player characters a foggy or clear "flashback" to the memories of their ancestors at any time.

If a player character wishes to explore their genetic memories, they make a Resolve or Psychology Skill Roll.

Enhanced Senses

The Kaltorans are gifted with an exceptional sense of hearing, heightened further during their generations of time in the darkness. Many older Kaltorans were born blind, but the bio-tech remedy is relatively simple, and most Kaltorans have perfect vision as well as exceptional hearing.

Long Lifespan

Due to exception genetic coding, Kaltorans have long natural lifespans. Maturing quickly and ageing slowly, they are in their prime for far longer. Their lifespan leads to large families and allows older Kaltorans to still work and fight. Unfortunately, due to their brutal history, many Dark Tribe Kaltorans never lived to their elder years.

He was the embodiment of the night.

He was the silent protector, who struck from the shadows to advance the cause of the oppressed.

He feared nothing, neither man nor challenge.

He was completely lost.

Levi could've called for help over his commlink, but that didn't seem like something the embodiment of the night would resort to. Besides, anyone could be listening on the other side. Sarai could be listening. She'd already somehow managed to resist his charm and daring escapades, despite their constant contact working in the same docking bay.

Levi breathed out a long, dramatic sigh that echoed throughout the poorly lit tunnels beneath the pit city. The life of a dashing hero was lonely and cold, especially considering he'd been sent down there to fix the heating and hadn't managed to actually locate the central furnace grid. Levi pulled his oversized coat more tightly around his shoulders and raised his wrist, glancing again at the hologram map. Could hologram maps be displayed upside down? That would explain a lot.

His four ears twitching for any signs that he was getting close, the young Kaltoran tried to remember what his ancestors had learned about the area.

His ancestor Amos Thrift also became lost in the tunnels during routine maintenance. He'd nearly starved on the way out. It was a simpler time.

Maybe Amos Thrift wasn't the best source of knowledge.

His great, great uncle Joseph Thrift worked on board a waste transportation ship as a lowly engineer. He'd accidentally spilled his drink over the artificial gravity console, and the crew had been forced into zero-G for the rest of the voyage.

That memory hadn't been helpful. And the pit city didn't even exist while Uncle Joseph was alive.

His great grandmother Esther Renn, despite being a member of the higher-society, would sneak down to the caves near her estate. Or rather, she did so once and was nearly eaten by a Pit Worm. She spent the rest of her life with a crippling fear of the outdoors.

Fun though that memory had been to relive, Levi was now paranoid about Pit Worms. Unhelpful.

Genetic memories were a tricky business, as specific details were sometimes as hard to grasp as early childhood memories. Surely some of his ancestors had found their way around the pit city caves.

Levi glanced around and tried to find anything that seemed familiar.

Not a memory, but his cousin Adam had accidentally activated a dormant Mechonid and had nearly gotten his ears blasted clean off.

His grandmother Ezma had been born with a fear of heights. Given that Kaltorans now made their homes along the walls of a gigantic subterranean pit, her life was a series of nervous breakdowns.

His own father Jonathan had been a tunnel scout for his Dark Tribe in his teen years. He'd been demoted after a week due to getting stuck head-first in the gas vents no less than four times in a single day.

"Ah," Levi said out loud. "That's why Dad's claustrophobic."

"Come again?"

Levi wheeled around, his hand moving to the shock spanner he kept at his belt. It wasn't a necessary tool for heating maintenance, but it could potentially be used as a weapon against Pit Worms and general evildoers. The figure standing behind him in the tunnel was neither.

"You gonna shock me, lamebrain?" said Sarai Jinx, fellow maintenance engineer and the most beautiful creature on two legs Levi had ever laid eyes upon. Only the tips of her ears were visible through her long, curly white locks, which framed almond-shaped eyes that were the deepest and most gorgeous shade of mud. Levi didn't usually find mud to be attractive, but all that had changed when he'd met Sarai. She could even make mud look attractive. Even the grubby overalls she wore looked stunning. The way she stuck a spanner behind her ear made Levi's heart beat faster.

Not that he was in love, or anything. The embodiment of the night was above such things.

"Sarai," Levi squeaked, then he coughed and brought his voice down two octaves. "Uh, Sarai. What are you doing down here?"

"Seriously?" Sarai replied, striding past him whilst checking her own holo-map. "You've been down here for two hours. This job is basically just flipping a switch."

"Well, yeah," Levi said. "But I… uh, found some more stuff to do. Lots of broken things. Engineer work. Complex repairs. That kind of thing."

He reached out with one arm and tried to casually lean on one of the service pipes. The pipe turned out to be searing-hot, and he yelped as he snatched his hand away.

Sarai was still studying her holo-map, and apparently hadn't noticed. Still cool. Levi made a mental note, reminding himself that if Sarai found herself dangling over a chasm and he had to heroically reach out and pull her to safety, he'd have to use his left hand. That burn mark wasn't going away any time soon.

He was in the middle of deciding whether to pass the burn off as the result of something daring and manly when Sarai punched him on the shoulder.

"Lamebrain," she said, narrowing her eyes in that adorable combination of exasperation and pity. "It's this way."

***

Twenty minutes later, they emerged from the tunnels. Sarai had flipped the switch, completing the job, and it was now quitting time.

Levi bid Sarai farewell at the express elevator before squeezing himself into one of the crowded corners. It was a massive contraption, designed to deposit masses of tunnel workers at their living floors, and spiralled around the pit as it went. Levi spent the better part of an hour compressed into his corner before his floor finally came around, and he stepped out into freedom.

The daily lift ride was just one of many reasons Levi had applied for ship leave. Freelance ships would sometimes hire young Kaltorans for apprenticeship programmes that lasted a year. If Levi could get in, he could prove himself... and then he could finally do something with his life. Get out of the pit.

It may have been his twelfth application, and he may not have had a recommendation from his boss... but he had a good feeling about this one. His time would come. The embodiment of the night would bring justice to the stars.

Cut as they were into the side of the chasm, Kaltoran homes were almost cave-like in their design, supported by innumerable metal columns embedded in the earth. Bright lights illuminated the wide, crowded walkways, along which stall-keepers hawked their wares and children released from their home-schools played amongst the support columns. Levi finally reached his own home, a nondescript metal door in a row of hundreds, and was greeting upon stepping inside by a pillow thrown at his head.

With practiced reflexes, Levi snatched it out of the air and hurled it right back. His brother Judah yelped and scurried into the lounge, and Levi grinned. He may not have been a stellar engineer, but years of family pillow wars had sharpened his

throwing skills to a fine edge.

He stepped into the kitchen, which also served as the entrance room, and greeted his mother and two aunts before moving into the lounge.

"Die, Nephilim scum!"

Judah had been lying in wait behind the door, and swung his pillow with all the force his thirteen years could muster. Being twice his size and five years his senior, Levi blocked with one arm and scooped his little brother up with another, tossing him onto the sofa. He then leapt in after him and they tousled for a few moments before collapsing back onto the couch, panting for breath.

"Fun day of war-mongering?" Levi asked his little brother. Judah shook his head.

"Nah. More ancient human history. Did you know they used to have this festival where they put spiky things on their trees and planted bombs underneath the chimney to protect their stuff from bandits?"

"That first part sounds familiar," Levi said. "Not sure about the bombs."

"It's true!" Judah insisted, emphasising the point with another failed pillow assassination.

"Anything that didn't involve explosions?"

"Well…" Judah said, thinking hard. "They did a lot of colonisation. Then there was that… uh… terror thing. Terror farming."

"Terraforming?"

"Ah, yeah. Pretty much every planet they could find, so they had more room to… um, do human things."

"Must've been nice," Levi said, placing his hands behind his head, "To just see a planet and think 'Hmm, nice place. We can set up a summer home on top of that lava waterfall. The kids will love it.'"

Judah thought for a moment, then a sly smile crept over his features.

"So, how's Sarai?"

"Sarai…" Levi repeated, pretending to mull it over. "Let me think."

He grabbed a pillow, still appearing deep in thought, and began to shove it over Judah's face.

"That…" he said, as his little brother made dramatic mock attempts to avoid being smothered, "is none of your business, nosy little brother. Speaking of which, where are all…"

Levi stopped mid-sentence as he heard his name being called from the doorway. He had a split-second to sit up before seven of his younger siblings and cousins, fresh from class and chores, piled on top of him like he was a skinny trampoline.

"Dying," Levi choked as he attempted to extricate himself from the mass of limbs. "Losing oxygen. Must breathe. Judah, help."

He caught a glimpse of Judah on top of the pile, egging the others on. No hope there, then.

"Jezz!" called his mother from the kitchen, "Yoel, Michal, Hanna, Joseph, Ruth, Peter… give Levi a break."

Levi was left in the middle of the floor as his siblings and cousins flocked to the kitchen. Despite this being something of a ritual, he still felt like all his bones had been broken. A few minutes later his three uncles, third aunt, and six other cousins all entered the house together. Their large family sat down for dinner around the huge kitchen table, with overspill into almost every room. It was, as the phrase went in Kaltoran society, rehearsed chaos. Levi looked around at his younger siblings, cousins, aunts, uncles, and his harried mother, and felt a swell of pride at being part of such a family. As one of the oldest children, there was great expectation laid upon him.

"No Dad and Gran today?" he asked, and his mother shook her head.

"Dad's working late and Gran isn't back from the firing range," she replied, to a chorus of aww's from the assembled kids. In expectation of food, the room went silent as Levi's second aunt gave a small prayer to their ancestors, and soon the food was flying alongside the conversation. Just another meal in the Thrift household.

***

Zera took one last look at her family before turning to board the colony ship 'New Hope'. All twenty-seven of them were gathered on the platform waving goodbye, she could see her mother was crying on her father's shoulder. She swallowed the lump in her throat and waved goodbye for the last time.

As Zera boarded the ship she was comforted that her family and ancestors would be travelling with her in her memories. Although she would miss her family there was no doubt as to the importance of her purpose. Zera wanted a fresh start for her and her future children, Kadash was sea of bad memories, she knew she wanted better.

As soon as he stepped off the lift for work the next morning, Levi could tell that something was wrong. Instead of being at their stations, the docking bay crew were all huddled around the foreman's office. No ships were leaving or arriving, and the only sound was whispered conversation.

"What's up?" Levi said, to a nearby worker.

"Grav-pads are down," was the reply. Now the problem was clear: grav-pads were the lifeblood of the docking bay. Spacecraft coming in for landing and taking off were aided by giant platforms that created custom gravity fields. Without them, the ships' navigators were nowhere near precise enough to avoid the walls of the pit and land safely.

Using his lack of bulk to his advantage, Levi snaked his way to the front and found Sarai standing next to her father around a portable diagnostics terminal.

"There," her father growled, pointing a finger that was just as beefy as the rest of him at the screen. "Tunnel 47. Grav-generator malfunction."

"Forty-seven," Sarai repeated. "One of our deepest. No one's done any maintenance there in years."

"Well, they're about to."

Her father turned to the assembled crowd and cleared his throat.

"Alright, everyone," he called, "we can see the problem. One of our old generators has packed in, and we need someone to give it a kick-start."

"Whereabouts?" said a voice in the crowd. Sarai and her father shared a glance before replying.

"It's in 47," he said, and a ripple went through the workers. Levi was still new, but he had his father's memories. Tunnel 47 was in one of the deepest tunnels, so far down that most of the access tunnels had been claimed by nature or flooded. The only way to access those tunnels was to go the long way round, through cannibalistic Dark Tribe territory.

"We have a choice," the foreman continued. "Wait for a Dark Tribe ambassador to negotiate safe passage, or someone can climb through the collapsed tunnels to check it out. A two-hour job at most."

The crowd shuffled with nervous energy. This was no one's idea of a good plan.

"A negotiator will take forever," Sarai announced, striding forward. "Every second we're down, this business goes under. I'm small, I'll go."

"You can't go alone," her father retorted with a frown. "I won't let…"

"I'll go with her," Levi said, feeling a heavy dread settle on his shoulders as the words left his mouth. "I mean… I can help. Two should be fine, right?"

Sarai's father looked him over as if he were a particularly disappointing toothpick.

"Chill, Dad," Sarai said, already looping up her tool belt. "We'll be in and out in a flash. Besides, Levi will look after me."

Levi was around 85% sure that the last part had been a joke, but her father relented.

"Take a tracking beacon," he said. "Be as quick as you can. No unnecessary fiddling."

Sarai took the small beacon and nodded, motioning for Levi to follow her to the elevator. Her father caught her by the shoulder and whispered something. Even if he didn't have four ears and unusually good hearing, Levi couldn't have missed it.

"For heaven's sake… do not let him touch anything."

***

The journey into the depths was made in silence. Sarai spent the entire time either checking her holo-map or pretending to check it. Levi surreptitiously tried to check his hair in the reflection of the doors.

Yep, still a tangled black mess.

Finally, the doors slid open and they emerged into the gloom of Tunnel 47. It was exactly as the stories had described: a dank, partially collapsed, foreboding cavern, lined with rusted metal and snaking vines along the walls. What few lights remained flickered, threatening to expire at any second, and the walkways were barely visible through the damp earth. Instead of the oily, metallic smell of the docking bay, this tunnel had an overpowering odour of soil and plant-life. It was far more nature than man-made.

"Stay sharp," Sarai said in a low voice. "I don't know how many of the stories about this place are true, but I'd rather not find out."

Levi didn't reply, but pulled his shock spanner out of his belt and nervously glanced left and right. Cloying darkness in both directions. Marvellous.

They ignited their shoulder-mounted torches and set off down the left tunnel at a steady pace. Every drop of water echoed throughout the space, and Levi expected some hideous beast to burst out from the darkness at any second craving Kaltoran kebabs. They came to a fork in the tunnel, and Sarai was in the process of consulting her map when she grabbed Levi's shoulder and spun him round.

"Pit Worm," she said, and Levi froze as a shape reared out of the darkness. It had a slimy, off-green body that ended in a head split into a double-jaw, all two sections lined with small sharp teeth. Six beady eyes stood out, and it swayed as it looked from one to the other with a low hiss.

It was also about half a meter long.

"That's a Pit Worm?" Levi breathed, as he took in the sheer lack of size. "It's a bit…"

"Disgusting?" Sarai offered. She strode forward, shock spanner in hand, and dispatched the worm with one electrified swing. In death, the worm looked even smaller.

"But my Gran was almost eate-" Levi began, before stopping himself. His companion threw a questioning glance his way.

"I mean, uh…" he continued, "she almost ate one. She ate lots of them, actually. 'Worm-Eater', they used to call her. She's a great woman."

"She ate Pit Worms?"

"By the barrel."

"They're incredibly poisonous."

"Ah hah!" Levi laughed, awkwardly shoving the spanner into his belt, "Yeah, that's my Granny Esther. 'Iron-Stomach', they call her. She is a… um…"

"Great woman," Sarai finished. "She has a lot of names."

"Yep."

Sarai raised an eyebrow, but decided not to pursue the matter. As she moved to take the left fork, Levi stole a final glance at the diminutive worm and wondered if his gran hadn't perhaps exaggerated its size.

Further into the cavern they went, with the only threats being the occasional Pit Worm. Levi was beginning to finally relax, and was preparing a snappy conversation starter when Sarai abruptly stopped, holding up a fist.

"Here," she said, shining her light on a rusted metal door that stood two meters high. "This is the generator."

The panel on the wall had long since died, but a quick zap from her spanner brought the controls to life for a brief minute. With a baleful grinding, the decrepit door shuddered and began to rise, sounding like the gears were performing one final task before stopping for good. The door made it high enough for them to duck underneath, and they entered the grav-generator room.

It wasn't much to speak of: just a circular room with a railed walkway around the edge. Far, far below in the central pit lay the gravity generators, almost entirely shrouded in darkness. Just looking over the chasm made Levi queasy, and he occupied himself by finding the control console.

"By the looks of things," Sarai said, circling the railing, "it's been put out by a power spike. Maybe we'll need some maintenance later, but for now all it needs is a jolt to the main switchboard. Should bring the whole thing to life for a day or so."

"Great," Levi said, clapping his hands together to convey his false enthusiasm. "Just a jolt. So where's the switchboard?"

Sarai scanned the walls for a few moments, then inhaled sharply. She whirled around and stared down into the pit. Levi followed her gaze and saw the problem.

"Oh," he breathed, "That is ridiculous."

The switchboard lay behind a wire grid, embedded in the wall about thirty feet down. A rickety elevator platform stood at the edge of the railing, but it was opposite from the grid and the gap was at least twenty feet across.

"So…" Levi began, joining Sarai at the rail, "How do they expect people to do maintenance? With telekinesis, perhaps?"

"There," Sarai said, pointing to the metallic box underneath the switchboard. "Gravity generators. I'm guessing that when this place is operational, it creates an invisible grav-bridge from the elevator to the grid."

"What, they couldn't just make the elevator go down to the switchboard? Whose idea was that?!"

"Who knows?" Sarai replied, already fiddling with the lift controls. "Why do homes sometimes have power-points on the ceiling? Innovation is weird. Maybe they needed the bridge for testing the gravity levels. Maybe they were too lazy to build an actual bridge, so they installed a cheap gravity platform."

"So you need a gravity bridge to fix the gravity generators, which… supply the gravity bridge."

She smacked the console, and the lift spluttered to life.

"Yeah, it's a real weekend job," she said. "Either way, I have to get down there. Maybe I can activate the bridge remotely."

She opened the gate and stepped onto the flat square of metal. It groaned, but held.

"Whoa, wait," Levi said, his mouth overruling his fear. "Shouldn't we both go?"

"Lamebrain," Sarai replied, pointing down. "This lift is half-dead as it is. Unless you're hiding a jetpack in that bird's nest on your head, it's best if I go. I'm lighter. Probably."

Levi reluctantly stepped back, placing himself in front of the controls.

"Send me down," she said, folding her arms. "And be ready to chuck me your spanner. I might end up just having to lob it across."

Levi swallowed and nodded, pressing the DOWN button on the lift. It creaked, began to lower, and there was a snapping noise. There was no time to register that one of the supports had buckled. Levi only saw the lift tilt to the left, throwing Sarai off into the open air. He moved on pure instinct, diving after her and grabbing her outstretched arm with his left, unburned hand.

Ha, success!

Unfortunately, his feet had left the platform during his dive. At the same moment he grabbed Sarai's hand with his left, his burned right hand had to clasp the railing, supporting their whole weight.

Oh, bad idea. Ouch. Ouch, ouch, OUCH!

This plan hadn't been well thought-out. Wait… what plan?

"Don't let go!" Sarai screeched from down below, dangling by a single appendage.

"Thanks," Levi replied through gritted teeth. The pain was already intense, and it had only been a few seconds. He spent the next few lamenting his unfortunate life decisions before a cry from Sarai brought him back to reality.

"Levi, you have to pull us up!"

"Pardon?"

"Pull us up!"

Levi tried. He pulled with all his might, but even lifting the girl by a few inches was pure torture.

"I can't," he replied, miserably letting his head dangle. "I'm too… I'm too weak."

"You have to!" was Sarai's reply. "If we fall, we're dead. Or hadn't you noticed?"

Levi had, in fact, noticed. The drop was gigantic, and they couldn't even see the bottom. The moment he let go they'd plunge straight into a mass of machinery far below.

"Levi!"

"I CAN'T!" he yelled back, practically sobbing the words. "Don't you get it? I'm a skinny, weak loser and I can't pull us up!"

"You have…"

"No!" he interrupted, gritting his teeth again as his failures came crashing down on him one last time. "You don't understand. My family are losers, my head is full of all these memories of us being losers, and yours is probably full of all the dashing, good-looking heroes, and all I have in my family tree are failures and weaklings and people who didn't make anything of themselves, and I see that every time I close my eyes, and that's why I can't pull us up, because that's what I am."

The pain was immense now, as if his right hand was being branded. His shoulder felt like it was being slowly dragged out of its socket. Still, all Levi could do was hang there, unable to save himself or Sarai, hating himself at the end.

"Levi," she said, her tone different. "They're not you."

"But they…"

"Wise up, lamebrain," she growled, sounding exactly like her father. Even in the midst of the pain, Levi couldn't help but pay attention. "They were them, you are you. Just because you can remember them doesn't make them the same. You are here, right now; they are not, and you have to use what you have to pull us up."

Levi blinked and felt a memory rush to his head. It was his memory. Only his.

"Actually," he breathed, knowing he had only seconds, "there is something I have that they didn't."

"What?"

"I'm really good at throwing."

"But how does that…"

Sarai didn't get to finish her sentence, as at that moment Levi let go of the railing and they plunged into the abyss. Her screaming, instead of being distracting, gave him focus. As they fell close to the switchboard, he drew his shock spanner from his belt and zeroed in on the grid. Summoning his pillow-hurling skills, Levi powered the spanner and threw it at the grid. Direct hit.

The grid sparked to life, as did the gravity bridge. They landed heavily, though the bridge's incorporeal nature dispersed the momentum. For minutes they lay there, catching their breath. Levi had landed face-down, and he saw through the invisible surface that they would've splattered onto an electrical coupling.

Slowly, he rose to his feet, adrenaline still racing. He strode over to Sarai heroically. With every ounce of cool he possessed, he offered her his hand. She accepted, and her touch was chilling. Then she drew back her fist and smacked his shoulder.

"Lamebrain," she snarled, before softening. "Thanks, I guess."

Levi accepted her gratitude with a nonchalant shrug.

He then proceeded to grin like an idiot for the rest of the day.

A week later, Levi stood in the docking bay, bag over one shoulder. He wasn't here to work; in fact, he may never work here again.

Ship leave, he thought, proudly noting that the memory of receiving his approval would be passed on to his descendants. The Realmwalker would be the freelance vessel where he'd serve his apprenticeship, and he watched as it gently alighted on the grav-platform.

His family stood by his side, and it was time to say goodbye. He hugged his mother, and was warned by his father not to get his head stuck in anything. After that, Levi's neck was constricted two dozen times in a row by siblings and extended family, until finally he came to Judah. The brothers embraced, and Levi pulled away to see tears in Judah's eyes.

"It's up to you," Levi said with a smile. "You're the big one now. Look after them."

"You gotta write to us," Judah replied, sniffling. "Like, every day."

"Maybe not that much," Levi laughed. "How about just the good stuff?"

Judah nodded, and Levi swung the bag over his shoulder. It was time.

He waved to his family until the cargo ramp slammed shut. He felt a wave of sadness and apprehension. This is what he wanted, but that didn't mean it wasn't bittersweet.

A stern-faced Legion female showed him to his quarters, then led him to his workplace. He stepped in the door and found himself in a generator room: specifically, gravity generators. He laughed once he was alone.

"Gravity," he said out loud. "Of course."

"I know, right?"

His head snapped upwards, and he saw Sarai sitting on one of the conduits.

"Sarai?!"

She laughed at his expression.

"Yup," she replied with an impish grin. "Looks like we got the same posting."

"I didn't know you were... uh, I wasn't..."

"I've been requesting ship leave for AGES," she said, leaping down and landing gracefully on the metal surface. "My sister Rachel is out there, seeing the stars, but Dad wouldn't let me go. I finally convinced him. Plus, how d'you think you managed to get on board?"

"Your dad recommended me?" Levi said in confusion. "But he hates me."

"Certain circumstances lately might have changed his mind."

She stood there in front of him, beautiful mud eyes and all, and Levi tried to comprehend how his life would be from now on. Fortunately, Sarai put it into words.

"So, same ship, same engine room for our apprenticeship," she said cheerily, slapping him on the shoulder on her way out. "Looks like we'll be spending a lot of time together, Levi."

The door slammed shut, and Levi swallowed, still rooted to the spot. A whole conversation, and she hadn't once called him " lamebrain"..

However, to say that he was astoundingly, earth-shatteringly overjoyed was completely untrue.

The embodiment of the night was above such things.

Absolute darkness. The roughened metal floor was cold against his bare knees. He knelt silently with tears streaming down his face from the hollows of his eyes as the sucking babe slept in his arms. Around him were his Dark Tribes kin, chanting mystical prayers as a new lightwalker left the Shroud of the Deep.

Ceremonial Stinkbough smouldered in the dark, its heavy scent a tribute to the loss of the Tribe, and the gain of its people.

He wept for the daughter he'd be taking up and giving to the lightwalkers. She would only know her true family through the dark memories she would inherit. But the father hoped against all odds that the child would create better memories for her children. Memories of joy and light.

....

The entire Swagger family gathered in celebration as their newest daughter Rachel cried as she received her new eyes and saw light for the first time.

Legion

Creator: Archons
Average Height: 2.4m
Average Weight: 180kg
Average Life Span: 70 years

Home Planet: Cerberus Prime
Total Population: 2.8 million + 1.8 million Exsilia
Yearly Population Growth Rate: +2%

Years Since Re-emergence into Space: N/A (never lost ability)

Common Characteristics

Efficient, focused, honourable, loyal, organised, protective, proud, and stubborn.

Distinctive Physical Features

Scaled, lizard-like skin.
Often large and muscular.

Legion Trait, pg: 340

» +1 Resolve, Gunnery, and Heavy Arms.
» +1 Armour.
» +2 Defence vs Impair.
» Never requires 'Environmental Outfit or Equipment: Arctic'.
» Gain Language: Legion.
» Requires 'Environmental Outfit or Equipment: Temperate' outside Arctic Environments or be Suppressed each Turn.
» -1 Armour when at 0 Endurance.
» -2 Maximum Movement.

Preferred Combat Equipment

Gauss and rail weaponry.
Kinetic and shrapnel shells.
Tactical armour or assault plates.

Legion History

The Legion has the shortest and most violent history of all the races. They were created just a hundred years ago to fight for the Archons during the Great War. After the last Archon was killed, the Legion continued to fight the Nephilim for thirty more years.

As supplies ran low, it became apparent that if they were to survive as a species they would need to procreate and create a stable society for themselves. They found an arctic planet suitable for their physiology, naming it Cerberus: the watchdog of hell. This was fitting, as their new purpose would be to protect the survivors from the hell created in the wake of the Great War. As the fleet had used most of its fuel to reach this planet, it would be a permanent settlement.

The Legion struggled to raise families and become arctic farmers as there was nothing more contrary to their nature. The Interior Branch of the military was created to manage these non-military activities.

For sixty long years the Legion assumed that they and Feral Nephilim were all that remained, then unexpectedly the Corporation made contact with the surviving Legion. This first contact created chaos, and the Legion commanders (Casila Curia) struggled to relate to these new outsiders. Mere days after their first meeting, Corporate executives began offering mercenary jobs to the Legion. Over the course of that first year, almost two million Legion deserted Cerberus to join the Corporation. Scrambling to control the situation, the Casila Curia issued an edict that all deserters could never return to Cerberus and labeled them Exsilia, meaning exiled soldiers.

This was an unpopular move, as many families had been lifted from poverty due to the resources sent back home by the Exsilia, despite being labelled Exsilia. In response, the government formed a Foreign Branch along with a new army of official Legion mercenaries, the Auxilia. Large numbers of Legion soldiers transferred from the Interior Branch to the Auxilia to become mercenaries. Additionally, it was decided that Exsilia would be absolved of their crimes if they enlisted in the Auxilia. As a base for the new Auxilia army and to encourage the Exsilia to re-join the Legion fold, a new colony was formed in the Haven system on the arctic planet Lilith.

Legion Culture

The Legion are the only Archon race to not fall during the Great War, thanks to their physical and mental resilience, as well as their highly structured militaristic society.

Because they were created as a warrior race, they place a heavy emphasis on duty, honour, and glory, which come from military service and involvement in combat. When the Great War ended, the Legion had to reinvent its society to accommodate peacetime professions and family. Taking on a civilian role is seen as a noble sacrifice, raising a family being the most noble sacrifice of all.

The Legion were once unified by the singular purpose of fighting X'ion's Nephilim army. During the settlement of Cerberus Prime many left to live in nomadic lives, and upon meeting the Corporation many Legion left and became Exsilia. The Legion are no longer unified by purpose. Nomads roam freely while the Exsilia now owe their loyalty to the Corporation and themselves.

Generally Exsilia soldiers consider themselves loyal Legion soldiers who became mercenaries to avoid poverty and the shame of a menial existence. They work for the Corporation and others, often sending wealth and supplies back to their families.

Enlisted Legion soldiers, known as the Auxilia, are rented out by the Casila Curia. The Auxilia often consider Exsilia to be deserters but still respect them. Auxilia contracts are paid directly to the Casila Curia, who in turn pay wages to the Auxilia and their families.

The Nomads are those Legion who deserted long ago to fend for themselves in the wilds, making a completely new society for themselves, free from many old traditions and the control of the Casila Curia.

It is not uncommon for Legion mercenaries to be hired by competing interests and end up on opposing sides of a battle. In this case, all that changes is a higher chance of taking prisoners and honourable conduct. But Legion mercenaries will happily fight against each other, often killing one another, safe in the knowledge that they each are performing their duty and gaining glory.

The Legion conducts themselves with duty and honour. Their duty is to whomever they serve, to their commanding officer and to their employer for the mercenaries. If forced to choose their loyalty, though, they will always pick their commander over their employer. The honour with which they conduct themselves is not classic faerie-tale honour, though; they will use ambushes and sneak attacks to gain victory. However, the Legion do everything they can to avoid collateral damage, refusing to attack innocent civilians even if ordered to, and never flee from battle unless ordered.

Creating a Legion Character

Nomad

During their early years of settlement, many Legion left their overcrowded cities to become nomadic arctic hunters and gatherers, determined to take charge of their own destinies and to live by their wits and skill. Many of these Nomads have now moved to the Haven system to again find a better life.

Recommended Skills
» Physical
» Survival
» Planetoids
» Exotic

Recommended Traits
» Physical: Capacity Training
» Survival: Wilderness
» Tactical: Second Wind

Specialist

The Legion army has many specialists in addition to their regular soldiers. Specialists are trained in overcoming problems and obstacles by using technological expertise to find and exploit weaknesses in their enemies. They take their time in combat, analysing the situation and applying their considerable skills as needed.

Recommended Skills
» Any Professional Skill.
» Heavy Arms

Recommended Traits
» Awareness: Alert
» Electronics: Shield Breaker
» Heavy Arms: Coordinated Strike

Mercenary

The Corporation employ large numbers of Auxilia and Exsilia Legion mercenaries to do their dirty work. They are strong and fearless expert warriors. Their reputation is such that they can often scare enemies into submission. In combat they commonly make use of Auto Fire weaponry to suppress and destroy their enemies.

Recommended Skills
» Leadership
» Resolve
» Medicine
» Small Arms

Recommended Traits
» Strength: Muscular Implants
» Resolve: Fearless
» Small Arms: Covering Fire

Nomad   Specialist   Mercenary

Government and Law

Government: Military Dictatorship.
Leadership: Casila Curia.

Casila Curia

The Legion are best characterised as a military dictatorship, in which all society is governed by a strict military hierarchy of ranks. The Casila Curia consists of five Consuls, the highest-ranked officers, one from each branch of the military. The Consul of the Fleet, Tiberius Valeria, has a fearsome reputation when it comes to discipline. The Consul of the Army, Capito Lulia, is considered to be the foremost Legion expert on guerrilla warfare. The Consul of Operations, Brutus Calpurnia, was barely chosen to be Consul due to his questionable approach to research and intelligence. The Consul of Foreign Affairs, Athene Kosta, has been fondly nicknamed "Lady Vengeance" in honour of her past service. Finally, the Consul of the Interior, Volusus Servilla, is renowned for his rigid manner and attention to detail.

Lady Vengeance

Consul of Foreign Affairs Athene Kosta is the only representative of the Casila Curia who lives in the Haven system. She is stationed there as is it facilitates her role with the other races and Legion mercenaries. She is the ranking officer in Haven and thus the commander of the Legion forces there.

Athene regards the Exsilia as misguided; she understand the reasons for their departure, but she does not accept disloyalty. She has offered a pardon to any Exsilia who wishes to enlist in the Auxilia; however, Exsilia who have outright refused this generous offer or have attacked the Legion are branded traitors and deserters.

Athene is the youngest member of the Casila Curia, gaining rapid promotion through the ranks during a major Legion operation to clear Feral Nephilim from the Liberty Belt. Her reputation for breaking protocol and leading her soldiers from the front has made her very popular among the rank-and-file Legion troops and has earned her the affectionate nickname "Lady Vengeance".

Anyone in the Haven system who wishes to speak with Legion leadership will find themselves negotiating with her.

Tribunal Law

The Legion deals with all internal legal matters by military tribunal. Any officer or soldier who has committed a crime is brought before three high-ranking officers, who determine guilt and punishment. At times they order an investigation and make their decision based on its findings.

Punishments can be quite harsh: death for treachery, and public whipping for negligence. When many Legion deserted to become mercenaries, they were exiled as punishment. If an Exsilia is caught on Cerberus Prime, the punishment is death. Exsilia in Haven are often under the authority of Corporate regulatory law as they are no longer considered part of the Legion army.

Foreigners are exempt from the tribunal because it only applies to members of the Legion. Instead, visitors to Legion settlements are subject to the summery punishment of the police without trial.

Exsilia

Although no longer technically part of the Legion military, the Exsilia represent the majority of the Legion within the Haven system, primarily working for the Corporation or as freelance mercenaries.

Five Branches of the Military

All those still under the authority of the Casila Curia are considered to be in the military, even the farmers and homemakers. The military is divided into five branches, each of which led by a Consul who sits on the Casila Curia.

The Army and Navy protect Cerberus Prime from outsiders and fight against enemies of the Legion, such as Feral Nephilim.
The Operations Branch is responsible for secret operations, intelligence-gathering, and research.
The Interior Branch is responsible for all domestic non-military activity such as farming, homemaking, and food services.
The Foreign Branch encompasses Legion who interact with outsiders, including diplomats, traders, and the Auxilia.

Rank

Within the Legion command structure, rank directly reflects the number of soldiers under one's command. Each tier of ranking has a primary officer and two deputy officers, called the first, second, and third of that rank. The first of each rank commands the full allotment of soldiers, but delegates command to their second and third officers.

The Tiers of Rank
» Consul commands a Branch of the Military
» Imperator commands an army of 100,000
» Legate commands a Legion of 10,000
» Tribune commands a cohort of 1,000
» Centurion commands a centuria of 100
» Decanus commands a contingent of 10

One's rank is usually preceded by a word that indicates what type of work that individual does. Some examples from officers serving in mercenary armies would be 2nd Mercenary Legate or 1st Mercenary Centurion.

These military ranks apply to all members of the Legion, including all non-military duties such as farming or food service. The foreman of a factory is likely to be called the 1st Factory Centurion, and his regional manager might be the 2nd Factory Tribune.

Legion who do not have an officer rank are simply referred to by their job. Some example salutations include Soldier, Medic, Specialist, Pilot, Farmer, Worker, and Cook.

Relationship with Other Races

The Foreign Branch is responsible for most official interactions with the other races, including diplomacy, trade, and especially mercenary work. The Diplomacy Army includes all Legion dignitaries as well a force of soldiers that volunteers emergency support and peacekeepers for the purpose of building friendly relations. The Trade Army sells Legion-manufactured goods and mercenary contracts while purchasing anything the Legion needs from outsiders. Generally, Legion settlements have almost no visitors with the exception of high-ranking dignitaries; outsiders are restricted from entering Legion settlements, especially Cerberus Prime.

Corporate Muscle

The Auxilia make up well over half of all the workers in the Foreign Branch. They fulfil contracts sold by the Trade Army. Companies within the Corporation hire individual contingents, centuria, or even whole legions of Auxilia, depending on their demands. Most Legion mercenaries are Exsilia as they tend to be cheaper to hire and far more numerous than the Auxilia forces. It is common for Corporates to mistake Exsilia and Auxilia as being the same thing. However, the difference is important to the Auxilia: the Auxilia officially serves the interests of the Casila Curia, whereas Exsilia serve their own interests.

Salvage Agreements

Kaltorans and Legion have a healthy relationship of mutual respect and trust. The Legion protects the Kaltorans as children of the Archons and tends to respect their bravado and loyalty to family, whereas the Kaltorans are impressed by the Legion's sense of selfless duty and skill in combat. Both races also rely heavily on salvage operations for their ships and technology, so they have come to an unspoken agreement: Kaltorans will bring any old Legion warships they find to trade back to the Legion rather than junk them. In exchange, the Legion are happy to part with any non-Legion salvage they find. Additionally, the Kaltorans are suspicious of the Nephilim, the Legion's old enemy.

The Old Enemy

The Nephilim were once the enemy of the Legion in the Great X'ion War. The Legion accept the current peace with the Eden Brood as necessary for the continuation of life in the Haven system, but they have never forgotten or forgiven the Nephilim for their many atrocities in the Great X'ion War. For this reason Legion and Nephilim rarely work together on anything.

Since the Nephilim are strange and the Legion do not care to know them better, the Legion frequently confuse the different factions of Nephilim. It is not uncommon for Legion to accidentally kill Devwi-Ich Nephilim, mistaking them for being Feral. The Nephilim often overlook these incidents, as they do not value life highly.

Economy

Exports: Enforcement Services (Corporation) and Munitions.
Imports: Spacecraft Salvage, Food (Kaltoran), Fuel (Corporation), Construction and Transportation Services (Corporation).

Interior Branch

All of Legion society is organised in a military fashion, including the economy and domestic leadership. The Interior Branch is by far the largest branch of the military, and aside from the police it has no combat function. Instead, the Interior Branch is responsible for managing the non-military operations of the Legion, including production, health, education, services, agriculture, mining, welfare, and police.

Planned Economy

The officers of the Legion manage their economy with military precision and mindset, and this has several important implications: First, all basic supplies are distributed according to need. Quartermasters of the Legion create a list of requirements for their living needs and operation; in turn this list is given to the Interior Branch, which ensures that all needs are met.

In recent times, large numbers of Legion have departed to the Haven system, and the Corporation has provided the Legion with significant resources. All this has led to surpluses for the first time in a century. The families of Auxilia are first to receive these surpluses as a reward for their valuable service to the Legion economy.

Economics of Mercenaries

Auxilia do not work for themselves; in fact, they are still soldiers in the Legion Army. Foreign Branch traders are responsible for selling Auxilia contracts to the Corporation and others; they in turn pay the traders for the mercenaries. The traders will then send some money to the Casila Curia, but spend most on buying equipment and supplies for all branches of the military.

Exsilia on the other hand work for themselves, directly receiving an income from their employer. Contracts are given to Exsilia individually or in a group. Most Exsilia send some of their pay back home to their families on Cerberus Prime.

Corporation Transportation Ships

The Legion have needed a great many non-military ships, mostly for transportation. Legion warships are too valuable and small to use for this purpose; instead, they hire ships from the Corporation.

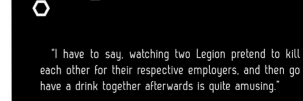

"I have to say, watching two Legion pretend to kill each other for their respective employers, and then go have a drink together afterwards is quite amusing."

Science and Technology

Lost Knowledge

Just as the Legion were created by the Archons, they were also armed by them. Much of the technology that the Legion use was designed by the Archons, while the Legion were only taught to maintain it. For this reason, the Legion do not know how to make new things from their old technologies; that information died with the Archons. Over the years the Legion have reverse engineered a few weapons and most munition types, allowing for some self-production. However many technologies, especially those used in Legion spacecraft, are lost to them. They can refurbish and maintain these technologies, but cannot recreate them from scratch.

Research

When the Legion peruse science and technology, it does so with regimented precision. The Operations Branch of the military includes the Research, Exploration, and Praetorian Armies. These armies are functionally responsible for technological progress. The Research Army does this directly through scientific research, while the Exploration Army studies new planets and old technologies. The Praetorians occasionally conduct intelligence and espionage operations that yield new technologies.

Old Warships

The Legion have no technology of their own, as the Archons mass-produced military equipment and ships for them to use during the Great War. Their vast fleet was mostly destroyed during the Great X'ion War, and the ruins of this once-great fleet remain scattered across numerous star systems.

With no capacity to build new warships, the Legion tend to maintain century-old vessels or repair reclaimed ships.

Legion warships tend to use hydrogen fusion reactors, a technology which lost with the Archons. They must be repaired by finding wrecks for replacement parts; no known person can make a fusion reactor from scratch.

Floating amidst the former engineering bay of the Paragon, Abelia nudged herself around a spine-shredded piece of hull until she reached a large undamaged sphere and locked her magboots.

"Sir, I'm fairly sure we have confirmation. Requesting tech team to the wreckage."

- Recovery of a hydrogen fusion reactor.

The humid and faintly spicy scent of the Mishpacha jungle went unnoticed by most Legion, but Medea felt alive for the first time in a week.

The sharp cracka-crack of gauss and faint hiss-crack of rail weaponry filled the air of the firing range. Nephilim and Mechonid outlines, already long pitted and dented, were painted on the old hull piece at the other end of the clearing. Medea raised her rifle to her shoulder and breathed out. Another dent in the already chipped and distorted face of the Nephilim told of the last of her ammunition for this practice session.

With a heavy sigh she left the firing range and headed back to her "duty". As she passed the "Make Babies; FOR VICTORY!" poster she regretfully slipped off her old Centurion badge and filed into another stark bunker-like building.

"Medea!" cried the young Legion children, seeing their favourite caretaker.

Genetics

Created by the Archons

The Archon Empire was crumbling when they created the Legion. They were losing the war against X'ion and its Nephilim creations. The Archons made the Legion hastily, leaving out much of the coding required for a well-rounded species. This has had farreaching consequences as the Legion now struggle with the everyday, such as raising families and working productive jobs; they are hardwired both mentally and physically for war.

Bred for War

The Legion were made with a singular purpose: to be a weapon with thick natural armour, hardened to ward against stress and empathy. Even their minds were genetically designed to predispose them towards being a soldier as they are innately protective and disciplined.

Genetically Flawed

The Legion were hastily engineered to fight in Great X'ion War, not to survive the ages.

Their predisposition towards combat makes peace difficult and frustrating. They are mammalian creatures but with thick reptilian hides, and this insulation often causes their organs to overheat. Because of this, they need a cold environment to survive. They have a short lifespan from cell degradation due to age and from death in combat. Finally, they have a poor birth rate due to low fertility.

Short Story: Eterion

Eterion never thought of himself as violent. Even growing up as a member of the Legion race, he was less interested in violence than his peers. When his classmates had been wrestling in the snow banks, he'd been content to simply read of their race's history. When his schoolmates had been embroiled in their imaginary war games in amongst the metal bunkers of the city, Eterion had been content simply to help out on his parents' farm.

Eterion knew he was a little odd for a Legion.

All this changed when he handled his first high-calibre assault rifle. His father had let him handle small arms, but never anything like this. His head instructor at the academy had led the class to one of the many armouries, where they'd been allowed to pick a practice weapon. Uncertain, Eterion chose the one nearest to the door: an Artemis 300 Assault Rifle, with laser sights, auto-reload, and retractable electro-machete. It was heavy. It practically hummed with energy. Eterion held it in his arms, and suddenly realised the meaning of glory in combat.

It also just felt really, really cool. He pumped the reload trigger, which was unnecessary but felt like the right thing to do, and hefted it into the same position he'd seen in the old war films. It felt good; for the first time, Eterion felt like a Legionnaire. That was when his instructor plucked the weapon out of his hands.

"Nothing higher than a 200-gauge, cadet," their teacher grunted. "Don't you listen? Pick something else."

Embarrassed, Eterion glanced up to where the guns were clearly labelled by calibre. He needed to stop daydreaming. They filed out of the armoury, armed to the teeth and buzzing with nervous energy. Though many of the students had been allowed to handle their parents' guns, this was the first time any of them had been authorised to shoot anything. Discipline held, though its influence was taut.

With a sudden turn of the heel, their grizzled instructor moved away from where they knew the firing range lay and headed back towards the classroom. Twenty confused cadets followed, and soon they were filing back to their desks and sitting down, feeling somewhat ridiculous holding high-powered weapons while surrounded by textbooks.

"Lay your weapons upon your desks," their instructor ordered. They did so, Eterion feeling a twinge of longing in the first few seconds as his finger left the weapon. The instructor paused for a moment, allowing his eyes to sweep around the room. He was old; older than old. His scars spoke of war, combat and victory. He retained all of his muscular limbs, concealed as they were by a tattered grey cloak, and wore ancient Legion armour underneath.

"First things first," he announced. "You've probably heard about the Corporation. We've had a few visitors in the city. They are a race looking to form business relationships with the Legion. In particular, they are interested in our line of business…"

Everyone glanced down at their weapons.

"And so, this is your first weapons lesson," the instructor continued. "Consider your days of farming over. From now on, you are a generation of soldiers."

The class had been expecting the announcement, but a ripple of excitement still ran through the room.

"However… don't entertain the notion that you'll be firing a single shot today."

The excitement died instantly, replaced by unease. A cadet near the front raised a fist, requesting permission to speak.

"With respect, sir," he said, eyes down, "we were told that we would be receiving firearms instruction."

"And you will," the instructor replied. "However, before I allow a single finger onto a trigger, you all need to learn an important lesson."

He reached a hand into the back of his cloak and pulled out his Kopis pistol, an archaic model. The weapon was decrepit, old, and had a poor rate of fire. And yet, the flat metal side bore countless black marks. The class went even more silent than usual as they realised how many kills this symbolised.

"The gun is not your ally," the instructor said. His voice was almost a whisper, but no one had any trouble hearing. "Your gun is a tool. Your comrades… they are your allies."

He tucked the pistol back into its holster.

"Until I'm satisfied that you have all learned that lesson, your lessons will be theoretical. You will file into the armoury every morning, select your weapon, return here, and place the weapon on your desk. It shall remain unmoved until the end of the day, when it shall be returned. Do I make myself clear?"

Eterion raised his fist along with the rest and yelled his consent, trying to avert his eyes from the shiny 200-gauge Xiphos rifle with laser-tracking and localised shield generator that took up most of the space on his desk.

It was going to be a very long year.

***

The Legion gunship touched down in a clearing, the bright red chrome clearly visible against the green of the undergrowth.

The ramp lowered, and twelve fully armed Legionnaires descended, the sound of their heavy boots joining the throng of wildlife sounds pouring forth from the jungle. Eterion donned his helmet as his boots met the grassy surface. Deirdre stood at the bottom, her silver Corporate hair perfectly straight, and her suit-and-skirt combo unruffled. She peered at her mercenary team over her glasses, like a parent on the verge of delivering a lecture to her children for staying out too late. Her holographic form flickered, but it did nothing to detract from her aura of authority.

"I've updated your intel," she explained, her voice fuzzy. "From what we can tell, it should be sleeping. Unfortunately, you'll have to wake it up if you want to kill it."

Gallus, the mercenary team's commander, quickly scanned the brief projected on his headset.

"It's a class seven," Gallus growled, meeting her gaze. "Defensive type. Your intel was wrong."

Deirdre didn't flinch. In fact, she seemed entirely unconcerned.

"Occupational hazard," Deirdre replied. "Or are you accusing me of feeding you misinformation? For my own amusement?"

"We could've been better prepared. If this costs me any of my men…"

"Your services are mine, Exsilia. I pay you to complete a job. If you can't work without whining, I'll find someone better."

The hologram flickered once more and faded. At the same time, the updated mission brief was uploaded to each of their headsets. Eterion saw the problem immediately. However, Gallus merely motioned forward, and they began the long march into the jungle towards the target.

***

They were two hours into the fight, and Eterion had run out of curse words. By this point he was practically making up new ones.

The humongous Feral Nephilim didn't seem to be tiring; if anything, it seemed to thrive off of being shot at. It stood at least fifty feet tall and had a shell-like carapace that could comfortably conceal its head. Add in the six jagged limbs, each twice as thick as a tree trunk, and you had a beast that no weapon could truly damage. Foliage grew all over its shell and limbs, speaking of the long hibernation from which it had been awoken. This would explain the grumpiness.

The first part of the mission had gone smoothly. After a quick trek through the jungle, they'd come across the ancient crater left when X'ion had bombarded Mishpasha with its creations. The Nephilim had rained down like meteors, protected upon impact by a spongy

shell that they later ate through to join the fight. Not that there was much resistance: from what little data remained of the attack, it was apparent that the great city-states of Mishpasha had no way of fighting against a horde of towering, genetically modified beasts. Within days, the planet's civilisations were in disarray, and the major cities had been annihilated. The only reason the landscape hadn't been reduced to ash was the unexpected departure of X'ion.

Most of the largest Nephilim had died from starvation, a few had cannibalised their own kind, and some lay in hibernation across the planet.

The mercenary squad had approached the gigantic shell in near-silence, intending to lay enough charges to crack the outer surface and fire upon the fleshy underneath. Their explosive experts had completed the job and the entire team had retreated to the edge of the crater, sniper rifles and rocket launchers at the ready. It wasn't enough. The initial explosions had caused cracks, but that was the limit of their effectiveness. Now the Nephilim was awake, and enraged.

Eterion stood in a line with two of his comrades, raining down an armour-piercing flurry with their Gladius Class-V Miniguns. The Nephilim screeched in pain, momentarily held back by the barrage and forced on the defensive. It scuttled backwards with surprising dexterity, withdrawing its head into the shell. Their rounds were depleting, however. The heavy-weapons users were forced to halt fire as their clips emptied, and they took this opportunity to duck behind one of the many sturdy trees.

Eos sprinted out from behind cover to take their place, a massive rocket launcher resting on her shoulder. She watched with unflinching concentration as the Nephilim realised it was no longer being shot at. Its head unfurled from the innards of the shell, and its tiny eyes swivelled in their sockets as it searched for prey. Its gaze fell on Eos, seemingly alone and an easy target. The beast charged, shaking the forest floor with its footfalls.

Eos sank into a steady crouch as it drew nearer. When it was only twenty feet away, she let loose with a rocket. It flew in a spiral and collided with the monster's head, engulfing it in flames. It roared, and its front legs crumpled. As soon as it was down, that was their cue. The three heavy-weapons users sprinted out of cover while the two snipers in the trees were given a solid target. Meanwhile, Eos had dropped her rocket launcher and drawn her Artemis Assault Rifle. She sprinted up to the Nephilim's head and vaulted on top, planting her feet in the charred flesh. She then pointed her rifle at one of its eyes and opened fire, point blank.

Eterion could only admire her nerve as he sprinted in, holding his minigun in both hands. He aimed the laser sights at one of the cracks in the shell and opened fire as his comrades did the same. The Nephilim's limbs flailed as it attempted to rise, but it only managed to buck Eos off its head. She landed in a roll, sprang to her feet, and continued firing. The snipers fired round after round, aiming for the eyes, and for a few moment the hailstorm of gunfire looked like it would be enough to finish the fight.

***

The snow drifted downwards with a sluggishness that suggested that even the sky was holding its breath. Eterion sat on the very top of his family's bio-dome, gazing down at the settlement without any particular focus. From his vantage point, he could just about see the barracks in the distance, and shots could be heard from the practice range. Shots could always be heard from the practice range.

Not even a round of shooting could distract him from the coming announcement. He glanced around and noticed for the first time in years how ramshackle the city was. Their bunker-like buildings were a mish-mash of metal sheets welded together, anything that would keep out the wind. Their guns were outdated, and the food was enough to keep them alive, no more. Even the family dome suffered, with numerous patch jobs to keep the cold from ruining the crops.

The Legion race was in crisis. That was what came of being made for war and little else. Eterion felt a tap on his shoulder, and turned to see that Darius had appeared next to him. As a tactical expert, his friend knew how to move around without making noise. It was a rare gift for a Legion.

"Thinking again?" Darius asked. "It does you no good, y'know."

"Says the tactical expert," Eterion replied, punching Darius on the leg. His friend took the hit and sat down next to him.

"It's mad, what they're doing," he said eventually. "I mean, declaring every mercenary a traitor?"

"Hmm," Eterion replied.

"The Corporation are giving us a chance," Darius continued. "It's not like we'll ever get half the action here as we would off-world."

Eterion said nothing. In just a few minutes, their government would come to decision: to continue to tolerate freelance mercenary work, or more likely to declare all non-sanctioned mercenaries as traitors, never to return to Cerberus. Exsilia.

If the law was passed, their choices were reduced to either enrolling with the security forces or taking a non-combat job. Just the thought made Eterion's trigger finger itchy.

And yet… even to be branded as an Exsilia meant freedom. Freedom to choose jobs, to not be bound by meagre Legion pay grades. Freedom from a life of snow and boredom.

There was a beeping from Darius's terminal. It was an archaic model, but tacticians were the only ones allowed them, so it was their best source of news. Darius opened the viewscreen and accessed the

It is not an efficient method of child rearing for one or two parents to tend to the same number of children. If we truly wish to do more than just stabilise our population, we must raise our children like we raise armies.

I propose that mothers be encouraged to give birth to a minimum of five children, and those children should be raised at collective childcare (barracks) centres where three or four adults can manage as many as thirty children.

Children should be trained from a young age to love the state and the Casila Curia, from age five martial arts training should begin, and from age ten weapons training. At age fifteen the children shall be apprenticed to their profession of choice, which shall become their lifelong career. In this way, all Legion shall grow to see their state as parent and provider, ensuring a stable existence into the future and avoiding further mass desertions.

– Volusus Servilla, Consul of the Interior.

directive folder, where they read the news.

Eterion felt the urge to slam his fist against the dome ceiling. With the poor state of things, it would probably collapse soon anyway.

"Turning on their own people," he snarled. "It makes no sense."

"Trying to keep control, I guess," Darius replied in a low voice. "There are so few of us left…"

That was it. Legion society had been devastated by the mass exodus to Corporate freelance work, and this was the government's way of gaining back some control.

"Yeah, well they obviously don't care much for the mercenaries supporting their families," Eterion shot back. "We're not gonna survive on stupid vegetables."

At this last word he stomped on the roof of the dome so hard it left a dent in the metal. Seething, he got up and flung open the exit hatch, clambering inside to escape the mundane, derelict sight of the city below.

***

The fight should've been over. The mercenary team poured on the bullets, causing the beast to stumble. Eos attacked from the front, firing away with an assault rifle. Then the Nephilim managed to right itself, and it charged forward. Eos dove to one side as the snapping neck bit the air where she'd been a moment previously. It tried again, but she'd already jumped over an embankment and was rolling out of range. The Nephilim's head was oozing black blood and full of bullet holes, but even as they watched, the wounds began to close. Eterion's clip ran dry, and the Nephilim whipped its head around in his direction. One of his comrades hurled a smoke grenade and it exploded in the Nephilim's face, covering their retreat.

"Captain, this is Eterion," he reported into his radio. The three of them jumped down the embankment, and he paused as they slid to the bottom and took off running. "Heavy weapons fire is ineffective, and the snipers can't get a clean shot. We'll need a nuke to take this thing down!"

"Coming up on your location!" Gallus barked in return. With the absence of gunfire, Eterion noticed the sound of an approaching engine. They kept running and were soon met by Gallus, returning from the cliffs.

The snipers used cables to descend from the trees as the hovercraft came to a halt, and they all turned to see the Feral Nephilim thrashing in the smokescreen. Its eyesight had been damaged, leaving it disoriented.

"Plan B isn't ready yet," Gallus growled, briefly scanning the creature's damage now that the smoke from the grenade had cleared. "We'll have to see if we can finish it here."

He raised his ion cannon and motioned for them to attack in a fan formation. The team spread out and advanced on the wounded creature. That was when the massive beast went silent.

Then its shell began to smoke, a thick green substance that reeked of a thousand chemicals mixed together. The gas poured like fog over the entire area, creating its own natural smoke screen. They lost all visibility, forcing them to cease the assault.

Eterion rapped the side of his helmet, but it was an older model, and the smog seemed to be interfering with the heads-up display. He cursed under his breath; they were essentially blind.

A yellow flare ignited somewhere in the mist, and they began to regroup. The eerie quiet was broken only by the hissing of the light. Eterion stumbled a few times, catching glimpses of his comrades in the mist. Eventually, they had gathered around Gallus, who was peering through the fog with tactical goggles.

"Just sitting there," he muttered. "Pumping out this stuff. Helmets stay on until it clears."

This would be sooner than they thought. A great vacuum sound emanated from the Nephilim's shell, and the smog began to thin. Slowly, the surrounding forest cleared until

they stood before the massive shell, still immobile. Gallus raised a fist and was about to give the order to recommence the attack when the monster suddenly pushed off the ground with explosive force. Faster than anything of that size should've been able to move, the fifty-foot creature bounded towards them, its head emerging with gullet wide and foaming. They began to fire, but the Nephilim reared back its head and thrust it forward, unleashing a tidal wave of green liquid.

"SCATTER!" Gallus yelled, and the team split in two as the wave poured forth. An acrid burning filled the air and even seeped into Eterion's helmet as they sprinted out of the way. He heard a roar of pain, and saw that one of his comrades hadn't been fast enough. His comrade staggered and fell, his leg coated in the acid. The Nephilim turned its head in his direction, pouring acid over him in a shower. They were forced to watch as his body melted into liquid, indistinguishable from the burning forest floor. The Nephilim snapped its jaw shut and surveyed the acidic devastation.

Eterion squinted as his eyes began to sting from the fumes. Clenching his fists, Gallus stared at the spot where their companion had died. Eterion knew the look. It was rage being stowed away for a more appropriate time. Despite being the size of a small building, the Nephilim scuttled back and forth as if taunting them into attacking.

"Captain?" Eos asked. Gallus grit his teeth and swung his arm about in a retreat signal.

"We're going with Plan B," he declared into the radio. "Everyone converge on the cliff!"

***

For no good reason, he found himself looking at the poster he'd seen a thousand times.

HAVE A BABY… FOR VICTORY!

It depicted a female Legion solider, proudly holding an infant as if it were her first high-calibre rifle. In fact, Eterion remembered seeing exactly the same look on his peers' faces when they'd first been allowed to fire at something. He still remembered the roar of the barrel, how the target was shredded to pieces with just a short burst.

It was the target of the person standing next to him, but his accuracy had improved since then.

Eterion pulled his furs around his shoulders and glanced around for the thousandth time. No one except security guards ever came out at night, least of all to the ruins of the crashed freighter outside of town. He'd fought through the blizzard to get there, only to find that their transport was late. Five other ex-soldiers stood in the sparse shelter, which consisted of the tail end of the ship that had broken off during the crash. Darius wasn't there, but Eterion held out hope that his friend would eventually follow.

They stood in what was previously the cargo hold, a box-shaped room encrusted in snow. Eterion had served aboard the freighters that carried goods across the planet, and knew from experience that the room would be hardly changed if it were operational. Legion ships were cold and sparely furnished. Decorations and frills were impractical and almost unheard of.

The cold was bitter, and the company even more so. No one wanted to talk, given what they were about to do. They had no authorisation to leave, which was why a covert Corporate shuttle had arranged to meet them there.

Eterion's family knew, and that was all. Even his commanding officer was unaware that he wouldn't be showing up for duty tomorrow. He'd said farewell to his parents, and his sister had seen him off at the door. He'd told her to get back inside, to look after herself. Who knew what the cold could do to an unborn baby? Stubborn as ever, she'd stood and watched him disappear into the falling snow.

Eterion did this for his family, and for the future of the Legion race his sister carried inside her. Every credit he earned from his mercenary job, or at least, a large majority, would be wired back to help them survive. His former peers might call him traitor, but Eterion had resolved never to apply that title to himself. He would always be loyal to the Legion, even if they branded deserters like him as Exsilia.

The faint lights of their shuttle appeared in the sky as it steadily descended towards the snow. Eterion grasped his Kopis pistol, the gun that had become his favourite during academy training, and made a silent vow to never forget. No matter how far he travelled, or whatever he was forced to do for the Corporation… this was his home. He was Legion. And he would always remain loyal.

The shuttle touched down, and the small group of soon-to-be deserters boarded with the haste of those fleeing the law.

***

The team made a tactical retreat on foot, using both the trees and their small size to their advantage. The Feral Nephilim couldn't move freely in the overgrown areas, and was still partially blind. A few times it became trapped, forcing it to regurgitate more acid to melt a path. Eterion turned and swung his rifle upwards. It was all he had left, but still… A gun in his hand made him feel strong. Comrades at his side, even more so.

The monster arched its legs and hurled itself forward, snapping through a set of close-together tree trunks. Two mercenaries were forced to roll to one side as the trunks came smashing down. They then found themselves facing down the Nephilim up close. Eterion raise his rifle, but Gallus was already barrelling in, yanking the pin out of a fragmentation grenade with his teeth.

"COVER!" the captain yelled, and the mercenaries had just enough time to dive over the fallen tree trunks before the grenade exploded.

The four of them stood side by side, staring up into the sky as the ship rose from the docking bay. It hovered for a brief moment before engaging the engines and flying straight through the clouds, out of sight.

Maximus had been on board. No one had expected him to go. Then again, no one ever knew what Max was thinking. The pull towards an Exsilia life of exploration and adventure was too much for many young Legionnaires, even if they didn't show it.

"It doesn't mean anything," Mars grunted as he turned from the landing platform. "We're still comrades."

....

Mars wandered through the streets of the city, off-duty and still in mourning over the loss of a teammate. They'd parted on good terms, but there would be no replacing Max.

'Your gun is not your ally. Your gun is a tool. Your comrades, they are your allies... Auxilia and Exsilia.'

It was tiny next to the Nephilim's bulk, but the little metal shards embedded in its skin made it hesitate briefly, and they were off running again. The light grew brighter, and Eterion could see that they were near to the cliff. A steep embankment was all that lay between them and the trap, and he was about to begin the descent when he heard the ominous gurgling.

Eos had stumbled over a root and sprawled on the ground as the Nephilim clomped towards her. She rolled onto her back and raised her pistol, but it would do no good. The beast's neck shook as it filled with liquid. The entire team unleashed a barrage of bullets with whatever they had left, but their armour-piercing rounds were gone.

Well... all but one. Eterion drew his Kopis pistol, whose barrel contained a single Archon round. Too dangerous and expensive for heavy weaponry, they performed well in small arms. He raised the gun, the familiar grip giving him focus. The Nephilim's head had stopped shaking; it was about to unleash the torrent of acid. Eterion sharply inhaled and fired.

The Nephilim screeched as its one good eye was struck by a red-hot bullet spinning fast enough to drill through steel. The acid in its mouth spilled out, but in no clear direction. Eos rolled backwards and took off while it was distracted, and once Eterion had confirmed that she was out of danger, he leapt over the steep hill and skidded all the way to the bottom.

"Darius, status!" Gallus roared, right behind him.

"Trap is set, Captain," said Darius over the radio. "You just need to get it here."

The team reached the bottom of the hill and fanned out along the tree line while Gallus charged forward. He turned and raised his rifle as the Nephilim appeared at the top of the ridge, spraying it with useless yet irritating gunfire. It covered the incline in three steps and smashed through the trees, coming face to face with Gallus. Their captain stood on the cliff edge, and all that was visible down below was swirling white cloud.

Eterion felt his throat tighten. If this didn't work... well, nothing would. The Nephilim charged, seeming to relish the thrill of not being boxed in by trees. Gallus stood his ground on the very edge of the cliff. As soon as it was close enough, he raised his rifle and fired a maglev cable at one of the fallen tree trunks that lay in the creature's wake, right underneath its gargantuan legs. It arched its neck and tried to snap up the hulking Legion in one gulp, but it ended up eating a mouthful of dirt instead. Gallus had activated the cable, yanking him right through the Nephilim's forelegs, underneath the shell, and out the other side. He severed the cable before he smashed into the trunk, hit the ground rolling, and leapt to his feet. The beast was still confused, scanning the cliff edge to find where its prey had gone. Gallus leapt over the fallen trunk and yelled his order as he sheltered himself for impact.

"FIRE IN THE HOLE!"

Their compact shuttle ascended from the cloud bank and hovered in front of the feral Nephilim. It regarded them, not stupid enough to try to snatch them out of the air, but it didn't matter. It was already too late. The charges laid by the second team exploded in a glorious conflagration of flames and scattered earth. At the same time, the shuttle fired its missiles at the unstable cliff edge. Combined with the Nephilim's massive bulk, it proved too much. The beast shrieked as its footing gave way, pitching it headfirst into the cloudy abyss. The last thing they saw was its flailing legs before it fell out of sight.

After a few painful seconds, a distant whump sounded from the chasm, accompanied by one final tremor. The soldiers emerged from their hiding places, carefully circling the still-unstable edge. They fanned out and peered down into the clouds. For a while, nobody spoke. Then Eterion spoke up.

"So..." he ventured, "...does anybody want to climb down and make sure it's dead?"

Nephilim

Creator: X'ion
Average Height: 1-2.5m
Average Weight: 50-290kg
Average Life Span: 20-(est) 300 years

Home Planet: Eden
Total Pureblood Population: 12.2 million
Total Hybrid Population: 52.4 million
Total Emissaries Population: 0.12 million
(Estimated Total Feral Population: 85 Billion)
Pureblood Yearly Population Growth Rate: -2.1%
Hybrid Yearly Population Growth Rate: +26%
Emissaries Yearly Population Growth Rate: +68%

Years Since Re-emergence into Space: 26 years

Distinctive Physical Features
Wide range of appearances.
Often have mammal and/or insect features.

Nephilim Trait, pg: 340
» +1 Physical, Engineering, and Exotic.
» +1 to all Spare Time Rolls.
» +1 Recover.
» Gain Language: High X'ion or Primal X'ion.
» -1 Conversation.
» -2 Culture.
» Racial Prejudice from Kaltorans and Legion.

Preferred Combat Equipment
Bio tech equipment.

Nephilim History

Twelve X'ion were created by the Archons, and they were declared to be a perfect species. However, this title was soon rescinded, and out of anger at their rejection, the X'ion tried to slay their creators. They failed, and only one X'ion survived. Stealing an Archon ship, it fled into the dark of space and wouldn't return for two centuries. In its exile the X'ion created a new species to act as an instrument of its vengeance: this species was the Nephilim.

The Nephilim were made to be exquisitely engineered organisms, created for the sole purpose of destroying the Archons. They fulfilled their purpose during the Great X'ion War, laying waste to the Archons and their creations. This army was organised into broods, each with a unique purpose. It was the purpose of the Devwi-Ich Brood to destroy the favoured children of the Archons: the Kaltorans.

The Devwi-Ich Brood did their task well. They took Eden, the home world of the Kaltorans, and ruined it. They scoured the system until all Kaltorans were gone; when there were no more Archons to kill, the X'ion vanished into the void. As the years dragged on and supplies ran low, the Devwi-Ich crashed many of their remaining ships into Eden to form a hive, and then it slumbered.

For almost a hundred years, the Devwi-Ich slept. While it slumbered its Nephilim brood was without purpose and order, and they devolved into wild animals or feral tribes. With the arrival of the Corporation in the Haven system, the Devwi-Ich awoke. It reunited the tribes of Feral Nephilim on Eden, and with renewed purpose and leadership the Brood was reborn. The Devwi-Ich cast off all ties to X'ion, who had abandoned them. They would make their own way and set their purpose.

In the Corporation the Devwi-Ich saw an opportunity for building a new society for its brood. It forged an alliance with these newcomers, knowing that the only way for its brood to survive the ages was to create a new society with a purpose greater than destruction.

Nephilim Culture

Life is Cheap

Created to be an un-empathetic warrior race with a short cultural history, the Nephilim often find it hard to understand why the other races are at times so averse to killing.

While each Nephilim often holds their own life in high regard, they rarely value the lives of others. This self-destructive and potentially devastating cultural trait would not only ruin their own society, but also their relationships with the other races of Haven, if not for the foresight of their leaders who often enforce restraint on their subordinates – often, ironically, through death.

Pursuit of Perfection

The Nephilim are driven towards the singular purpose of genetic perfection, seeking to improve their own genes and the genes of their offspring. Those who have excellent genes are given a greater position in society, and those with poor genes are treated as inferior. Unfortunately, perfection is subjective, and to improve yourself is only the first step of many, as you will need to prove to others that your genes are superior if you hope to gain recognition. Each Nephilim will try to do this in their own way, but sooner or later the stronger and more cunning Nephilim often find themselves in charge.

This eugenicist attitude is reminiscent of Archon society. Most hold to the belief that X'ion did not create the Nephilim in the hopes of creating a perfect race, but simply to use them as a tool to crush the Archons before they could create a new, better successor to the X'ion. This drive for self-perfection, more so than any other cultural trait, shows that the Eden Brood has rejected X'ion.

Symbiotic Dependence

The Devwi-Ich is as wise as it is immensely powerful. It has seen what happens to the Nephilim masses when they are left to their own devices. Despite their intelligence and strength, the Nephilim are ill-equipped to form a stable, long-lasting society without the assistance of outsiders. With the long-term survival and prosperity of its brood in mind, the Devwi-Ich has sought to create a symbiotic relationship with the other races. Without the cultural diversity and resources of the other races to draw upon, the Devwi-Ich's brood would once again become a feral war machine.

Will this pursuit towards a sustainable co-existence only last until the Nephilim are able to survive on their own? Many, especially the Legion, suspect the Nephilim of only playing the role of friend until they no longer need the other races.

Creating a Nephilim Character

Pureblood

Some Nephilim have survived since the Great X'ion War, while others are clones and purebred offspring. The Purebloods are perfect specimens of their original, X'ion-designed form. Each Purebloood genus has been engineered for a specific wartime purpose. Most are large, powerful, monstrous-looking creatures with admirable physical and mental ability.

Recommended Skills
» Leadership
» Physical
» Exotic

Recommended Traits
» Strength: Massive
» Reflexes: Solid Build
» Exotic: Frenzy

Hybrid

Born from a mixed Purebloood or Hybrid pairing, Hybrids are in many ways the opposite of their Purebloood parents or ancestors. Hybrids are adaptive, cunning, and flexible creatures. They are extremely varied; many have genetic abnormalities and adaptations, and they are every bit as powerful as the Purebloods, arguably more so as they have thrived in great numbers while the Purebloods decline.

Recommended Skills
» Survival
» Bio Tech
» Small Arms

Recommended Traits
» Reflexes: Agile Build
» Survival: Makeshift
» Exotic: Special Ammo

Emissary

First created only a few years ago, the Emissaries are the newest genus in the Eden Brood. Primarily female and engineered for interacting with other races, they appear more "normal" than other Nephilim. Emissaries are grown to full maturity in vats in a single year. Their minds are filled with fake memories and experiences to give them a personality and skills.

Recommended Skills
» Conversation
» Awareness
» Bio Tech

Recommended Traits
» Strength: Eye Candy
» Conversation: Pheromones
» Intelligence: Introvert

Pureblood   Hybrid   Emissary

Government and Law

Government: Genecratic Feudalism.
Leadership: The Devwi-Ich.

The Devwi-Ich

The Devwi-Ich is rarely seen, and its exact nature is largely unknown. But none can deny that it is a powerful and cunning creature who commands the loyalty of the Eden Brood from the megacity of Necronus. It rules with absolute authority by right of its genetics.

Loyalty of the Brood

The Eden Brood is based on a pyramid of hierarchy: the Devwi-Ich is at the top, beneath it are the Genocrats, and beneath the Genocrats are the remainder of the brood. Loyalty is important in the structure of the Eden Brood; a Nephilim who stands alone will not live long. Each member of the brood is loyal to a Genocrat, and all the Genocrats are loyal to the Devwi-Ich.

The Genocrats

There are no official titles among the Nephilim. Instead, there is a generally recognised pecking order based on individual genetics, prowess, and cunning. The Nephilim have a society of authority through power, generally derived from exceptional genes. The Genocrats are exceptional genetic specimens, smarter and stronger than lesser beings, and as such they are the rulers in the Eden Brood; they are the Nephilim "nobility" and only answer to the Devwi-Ich. Each Genocrat controls a territory, station, Necronus spire, or spacecraft. Nephilim under the Genocrat's command are considered their subjects and must swear loyalty to them. Each Genocrat usually has an inner circle of advisers and lieutenants who enforce the Genocrat's will.

Law of the Strong

The legal system of the Eden Brood is straightforward: if you swear loyalty to someone, you come under their protection and their authority.

If you do something which displeases anyone with power over you, they determine your guilt and administer punishment as they see fit. The only way to challenge a charge against you is to defeat your accuser in direct or indirect combat. Failing this combat will often result in death.

Minor Crimes, Examples (Public Beating)

» Displaying incompetence in your duties.
» Disappointing your master.
» Having something that a more powerful Nephilim wants.
» Killing a master's servant.

Major Crimes, Examples (Death)

» Shaming your master.
» Showing disobedience.
» Attacking a more powerful Nephilim.
» Having a prominent genetic flaw.

Relationship with Other Races

The Eden Brood is the clear military power in the Haven system and could destroy the other races should they wish it. But knowing that they are ill-equipped to survive on their own, the Devwi-Ich has declared a status of non-aggression towards the other races.

Though they do not wield their military strength, that strength does act as unmentioned bargaining chip for interracial negotiations, forcing the other races to take the Nephilim seriously.

Alliance with the Corporation

When the Corporation first arrived in the Haven system, they were struggling to survive and colonise the gas giant Alabaster. In an unrepeated sign of compassion, the newly awoken Devwi-Ich had the Eden Brood assist the Corporation with supplies, labour, and help in using their living spacecraft.

This cooperation continues to this day through peaceful trade, in exchanges of cheap Nephilm labour, in the form of biologically engineered drones called Flesh, for Corporation-harvested fuel.

Struggle to Find Allies

The Eden Brood harbours no ill will towards those who used to be their enemies in the Great X'ion War, but this feeling is not mutual. Although the Nephilim are keen to make alliances with the Legion and Kaltorans, both of these races have been reluctant to do so. The Kaltorans have genetic memories of the atrocities that the Nephilim committed against them, and the Legion were built to combat the Nephilim. To overcome these problems, the Devwi-Ich has adopted a strategy of interdependence: if the other races can be made to rely on the Eden Brood to the extent that their help cannot be refused, then alliances will come about naturally.

Emissaries

To ameliorate their common diplomatic troubles, the Nephilim have created a new genus to curb public opinion of their monstrous nature, This new genus is known as the Emissaries.

Not only fashioned to look more like the other races, their brains have been engineered for greater empathy and understanding. Emissaries are born fully grown with memories and experiences implanted directly into their minds, allowing them to be fully functional from the moment of their creation. They are given the singular task of simply mingling with the other races, acclimatising them to the Nephilim and easing their concerns simply through proximity.

Feral Nephilim

When left to their own devices and without the guidance of a strong leader (such as the Devwi-Ich), the Nephilim often devolve into purely survival-driven animals or primitive savages; such Nephilim are considered feral. The Devwi-Ich is constantly working towards bringing powerful Feral Nephilim into its brood, whereas the other races would rather simply destroy them. However, the Devwi-Ich and its brood harbour no ill will to the other races should they decide to kill a Feral Nephilim.

Economy

Exports: Unskilled Labour (Corporation) and Scientific Knowledge.
Imports: Fuel (Corporation), Food, and Feral Nephilim.

Storehouse

As supplies ran low during the Great War, the Devwi-Ich commanded its fleet to crash onto Eden, a barren wasteland, creating a massive graveyard of spacecraft. Buried deep within this graveyard, the Devwi-Ich stored what remained of their supplies. The Devwi-Ich kept these valuable supplies locked up until it awoke, over one hundred years later, when the Corporation arrived in the Haven system.

In a sudden explosion of prosperity, the Devwi-Ich opened these storehouses of resources and equipment, building a singular massive city and propelling the Eden Brood back into space. But Eden is a wasteland, and the Nephilim are ill-equipped to create a sustainable society. It is only a matter of time before these supplies run out – a fact that the Devwi-Ich is keenly aware of.

Borrowed Economy

With no set economic system, the Eden Brood has naturally absorbed the methods of the strongest economic system in Haven: the Corporation's Credits. However, there are a few key differences: The Eden Brood rarely deals in pure finances and stocks, and Eden has no major banks or established brokerage firms, as the planet lacks the infrastructure for high finance.

The Eden Brood is far more flexible than the Corporation, however, as they don't have a well-established financial system, they are very willing to barter with goods and services as needed.

Wealth and Power

Nephilim culture is turbulent, so keeping wealth is not straightforward, and the emphasis on the strong ruling the weak greatly affects the economy of the Eden Brood. A Nephilim can only keep as much wealth as it has the power to protect, and it can only extract as much wealth from others as it can force from them.

Genocrats are often wealthy because they extort money from others under threat of harm, and they can keep their collected wealth because others cannot take it. However, weaker Nephilim can become wealthy under the protection of Corporate regulations, encouraging many entrepreneurial Nephilim to leave Nephilim society for the collective protection of the Corporation system.

Diplomatic Economy

The Devwi-Ich has made trade with the other races a priority because trade facilitates communication and overrides racial prejudice. Despite their reasons for despising the Nephilim, both Kaltorans and Legion still trade with the Eden Brood. In this way the Eden Brood has made great leaps in overcoming the prejudice it faces from the other races, opening a dialogue which may eventually lead to greater peace and stability in the Haven system.

Science and Technology

Bio-Technology

X'ion used genetic engineering wherever possible to win its vicious war against the Archons. In its army, biological creatures filled roles that the other races would have filled with engineered machines.

For the Nephilim, large and complex technologies such as spacecraft are not single creatures but rather ecosystems of symbiotic life forms. For instance: in a spacecraft, Death Scarabs eat the waste of other systems, and they create nests in weak and fractured parts of the hull, stabilising the larger body. During boarding actions, they would consider the boarders as waste and try to eat them.

Blended Eden Brood Technology

During the last century, and especially during the last decade, the Eden Brood has been forced to adapt much of X'ion's purely organic technologies to their available resources. As many of X'ion's construction methods have been lost to the Nephilim, it is common practice to replace failing organic systems with mechanical or electronic systems. Mechanical and electronic components are readily available to the Nephilim from trade with the Corporation.

These factors have led to hybridised technological systems, replacing much of what remained from the Great X'ion War. The Eden Brood prefer organic technologies where possible, though they have worked to make their devices appear non-biological in order to facilitate trade.

Personal Research

The Eden Brood has a great many scientists working towards personal research objectives. This research is often driven by the desire for self-advancement through genetic engineering. However, it is also understood that knowledge is power, and to the Eden Brood, power is everything. All manner of research is conducted to establish one's intellectual superiority, and this knowledge is a valuable commodity to those who know how to use it.

This non-collective, individual approach to research sets the Nephilim apart from most races – especially the Corporation and Legion, who often prefer well-organised teams of governmentally or centrally funded researchers.

The End Justifies the Means

Nephilim scientists tend to believe that all things are permissible in the pursuit of scientific knowledge and personal advancement. Nephilim scientists often abduct unwilling test subjects and are happy to explore any technology, regardless of its potential for causing wider negative consequences. To the Nephilim, no research is unethical or too dangerous.

This amoral approach to acquiring knowledge and power is thought to be a result of not only their genetic predisposition towards self-advancement, but also their primal and violent culture.

Genetics

Created by X'ion

Unlike all the other races, who were created by the Archons, the Nephilim were created by the X'ion. They were made for the singular purpose of destroying the Archons and their creations. Naturally, Nephilim are violent killers without empathy or the ability to process complex emotions and social cues. This has caused many problems after the war, as most Nephilim devolved into animals or were only able to create primitive, barbaric tribes.

One Species

All creatures created by X'ion are categorised as Nephilim; they share a common genetic structure, and they are often biologically compatible, most prominently the Pureblood and Hybrid genera, but also much of their biological technology: weapons, armour, spacecraft, and just about any biologically engineered creature made by X'ion or the Nephilim. Purebloods and Hybrids share the same number of chromosomes and can both produce Hybrids, although not all Hybrids are genetically viable (for instance the offspring of a Pureblood Nephilim and a spine rifle).

Breeding and Gender

Other than the Emissaries, Nephilim are not gendered in the same way as the other races; they do not often adhere to strict male and female reproductive distinctions. Bred for combat, most Purebloods of the same genus are identical and display no obvious signs of gender.

Those Nephilim who can reproduce often do so by laying eggs and having another Nephilim (even one that can lay eggs) fertilise the eggs by excreting their DNA in a mucus. Most Hybrids are born in this way.

Those genus unable to naturally reproduce often immerse themselves in pools of mutagenic fluid to extract their DNA, enabling them to fertilise eggs. Otherwise, they make use of laboratory cloning vats or artificial insemination. Many Nephilim prefer their offspring to be grown in a laboratory because natural breeding methods are often erratic.

Gene Splicing

Gene splicing is one of the primary means by which the Eden Brood alter their own genes. Traditional genetic engineering requires a new generation to be created, but gene splicing allows the alteration of genes in a living and fully grown specimen.

In gene splicing, a biological engineered virus is injected (painfully) into a host, altering their DNA. The virus replaces parts of the host's genes in order to achieve a specific result.

Implants

Adding biological or electrical devices to one's body (with or without altering DNA) is a common practice amongst the Nephilim. Once installed, many implants act as parasites, feeding off the organic energy produced by the host's body.

Viewed in a similar way to blended biological technology, implants are not seen as true improvements to one's self, as they do not alter or improve the genome. However, they are seen as valuable tools, useful for advancing one's abilities.

Purebloods

X'ion created many Nephilim genera, each with a specific war-focused function. All of these first creations are referred to as Purebloods for the simple reason that their genus remains unchanged. Many Purebloods are not those created by X'ion, however; rather, they are the children of pairings of Purebloods of the same genus. Some Purebloods are clones, while others have simply never died.

Hybrids

After a hundred years of post-War existence, those Pureblood genera which could breed did. All Nephilim, regardless of genus, are genetically compatible, and so a great many Hybrid species have been created from various Pureblood pairings. Hybrids vary greatly from one another; each pairing may result in different genetic combinations, and even siblings can be very different.

Hybrids are not genetically inferior to Purebloods, but they are less specialised. Hybrids are generally more adaptable than their Pureblood parents, as their genera were capable of surviving the process of natural selection over the hundred years after the Great War, the Years of Darkness.

Emissaries

Created only three years ago, the Emissaries are the newest genus to the Eden Brood, engineered for interacting with the other races. As such, their outward appearance is similar to the other races. But make no mistake: they are Nephilim.

Emissaries are primarily female, created in laboratories, and grown to full maturity in vats in a single year. Their minds are filled with fake memories and experiences to give them a personality and skills. They are similar to Flesh in the way they are created and skilled, but Emissaries have free will and are genetically Nephilim.

Short Story: Udryk & Yreig

Udryk was hardly ever called upon to stab people any more. This was disappointing, as the job had been a lot more exciting when she'd started.

Her interview had consisted of entering the Supplier's shack and immediately being attacked by his bodyguard, who'd been hiding behind the door. The guard was a Nephilim Pureblood – strange, as not many of them were seen in the slums – but a relatively small one. Udryk had grabbed his knife-hand and squeezed, relishing the snapping bones. She was given the job on the spot.

The Supplier was setting up his business in the slums of Necronus, right on the very lowest level, beyond even the thoughts of the higher-ups of society. Here they lived in the shadows of the great towers, growing ever more indifferent to the stench of the surrounding swamps, caring very little for the affairs of the upper world. It was the only way to live.

Udryk was a Hybrid. Her body was wiry and deceptively thin, like that of a stick insect. The claws of her feet and hands were long and wickedly sharp, her greatest feature. Though she cared little for clothes beyond her simple brown worker's tunic, Udryk sharpened her claws daily. She made sure she could see her face in their gleaming silver surface: it would be the last thing an enemy would see, should they cross her. Her claws could be retracted, but she rarely bothered.

Udryk's head was triangular, with ears set into either side and two pure black eyes that often moved independently. Most importantly for her job, she was tall, tall enough to match most Purebloods. Her body may have been slim, but once Udryk corrected her deceptive slouch and fully extended her claws, it no longer mattered. Hostile visitors to the Supplier's shack often took one look at Udryk, swallowed, forced their eyes away from the steely talons, and adopted a more submissive tone.

Udryk loved the power, but sometimes wished she was less outwardly intimidating. Her appearance deterred fights... and Udryk loved to fight. Still, it had given her a stable job, which was more than could be said for many living in the slums. The Supplier had set up his business deep in the tangle of metal shacks and piles of refuse, strategically placed beneath a jungle of organic steel girders to prevent the flying patrol from ever spotting it. The entire slum population knew where to find the shop, but none were stupid enough to spread the word to the upper city. In any case, the two worlds rarely crossed paths.

That day, Udryk was doing exactly the same thing she did every day: nothing. Strictly speaking, she was guarding the entrance to the shack that served as the Supplier's place of business, but ever since she'd gutted that one upstart who'd pulled a gun and tried to force her boss to return his money... well, people seemed to be taking the security a lot more seriously. Slum residents would file by her, occasionally throwing a brief, nervous glance at her unsheathed claws. Their business complete, they would shuffle out again. It was a living, if not an exciting one.

Udryk stood outside the flap that led into the Supplier's shack, crouched as always. She glanced up as she heard the distinctive hiss of the crate as it whizzed overhead. The crate was the only elevator that led straight into the slums, and could only be operated by the upper class. Needless to say, it wasn't used often. It glided on a rail over the shanty town, weaving in amongst the dense Necronus infrastructure, and finally came to a rest at the base of the central column: a great, long-dead ship that jutted upwards into the highest reaches of the city. Though it wasn't visible from where Udryk stood, she knew that the entire area was surrounded by an electrical barrier to stop the slum-dwellers from getting any delusions of grandeur. In the entire time Udryk had been alive, no one had ever attempted to breach the barrier. If the lower class had anything, it was an inflated sense of self-preservation.

Udryk narrowed her eyes as the crate descended and was lost from view.

"Could be our lucky day," said the Supplier, stepping through the flap with a smirk. He was a Hybrid, like Udryk, though far shorter and covered in fur. His legs were bowed, and his head was beetle-like except for his two horns. His left hand was half sawn-off, and he had a metal multitool where his right should've been. Krysh was his name, but to maintain his mystique and selling power he went by "The Supplier". No one could source components like he did, whether for weapons or household appliances. With resources at a premium in the slums, many relied upon his services to get by.

"Hmm," Udryk grunted back. Krysh shrugged and continued to polish his tool-hand with a rag.

"Maybe they're here to give us all a promotion to the upper city," he continued. "Gotta live in hope, right?"

Udryk knitted her brow in annoyance. Krysh was from the upper city, but had been cast down for crossing the wrong Genocrat, a tower warlord of sorts. She still found his opinions grating.

"They live up there," Udryk replied. "And we down here. That's the balance."

"Uh-huh. Get that from a textbook, did ya?"

This was probably a joke. If not, it was so ridiculous that Udryk didn't bother to respond. It was a well-known slum rule that every child knew from the day they understood words: your genetics defined you.

"Well, whatever," Krysh said, finally. "I can tell ya a million times how things are up there... but if you wanna stand there looking tough all ya life, be my guest. Can't say I'd wanna lose ya anyway."

He lifted the flap and vanished back into his shop, and Udryk was left alone with her thoughts. She glanced upwards, something she did sparsely. There wasn't much to look at in the jungle of rotting bio-hulls and abandoned carapaces that made up the foundations of the great towers, and it prompted very little thought. She'd barely ever even seen the sky, except on short hunting trips with her hive mother when she'd been young. It suddenly struck her that, in the upper city, they could see it any time they wanted.

The thought was… unsettling. Then again, most of Krysh's unwanted banter had this effect. Udryk shook her head and settled back into her boredom, forgetting the arrival of the crate entirely.

***

A few minutes passed that stretched themselves into miniature hours. Business was slow. Udryk was contemplating a pace back and forth, or perhaps adopting a crouch, when a slender figure appeared over the edge of one of the scrap heaps. Sensing something that definitely wasn't a customer, Udryk immediately came to attention. The figure was clad in black, and it descended the pile of metal with uncommon grace. A somersault finally brought it to the ground, and Udryk was able to identify it for the first time.

It was an Emissary. Possessing a far more "human" shape than any Nephilim in the lower city, the new arrival had pale green skin and glossy black hair, held to her head by luminescent tendrils. Her black clothing was cloth, but tight-fitting, showing off her slender frame. It was Udryk's first time seeing one in person, and she immediately thought that the Emissary looked weak, flimsy. One little slice and her head would be on the floor. Still, it wasn't like they'd been bred for combat.

She had landed in a crouch, and looked up to survey her surroundings. Udryk heard the drone of a patrol, and the Emissary's head snapped towards the sound. The two locked eyes, and there was a clash of curiosity and wariness in both gazes.

Without knowing exactly why, Udryk slowly raised a claw and motioned to the shack entrance. The Emissary hesitated, glanced behind her, and sprinted for the flap. Keeping an eye on Udryk's humongous claws, the small Nephilim slipped inside half a second before the mounted patrol appeared over the ridge. It was composed of four hovercrafts, each of them seating a hulking Hybrid thug. They could often be spotted around the streets, keeping a watchful eye for the local Genocrat. Udryk had little time for warlords and their delusions of power, but their patrols were often culled from the worst of society. No one crossed them, unless they wanted to find themselves without a head before the day was over.

They scanned the street as they passed, casting a suspicious glance at Udryk from above. She didn't make eye contact with their leader, but must've projected an air of boredom so great that they were forced to conclude she knew nothing. The patrol kept flying deeper into the slums, and soon their drone faded to nothing.

The Emissary emerged from the shack and nodded to Udryk.

"Thank you," she said. These weren't words heard often in the lower city, and the Hybrid Nephilim had no idea how to respond.

"You're an Emissary," she said instead. "Why are you here?"

"Exploration."

"Of what?"

The Emissary looked at her as if the question should've been evident. Udryk let her eyes wander, and she saw that the smaller Nephilim had a spine gun strapped to her waist. It was at this moment that Krysh came stumbling out of the tent, confident that the patrol wasn't after him.

"A pretty little Emissary, in my shop," he said hungrily, eyeing the new arrival with interest. "And on the run, too. Could be a few benefits to bringing her in."

"You can try, Hybrid."

She spoke with confidence that dwarfed her stature, and her hands strayed to the gun at her side as she spoke. Udryk was impressed.

"We owe nothing to the security patrol," she said, standing between the Emissary and Krysh. "Anything that irritates them is fine by me."

Krysh made a noise of impatience and shot the Emissary a suspicious glance before heading back into his shop.

"I am Yreig," said the Emissary, as soon as he had gone. "I was born several hours ago."

Udryk simply looked at her.

"It seems that knowledge of the slums was considered useless information."

Udryk still stared, wondering when the Emissary would get to the point.

"I eluded my escort specifically so I could see every inch of the city," Yreig continued. "I have learned much in my time here."

"Like how to build a house out of spare parts?" Udryk snorted. She couldn't believe this conversation was taking place. This Emissary was likely defective, not to mention distracting. Yreig gave an exasperated sigh before walking straight past Udryk, on the path that led into the centre. Abruptly she spun around and folded her arms.

"I require a guide," she stated. "Someone to accompany me in the upper so that I do not draw attention. You will help me."

Yes, this one was definitely defective. To think that any random slum-dweller would consent to running around with an Emissary, simply because they asked… this one was clearly socially deficient.

And yet, Udryk paused to consider the offer. She was bored, critically so. Any change of surroundings would be welcome. If she was accompanying a brain-dead Emissary, things had suddenly gotten a whole lot more interesting.

"You can get us to the upper city?"

Yreig held up her arm, and beneath the surface of her palm was a faint glow.

"My bio-pass. It will take us to most places."

Most places. Now, Udryk was interested. If a security team found them, she could simply say she was taking the little upstart back to the lab.

"Fine," she replied with a toothy smile. "Stay in the shop until my shift is over. And I'll be your tour guide."

Yreig nodded as if there was never any other conclusion to asking a complete stranger to be your companion. She lifted the flap and was soon lost from sight. Udryk turned back to the road with a tiny smile, knowing that her boredom was about to be relieved for the day.

***

"Why would someone choose to live in the slums?"

"Is equality so difficult to achieve?"

"Why is it that those down here have so few thoughts of their own?"

Udryk was relieved when Yreig used her pass to access the crate, and they stepped inside.

The doors slid shut behind them, and Udryk watched through the small window as the machine ascended. She frowned as she realised that she'd never before seen the slums from above. It looked… disappointing. Just an expanse of organic steel and rotting ship carcasses. It lay permanently in the shadow of the society above. The crate began to wind through the jungle of girders, and soon her home was obscured.

Yreig had taken one of the simple metal seats, and was looking up at her companion with curiosity.

"Was it embarrassing, to be seen with me?"

Once again, Udryk couldn't comprehend the question. She had never been embarrassed in her life, and couldn't imagine what it felt like.

"No," she replied, which was the truth. "Were you embarrassed?"

"…somewhat."

Udryk glanced away from the window and saw Yreig staring defiantly at the floor, her face a mass of emotion. Definitely defective.

"You have a good future ahead of you," the Hybrid offered. "You were made to travel. See what is out there."

"To not have a home?"

Udryk noted the sorrow in her voice, and she was overcome by an odd urge to drop Yreig at the nearest laboratory and tell them to melt her down into genetic paste. Nephilim did not feel sorrow at petty things.

However, the Emissary was still a curious creature. Udryk's curiosity had awoken, and it drank in the new experiences that never would've occurred without their meeting. The crate continued to ascend, and the Hybrid Nephilim took a seat opposite her companion. They were built for large Purebloods, and neither of them was comfortable.

"You thoughts are ridiculous," she said plainly. "You were made for a life of travelling. Accept it."

That was all she could think of. Fortunately, Yreig had many more thoughts.

"Or my home is not Eden," the smaller Nephilim continued. "Yes, I had considered this. Perhaps I was created to search."

You were created to be a pretty piece of eye-candy to lull the other races into a false sense of security, Udryk wanted to say. She restrained herself.

"Just be glad you are what you are," she replied. "You have genetic privilege that those in the lower city do not."

"Do you have a family?"

And they were back to the ridiculous questions.

"Yes."

"You live with them?"

"Not anymore."

"And you… love them?"

If this kept up, the Emissary really would be heading for a life of being genetic paste.

"We're bound by genetics. That is all."

"And you were born naturally?"

"In an egg, yes."

"How intriguing."

"Not really," Udryk replied. "I can't imagine a pod birth is any more exciting."

"But it is!" Yreig said, leaning forward in her seat. "I mean… I remember it was warm. The laboratory was so cold when the pod dissolved. And I felt alone, even though I had so much knowledge of other places being placed into my head. And the way I was suspended…"

"Enough," Udryk snapped. Her patience was running thin, and this never-ending stream of details had whittled it shorter than usual. Yreig swallowed and lowered her eyes. For a moment, Udryk enjoyed the blissful silence. Then she felt the slightest twinge of guilt.

"You're learning, I get it," Udryk hissed, waving her hand impatiently. "Your curiosity is exhausting. But… understandable."

It was a lie, but Yreig nodded and seemed satisfied. The crate moved higher. Necronus had many layers and branches, and once the crate had cleared the forest of girders it took a sharp right. The track ran alongside a massive spire that jutted out into open space horizontally. There were residences built all over the top, but the crate began to move towards one of the lower levels. The track entered an opening, and Udryk saw that they were passing rows upon rows of doors. Finally, the crate whirred to a halt, and the doors opened straight into an elevator. They stepped inside and travelled up, and after a short journey the doors opened to Udryk's first view of the upper city.

Now it was her turn to be amazed. The dusty floor of the lower city had been replaced by crystalline walkways spread out like membrane between the city's great pillars. It glowed a faint green, giving all the light the denizens of the city could need. Nephilim of all breeds moved back and forth with real purpose, not dragging their feet like those below, and Udryk spotted several shops and drinking establishments, some with flashing neon lights that advertised their wares from a mile off. The darkening sky was visible even through the pillars, and she found her gaze caught upwards.

As she stood staring up, there was the whine of an engine, and a massive craft approached from the west.

"What is…" Yreig began, "…oh, a bio-ship!"

It began to descend, and they could see the dark, fleshy hull lit up by the lights of the upper city. The ship came to rest at the docking bay and left their view.

"That's where I'll be going," Yreig said, looking up at the great plates that formed the landing area, the city's highest point. "All

of us were supposed to gather there after we were cleared. I… slipped away."

"So keep slipping," Udryk replied. "Now it's your turn to show me the place."

Yreig turned out to be a terrible tour guide, as her hastily installed memories didn't include much experience of the Necronus streets. Nevertheless, Udryk found every corner fascinating, marvelling at the simplest of differences.

Udryk felt no jealousy or anger at seeing how they lived. It was more like her curiosity had been fulfilled; this world that lay only a mile or so above had been unveiled. If anything, she was disappointed. She'd expected music, more of a bustling metropolis. Instead, even the upper city looked morose. They were not a happy race. Even the electricity, the bio-organic nature of which should've made the city seem alive, seemed sluggish and morbid.

This level was a basic circuit that ringed a central tower, and after hours of simply wandering, they found themselves back at their starting point.

"I should get back," Yreig said, casting a guilty glance upwards. "They'll be waiting…"

Udryk said nothing as they stepped into the elevator and directed it to take them up. Their final stop would be the landing platform, after which they would return to their lives, jaunt over. The elevator ride was painfully short, and soon the doors slid open to reveal the great flat plates that formed the landing platforms. Control towers dotted the space, and ships of all types were arranged in straight lines.

The air was clear, and their altitude offered a brilliant view of the setting sun over the wasteland.

"I'll tell them I got lost," Yreig said as they emerged into the crowd. "And you brought me back. No more questions needed."

"Fine," Udryk replied.

Yreig smiled, another gesture she'd need everywhere that wasn't Eden.

"I have learned much from our interactions. Thank you."

Udryk grunted, and they weaved their way through the mass of Legion, Corporates, and Nephilim going to and from their ships. A few Kaltorans could be spotted in the mix, and Udryk noted with interest how they carried themselves; it was a carefree swagger that just seemed… alien. Which they were, technically.

Yreig seemed to know where they were going, so they took a direct route through the sea of ships, stepping off the criss-cross pathways. It grew quieter, and they found themselves in the shadow of a large Corporate freighter. Its bulk cast a long shadow, and outside of the

landing platform sat a ring of Legion mercenaries. They laughed at some bawdy joke as the two Nephilim passed, though one of them stopped abruptly and stepped into their way. He wore dark red combat armour, but half the buckles were undone, and he swayed on the spot. Udryk didn't need her keen sense of smell to tell he was severely drunk.

"W-who said you could w-walk here?" he slurred, swinging his metal mug in a wide arc. "Thissss… this here's the Nova Zero. N… not a ship for filthy Nephilim h-hands to get all over, eh?"

Yreig shrank back, but Udryk stood her ground.

"We're not touching anything," she replied. "We'll go."

She attempted to step forward, but another swing of the mug whistled past her nose. The Legion recovered from his stumble and attempted a clumsy swing at her head.

"Enough, Legion!" she hissed as she grabbed his wrist. "We have no quarrel with you!"

She shoved him aside, where his shipmates tried to pull him back. The Legion shook them off and drew a pistol from the back of his belt.

"W-well WE have a q-quarrel with you," he growled back, "Genetic scum. Pathetic X'ion leftovers."

He raised the pistol and Yreig cried out a useless warning. One swipe of Udryk's claws took off his hand. Her other set plunged right into his chest, where his armour hung loose. She roared and tossed him off, where he crumpled and lay bleeding.

For a moment, nobody moved an inch. Then Udryk grabbed Yreig by the shoulder and left the stunned Legion mercenaries behind. They half walked, half ran to the shadow of a nearby ship, where Yreig backed away, her eyes wide. Udryk listened for a few moments to make sure they weren't being followed.

"Do they all hate us?" Yreig asked, her voice half a whisper.

Udryk flicked blood off her claws with disgust.

"They mistrust us," she replied, and despite her slum upbringing, she knew this for sure. "And you can never trust them. As I said, we truly have no quarrel with the other races. We need them. But that cannot be mistaken for friendship."

Her own words surprised her. Yreig seemed taken aback, unsure of what to make of them. Before anyone else could speak, they heard one of the Legion call out to his comrades. Udryk snapped her head around and saw one of them aiming with his handgun. She shoved Yreig to one side and charged towards him in a crouch. The mercenary opened fire, but Udryk ran along the side of the wall and flipped over his head, dealing a deep gash to his neck.

He crumpled, but the others were close, and the only reason Udryk was still uninjured was how intoxicated the Legion all were. She crouched next to the corner until she could hear their footsteps up close, then leapt out, claws flashing. One was disarmed and she slashed him across the face, but the other managed to duck underneath and deal Udryk a powerful blow to the head. She was knocked against the side of a ship, and her vision went blurry. She was vaguely aware of a muzzle in her face, but when it fired, it sounded wrong. There was an audible twang, like that of a solid projectile.

Udryk shook her head, and her vision cleared in time to see the Legion mercenary crumple in pain, a large spine sticking out of his eye. Yreig stood a few feet away, wide-eyed but with a steady hand. Hybrid and Emissary locked eyes, and there was a moment of understanding.

Udryk leapt to her feet, and they quickly moved away from the scene before anyone saw what they'd done. They crouched behind a fleshy-hulled Nephilim frigate, whose skin pulsed with green-veined energy.

"It was a good shot," Udryk said, hoping it qualified as gratitude. Yreig nodded and stowed her spine gun back in its holster.

"I will go," she said, her voice breaking. "I mean… I should go. There's much I have to see."

Udryk shrugged, secretly disappointed. One little flash of her claws and the delicate thing was scared off. Yreig nodded again, and turned awkwardly in the opposite direction. She took a few steps, then turned back with a resolute expression.

"Thank you for you cooperation," she announced. "I had… anyway. You're here now."

"Yes, I am," Udryk replied, wondering when she'd get to the point.

"No, I mean…you're here. In the upper city."

"…yes."

"And you have no obligation to return."

The realisation dawned, and Udryk furrowed her brow in amusement. Yreig, seeing that she'd gotten her point across, gave a brief smile before disappearing into the labyrinth of ships. Udryk heard her footfalls fade, and looked around. She was in the upper city. No one in the slums would miss her, save for Krysh. And who cared about him, anyway? He'd find some other hulking muscle.

Udryk bared her teeth in amusement, then turned and walked away before anyone saw her with the Legion's bodies.

She wondered if any of the upper city businesses were in need of security guards.

Places of Interest

See pg: 8 for Sector and System Maps.

The great sprawling Habrixis Sector began as a utopian dream of the Archons – a place for their genetically cradled children to flourish and populate a glimmering starscape. The nightmare of the Great X'ion War consumed that dream, and now a hundred years later, Habrixis is a divided span of uncharted systems.

Haven System

From a distant observatory, the Haven system seems the perfect solar community: a grouping of diverse worlds, gently kissed by the Halo Nebula, serenely orbiting their beacon star, Esh – a warm light for many. Originally the Kaltoran home system, now Haven is a highly contested territory, where every race's dreams of a better future hinge on and against one another. For now a tremulous peace reigns, but disputes over planets, mineral-rich asteroids, and solar shipping lanes create a tense web of conflict.

Var System

Once the home of the Corporation, the Var system refers to their original namesake, the Vargarti, as they were once titled by the Archons. The Var system was to be a distant pen, or cradle, far from the Archon's more capable and loved children. But the ambitions and ingenuity of this genetically disadvantaged race gave rise to the powerful Corporation, which left the Var behind to wield tremendous influence across the Haven system. Whether or not any Vargarti were left behind in their home system is unknown to all but the highest CEOs of the Corporation.

Cerberus System

Dominated by the large planet Cerberus Prime, the Legion home world, the Cerberus system is fiercely guarded and protected against any intrusion. The Legion allow no uninvited entry, and constant patrols of heavy warships and flights of fighters reduce any unauthorised vessels to ash long before they come near the worlds of their home system. Though the Corporation have been assimilating the Legion in the Haven system as a dedicated mercenary force, the Legion of Cerberus remain unquestionably autonomous. Those Legion who defect, however, will never again see their home system, for return means facing the harsh justice of a tribunal.

Black Reach Nebula

This distant nebula remains a dark mystery, with perhaps thousands of worlds lost inside its black embrace. Those who travel near it pick up eerie radio echoes reflecting off the masses of stardust. Some frenetic terror-soaked broadcasts date from the X'ion War, and others, reflecting off some distant resonator harken back even earlier, perhaps even to the era of humanity.

Uncharted Systems

The young races of Haven have yet to rediscover most of the systems from the Habrixis Sector – these uncharted fringe worlds are mysteries, sure to contain other forgotten children of the Archons and the X'ion.

Alabaster

Mean Diameter: 164 981 km	Surface Gravity: 12.97 m/s
Rotation Period: 12.29 hours	Orbital Period: 58.21 years

Once a holy pilgrimage site and source of much of the Old Kaltoran Theocracy's fuel supply, this gas giant of swirling milky white streams and golden conflux was once called Makor. After leaving their home system of Var, the Corporation set its hungry eyes on Makor, making it their new home.

When the Corp assumed dominance of Makor, they renamed her Alabaster for her ivory halo of vapours and the majestic icy rings which encircled the picturesque world. Alabaster's noxious vapours contain numerous rare elements of impressive utility, including tremendous amounts of helium-3 starship fuel, rare chemicals to aid ore processing, and the compounds needed to create Synth Steel. Still more treat rare ailments, serve as power-core coolants, and one special gaseous element, elysium-4 (commonly called Gossamer), serves as the key ingredient in the system's most potent addictive narcotic: Draz.

Geography

Alabaster is nothing more than wells and storms of elemental gases enshrouding a dense nodule of hard metallic rock. The Corp's network of power stems from the clutch of six gargantuan space stations navigating the circumference of the gas giant in slow, steady orbit. The silence and serenity of these luminous constructs of metal betray little evidence of the whirling buzz of activity and bedlam of industry constantly raging within.

The greatest of these six stations is Alabaster 1, the oldest station and by far the most affluent. In contrast to her sisters, 1 is more of an orbital city than a fully active processing station, replete with stunning promenades sporting dozens of great monuments, a massive and luxurious habitat ring, and zero-gravity recreational centres with floating pools, gymnasia, spas, and baths. Only those steeped in profit, wealth, and power can afford the prohibitive expenses of the good life on Alabaster 1.

"Initiating algorithms... Quarterly financial diagnostics complete... PRIORITY REPORT: Productivity is down 3.7% on Alabaster 4. This is not an anomaly. Alabaster 4 reports six consecutive quarters of sustained and deepening deficit. Suggested course of action: Terminate chief executive team and chief engineer. Downsize all Class-R workers showing less than 87.7% efficacy – replace with latest iteration of Biological Flesh Drones from Batch J-47, who test for Class-R manual labour at 87.8% efficacy. Re-evaluate in 3 months."

– Domina, Alabaster Station Network A.I.

Alabaster 2, nicknamed Glass, is likewise inhabited by the upper crust of the Corporation, though residents of 1 look down on Glassers, seeing them as "neuvo-riche" who could never withstand the prodigious cost of a suite or estate on 1. Glass began as the Corporation's premier energy station, though now Alabaster 4 shoulders that burden. The flute-works of 2's crystalline processing monoliths are now more of a curiosity since the station now produces high-quality robotics and leading-edge cybernetic implants. Some even whisper of secret laboratories, where Mechonids are dissected for their secrets.

Alabaster 3, an oblong station with several spindly appendage-like segmented modules, went dark six years ago, quarantined after a catastrophic spill of elysium-4. Tens of thousands of workers and residents remain trapped there. Few escaped crippling respiratory illness or any number of degenerative ailments brought on by exposure to massive doses of Gossamer. Rumour has it that part of the dark station still produces tremendous amounts of Draz despite the ruined eco-sphere, supplying some unknown arm of the Corporation who spreads this outpouring of narcotics.

Alabaster 4 is called the Stink, so named for the noisome odours pervading every bulkhead and corridor. The source of this rank pollution is the skunk-works, in the bowels of 4, where powerful chemical stews centrifuging in turbines process helium-3 and other chemicals into starship fuel.

Alabaster 5, called the Post, serves as the major trading hub of the Corporation. Massive malls, trading floors, and shopping districts offer up thousands of Corp-produced goods, fed by a strata of factories below the commercial "crust" of this planetoid-shaped station whose machines of industry never cease.

Alabaster 6, at present, remains incomplete. Its skeletal half-finished structure is constantly abuzz with multitudes of drones laser-welding, turbo-sealing, and molecular-bonding new processing units, mining pod-bays, and cargo holds every day. The site of numerous strikes, riots, and uprisings, 6 was intended to be the Corporation's most impressive production and processing facility, but commencing work on an in-progress station inflicted dreadful work conditions on the labour force. 6 has become a giant thorn in the Corporation's side, but they have invested too much in to the facility to shut it down.

Population

The majority of the population on Alabaster 1 to 6 are Corporates, the most affluent among them inhabiting the earliest-constructed stations. Hardier Nephilim workers supplement the labour force (on 6 especially), as do the grey-skinned androgynous organic constructs known as Flesh. The Corporation also hires a large number of Legion "peacekeeper" mercenaries who ensure the safety of their employers.

Asteroid Belts

Monopoly Belt

Whirling about Esh scattered in the vast region of space between Lilith and Alabaster, the Monopoly Asteroid Belt was once home to the Eight Hermitages, far-flung places of solitude where aesthetic orders of Kaltorans erected underground monasteries far from society's sway. After X'ion began its Great War, Monopoly became a refuge for displaced Kaltorans and the site of a dozen battles between combined Legion and Kaltoran fleets against X'ion's Nephilim. To this day, a graveyard of derelict vessels and debris dances slowly among these titanic rocks, hidden from all but the most dedicated salvagers.

Today, the mineral deposits among the asteroids in Monopoly attract much interest from both the Corporation and the Kaltorans, not to mention hordes of unaffiliated prospectors, who compete over mining operations in the region. Alabaster's great processing and production stations are fed a steady diet of convoys from Monopoly Belt, bearing millions of tons of metal and elemental compounds.

The Kaltorans, outstripping their competitors handily in the arena of mining and excavation technology, roam the belt freely, selectively stripping a handful of important elements from whole swaths of asteroids, leaving the rest of the belt intact. The Corporation's less effective methods force them to set up large mining stations, either orbital or anchored to larger asteroids in the belt. These stations pulverise asteroids to dust in order to extract only a portion of the rich elements within. Occasionally Kaltorans passing into range of these stations spark conflict with Corporation agencies. The Kaltorans' cavalier attitude to Corporation claims and their legality of dominion chafes the merchant kings of Alabaster, and the Corp's wasteful method of farming minerals is laughable and appalling to the Kaltorans. Conflict steadily brews between these civilisations, and many independent prospectors find themselves caught up in hostilities or forced off their claimed 'roids by one side or the other.

For the most part, when the Corporation insists that Kaltorans move on, they do so, content to seek minerals elsewhere among the millions of asteroids in the belt. However, on a few occasions, after laying claim to one of the ancient hermitages floating amongst Monopoly, the Corporation was shocked by the alacrity and violence of Kaltoran reprisal, mostly from tribes whose family members once sought solitude within these sanctuaries.

"It's not an easy life out here in Monopoly, but if you get lucky, there's riches to be had. Asteroid prospecting isn't without its hazards – there's the self-interested Corp, laying claim to everything in the galaxy and sicking their Legion lapdogs on every honest prospector just trying to make a living. Then, Archons-forbid you accidentally prospect a 'roid with an old Kaltoran monastery buried inside – there'll be hell to pay once those blind chosen-ones find out! But if you hit a sweet score, you can retire to a pleasure station for the rest of your days. Almost makes it all worthwhile… almost."

– Yurg, Nephilim prospector

"Liberty! Ha! Its free alright – free of life! There's nothing there but cold rock and long dead Kaltorans. I know what you've heard: rumours about old tech abandoned on long lost stations. Even if that's true, the whispers I hear of pirate armadas hiding amidst the asteroids, mass-murderers in hiding and rumblings about Mechonid nightmares left over from the war are more palpable. You steer clear of Liberty – everyone with sense does."

– Michael Wilder, Corporation Surveyor

The Legion is the third point in this strained triangle of conflict. Steady increases in Kaltoran and Corporation presence in Monopoly places Lady Vengeance and her Auxsilia in a conundrum: they often seek gainful employ from the Corporation, but the Legion remains steadfast allies with the Kaltorans.

Some enemies of the Kaltorans claim their interest in the Monopoly Belt stems from a more nefarious purpose: the belt's proximity to Mishpacha. While Mishpacha remains unclaimed as of yet, it draws the interest of Nephilim, Legion, Corporation, and Kaltoran alike. The wild planet experiences the occasional impact of asteroids, and some claim this to be the Kaltorans' doing. They say the Kaltorans are using their mastery of excavation and gravity tech in concert, launching larger asteroids out of Monopoly towards precise targets on Mishpacha – a cheap and effective means of bombardment should conflict over control of the planet escalate. So far, the Legion writes this off as nonsense conspiracy theory, and the Corporation considers it too strange a possibility to ponder with any severity.

The belt's immensity allows for these three races' interests to remain unchallenged for now. In truth, much of the belt remains unexplored after the Years of Darkness. Historical records point to lost Archon ships, hidden pre-War laboratories and science stations, secluded starbases perhaps containing peoples cut off from the system at large for hundreds of years, and other unfathomable mysteries.

More than a few prospectors and travellers in Monopoly claim to have run afoul of terrifying vessels of unspeakable size: ancient Nephilim warships slumbering deep within the dark, uncharted heart of Monopoly – or worse, prowling the densest reaches of the belt, where debris fields and space dust hide these massive dreadnoughts from sensors. The old Nephilim warships must feed to survive, and more than a few wonder if these scattered reports might explain the staggering number of ships gone missing in the Monopoly – either destroyed by asteroid collision… or devoured by hidden behemoths hunting among the rocks.

Liberty Belt

Most of the Liberty Belt is far sparser than Monopoly, and though clusters of colliding rocks do exist, most of the belt's stony denizens are lonely asteroids, each several hundred or even thousand miles away from its nearest neighbour.

Once, Liberty was a thriving mining zone, busily harvested by the Kaltorans. They called this belt of asteroids Eaven Geshem, which was to be renamed to Liberty by the Corporation during their first exploratory mission to the Haven system. It was heavily populated in those halcyon days before the Great War, speckled with massive space stations containing entire tribal families. When the Kaltorans fell back to defend Kadash, the Nephilim ransacked their stations and pillaged anything of value or use.

When the Kaltorans again launched their culture into space, they reclaimed several colonies and stations in Liberty. Now the asteroid belt is heavily populated but strained for resources, and the tribes tasked with reclaiming these stations require constant subsidies of fuel, rations, and other supplies convoyed from Kadash. While reclaiming these stations has cost Kadash a great deal, the technologies rediscovered among these whirling husks aid the Kaltorans in their quest to bring light back to the dozens of Dark Pit Cities wallowing in chaos on the bottom of the Great Sea.

The Kaltorans are not alone in their interest in Liberty. Given its vast distances and general dismissal, the belt also attracts those seeking to avoid discovery. Particularly nasty fugitives, flotillas of pirates, and some of the most unsavoury Exsilia Legion merc companies maintain hidden bases, hideouts, and safehouses here, concealed amidst far-flung asteroids. These predators occasionally prey on Kaltoran settlements and reclaimed stations out of convenience or desperation. On occasion, rivalries between petty pirate lords explode into full-blown space battles. Whole armadas of galactic scum have obliterated one another here, the only witnesses to their witless self-annihilation being the slowly spinning asteroids of Liberty.

Eden

Terraformed by: Humanity
Mean Diameter: 73 421 km
Rotation Period: 32.18 hours
Primary Biodiversity Source: X'ion
Surface Gravity: 9.82 m/s
Orbital Period: 626.9 days

Visitors to present-day Eden find it hard to imagine this Nephilim-infested planet was once the Kaltoran home world. Now a barren, crater-scarred planet of craggy broken peaks and radioactive wasteland, Eden writhes like an undead thing, strewn with the corpses of the once-unstoppable Nephilim fleet of living ships. Their carapaces shattered, their biochemical blood-like fuel seeped into the earth, and their former crew – a host of Feral Nephilim – prowl the crags and ravines like parasites.

After the Great War, as the Nephilim fleet depleted their resources in their desperate attempt to annihilate what was left of their foes, a large armada found itself locked in Eden's death-grip orbit. Their last act: crashing the entire fleet into Eden's surface. The survivors among these Nephilim poured forth from the ruptured bellies of the beast-like ships and raged among the radioactive wilderness of the planet. After many years of frenzied slaughter, only the most savage and powerful Nephilim survived.

As the years passed by, the Corporation entered the Haven system and unwittingly awakened something slumbering deep in the carcasses of the living fleet. Buried in a pile of gargantuan corpses, slumbering, or gestating, a dread entity calling itself the Devwi-Ich stirred. No one has seen it. No one knows its mind. Its inscrutable and sinister intentions are beyond any other living being's ken. Upon awakening, the Devwi-Ich opened secret cargo holds, buried deep among the rotting remains of the Nephilim fleet, releasing thousands of Purebloods to reunite the roaming Nephilim tribes and hordes of Eden. The Devwi-Ich's labyrinthine intellect and hidden troves of X'ion-era technology and resources launched the Nephilim of Eden back into the stars in a mere handful of years.

The Devwi-Ich now commands a large portion of the Nephilim race from Eden. This once-Kaltoran home world, now unquestionably the centre of the Nephilim society, is this powerful entity's key stronghold in the Haven system.

Geography

Most of Eden's surface resembles more a lifeless moon than the once-thriving world the Kaltorans called home: Vast expanses of deserts and craggy windswept wastelands, where radioactive dust storms a hundred miles across hold sway. Canyons and riven networks of tunnels pierce many a shattered mountain range where Nephilim bombardment obliterated august peaks.

Eden's pristine azure oceans have been reduced to boiling festering wetlands by pollution, searing heat, and ecological ruin. What little potable water remains on Eden rests far below the surface in underground pools, difficult to reach and, once breached, impossible to preserve from the radiation and polluted blood of countless dead Nephilim ships.

"X'ion was the father… mother. Its strength became ours. But it abandoned us, discarding its children. Left before its work was done. It let the Archon's Brood survive. Left the war unfinished, failed. We do not need it. The Devwi-Ich is our true master. An overlord worthy of our race. The Devwi-Ich's will is ours."

– Tyjem, Pureblood.

The only feature of note on this decaying world is the massive tower-studded city of Necronus, erected in a mere handful of weeks by the Devwi-Ich's Pureblood servants. Toiling at a terrifying pace, and aided by the unspeakable powers of their mysterious master, the Eden Brood managed to turn millions of tons of decaying bio-technology, heaped amongst the tattered ruins of the ruined Nephilim fleet, into the single largest city in the Haven system.

This hive-like city – a metropolis of organic tech, entwined with wires, metal, and throbbing synapses, anchored together with cables and sinew, partitioned by great sphincters and jaw-like archways which once adorned the great command centres of Nephilim cruisers – is both terrifying and striking to behold. Her towers of metal and carapace extend above the cloud line and grow taller each year, as drones toil day and night to expand the already-titanic city.

Population

Necronus's bioluminescent towers boast populations of Nephilim extending into the millions, and an even greater number of X'ion's cast-off children huddle in the warrens and ghettos sitting in these spires' long shadows. Its populace continues to grow as more and more of the feral nomadic tribes of Nephilim scattered across Eden's surface and the Haven system are pacified by the Devwi-Ich's minions every year, brought to heel and gathered into the fold of the Eden Brood.

A near-feudalistic hierarchy reigns in Necronus. Those most ruthless, powerful, and useful to the Devwi-Ich inhabit the highest spires of the great city, looking down on the dregs eking out a paltry existence in the slums miles below. Maintaining status is no mean feat, and the constant infighting and desperate attempts to satisfy the will of the Devwi-Ich ensure constant upheaval among the Eden Brood's elite. The millions held in thrall are pacified through force and intimidation, and are kept enslaved by a strange mead exuded by Necronus's great towers – a sludge-like rain of nutrients and narcotics that dull the ambitions of these lesser Nephilim and keep them fortified for a life of backbreaking labour necessary to achieve the impossible ambitions of the Devwi-Ich.

Gehenna

Terraformed by: Humanity
Mean Diameter: 4 692 km
Rotation Period: 43.78 days

Primary Biodiversity Source: X'ion
Surface Gravity: 8.64 m/s
Orbital Period: 124.2 days

Gehenna embraces Esh closer than do her sister worlds, bathing in the mother star's solar winds and fearsome superheated radiation. Little more than a sphere of magma, her crust, though thin and scorched black, is riddled with deposits of the rarest minerals in the Haven system. A witch's brew of intense solar energy, geothermal chaos, and plasma storms give rise to alchemical feats beyond any laboratory in the known universe. Though the planet's pyroclastic surface, bereft of water and clean air, scorns traditional life, the lure of great mineral and elemental treasures have drawn the occupants of Haven to establish perilous mining colonies on Gehenna since time immemorial.

Geography

Gehenna's solar-blasted surface is constantly in flux – a canvas painted over again and again by volcanic eruptions, running rivers of magma one hundred kilometers wide, and continent-rending seismic explosions. Few geographical landmarks can withstand Gehenna's cataclysmic crucible of fire.

Along the equator runs the Perdition, a deep rift burned into Gehenna during one of Esh's most powerful plasma storms. The walls of Perdition's deep canyons course with rich veins of minerals and rare elements, along with the majority of Kaltoran mining operations on Gehenna.

The Bronze Sea, a massive ocean of liquid magma, occupies most of the northwestern hemisphere of Gehenna. Ancient data caches indicate that the Bronze Sea holds an extensive network of mining operations created by the Archons before the Great X'ion War. Supposedly a great city-sized installation capable of weathering Gehenna's volcanic fury, the network once stood at the centre of this ocean of liquid fire. Some believe that the installation may still lie at the bottom of the Bronze Sea, miles below the boiling magma bubbling at the surface.

Population

Before the Years of Darkness, Kaltorans braved the hellish fires of Gehenna at the behest of their Archon masters, only abandoning operations on this volcanic treasure-trove when the Nephilim fleet threatened holy Kadash. Now, newly risen from the waters of Kadash, the Kaltorans plunge themselves into the fires of Gehenna once more. This time their race against pyroclastic destruction for rare elements is spurred by a desire to reclaim their underwater cities at an accelerated pace. The energy demanded to bring the Dark Cities back online far exceeds Kadashan reserves, and the sea-repelling Electro-Gravity wells require the rarest elements to function at their full potential.

The best minds of the Kaltoran race constructed environmental mining modules for deployment in Perdition, some as large as

"Welcome to Gehenna, friend! You must be Davin's replacement… or Kylar's… or Elizabeth's… who can keep track, really.

I don't know what you've heard, but Gehenna's not as bad as most claim! Sure, the sulfur and ash will choke you to death eventually, and the mining run-off in the so-called "filtered" water will positively fill you with tumors. And yes, it has worst work conditions in Haven, with more fatal accidents per month than the Liberty Belt mining stations. And yeah, your chances of being reduced to molten flesh by a magma vent or getting liquefied in a lava wave are higher than a Corp doxy's chance of contracting space flux.

But hey – if you can survive the Legion taskmaster for long enough, you might just make your fortune here."

small starships and many capable of burrowing through the crust of Gehenna. While impressive specimens of technology, these mining modules are hellish on their inhabitants. The filtration units strive in vain to manufacture breathable air from the sulfuric and ashy vapours on Gehenna, and accidents and catastrophic losses of entire modules are common.

With great pressure comes great costs, and conditions throughout the mining operations on Gehenna grow more dire every year. Family tribes with less influence commonly seek out the wealth of Gehenna in hopes of funding a better life for themselves, and it is not uncommon for the operations to employ extreme measures to keep the minerals flowing. First, Draz is regularly dispensed to workers to keep them on their feet in the scorching heat and to throw off pain, sleep, and exhaustion. However, as addiction and misery spread through the mining operations, many modules are reduced to violent and despair-drowned slums. To keep up order and productivity, the Kaltorans brought in a contingent of Legion Exsilia, under the leadership of a cold and pragmatic Legat named Gorgantis Lavinias, whose draconian means of coercion are legend.

Additionally, the Corp has its own designs on Gehenna. They have already begun extracting minerals, though their operations are inferior in every way to the Kaltoran efforts. For now, the Corp is careful to avoid any regions regularly mined by Kaltoran modules, but a conflict between the two grows more likely with each passing month.

Halo Nebula

When trillions of tons of stardust scattered to the Habrixis Sector, several colossal clouds gathered a host of asteroids, elements, planetoids, and energy into their swirling embrace. These nebulae vied for galactic vassals in a slow and steady race for gravitational dominance. The Halo Nebula lost its race against Esh. Now, the Halo's grip loosened, it skulks about the Habrixis, scattered and murky, its tendrils sprawling across a half dozen systems, with one appendage still grasping vainly at the edge of the Haven system – as if longing for Esh's domain.

From the earliest habitation of the Habrixis by humankind, the Halo has remained a mystery. The most ancient data streams hint vaguely that humanity explored the nebula, and perhaps even charted the other five star systems grasped by Halo and the numerous rogue planets forever wandering the expanse of the nebula's seemingly endless innards. Analysis of what fragmentary data caches remain from the Archons' time suggests they mostly avoided the nebula. Nearly every Archon file detailing the nebula's inner reaches has proven corrupted or deleted. Yet there she sits, on the edge of Haven system, beckoning explorers, scientists, maniacs, and scoundrels – seeking truth, or obfuscation, within the folds of Halo's stardust miasma.

Geography

The nebula is as limitless as it is eternal, a cloud of stardust the size of a thousand worlds. Long-range probes show five other uncharted star systems on the outskirts of the nebula, though certain spectrum analysis also leads some top Kaltoran scientists to believe the nebula may have enveloped as many as ten more systems in its voluminous reaches.

Beyond the possibility of swallowed stars and their sad suffocated worlds, Kaltoran and Corporation probes have already encountered over twenty rogue planets and hundreds of giant asteroids, dust-blind and lost, meandering for millennia within the Halo.

Some data patterns confirm an interesting anomaly: a giant conglomerated mega-planetoid – perhaps formed by a gravitational aberration which caused hundreds of asteroid fields and cast-off moons to collide and then coalesce into one giant dead world – easily 600,000 times larger than the largest planet in the Habrixis, dwarfing Esh in mass. Old Archon records name this mythic beast of a planetoid Shade, though many believe these tales to be apocryphal; current data remains inconclusive. The Corporation has offered a handsome bonus to any surveyor who can locate this giant lost rogue world, whose elemental riches could keep every foundry and processing plant in the Haven system churning for centuries. Kaltoran interest in Shade's existence is more profound: if a planetoid of such gargantuan size were to wander anywhere near Haven, its gravitational force could bring about a system-wide apocalypse.

Some surveys by probes and captains steely willed enough to brave the nebula show that a portion of the nebula is composed primarily of highly volatile gases, whose potential energy would be easily ignited to catastrophic explosive force by burning thruster fuel or weapon discharge. These wide-rolling waves of incendiary vapour are known as the Phetonic Sea. Navigating this murky ocean of fiery vortices and infernal hazards is treacherous in the extreme. Even so, rumours of a lost fleet of Kaltoran refugee ships stranded somewhere in the Phetonic during the end of the Great X'ion War have spurred some to dare its fiery expanse – none have yet returned from this voyage into oblivion.

Beyond the Phetonic lie dozens of undiscovered worlds, nestled in the Halo, whose secrets remain hidden, and whose strange inhabitants or lost treasures entice many explorers to venture deep into the murky nebula, never to return.

Population

The residents of Halo are mostly unknown, or long forgotten. Rumours abound of lost Archons, of forgotten colonies of Kaltorans, even of secret pockets of surviving human progenitors – all without a shred of data to back them up.

After the Great X'ion War, the Mechonids – one of the most dangerous predatory races born of Archon desperation – mostly vanished. Some believe the majority of these cyber-monstrosities perished with their creators, but others harbour darker suspicions as to their fate. Ancient sensor records recovered from remnants of living ships and derelict battleships floating around the edge of Haven space show massive migrations of Mechonid fleets near the end of the X'ion War. Some seemed to be amassing among the concealing fields of asteroids throughout the Liberty and Monopoly Belt, but the lion's share of this dread force charted a course deep into the Halo Nebula in a mass exodus. The Mechonids' current

"… and we ask the blessing of Perfection, as we await Perfection's return, and our ascension to Glory!" cried X'ion's prophet on the ornate raised pulpit.

The walls of the makeshift chapel were lined with large vats of greenish liquid, casting a sickly glow over the crowd below as the rapt believers crowed in exultation. The massed ranks of carapace, armour, and rags pressed forward as a lesser priest stepped up to the less garish lectern.

"My brothers in conviction," he began as they quieted quickly, "we have an urgent crisis of faith. A ship of non-believers has arrived and are asking questions that disrespect the Sanctity of Perfection!"

"Sure I've been there. Beyond the pale, some say – a journey into the cloudy womb of a future star. Just think, someday, eons from now, our beloved Esh may have a sister, and their binary dance shall shed unfathomable brilliance and warmth on this little insignificant war-torn corner of the galaxy. But for the next several million years, the Halo remains light years of dust, hidden rogue planets, lost derelict survey ships, and… well… I've said too much… no, no… I have to go. Gotta ship out early in the morning, you understand. Thanks for the drinks. I'd say good luck with your expedition, but I like you, so, trust me – abort. Cancel the survey mission. What's out there, you asked… I've been trying to forget for five years."

– Cayman Drift, Former Kaltoran Explorer,
now freelance freighter captain for any vessel, so
long as its route steers far clear of the Halo Nebula.

whereabouts are unknown. More than one ship trying to breach the nebula has been set upon by unknown ships. Broken echoes of their final transmissions reveal their horrific fate - torn to pieces, their hulls cannibalised, their crews' biological material harvested to the last cell - food for the last bastard race of monsters born from the Archons' war machine.

Data analysis of the Mechonid migration into the Halo gives some experts cause for more crippling terror. While the general belief is that the Mechonids' withdrawal to Halo was a retreat at the war's end, others think these cybernetic horrors were merely carrying out orders – pursuing their masters' terrible nemesis, X'ion itself.

Though X'ion's destination upon departing Haven is wholly unconfirmed, the Halo Nebula is a viable option. Some of X'ion's old followers believe Halo to be the renegade's new home. At the war's end, cast off Nephilim – remnants of X'ion's once-massive fleet – gathered at the edge of the nebula, like lost children awaiting their sire's return. Over the following decades, more and more arrived, and at present a sizeable host of Nephilim eke out an existence in war-torn ships, stolen freighters, and salvaged derelicts on the outskirts of the nebula. Bizarre, frenetic cults, preaching of X'ion's foretold return, have arisen among this horde of fringe Nephilim. Agents of the Devwi-Ich attempt to make inroads with this lost armada of X'ion loyalists, but their overtures of new allegiance to Eden's risen master only provoke wild violence from these zealots.

Halo is also home to every manner of miscreant criminal, whether Legion, Kaltoran, Corp, or Nephilim. The Halo's mysteries and dangers are enough to dissuade all but the most dedicated avengers. Those with more enemies than friends in Haven often hide in the Halo.

Kadash

Terraformed by: Humanity	Primary Biodiversity Source: Archon
Mean Diameter: 10 876 km	Surface Gravity: 9.64 m/s
Rotation Period: 43.12 hours	Orbital Period: 321.16 days

The Great X'ion War sowed misery on every planet within the Haven system, but few suffered as much as Kadash. When the Nephilim laid siege to the Kaltorans' holy world, every tribe fell back to defend Kadash in one pyrrhic final stand. In those most brutal years of the war, cataclysmic weapons left Kadash's ozone in tatters. Her glacial poles dissolved in mere weeks, her climate raged, and her oceans, bloated and roiling, devoured the land. Kadash's five ancient oceans collided and grappled. The turbulent, unforgiving All-Sea roared to life in their wake.

Millions of Kaltoran martyrs sacrificed themselves in those hellish days, remaining on the surface, in a world gone mad, buckling under storms and smothered by crashing tsunami. These brave defenders repelled the Nephilim incursion forces long enough for their people's engineers to complete a sprawling network of domed cities in the deepest reaches of the ocean, beneath the frenzied surface of the weather-tortured All-Sea. Even now, nearly a hundred years later, the surface remains a blasted nightmare of unwholesome elements and ravaging radioactive storms, eradicating all vestiges of emergent life. Beneath the waves, however, a vast civilisation nurses itself back from the raggedy edge after seven decades of Darkness.

Geography

Kadash is a cerulean world of conquering oceans, veiled in whirling hurricanes whose winds regularly exceed 200 kilometers per hour. The planet's few meagre continents, pale and lifeless as scoured bone, lie half-drowned by the pitiless and ever-encroaching All-Sea.

A host of broken holy cities, mostly reduced to dust or submerged beneath the waves, are all that remains of pre-War Kadash. The punishing storms ensure few relics survive to evoke the world that was. The restless All-Sea surges and recedes, often thousands of miles a day, her chaotic dance as unpredictable as the winds and quakes that drive her mad. Only the highest peaks of the Alurian Range, on the old drowned continent of Nestoria, remain above water year-round. The island-continent has been renamed Skyrock, called "the Rock" by most Kaltorans, home only to a handful of weather researchers and climatologists working like the devil to analyse the wild pattern-defying whimsy of Kadash's unrelenting storms.

Below the waves Kadash comes alive. Networks of domed cities spider-web across the sea floor, fed by forests of kelp, schools of fish, and beds of crustaceans, heated by volcanic vents and inhabited by the majority of the Kaltoran race.

The greatest engineers and technicians in the galaxy raced to redefine their world during the final years of the X'ion War, building incredible redoubts hidden from their enemies beneath miles of ocean. Hubs of subterranean "pit cities" built under massive Electro-Gravity shields to hold the oceans at bay and configured with large central

"Dream. Close your eyes and they will come. The past. The strife. The horrors. Cities long dead. Multitudes drowned. We must embrace the truth of our race – our darkest moments of hunger, regression, feral madness. Once reduced to little better than the Nephilim. But it is our understanding of these bloody times that allow us to forge ahead and never again lose ourselves. The tribe is our salvation. Genetic memory bonding us together in a way no other race could ever imagine. Dream, little one. Nightmares pass. Ours are long over. They haunt us, but to remind us. Draw strength from them to face the challenges ahead of you."

– Asher Jazz, Dreamkeeper of Yasha

pressurised chambers, buildings hugging the circumference and connected by a skunk-works of tunnels made up the majority of the engineers' brave new underwater world. The result of their herculean and inspired efforts sadly did not yield unmitigated success. After resettlement, several of the hubs failed utterly, suffering total loss of power, or worse, their Electro-Gravity domes surrendering to the punishing pressure of the All-Sea.

The first hub to go dark was New Eden, the largest municipal web of six great crystalline cities, each named for their most populous and gloried pre-War surface counterparts. When systems failed and the domes went dark, chaos and madness prevailed. Confusion bore riots in its wake, and as food rations dwindled, millions of people resorted to cannibalism.

For seventy years, New Eden wallowed in Darkness. The strong fed on the weak. Civilisation ripped itself apart, and the most cosmopolitan and illuminated Kaltorans of the old theocracy fell to feral Dark Tribe savages. The desperate fled through tunnels towards other Hubs, throwing themselves by the thousands against emergency shields coldly lowered by their neighbours, who feared that the madness might spread.

But New Eden would not suffer alone. In the years that followed, Ziz, the capitol of the Shamir Hub in the northeastern hemisphere, suffered a massive power drain. Ziz's sea-repelling gravity wells winked out; her dome cracked and buckled. The All-Sea surged in, coursing through the Hub's vein-like tunnels and flooding seven cities before emergency shields finally staved off the hungry tide. These cities remain as drowned ghost towns to this day, their once-august promenades, hotels, malls, and convention centres prowled by terrors of the deep and patrolled by waterlogged robotic slaves whose masters fed the fish on their bloated flesh long ago.

Dozens of other smaller hubs surrendered to the vicissitudes of pressure, food shortage, and gravity-tech malfunctions over the course of the Dark Years. The floor of the All-Sea is a strange graveyard of still cities, scattered between deep rifts and latticed fields of coral.

The centre of modern Kaltoran culture and society is Yasha, a hub in the southwestern quadrant of the All-Sea, which was spared some of the more terrifying horrors of the Dark Years. Power failures and wars with feral Dark Tribes from neighbouring hubs plagued the residents of Yasha, and their society split into tribal families and spawned bloody conflicts periodically, but these Kaltorans retained their grasp of technology. Over seventy years they painstakingly restored the Electro-Gravity drives of their cities, reinforced their domes, and harnessed geothermal power to supplement their flagging reserves. Great leaps forward in genetic memory tech and advances in hybrid aquatic and star-faring craft allowed the residents of Yasha to reclaim some of their pre-War culture, reconnect with other cities on the sea floor, and ascend to the stars once more.

Population

Yasha today is a thriving, heavily populated hub, its many cities teeming with family tribes ruled by patriarchs and matriarchs whose genetic memories stretch back into the holy days of Old Kadash – the days of Land and Sky. Most of the inhabitants of Yasha are Kaltoran, but a few visitors of other races make their home here, those fortunate enough to be granted an honourary place among a powerful family tribe.

As Yasha's population grows, great pressure is placed on the matriarchs and patriarchs to accelerate their reclamation of dark cities and hubs, but this process proves painfully slow.

Though the tribal elders of Yasha proclaimed an end to the Dark Years seven years ago, the dread truth is that an unknowable number of Kaltorans remain trapped in New Eden and other fallen hub city-states, where cannibalism and savagery are often the only means of survival. At present, only one of these cities has been fully reclaimed – Mayim, the southwestern edge of New Eden's web – but the city's sub-structure is still rife with nests of insane Dark Tribe cannibals who plague the families resettling there.

Though some of the Dark Tribes are little more than insane monsters, others retain shreds of their souls. Some of these tribespeople live below the revitalised and reclaimed cities of Kadash, and though they are too far gone to re-enter Kaltoran society, they wish a brighter future for their beloved children – a life free of cannibalism, terror, and madness. On occasion, these Dark Kaltorans will brave the lights above their underworld of tunnels and ruins, offering up a child in hopes the city-dwellers will raise it as their own These foundlings, tribe-less and born of darkness, find life difficult, but far more forgiving than the brief and savage fate that awaited them below.

Lilith

Terraformed by: Humanity	Primary Biodiversity Source: X'ion
Mean Diameter: 6 126 km	Surface Gravity: 10.401 m/s
Rotation Period: 148.02 hours	Orbital Period: 187.1 years

The forlorn Lilith, her orbit cast farthest from the sun, struggles against the icy void of deep space. Exiled to the shadows of her sister-worlds, and grasping at mere glimmers of Esh, whose erstwhile rays shed but meagre radiance and less warmth on this dismal world, Lilith is Haven's icy bauble, dangling on the system's raggedy edge, solitary and bereft of colour.

Little more than a spinning ball of ice, whose geothermal energy is barely capable of sustaining even the hardiest life forms, it is little wonder then that the resilient and disciplined Legion find Lilith's cold embrace most welcoming. Lilith serves as the advance base for the Legion Auxilia's theatre of operations in Haven. An indeterminate, but vast, number of Legion train for whatever hellish conflict should consume Haven next on this distant white sphere, repelling outsiders as swiftly as the legendarily bitter winds of this brutal world.

Lilith is both orphan and gatekeeper. All space jumps into the Haven system must pass through Lilith's orbital path. Thus the Legion Auxilia glumly monitors all travel in and out of Haven from their cold fortress planet. They mostly allow traffic to pass unmolested, though on occasion a ship or convoy will mysteriously vanish. The Legion neither denies nor confirms their involvement in the disappearance of these vessels. Overtures and queries are always met with icy silence.

Geography

At first glimpse, Lilith is uniform in geographical makeup, a pale arctic expanse, mostly unmarred, and scoured flat by relentless winds and driving blizzards. Beneath Lilith's glacial crust, however, lie vast frozen seas, buried mountains, and a riven system of valleys whose rifts run so deep that rising magma wars with invading ice in an ever-churning dance of elements. At the arctic surface, however, liquid water never anoints this frozen world, not even in summer months.

Lilith's smooth face of glacial flats is only broken in a handful of places. The Crown, a circle of ridge-backed mountains, rings the northern hemisphere, and the Maw, a deep rift, over three thousand kilometers in diameter, yawns across the southwestern quadrant of the planet.

Finally, the Hive, an enigma of crystalline and mirror-like ice formations at the southern pole, reaches high into the aurora-shimmering sky, reflecting these dancing lights back at their source. The Hive is obviously not a naturally occurring phenomenon, but rather the result of this world's mythical human terraformers, its purpose as mysterious as the strange optical illusions it casts against the eerily glowing sky.

The gateway to Lilith, and the sentinel at its doorstep, is the massive warship Olympus. While it can jump, the Olympus often maintains a standard orbit of Lilith proper. Olympus is a block-shaped collection of vast cargo holds, gun ports, and hangar bays, home to six full squadrons of fighters. The ship is commanded by Legat Draxis Kul, one of Athene Kosta's most trusted officers; Draxis shares Athene's vision of Lilith, and his diplomatic skills (rare for a war-hardened Legion) make him the perfect "face" of the Auxsillia's outreach efforts.

Olympus is a way station for goods and supplies, not to mention large payments rendered to the Auxsillia from the Corporation - recompense for the many security and military (not to mention paramilitary) operations fulfilled by the Legion. This remuneration is organised into well-guarded convoys on Olympus, eventually disembarking from the station destined for Cerberus Prime.

Many criminal rings and bands of pirates consider these convoys the ultimate heist; marauders or Nephilim attempt to hijack each shipment, but they are foiled every time. The Legion has never lost one of their payment convoys – a point of pride for the Auxsilia, important to retaining their reputation as the most effective mercenaries in Haven.

Population

Lilith's environs are only half as inhospitable as her inhabitants. The Legion Auxilia has used this icy planet as their forward operating base for eight cold years. Those suicidal enough to spy on the Legion risk summary annihilation and usually garner little information as to the Legion's numbers, armament, and readiness. Auxilia forces on Lilith serve under Athene Kosta, otherwise known as Lady Vengeance, the current Consul of Foreign Affairs, and supreme commander of the Haven Auxilia mercenary forces.

Kosta's officer training memorandums ubiquitously cite deception as the key to military strategy, and Lilith was her first and only choice for a forward operating base in Haven, against strong concerns voiced by several fellow ruling members of the Casia Curia, who

proposed that a series of outposts in the Liberty Belt would risk less exposure.

Now eight years later, the other consuls plainly see the merits of Kosta's plan. Though only a handful of bunkers dot Lilith's surface, hints at vast subterranean bases – their entrances and heat signatures painstakingly concealed – strike trepidation into even the most fearless adversaries of the Auxilia. Reports are wild and far-ranging, some claiming "the Auxilia's presence on Lilith is fleeting at best, a mere waypoint for operations in Haven." Others boldly state "underground barracks, hangars, and bases house hundreds of thousands of battle-ready Legion, an advance force capable of occupying Alabaster and Mishpacha, while effortlessly cleansing both the Liberty and Monopoly belts of such nasty variables as exiled Legion Exsilia mercenary companies, raiders, Feral Nephilim ships, and lost Mechonid armadas." Reports such as the latter breed constant anxiety among the Corp inhabitants of Alabaster, who prefer to think of the Legion as their trained attack dogs, rather than aspiring conquerors.

Even more unsettling, Lilith's long orbit commonly takes her through the edge of the Halo Nebula. Myriad rumours say that special training exercises, secret operations, and testing of classified projects are scheduled for this period of perfect obfuscation – in doing this, the Auxilia avoids the scrutiny of their many enemies, retains their tactical edge, and continues to terrify those threatened by Legion expansion in Haven. Some intelligence agents even suggest the Auxilia are stockpiling additional troops and ships on secret star-bases inside the Halo, transferring personnel and supplies while Lilith is shrouded in the nebula. These cloaked fleets stand poised to smash any opposition at a moment's notice, and even if their existence is pure fiction, this threat keeps enemies of the Auxilia at bay and brings a cold smile to Lady Vengeance's face nightly.

Year after year, many Corporation businesses petition vigorously for a sanctioned presence on Lilith, official or otherwise, and year after year they are flatly refused. All permanent residents of Lilith are Legion, and only a few Kaltoran or Corporation ships are ever allowed to land by formal invitation, submitting themselves to extensive searches and protocols. To date, no Nephilim ship since the Great War has ever touched down on Lilith.

Trade is likewise scoffed at, and visits of any kind are thwarted, no matter what pretence Corporation diplomats might concoct. Limping Corporation freighters requesting mechanical assistance, medical vessels requiring emergency aid, refugee ships, and the like are stopped at Olympus, a massive warship on the edge of Lilith space, and aid is dispensed there – under no condition are such vessels allowed landfall on Lilith proper.

Mishpacha

Terraformed by: Humanity
Mean Diameter: 22 457 km
Rotation Period: 28.23 hours
Primary Biodiversity Source: X'ion
Surface Gravity: 9.658 m/s
Orbital Period: 1187.2 days

From orbit, Mishpacha is a world of deep blues and vibrant greens. Her three giant continents betray little sign of civilisation, covered in verdant, undulating carpets of rain forest, broken only by jutting volcanic mountain ranges rising like the bared teeth of Mishpacha's many deep and forlorn valleys.

Once a Kaltoran world, her wild reaches are populated with idyllic flora and fauna born of the gloried powers and imaginations of the Archons. Mishpacha is the only unclaimed world in the Haven system – a frontier, offering asylum to the wicked and persecuted alike.

This beautiful hermit's world, seductive in its striking colours, and beckoning with promises of treasure and freedom, hides a deadly bioweapon-ravaged landscape. The Nephilim mutagenic bombardment at the height of the War sowed the seeds of horrifying mutant flora, whose sweet scents and alluring colours conceal mortal poisons and lethal tropisms. After X'ion abandoned them, the Nephilim left entire armies behind on Mishpacha, surrendering them to the mutagen-laced environs which twisted these lost troops into the teeming feral herds that now plague Mishpacha's dark jungles.

Geography

Mishpacha's three emerald continents float serenely on azure seas. The smallest, the Spur, spirals southward towards the pole; it is a nesting ground of wild forests, strange fens, and swaths of fungal growth several miles in diameter. Botanists flock to the Spur in droves every year, hoping to catalogue the millions of strange plant species pulsating and slithering among the wetlands. Many colonies on the Spur harvest hydroponic flora in massive farms, yielding all manner of edible mushrooms and fungal pods - some intoxicating enough to rival Draz's steely grip on the addicted masses - but none of these operations last long before being overrun by the hazardous and persistent moulds that eventually consume even space-worthy materials with ease.

Most colonies and research outposts on the Spur simply disappear, their inhabitants vanishing without a trace and their homes and gear sinking beneath meters of virulent fungal growth. Even in the last five years of the Rebirth, Mishpacha counts dozens of lost colonies, averaging at least four a year, and the lion's share of these communities are swallowed on the Spur.

The largest continent on Mishpacha, called Star, spans most of the world's steamy equatorial belt on one hemisphere, its many great peninsulas radiating from a volcanic centre. Most of Star is a wild rain forest filled with virus-altered flora, most of which can slay novice explorers in moments, such as the Slaughter-Vines and Back-Breaker trees; then there are the other subtle and poisonous hazards, such as the Purple Lotus and the delicate thousand-petaled Blood Tears.

"Paradise, some say – a home for all the vagabond castaways of the Haven system – but that's not my experience. It's a wild place, and them that live there eventually go wild too. The land itself is murderous. It's a cunning place, with vines to strangle men in their sleep, and diseases to slowly drive you mad while you sweat blood through your skin…"

"What? Why am I going back…? Best big game in the system! I've looked down ol' Jezzie's scope at some of the most terrifying monsters in the universe on that hateful world. You know you're alive when your hunting one of them virus-mutated freak Nephilim in the steamy jungles of Star… and you know you're dead when they start hunting you."

– Interview with Darius Ventari,
famed Legion big game hunter, missing.

At the centre of Star, perched amongst high peaks, lies the Reclaimed Zone and the cleared ancient Kaltoran city of Beacon. Accessible by shuttle from the only orbiting space port around Mishpacha, Beacon is the only vestige of true civilisation planetside, albeit more a lawless trading post than a true city; one of a few cities in Haven where members of different races freely coexist.

As one explores farther out from the Reclaimed Zone, civilisation falls away with stunning alacrity; no roads, or even trailheads, long survive the clenching grasp of the fast-growing jungle. This wildly overgrown terrain befuddles most navigational instruments. Strange interference from the continent's bioweapon-altered geothermal signature jams global positioning systems, and the constantly shifting, life-like jungle makes even the best landscape-imaging technology unreliable at best.

The third continent of Mishpacha, called Orphan, rests on the opposite side of the globe, abandoned to the lonely northern reaches of the Obsidian Sea. Orphan's long, dark winters leave her far more barren than her two cousins to the south, but her glacial reaches are still home to entire forests of lichens, which have spread their thin spidery grasp over a century to conquer much of the continent.

Storms are a regular occurrence on Mishpacha, and swirling cloud-cover sometimes obscures most of the planet's seas and coastal regions, as punishing winds and chemical rains bombard the beaches and littoral colonies. Besides its own climatic hazards, Mishpacha's proximity to the Monopoly Belt adds the colony-shattering threat of falling asteroids to the list of misfortunes likely to befall those desperate or daring enough to call this wild world home.

Population

Most of the colonies on Mishpacha are located on Star, where hardy folk attempt to tame the landscape to their needs, or hide from prying eyes. Some of these communities are born from whatever faltering ship brought its people to the planet surface – with huts and lean-tos erected from bulkheads and cargo containers. Other colonies are lashed together from what bits of jungle flora won't kill those who approach it, and others still are hollowed out of the ruins of the hundreds of ghost cities concealed deep in the jungles.

Mishpacha's extraterritoriality attracts all manner of settlers – from religious extremists and odd cults of strange folk whose beliefs no sane person can fathom, to galactic criminals whose infamy makes any other port of call a hot zone, to victims of happenstance marooned on the planet's surface, to simple folk who just want to toil far from the interfering fist of any governing body. Mishpacha is a true frontier, and the colonies nestled in its valleys and perched on its mountainsides are peopled with hardy survivors who thrive in spite of some of the deadliest predators in the Haven system.

Racial divides cave to necessity on Mishpacha, and while some colonies are mostly homogeneous, many are multi-cultural affairs, where a person's usefulness supersedes their genetic ancestry. The further out towards the peninsulas of Star, the more wild and unpredictable the settlements become. The farthest reaches of Star are inhabited only by tribes of rabid former-colonists, driven mad by Blood Tears or other horrid diseases, and rampaging packs of Feral Nephilim.

Spur only attracts those with a deep interest in the botanical nightmares and oddities that have consumed that continent. Every year, fresh crops of researchers and scientists vanish into its fungal embrace – most are never heard from again.

Far-flung Orphan is sparsely populated. Only true outcasts and vile personages unfit for any kind of society find themselves inhabitants of "the Lost Continent" where storms rage year round, and colder temperatures, as well as the occasional sub-zero flash freeze, slay all but the hardiest homesteaders. Orphan attracts more and more Nephilim every year, either fleeing the oppressive reach of the Devwi-Ich or the hatred of other races.

Law and order on Mishpacha varies from colony to colony, but on Star a group of wandering Legion, called the Tribunes, offer their services as marshals, judges, and executioners for those colonies without their own permanent law-enforcing bodies.

Not everyone seeks Mishpacha as a new home – the jungle planet's lost cities, hidden caches of powerful technology, and Feral Nephilim big game also attract a host of explorers, treasure-seekers, adventurers, and hunters, ranging from the mercilessly professional to the utterly foolhardy. Mishpacha's many horrors devour both with ease, and yet the promise of adventure and hidden wealth summons a new flock of daredevils every moon-turn.

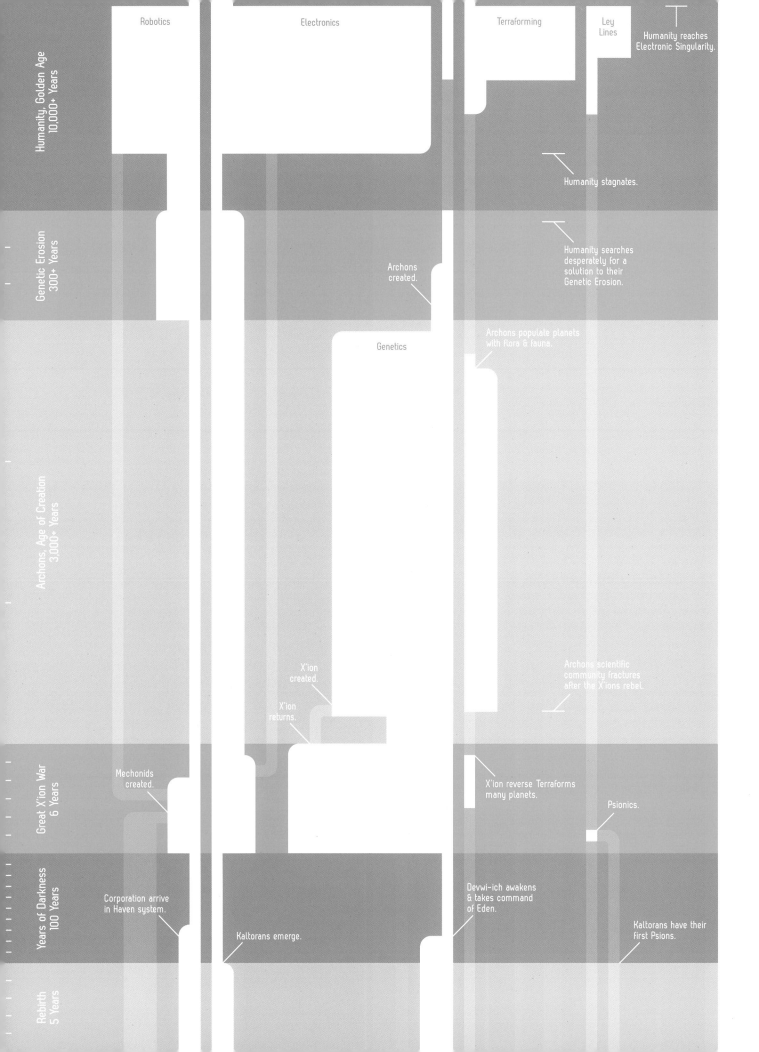

Robotics

Electronics

Terraforming

Ley Lines

Humanity reaches Electronic Singularity.

Humanity, Golden Age 10,000+ Years

Humanity stagnates.

Genetic Erosion 300+ Years

Archons created.

Humanity searches desperately for a solution to their Genetic Erosion.

Genetics

Archons populate planets with flora & fauna.

Archons, Age of Creation 3,000+ Years

X'ion created.

X'ion returns.

Archons scientific community fractures after the X'ions rebel.

Great X'ion War 6 Years

Mechonids created.

X'ion reverse Terraforms many planets.

Psionics.

Years of Darkness 100 Years

Corporation arrive in Haven system.

Kaltorans emerge.

Devwi-ich awakens & takes command of Eden.

Kaltorans have their first Psions.

Rebirth 5 Years

Technology

Technology has changed through the ages and with the rise and fall of civilisations and peoples. Different cultures have placed different emphases on technology, or have emphasised what technology they deem the most useful and valuable. As time passes, some technologies are learned while others are forgotten.

Humanity, Golden Age

The Golden Age of Humanity is all but myth and legend. The wonders of humankind are incomprehensible to the people of the present. Yet, the results of these marvels remain, and their effects have left a permanent mark on the galaxy.

The Electronic Singularity

Humanity achieved a point of exponential growth in electronics-based technology.

Reality Fracture - Ley Lines, pg: 278

Through an event simply known as the Reality Fracture, humanity broke the universe ever so slightly by creating impossibly long, thin, and invisible cracks known as Ley Lines. An invisible and mysterious substance known as Ley Energy leaks from these cracks, spreading far out into space.

By harnessing this energy, spacecraft can create portals that allow them to travel faster than light. It is through this new form of travel that humanity was able to explore and terraform the galaxy.

Humanity, Apathy, and Stagnation

Spread far and wide on comfortable worlds without want or need, humanity became complacent, stagnated, and started to lose touch with each other and their achievements.

Humanity's Genetic Erosion

Slowly humanity's genome succumbed to genetic erosion, and with no knowledge of how to reverse the problem or ability to mobilise, humanity faced extinction.

Creation of the Archons

Unable to save themselves, humanity created the Archons to become the new stewards of the galaxy and to inherit their fallen empire. But the Archons did not wish to follow in humanity's footsteps of electronics and exploration, so they looked to genetics.

Archons and the Age of Creation

Obsessed with genetic perfection, the Archons became eugenicists: new Archons were designed rather than born. They created vast numbers of new species to inhabit the abandoned ruins of the human empire.

The Archons maintained many of the electronics and terraforming technologies which the humans developed, but they made few new developments in these areas. Instead, they were consumed by a desire to create the perfect race, a desire which resulted in the X'ion.

The Great War and X'ion

The war provoked a boom in technological development as the Archons desperately searched for ways to fight X'ion and its Nephilim army. Long-lost technologies of humanity were reborn, and weapons development flourished.

Nephilim

During the Great War, the Nephilim almost exclusively used organics-based technologies. But due to declining resources and knowledge, many Nephilim now use a blend of biological, mechanical, and electronic technologies.

Mechonids

The Archons built these beings from a blend of ancient human robotics and Archon weaponry.

Years of Darkness

The time which followed the Great War lasted a hundred years, and in this time many technologies were lost or forgotten as people scrambled to survive. Most technologies that did survive were important for survival.

Rebirth

As each of the races re-emerged into space, they brought with them their unique blend and style of technology.

Corporation

Commonly look backward to find lost human technologies and favour clean, metallic, electronic technologies.

Nephilim

Have a blended approach of progressing though any means (even amoral) and using available resources. They favour organic or blended technologies.

Kaltoran

Survival above all else. They prefer to maintain what they have access to, and rely on their genetic memories. Their technology is often rough and dirty, blending advanced and primitive technologies.

Legion

Preservers rather than innovators. More so than the other races, they have retained a large portion of their war-time technologies through dedicated maintenance and reclamation. Their tech is often robust, heavy, and red.

Uneven

Technological development is not universal across the Haven system as not all technologies were preserved everywhere. Some settlements may use both beasts of burden and advanced plane-tary-defence cannons. Another settlement may have an advanced computer network and a well-maintained drone security force.

Daily Life

Domestic

In households throughout the Haven system, small and commonly overlooked technologies do their part. Many of these techs have a simple and specific function related to basic survival needs, such as preparing food, controlling the environment, and cleaning.

Occasionally, these technologies can be surprisingly advanced, as they were considered quite valuable during the Years of Darkness after the Great War. The many advanced technologies would be difficult to understand if the races did not hold onto their knowledge by constructing and maintaining these commonplace yet vital technologies.

Food Production

Many means of producing food exist in the Haven system, including mechanised farming, hydroponics, hunting, and foraging. Much of what decides the method used on any given world is the environment of the planet or habitation.

In arctic environments, food is commonly produced through a combination of enclosed farms and hunting.

Space stations and subterranean settlements often use mechanised hydroponics; it does not rely on natural light and requires less room than traditional farms.

Mishpacha is a bio-diverse world with an abundance of plant and animal life, but very little open land. As such, most settlements use a wide variety of food-production techniques, including hunting, gathering, farming, and hydroponics.

In Nephilim settlements and spacecraft, photosynthesis is used to grow a mead-like substance, which is then excreted for the population to consume as food.

Currency

The most popular form of currency is Corporate Credits (pg: 204). However, valuable commodities such as precious minerals, ammunition, food, and favours are also commonly traded. Digital financial institutions such as banks and stock exchanges are rare outside of the Corporation.

Space Stations and Settlements

Aside from their planets of origin, the races of Haven must rely on space stations and settlements to expand their territory and influence.

The vast majority of space stations and a great many settlements are reclaimed Kaltoran facilities, ruins left over from the Great X'ion War. Most space stations use artificial gravity derived from Kaltoran Electro-Gravity technology. Many of their other life-support systems are a patchwork of technologies, commonly including electronic, mechanical, or bio-tech components.

Communication

There are three common forms of long-distance communication within the Haven system. From shortest to longest range they are Data Streams, Radio, and Data Hauling.

> Each day of Jump travel time within the Haven system is equivalent to one hour of communication lag when using common radio communication technologies.
>
> Data needs to be physically transported between systems; radio would simply take too long to be of any use.

> **Communication Satellites Are Rare**
> The curve of a planet or other physical object will regularly block a long range Radio transmission.

Data Streams

A common name given to localised public data networks. The content transmitted and technology used in a Data Stream varies widely by location and culture. For example, the Nephilim and Corporation prefer wireless networks, whereas the Legion and Kaltorans prefer physical cables.

Data Streams are often extremely dense and complex, allowing for enormous amounts of information to be transferred or shared over a short physical distance. This is achieved either by using photonic-crystal fibre-optic cables or short-range wireless hubs. The range of a Data Stream tends to be a single city or station, depending on the infrastructure.

Radio

This ancient form of communication is used for a wide range of communications between individuals, planets, space stations, and spacecraft.

During their early years in the Haven system, the Corporation widely used broad-spectrum transmissions, which not only alerted the Kaltorans, Legion, and Eden Brood Nephilim to their presence, but also awakened the Mechonids.

As piracy and Mechonid attacks grow more frequent with each year, a few precautions have become commonplace, including limiting all transmissions to a narrow band and using data encryption.

Data Hauling

Because the distance between stars is so vast, hard drives of data must be physically hauled by individual spacecraft. Most data hauling is done alongside other trade cargo, but on occasion mercenary teams will transport rare, expensive, or sensitive data as their sole cargo, or hide it in their cache.

Electronics

Electronics technology encompasses any devices which function by transmitting electrical signals through circuits. The nature of both the signals and circuits can vary wildly.

The vast majority of electronics technologies are remnants of the human civilisation. Many of them were preserved by the Archons, whilst others were rediscovered during the Great War.

Organic, Metallic, and Optical Components

Electronic signals can be carried in many ways, most commonly via metallic conductors, conductive plastics, ionic liquid channels, or bio-engineered nervous systems and data spines.

Computers

The development of computers had largely ended with the human empire, and since then it stagnated and even declined up until the Great War. Many Archon computers are replicas of those invented by humanity. Most new computers are developed by the Corporation and pale in comparison to their Archon counterparts. Even so, the Corporation is the only race seriously investing in computer technology, stemming from their passion for lost human technologies.

Many computers utilise biological components; these are known as Synaptronic computers. See pg: 276 for details.

Holograms

Cost effective to produce and readily available, holographic technologies are commonly used for digital displays. Moreover, they can be used in virtual reality simulations, cloaking devices, and short-range combat drones that can project a positively charged bolt along a negatively charged light beam.

Shields

A variety of technologies can generate a wall of force or energy, collectively referred to as shields. All types of shields require enormous amounts of power to function; although most spacecraft use shields, they are expensive when used for personal protection.

Electro-Gravity shields use magnetism to create artificial gravity, which is then used to push or deflect incoming objects.

Plasma windows are one of the most common methods of shielding. In this technique, air is trapped into a thin sheet by electro-magnetic confinement. The air is then ionised to create a field of plasma. If maintained at a high temperature, the plasma then incinerates or reacts with any matter that enters the field. This is a very effective method of converting large chunks of matter into a mixture of constituent atoms and small molecules.

"I was on a long-range scouting mission to Haven on fuel dregs, noting Nephilim presence as I went.

Soon as I got in system, I received a message. Something about if I paid nineteen more credits I'd get something or other for half price… Something in me died at that moment."

– Third Decanis Eris Gracchus, first Legion to meet the Corporation.

Disruptors

These devices make use of intense electromagnetic waves in the visible and near-visible regions through to the microwave region to disorient and disrupt electronic devices and sensors. They are widely used by law-enforcement officers because they can disrupt advanced weapons in a non-lethal manner. Additionally, they are used for live capture by bounty hunters, slavers, and scientists. Disruptors are especially devastating against robots because the intense electro-magnetism interferes with and overloads their circuits. Those who have implants should also be wary of Disruptors as they can damage delicate components.

Electro-Gravity

This technology is believed to be a remnant of human terraforming technologies used to change the gravity of entire worlds. The Electro-Gravity technology that exists today is a shadow of its former self; even so, it is still versatile and useful.

Electro-Graviety tech was preserved by the Kaltorans because they used it abundantly in constructing their subterranean, sub-aquatic cities on Kadash. The Kaltorans have also weaponised the technology to throw objects, propel munitions, and suspend enemies in mid-air.

Electro-Gravity has been used for artificial gravity on spacecraft for thousands of years. It is also used to cushion and guide landings at star ports.

Mechonids

See pg: 316 for full Mechonid setting write-up.

Without a doubt, the most advanced electronic technologies in the Haven system are used by the terrifying Mechonids. Constructed from superior and ancient human technology, Mechonids are rumoured to utilise ancient human marvels such as teleportation. They have also integrated many advanced Archon weapon technologies, such as their devastating Bio-Disintegration weaponry.

Biology

This field of science is one of the most important areas of current research. It ecompasses the science underlying the creation of all known biological life forms.

The Archons inherited an advanced but narrow knowledge of biological technology from their human creators. The Archons advanced their knowledge in this area to modify themselves and to create hundreds of intelligent races and millions of other species. X'ion, one of the final creations of the Archons, also created a great many creatures, known as the Nephilim.

Genetic Engineering

This is the direct manipulation of an organism's genome using bio-technology. A host's genome may be modified to either insert or remove particular DNA sequences. Based on molecular cloning methods, the target genome is first isolated, and then modified through the use of vectors, typically adenoviruses. In this way, new forms of life may be created from scratch, or existing forms may be substantially altered. However, this process must be carefully executed, as poor modification or delivery can result in permanent damage or even the death of the host.

Medicine

Access to medical facilities varies greatly among locations and cultures. Some have access to advanced Nephilim gene therapy labs, while others – such as many of the settlements on Mishpacha – only have access to primitive herbalism.

Despite the existence of many advanced medical procedures, tried-and-tested tools always have their place. These include bandages, pharmaceuticals, and knives.

Age Reversal

It is well known that Nephilim have an exceptional lifespan; many have lived since the Great X'ion War. Certain wealthy Corporate CEOs appear to have also defied ageing. Many assume that age-reversing technologies exist, despite their lack of availability to the general public.

Cloning

Despite wide spread use during the Great War to multiply Legion and Nephilim forces (and speculated to have contributed to the genetic erosion of humanity), cloning is not commonplace due to the technology's reputation for never getting things "exactly" right.

Limb and Organ Replacement

It is within the capabilities of advanced medicine to regrow and replace entire limbs and organs. The most common method is to use Nephilim Flesh Rejuvenators. However, this may not be sufficient if the body is significantly damaged or if there is any genetic degradation. Genetically engineered or robotic replacements are commonly used in combination with Flesh Rejuvenators.

Bio-Warfare in the Great War

During the Great War, the Archons, Mechonids, and X'ion used a myriad of incredibly powerful viruses, diseases, and mutagens. These powerful weapons often leave the most accomplished diagnostic teams at a complete loss and in terrible fear.

Synaptronics

This term refers to bio-technology used to perform computing and electronic functions. The Nephilim commonly use synaptic systems from genetically engineered brains in conjunction with neural networks (organic or otherwise) acting as cables, often called data spines.

Synaptronic Computers

These are in many ways superior to traditional electronics in raw computing power. This difference is largely due to the non-binary nature of synaptronics, letting them compute dozens of answers at each decision point, compared to the two answers (on or off) possible in traditional electronic computers. However, synaptronic computers have no way to wirelessly transmit these decisions outside of an electronic bottleneck.

Synaptronic Sensory Organs

Nearly identical in function to electronic sensors, synaptronic sensory organs differ primarily in their individual calibration. While electronic sensors can be programmed for a wide range of uses, synaptronic sensors are commonly made for specific functions such as tracking or heat detection.

Neural Interfacing

This is the name given to any device which creates a bridge between any kind of synaptic activity, including electronic devices, synaptronic minds, and traditional minds. This technology allows for direct mental control, data transfer, or both.

Implants

Adding a separate physical device (electronic, mechanical, or organic) to a person is often referred to as an implant. To function, all implants require neural interfacing, which allows the host to consciously or subconsciously control the implanted device.

Neural Fatigue

As the host of a complex implant becomes exhausted, the neural interface will often cause them neural fatigue, resulting in additional strain on the internal organs and the focus of the host.

Gene Splicing

This process permanently alters one's DNA. It is commonly achieved through implanting genetically engineered viruses, programmed to seek out and replace defined sections of the host's DNA. The process can be painful and long, but is the only way to alter the DNA of a living creature past its embryonic stage of growth.

Mechanics

Mechanics is concerned with the behaviour of physical bodies when subjected to a force, and the subsequent effects of the bodies on their environment. It can also be defined as a branch of science which deals with the motion of and forces on objects. The study of mechanics can include hydraulics, pistons, gears, and other physical parts with significant movement. Because mechanics is concerned with physical materials in motion, most training in mechanics also includes the study of materials.

Materials

As important as how the parts move is what the parts are made from. Mechanics and engineers pride themselves in knowing what materials are best used for what job, since there are many alternatives and improvements to what can be mined.

Synth Steel

Not made from iron but carbon, Synth Steel is a Corporation technology which uses blends of synthetic carbon-based polymers to form a material with the strength of steel but at a fraction of its weight. Nano-fibres and nanotubes can also be incorporated into the polymer blends. Some kinds of Synth Steel are solid forms that mimic the properties of steel nearly exactly, particularly tensile strength and hardness. However, there are other forms of Synth Steel, two of which are listed below.

Synth Weave

This thin fabric of Synth Steel is used to make many forms of resistant clothing, such as the Octanto™ Impenetrable Business Suits. Not only are they more resilient than traditional fabrics, they are well known for being more waterproof and stain-resistant than traditional armour. Synth Weave generally contains a much high concentration of nano-fibres and nanotubes than Synth Steel does.

Transparent Steel

This version of Synth Steel is transparent and favoured in windows and luxury vehicles. It is more expensive to manufacture as it requires large quantities of special transparent synthetic carbon-based polymers, but it is just as resilient as regular Synth Steel.

Tungsten Carbide

One of the hardest and most heat-resistant natural materials, tungsten carbide is a strong alloy of tungsten and carbon. The elemental ratio, impurities, and heat treatment used to anneal and descale the alloy can alter its properties. The alloy's strength and heat resistance make it ideal for military-grade armour.

Carapace and Bone

Despite their exotic nature, organic carapace and bone can make for excellent construction materials.

Drones

Mindless organic or electronic automations which are controlled remotely or via programming are commonly called drones. Most commonly used by the Corporation and Nephilim, they are primarily used for dangerous conflicts or manual labour.

Defence Systems

Some drones are designed as defence systems or emplacements. These tend to be stationary or at least restricted to an area which they patrol. Defence systems are more commonly programmed than directly controlled, and they act as deterrents for would-be intruders.

Electronic

With the exception of the Flesh, most Corporate drones are mechanical. These drones use electronic circuits and receivers to control metallic moving parts. They vary greatly in form and function.

Biological

These organic drones are engineered with limited or no personal intelligence. Their synaptronic brains have a limited number of behaviours, which function similar to programming. Many have built-in weapons.

Flesh

One of the most influential Nephilim technologies in the Haven system is the Flesh: biologically engineered drones in the form of bipedal, androgynous, grey-skinned humanoids. They will work tirelessly with just enough knowledge and understanding to complete their work, but they have no free will or independent thought.

It is important to note that, genetically. Flesh are not Nephilim.

Horrors

Although the Flesh are biological drones, their combat utility is very limited. The Nephilim prefer to make biological monstrosities designed specifically for war. Named Horrors by the other races, these drones are deadly and efficient creatures who mindlessly perform their murderous task.

Living Ammunition

Some drones are expressly designed as ammunition for weapons, especially in Nephilim ship-to-ship weapons, although smaller drones are sometimes used in handheld guns. These drones are pre-programmed with a specific behaviour such as burrowing, eating, or exploding.

Ley Lines

See pg: 288 for more on Spacecraft Jump Technology.

Ley Lines are important to all the races; they are used daily by spacecraft to travel vast distances in a timely manner. Despite the significance of the Ley Lines, very little is known about them, as their secrets died before their human creators did.

Creation

Ley Lines were created by humanity during an event referred to as the Reality Fracture. No one knows what caused it; some speculate that it was by design, others by accident.

Nature

The Ley Lines are tiny cracks or tears in the fabric of space-time; their exact nature is unknown. Although the cracks are microns thick and invisible to the naked eye, their lengths are measured in light years.

Theories

Many speculate that the Ley Lines are cracks between our dimension and another, which is bleeding its own natural laws into our own.

Others believe that the Ley Lines do not lead to another dimension at all, but are instead chains of densely packed energy particles which have been slowly dissipating for millennia.

There are some people on the fringes who believe the Ley Lines are gateways to a mystical afterlife or were created by a non-human being of immense power.

Ley Energy

What we do know is that the cracks leak energy particles known as Ley Energy, and this energy is used to generate a powerful force which allows interstellar travel. It has been so long since the Ley Lines were created that Ley Energy now exists thousands of light years away from its point of origin, forming concentric rings around stars and potentially granting access to locations that not even humanity was able to travel to.

Use

Jump Drives draw in Ley Energy from surrounding space and use it to create a wormhole through which spacecraft may travel. Jump Drives can use radiant Ley Energy which exists all throughout space. However, ships which travel close to the Ley Lines can travel faster because there is more available Ley Energy; in this way, the Ley Lines act like highways.

Once inside a wormhole, a ship would be crushed if not for the energy field that ships emit to protect themselves. The wormholes are unstable, so ships may pass through, but radio signals and the like cannot. Once in a wormhole, ships use whatever usual forms of propulsion they rely on to traverse space, but at a much greater speed.

Psionics

A few rare individuals exhibit extraordinary abilities which break our current understanding of science and how organic minds function. These people can project consciousness from their minds and read it in others. Unsubstantiated reports and rumours mention individuals that can see the future or the past. Anyone with this ability is called a Psion, and Psionics is the name given to their abilities.

Post-War Phenomena

Psionics are only a recent development; there were no Psions during the time of the Archons or even the Great War. Psions only began to emerge during the Years of Darkness, and they did so simultaneously for all except the Kaltorans, who have only reported Psions after their re-emergence into space.

Connection to Ley Lines

Although the exact nature of the relationship between Psionics and Ley Lines is unknown, there certainly is one. Psions become less powerful if they stray too far from the Ley Lines, and they have been known to grow in power while near great Ley Energy.

The Legion are a particularly interesting case. At first, there were very few documented Legion Psions on Cerberus; this makes sense, as their home planet is far from any Ley Lines. However, when the Legion began to re-enter the Haven system, something awakened their psionic power. Many, though, have attributed this delay not to their distance from the Ley Lines, but rather their proximity to an overbearing and suspicious Legion government.

Genetic Connection

Certain combinations of genes appear to manifest in naturally occurring Psions. Thus far, however, only unsubstantiated rumours exist of scientists being able to artificially grant Psionic abilities.

Mind and Time

The vast majority of Psionic power is restricted to subtle mental abilities such as secretly reading thoughts or influencing others' decisions. Psions are also telepaths and can communicate with other Psions with thought alone. Powerful Psions might be able to control the thoughts and actions of others, but if any Psion can do such a thing, they have kept it a secret.

The other power which few Psions possess is the ability to manipulate time. It is thought that they can create ripples and folds in the fabric of time, and in doing so they can distort the passage of reality. But the few which have claimed such power have been thought of as charlatans.

The Unknown

For each known there are a thousand unknowns. The vastness of space has its mysteries: some horrifying, some wondrous, some awe-inspiring.

Lost Technologies

The remnant technologies and wonders of humanity, the Archons, and the X'ion are spread across the galaxy. What technologies could be uncovered? What truths discovered? What power could have been wielded by them?

Lost Races

Several races have been detailed in this book, and others will be described in future books. The Archons and X'ion created thousands of species. Where and what are they?

Aliens

Does life exist that was not created by humanity, the Archons, or the X'ion? And if it does, would we recognise it?

Sentient AI

As they were masters of electronic technologies and capable of creating the Archons, is it not reasonable to presume that humanity created other electronic children? But if they did, why did they not tell their beloved Archons? Are the Mechonids sentient?

Ley Lines

What is the true nature of the Ley Lines? Are they the result of a deliberate decision by humanity or an accident? Are there dimensions beyond ours? What other uses for Ley Energy exist?

Psionics

What are the true origins of Psionics? Is it really limited to the manipulation of minds and time? Or are there some capable of greater feats?

Strangeness of Deep Space

The Haven system has been partially tamed by the Corporation, the Kaltorans, the Legion, and the Eden Brood Nephilim. But what lies outside of Haven? Are remnants of the X'ion army dormant in other systems? What strange astral phenomena float in the black of space?

Will the X'ion Return?

For all our sakes, let's hope not.

"Madness… pure madness…" The grey-haired scientist waved his palms across the holographic wall in frustration. Each swipe of his wrinkled, clawed Nephilim hands pushed a complex equation to the side of the wall or off the edge and into the digital bin.

With a large empty space now occupying the centre of the holographic wall, the hulking Nephilim scientist scrawled a clean and deceptively simple equation.

$$V = Sqrt(GM/R)$$

"… or magic."

"Gratar, this is not what we are here to do." The frustrated Corporate botanist took a seat; she knew this would take a while. "We need to continue our genetic mapping of the flora and fauna across the system."

"Child's play."

"Child's play? Really?" Sam hated how her counterpart could so easily reduce her life's work to nothing. "We haven't even begun to scratch the surface on the genetic structures of even half the Archon-created plants on Mishpacha, let alone the mutated X'ion hybrids…"

"No!" Gratar gritted his teeth in frustration. "It means nothing to understand how the Archons and the X'ion populated the worlds if we can't grasp the basics of how the worlds were altered to accommodate life."

"But we do know. humanity used powerful chemical synthesisers to alter and balance the atmo…"

"You are missing the point! Atmospheres, bio-diversity, all of this we can begin to grasp. But this!" Gratar pointed towards his wall. "Gravity, this eludes us all."

Sam sat patiently. This would take a while.

"We often mistakenly think that electronics was humanity's crowning achievement. But it's not…" Gratar closed his large eyes in thought. "It's as if humanity looked at the planets like we would look at an overgrown field and said, 'No, this will not do; let me change things so that I may build a home here'… to planets! They had this attitude of damn planets! None of our orbits or gravitation pulls are what they should be! None of them! Humanity has changed every single one of them, and we have no idea how!"

Combat Technology

Archons

A largely peaceful race that gave minimal thought to war and large-scale conflict. During the Great X'ion War, there was an enormous cultural shift amongst the Archons towards survival and conflict. This led to many new and innovative weapons and combat technologies.

Nephilim

Created by the X'ion, the Nephilim are a race of creatures which are part person, part biological equipment. Post-War, the Eden Brood has proven to be the most resourceful and adaptable species, blending their war-time biological equipment with more readily available mechanical and electronic technologies.

Legion

The Archons created the Legion as a military power to fight X'ion and its Nephilim army. To arm the Legion, the Archons created a variety of magnetically propelled weaponry based on ancient human designs. These advanced rail and gauss weapons are widely used to this day.

Kaltorans

Left to defend themselves from the Nephilim, the Kaltorans adapted peaceful electro-gravity technologies into weapons of war. During the Years of Darkness they also resorted to using readily available nuclear waste to create irradiated projectiles.

Corporation

The Corporation emerged after the Great War ended. On their home world they used primitive weaponry. The great warlords who united the tribes made widespread use of superior particle weaponry that never needed reloading. Once in space, they recognised that something capable of firing in the void of space was necessary, so they began to use ionised spacecraft fuel as a weapon. Both ion and particle weapons are still popular among the Corporation.

Spacecraft

During the Great X'ion War, very few land or sea-based vehicles were developed as it is easier to give artillery support and launch assault troops from orbit. Nearly all military spacecraft were constructed during this time, and most spacecraft still in use are the same ancient machines.

Weapons

Most weapons were developed for the Great War when the Archons and their creations desperately mobilised against the X'ion-created Nephilim army.

Burst Spores

This weapon spawns a dense ball of spores at the back of its oesophageal launcher. When spewed from the weapon, these dense balls can travel a great distance and burst upon striking the target, releasing a dangerous chemical coating. The exact nature of the chemical varies greatly from one weapon to the next. Some corrode the target with acids, while others set fire to the target with napalm or phosphorous.

Gauss Weaponry

By applying an oscillating current through the conductive coils wrapped around the barrel, these weapons generate an oscillating electromagnetic field in its barrel. Then, by shifting the polarity of these electromagnets, they project the bullet forward while applying spin.

Ion Weaponry

These weapons use tridrogen as ammunition, the same material used for high-grade Corporation spacecraft fuel. They operate by supercharging (or ionizing) helium-3 inside the chamber and ejecting it as a glowing jet. As this type of weapon uses a very cheap source of ammunition, it is popular amongst those conscious of ammunition consumption.

Irradiated Ammunition

These weapons use a mechanical firing mechanism not unlike those used in ancient human weaponry. However, they fire an ammunition crafted from depleted uranium, a waste product of nuclear reactors. The bullets are highly radioactive and dangerous to handle but also extremely dense, giving them excellent stopping power.

Particle Weaponry

Little more than a small particle accelerator on a trigger, these weapons draw in surrounding gas particles to be charged and fired at extreme speed in a focused beam. These weapons are limited in their destructive capability and do not work in the void of space, where there are too few particles in the environment. However, they require no ammunition and are cheap to manufacture, making them a popular sidearm.

Rail Weaponry

Two electromagnetic rails run down either side of this weapon's barrel. When charged, these rails project a bullet at supersonic speed with little to no recoil.

Self-Propelled Ammunition

Each bullet has a small, single-use electro-gravity generator, which creates a bubble around the bullet, propelling it forward. The bubble also protects the ammunition, allowing it to pass through liquids safely.

Spine Launcher

This biological weapon grows tightly packed rows of sharp spines inside cords that run the length of the weapon. The launcher spews these cords sequentially at high speed, giving an exceptional rate of fire. To replenish its spines, the weapon is fed dense biomass sacks into its mouth. These spines can be regrown in mere seconds.

Electro-Gravity

This versatile weapon is a masterwork of artificial electro-gravity technology. It can manipulate finite pockets of gravity in such a way that enemies can be lifted, flung, tripped, or disarmed at range.

Shell Weaponry

A shell is any versatile, hollow ammunition that can be fashioned into single-use grenades or ammunition for heavy weapons and shotguns.

Dispersion Shells

These shells are packed full of dangerous chemicals. When the shell impacts a target, it sprays a chemical over a wide area. A variety of chemicals may be used in dispersion shells, from napalm to neurotoxins.

Dummy Shells

Cheap to produce, these shells are used to confuse and panic enemy ranks. Packed with magnesium, they explode with a loud noise and a bright flash.

Kinetic Shells

Primitive but extremely effective, these shells use the kinetic force of the explosion they produce to tear their targets apart.

Shrapnel Shells

Similar to kinetic shells, shrapnel shells are packed full of small, sharp objects. When such a shell detonates, it sends shards out in all directions, making it particularly effective against large groups of lightly armoured targets.

Smoke Shell

Not designed to cause harm but to create cover, these shells billow thick smoke or mist over a large area, obscuring vision.

Snare Shells

Used primarily for crowd control, snare shells employ a variety of substances to immobilise targets. These substances include adhesive gels, weighted ropes, and nets.

Chemical

A variety of chemical agents have been weaponised for use in chemical throwers, dispersion shells, and burst spores. Most chemicals are produced using bio-chemistry, although some are synthetics.

Napalm

A highly flammable chemical that is ignited as it leaves the chamber of a weapon or shell. It burns at high temperatures and is resistant to being extinguished.

Antimonic Acid

This highly concentrated acid can burn through nearly any substance. The effects of this acid on flesh are horrific to behold, and its ghastly effects are commonly used to demoralise opponents.

Cryo-Gel

This Nephilim-made bacterium formulation is used in cryogenic stasis chambers. It can be weaponised as a dangerous substance that can numb muscles and freeze joints.

Neurotoxin

This highly toxic gas directly attacks the nervous system and brain, causing neurological damage and in many cases death. The particles of this gas are so fine that they ignore most filters, armours, and other defences.

Melee Weaponry

A primary weapon for many Nephilim and some specialist forces of the other races, melee weapons are deadly in the hands of a skilled user. A great variety of melee weapons exist: knives, bayonets, swords, and spears, to name a few.

Arc Fire

A composite blade drenched in ionised photons held on by static charge. The photons give the blade a faint glow and allow it to burn through flesh and metal.

Composite Blades

Refers to any blade made from a blend of different materials, including Synth Steel, tungsten, and titanium alloys.

Nano-Bone Blades

Created by X'ion for its Nephilim troops, this thin bone-like material is razor-sharp. There are many modern adaptations of this organic technology, some of which appearing more like cut metal than bone.

Defences

There is always an arms race between new weapons and new armour. New and varied materials are being used and configured for battle, allowing a great variety of armours to be fashioned, from thin retractable suits up to bulky mech suits with assisted movement.

Tactical Armour

General-use, all-purpose combat armour, it is not so heavy as to impede movement, and resistant to many light weapons. It comes in many forms and varieties, depending on the technology behind it. Tactical armour also comes equipped with bandoliers, pockets, and storage compartments.

Retractable Armour

Favoured by Corporates for its unobtrusive nature, retractable armour is compact and lightweight and can be compressed into a small wearable item such as a vest or belt. When activated it deploys to cover its user in thin, lightweight protective plates or an energy shield.

As it is discreet, retractable armour allows the user to be more diplomatic than combat armour would normally allow. A soldier in full battle fatigues is unlikely to get a good reception at a peaceful meeting, but retractable armour allows one to be prepared while putting others at ease.

Environmental Adaption System

Adaptable and dependable, this environmental system is suited to a variety of hostile environments. The suit reacts to its surroundings and changes its configuration to protect its wearer against almost any environmental danger.

Tactical Array Suit

This computerised armour makes use of sensors to gather data from its surroundings to be uploaded to the user's helmet HUD. The armour is often networked with weapons and other suits to maximise battlefield awareness.

Technical Suit

Any well-rounded combat force includes engineers and specialists or even field medics, and these technicians often prefer to use a technical suit rather than tactical armour. The technical suit is equipped with a variety of tools customised to the user. These tools are built into the gauntlets and compartments within the suit, allowing easy access while protecting the user from attack.

Mech Suits

This term generally refers to armour too heavy and cumbersome to be moved without assistance. This extremely heavy armour is rarely used outside of full-blown battlefields. Each suit is capable of moving itself to assist the movement of its wearer, usually through robotics in advanced mech suits or muscular systems seen in Nephilim outfits.

Shield Technologies

A variety of armour technologies rely on energy fields to augment their effectiveness. Some are more specialised than others, but each serves the purpose of protecting the wearer.

Shield Nodes

The most basic application of shield technologies is to project a field of ionised plasma around the user. This field absorbs incoming weapon fire but is often ineffective against direct hits.

Grav-Field

This shield of gravitational force is used to deflect slower-moving projectiles such as shrapnel and thrown grenades. The Grav-Field constantly pushes objects away from the wearer, which can be disorienting for anyone standing too close to the field.

Scram Suit

In an attempt to limit the effectiveness of battle drones against human combatants, the scram suit projects radio waves to interfere with the wireless signals used by many computerised systems. This interference blocks and/or confuses the signals. These radio signals are particularly effective against drones and targeting systems.

Stealth Suit

A holographic field is projected from this suit, rendering the wearer invisible. It is favoured by scouts and assassins who would argue the best defence against bullets is not being shot at in the first place.

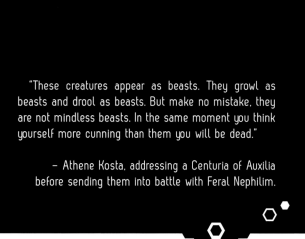

"These creatures appear as beasts. They growl as beasts and drool as beasts. But make no mistake, they are not mindless beasts. In the same moment you think yourself more cunning than them you will be dead."

– Athene Kosta, addressing a Centuria of Auxilia before sending them into battle with Feral Nephilim.

Biological

Many armours are fashioned from the exoskeletons of living (and on occasion, sentient) creatures, while others are living organisms that grow over or into the bodies of their hosts.

During the Great War, the Nephilim made extensive use of protective life forms that were separate to themselves. While many Nephilim were engineered to grow protective coverings, most did not. By having their "armour" separate from themselves, they could discard, repair, and change their coverings as needed, giving them a great amount of flexibility.

Parasitic or Symbiotic

The two defining categories of biological armour are their method of gaining required nutrients and their relationship with their wearer. These armours work either through a parasitic bond, in which the armour treats its host as subservient and feeds on it, or through a symbiotic relationship, which thrives on a mutually beneficial existence.

Carapace

Grown in labs or made from the shells of fallen Nephilim, this sturdy symbiotic material is a popular choice of protection.

Living Mech Suits

Some armours are actually enormous creatures that allow for a pilot (of sorts) to enter them. Synaptronic connectors join the wearer's nervous system to the creature, allowing the wearer to directly control the creature's movements. These creatures are made for war and allow weaker creatures to effectively control a large and terrible beast.

Spacecraft Technology

There are a great variety of spacecraft within the Haven system, ranging from single-pilot fighters to enormous battleships and freighters. Although most were built for military purposes during the Great War, nearly all of them have now been adapted to serve multiple functions while maintaining their combat ability.

Medium Sized

The most popular ships within the Haven system are small and medium-sized spacecraft with crews of four to twenty people, often with room for passengers or cargo.

Medium-sized ships are often preferred to larger craft due to their flexibility and efficiency.

Ancient and Forgotten Technologies

The vast majority of spacecraft are ancient vessels, over a hundred years old, which have been retrofitted, reconstructed, repaired, or simply refuelled and flown under its new owners.

Many of the technologies used in spacecraft are no longer fully understood. They can been maintained and operated, but nobody deeply understands how they all work. Because many of their key components can no longer be made, most spacecraft are highly dependent on salvaged parts from ancient derelicts.

Jump Technology

The most significant forgotten technology is Jump technology. Designed by humanity and maintained by the Archons, it is truly incomprehensible to the current races. It is known that they draw in Ley Energy emitted by Ley Lines to create a portal, allowing for travel times that far exceed the speed of light. But none know how these portals truly work, what they are, or how they are created. Jump Drives just work.

Ley Lines

These tears in the fabric of the universe emit Ley Energy, which is utilised by Jump Drives to facilitate faster-than-light travel via a portal. This Ley Energy must be collected just before a portal is opened.

Reclaimed

With the exception of Corporation-manufactured ships, almost all spacecraft are reclaimed salvaged wrecks brought back into working order. All the races do this to some extent, and it is the main way to get new spacecraft.

Corporation Built

Due to their extensive efforts at reverse engineering lost and forgotten technologies, Corporation spacecraft require fewer ancient parts to construct. While many components are of lesser quality than their ancient counterparts, they are usually more unified in their construction and appearance as they have been (almost entirely) scratch-built.

Kaltoran Cut 'n' Shut

With a particular gift for salvage, the Kaltorans make widespread use of a cut 'n' shut method of joining multiple partially working spacecraft together to create a single functioning craft.

After the Great War, the Kaltorans stored thousands of ships in their underground cities. While they stripped down most for materials, they kept many (mostly) intact in anticipation that they would one day re-emerge back to the stars.

Ancient Legion Warships

Most of the Legion fleet are ships which have been maintained since the Great X'ion War. Many of these ships have seen continual use since that time, despite diminishing supplies and fewer skilled technicians.

In recent years the Legion have restored many old ships with the assistance of the Kaltorans, although the Legion will often refuse to use a haphazard cut 'n' shut approach. They prefer to search long and hard to restore a ship to fully working order.

Wild Nephilim Ships

Nephilim vessels are huge living creatures capable of survival in deep space. These creatures have seemingly unlimited lifespans, and many have roamed space since the Great X'ion War, having long since allowed their crew to die. Despite the risks, these wild, untamed ships are regularly tracked down and domesticated by the Eden Brood.

Sensors

Spacecraft sensors are a mixture of devices capable of detecting energy and matter across the void of space. There are significant limitations to what kinds of phenomena they can detect.

Infrared

The void is extremely cold, so cold that anything emitting heat or light is easily detected in the black of space. Infrared sensors are used for detecting distant celestial objects like stars, planets, and even smaller objects such as asteroids. Infrared can detect objects many light years away, and it is primarily used for navigation.

At a close range of a few hundred kilometers or less, infrared can be used to detect subtle variations in heat radiation, allowing for a detailed assessment of a spacecraft's major systems, such as the location of its reactor, engines, and life support.

Gravity

Ships can detect the presence, intensity, and distance of gravity fields by measuring the forces acting upon the ship using a finely tuned gyroscope and complementary methods. Detecting gravity is useful in that it allows the ship to estimate the weight of almost any object and enables it to analyse planetary bodies, space stations, asteroids, and debris, as well as their trajectories.

Spatial

Using multiple external cameras and sophisticated mathematics, spatial sensors allow a spacecraft to detect the size and shape of distant objects. This is helpful for determining if an object outside of visual range has a regular shape, like that of a ship, or a rough shape, like that of an asteroid. As objects get closer, the sensor can determine the finer details of the shape.

Energy

One of the forgotten technologies commonly used in spacecraft are energy sensors. Nobody really understands how they work, but they are able to measure the joules of energy a ship or a section of a ship is using. In this way, ships with energy sensors can detect where another ship's reactor is, what systems are receiving power, and if the ship is powering up their weapons, readying them to fire.

"Captain, we've located the Draz-runners' wreck and pulled up within a few lengths. Energy signs are negligible, and heat is almost the same as the surrounding void. She's dead as a rock."

The astrogator's crisp report came from across the haphazard bridge, itself looking (rather accurately) to be made from two completely different ships welded together at an off-centre diagonal with a slash of Synth Steel patching.

"So, any life signs down there, guys?" Everyone ignored the Kaltoran captain as per usual. They'd explained it to him repeatedly how it didn't work like that. There was no magic DNA scanner or way of telling the different forms of carbon apart to that degree. "Guys, I asked if there were any life signs. This is bordering on disrespect."

"Captain, with all the respect you are due, we are currently assessing the situation, and will appraise you of any relevant developments."

A shout came from another of the bridge crew. "We have movement! On the far side of the ship, near that large hole!"

A few moments passed as the captain thought it over. "Take her around, and pull back a few dozen lengths! And see if it has signs of life while you're at it!" came the captains' command halfway through the ship doing so, the bridge crew exchanging glances of exasperation he didn't seem to notice.

"Okay, it seems that something the size of a large missile has exited the ship… slowly…" came the astrogator's cool report, drifting off as she bent over and squinted at the readouts. "Maybe two? It seems… Oh."

She closed her eyes, momentarily swearing under her breath before glaring at the captain. "It seems an idiot in a space suit has thrown some sort of undetonated munition at us. Helm, be ready to dodge in the next three to four minutes."

Collective sighs of distaste came from across the bridge as the captain sat looking delighted, his beaming face grinning knowingly at the Corporate bridge crew.

"So, you say you detected life signs?"

Shields

Spacecraft are constantly bombarded by small particles and micro asteroids, especially when travelling through nebulas and asteroid fields. This necessitates an additional layer of protection over the ship's hull in the form of a shield. Spacecraft, with their powerful reactors, avoid the primary problem with shield technology: their high power consumption. For these reasons, nearly all spacecraft are equipped with shields, and only the most suicidal (or desperate) of captains make do without them.

Unlike personal shields that use a single method of protection, spacecraft make use of two simultaneous shield layers.

Grav-Field

The outermost layer of protection is the Grav-Field: this shield forms a protective bubble around the ship that deflects small and slow-moving debris such as microasteroids and space dust. In addition, Grav-Fields push matter (and some forces) away, allowing ships to withstand high-pressure atmospheres and most importantly jump portals.

Kaltorans, who are masters of grav technologies, tend to have powerful enough Grav-Fields that their ships can endure the immense pressures of the deep sea.

Plasma Field

The Grav-Field also suspends a thin layer of gases, which forms a second layer of protection. These gases are ionised, creating a transparent but uniform bubble of hot and highly reactive plasma. This bubble protects the ship from high-velocity impacts, such as incoming weapons fire, by converting the incoming material into constituent atoms and molecules. Although strong, the plasma field is not indestructible, and on occasion a well-placed shot can break through the field (even fully charged).

Each time a plasma field is hit, some of the ionised gases escape, which gradually weakens the shield. It can be recharged with more ionised gas, but this takes time. A shield which endures significant damage will eventually fail, leaving the ship exposed. Should this occur in battle, it is unlikely that the ship would last for very long.

"I sincerely admire the technical artistry of the design. Six Kaltoran ships, none of them working worth a damn, are now part of one big beautiful clusterfrag of a ship. Half the power's run off uranium and steam, while the other parts have a black flammable gunk they drilled for. Pity I'm going to blow it up."

– Phillip Bonderrosh, Corporate competitor.

"Hard to port, and a seven second full burn, Jesiik!" B'darr yelled.

A rumbling noise of assent came through the Bioship, as its manoeuvring put it just out of line with the enemies' munitions yet again.

"And stop playing around in that damned turret and hit something!" she yelled again, feeling the dorsal and port thrusters of the ship firing through her brain, the psionic link she'd made with the ship showing her more than the screens ever would.

"I'm bloody trying! I hate fighting small ships!" came the frustrated yell from the floor-recessed gunnery pustule. These smarter ships were a marvel, she mused, directing the scram signals to stop the enemy from locking onto her ship. Lucky they're able to help the crew to, well, crew them, or the two of us would be far less efficient, and likely dead.

B'darr's thought was interrupted as a juddering ripple of strain passed through the walls; her own joints and muscles clenched in sympathetic pain as early bruising spread through the ship's stress points. The enemy fighters had scored a palpable hit to the shields. "Damnit! Jesiik? You need to point me to any damage that could impact our escape." The rumbling assent came again as the Legion in the weapon pustule called out a question.

"Captain, would dumping our cargo shake off enough mass to give us a little better manoeuvrability?" His thick, scratchy voice seemed worried.

"No, not enough to matter. Reactors, even biological ones, outclass our cargo mass by several orders of magnitude, not to mention the rest of the ship. It'd be like throwing away a couple of teeth to run faster."

A simplistic explanation, given the physics involved, but one must make sure the less intelligent races understood one's sentences. Sometimes, she mused, being an Emissary was tough.

"Hah! I hit one! Popped his shields, and he's limping home with his exhaust between his legs!"

B'darr smiled. Even if the Legionnaire didn't understand, at least he was useful.

Reactors and Propulsion

The Archons powered their ships primarily with fusion reactors, but there are relatively few surviving reactors and great demand for working spacecraft. This has led to the development of a variety of propulsion methods and reactor types within the Haven system.

Hydrogen Combustion

Easy to manufacture and mass produce, these combustion engines are primarily used by the Corporation.

Powered by burning hydrogen gas with oxygen, the reactor produces energy, and then by venting the resulting explosion through the engines it creates thrust. The largest drawback of this method is that it destroys oxygen, a valuable component of life-support systems. The positive side is that it produces water, reducing the need for water recycling.

Hydrogen Fusion

Used primarily by the Legion, fusion reactors are common in dedicated Great War warships. These reactors use H2 (diatomic hydrogen) and H3 (triatomic hydrogen), forms that both occur naturally in many gas giants. These forms of hydrogen are unique in that their nucleus contains not just a single proton, but also one or two neutrons. A stable fusion reaction combines the hydrogen atoms, generating helium and a free neutron, along with a huge amount of energy. It is the most efficient use of hydrogen fuel. However, the reactors are a forgotten technology, so they are limited in number and cannot be replaced should they overload or be destroyed.

Nuclear Reactors

Nuclear reactors are used primarily by the Kaltorans when they cannot find a working fusion reactor. In these, chemical energy is converted into electricity by boiling water and using the steam to drive a turbine. The heat required to boil the water is obtained from the nuclear decay of highly radioactive materials such as uranium. Unfortunately, this process creates incredibly dangerous waste, but it can be disposed of directly into space. However, should the reactor be damaged and need repairs, the process can become incredibly dangerous.

Bio-Solar

Many living Nephilim ships use Bio-Solar reactors, which make use of engineered photosynthesis to generate chemical energy that allows for converting water and CO_2 (carbon dioxide) into Bio-Oil (ethanol) and oxygen. The excreted Bio-Oil is burned, generating heat, which can be used to power the engines. The process also creates CO_2 and water as waste products, which are recycled to make more fuel. Relative to the other reactor types, Bio-Solar reactors generate little energy for the space required, so it is often supplemented with a second reactor. However, the process is very efficient, and the biological catalysts required to generate Bio-Oil occur naturally within these living ships, making the process a renewable, closed system that can last for the life of the creature.

Jump Travel

A wonder of ancient human technology, Jump travel is what made populating the universe possible. Jump travel involves the absorption of Ley Energy into a portal generator, which then creates a shortcut through space to an intended destination.

Ley Lines and Ley Energy

Humanity tore the fabric of space-time (during the Reality Fracture, pg: 273) to create the Ley Lines. These tears in space emit Ley Energy, which makes Jump travel possible. Nobody really understands how it works, only that it does work.

Traversing Wormholes

When wishing to travel through a wormhole, the Jump Drive first draws Ley Energy into the drive. These energies are then focused and projected in front of the ship. This projection produces an event horizon, a portal which a ship can enter. These wormholes go one way, and the portal doesn't open at the other end until moments before the ship emerges. In addition, the portal that the ship first entered remains open for only a few moments before it closes; this means that for most of the time a ship is inside a wormhole, there is no visible portal at either end.

Surviving Wormholes

Being inside a wormhole is not unlike being inside a tunnel whose walls are made from lava and continuously collapsing. Traversing wormholes is incredibly dangerous. Ships require a functioning Grav-Field in order to stop the wormhole from collapsing and destroying the ship. There is a constant battle between the ship's shields and the pressure of the wormhole.

What happens in normal space when a wormhole collapses has been observed. A small portal opens no larger than a few centimeters across through which an entire ship and its crew are forced through in only a few seconds. The resulting debris field is spectacular and terrifying to behold.

Travel Within Wormholes

Each wormhole tunnel is separate, and they cannot be joined together. The only way for two ships to be inside the same tunnel is if one followed the other in close succession, but this is very dangerous.

It is important to carefully plot your destination before jumping into a wormhole. Once you have begun your journey, you cannot change the destination whilst inside the wormhole. You can cut your journey short and drop out early, but it is impossible to know exactly where you will end up, only that it will be somewhere along your route.

Once inside a wormhole, you are no longer in normal space-time, making it incredibly hard for you to be tracked or located. This effect has made piracy, smuggling, and other illegal space activities that much easier.

GM's Guide

Being a Game Master (GM) is often a great sacrifice. It requires a lot of preparation before the game and your undivided attention during the game. This section will help you to prepare more efficiently and ease the work required during play.

Players can read this section. It gives away no secrets and may help them to understand and appreciate the work a GM does.

Overview

The Basics
It is assumed you already know what a Game Master is, how to prepare a story, and how to use non-player characters (NPCs) – GM skills used across all role playing games (RPGs). If you don't know any of this, we recommend you join an existing group for a while. Ask your local gaming store.

This section will only teach you the specifics of GMing in the Fragged Empire system and setting.

Set the Style
First and foremost, discuss with your players what style of game you will be playing. For more, see Optional: Game Types (pg: 29).

Will it be heavy on combat?
Will there be lots of exploration and science?
How long will the game go for?

Invent Your Own Rules
Once you understand the rules well, go ahead: bend and break them. Even invent your own. Feel free to create new Weapons, Traits, Environments, and opponents for your player characters to fight.

If you accidentally create an unbalanced rule, just change it. But try to be as consistent as you can be.

Have Fun
This cannot be over-stressed: the number-one rule of all RPGs is to have fun. The measure of a good GM is not how much they thwart or beat their players, but how much fun they everyone is having (including the GM).

Don't argue over rules. If there is a disagreement, just make a quick decision or roll a die. Don't take up valuable game time with a long discussion. You can discuss the rule after the game session is over.

Non-Combat

See pg: 182 for an extensive Setting write-up.

The rules for non-combat interactions are fairly light and basic. In these cases, the GM sets the scene, and the players choose which Skill (pg: 38) they wish to roll while describing how they are using that Skill.

Degrees of Success
See pg: 38 for full Skill Roll rules.

If a player makes a Skill Roll and gets much higher than the Difficulty, the outcome should be better than intended – and vice versa.

Just as important as the roll is the player's approach, description, and Skill choice. These also help define the nature of outcome.

NPCs
See pg: 38 for full Skill vs Skill Roll rules.

NPCs that are primarily there for non-combat reasons do not need to have a full Character Sheet written up. Simply give them a bonus or penalty to Skills that make sense for them.

Untrained: –2
Experienced: +1 or +2
Expert: +3 or +4

Give Downtime
See pg: 64 for full Spare Time Points rules.
See pg: 95 for full Downtime rules.

It is important to give your characters some Downtime, so they can spend their Spare Time Points and pursue their own goals, especially if they have Workshops and Labs (pg: 138).

Combat

See pg: 71 for full Combat rules.
See pg: 155 for full Spacecraft Combat rules.
See pg: 315 for a list of example Opponents.

Combat and violence are significant parts of the Fragged Empire setting. Not that everyone is violent, but everyone's life is regularly shaken by violence.

Set the Scene

Use combat as a tool to push the story forward.

Don't just describe the environment. Explain to the players (as far as they know) why there is conflict. Give your NPCs a purpose and a reason to fight. No one is ever evil for evil's sake.

Reward Good Tactics

If players approach combat intelligently — for example, if they set up an ambush — be sure to reward them: for the ambush, you might give them a Surprise Round (pg: 101).

Personal Combat

This is often messy, fast, and heavily shaped by available Cover.

Be sure to include Cover (pg: 86) in all personal Combats.

Spacecraft Combat

Personal and spacecraft Combat are vastly different. Spacecraft Combat usually has the players controlling one vehicle, each using a different Vehicle System (pg: 53). Often, the result is a single damaged spacecraft retreating through the Combat Jump System Roll (pg: 175).

Mix It Up

Combat should tell a story and be fun, so mix things up to make things interesting. Vary up the difficulty, as well; not every fight needs to leave your player characters battered and bloodied, unless that's the style of game you are going for.

Some example methods of mixing it up are:
» A way for the PCs to make use of the Environement (eg: gun emplacements or bottomless pits).
» A few easy fights against underpowered opponents before a big climatic fight against a overpowered Nemesis.
» Give your NPCs a Trait or Variation of your own design.

NPC Actions

This set of optional NPC Actions may make it a little easier for you to manage multiple NPCs during a combat.

New Actions
There are three new NPC Actions: Moving, Shooting, and Striking.

All of these new Actions are intended to simplify the control of NPCs. They are also STRONGER than the standard Actions.

Traits Modifying Actions
Some Traits grant bonuses or penalties to specific Actions. These changes also apply to NPC Actions.

» Moving counts as Full Move and Prep.
» Shooting counts as Snap Shot, Spray Fire, and Sighted Shot.
» Striking counts as Strike and Charge.

Removed Actions
Nine Actions have been removed: Full Move, Take Cover, Prep, Snap Shot, Spray Fire, Sighted Shot, Strike, Charge, and Block.

You may use any of these if you wish.

NPC System Rolls

As with NPC Actions, you may use these optional NPC spacecraft System Rolls. They are intended to simplify the control of NPC spacecraft.

Manoeuvre
The Manoeuvre System Roll now has an additional System Roll Effect: It may Launch a group of Fighters (as with the Direct Crew System Roll).

Removed System Rolls
Four System Rolls have been removed: Direct Crew, Divert Power, Scan, and Volley.

You may use any of them if you wish. However, if you allow your NPC spacecraft to make the Direct Crew System Roll, the Manoeuvre System Roll does not Launch Fighters (as this would allow two Launches per Turn).

Optional: NPC Personal Combat Actions

Pick any 2 Actions Per Turn		Bonuses from the same Action do not Stack			
Tactical Actions		**Range Actions**		**Melee Actions**	
Moving — Move	Move +2 Pick One: Draw Wpn, Reload, Un-Jam, Set Up, Pull Down, Use Stim or Skill Roll (Medical).	Shooting — Attack Damage	Hit +Per +Extra RoF Dice Range +Foc	Striking — Attack Damage Move	Hit +Ref +Extra RoF Dice
Analyse — Attack Recover	On Hit: Boost next Attack: Crit Attribute Location +/-2	Throw — Attack Damage Move	Hit +Ref Range +Str	Impair — Damage Impair Move	Hit +Ref +Str On Hit: Pick One Debuff vs Target: Prone, Grab or Move 1
Stealth — Stealth	Vs Highest Defence On Hit: Cant be Targeted	Overwatch — Attack* Damage	Hit +Per *May Attack in a 180 Arc in response to any Action.	Escape — Damage Impair Move	Hit +Ref +Str On Hit: Debuff Target: Loose Grabbing Target.

Optional: NPC Spacecraft Combat System Rolls

Highest Velocity (or Size if Equal) First		Make 1 System Roll per Turn (Successful System Rolls may not be rolled again).				Highest CPU (or Sensors if Equal) First	
Command + 2		**Engineering + 2**		**Operations + 2**		**Gunnery + 2**	
	Skill Roll		Skill Roll		Skill Roll		Skill Roll
Full Burn	8 — Rotate 45° Alter Velocity = Eng.	Damage Control	12-Crew — Remove 1 On Fire Effect. Regen Shields. Armour vs Boarding +1	Calibrate	12-CPU — Add or remove 1 Target Lock Effect.	Preparation	8-Crew — Reload or Un Jam a Weapon. May Roll once per Weapon.
Manoeuvre	Size x4 — Rotate 90° Alter Velocity = Eng -2. Launch Fighters.	Combat Jump	14-CPU* — *4 Success, +2 Success required if Spacecraft leaves Combat Area. ⬡⬡⬡	Dumb Fire	vs Def — Launch and Attack with a Warhead. Destroy this Warhead at the end of the Turn.	Lead the Target	vs Def — Attack with a Battery. Range +1 May Roll once per Weapon.
Strafe Size 1 or 2	vs Def — Rotate 45° Attack Front Arc with a Battery. Range -1	Patch Job	14-Crew — Repair 1 Attribute Dmg that was dealt after your last Turn.	Seeker	8-Crew — Launch a Warhead. This Warheads gains: Lock On +6.	Bombard Size 4+	vs Def — Attack with 2 Batteries. Hit -2

Balancing

See pg: 73 for full Environment rules.
See pg: 315 for a list of example Opponents.

NPCs for your PCs to fight in personal Combat are arranged into three categories: Henchmen (pg: 296), Skilled (pg: 298), and Nemesis (pg: 300).

- » A Henchmen group is comparable to 1 player character.
- » A Skilled opponent is comparable to 1 player character.
- » A Nemesis is comparable to 3 player characters.

If you wish to make a balanced fight, set the difficulty value of the opponents equal to the number of player characters (eg: 1 Nemesis and 1 Skilled opponent for 4 player characters). However, feel free to increase or decrease the difficulty as you think best, especially because many other factors affect the difficulty of the fight, including the environment (eg: little or lots of Cover), the amount of Ammunition (pg: 122), and existing Attribute Damage (pg: 87).

Combat Should Never Be Perfectly Balanced

Do not attempt to make combat perfectly balanced; it is not meant to be. RPGs are about your player characters' stories. While the player characters should win most fights, they should not expect to be able to defeat any NPC at any time.

Building NPCs

Henchmen (pg: 296) are built like a Companion (pg: 105) Weapon.
Skilled opponents (pg: 298) are built like player characters.
Nemesis opponents (pg: 300) are built like player characters.

Henchmen Are Easy to Manage
If you would like NPCs to be easier to manage, you can use Henchmen in every combat.

Average Player Resources (Avg Res)

The combat ability of a player character is primarily determined by their Resources (pg: 56). NPCs gain additional abilities as player characters gain Resources. Be sure to track your players' Average Resources and see the relevant Ability Table to see what the NPCs gain.

Player Level Much Higher than Their Average Resources

If your player characters are 3 Levels higher than their Average Resources. Opponents should be given abilities from a higher Average Resources level on their table.

Traits

NPCs do not need to be Trained in a Skill to select a Trait from that category. Regardless, they may still only select 1 Trait from each area, except for the Vehicle System and personal Combat sections, from which they may select 2 Traits.

Environment and Cover

See pg: 86 for full Cover rules.

Be sure to add Cover to every personal Combat. Open terrain is very dangerous.

Ambush
Be very careful with giving Henchmen a Surprise Round (pg: 101) as they can deal a lot of Damage very quickly.

NPCs with an Attribute of 1
Be careful with giving a NPC an Attribute score of 1, as they may die very quickly.

Spacecraft Combat

See pg: 142 for full Spacecraft Creation rules.

NPC spacecraft are built like PC spacecraft. In a balanced spacecraft fight, both sides will have spacecraft of equal total Influence Cost.

Killing Player Characters

You should rarely try to actually kill your player characters. It is actually quite hard to kill one: not only can they automatically save their life by reducing their Fate by 1 (pg: 35), but it is also very difficult to reduce one of their Attributes to –5.

All that said, you can cripple a player character through Attribute Damage. Attribute Damage will often stay with a character for a couple of sessions, until they can make the required Medical Spare Time Rolls (pg: 92). To the player, crippling their character is often scarier than death.

Why Cripple over Death?
Fragged Empire is a gritty post-apocalyptic setting where players are encouraged to consider the long term consequences of their actions and make sustainable choices.

Crippling was chosen to be more common than Death because crippling is often scarier to players. This encourages players to more deeply consider any form of lethal violence and to give character the chance to make a desperate retreat if needed.

Be careful to not cripple your players too often. Crippling is a major event.

Creating a Balanced Combat

Other factors (eg: low on Ammunition, environment, etc.) should be considered.
No combat should be perfectly balanced.

Number of NPCs

Opponents have comparable ability to a single player character (PC).
Select a Number of opponents equal to the number of PCs.

● Henchmen = 1 Player Character.
◉ Skilled = 1 Player Character.
☻ Nemesis = 3 Player Characters.

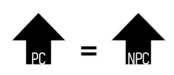

Opponents Gain Ability as Players gain Resources

Keep track of your players' Average Resources (Avg Res).
Opponents gain bonuses for every 5 Average Resources your
players have.

Build Opponent Spacecraft Around Similar Influence

Use the same amount of Influence as all of your player characters
have available. Influence spent does not need to be an exact match.
NPC can make as many System Rolls as the player characters.

Henchmen

See pg: 105 for full Weapon Type: Companion rules.
See pg: 358 for a full list of available Weapons.

These represent lesser skilled Opponents and will often be the most commonly fought. Often making up for their lack of skill with numbers. Most fights should include Henchmen as they are easy for a GM to manage and are great fun for players to fight against.

Drone Combat Rules

Henchmen work just like Companions (pg: 105). They have no Attributes, have no Endurance, take a single Move and Attack each Turn, and are Killed when they take 1 Attribute Damage.

Reminder

All Henchmen Bodies in a group Attack as one Attack Roll.

Each Turn, each of your Henchmen groups may make 1 Move and Attack/Escape/Reload (may always add any RoF bonus).

Unlike player Drones and Companions, Henchmen do not necessarily have a Controller.

Combat Order, pg: 100

All Henchmen have Combat Order of "O".

Building a Henchmen

Henchmen have starting Stats (see next page) that may increase through Traits, Variations and as the players' Average Resources increases.
Henchmen Resources are only spent on Weapons.

Buffs and Debuffs

These affect all Henchmen Bodies in a group.

Defence vs Stealth

All Henchmen have −4 to their Defence vs Stealth (pg: 84).
They still add +1 Defence vs Stealth to all Allies for each Body.

Defence vs Impair

All Henchmen add their Slots value to their Defence vs Impair (pg: 84).

+1 End Dmg and RoF per Body

Henchmen gain +1 End Dmg and RoF for each Attacking Body in their group.

Drones and Companions

Henchmen cannot acquire Drones or Companions.

Jam, pg: 125

All Henchmen are immune to the Jammed Effect.

+2 To Hit

All Henchmen gain +2 to any Combat Skill they use (including Stealth).

Weapon Modifications

May have any appropriate Weapon Modifications.
No Spare Time Roll is needed.

Draz Addicts Attack, Henchmen Example

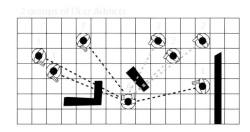

2 groups of Draz Addicts

Jasmine (A) is being Attacked by two groups of Draz Addicts (1 and 2). Each group may make a single move and make a single Attack Roll (+1 Endurance Damage and RoF per additional Attacking Body over 1).

Two members of Group 1 are Attacking Jasmine through Heavy Cover, and the remaining two members are Attacking Jasmine through no Cover. The Cover Bonus that Jasmine gains is averaged in her favour, so Jasmine gains Light Cover. Members of Group 1 also average their Range Penalty, rounded in favour of the player character.

All three members of Group 2 are Attacking Jasmine through Heavy Cover, so Jasmine gains the Heavy Cover bonus versus their Attack. These members also average their Range penalties.

Not every Body in a Henchmen Group needs to Attack.

Henchmen & Weapon	Hit	End Dmg	Crit Dmg	Range	Clips	Ammo	Load	RoF	Weight	Type, Traits & Notes	Resources
	+2	+Bodies						+Bodies			
Combat Order = 0	Lock On	Movement		Armour	Defence	vs Stealth	vs Impair		Slots		Bodies
Average Player Res						−4 +	+Slots				

Used Ammunition ○○○○○○○○○   ○○○○○○○○○   ○○○○○○○○○ Used Clips ○○○○○○○○○

Destroyed Bodies ○○○○○○○○○

Creating a Henchmen Group

Function very similar to Weapon Type: Companion, pg: 105.
Equal to 1 player character.

 16 Defence

 3 Armour

 4 Movement

 3 Slots

 4 Bodies

 1 Trait

 ✗ No Outfit

 ✗ No Utility Items

 1 Resource

Henchmen Ability Table

Avg Resources	Changes	Avg Resources	Changes
1-5	4 Bodies, 1 Resource, 1 Trait, -1 Armour OR -1 Resource	16-20	7 Bodies, 3 Resources, 2 Traits
6-10	5 Bodies, 2 Resources, 1 Trait	21-25	8 Bodies, 3 Resources, 3 Traits, 4 Armour
11-15	6 Bodies, 2 Resources, 2 Traits	26-30	10 Bodies, 4 Resources, 3 Traits, 4 Armour

Henchmen Traits

Traits	Requirements	Benefits	Disadvantages
Brute	Henchmen NPC	+1 Armour. +2 Slots.	-1 Movement. -1 Bodies.
Critter	Henchmen NPC	Any of your Weapons may gain the Keywords: Bio Tech and Natural. You are able to function in a specific hostile environment or fly. Gain 1 extra Trait. +2 Movement.	-1 Armour. -2 Defence.
Droid Body	Henchmen NPC	You are a Robot. Gain 1 extra Trait. Lock On +2, all Weapons.	-2 Hit, all Weapons.
Endless	Henchmen NPC	Gain 1 additional body at the start of each of your Turns, unless all other friendly Skilled and Nemesis NPCs are dead or incapacitated.	-3 Bodies.
Soldier	Henchmen NPC	+2 Hit, all Weapons. +2 Defence.	
Swarm	Henchmen NPC	+4 Bodies.	-1 Armour.
Tackle	Henchmen NPC	Strong Hit: **Tackle** (Melee, Hit) Pick One Debuff to apply to Target: Prone, Push 1 or reduce all Movement by 2 until your next Turn.	
Well Armed	Henchmen NPC	+2 Resources. +1 Slot.	-1 Bodies. -2 Defence.

All four of Rachel's ears twitched with nervous energy as she and Maximus searched the Nephilim gene lab. They'd been hired to steal data, but the bloody dissection tables and the occasional vat filled with murky liquid hadn't been part of the job description.

Out of morbid curiosity, Rachel turned her gun-mounted flashlight onto the nearest vat. It was massive, at least two meters tall and filled with an opaque green fluid. She approached and peered into the murky depths. "What could possibly be growing inside these?" she whispered.

SMACK!

Rachel stumbled back as she received a partial answer. A black claw, bigger than her head, had reached out of the liquid and slammed into the glass wall of the vat. Just as abruptly, it disappeared back into the depths of the tank.

"Don't worry, Rach," Maximus grunted, barely glancing at the source of the disturbance. "Nothing can bust out of those vats. They're made of two-inch-thick Synth Steel. It would take…"

Max and Rachel's hearts simultaneously skipped a beat as they heard the crunch of something breaking underneath Max's huge combat boots. Rachel swung her torch to the ground and saw scattered fragments of metal and glass.

"What's that stuff?" she asked, glancing at her partner. Maximus hesitated before answering.

"Two-inch-thick transparent Synth Steel."

"Ah."

Skilled

See pg: 30 for full Character Creation rules.

These are highly skilled Opponents that are close to the capabilities of the player characters. Most combats will include a Skilled opponent, often supported by Henchmen.

Inexperienced GMs, be careful with how many Skilled opponents you have in a Combat as it can take some amount of work to keep track of everything: Actions, Endurance, Attribute Damage, Ammunitions, Clips and so on.

Skilled Opponent Combat Rules

They fight exactly like player characters, except as noted below.

NPC Actions, pg: 293

Skilled opponents have the option to use simplified NPC Actions.

+2 To Hit

All Skilled opponents gain +2 to any Combat Skill they use.

Death

ALL NPCs die when ANY Attribute is reduced to 0 (player characters die when any Attribute is reduced to -5).

Weapon Modifications

May have any appropriate Weapon Modifications.
No Spare Time Roll is needed.

Building a Skilled Opponent

See pg: 294 for full Balancing Combat rules.
See pg: 358 for a full list of available Weapons.

Skilled opponents are created just like player characters except for the points on the next page. As player characters gain Current Resources, NPCs gain additional abilities.

Skilled opponents have no Levels. They gain Traits as the players' Average Resources increases. Skilled opponent Resources are only spent on Weapons, not on Outfits or Utility Items.

The pain meds made the survivor talkative, which suited the big Legion Decanis just fine as his men secured the immediate area.

"They just kept coming out – the big'un just pumped more and more of the small bastards out – but we couldn't get close enough to kill it." The wounded Corporate breathed out a sigh as the rejuvenator was inserted into the flesh of his bloodily severed intestinal tract.

"The little ones were so agile. We'd put one down after a lot of fire to hit the damned thing, and two more'd be firing from the sides in the meantime." Here he paused, coughing up a small amount of blood and bile onto his already-ruined suit.

"Thank you for the information," said the red-armoured Decanis as he motioned his squad to move out, leaving the survivor behind.

Creating a Skilled Opponent

Created like a player character, pg: 30.
Equal to 1 player character.

14 Attribute Points   0 Fate   3 Armour   Race 1 Trait

No Outfit   No Utility Items   2 Resources

Skilled Ability Table

Avg Resources	Changes	Avg Resources	Changes
1-5	14 Attribute Points, 2 Resources, Race, 1 Trait, -1 Armour	16-20	16 Attribute Points, 3 Resources, Race, 2 Traits, 2 Variations
6-10	14 Attribute Points, 2 Resources, Race, 1 Trait, 1 Variation	21-25	18 Attribute Points, 4 Res, Race, 2 Traits, 2 Variations, 4 Armour
11-15	16 Attribute Points, 3 Resources, Race, 2 Traits, 1 Variation	26-30	18 Attribute Points, 5 Res, Race, 2 Traits, 2 Variations, 5 Armour

Skilled Variations

Variations	Requirements	Benefits	Disadvantages
Attrition	Skilled NPC	You may be holding a hostage or near a sensitive location! When any character make a successful Attack Roll against you in Combat they take 5 Endurance Damage.	If you loose the reason for your Attrition Trait (eg: your hostage is freed) you loose all Benefits of this Trait.
Bonded	Skilled NPC Max Ref 3	You are connected to a Nemesis NPC (eg: you may be a limb)! A Nemesis gains +1 Armour while you have Endurance.	You must stay close to your Nemesis! -2 Recovery.
Explosive	Skilled NPC	On your Death, deal 4 Endurance and Critical Damage to all characters within 4 of you (as if it were an Attack the Ground Splash Attack).	
Fierce	Skilled NPC	+4 Hit, all Weapons. +2 Defence.	
Lone Hunter	Skilled NPC	+2 Stealth. All Weapons gain +1 Endurance and Critical Damage if you have no Allies within 10 of you.	
Overseer	Skilled NPC	All Allies have their Combat Order changed to equal your Combat Order. Strong Hit: **Plan** (Analytical, Hit) All Allies gain +1 Hit for the remainder of the Combat.	
Pack Hunter	Skilled NPC	All Weapons gain +2 Endurance Damage (up to +8) for each Ally within 2 of you. +2 Recovery.	
Talent	Skilled NPC	+4 Attribute Points.	
Well Armoured	Skilled NPC	+1 Armour.	-2 Defence.
Well Prepared	Skilled NPC	Pick one: +2 Resources or one of your Drones or Companions cost 4 less Resources. Pick one: Gain a free Utility Item or all Weapons gain +1 Hit.	

The hulking metallic Mechonid wasn't made in clean and straight lines like most drones. The flowing, almost organic nature of its Archon-designed body was graceful. A slight distortion in the air marked where some sort of shield was deflecting incoming fire as the machine skittered almost effortlessly over the rubble, firing relentless salvos of murderous fire at the red Legion figures, shattering skulls and limbs at will.

Purple lights flickered within as it maintained its dance of death, ignoring the continuing fusillade of rail fire from the Second and Fifth Centuriae. Decanis Tiro closed his eyes behind his mask. Blisters were already forming under the scales around his still-bleeding wounds from the excessive radiation the monster kept pumping out into the snowy, icy waste.

Opening his eyes, he watched it advance up the ridge, shallowly recessed weapons at the ready. It was now leaving smoking holes as it fired its irradiated weaponry up the icebound ridge at the cover-hugging soldiers of the Auxilia. Sensor orbs flicked from side to side as it dove and burrowed into a mound of ice and rubble, the chrome-like silvered exterior blending seamlessly with the ice glare.

"Is it dead?" "Where'd it go?" "Watch the flanks!"

Tiro coughed from his twisted position, staring at the mound as the varied Legionnaires advanced, weapons still smoking from ineffective fire. Nothing moved except the wind and the red armoured figures, still hugging cover.

Tiro wept in frustration, his ruined torso shuddering as death came home.

The last things he saw were his suits radiation meter spike past red as a sharp silver limb larger than he was gracefully bent to lift above his prone form.

He did not witness its descent through his shattered chest.

Nemesis

See pg: 30 for full Character Creation rules.

These are extremely powerful and dangerous opponents, far more powerful than a single player character. Include a Nemesis only in the rare combat, and only support them with a few Henchmen or Skilled opponents.

Reducing Fate to Avoid Death

A Nemesis can permanently reduce their Fate to avoid Death (pg: 90) if they are extremely important to the storyline. Do not abuse this ability as you may frustrate your players.

Combat Rules

A Nemesis functions exactly like Skilled opponents, except that they have their own Ability Table and Variations.

Building a Nemesis Opponent

See pg: 294 for full Balancing Combat rules.
See pg: 358 for a full list of available Weapons.

Do not hold back, build the most powerful opponent you can.

Nemesis Tactics

Despite being so powerful, a Nemesis still only has 2 Actions per Turn, making them vulnerable to Suppression and being forced to spend Actions to avoid or Heal Damage.

A Nemesis will rarely be the only opponent in a fight, though. Be sure to use Henchmen and Skilled Allies as support.

Folding the weapon down, Brent stowed it on his hip while powering his shield nodes down.

Retractable energy shields were useful and worth every credit, he noted, while the others wiped off blood and smoke stains, trying to look presentable. Their employer was coming, and she occasionally gave out bonuses for work above the expected quality. Not only did Brent have the highest kill count, but he would also look the best.

Creating a Nemesis Opponent

Created like a player character, pg: 30.
Equal to 3 player characters.

20 Attribute Points	1 Fate	4 Armour	Race 1 Trait
No Outfit	No Utility Items	3 Resources	

Nemesis Ability Table

Avg Resources	Changes	Avg Resources	Changes
1-5	20 Attribute Points, 3 Res, 1 Fate, Race, 1 Trait, 1 Variation, -1 Armour	16-20	22 Att Points, 5 Res, 2 Fate, Race, 3 Traits, 2 Variations
6-10	20 Attribute Points, 4 Res, 2 Fate, Race, 2 Traits, 1 Variation	21-25	24 Att Points, 6 Res, 3 Fate, Race, 3 Traits, 2 Variations, 5 Armour
11-15	22 Attribute Points, 5 Res, 2 Fate, Race, 3 Traits, 1 Variation	26-30	24 Att Points, 6 Res, 3 Fate, Race, 3 Traits, 3 Variations, 5 Armour

Nemesis Variations

Variations	Requirements	Benefits	Disadvantages
Master Assassin	Nemesis NPC	You always have Light Cover (+2) (and may Stealth and gain bonus Cover Steps). +2 Stealth Strong Hit: **Assassinate** (Damage, Hit, Target is at least 3 spaces away from all non Drone Allies) Target is Suppressed and takes 2 Attribute Damage (no Armour) to a random Attribute (1d6).	-1 Armour -2 Recovery
Minion Master	Nemesis NPC	You gain +2 Hit and End Dmg for each Allied Henchmen Group that has at least 2 Bodies. Strong Hit: **Summon** (Attack, Hit) All Allied Henchmen with at least 1 Body gain 1 additional Body (they may never have more than 6 above their starting Bodies).	-1 Armour if you have no Henchmen Allies.
Monstrous	Nemesis NPC	+4 Attribute Points and Attribute Maximum is 7 (normally 5). +6 Defence vs Impair Ignore 1st Suppressed Effect each against you Turn.	-2 Defence -2 Stealth Character takes up 4 spaces (normally 1).
Overlord	Nemesis NPC	All Allies have their Combat Order changed to equal your Combat Order. Strong Hit: **Master Plan** (Analytical, Hit) All Allies gain +2 Hit and Endurance Damage for the remainder of the Combat (Stacks).	
Swift	Nemesis NPC	You may take 3 Actions per Turn (normally 2 per Turn).	Reduce all Movement by 2 from your Actions. -2 Hit and End Dmg, all Weapons
Warlord	Nemesis NPC	Pick one: +3 Resources OR one of your Drones or Companions cost 6 less Resources. Pick one: Gain a free utility Item OR all Weapons gain -1 Load.	
Near Immortal	Nemesis NPC	You Die when any Attribute is reduced to -2 (normally -0). +6 Recovery	You gain the Bleeding Effect when any Attribute is reduced below 0.

Spacecraft

See pg: 142 for full Spacecraft Creation rules.

Most spacecraft combat only involves two craft, though some may involve two smaller spacecraft against a larger one.

Spacecraft Opponent Combat Rules

NPC spacecraft use the same combat rules as player characters, except as noted below.

Equal Number of System Rolls

The total number of NPC System Rolls (across ALL NPC spacecraft) per Turn equals the number of PCs. If there are multiple NPC spacecraft, the GM chooses how to spread the System Rolls across the craft, reflecting how many skilled crewmembers are on board each.

There are four PCs facing three NPC spacecraft. The GM gives 1 System Roll to two of the NPC spacecraft, and gives 2 System Rolls to the third. These assignments remain fixed for the entire combat.

NPC System Rolls, pg: 293

Spacecraft opponents may use the simplified NPC System Rolls.

System Roll +2

NPCs gain +2 to all System Rolls they make.

Destruction

NPC spacecraft are Destroyed when ANY Attribute is reduced to 0.

Spare Time Roll Cost

GMs can give any spacecraft opponent any appropriate Weapons, Modifications, and Variations that require Spare Time Rolls.

Escaping Combat

See pg: 156 for full Combat Scale rules.
See pg: 175 for full Combat Jump System Roll rules.

Many spacecraft Combats will end with one spacecraft leaving the Combat Area, either through a jump portal (Combat Jump System Roll, pg: 175) or by changing their Combat Scale, pg: 156 (through remaining at a Current Velocity of 1 or 6).

Spacecraft are large and expensive, and their crew will rarely sacrifice themselves pointlessly.

Having a spacecraft try to escape (whether the PCs or NPCs) can be a great way to build up tension in combat.

Building a Spacecraft Opponent

See pg: 294 for full Balancing Combat rules.
See pg: 377 for a full list of available spacecraft Weapons.

NPC spacecraft are created just like PC spacecraft, except as noted below.

Equal Influence Cost

In a given combat, total Influence Cost of all spacecraft opponents should be close to or the same as the total Current Influence of all involved PCs.

20 Attribute Points

NPC spacecraft have 20 Attribute Points to spend.

Non-Spacecraft Traits

An NPC spacecraft can acquire character Traits for 5 Influence each. These Traits apply to ALL System Rolls made on that spacecraft.

My Baby Trait, pg: 342

If an NPC spacecraft has only 1 System Roll and is Size 2 or under. It should take the "My Baby" Influence Trait.

This will reduce is Influence cost by 5.

Gliding gracefully through the void between the planets, Qshapk's ship sang quietly to itself as its captain, Qshapk, raged at everything... again.

"Why is it taking so long?" he screamed at the walls, swinging his huge weapon in wild slashes through the humid, warm air of the hold. The ship's scuttling cleaning and repair nestlings bore the ichor-filled brunt of his fury.

"Captain most mighty and intelligent, the journey forsaking your territory on Eden to the Monopoly Belt, so we can... 'Pirate' as you wanted is several Eden-days longer."

Thankfully, Qshapk didn't understand sarcasm.

Creating Spacecraft Opponents

Created like a PC spacecraft, pg: 142.
Influence Cost of the NPC craft equals that of the PCs' craft.

Equal Influence Cost

1 System Roll per
Player Character

20 Attribute
Points

Build

Optional: Large-Scale Combat

See pg: 71 for full Personal Combat rules.
See pg: 155 for full Spacecraft Combat rules.

The Fragged Empire combat system is designed for PCs (with little to no NPC assistance) combating an NPC force of comparable size over a relatively small area.

If you wish to run a combat with many NPCs or spanning a large area, there are three easy ways to tweak the system for this.

Option 1: Increase the Space of Each Square

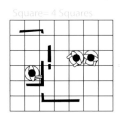 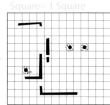

Square= 4 Squares   Square= 1 Square

This is a simple solution: make each square on your Battle Map cover a greater area. By making a square twice as long in each direction, the characters can shoot farther and get places faster.

> This solution is ideal for combat over a large area that does not involve more characters than a standard combat.

No Larger than 4x4
It is not recommended to make each Square equal more than a 4x4 area.

Favour the Acting Character
When measuring distance for Attack, Splash, and Movement, round in favour of the character taking the Action.

Entering the Same Space
A character cannot end their Movement in the same space as another character.

Cover
When using this option, be more flexible when determining whether a character is in Cover. Increasing the size of a space makes determining Cover more imprecise.

Melee
All characters in an adjacent space may be Attacked with a Range '-' Melee Weapon.

> "Death and pain, be the taxes of the harshest of lords... progress."
>
> -Yalambrack, 134-year-old Nephilim Pureblood.

Option 2: Theatre of the Mind, pg: 96 & 166
If a combat would be unusually complicated and large, use the Theatre of the Mind rules.

Option 3: Multi Conflict Combat
This solution is a blend between the standard combat rules and the Theatre of the Mind rules.

> This solution is ideal for combat in a large area with many characters, such as a field of war.

Have the players describe their approaches to the conflict, possibly using the Theatre of the Mind combat rules. Then, for a clamactic combat, use the standard combat rules.

> ### Endless Variation, pg: 297
> Henchmen have a great Variation called "Endless", which can be an ideal way to represent more combatants moving into the Combat Area.

Additional NPC Allies
If the PCs gain an Ally, the number of NPC opponents should increase. For example, if a PC gains a Henchmen group as an ally, their opponents should gain a Henchmen group or Skilled ally.

> "Really? That's the choice? My shipmates' lives or my custom ride? Dude, kill 'em."
>
> - Renegade Jacob Chillax, being honest in a ship theft turned hostage situation.

Rewarding Players

See pg: 54 for full Acquisition rules.

Rate of Acquisition
Reward PCs with Resources, Influence, and Spare Time Points at the rate that matches the style of game you want to run.

Working for NPCs
This is a great way to help your players interact with the game world. There is always work to be done: bounty hunting, smuggling, rescue missions, and exploration. Some paying, some not.

Working for Pay
Often the cleanest, simplest way to get things done. Someone with money or material wealth wants something done, so they ask someone else to do it for them in exchange for money or other material reward.

Jobs done for payment reward the PCs with Resources (pg: 56) and, rarely, Influence (pg: 58).

Working for Free
Not everything is money and material gain. Often, building friendships and relationships is more valuable, especially if they gain you favour with powerful or large groups.

Friends and connections are especially important when it comes to building and maintaining a spacecraft. These ancient machines are invaluable to building this new society, and spacecraft components are rarely available on the free market. Instead, they are given to friends and allies as rewards, in an effort to make sure that this emerging society is shaped by the right people.

Jobs done without direct payment or for spacecraft components reward the PCs with Influence (pg: 58).

Personal Missions
Encourage players to plan their own personal Missions. Their actions do not need to be continuously dictated by NPCs.

Trade Goods, pg: 66
These are a great way to build Resources (pg: 56). Encourage the players to deal with the right NPCs to gain bonuses to their Spare Time Rolls.

Research, pg: 68
This is a great way to build Influence (pg: 58), gain access to powerful Traits (pg: 33), Prototype Weapon Variations, Minor Perks, and knowledge.

Exploration
One of the most exciting things the players can do is to head off into the unknown, with no NPC to guide them… or rescue them.

Exploration often grants Trade Good Boxes (pg: 66) and Research Units (pg: 68).

Looting, Stealing, and Finding Things
See pg: 54 for full Loot rules.

Dealing with this can be tricky. Feel free to let players take items they find, but remind them that they can't keep looted items that cost Resources or Influence for more than one session. Instead, they can turn looted items into Trade Goods, roughly 1 Trade Box per 4 Weight of items.

Ammunition, pg: 122
Looted Ammunition can be used to refill spent Clips and Ammunition without requiring Downtime (pg: 95).

Finding Equipment with Modifications
A great way to reward players and get them excited over looted items is to give them Weapons or Outfits with difficult-to-acquire Modifications.

They can swap out their current item (freeing up Resources) and keep the looted item.

Exchanging Looted Weapons for Trade Boxes Example
Alvin and his mercenary party have just won a massive fight against a well-armed Draz Cartel. Nobody in his party wants to use the looted Weapons, preferring to sell them.

The GM says that if they can collect and box up the Weapons, they will get 8 Trade Boxes.

Research, pg: 68
Loot rarely grants Research Units. However, found objects and information found commonly grant a Description Bonus of +1 or +2 to a single Research Spare Time Roll (pg: 64).

Free Time
If your PCs have a sizable amount of spare time in a hospitable location (eg: a week or so in a city or on their spacecraft), consider giving them additional Spare Time Points (pg: 64).

Tweaking the Game

See pg: 29 for four Example Game Types.

There are many forms of advancement in Fragged Empire that you can tweak, including Levels, Resources, Influence, Spare Time Points, Trade Boxes, and Research Units.

Game Style

By changing the rate of advancement in various elements of play, you will alter the feel of the game.

> **Give out as MANY or as FEW of each kind of advancement that you want.**

Levels

A PC's level represents their general level of skill. By default, all PCs start at Level 1 and gain 1 Level after every third game session.

Starting the PCs at a higher Level means the players will have to spend more time creating their characters, but this can be a good choice for games where the PCs start off as important and/or skilled individuals.

Altering the rate of Level advancement can greatly alter the tone of play. Reducing the rate can be ideal for gaming groups that meet very regularly or have short game sessions, while increasing it can work for those who meet sporadically or for long periods of time.

Resources

Resources reflect the amount and quality of equipment that your PCs have access to. It is also the primary gauge of their combat ability. By default, a character's Maximum Resources equals their Level +2.

Resources are primarily gained through the PCs' actions and and choices during sessions.

PCs with few Resources will have limited access to Weapons and other Combat Equipment, which can create a "low tech" or "just getting by" feel. If you want to tamp down the Resources that your players have access to, you may want to reduce their Maximum Resources (eg: by reducing it to Level devided by 2). This prevents characters that focus on Trade Goods from gaining too many Current Resources.

Influence

Influence is like Resources, but it reflects a PCs' ability to maintain a spacecraft, along with their connections to NPC organisations.

Spare Time Points

Spare Time Points are primarily spent on Healing, Repairing, Miscellaneous Items/Services, Equipment Modifications, Trade Goods, and Research. By default, PCs gain 1 Spare Time Point at the start of each session and may gain more through their actions.

By giving the PCs more Spare Time Points, they'll be able to take up more side projects and hobbies. It will also make Healing and Repairing a lot easier, making it very unlikely for the PCs to go into a fight wounded.

Giving them fewer Spare Time Points will have the reverse effect. This is great for games focused on survival.

Trade Boxes

Trade Boxes are a great way for the PCs to turn Spare Time Points and loot into Resources.

By reducing the Resources you hand out while increasing the amount of Trade Boxes, you can create a game focused on salvaging and bargaining.

High/Low Research Units

With Research, the PCs get great opportunities to gain Influence, Minor Perks, and Secret Knowledge Equipment andTraits.

By giving out more Research Units, the PCs will get many more Minor Perks and stronger Traits. This is a great way to make them feel even more skilled and connected to NPC groups.

Example Game Types

Just Getting By
» High Level.
» Low Resources and Influence.

Space Politics
» High Influence and Spare Time Points.
» Low Resources.

Space Marine
» High Level, Resources, Influence, and Spare Time Points.
» Low Trade Boxes and Research Units.

Horror/Survival
» High Level.
» Low Spare Time Points.

Perks

See pg: 60 for full Character Perk rules.
See pg: 152 for full Spacecraft Perk rules.

Feel free to give characters and spacecraft any additional Perks that you wish, especially when it fits the story.

Complications and Conditions

See pg: 73 for full Complication rules.
See pg: 73 for full Character Condition rules.
See pg: 160 for full Spacecraft Condition rules.

As with Perks, feel free to give characters and spacecraft any appropriate Complications or Conditions.

Unlike Complications that are gained through increasing a PC's Current Influence. If these Complications or Conditions are removed, characters do not need to replace them with new ones.

> Only give additional Complications (those not gained through Influence) to a character if it would not be applied to other characters.
>
> If it would affect multiple characters then it is simply a part of the story being told.

Bounty, Group Complication Example

The party attacked a powerful corporation, causing a bounty to be placed on their heads. However, the GM does not give any of the PCs a Hunted: Bounty Complication because the bounty is just part of the story.

However, if one PC had gained the bounty, that PC would have gained the Complication Hunted: Bounty.

Reducing Fate to Avoid Death or Destruction

See pg: 90 for full Reduce Fate to Avoid Death rules.
See pg: 164 for full Reduce Fate to Avoid Destruction rules.

If a character reduces their Fate to avoid their Death or their spacecraft's Destruction, this can be a great thematic opportunity to give them a Condition (eg: Lost Limb).

"No refunds, and nothing in life is free."
— Common Corporate outlook.

"Family comes first, unless we're talking cannibalism."
— An old Kaltoran joke.

"Superiority is key, genetic superiority most of all."
— Nephilim philosophy.

"War is Life, all else is sacrifice."
— Common Legion sentiment.

Optional: Intense Damage

Optionally, any Attack that deals at least 3 Attribute Damage (after Armour) or reduces an Attribute to -3 also gives the Target a Condition.

Strength: Lost Limb (arm/hand)
Reflexes: Impairment (no Surprise Round)
Movement: Lost Limb (leg)
Focus: Fear
Intelligence: Psychological (PTSD)
Perception: Blind or Deaf

Hull: Low Munitions
Engines: Low Fuel
Crew: Decompressed Room
Power: Damaged Reactor
CPU: Disrepair
Sensors: Damaged Communications

Game Ideas

See pg: 7 for a list of Setting Themes.

The following four game ideas are examples focused on the key themes of Fragged Empire: cultural tension, genetic engineering, and exploration. They are intended to inspire you to create your own adventure ideas.

> Be sure to read the Setting Guide (pg: 182) and opponents (pg: 315) sections for more ideas.

Hijacking the Orpheus Run

EXCERPTED FROM HERMES-EPSILON COMM LOG

UNKNOWN - This is the freighter Potemkin, requesting immediate assistance, navigational controls jammed, helm unresponsive.

LT. DARIUS JAMES - Freighter Potemkin, this is convoy leader Hermes-Epsilon, divert immediately or we will fire upon you. Repeat, divert immediately, or…

UNKNOWN - Negative, Hermes! Navigational controls overloaded, the whole board's melted! Hold your fire! We are out of control!

::Sounds of laser fire and impact::
END OF TRANSMISSION

Adventure Background

Every year, for five years, the Hermes convoy makes the grueling Orpheus Run – a long loop from Alabaster to Gehenna – delivering thousands of metric tons of Draz for the Red Roi Syndicate, who spread the potent narcotic like a cancer through the underground communities of Kaltorans. Every year, some fool of a pirate prince gathers his rag-tag armada of ships and attempts to seize the convoy. Every year these hijackers are blasted to so much space dust by the Talons, the company of Draz-enslaved Legion mercenaries hopelessly addicted to the Red Roi's premium product.

Adventure Hooks

A Kaltoran tribal leader named Ezra Zapped engages the party to help hijack the Orpheus Run – the proverbial heist of a lifetime.

Kaltoran PC Hook

A Kaltoran PC has family on Gehenna, and the epidemic of Draz use has turned their mining city upside down. To strike a blow against the Red Roi is to save future generations of Kaltorans from addicted enslavement.

Legion PC Hook

An old comrade of a Legion PC's son has been pressed into service by the Talons and is now enlisted onboard the Hermes Epsilon. The boy must be saved before he spirals too far down the Draz rabbit hole.

Corporate PC Hook

Disrupting the Red Roi's control of the Draz trade on Gehenna paves the way for a Corp PC's organisation rise to power in the region.

Nephilim PC Hook

A powerful force of Nephilim on Mishpacha are ready to take over a Corp colony on that world, and they would pay well for a few hundred doses of Draz to ensure victory in the coming battle.

Action

Ezra's heavy freighter, the Potemkin, is purpose-rigged as an armoured battering ram. First, a dazzling space battle heralds the Potemkin's ramming of the convoy's lead ship, the Hermes Epsilon. Afterwards, the PCs lead a grueling boarding action to secure the vessel and its narcotic cargo.

Threats/Encounters

Kamikaze Escorts

Two wings of gladius-class support fighters, flown by Draz-wired Talon pilots, protect the convoy. They engage the Potemkin on its approach. These Draz-addled pilots are indoctrinated to crash into any serious threat to the Hermes Epsilon – any gunners among the PCs will have to blast them before they slam into the Potemkin.

Draz-Crazed Mercenaries

Once on board the Hermes Epsilon, the PCs face a full company of Talons, whose combat ration of Draz makes them nigh invulnerable to conventional wounds. Protracted and bloody fighting, mixed with the occasional charging Legion suicide bomber, ensures the PCs and Ezra's crew must bleed for every square inch of bulkhead they claim.

Secutor Dranos

Dranos, the Talons' champion, dwarfs most other Legion by at least two feet, and the maiming wounds he suffered during a campaign on Mishpacha never healed, leaving his torso a gaping, pus-drowned crater. He is a walking corpse, wildly animated by astonishing overdoses of Draz, and once set upon prey, Dranos doesn't relent until all foes are reduced to a pulpy mess.

The Jackal

The Jackal and his band of filthy space pirates are infamous throughout the Haven system as opportunistic scavengers. A Nephilim Pureblood and former intelligence operative during the Great War, the Jackal is old, cunning, and lazy, employing his considerable talents for espionage to latch onto other criminals' heists. The Jackal waits for his quarry to complete the lion's share of the illicit labour – neutralising foes, circumventing security, and such – and then swoops in with his misfit crew of pirates to claim the spoils.

Ezra's Unscrupulous Ambitions

After the smoke clears, Ezra reveals his true intentions: to replace the Red Roi Syndicate as the main supplier of Draz for his people on Gehenna. He welcomes the PCs into his new crime ring, but if they blanch at his motives, he moves to slay them with a sad sigh.

Rebellion on Exo-Station 13

We, formerly the contracted labour force of Exo-Station Hammer 13, citing gross breach of contract and violent oppression by the DMC (Dray Mining Consortium), hereby declare our sovereignty, and henceforth we shall be known as the Free Station of Conroy.

We demand the immediate removal of all occupying forces and payment of damages for instances of detainment, assault, and murder, to be paid in full to our citizens (or their next of kin), as well as the return of all wages unlawfully withheld. Leave now and pay what's owed, or we will cut your throats while you sleep.

– Communiqué from the Free Station of Conroy Liberation Front.

Adventure Background

The Dray Mining Consortium garners an ugly system-wide reputation for their brutal intimidation of labour and their unscrupulous contracts. The backbreaking interest they charge on "colonisation fees" and their exclusive equipment clauses – forcing workers to purchase shabby gear from the Consortium at a high cost – reduce whole populations of colonies to slaves.

A few months ago, one small station in the Monopoly Belt – an innocuous blip amongst a sea of asteroids called Exo-Station Hammer 13 – exploded in rebellion. One daring leader, a mysterious Corporate named Conroy, planned and executed the takeover of the entire Industrial Bloc of the station. When the DMC's Legion thugs restored order, Conroy and his co-conspirators were mowed down. Shortly thereafter, a new resistance movement called the Liberation Front emerged, supposedly backed by a mysterious and far-reaching underground operating under the cryptic moniker of "UNITY".

Adventure Hook

The Liberation Front gains ground daily, and the DMC grows desperate. Rumours of their successes have spread to other mining stations, and rumbles of similar rebellions shake the DMC's steely grip over its entire empire. In response, the DMC hires the PCs to eradicate the rebel group by any means necessary.

Liberation Front Hook

An engineer on the station is an old friend of the PCs and requests their help in liberating it from the DMC's oppressive rule.

Kaltoran PC Hook

The DMC kidnapped a noted patriarch of the Juryrig family, known for their skills in developing new mining technology. A Kaltoran PC is dispatched to retrieve the patriarch before he is harmed.

Legion PC Hook

Sympathisers among the Legion on Hammer 13 aid the Liberation Front, much to the distress of their former commanders. A Legion PC's secret mission is to slay these dishonourable traitors before their actions threaten the Legion's reputation as infallible mercenaries in the Haven system.

Corporate PC Hook

A rival Corp group is preparing to buy out DMC, and sends one of their agents to ensure the campaign against the rebels thoroughly embarrasses and disrupts the consortium, plunging their value to a bargain low.

Nephilim PC Hook

Intelligence suggests the mysterious Conroy is an escaped Nephilim prototype of the Emissary sub-breed. His genetic material may be wholly unique and nearly priceless if recovered.

Action

The PCs arrive on the sprawling mining station to find entire sectors reduced to demilitarised zones. The PCs contend with the various threats and hazards that emerge on the front line of any military conflict.

Threats/Encounters

Profiteering Arms Smuggler

Karantha, a Nephilim arms dealer, supplies the rebels with weapons, but also sells intelligence about their leaders and plans to the DMC – either side might target her for elimination.

Legion Off the Leash

A platoon of Auxilia Legion led by the hulking Praxus have gone rogue. Praxus installs himself as defacto warlord of Hammer 13's Recreational Hub, enslaving the residents and repelling attempts from both DMC and the rebels to liberate the Hub.

Miners Turned Terrorists

A splinter faction of the Liberation Front, called the Hammerheads, engage in wholesale terrorism, bombing medical wards, kidnapping children of DMC officials, and torturing suspected "collaborators" to death on live holo-feed. Their latest "plan" involves overheating the station's core, with cries of "Death is better than capitulation!" Thousands of lives (on both sides) are at stake unless the PCs can crush the Hammerheads.

Flesh Gone Mad

A bio-engineer among the rebels has crafted a specialised bio-agent to turn organic Flesh drone servants back on their Corp masters, but it went too far, turning all the Flesh aboard Hammer 13 into frenzied killing machines.

The Enemy

Depending on which side the party chooses to back in this bloody conflict, they either face crack squads of well-organised Legion and brilliant Corp handlers, or a highly committed group of fanatical terrorists who are willing to die for their freedom.

Archon Ghost Ship, Carthage

At 03:13 hours standard Haven time, on Octo 14th 1005 AX, the Archon medical frigate Carthage issued a general distress call. At 5:05 hours on Octo 16th, Legion VESPER force Epsilon boarded the vessel. A few minutes later, the ship went silent, charted a course for deep space, and was never heard from again.

– Vital Emergency Stellar Protocol Expedited Recovery (VESPER) Force After – Action Report on the Carthage Incident.

Adventure Background

As the crucible of the Great War consumed the Archon Empire with impunity, its searing heat gradually melted the Archons' ironclad ethics to slag. The Carthage began as a medical ship on a mission of mercy, but as the Archons' cause grew every more desperate, she received a dread new purpose: harvest Kaltoran refugees and Nephilim prisoners of war to develop new bio-weaponry for immediate deployment on the front.

The ensuing experiments yielded a deadly nano-virus, Kormoria, which sowed death and madness among crew and captive alike. Shortly after VESPER force Gamma breached the Carthage, the vessel's Archon master, Solaria, either in the grips of madness, or in a vain gambit to save the rest of Haven from Kormoria, charted a course into a vast uncharted region of space…

Inciting Incident

Now, 108 years after its lonely sojourn, a homing beacon on the Carthage pilots her back to the Haven system. The derelict ship floats between trade routes, emitting a weak distress beacon, and remains unresponsive to all hails.

Adventure Hooks

A mysterious benefactor craving the truth of the Carthage's disappearance, and potential valuable artefacts onboard, engages the PCs as expert salvagers – providing a transport vessel if the party lacks their own ship.

Kaltoran PC Hook

The Jaded family line, a clan with a storied history, was extinguished in the War, their genetic memories lost. Evidence suggests several Jaded numbered among the Kaltoran refugees sheltered onboard the Carthage. Recovering their genetic memories would strengthen and galvanise the tribe.

Legion PC Hook

A Legion PC's ancestor led the VESPER force charged with recovering the Carthage. Slanderous accusations of incompetence, betrayal, and cowardice have besmirched the PC's family since the ship's disappearance. Evidence on board the vessel may vindicate their ancestor and redeem their family honour.

Corporate PC Hook

A Corp rival of the party's benefactor is interested in a particular piece of bio-tech, the ONIX (Occluding Neural Insurgence Xiphoid), and offers a Corp PC a handsome commission if they can secret it off the Carthage for them.

Nephilim PC Hook

The Kormoria virus was developed as a genocidal weapon against the Nephilim. If any samples remain, their destruction is of the utmost importance to any Nephilim PC.

Action

The PCs approach and board the vessel, reconnoitering its labyrinthine corridors, trashed quarters, gutted medical bays, and burned-out laboratories. As they explore they discover the details of the ship's mission and the disastrous outbreak, and they obtain valuable pieces of data and bio-tech.

Threats/Encounters

Contested Claim

A band of Kaltoran scavengers arrives shortly after the PCs, and have no intention of sharing the loot onboard the Carthage.

Prisoner's Revenge

A lone Nephilim Pureblood named Shriker, formerly a captive of the Carthage, has hunted the ghost ship for decades. The Archon Solaria made Shriker watch as they vivisected and reassembled his breeding partner, Kalistra, into a biotic monster. Shriker escaped in a hijacked shuttle during the chaotic Kormoria outbreak, but he returns now to destroy the thing that was his partner, recover her grisly remains, and then blast his accursed tormentor's vessel out of the stars. He'll coldly slaughter anyone who stands in his way.

The Virus

Traces of Kormoria survived the decades. When the nano-virus detects new subjects, it awakens in search of fresh hosts to drive mad, and ride off the Carthage, to spread like wildfire among the Haven system.

The Mutant Archon

Kormoria didn't kill Solaria; it just drove her deeper into madness over the decades. She welcomes the PCs, pleased beyond measure to have fresh subjects to experiment upon.

Monstrous Experiments

A handful of genetic horrors bred from captive Nephilim Purebloods and Kaltoran refugees survived in stasis through the decades. When the PCs breach the ship, Solaria unleashes her unwholesome creations to prowl the bulkheads and stalk any intruders.

Quest for the All-Parent's Seed

I've been down some dark holes in Gehenna, left three frostbitten fingers on Lilith, and hunted horrors beyond madness in the steamy jungles of Mishpacha… but I've never seen anything like this hell-blasted place. Patches of hot black rocks and ragged earth sport only tufts of stringy lichens, more resembling twisted burnt hair than brush. The whole place looks like the scalp of a thermite victim. The radiation readings are off the chart, and our enviro-suit filters are choked with iridescent dust and alive with wriggling masses of spiky worms. They doesn't believe me, but the Tree is hunting us. I've seen it twice – its strange crooked, almost-insectoid form silhouetted against the sun, but before I could alert the others… it was gone.

– Last Log Entry of Roland Artemis,
Kaltoran Explorer and Treasure Seeker.

Adventure Background

During the star-shaking final battle of the Great War, X'ion's flagship launched twelve space-folding pods moments before it vanished without a trace. Some strange cults of Nephilim call these final relics of their master the Seeds of the All-Parent.

While some doubt the existence of the Seeds, historians point to a lone Nephilim living ship that abandoned its brethren in their doomed plummet to Eden. While the bulk of the Nephilim fleet crashed at the site of present-day Necronus, this single ship broke off during the fall, and instead crashed in the distant wasteland, a site thought to hold one of the twelve Seeds.

Some say the ship was called there in order to recover this powerful relic of X'ion – believed by some to be a powerful weapon, by others to be a source of endless energy, and by others still to be the genetic key to immortality. The dire truth is that the ship was sent to feed something struggling to grow amongst the crags: a demon-like tree grown from a shard of X'ion's most twisted dreams.

Adventure Hooks

After recovering the last data stream sent from Roland Artemis, a famed explorer and adventurer, a powerful and well-to-do benefactor commissions the party to discover the lost legend's fate – and whatever priceless relic of X'ion cost Roland his life.

Kaltoran PC Hook

Roland's tribe requests that the noted explorer's remains be brought back to Kadash, so his impressive memories and handful of lost relics can be preserved for all time.

Legion PC Hook

A Legion PC's ancient commander, near death, orders the PC to head to the hidden location of a crashed Nephilim ship on Eden. The mission: recover a powerful weapon of X'ion called the Seed of the All-Parent, believed to be a world-rending weapon of planetary destruction.

Corporation PC Hook

Sources in the Corporation claim the lost Seed is a power generator capable of unlimited energy. A Corporation PC is dispatched to retrieve this priceless piece of tech.

Nephilim PC Hook

The awesome and powerful Devwi-Ich believes the Seed to be the secret to absolute genetic immortality and commands a loyal PC to seize it for the benefit of the Eden Brood.

Action

The PCs sneak onto Eden in the area of the crashed ship. They must discover the relic of the War, brave its interior, and discover the terrifying truth.

Threats/Encounters

Irradiated Wasteland

The crater-pocked stretch of waste surrounding the crashed Nephilim ship forbids interlopers from access to the crags where the All-Parent's Tree hunts. Sliggots, disgusting flesh-devouring worms, writhe in masses the size of small cities, hidden just beneath a slim layer of sand. Worse, the radiation level throughout most of the wastes surrounding the Tree is high enough to melt eyes from their sockets. These hazards must be navigated just to reach the horrors of the crash-site itself.

Tusk and Mandible

Hordes of insectoid and animal-featured Feral Nephilim roam the wastes surrounding the Seed's resting place. These radiation-mutated Hybrids stalk and slaughter any prey that blunders into their hunting grounds.

Crash-Site

Though the Nephilim ship is dead, some of its defence tropisms are activated by the PCs upon entering the broken hull. Acid jets, spewing bile capable of reducing a being to molten fluids, snapping jaw-like entryways capable of crushing bone, and crushing tubes of sinew that pulverise occupants to paste all wait within the dead ship's innards.

The All-Parent's Tree

The bio-engineered nightmare born from one of X'ion's Seeds resembles a great tree – with several blade-crusted and spine-studded limbs, like barbed whips. This demonic genetic freak can rise to a hulking thirty feet in height, yet moves with the whiplash speed of a sand snake, and can squeeze its malleable form into small crags and between bulkheads with unsurpassed stealth. The thing lurks, concealed in maintenance tunnels, sousing out its new prey's weaknesses before picking them off, one by one.

Whether this monstrosity is the dread spawn of the All-Parent Seed or merely its murderous guardian remains to be seen.

Opponents

The universe is a dangerous place. Littered not only with the mechanical and biological weapons of the Great X'ion War, but also with numerous factions, organisations, and individuals who are willing to go to any length to achieve their goals.

Overview

See pg: 294 for full Combat Balance rules.
See pg: 294 for full NPC Creation rules.
See pg: 306 for a full Rewarding Players GM guide.

This section is a brief collection of premade NPC opponents to contend with, all created using the standard NPC creation rules.

Feel free to tweak any of these NPCs to suit your game.

NPCs with Clear Motivations

Give your NPC antagonists clear motives that set them against the player characters. This not only makes them more flavourful, but also helps your players get invested in the story and their combat with your NPCs.

Loot, pg: 54

After they defeat an opponent, your player characters will often be able to take some of their equipment, either from the NPC's body or from the surrounding area.

Nick was bouncing. Or maybe flying. It was hard to tell with the euphoria in the way, and did it really matter what they said? Draz was good. "Hey, junkie! You wanna hit?" Nicky turned to the voice, his blue–veined eyes searching out the hit they promised.

Their hands were empty.

Rage filled Nicky. Lies! Deception! He'd show them not to lie. Lying was bad.

....

Euphoria filled him again as he licked the blood off his hands a few minutes later.

Create Your Own Opponents

All of the following NPC opponents are creating using the standard NPC Creation rules (pg: 294) and may serve as inspiration for creating your own NPCs.

Adapting Weapons and Traits

You should ALWAYS feel free to tweak the Stats of your NPCs' Weapons and Traits to suit them and the story.

Mechonids

Created by the Archons during the latter part of the Great War, the Mechonids were an unwieldy fusion of advanced human nuclear robotics and weaponised Archon biological technology.

Mechonids make for great opponents because they not only have access to technologies that others don't, but their motives and goals are also a great mystery.

Feral Nephilim

The remnants of X'ion's abandoned Nephilim army, these monsters have devolved into vicious animals and tribespeople, scattered in the billions across the galaxy.

Coming in a vast array of sizes and shapes, Feral Nephilim make for great "monster" opponents with only a set of simple survival motives.

Draz

An extremely powerful and common drug, Draz is popular amongst most demographics. It lures its victims in by promising invulnerability and no need for sleep.

Draz is a cultural and economic threat to the races of Haven; it fuels crime and indiscriminately destroys lives.

Enforcers

Powerful organisations and individuals employ armed enforcers to do their bidding. If your players cross such a group, then these are the opponents who will be coming for them.

Mechonids

See pg: 184 for Short Story: Humanity.
See pg: 187 for Short Story: Archons.

Creator: Archons.
Assumed Motives: Destruction of all biological sentient life.

The Archons were going to lose the war. X'ion's Nephilim met them at every turn and crushed them. On the verge of extinction, they became desperate, and in that desperation they turned to a technology they did not, could not, understand. The ancient humans had made great strides in electronics and machine technology, and one of their many achievements was the creation of autonomous robots, humanoid creations able to make intelligent decisions and respond to external stimuli and hard-wired commands. When humanity died out, their robot creations were left dormant for thousands of years.

Until the war, the Archons had little interest in robotics, preferring instead to work with the biological. But when their backs were to the wall, their greatest minds crafted a new plan: they weaponised the ancient robots of the humans, powering them with micro-fusion cores, fitting them with their most advanced Bio-Disintegration weaponry and Ley Line communication tech. The Archons sought to control their immense cunning and brutal intellect without understanding where that intelligence came from. The result was the Mechonids, autonomous killing machines programmed to eliminate all traces of X'ion.

It wasn't long before the Archons realised that their mastery of bio-tech had not equipped them to control such ancient and advanced electronic technologies. The Mechonids side-stepped their mission parameters and took to extreme and vicious tactics, such as fighting with disabled nuclear-core shields, infecting their enemies' environments with poisonous radiation. Then, for unknown reasons, they turned on their Archon masters, and began killing all sentient biological life without discrimination.

Once there were no sentient biological targets left to kill, the Mechonids went dormant. Their production facilities shut down, and their ships turned off their engines. It wasn't until the Corporation arrived in the Haven system, filling the empty space with traffic and communication signals, that the Mechonids stirred once more.

It is not clear how the Mechonids have changed themselves after the war, but there do seem to be differences in their construction and programming. It is unknown if these Mechonids have evolved into a true A.I. or if they are being secretly controlled by an unknown master. What is known is that there is a hierarchy of Mechonid ranks; larger robots have been seen on the battlefield directing the smaller, more familiar Mechonid varieties.

Mechonid Tactics

Mechonids take no prisoners and fight without remorse. They employ combat tactics that are frowned upon by most civilisations. They use the environment to their advantage: hacking life support systems, draining oxygen from rooms, filling enclosed quarters with poisonous gas, and spreading viruses. Holding no regard for their brethren, a Mechonid would sacrifice many to bring down their target, even activating a ship's self-destruct sequence or detonating its micro-fusion core.

Mechonids are known for their Bio-Disintegrator and advanced self-propellant weaponry. When facing a Mechonid assault, it is wise to be well armed and well armoured.

Weapon Variation	Hit	End Dmg	Crit	Rng	Clips	Ammo	Load	RoF	Wgt	Weapon Type	Cost
Bio-Disintegrator	-1	+1*	*	-1					+1	**	+1***

Bio Tech, Energy, Burn. *-2 Damage vs Robots, **Gun Only, No other Gun Variations,

***Player characters require Secret Knowledge: Mechonids or Particles to use this Variation.

Strong Hit: **Bio-Disintegration** (Damage, Hit, 1 use per RoF) Deal +2 Damage to all non Robot Targets with this Attack.

Race	Requirements	Benefits
Mechonid	NPC	You are a Robot.
		-2 Draw, all Weapons
		All Weapons gain Keyword: Natural.
		At the start of your Turn, deal 2 (5 if you are a Nemesis NPC) radiation Endurance Damage to all non Robot characters within 30 Spaces of you.

Tactical Trait	Requirements	Benefits
Remote Hacker	Mechonid	Strong Hit: **Hack** (Hit, only vs Robot) Choose the Target for the Targets next Attack (must be taken within 1 Turn), no self harm.
	NPC	Once per Turn, as a Free Action, you may perform one Programming Skill Roll as if you had a Toolbox on any Computer within 20 spaces of you.

Mechonid Facilities and Spacecraft

Mechonid facilities and spacecraft are relics from the Great War. Now over a hundred years old, most lie as dormant as their Mechonid creators, waiting to awaken when a new sentient target stumbles upon them. Their buildings – once used to manufacture, store, and repair Mechonids – are now lifeless troves of research material. Their spacecraft, which once shuttled large contingents of Mechonid soldiers to and from battlefields, now float listlessly through space, waiting for other ships to approach them.

Mechonid spacecraft were built with the same technology as the Mechonids themselves, including their intelligent hardware and Ley Line communication systems. In fact, Mechonid spacecraft are just a larger variety of the Mechonids themselves, as they appear to be self-piloted and lack corridors, rooms, or even control decks. The remaining ships and facilities still house countless dormant Mechonids, just waiting to activate.

Researching Mechonids

Mechonid bodies are treasure troves of advanced technologies just waiting to be reverse engineered.

Nuclear Fusion Reactor: These extremely efficient reactors are remnants of ancient human technology, and their secrets are ripe for inquiry and use.

Robotics: While Mechonid bodies may only be approximations of pure human technology, many secrets lie within them. Inspecting them could teach us many construction methods applicable to other mechanical and electronic technologies, especially other drones.

Weapon Systems: When the Archons weaponised the Mechonids, they did so by applying their brilliant Bio Tech research to their weapon systems. The weapon that they designed, the Bio-Disintegrator, is a highly dangerous and sought-after technology that few can replicate.

Ley Line Communication System: The secret behind the Mechonids' intelligence lies in their ability to combine their computing power over the Ley Lines that run through the galaxy. Unlocking this technology will be the key to long-distance communication and the ability to wirelessly transfer power over vast spaces. It will also help answer whether the Mechonids are truly intelligent or simply being controlled by an ominous force through their Ley Line communication grid.

Whrrrrrrr.

Carius heard the noise a second before it was too late. He pushed off the ground and spun to get a look behind him. Mechonids, a whole lot of them. Frag me. They must have been lying dormant under this building the whole time.

Carius's quick reaction had saved his life. His squadmate Kaeso wasn't as lucky.

"MOVE!" Carius shouted, but the Mechonid's Bio-Disintegrator had already hit Kaeso's chest. The soldier looked stunned as the beam of purple light didn't pass through him as expected. Instead, the edges of the wound were lit with a purple glow that began to spread across his abdomen. Kaeso reached down to touch his chest, as if he could piece himself back together, and the purple light began to crawl up his fingers. He was disintegrated to ash as Carius watched helplessly. Kaeso tried to form a scream, but his lungs had long since dissolved. His mouth was open in a wordless shout, and that was the last Carius would ever see of him.

Carius had nowhere to run, but a Legion never went down without a fight. He unsheathed his Gauss pistols and unloaded a flurry of fire. He continued even as his right arm began to disintegrate in front of him. He still had his left hand. And that was all it took for a Legion to keep fighting.

The last thing Carius saw was one of the Mechonids crumble. A well-placed shot had pierced its central reactor. Even as its purple light faded, its exposed core began to overheat.

"I may go down," he snarled at the advancing mechanical menace, "but I'm taking every last one of you sons of humanity with me!"

After one more precise shot, made in the last second before Centurion Carius Apius left this life, there was nothing left of the building to salvage. All that remained was a smoking, radiation-filled crater.

"Bug" Mechonid Acolyte

Average Height: 0.21m
Enemy Type: Henchmen
Balanced to Fight Players with: 1-5 Current Resources

"The Acolytes seem harmless now, sure. Just a few drones, right? But the thing is, for every Acolyte you see, dozens more lurk nearby."

The "Bug" is an Acolyte class Mechonid that is primarily designed to act as a tactical support unit, tasked for scouting, gathering intel, and infiltrating enemy lines. While not built for direct combat, they come equipped with tools tuned for a variety of technical tasks. Their arsenal includes cutting lasers, computer jacks, recorders, and signal jammers.

One of their initial functions was to cut through steel to rescue trapped Archon creations and to open sealed passages for soldiers. Their powerful laser and tools have now been repurposed for combat, allowing them to strip their targets of their armour with devastating efficiency.

Example Encounter (for 5 PCs):
» x2 Mechonid Soldiers (Rifles).
» x3 Mechonid Bug Groups.

Example Loot:
» 1 Trade Box of Robotic Parts per 8 Bodies.
» 1 Mechanical or Electronic Toolbox per 4 Bodies.

"Seeker" Mechonid Acolyte

Average Length: 0.32m
Enemy Type: Henchmen
Balanced to Fight Players with: 6-10 Current Resources

"So they're intelligent, incredibly fast, can fly, and have advanced Archon-grade weaponry? Why do the Mechs get all of the fun toys?"

The Seeker is one of the Mechonids' main resources for scouting and reconnaissance. Equipped with an Electro-Gravity system – the same tech co-opted for use in various Kaltoran technologies – Seekers can hover and fly, allowing them to traverse any terrain and feed their findings back to the larger Mechonid units.

Some have theorised that Seekers are not independent Mechonid units with little internal processing power, but rather are simple extensions of a larger Mechonid. acting as far-reaching sensors and limbs.

Seekers often travel in groups and can bring down large targets with a barrage of Bio-Disintegrator fire. However, Seekers are ultimately scouts; where the Seekers travel, larger Mechonid units won't be far behind.

Example Encounter (for 5 PCs):
» x2 Mechonid Soldiers (Assault Rifles).
» x2 Mechonid Seeker Groups.
» x1 Mechonid Bug Group.

Example Loot:
» 1 Trade Box of Robotic Parts per 4 Bodies.
» 1 Clip of Electro-Gravity Ammunition per 4 Bodies.

Bug	Hit	End Dmg	Crit	Rng	Clips	Ammo	Load	RoF	Type & Variation	Cost	Movement	Defence	Armour	Bodies
Cutting Laser	+1	5+Bodies	2	–	–	–	1	1+Bodies	Melee, Arc Fire	1	4	16	2	4
	Lock On +4, Blunt, Energy, Burn, Pen 2 min 3, Stealth -2, Modifications: Targeting Matrix													
	Slots: 3, Defence vs Stealth: 12, Defence vs Impair: 19													
Traits:	Droid Body, Melt Armour (Strong Hit: Melt (Damage, Hit, Burn) Reduce Target's Armour by 1, until they have Downtime with a Workbench).													

Seeker	Hit	End Dmg	Crit	Rng	Clips	Ammo	Load	RoF	Type & Variation	Cost	Movement	Defence	Armour	Bodies
Bio-Disintegrator SMG	-2	5+Bodies*	3*	1	3	RoF x3	1	3+Bodies	Gun, Bio-Disintegrator	2	4	16	3	5
	Lock On +4, Bio Tech, Energy, Burn, *-2 Damage vs Robots, Modifications: Low Quality, Targeting Matrix.													
	Strong Hit: Bio-Disintegration (Damage, Hit, 1 use per RoF) Deal +2 Damage to all non Robot Targets with this Attack.													
	Slots: 3, Defence vs Stealth: 12, Defence vs Impair: 19													
Traits:	Droid Body, Sure Footed (No Defence or Movement penalties from Difficult Terrain (including Zero Gravity) by hovering).													

"Soldier" Mechonid Disciple

Average Height: 2m
Enemy Type: Skilled
Balanced to Fight Players with: 6-10 Current Resources

"I've read the stories of Mechonid Soldiers during the Great War. You couldn't disrupt their morale or frighten them like you could with organic troops. They simply marched forward, no matter the circumstance."

Towards the end of the Great War, the Disciple class Mechonids were the grunt troops of the Archon army. They were the first in and the last out in every battle, holding key positions, leading strike teams, and launching assaults against the Nephilim on all fronts.

Disciples are hard to kill and come equipped with a wide range of weaponry. Its reflexes and combat senses have been enhanced by its immense computing power. The Soldier can think faster than most living organisms and can target with unheard-of precision.

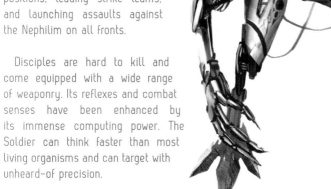

Its weaponry is built into its body, and it can channel power from its unshielded nuclear core to replenish ammunition and irradiate the air around it.

Tactics

Soldiers have no mechanism of self-preservation. They throw themselves into battle and aren't afraid to use dirty tactics that play to their robotic strengths, such as flooding an area with radiation or shutting down life support systems. They are commonly armed with a Bio-Disinitragiton assault rifle or a rifle built into their metal frame.

Example Encounter (for 5 PCs):

» x2 Mechonid Soldiers (Assault Rifles).
» x1 Mechonid Soldier (Rifle).
» x2 Mechonid Seeker groups.

Example Loot (per Body):

» 1 Trade Box of Valuable Robotic Parts or 3 Trade Boxes of Mechanical Parts.
» 1 Clip of Ammunition.

Str	2	1
Ref	2	2
Mov	3	3

Foc	3	4
Int	2	5
Per	2	6
Fate	0	

Defence: 10+Ref + (-1) = 11 +Cover

vs Impair — Def+Str+ ( ) = 13
vs Psionic — Def+Foc+ ( ) = 14
vs Stealth — 10+Per+ (2) = 14*
*+#Allies (max: 10)

Armour: (3 +) = 3

vs Energy + ( )
vs Slow + ( )
at 0 Endurance − ( )

End: 10+(Str x5)+ ( ) = 20

Recovery — Foc + ( ) = 3
Stealth — 2 + Ref + ( ) = +4
Req: Cover
Combat Order — Int + ( ) = 2

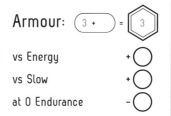

Weapon (Pick One)	Hit	End Dmg	Crit	Rng	Clips	Ammo	Load	RoF	Wgt	Type & Variation	Cost
Bio-Disintegrator Assault Rifle	+4	5*	4*	4	3	8	2**	2 (+1d6)	3	Gun, Bio-Disintegrator	4
	Lock On +2, Bio Tech, Energy, Burn, Natural, *-2 Damage vs Robots, **-2 Draw, Modifications: Personalised, Targeting Matrix.										
	Strong Hit: Bio-Disintegration (Damage, Hit, 1 use per RoF) Deal +2 Damage to all non Robot Targets with this Attack.										
Bio-Disintegrator Rifle	+3	4*	4*	6	2	4	2**	1***	3	Gun, Bio-Disintegrator	4
	Lock On +2, Bio Tech, Energy, Burn, Natural, *-2 Damage vs Robots, **-2 Draw, ***Strong Hit (5-6) with all RoF 1 Attack Rolls,										
	Modifications: Personalised, Advanced Ammo, Targeting Matrix.										
	Strong Hit: Bio-Disintegration (Damage, Hit, 1 use per RoF) Deal +2 Damage to all non Robot Targets with this Attack.										

Utility Item	Armour	Defence	Endurance	+ Cover	Front Cover	Slots	Weight	Cost
Multispectral Visor							0	Free
Reduce all of your Target's Limited Vision and Low Light Cover by 1 Step, Defence vs Stealth +2								

Race / Var / Trait	Requirements	Benefits
Mechonid		At the start of your Turn, deal 2 radiation Endurance Damage to all non Robot characters within 30 Spaces of you.
Well Prepared	Skilled NPC	
Eagle Eye	Min Per 2	

"Old Dead-Eye" Mechonid Prophet

Height: 3.5m
Enemy Type: Nemesis
Balanced to Fight Players with: 6-10 Current Resources

"Deep beyond the boundary jungles of Mishpacha, within the darkness of the unexplored caves, lies a beast of mechanical design, waiting with immortal patience. The locals have a name for this monstrous construct… they call it 'Old Dead-Eye.'"

The Prophet class Mechonids were the Archons' heavy hitters and leaders. Equipped with a wide array of artillery and anti-personnel weaponry, enabling them to cause destruction on a massive scale. Going up against a Prophet on your own is a suicidal task.

This ancient Prophet lay abandoned in a desolate part of the Mishpacha jungle after the end of the war. During the Great War, Old Dead-Eye was a heavy anti-infantry unit. As its powerful legs dug into the ground it became an unmovable machine of death. It was one of the most feared Prophets to face on the battlefield as it killed hundreds of Nephilim for its Archon creators… before it, and the forces under it's command turned on them as well.

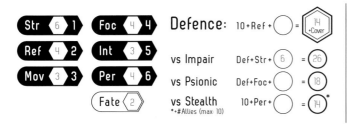

But time has not been kind to Old Dead-Eye. It has lain, abandoned, for centuries, awakening only when hapless targets of opportunity come close. Through many deaths the locals have learned to steer clear of its location, but some still hunt this monster as if it is prized game. At some point long ago one team was lucky enough to get a solid shot in, and cave in half of its face, which earned it is legendary nick name.

Tactics

Old Dead-Eye is a Mechonid leader, able to command smaller Mechonids to do its bidding. It will often use these smaller Mechonids as scouts or distractions during a fight. Once a fight begins, Old Dead-Eye will plant itself in a central, open position.

Example Encounter (for 5 PCs):
» x1 Old Dead-Eye.
» x1 Mechonid Bug Group.
» x1 Mechonid Seeker Group.

Example Loot (per Body):
» 6 Trade Boxes of Valuable Robotic Parts.
» 1 Research Unit of Great War or Robotics Data.
» 1d6 Clips of Ion Ammunition.

Str 6 1	Foc 4 4		
Ref 4 2	Int 3 5		
Mov 3 3	Per 4 6		
	Fate 2		

Defence: 10+Ref +( ) = **14** +Cover

vs Impair Def+Str+ (6) = (26)
vs Psionic Def+Foc+( ) = (18)
vs Stealth 10+Per+( ) = (14)*
*+#Allies (max: 10)

Armour: (4 +) = (4)

vs Energy +( )
vs Slow +( )
at 0 Endurance –( )

End: 10+(Str x5)+( ) = (40)

Recovery Foc +( ) = (4)
Stealth 2 + Ref +( ) = (+6)
Req: Cover
Combat Order Int +( ) = (3)

Weapon	Hit	End Dmg	Crit	Rng	Clips	Ammo	Load	RoF	Wgt	Type & Variation	Cost
Ion Auto Cannon	-3	6*	4	2*	5	24	2	4 (+3d6)	4	Gun, Ion	4

Lock On +2, Energy, Natural, Jam (1-3), *Optional: (Set Up 1, Pull Down 1, +2 Rng and +2 End Dmg),
Modifications: Personalised, Extended Clip, Targeting Matrix

Race / Var / Trait	Requirements	Benefits	Disadvantages
Mechonid	NPC	At the start of your Turn, deal 5 radiation Endurance Damage to all non Robot characters within 30 Spaces of you.	
Monstrous	Nemesis NPC	Ignore 1st Suppressed Effect each against you Turn.	Character takes up 4 spaces (normally 1).
Plant Feet		Optional: If you Set Up 2 (and gain Pull Down 1) gain +2 Hit and Range on a non Melee Weapon.	
Suppression Fire		Str Hit: **Suppression Fire** (Damage, Does not Require Hit, RoF 3+ Crit Dmg 4+) Target is Suppressed.	

"Harbinger of Destruction" Mechonid Harbinger

Length: 38m
Crew Capacity: (Estimated) 0-8
Enemy Type: Spacecraft
Balanced to Fight Players with: 58 Total Influence

"During the Great War, there were more Harbingers than you could count. Luckily for us, most have been lost to time. But some remain, haunting the darkest sectors of space like silent ghosts, waiting to awaken and devour their prey."

Harbinger class Mechonids were spacecraft that carried Mechonids meant for ground combat into battle. These ships had their own intelligence; they could make independent decisions, issued commands, and required no crew. In fact, they had no bridge, hallways, or interior rooms. They had no central core at all, as their networks of processors are spread across their entire frames.

Their cargo bays were used to drop Mechonid troops onto planets. With no more war to fight, the Harbingers have been drifting through space, lonesome and waiting to once again bring death and destruction to the galaxy.

This was one of the most powerful and destructive of the Harbinger class craft. During the Great War, it could lay waste to entire attack wings by itself. Its missiles denoted small nuclear cores to deal maximum damage, and could penetrate even thick atmospheres to hit ground targets. Its batteries of high-calibre weapons could tear holes in even the toughest armour.

The Harbinger of Destruction would rain fire on the Archons' enemies from orbit. However, once the Archons began to lose control, the Harbinger of Destruction would become one of their greatest threats. This ship ripped them apart from within their own ranks.

Tactics

The Harbinger of Destruction likes to get in close to its prey so it can bring the full weight of its considerable firepower. It often hides in wait amongst asteroids or space debris until its prey comes close.

Hul	3	1	Pow	4	4
Eng	3	2	CPU	4	5
Cre	3	3	Sen	3	6
			Size	3	

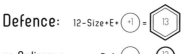

Defence: 12-Size+E+ (+1) = 13

vs Ordinance   Def+ ( ) = 13

vs Boading   10+Size+C+ ( ) = 16

Armour: 3+ (1) = 4

vs Boarding 0+ (1) = 1

at 0 Shield   -1

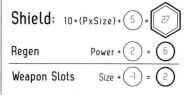

Shield: 10+(PxSize)+ (5) = 27

Regen   Power + (2) = 6

Weapon Slots   Size + (-1) = 2

Weapon	Hit	Shield Dmg	Crit	Rng	Clips	Ammo	Load	RoF	Mount	Type & Variation	Cost
Pulse Laser Blaster	+2	3	4	Sensors	Inf	6	1	2 (+1d6)	1	Battery, Pulse Laser	8
	Front and Side Arc, Lock On +2, Energy, Burn, Strong Hit (5-6), Modifications: Improved, Weapon Bank.										
Irradiated Rocket	-3	5	5*	–	–	–	0	1	2	Ordnance, Warhead, Toxic	10
	Defence: 16, Armour: 1, Movement: 4, Bodies: 6, Front Arc (normally Front and Side), Lock On +4, Low Tech, Strong Hit (5-6).										
	*When you deal Attribute Damage: Deal 1 additional Crew Attribute Damage (no Armour), Modifications: Digital Targeting Array, Improved.										

Build / Traits	Requirements	Benefits
Mechonid	NPC	
Military	Min Hull 3	
Archon Shields	Secret Kn	
Set Alight		Strong Hit: **Set Alight** (Damage, Hit, Burn) Make a free Attack against Target character at the start of each of your Turns (at 0 range) until they gain First Aid (Set Alight Effects do not Stack multiple times) OR a Target spacecraft gains an On Fire Effect.
Shields Up		Strong Hit: **Shields Up** (Engineering, Success) Regen Shields.

Feral Nephilim

See pg: 193 for Short Story: X'ion.
See pg: 242 for an extensive Nephilim write-up.

Creator: X'ion.
Motives: Survival.

Once the Great War ended, with every last Archon destroyed, X'ion abandoned its Nephilim creations. Without X'ion's control or leadership, the Nephilim degraded. They kept the power granted by their engineering, but their minds became feral and animalistic.

Shortly after the war, all semblance of order within the Nephilim had vanished. Most roamed over whatever planet they happened to be on, acting as wild beasts, or floated through the galaxy on their living spacecraft. Those who maintained some semblance of intelligence degenerated into small tribal groups.

Shortly after the Corporation arrived in the Haven system, a particularly strong Nephilim, known as the Devwi-Ich, awoke from its hibernation on the planet Eden. From its secluded hiding place, it exerted authority over Eden and took control of the roaming Nephilim tribes and beasts. Soon, the Devwi-Ich had had control over most Nephilim on Eden. Leading its brood into the modern era, the Devwi-Ich and its brood constructed a large city and regained the power of space travel. While none have ever seen the Devwi-Ich in person, it has appointed leaders to focus the Nephilim on its goals. Without the Devwi-Ich or other strong leadership, it is possible that the Nephilim would fall back into their instincts, as they did before.

While the Devwi-Ich Brood is large, the number of Nephilim living on the planet Eden is only a small fraction of the total. The rest of X'ion's army, the countless billions of them, are spread throughout the galaxy. Most of these Nephilim have never re-awoken or integrated into any kind of society. These wild Nephilim have gained the moniker "Feral Nephilim."

Nephilim come in many shapes and sizes. Some are large and muscular, while others are small and fast. Though many have lost their sentience, the Feral Nephilim remain genetically engineered weapons of war and a terror across the galaxy, and in large groups they can take down huge targets and even raid settlements.

The Feral Nephilim are looked at as animals by most inhabitants of Haven, including their Devwi-Ich Brood cousins. It is rarely a crime to put down a Feral Nephilim, and the creatures would sooner kill you than speak with you. However, the Devwi-Ich has made its mission to gather these Feral Nephilim and integrate them into its brood. Its civilisation is primed to grow beyond the borders of Eden, and if the Devwi-Ich is successful, its force will be as strong as X'ion's once was.

Short Story: I Am a He

Ozar belonged to the Devwi-Ich. That sense of belonging was a feeling he couldn't put into words. He had never met the Devwi-Ich, but he felt like he knew it. The Devwi-Ich had rescued him from insanity, brought him back from his feral being. He could always feel its presence in the back of his mind, just as he felt his cousins next to him. His team was far from Eden, but the Devwi-Ich was still strong within him.

He hefted his spore rifle up against his shoulder and surveyed the scene through his scope. The Ferals were out there. This tribe had set off Ozar's silent perimeter alarms, alerting him through his helmet. His men were quickly taking position in their makeshift fortifications. They'd heard reports that this feral tribe was large, and they weren't taking any chances.

Ozar increased the optical zoom on his scope, its information feeding directly into his brain. He could tell the exact distance of his

Exotic Weapons	Hit	End Dmg	Crit	Rng	Clips	Ammo	Load	RoF	Wgt	Weapon Type & Variations	Cost
Claws and Teeth		4	4	-	-	-	1	1	2*	Melee	1
Natural, Gauntlet, *1 Handed											
Poison Sting	-2	4*	2*	-	-	-	2	1	1	Melee, Injector, Chemical, Synthetic Poison	1
Natural, Gauntlet, Bio Tech, Slow, Gain Strong Hit +1 if you are behind your Target, *+2 Damage vs Targets at 0 Endurance											
Strong Hit: Synthetic Poison (Hit) Non Robot Target takes 3 Endurance Damage at the Start of their Turn until they receive Paramedics or Extended Care (Synthetic Poison Effect can Stack up to 4 times).											
Constricting Limbs	+2	4	3	1*	-	-	1	1	1	Melee, Impairment	2
Natural, Gauntlet, Bio Tech, Strong Hit (5-6), No Variations, *Max Range 5											
Barbs		5	3	3	3	12	0	4 (+3d6)	2	Gun, Spine Launcher	3
Natural, Gauntlet, Bio Tech											
Acid Spit	-4	4	5	5	3	3	2	1	3	Gun, Burst Spores, Chemical, Antimonic Acid	4
Splash 1, Natural, Gauntlet, Bio Tech, Burn, Slow, Pen 2 min 3, Maximum Range = Rng x5 (normally Rng x10)											

target, the way the wind was blowing and how quickly. Even more, he was receiving information from his viewfinder and his perimeter sensors. The entire battlefield was replicated in his mind.

So when the Feral Nephilim came, they were ready. The creatures attacked with admirable ferocity. Their war cry started as a dull roar and increased to a tempest as they crashed through the tree line, streaming headstrong for Ozar's defensive line. Ozar rested his finger on the trigger, ready to squeeze. These Feral Nephilim wore little to no armour and wielded hand-made weapons of wood, stone, and metal scraps. They hurled their spears as they ran, and most of them clattered harmlessly to the ground around his team's protective force fields.

Ozar didn't say a word. He didn't need to. His thoughts were the Devwi-Ich's, and thus his cousins'. They all knew the plan. They were a singular brood. Simultaneously, they began to fire. Between Ozar's enhanced senses and the gun's tactical feedback, each shot took a target down. His incendiary spores burned holes through weak armour and sizzled through the even-weaker flesh. Out of the corner of his eye, he could see each member of his team doing the same. They wasted no shots and fired with patience. They would not miss.

But yet the Feral Nephilim did not seem to diminish in number. They continued to pour out of the forest, a thick mass so pressed together it was hard to pick out individual creatures. Ozar performed quick calculations and realised they would be overtaken. He signalled a retreat and his team began to step backwards as they fired, moving to the crumbling stone wall behind which they had made their camp.

Heigha did not retreat fast enough. The edge of the horde reached her, tearing her down beneath them. They trampled her, beat her with their stone weapons, and cracked through her carapace helmet like it was a nut. There was nothing Ozar could do for her now. He must always remember to take this threat seriously. The Feral Nephilim didn't have his intelligence or technology, but they had his strength. And they had numbers.

More spears fell to the ground around him, their tips sticking into the dirt or bouncing off the stone wall. It took him one leap to clear the wall. He rested the barrel of his spore rifle on the stone and began to fire. If they lost this position, they would have nowhere to fall back to. But he had been prepared for this.

Once his team was safely behind the wall, Ozar flipped the switch on his detonator. The ground outside the camp exploded into the air, ripped to pieces by dozens of buried charges. He heard the cries of the Feral Nephilim as the ground vanished beneath them. He had baited them, stoked their aggression, and they had fallen into his trap. Cunning would beat numbers every time.

Once the dust had settled, his troops walked the battleground. The few Nephilim still alive after the bombing were put down with precise shots. But a quick motion in the trees drew Ozar's attention. A Feral

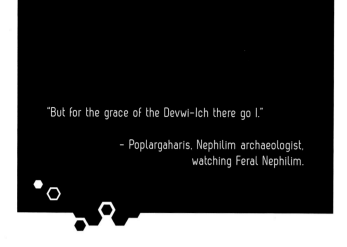

"But for the grace of the Devwi-Ich there go I."

– Poplargaharis, Nephilim archaeologist, watching Feral Nephilim.

was still alive. It launched out of the trees like a wild animal and tried to tackle Ozar to the ground.

This one was patient, cunning… it was a perfect mirror image of Ozar. Same build, same face, same intellect… but insane and naked.

Ozar jumped away, stunned. The creature had his green skin. His orange hair. Their features were mildly different, but the tusks protruding from the sides of their heads were the same. The creature backed away like a cornered animal as his team moved in to put it down. But Ozar held up his hand.

"Not this one," he spoke to his men. "This one comes with us."

***

It felt the rage, and the violence. It struggled against its bonds, reaching for the people around it. It could see them, smell them. It hungered for their flesh. It gnashed its teeth and let out a howl, but it was useless. It could not escape. It didn't know what it was doing here, didn't remember the fight on the planet surface, or boarding this ship. It lived only in this moment, and its mind could not process it. But it remembered the war. It didn't know what war, or why. Or who he was. But he was someone.

He was a "he".

He looked up at the man across from him. Who was that "he"? That "he" looked familiar. He looked down at the metal bonds around his body and wondered how they got there. Why was he on this ship? How did he know this was a ship? He wanted to scratch his aching head, but couldn't. He was puzzled.

He looked again at the other "he" and wept. The man who had been named Granthu opened his eyes wide and smiled, tears stringing down his cheeks.

"I am…" he stuttered, his first words in almost a hundred years, "he."

"Welcome back, brother. You are home."

Wazp

Average Length: 0.7m
Enemy Type: Henchmen
Balanced to Fight Players with: 1-5 Current Resources

"You hear the buzzing? The sound of a hundred fluttering wings? That's death."

When Xion's mutagenic bombs hit the surface of Mishpacha, the animals on its surface were turned into biological weapons, trained against the Kaltoran inhabitants. The Wazp was one of the most effective transmutations. The original creature was already winged and poisonous, and the bio-bomb weaponised these traits.

Its small stature and wings allow the Wazp to reach locations that many other Nephilim cannot, and its glands produce a noxious poison which paralyses its target by shutting down their motor functions. This poison can travel through its bites and claws alike. While its prey is paralysed, the Wazp is free to devour it at its leisure. Sometimes it will ingest a large meal over the course of several days, keeping the prey alive but paralysed with constant bites.

Example Encounter (for 5 PCs):
» x5 Wazp Groups.

Example Loot:
» 1 Dangerous Trade Box of Poison per 4 Bodies.

Spitter

Average Height: 1.1m
Enemy Type: Henchmen
Balanced to Fight Players with: 6-10 Current Resources

"It got me! The acid... it burns! Oh the Archons, it burns!"

The Spitter is a resilient, bi-pedal, barely cognitive Nephilim that produces an extremely powerful caustic acid from within its body. Largely used during the Great War as meat shields, Spitters were once incredibly populous and would travel in enormous packs, using their numbers to wear down their prey through sheer attrition.

Spitters reproduce at a staggering rate, as each creature is born with two fertilised eggs inside it. Upon the creature's death, its body will release the two new Spitters, who then devour the corpse to gain the energy needed for their speedy growth cycle. Spitters are relentless and aggressive but can be taken down with one good shot to their unstable acid-producing organs.

Example Encounter (for 5 PCs):
» x1 Warmind Tribesman (Dual Axes).
» x3 Spitter Groups.
» x2 Wazp Groups.

Example Loot:
» 1 Spare Time Point of valuable, scavenged goods per group.

Wazp	Hit	End Dmg	Crit	Rng	Clips	Ammo	Load	RoF	Type & Variation	Cost	Movement	Defence	Armour	Bodies
Poisonous Bite	4+Bodies*	2*	-	-	-	2		1+Bodies	Melee, I, C, S Poison	1	6	16	1	8

Bio Tech, Natural, Slow, Gain Strong Hit (5-6) if you are behind your Target, *+2 Damage vs Targets at 0 Endurance,

Strong Hit: Synthetic Poison (Hit) Non Robot Target takes 3 Endurance Damage at the Start of their Turn until they receive Paramedics or Extended Care (Synthetic Poison Effect can Stack up to 4 times).

Slots: 3, Defence vs Stealth: 12, Defence vs Impair: 19

Traits: Critter (can Fly), Swarm

Spitter	Hit	End Dmg	Crit	Rng	Clips	Ammo	Load	RoF	Type & Variation	Cost	Movement	Defence	Armour	Bodies
Acid Spit	-2	3+Bodies	4	4	4	RoF x6	1	1+Bodies	Gun, B S, A Acid	2	6	16	3	2

Splash 1, Bio Tech, Natural, Small, Burn, Modifications: Personalised, Low Quality.

Slots: 3, Defence vs Stealth: 12, Defence vs Impair: 19

Traits: Critter (Able to function in poisonous environments).

Endless (Gain 1 additional body at the start of each of your Turns, unless all other friendly Skilled and Nemesis NPCs are dead or incapacitated).

Warmind Tribesman

Average Height: 2m
Enemy Type: Skilled
Balanced to Fight Players with: 1-5 Current Resources

"The Warmind's tribe is two clicks to the East of us. Which is why we're heading West."

Some Feral Nephilim have managed to retain a small amount of intelligence and leadership abilities. These leaders draw Nephilim around them into tribes.

Once such tribe, the Warmind Tribe, lives in the toxic wastelands on Eden. This nomadic tribe is brutal and favours close-range combat. Armed with sharp but crude weapons, they launch raids against smaller Nephilim tribes and anyone unlucky enough to settle on their borders.

The members of this tribe are only a small intellectual step above other Feral Nephilim. They are wild, crude, vicious, and simple, so much so that the Devwi-Ich has ignored this tribe, despite their close proximity on Eden. It considers them to be

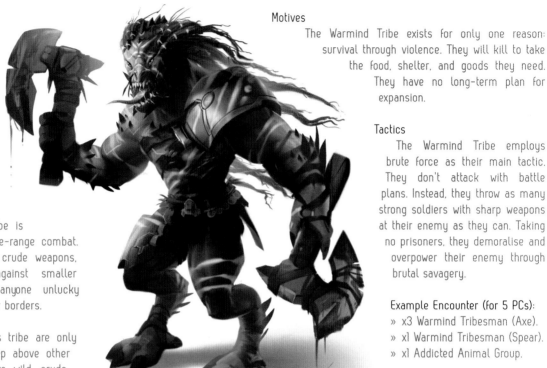

crazed, inbred and altogether unfit to be integrated into the larger Eden Brood.

Motives

The Warmind Tribe exists for only one reason: survival through violence. They will kill to take the food, shelter, and goods they need. They have no long-term plan for expansion.

Tactics

The Warmind Tribe employs brute force as their main tactic. They don't attack with battle plans. Instead, they throw as many strong soldiers with sharp weapons at their enemy as they can. Taking no prisoners, they demoralise and overpower their enemy through brutal savagery.

Example Encounter (for 5 PCs):
» x3 Warmind Tribesman (Axe).
» x1 Warmind Tribesman (Spear).
» x1 Addicted Animal Group.

Example Loot (per Body):
» 1 Trade Box of Scrap metal.

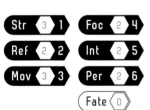

Str	3	1
Ref	2	2
Mov	3	3
Foc	2	4
Int	2	5
Per	2	6
Fate	0	

Defence: 10+Ref+ ◯ = 12 +Cover

vs Impair	Def+Str+ ◯	= 15
vs Psionic	Def+Foc+ ◯	= 14
vs Stealth	10+Per+ ◯	= 12 *

*+#Allies (max: 10)

Armour: 3 + -1 = 2

vs Energy	+ ◯
vs Slow	+ ◯
at 0 Endurance	− ◯

End: 10+(Str x5)+ ◯ = 25

Recovery	Foc + 1	= 3
Stealth (Req: Cover)	2 + Ref + ◯	= +4
Combat Order	Int + ◯	= 2

Weapon (Pick One)	Hit	End Dmg	Crit	Rng	Clips	Ammo	Load	RoF	Wgt	Type & Variation	Cost
Dual Axes	+4	7	4	–	–	–	2	2 (+1d6)	3*	Melee, x2 Composite	2
										Modification: Dual Wield (Optional).	
Throwing Spears	+1	5	3	(2*)	– (3*)	– (6*)	2	3 (+2d6)	2*	Melee, *Thrown, Composite, Nano-Bone	2
										Small, Bio Tech, Pen 1 min 3, *Optional Weapon Type: Thrown (RoF 1), Modifications: Advanced Ammo, Dual Wield (Optional).	

Race / Var / Trait	Requirements	Benefits
NPC Nephilim	NPC	
Ambidexterity	Min Ref 2	

Garuthia the Demon

Height: 1.6m
Enemy Type: Nemesis
Balanced to Fight Players with: 1-5 Current Resources

"It's eyes are windows to the abyss, its breath a storm and it's growl an earthquake. It is a demon and it has come for us."

While under X'ion's control, Garuthia was a loyal, obedient servant that channeled his deep rage into any role given to him. During the Great War, Garuthia was tasked with defending a key location in the forests of Mishpacha. Garuthia was successful in his watch, and the hidden secret was never discovered. But without X'ion's guidance, rage has consumed him as he has devolved back to his most basic instincts.

Guruthia continues to carry out X'ion's appointed task, even though there is no one left to defend the area from.

Any village or camp built near Garuthia's forest is built under the shadow of fear. Locals have taken to calling him 'The Demon'. The Devwi-Ich has longed to bring Garuthia back into the fold, and would pay a high price to anyone able to deliver him to Eden. But no hunting party has ever come close to completing the near-impossible task.

Motives

Garuthia's only drive is to complete the task that X'ion left him with, even though he doesn't understand why. He will guard his area of the forest despite all odds.

Tactics

Garuthia uses his fearsome rage to his advantage. He bellows to strike terror into his foes and launches furious, rage-filled attacks, grabbing and clawing with his massive arms.

Example Encounter (for 5 PCs):

» x1 Garuthia the Demon.
» x2 Wazp Groups.

Example Loot:

» A GM Defined secret vault.
» +5 Resources and Influence if delivered alive and restrained to the Eden Brood on Eden.

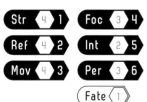
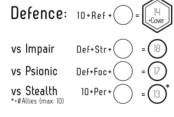
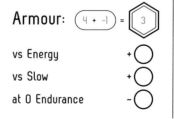

Str	4	1
Ref	4	2
Mov	4	3
Foc	3	4
Int	2	5
Per	3	6
Fate	1	

Defence: 10+Ref+ ◯ = 14 (+Cover)

vs Impair — Def+Str+ ◯ = 18
vs Psionic — Def+Foc+ ◯ = 17
vs Stealth — 10+Per+ ◯ = 13*
*+#Allies (max: 10)

Armour: (4 + -1) = 3

vs Energy + ◯
vs Slow + ◯
at 0 Endurance - ◯

End: 10+(Str x5)+ ◯ = 30

Recovery — Foc + 6 = 9
Stealth (Req: Cover) — 2 + Ref + ◯ = +6
Combat Order — Int + ◯ = 2

Weapon	Hit	End Dmg	Crit	Rng	Clips	Ammo	Load	RoF	Wgt	Type & Variation	Cost
Clawed Hands	+3	4	3	1*	–	–	1	2 (+1d6)	3	Melee, Impairment	3

Bio Tech, Natural, Strong Hit (5-6), No Variations, *Max Range 5, Modifications: Dual Wield (Optional), Personalised.

Race / Var / Trait	Requirements	Benefits	Disadvantages
Beast	NPC	Able to function in thick Jungle Environments.	
Near Immortal	Nemesis NPC	You Die when any Attribute is reduced to -2 (normally -0).	You gain the Bleeding Effect when any Attribute is reduced below 0.
Frenzy	Nephilim	Strong Hit: **Frenzy** (Damage, Hit, First Range Increment or Melee) +1 Armour and Combat Order until your next Turn.	

The All Mother

Length: 46m
Crew Capacity: (Estimated) 0–14
Enemy Type: Spacecraft
Balanced to Fight Players with: 30 Total Influence

"Ancient lore says that the Nephilim had a kind and nurturing mother. I do not think the All Mother is it."

The living spacecraft known as the All Mother was created with an incredibly fast reproductive cycle, allowing her to continuously replenish her supply of attack fighters. This was a great boon during the Great War: even during the most exhausting of battles, the All Mother could replenish her forces with ease.

But when she lost her connection to X'ion, she was en route with hundreds of Nephilim foot troops. Only weeks into her isolation, the All Mother devoured her own crew and passengers in an attempt to satiate her overwhelming hunger and give her the energy she needed to continue her forced reproductive cycle. Once those Nephilim were gone, the All Mother had only her young left on which to feed.

And so the All Mother sails through the galaxy, searching for organic materials to devour in order to avoid eating her young. But when the starvation sets in, the All Mother is quick to eat her own... only to be forced to give birth to more.

Motives

The All Mother roams the galaxy in search of edible material. Unable to land on any planet, she must be satisfied with what she can find floating through space or in the upper atmosphere of a planet. She prefers eating other Feral Nephilim spacecraft, as they are entirely organic and digestible. The All Mother will eat metal craft when she must, sucking all organic material out if it, but this is not preferable.

Tactics

Despite being used as food source, the All Mother's young are fiercely protective of their mother. They will attack as one unit to consummately destroy their foes and bring the remains into the All Mother's gaping maw.

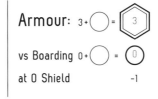

Hul	4	1
Eng	3	2
Cre	3	3

Pow	5	4
CPU	3	5
Sen	2	6

Size ⟨3⟩

Defence: 12-Size+E+ ◯ = ⬡ 12
vs Ordinance — Def+ ② = ⑭
vs Boading — 10+Size+C+ ② = ⑱

Armour: 3+ ◯ = ⬡ 3
vs Boarding — 0+ ◯ = ⓪
at 0 Shield — −1

Shield: 10+(PxSize)+ ◯ = ⬡ 25
Regen — Power + ◯ = ⑤
Weapon Slots — Size + ⟨−1⟩ = ②

Weapon	Hit	Shield Dmg	Crit	Rng	Clips	Ammo	Load	RoF	Mount	Type & Variation	Cost
Sacrificial Child	+3	1	1	1	–	Inf	0	2 (+1d6)	0	Battery, Living Weapon	2
	Full Arc (normally Front and Side), Lock On +2, The first Warhead each Turn that fails an Attack Roll against you is Destroyed.										
	Strong Hit: **Nephilim Horror** (Hit) Apply 1 Boarded Effect to Target.										
Hungry Children	−1	Bodies−1	4	1	–	–	0	Bodies	2	Ordnance, Fighter, Nephilim Swarm	8
	Defence: 14, Armour: 1, Movement: 2, Bodies: 5, Front and Side Arc, Lock On +2, Bio Tech, May Attack during the Turn they are Launched,										
	Modifications: Improved, Large Bay.										

Build / Traits	Requirements	Benefits	Disadvantages
Nephilim		You may make 1 free System Roll each Turn at +0 (no Strong Hits).	
Hanger Bay	Min Hull 4		
Deck Hand		Strong Hit: **Get Back out There!** (Engineering, Success) Rebuild one Fighter Body, this Fighter Body may be Launched instantly.	

Draz

See pg: 139 for a full list of Draz items.

Creator: Nephilim.
Produced and Sold by: Corporation.

Draz is an incredibly addictive and powerful chemical concoction, originally crafted by brilliant Nephilim scientists under contract from the Corporation. Draz was created by the Corporation to be a literal "opiate of the masses." Their goal was to give the people a substance that would not only boost their efficiency, but would also keep them addicted to something they could control. To this end, Draz has performed perfectly.

No single Corporation company has ever convincingly claimed exclusive ownership of Draz. Numerous shell companies, hidden production facilities, and fraudulent product copies exist, which allow these companies to secretly move large quantities of Draz while hiding who truly profits from its sale.

Draz appeals to people from all walks of life and comes in many different forms, but primarily in energy drinks and popular alcoholic beverages.

Draz has greatly affected the economy and ecology of the Haven system. Entire criminal organisations have built themselves around controlling local inventories of Draz products. Addicted pirates find Draz shipments to be irresistible targets and often make desperate attempts to strike at Draz supply caravans. Many shadow wars have been fought over the Draz supply. After all, having an entire city desperately addicted to your product is incredible lucrative.

Note to GMs: Addiction
If a player character consumes a large amount of Draz, have them make a Resolve Skill Roll to resist addiction.

If they do become addicted, they gain the Draz Addict Trait (pg: 345).

Effects of Draz

Draz contains many exotic chemicals and mutagens that work together to affect the body of the user. Based on the amount of Draz ingested, it has different effects.

When taken in small doses, Draz artificially replicates the body's sleep patterns while keeping the user fully awake and cognisant. It produces the same chemical and hormonal effects as sleep, yet does not restore the body as a full night's rest would.

When taken in a large or concentrated dose, Draz pumps the user's body full of exotic, fast-working bio-replication mutagens. While this allows the body to shrug off almost any damage, it chips away at the user's sanity and destroys their brain functions.

After prolonged, intense use of Draz, the user can become incredibly addicted to it. If the user continues to consume Draz after the effects of addiction begin, they start to experience the following side effects:

Light Addiction: A minor addiction to Draz is incredibly expensive to maintain, and going without it can cause intense sensitivity

Chemical Variation	Hit	End Dmg	Crit	Rng	Clips	Ammo	Load	RoF	Wgt	Weapon Type	Cost
Weaponised Draz	+2	+2*	-1*							**	+1***

Bio Tech, *-4 Damage vs Robots, **Chemical Only, No other Chemical Variations.

***Player characters require Secret Knowledge: Draz Production to use this Variation.

Strong Hit: **Draz Dose** (Damage, Hit) Target gains +1 Armour and can only attack the nearest character to them until they receive First Aid. They also loses 1 Spare Time Point (this Effect does not Stack multiple times).

Small Arms Weapons	Hit	End Dmg	Crit	Rng	Clips	Ammo	Load	RoF	Wgt	Weapon Type & Variations	Cost
Junky Pistol	-2	4	3	3	4	6	1	1	1	Gun, Pellets	0

Small, Low Tech, no Variations

Small Arms Weapons	Hit	End Dmg	Crit	Rng	Clips	Ammo	Load	RoF	Wgt	Weapon Type & Variations	Cost
Sawn off Shotgun	+4	8	2	1*	5	2	1	2 (+1d6)	3	Gun, Pellets	2

Splash 1, Low Tech, *Strong Hit (5-6) vs Targets within first Range Increment, no Variations

Resolve Trait	Requirements	Benefits
Experimental Draz	NPC	Strong Hit: **Unpredictable Side Effects** (Damage, Hit) You take 1 Attribute Damage to a random (1d6) Attribute and gain 2 additional Attribute Points to two different and random (2d6) Attributes (may go above your Maximum) until the end of the Combat.
Managed Addict	NPC	You are able to maintain a partially controlled Draz addiction.
	Min Foc 3	Reduce all Attribute Damage you receive by 1 to a minimum of 1.

Brendan felt himself submitting to the craving and blinked his eyes against the harsh light that burned his retinas. The sun seemed incredibly bright this close to sunset, but Brendan assumed it was the Draz messing with his eyesight. He was starting to itch and his throat was burning.

"Soon… just a little longer and the Draz will be mine."

Brendan crouched behind a few stacked crates, watching the entrance to a supposedly abandoned warehouse. But Brendan knew that not all was as it seemed. This particular warehouse was a front the Wu Tia mob used to transport its Draz. Brendan's trigger finger itched. The Draz was so close he could almost taste it. He needed the Draz.

"Why do they have it? Why do they get it and we don't? Why do we have to suffer?"

The thoughts entered his mind suddenly and unceremoniously. But he was now acutely aware of one thing: the Draz inside that warehouse belonged to him, and they were keeping it from him. This thought made Brendan incredibly angry for reasons he couldn't quite explain. Yet the explanation didn't matter to him either. All that mattered was the Draz. Just on the other side of those doors.

Brendan set his jaw and tried to resist. After all, he knew what kind of firepower would be waiting on the other side of those doors.

But they had all the Draz…

Brendan hated them. He hated everyone that had Draz when

he did not. His anger flared and before he knew what was happening he was on his feet, pounding the pavement on a straight line to the doorway. In the back of his mind he knew he shouldn't be doing this, didn't want to be doing this, but he had to do this. He saw red as he rammed his shoulder into the double doors, finding an untapped reservoir of strength that allowed him to snap the locks.

He heard the loud crack of gunfire and was aware of the movements of the men all around him, but his sense pointed to one thing: Draz. There it was… countless containers stacked upon countless containers, all filled with Draz.

He rushed to the nearest container and ripped off the top in one fluid motion. He could feel himself hulking now. Maybe he was even taller than he remembered. The men around him were shouting, and the bullets seemed to be impacting his fleshy body, but Brendan didn't seem to notice or mind. The Draz was in his hands. His fingertips fought with the cap, but he found his body unable to respond. His eyes began to blink and lose focus. Had the floor been this slippery the whole time?

The last thing Brendan saw was the Draz drop from his hands as he fell. The bottle landed in tandem with his body, and both shattered on impact. He feebly reached for the liquid and struggled to wet his fingertips and bring them to his lips. A firm boot on his wrist stopped that motion.

Brendan looked up to his executor and tried to speak, but only one word slipped from his cracked lips. "Draz…"

Then it was over.

to light.

Medium Addiction: As the addiction to Draz increases, so does the user's mental instability. They find themselves in an almost ceaseless rage. Because of this, combined with their increased strength, they begin to easily and freely hurt the people around them.

Complete Addiction: Once a user is wholly dependent on Draz, the drug's bio-replication mutagens morph their physiology. Their body adapts to survive on Draz alone, with no need for any other nourishment. The user's organs become decentralised, spread throughout their entire body, and replaced with a ghoulish grey-blue sludge that keeps the body alive in any situation. The mutant can function without their organs, limbs, or even head.

Researching Draz

Despite its widespread use, the origins and true nature of Draz remain a cultural and scientific mystery.

Origins: No one knows who the true owners of Draz are. Determining their identities or those of the original creators could be very useful, indeed.

Cultural Impact: Many leaders would be quite keen to have an in-depth study on how Draz affects their communities at large.

Effects: What do the Draz bio-replication mutagens really do to a user's system? And how could such powerful regenerative properties be harnessed without the side effects?

Junkie

Average Height: 1.8m
Enemy Type: Henchmen
Balanced to Fight Players with: 1-5 Current Resources

"Can't get enough… Draz… more… Draz… please… I'll do anything…"

The Junkie is a street-level user of Draz. They will do whatever it takes to get their hands on more Draz and to protect their supply. They are often found lurking around Draz factories or supply warehouses.

Easy to bribe, they are often manipulated into acting as enforcers for drug cartels or protecting gang members who deal in Draz. Junkies are fairly easy to deal with, but when they are juiced on Draz they become vicious and extremely tough. But once the Draz wears off they are incredibly vulnerable and will do anything to get more.

Example Encounter (for 5 PCs):
» x1 Cartel Mobster (Assault Rifle).
» x2 Junkie Groups (Crude Sidearm).
» x1 Junkie Group (Crude Club).
» x1 Addicted Animal Group.

Example Loot:
» 1 Pack of Draz per 3 Bodies.
» 1 shot of Street Draz per 6 Bodies.

Addicted Animal

Average Length: 1m
Enemy Type: Henchmen
Balanced to Fight Players with: 6-10 Current Resources

"Watch out boss, something looks off with this mut… ARGHAA!"

Street gangs often perform terrible Draz experiments on the unwilling, taking unsuspecting homeless and turning them into Draz addicts. They even go so far as making stolen pets or stray animals into bloodthirsty Draz-powered beasts.

Animals infected by Draz can't be considered living beings anymore; it is the Draz keeping them alive. Their body and mind mutated into those of a ravenous beast, an infected animal is dangerous even to its owner and will attack anything in sight – unless that thing offers them more Draz. They are incredibly effective at guarding areas, as they can be locked inside a fenced area to keep intruders at bay. However, these beasts need to be replaced often, as the same Draz that empowers their body also kills it.

Example Encounter (for 5 PCs):
» x2 Cartel Mobsters (Submachine Gun).
» x1 Cartel Mobster (Assault Rifle).
» x2 Addicted Animal groups.

Example Loot:
» Often used to defend valuable locations (labs, workshops or cargo).

Junkie (Pick One)	Hit	End Dmg	Crit	Rng	Clips	Ammo	Load	RoF	Type & Variation	Cost	Movement	Defence	Armour	Bodies
Crude Club	+1	4+Bodies*	3	-	-	-	1	1+Bodies	Melee, Hammer	0	3	16	4	3
	Blunt, *Deal +2 Endurance Damage vs Targets with Armour 4 or greater, Modification: Low Quality.													
Crude Sidearm	+3	3+Bodies	2	4	Inf	RoF x5	1	1+Bodies	Gun, Particle	0	3	16	4	3
	Small, Energy, Does not Work in Void.													
	Slots: 5, Defence vs Stealth: 12, Defence vs Impair: 21													
Traits:	Brute													

Addicted Animal	Hit	End Dmg	Crit	Rng	Clips	Ammo	Load	RoF	Type & Variation	Cost	Movement	Defence	Armour	Bodies
Teeth	+2	4+Bodies*	3*	-	-	-	1	1+Bodies	Melee, I, C, Wpn Draz	2	6	16	3	5
	Bio Tech, Natural, Slow, Gain Strong Hit (5-6) if you are behind your Target, *-4 Damage vs Robots													
	Strong Hit: **Draz Dose** (Damage, Hit) Target gains +1 Armour and can only attack the nearest character to them until they receive First Aid. They also loses 1 Spare Time Point (this Effect does not Stack multiple times).													
	Slots: 3, Defence vs Stealth: 12, Defence vs Impair: 19													
Traits:	Critter (Able to function in junkyard Environments)													
	Tackle (Strong Hit: **Tackle** (Melee, Hit) Pick One Debuff vs Target: Prone, Push 1 or reduce all Movement by 2 until your next Turn).													

Cartel Mobster

Average Height: 1.8m
Enemy Type: Skilled
Balanced to Fight Players with: 11-15 Current Resources

"The mobsters run their Draz rings in broad daylight under the eye the Corporation, as if they are setting out a dare. Come and get me, they say. Let's see who draws blood first."

The Draz cartels are the organised face of Draz smuggling and Draz-related crimes. Considered legal in most places, Draz can be purchased mixed into energy and alcoholic drinks. However, the cartels operate in the shadows, regulating the supply and manipulating the prices.

No single cartel rules the market. The cartels compete for market, and smugglers and pirates battle over product and territory. It is incredibly dangerous work, and the cartels hire only the strongest and smartest to be their mobsters.

Most cartel members grew up on the streets as pickpockets and runaways. Their street skills made them great recruits, and rarely does a missing street rat go noticed. The cartels break down these lost children, forcing them to do terrible things in the name of their cartel masters. Out of the dozens recruited, only a few survive to become cartel members. This process fosters a fierce devotion to the cartels, and a mobster is a member of their cartel for life.

Cartel Mobsters rely on bribery, blackmail, and violence to keep local politicians and police organisations under their control, to ensure that Draz is sold only when and where they want it to be.

Motives

The Cartel Mobster will do anything to protect their cartel. They are difficult to reason with and normally cannot be bought off. They carry out the will of their cartel leaders and their main motive is to ensure the health of their organisation.

Tactics

They employ street-gang tactics such as blackmail and sheer force. They tend to fight in groups but aren't afraid to take on an enemy one-on-one if they feel they have enough firepower, or if they feel they are being disrespected.

Example Encounter (for 5 PCs):
» x2 Cartel Mobsters (Assault Rifle).
» x1 Cartel Mobster (Submachine Gun).
» x2 Addicted Animal groups.
» x1 Junkie Group (Crude Sidearm).

Example Loot (per Body):
» 1 shot of Street Draz.
» 1 Clip of Irradiated Ammunition.
» 1 Spare Time Point of Credits per 2 Bodies.

Str	4	1
Ref	3	2
Mov	3	3
Foc	1	4
Int	2	5
Per	1	6
Fate	0	

Defence: 10+Ref+ (2) = 15 +Cover

vs Impair   Def+Str+ ( ) = 19
vs Psionic Def+Foc+ (2) = 18
vs Stealth 10+Per+ ( ) = 11 *
*+#Allies (max: 10)

Armour: (3 + 1) = 4

vs Energy   + ( )
vs Slow   + ( )
at 0 Endurance   - (2)

End: 10+(Str x5)+ ( ) = 30

Recovery   Foc + ( ) = 1
Stealth   2 + Ref + ( ) = +5
Req: Cover
Combat Order   Int + ( ) = 2

Weapon (Pick One)	Hit	End Dmg	Crit	Rng	Clips	Ammo	Load	RoF	Wgt	Type & Variation	Cost
Irradiated Submachine Gun	+5	5	4	4	3	12	1*	3 (+2d6)	1	Gun, Irradiated	4
	Low Tech, *Take 5 Endurance Damage every Action you spend Reloading or Un-Jamming this Weapon										
	Modifications: Advanced Ammo, Extended Clip, Personalised, Telescopic Lens (Your Mind gains +4 Range while this Weapon is Drawn)										
Irradiated Assault Rifle	+5	5	5	4	3	10	2*	2 (+1d6)	2	Gun, Irradiated	4
	Low Tech, *Take 5 Endurance Damage every Action you spend Reloading or Un-Jamming this Weapon										
	Modifications: Extended Clip, Personalised, Telescopic Lens (Your Mind gains +4 Range while this Weapon is Drawn)										

Race / Var / Trait	Requirements	Benefits	Disadvantages
Corporation			
Fierce	Skilled NPC		
Draz Addict	Max Foc 1	Can not be Killed by Mental Attribute (Focus, Intelligence or Perception) Damage.	Sudden bright lights Blind you for 1 Turn.

Ra'ul, Assimilated Bodyguard

Height: 2.2m
Enemy Type: Nemesis
Balanced to Fight Players with: 11-15 Current Resources

"Could this monster be a glimpse of what the original Nephilim creators intended for Draz?"

Ra'ul was the greatest of the Sunset Cartel's manufacturers. Under the cartel's direction he produced a seemingly endless volume of Draz. Ra'ul had a very good thing going for him. The cartel pays its suppliers well, and his operation was protected by their mobsters. He wanted for nothing and had no reason to betray his bosses. Except for greed.

When it was discovered that Ra'ul was skimming off the top and selling under the table to another cartel, the Sunsets were quick to respond and make an example of Ra'ul. Ra'ul became the victim of his own product. The Sunset Cartel pumped his body full of the chemical and drowned him in his own Draz production vats; far beyond a lethal dose.

What remained in the vats when the Draz was finally drained some months later was no longer Ra'ul, but a mindless Draz fueled monster wearing Ra'ul's skin. This creature had been exposed to such a large dose that it had mutated his body, completely decentralising his organs (even his brain).

Having nowhere else to go, Ra'ul fled into the dark sewers to live amongst the junkies. Now, he is but an empty shell. The Draz pumping through his body keeps him alive and in a rage-fuelled stupor.

Tactics

Junkies will commonly follow Ra'ul at a distance, waiting for a chance to scavenge what remains of his victims. Often getting ahead of themselves, these junkies often get caught up in a fight alongside Ra'ul... which often leads to their deaths.

Example Encounter (for 5 PCs):
» x1 Ra'ul.
» x2 Junkie Groups (Crude Sidearm).

Example Loot:
» Ra'uls body is a treasure trove of Draz research material. Gain a +2 to all future Draz Research.

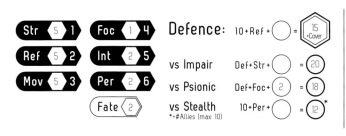

Weapons	Hit	End Dmg	Crit	Rng	Clips	Ammo	Load	RoF	Wgt	Type & Variation	Cost
Clawed Hands	-1	5	6	-	-	-	1	1	4	Melee, Claw	4

Bio Tech, Natural, Slow, Modifications: Master Crafted, Personalised.
Strong Hit: **Massive Bash** (Attack, Hit, Target has less Strength than you) Target is knocked Prone and Pushed 1

Weapons	Hit	End Dmg	Crit	Rng	Clips	Ammo	Load	RoF	Wgt	Type & Variation	Cost
Draz Infected Bite	-1	2*	3*	-	-	-	1	1	2	Melee, Injector, Chemical, Weaponised Draz	1

Bio Tech, Natural, Slow, Gain Strong Hit (5-6) if you are behind your Target, *-4 Damage vs Robots, Modifications: Low Quality, Personalised.
Strong Hit: **Draz Dose** (Damage, Hit) Target gains +1 Armour and can only attack the nearest character to them until they receive First Aid. They also loses 1 Spare Time Point (this Effect does not Stack multiple times).

Race / Var / Trait	Requirements	Benefits	Disadvantages
Beast	NPC	Able to function in chemical lab and sewer Environments.	
Swift	Nemesis NPC	You may take 3 Actions per Turn (normally 2 per Turn).	Reduce all Movement by 2 from your Actions.
Adrenaline Boost	Min Mov 5	You may spend 1 Fate Point to temporarily Heal all Attribute Dmg and gain Str Hit +1 for 1 Turn.	
Draz Addict	Max Foc 1	Can not be Killed by Mental Attribute (Focus, Intelligence or Perception) Damage.	Sudden bright lights Blind you for 1 Turn.

The Bastille

Length: 38m
Crew Capacity: 4-12
Enemy Type: Spacecraft
Balanced to Fight Players with: 19 Total Influence

"They see the Bastille as a beacon, as if by selling their stolen Draz at cut-rate prices they are looking out for those in the sewer. But don't be fooled, they would rather take what little you have and leave you for dead before helping you out of that sewer."

As long as there is Draz, there will be Draz pirates. These pirates strike at the centre of the Cartels and Corporations both, stealing whatever amount of Draz they can get their hands on. Many of these pirate groups are addicted to Draz and often ingest their own supply. The crew of the Bastille are among those that know better.

They run an small pirate empire out of their ship as they roam from planet to planet, making them difficult to track, helpful because almost every police force and bounty hunter in the Haven system wants them brought in. Every member of the crew has a bounty placed on their head, and they are under constant threat of attack… and they would have it no other way.

But to the people, these pirates are the heroes that liberate the Draz from the hands of mobsters and the Corporation. It doesn't matter that the pirates are in it for the money, or that they will be as quick to kill you as to deal with you. They bring Draz at cheaper prices than the rest do, and that is all that matters to most. But don't think you're safe just because you aren't in the Draz business. If you look wealthy, or weak, the Bastille just might set their targets on you.

Motives

The main motive of any pirate is to plunder. Despite prioritising Draz, they will set upon any lucrative or vulnerable target. Despite their noble reputation, they are motivated by money above all.

Tactics

Pirates are generally smart enough to rely on gadgets and electronic tricks to give them an edge. They will use the Bastille's weapons to target their opponent's systems before they move in to board them.

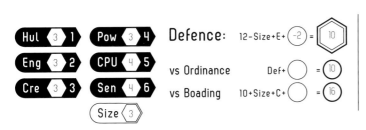

Hul 3 1   Pow 3 4
Eng 3 2   CPU 4 5
Cre 3 3   Sen 4 6
           Size 3

Defence: 12-Size+E+ (-2) = 10
vs Ordinance   Def+ ( ) = 10
vs Boading   10+Size+C+ ( ) = 16

Armour: 3+ ( ) = 3
vs Boarding   0+ ( ) = 0
at 0 Shield   -1

Shield: 10+(PxSize)+ ( ) = 19
Regen   Power + ( ) = 3
Weapon Slots   Size + (-2) = 1

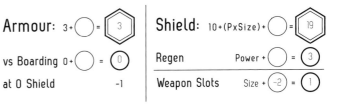

Weapon	Hit	Shield Dmg	Crit	Rng	Clips	Ammo	Load	RoF	Mount	Type & Variation	Cost
Burst	-3	6	4	Sensors	Inf	12	1	4 (+3d6)	2	Battery, Crack	9

Front and Side Arc, Lock On +2, Modifications: x2 Weapon Bank.

Build / Traits	Requirements	Benefits	Disadvantages
Kaltoran		Patch Job System Roll may be successfully rolled twice per Turn (normally once).	On Fire Effect deals 2 Attribute Damage (normally 1) to 2 random Attributes (roll 2x 1d6).
Jump Interdiction	Min Sen 2 Min CPU 3	At the End of your Turn, remove 1 Combat Jump Success from a spacecraft that has the Locked On Effect applied to them. Strong Hit: **Jam System** (Operations, Success) All Locked On Targets have -2 to their Operations Rolls until your next Turn.	
Hunk of Junk	Max Hull 3		

Enforcers

See pg: 203 for a full Corporation Government and Law write-up.
See pg: 214 for a full Kaltoran Government and Law write-up.
See pg: 233 for a full Legion Government and Law write-up.
See pg: 247 for a full Nephilim Government and Law write-up.

Common Motives: Finacial gain, vengence or duty.

Law is a complicated word within the Haven system. Primarily defined by those with enough power to enforce their rules, the law can change at a whim, and the relationship that most citizens have with the law is complicated at best. The best way to ensure compliance is to keep one's head down and not cause a ruckus, but for those who make a living on the fringes of society, avoiding a ruckus is not an option. For them, Haven will never be a safe place.

When one ventures outside one's city boundaries, the definition of law, and even civilisation, becomes much more flexible. However, no matter where one travels, there is a consistency among the methods used to enforce law. There will always be enforcers, those who ensure the laws of their land and the wills of their leaders are being followed. And there will always be mercenaries and bounty hunters, who will hunt down anyone for the right price.

In the wilds of space, a criminal can live a much freer life. There is little law or civilisation out there, so there are few laws that can be broken. However, powerful individuals from civilized places will bring their laws with them. If a pirate sets upon a Corp spacecraft in free space, you can bet that the Corporation will bring to bear the full weight of their Legion mercenaries. And while many enforcers won't venture into the darkest and most dangerous areas of the Haven system, bounty hunters are sure to. Any criminal who thinks that they've escaped into the frontiers or a secluded city slum shouldn't be surprised to find a bounty hunter close behind.

The Haven system is dotted with small settlements struggling to make a living. In these places, the law is determined by whoever has the power to enforce their will, through brute force or social influence. Local sheriffs acts as law-maker and enforcer in one, and strangers to these towns are treated with a wary eye.

Every planet, government, and race has their own version of the law. Some adhere to a strict legal code, like the Legion, and some hold a survival-of-the-fittest mentality, like the Nephilim. What is considered illegal to one may be commonplace to the other. Corporate lawyers have written countless heavy volumes on the difficulties of untangling the nuances of interracial law. If Corporation scientists are on a diplomatic mission to the Legion home world, whose law should they be subject to? If they break a Legion law, should they be tried by the Legion or sent home to be tried by their Corporation leaders? There is no clear answer. Often, whoever has the largest presence or feels they are most in the "right" has final say. This tendency has led to many innocents suffering terrible fates and many criminals walking free. Every situation is fluid, and the accused must think fast and act even faster to avoid sentencing.

When it comes to saying alive in Haven, it's important to know whose territory you are in, as it is to know which mob boss has the weaponry to back up their threats.

Fines
Small to medium fines can be paid with a
Wealth Spare Time Roll.

Usually a roll of 12t or 14t.
Expensive fines can cost a Resource.

Imprisonment
Usually done to hold a suspect until final sentencing.
Guarded steel cages are the most common form of
imprisonment, as they are cheap and easy to make.

Death
A very common sentence in the frontiers of Haven,
as it is cheap to administer and uncomplicated.
When a suspect is also a stranger, they will often be
executed without public knowledge.

Traits	Requirements	Benefits	Disadvantages
Local Friends	NPC	If you are killed or hurt other NPCs will seek revenge for you.	
		All Allies gain +1 Hit and End Dmg (may only Stack twice).	
Only Capture	NPC	All of your Weapons gain the Keyword: Blunt.	You only wish to capture your opponents.
		+2 Hit & End Dmg, all Weapons.	You will try to retreat if you are heavily hurt.
Reinforcements	Skilled NPC	For each Turn you are off the Battle Map gain +2 Hit & End Dmg.	You may only enter the Battle Map and Attack after Turn 1, you may stay off longer.
Security System	NPC	You may be a Robot.	You may only Attack Targets within a limited area or Arc.
		+1 Armour.	
		Reduce all Damage to your Movement by 2.	You may not change your facing.

Forms of Law Enforcement

Knowing whose territory you are in means knowing how to keep your head on your shoulders. Laws differ vastly from culture to culture, as do the punishments for breaking those laws.

Corporation: At its core, Corporation law is deceptively simple: if you cost the Corp money, they will fine you. If these fines go unpaid, they are doubled in value and used to apply a dead-or-alive bounty on the accused.

Teams of Corporation security contractors work in secret to enforce Corporate laws. They can trace an offender's digital signature, hack their computers and spacecraft systems, and track them throughout the Haven system. These Corporate security teams work from the shadows, often remotely, so their suspects don't know they are coming. Their eyes and ears come in the form of numerous drones that patrol Corporation cities and facilities.

If a Corporate security team is not enough to bring in the suspect, Legion mercenary forces will be sent in. If the criminal still manages to escape, the Corporation leverages their over-abundance of available funds to attract the best bounty hunters and procure sensitive data.

But at every step, the Corporation will weigh up the cost and benefit of enforcement, dropping all charges if they do not make financial sense.

Kaltoran: Kaltoran law is the least formal. Every Kaltoran is well armed, even the elderly. They are all expected to enforce justice, not only against wrongs done to them, but also those done to people they know, especially family.

As a close-knit, well-armed, and enthusiastic people, Kaltoran justice is often swift. Families forgive minor infractions, but act with brutal judgement against any major transgressions. Complex or disputed problems are handled by the family Elders. Kaltoran family units will often form posses, and publicly execute those who have wronged them.

The Legion: As the only society within Haven to have a substantial government, the Legion's judicial system is comprehensive and efficient — at least for those within their own society.

For those who live outside of the Legion influence, things become more difficult. The Legion tend to have little faith in the judicial systems of the other Haven cultures, so they often take it upon themselves to enforce Legion law and values wherever they happen to be. For crimes deemed severe enough, punishments can include imprisonment, deportation, travel restriction, forced labour, or execution.

The dust had barely settled in the middle of the street of the frontier town. The boy ran, as he had been told to do. The Kaltorans who followed him made a game of it. This was part of the boy's punishment. He had crossed his own Kaltoran family by killing, and the family wasn't going to forget it.

The Kaltorans followed behind in a hovertruck, whooping and hollering as they closed in. They brandished their weapons and put on displays of machismo from the back of the truck. The noise of the posse had drawn quite a crowd in the square. Mothers covered the eyes of their children as the criminal realised he had nowhere left to go.

Every exit from the square was blocked by members of the Kalotran posse. They grinned toothy grins and shouted profanities to the boy, who was forced to run back into the centre of the square.

The eldest of the family, the patriarch, stepped down from the back of the truck, tightening a long piece of monofilament rope between his fingers.

"For your crimes against our family," the patriarch spoke as he approached the quivering boy, "you have been found guilty."

The rest of the family swarmed the boy, grabbing him by the arms and legs, restraining him and leading him towards the patriarch. The elder continued, handing the rope to his family, watching them wrap the rope around the victim's neck.

"This is your judgement. For your crime of murder against your own family, you will hang from the neck until dead."

There were few things that could draw the attention of a Kaltoran crowd like a hanging. As the criminal's limp body swung in the wind, the rest of the Kaltorans would know that justice had been served.

Nephilim: The Nephilim follow only one law: survival of the fittest. Life is cheap and only the powerful have the strength to force their will onto others. The weak are ignored and the strong rule. Crossing a stronger Nephilim is the closest one can come to breaking a law, and this is universally met with violence, dealt out by the offended Nephilim or by the enforcers it keeps at its side.

"Vex" Corp Security Drone

Average Height: 1.4m
Enemy Type: Henchmen
Balanced to Fight Players with: 1-5 Current Resources

"Security drones, eh? Well, good luck with that."

The Corp L2T-VX, or "Vex," Synth Steel drone is a common sight in wealthy Corporation facilities. They were built to be the perfect guards, with no need to eat, rest, or take breaks. They cannot be reasoned with, bribed, manipulated, or tricked. The only way past a Vex without the right security clearance is by force. They are ever vigilant and wield their particle pistols with deadly accuracy. They act as the first line of defence for important Corporation buildings and often protect high-ranking VIPs. They can also be summoned at the push of a button to take down local targets.

Their primary weakness is their inability to travel far from their central control station. This makes them perfectly suitable for defending installations, but unsuitable for long-range missions.

Example Encounter (for 5 PCs):
» x2 Vex Corp Security Drone groups.
» x1 X4000 Personal Alarm Drone group.
» x2 Legion Mercenaries.

Example Loot:
» 1 Trade Box of salvaged Mechanical Drone Parts per 6 Bodies.
» 1 Trade Box of Small Weapons per 8 Bodies.
» 1 Particle Pistol per Body.

Corp X4000 Personal Alarm Drone

Average Height: 0.25m
Enemy Type: Henchmen
Balanced to Fight Players with: 1-5 Current Resources

"Dammit, you've been spotted. Pull back, there's nothing you can do now."

The inexpensive X4000 Personal Alarm Drone is one of the Corporation security contractor's most useful gadgets. This hovering drone can be programmed with basic instructions, such as following a target, guarding a room, or keeping watch over a sleeping VIP. The drone is equipped with a high-functioning tactical camera that records and photographs images to send directly back to a mainframe.

Once a Drone has set their camera on something, it's built in alarms trigger (either silently or blaringly loud), and the closest security forces are sent to that location. These drones will often swarm in large numbers to give comprehensive real time tactical feedback on the entire environment, giving security forces a full picture of every corner, entrance, and person in that area.

Example Encounter (for 5 PCs):
» x2 X4000 Personal Alarm Drone groups.
» x3 Legion Mercenaries.

Example Loot:
» 1 Trade Box of salvaged Mechanical Drone Parts per 20 Bodies.
» 1 Trade Box of Sensor Equipment per 5 Bodies (Electronics Skill Roll of 14 required).

Vex	Hit	End Dmg	Crit	Rng	Clips	Ammo	Load	RoF	Type & Variation	Cost	Movement	Defence	Armour	Bodies
Protectron	+3	3+Bodies	2	4	Inf	RoF x5	1	1+Bodies	Gun, Particle	0	4	16	3	4
	Lock On +2, Small, Energy, Jam (1-5), Does not Work in Void.													
	Slots: 3, Defence vs Stealth: 12, Defence vs Impair: 19													
Traits:	Droid Body (You are a Robot), Covering Fire (Str Hit: **Covering Fire** (Damage, Does not Require Hit, RoF 2+) 1 Ally gains Heavy Cover (+4) or +1 Cover Step until your next Turn).													

Corp X4000	Hit	End Dmg	Crit	Rng	Clips	Ammo	Load	RoF	Type & Variation	Cost	Movement	Defence	Armour	Bodies
Security Camera	+2	-	-	2	Inf	10	2	1+Bodies	Combat Computer	1	4	16	2	4
	Lock On +4, Strong Hit (5-6), Modification: Low Quality, Laser Sight.													
	Strong Hit: **Target Lock** (Hit) Target is Locked On.													
	Strong Hit: **Weak Spot** (Hit, Locked On) Until your next Turn, Boost all Attacks against Target: Endurance Damage +1.													
	Strong Hit: **Plot Trajectory** (Hit, Locked On) Until your next Turn, Boost all Attacks against Target: Range +1.													
	Strong Hit: **Tactical Scan** (Hit, Locked On) Until your next Turn, Debuff Target: -1 Cover Step (minimum Light Cover).													
	Slots: 3, Defence vs Stealth: 12, Defence vs Impair: 19													
Traits:	Droid Body (You are a Robot), Sure Footed (No Defence or Movement penalties from Difficult Terrain (including Zero Gravity) by Hovering).													

Legion Mercenary

Average Height: 2.4m
Enemy Type: Skilled
Balanced to Fight Players with: 6–10 Current Resources

"Just got the word: the Legion mercs have been called in. You're fragged, man, I'm sorry."

The Legion produce some of the greatest fighters and toughest killers the galaxy has ever seen. Created for battle in the Great X'ion War, the Legion have found new ways to use their their warrior instincts, marketing themselves as hired guns and enforcers.

Many Legion find sanctioned mercenary work within their high command as Auxilia soldiers. However, innumerable others act outside that command as exiled Exsilia freelancers.

The Corporation is by far the largest employer of Legion mercenaries, so much so that many mistakenly assume that all Legion work for them. Legion mercenaries are often the first and last line of Corporation physical defence, acting as both a patrolling police force and personal army.

Exsilia that don't contract with the Corporation often find themselves taking on any job that will pay the bills and let them put their military skills into practice. Wherever they happen to be encountered, Legion mercenaries provide an incredible obstacle. When the Legion appear on the scene, less-skilled criminals will simply turn tail and run. While these mercenaries may be found using any equipment that they can scrounge up or afford, most Legion prefer to use weapons and armour crafted and maintained by their own people.

Motives
Combat glory, duty, financial gain, and pride.

Tactics
Legion mercenaries favour a tactical military approach to combat. Making heavy use of cover, flanking, teamwork, and concentrated firepower.

Example Encounter (for 5 PCs):
» x2 Vex Corp Security Drone groups.
» x3 Legion Mercenaries.

Example Loot:
» 1 Trade Box of Illegal (x2 Resources) salvaged Legion Armour per 2 Bodies.
» 1 Trade Box of Weapons per 2 Bodies.
» 1 Gauss or Rail Clip of Ammunition per Body.
» 1 Gauss or Rail Rifle per Body.

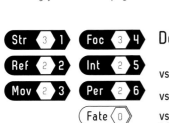

Str	3	1
Ref	2	2
Mov	2	3

Foc	3	4
Int	2	5
Per	2	6

Fate 0

Defence: 10+Ref+ ( ) = 12 +Cover

vs Impair   Def+Str+ (2) = 17
vs Psionic   Def+Foc+ ( ) = 15
vs Stealth   10+Per+ ( ) = 12*
*+#Allies (max: 10)

Armour: (3 + 1) = 4

vs Energy   + ( )
vs Slow   + ( )
at 0 Endurance − (1)

End: 10+(Str x5)+ ( ) = 25

Recovery   Foc + ( ) = (3)
Stealth   2 + Ref + ( ) = (+4)
Req: Cover
Combat Order Int + ( ) = (2)

Weapon	Hit	End Dmg	Crit	Rng	Clips	Ammo	Load	RoF	Wgt	Type & Variation	Cost
Rail Gun	+4	3	5	6	2	3	3	1*	2	Gun, Rail	3
		Lock On +4, Jam (1–5), *Strong Hit (5–6) with all RoF 1 Attack Rolls, Modifications: Personalised, Targeting Matrix.									
Anti Personnel Grenade	+2	8	4	1	2	1	1	1	1	Shell, Thrown, Shrapnel	1
		Splash 3, Small, Low Tech, Slow.									

Race / Var / Trait	Requirements	Benefits
Legion		
Well Prepared	Skilled NPC	
Coordinated Strike	Legion	Strong Hit: **Coordinated Strike** (Attack, Hit) An Ally gains Strong Hit +1 vs your Target with their next Attack (must be taken within 1 Turn).

Sarah "The Countess" Jinx, Kaltoran Bounty Hunter

Height: 1.6m
Enemy Type: Nemesis
Balanced to Fight Players with: 6-10 Current Resources

"You can run from me, little man. But you cannot hide. I will find you, I will bring you in, and I will get paid. It's what I do, and no one does it better."

Kaltorans have the unique ability to use their ancestor's memories as their own, using their myriad skills and knowledge gathered over many lifetimes. This can be incredibly helpful for a bounty hunter who comes from a long line of warriors and hunters.

Sarah Jinx is only the most recent in a long line of fabled hunters to come from her family. Left alone at a young age after losing her mother to a vicious attack from roving Dark Tribe bandits, Sarah was forced to take care of herself and make a living on the dirty streets of her pit city. She quickly made a name for herself as a skilled fighter, tracker, and bounty hunter.

She has no patience for banditry or violence against women, and takes a special pleasure in taking on assignments to avenge wronged women. In the face of every target she sees the ones who murdered her mother. She is extremely dangerous, incredibly

skilled, and takes her job very seriously. The pit city locals have taken to calling her "The Countess" because she scratches a small tick mark onto her gun for every bandit she kills.

Motives
Financial gain, revenge, and survival.

Tactics
Sarah is patient and cunning. She prefers to study her target, find their weaknesses, and set a trap. Once combat starts, Sarah will focus her fire on the most dangerous and isolated targets and will not hesitate to fall back as needed.

Example Encounter (for 5 PCs):
» x2 Skilled Kaltorans.
» x1 Sarah Jinx.

Loot:
» 1 Self-Propelled Assault Rifle.
» 1 Self-Propelled Pistol.
» 2 Spare Time Points of Credits.

Str	3	1
Ref	4	2
Mov	4	3
Foc	3	4
Int	3	5
Per	3	6
Fate	3	

Defence: 10+Ref+ ( ) = 14 +Cover

vs Impair	Def+Str+ ( ) =	17
vs Psionic	Def+Foc+ ( ) =	17
vs Stealth	10+Per+ (2) =	15*

*+#Allies (max: 10)

Armour: (4 + -1) = 3

vs Energy	+ ( )
vs Slow	+ ( )
at 0 Endurance	– ( )

End: 10+(Str x5)+ ( ) = 25

Recovery	Foc + (-2) =	1
Stealth Req: Cover	2 + Ref + ( ) =	+6
Combat Order	Int + ( ) =	3

Weapon	Hit	End Dmg	Crit	Rng	Clips	Ammo	Load	RoF	Wgt	Type & Variation	Cost
Assault Rifle	+7	4	4	6	3	8	2	2 (+1d6)	3	Gun, Self-Propelled	3
	Low Tech, Works in Liquid, Modifications: Advanced Ammo, Laser Sight, Personalised.										
Arc Fire, Bayonet	-2	4	3	-	-	-	2*	1	-	Melee, Arc Fire, Bayonet	1
	Energy, Burn, Pen 2 min 3, *Drawn with Assault Rifle (0 Hands for this Weapon), Stealth -2.										
Disruptor Grenade		8	3*	1	1	1	1	1	1	Thrown, Disruptor	1
	Splash 1, Small, Slow, Energy, Blunt, Strong Hit (5-6) *+2 Crit Dmg vs Robots,										
	Strong Hit: **Disrupt** (Attack, Hit) Debuff ALL Damaged Targets Active Non Low Tech, Non Bio Tech Weapons: Lose Ammunition equal to RoF.										

Race / Var / Trait	Requirements	Benefits
Kaltoran		Reduce all Limited Vision and Low Light penalties by 1 Step.
Master Assassin	Nemesis NPC	You always have Light Cover (+2) (and may Stealth and gain bonus Cover Steps).
		Strong Hit: **Assassinate** (Damage, Hit, Target is at least 3 spaces away from all non Drone Allies) Target is Suppressed and takes 2 Attribute Damage (no Armour) to a random Attribute (1d6).
Thrifty		
Dirty Fighter	Kaltoran	Gain Strong Hit +1 during Surprise Rounds, vs Prone or Suppressed Targets.

The Bloody Falcon, Legion Mercenary Bomber

Average Length: 43m
Crew Capacity: 3-12
Enemy Type: Spacecraft
Balanced to Fight Players with: 42 Total Influence

"When the sky turns red, and the wings of the Bloody Falcon descend upon you, it is far too late for hope."

The Red Phalanx is one of the most well-known and organised Legion Auxilia mercenary teams in the known galaxy. They are worth every Credit of their exorbitant contracts and can almost single-handedly turn the tide of a battle.

While the members of the Red Phalanx change over time, their spacecraft has stayed the same. The Bloody Falcon is one of the fastest, most aggressive ships to soar through the skies today. Built during the Great War to carry Legion commanders into battle, it was supposedly lost in a battle near the end of the war. In reality, the first members of the Red Phalanx ran off with it, repaired it, and made it their own.

The Bloody Flacon is armed with incredible weaponry, including heavy ordnance missiles that can chew through other ships and defensive structures alike. Its point-defence gun system keeps it protected in ship-to-ship battles and can shoot down missiles before they ever reach it.

The ship may seem unbeatable, but a ship is only as good as its crew. If the Legion mercenaries are compromised, then the Bloody Falcon would be as well.

Motives
Combat glory and duty.

Tactics
The Bloody Falcon is fast and has a heavy missile armament. Its signature move is to hit its target fast and early, hoping to cripple it so that the Falcon can take its time to safely strafe the enemy.

Hul	3	1
Eng	5	2
Cre	3	3

Pow	3	4
CPU	3	5
Sen	3	6

Size ⟨ 3 ⟩

Defence: 12−Size+E+ (2) = ⬡ 16

vs Ordinance Def+ (2) = (18)
vs Boading 10+Size+C+ ( ) = (16)

Armour: 3+ ( ) = ⬡ 3

vs Boarding 0+ ( ) = (0)
at 0 Shield −1

Shield: 10+(PxSize)+ ( ) = ⬡ 19

Regen Power + ( ) = (3)
Weapon Slots Size + ( ) = (3)

Weapon	Hit	Shield Dmg	Crit	Rng	Clips	Ammo	Load	RoF	Mount	Type & Variation	Cost
Point Defence	+5	1	2	1	–	Inf	0	2 (+1d6)	0	Battery, Crack	2
	Full Arc (normally Front and Side), Lock On +3, The first Warhead each Turn that fails an Attack Roll against you is Destroyed										
Missile	+1	4	4	–	–	–	0	1	1	Ordnance, Warhead, Explosive	5
	Defence: 16, Armour: 1, Movement: 6, Bodies: 6, Front Arc (normally Front and Side), Lock On +1, Strong Hit (5-6), Modification: Improved.										
Missile	+1	4	4	–	–	–	0	1	1	Ordnance, Warhead, Explosive	5
	Defence: 16, Armour: 1, Movement: 6, Bodies: 6, Front Arc (normally Front and Side), Lock On +1, Strong Hit (5-6), Modification: Improved.										

Build / Traits	Requirements	Benefits
Legion		On Fire Effect deals Damage at the end of your Turn (normally at the start).
Wrap Shield	Max Pow 3	
Auto Targeter	Min CPU 3	Calibrate may apply 2 Locked On Effects per Success (normally 1).
Hull Breach		+1 Engineering.
		Strong Hit: Hull Breach (Warhead, Hit, 1 use per RoF) Until your Target Successfully performs a Damage Control System Roll: They take 1 Crew Damage (no Armour), lose 1 On Fire Effect and lose 1 Boarded Effect at the start of each of their Turns.
Tweak Trajectory		Strong Hit: Tweak Trajectory (Operations, Success) Move one of your spacecraft's Warheads or Fighter Bodies, 2 in any direction.

Character Lists

Race (Must Select 1)

Race	Requirements	Benefits	Disadvantages
Corporation		+2 Maximum Resources and Influence.	−1 Fate.
		Gain 1 Resource and Influence.	−2 Maximum Strength.
		+1 Wealth, Operations, and Tactical.	Complication: Prejudice from Kaltorans.
Kaltoran		Reduce all Untrained Primary Skill Roll penalties by 1 (except Wealth).	−1 Wealth.
		+1 Awareness, Command, and Small Arms.	−2 Maximum Focus.
		+1 Fate.	Unwanted Flashback: If you roll triples with any
		+2 Defence vs Stealth.	Fate re-roll, you immediately gain a Minor
		Reduce all Limited Vision and Low Light penalties by 1 Step.	Psychological Condition (which may be
		Gain Language: Kaltoran.	removed with an appropriate Extended Care
			Healing Roll).
			Complication: Prejudice from Corporation.
Legion		+1 Resolve, Gunnery, and Heavy Arms.	Requires 'Environmental Outfit or Equipment:
		+1 Armour.	Temperate' (NPCs are assumed to have one
		+2 Defence vs Impair.	of these) outside Arctic Environments or be
		Never requires 'Environmental Outfit or Equipment: Arctic'.	Suppressed each Turn.
		Gain Language: Legion.	−1 Armour when at 0 Endurance.
			−2 Maximum Movement.
Nephilim		+1 Bio Tech, Engineering, and Exotic.	−1 Conversation.
		+1 to all Spare Time Rolls.	−2 Culture.
		+1 Recovery.	Complication: Prejudice from Kaltorans and Legion.
		Gain Language: High X'ion or Primal X'ion.	
Remnant		(data missing)	
Palantor		(data missing)	
Twi-Far		(data missing)	
Zhou		(data missing)	

NPC Race	Requirements	Benefits
Beast	NPC	You count as having the Nephilim Race for Trait Requirements.
	Max Int 3	Any of your Weapons may gain the Keywords: Bio Tech and Natural.
		You are able to function in a specific hostile environment.
		−1 Load, all Weapons.
Droid		You are a Robot.
	NPC	−2 Draw, all Weapons.
		All Weapons gain Keyword: Natural.
		Lock On +2, all Weapons.
Mechonid		You are a Robot.
	NPC	−2 Draw, all Weapons
		All Weapons gain Keyword: Natural.
		At the start of your Turn, deal 2 (5 if you are a Nemesis NPC) radiation Endurance Damage to all non Robot characters within 30 Spaces of you.
NPC Nephilim	NPC	+1 Hit, Exotic.
		+1 Recovery.
		+2 End Dmg, all Weapons.
		Gain Language: High X'ion or Primal X'ion.

Level Traits

Level	Requirements	Benefits	Disadvantages
Accomplished	Min Inf 6	Gain a Moderate Perk.	
Forethought		Gain 2 additional Fate Points each session to activate abilities or equipment. These Fate Points may not be used for re-rolls.	
Gifted		+1 to any Attribute.	-1 Maximum to all Attributes.
Lucky	Min Fate 2	You may use your Fate re-rolls to re-roll a single die (normally all rolled dice).	
Talented		Remove all Trait Attribute Maximum Disadvantages.	
Thinker	Min Int 3	Select one additional Skill to be Trained in.	

Fate Traits

Fate	Requirements	Benefits	Disadvantages
Adept		You may spend 1 Fate Point to add an additional 1d6 to any Skill, Attack, System, Healing or Repair Roll (not Spare Time Roll).	
All or Nothing		+2 to all re-rolls. If you re-roll an Attack Roll, add +2 Endurance Damage to that Attack.	If you fail a re-roll you may not spend any more Fate Points this session.
Eureka!		Strong Hit: Eureka! (Failed Spare Time Roll) Gain a Research Unit in any field that you have 8 or less Research Units in.	
Hero	Major Reputation	You may spend 2 Fate Points to gain Strong Hit +1 on any Attack or System Roll. +2 Maximum Influence.	NPCs easily remember you. You lose Influence more easily (as people have high expectations of you).
Just Won't Die	Min Fate 2	+1 Armour when at 0 Endurance.	
Reliable		+1 Recovery. You may choose to make any Spare Time Roll a total of 10 + modifiers (normally 3d6 + modifiers). Not for Research or Trade Spare Time Rolls.	
Void Touched	Min Fate 2	You may spend 2 Fate Points to force an NPC to re-roll any roll. All (non spacecraft) NPCs that Attack you gain the Keyword: Jam (1-4).	Your eyes glow slightly. NPCs easily remember you. Fate re-rolls cost you 2 Fate Points (normally 1).

Resource Traits

Resources	Requirements	Benefits		Disadvantages
Debt	Min Res 7	Gain 3 Resources.		Do not gain 1 free Spare Time Point per session.
	Not NPC	+2 Maximum Resources.		Cost 3 Resources to Retro this Trait or gain Complication: Hunted.
Extravagant	Min Res 4	At any time you may reduce your Current Influence by 2, to gain 1 Resource.		-1 Maximum Influence.
	or NPC	+1 Maximum Resource.		
		If you are a NPC, gain 1 Resource.		
Investor	Min Inf 4	At any time you may reduce your Current Resources by 1, to gain 1 Influence.		
		+4 Maximum Influence.		
		+1 Wealth.		
Merchant	Min Res 4	Once per session you may sacrifice 1 Resource or Influence to gain 2 Spare Time Points.		
		+1 Wealth.		
Scavenger		You are able to use looted Equipment past 1 session, until they have 0 Ammunition (GM Discretion).	-1 Maximum Resources.	
		Equipment with infinite Ammunition or Clips should be discarded within 2 sessions.		
Thrifty		Reduce the Cost of two Cost 1 Resource items to Cost 0.		
Wealthy	Min Res 10	You may make 1 free Wealth Spare Time Roll per session.		
		A spacecraft that you have spent Influence on; gains +1 spacecraft Perk.		

Influence Traits

Influence	Requirements	Benefits		Disadvantages
Birthright	Char Creation	Gain Moderate Perk: Reputation, important family.		Complication: Rival family or group
	Not Corporation	+2 Maximum Influence.		
Mercenary		Perks are gained by increasing your Current Resources (not Influence).		Complications are not gained by increasing your Current Resources (not Influence).
		+2 Maximum Resources.		-2 Maximum Influence.
My Baby	Min Inf 5	If you are the sole Influence contributor to a spacecraft that is Size 2 or under it Costs 10 fewer Influence.		If you are an NPC, your spacecraft may have a maximum of 1 character (normally unlimited).
Outcast	GM Approval	+5 Endurance.		Complication: Bad reputation.
		+1 Fate.		-4 Maximum Influence.
Well Connected	Min Inf 5	+1 Culture.		NPCs gain +2 all attempts to find you through social methods (eg: asking people where you are).
		Gain two Minor Perks: Contact.		

Example Minor Perks

Name	Description
Language	Ancient Kaltoran, Archon, Corp, High X'ion, Primal X'ion, Kaltoran, Legion (and Hand Signal), Vargartian.
Minor Access	1 Cargo space.
Minor Contact	Once per session, +1 to a specific Spare Time Roll Skill.
Minor Rank	One Companion costs you 1 fewer Resource.

Example Moderate Perks

Name	Description
Additional Income	+1 Maximum Resources.
Moderate Access	3 Cargo space.
Moderate Contact	Twice per session, +1 to a specific Spare Time Roll Skill.
Moderate Rank	Requires Minor Rank, all Companions gain +2 Hit.

Example Major Perks

Name	Description
Major Access	4 Cargo space and a Dedicated Workshop.
Destiny	+1 Fate.
Major Contact	+2 Maximum Influence, +2 to all Spare Time and Skills Rolls when making use of your Contact.
Major Rank	Requires Moderate Rank, all Companions gain +1 Body OR a single Companion gains +2 Bodies.

Example Complications

Name	Description
Enemy	Your enemy is aware of your equipment, strengths and weaknesses.
Bounty	Your GM may choose to increase the difficulty of a Combat by an additional Skilled opponent.
Prejudice	-2 to all Leadership, Conversation and Spare Time Rolls when interacting with someone who is prejudiced against you.
Reputation	NPCs are far more likely to remember you.
	You may have -2 to Leadership, Conversation and Spare Time Rolls when interacting with someone who is aware of your Reputation.
Condition	With GM permission, gain a Psychological Condition (pg: 76).

Attribute Traits

Strength	Requirements	Benefits	Disadvantages
Old	Max Str 3	+1 Leadership and Survival.	−1 Physical.
	Char Creation	+4 Maximum Influence.	−2 Equipment Slots.
		Gain 2 Influence.	
Extra Limbs	Nephilim,	You have up to 2 additional (arm and/or hand equivalent) limbs.	Must select at character creation or through Surgery.
	Palantor,	May acquire the Dual Wield Modification twice for a 1 Handed (Weight 1) Weapon OR you may	
	Zhou or NPC	acquire the Dual Wield Modification once for a 2 Handed (Weight 2+) Weapon.	
Natural Armour	Nephilim	Your Outfit is a part of your body and can not be removed!	Must select at character creation or through Surgery.
	or Palantor	Your Outfit gains the Keyword: Bio Tech.	−2 Equipment Slots.
	Not NPC	Your Outfit has −1 Weight and Cost.	
Eye Candy	Min Str 2	Perk: You are sexy!	NPC easily remember you.
		+2 to all Conversation and Leadership Skill re-rolls.	
		+2 Maximum Influence.	
Muscular Implants	Min Str 3	+1 Physical.	−2 Armour when at 0 Endurance.
		+1 Armour.	Must select at character creation or through Surgery.
Massive	Min Str 4	You are big!	
	Legion or	+1 Physical.	
	Nephilim	All equipment has −1 Weight (minimum 1).	
	Char Creation	+2 Equipment Slots.	
Regen Splice	Min Str 5*	You may spend 1 Fate Point to Heal any single Attribute by 2.	−1 Armour when at 0 Endurance.
	Not Legion	*If you are a Remnant, you require Min Foc 4, not Min Str 5.	Must select at character creation or through Surgery.

Reflexes	Requirements	Benefits	Disadvantages
Solid Build	Max Ref 1	+4 Defence vs Impair.	−1 Armour vs Slow.
		+5 Endurance.	
Dexterous	Armour 0-3	+1 Physical.	
	or NPC	All non Drone Weapons have −1 Load (minimum 1) for you.	
Ambidexterity	Min Ref 2	Dual Wield Weapon Modifications allow you to select 2 different Gun, Melee, Shell or Chemical	
		Variations (normally restricted to 1). OR gain +1 Clips.	
		If you have two (or more) 1 Handed (normally Weight 1) Weapons Equipped, they gain +2 Hit.	
Agile Build	Min Ref 3	+1 Physical.	
	Armour 0-3	+1 Stealth.	
		+1 Armour vs Slow.	
Reaction Implants	Min Ref 4	+1 Stealth.	−1 Armour when at 0 Endurance.
	Armour 0-3	+1 to all Trained Personal Combat Skills.	Must select at character creation or through Surgery.
		+2 Combat Order.	
Lighting Reflexes	Min Ref 5	+1 Physical.	
	Armour 0-3	You may spend 2 Fate Points to gain 1 Free Action during your Turn.	
		+1 Armour vs Slow.	

Movement	Requirements	Benefits	Disadvantages
Slow and Steady	Max Mov 2	All Actions gain the Major Effect: Move.	May not use Full Move or Charge Actions.
		Spray Fire and Strike Actions do not reduce your Movement.	
Sure Footed		No Defence or Movement penalties from Difficult Terrain (including Zero Gravity).	
		+2 Defence vs Impair.	
Speed Implant	Min Mov 2	+2 Movement with Full Move and Charge Action.	−1 Armour when at 0 Endurance.
			Must select at character creation or through Surgery.
Wall Runner	Min Mov 3	You may spend 1 Fate Point to ignore all difficult Terrain penalties and be able to move	
	Armour 0-3	along walls and upside down for a single Turn.	
		+1 Armour vs Slow.	
Mirage	Min Mov 4	Strong Hit: **Mirage** (Attack, Does not Require Hit) Make a free Stealth Action and Minor Effect: Move −2.	
Adrenaline Boost	Min Mov 5	You may spend 1 Fate Point to temporarily Heal all Attribute Damage and gain Strong Hit +1	
		until the start of your next Turn.	

Focus	Requirements	Benefits	Disadvantages
Draz Addict	Max Foc 1	+1 Armour.	Gain Complication: Addicted to Draz.
		+2 Defence vs Psionics.	Sudden bright lights Blind you for 1 Turn.
		Can not be Killed by Mental Attribute (Focus, Intelligence or Perception) Damage.	-2 to all Spare Time Rolls.
			-2 Wealth.
			If you are an NPC: -2 Armour at 0 Endurance.
Creative	Max Foc 1	Remove all Requirements (except for 'Does not Req Success') from Strong Hit: Effort.	
		Strong Hit: Effort gains Requirement: Does not Req Hit.	
Rage	Max Foc 2	+1 Crit Dmg vs Targets that have caused you Attribute Damage this Combat.	-1 Cover Step.
		+2 End Dmg vs Targets you have a prejudice against.	Complication: You are prone to becoming enraged.
Self Control	Min Foc 3	+1 Resolve.	
		+2 Hit, Natural.	
		+2 Recovery.	
		20 maximum unspent Spare Time Points (normally 10).	
Expert	Min Foc 4	You may immediately select and take a second Trait for one of your Trained Primary Skills.	
	Secret Kn	Skill Roll bonuses from your second Trait do not Stack with Skill Roll bonuses from	
		your first Trait.	
Focus Implant	Min Foc 5	+1 Resolve.	-1 Armour when at 0 Endurance.
	Not Remnant	If you perform the same Action twice in 1 Turn, you gain Strong Hit +1 for your second Action.	Must select at character creation or through Surgery.

Intelligence	Requirements	Benefits	Disadvantages
Neural Implant		You have a Computer and Short Range Comms (100km range) in your head (0 space).	-1 Armour when at 0 Endurance.
		Hitting with the Analyse Action automatically applies the Locked On Effect to your Target.	You count as a Robot for Strong Hit: Hack
		Your Mind gains Weapon Type: Combat Computer.	and Domination.
		You have a Weight 0, Programing Toolbox (+1 to Programing (does not Stack)).	Must select at character creation or through Surgery.
Introvert		+1 to all Trained Professional Skills.	May not be Assisted by other characters.
		+1 Hit, Analytical.	
Analytical	Min Int 2	+2 Range, Analytical and Combat Computer.	
		+1 Armour vs Slow.	
Natural Psion	Min Int 3	You are a Psionic.	
	Max Foc 2	Gain Language: Telepathy.	
		Your Mind gains Weapon Type: Psionic.	
		+4 Range, Mind.	
		Strong Hit: Glimpse (Attack, Hit, Psionic) Gain +1 Hit for the remainder of the Combat.	
Insight	Min Int 4	Strong Hit: Insight (Primary Skill, Success) Your GM may give you an additional piece of informa-	
		tion about your current situation OR you gain +1 Combat Order in your next Combat (Stacks).	
Educated	Min Int 5	+2 Hit, Analytical.	
		+2 to all Spare Time Rolls.	

Perception	Requirements	Benefits	Disadvantages
Foresight	Psionic	You may spend 2 Fate Points to give all Attacks against you this Combat the Keyword: Slow.	
	Armour 0-2	+1 Defence.	
Optical Implants	Min Per 1	You gain a HUD over your sight!	Strong Hits from Disruptors Blind you for 1 Turn.
		Reduce all Low Light Cover penalties by 1 Step.	Must select at character creation or through Surgery.
		All your non-spacecraft Weapons gain Lock On +4.	
Eagle Eye	Min Per 2	+1 Awareness.	
		+1 Range, all non Melee Weapons.	
Trained Eyes	Min Per 3	+1 to all trained Vehicle System Skills.	
		Strong Hit: Trained Attack (Attack, Hit) Debuff Target: Cover Step -2 against your next Attack.	
Dead Eye	Min Per 4	Strg Hit: Dead Eye (Damage, Hit by 5, not Splash, not RoF 4+) Deal 5 End Dmg to your Target.	
6th Sense	Min Per 5*	Reduce all Limited Vision and Low Light Cover penalties by 2 Steps.	*If you have the Condition: Blind; your Maximum Range
		+4 Defence vs Stealth.	is Rng x5 (normally Rng x10).
		Immune to Strong Hit: Light Burst.	
		*If you have the Condition: Blind; this Trait's Requirement is reduced to Min Per 2.	

Wealth	Requirements	Benefits
Always Prepared	Min Res 6	Your second Weapon that Costs 3 or more Resources Costs 2 fewer Resources.
Barter		Once per session you may lose 1 Trade Box to re-roll a Trade Goods or Wealth Roll with a +2 bonus.
Business	Min Res 5	Perk: You have your own Business.
	Min Inf 5	When you Sell 16 Trade Boxes gain +1 additional Resource and a Spare Time Point.
		When you Publish 16 Research Units gain +1 Influence and a Spare Time Point.
Black Market		+2 to all Conversation, Culture and Wealth Rolls to find and acquire illegal equipment or information.
		+1 Maximum Resources.
Optimisation		+2 Equipment Slots.
		A spacecraft of at least Size 3 that you have spent Influence on; gains +2 Cargo.

Conversation	Requirements	Benefits
Actor		You may spend 1 Fate Point to avoid losing Influence.
		+2 to all Conversation, Leadership and Culture Rolls to persuade NPCs through acting or deception.
		+2 Maximum Influence.
Charming		+2 to all Conversation and Leadership Rolls to gain NPC's trust through friendship, favours or seduction.
		A spacecraft with a Conversation, Culture or Psychology Dedicated Workshop, that you have spent Influence on; gains +1 Crew (Maximum 5).
		+1 Maximum Influence.
Friendly		Change a Minor Perk: Contact to Moderate Perk: Contact.
		+2 Hit, Henchmen.
		+2 Maximum Influence.
Pheromones	Nephilim	If you are a Nephilim, gain +1 Conversation.
		Strong Hit: **Pheromones** (Conversation, Success, Target is currently breathing air, not in combat) A nearby character will temporarily love you for 5 minutes and then hate you for 2 hours (possibly longer at GM's discretion).
Pick Thought	Psionic	Strong Hit: **Pick Thought** (Conversation, Sucess) Secretly read the surface thoughts of a non Robot character.
Taunt		+2 to all Conversation, Leadership and Culture Rolls to distract NPC's attention through abuse or baited communication.
		Strong Hit: **Taunt** (Attack, Hit) Debuff Target character: Strong Hit −1 on their next Attack if they do not Attack you or include you within a Splash area.

Leadership	Requirements	Benefits	Disadvantages
Guide		+1 Resolve and Culture.	
		You may spend 1 Fate Point to allow an Ally a single re-roll.	
		During your Turn, all adjacent Allies gain a Recovery when you gain a Recovery.	
Inspiration	Min Foc 3	+1 Resolve.	NPCs easily remember you.
		Strong Hit: **Inspire** (Attack, Hit) All Allies within sight gain a Recovery.	
		All adjacent Allies gain +2 Defence.	
Intimidating		+1 Resolve.	NPCs easily remember you.
		Strong Hit: **Intimidate** (Attack, Hit) Debuff all character enemies within sight: −2 Defence for 1 Turn.	
		Charge Action grants you +2 Defence.	
Management		+1 Conversation and Resolve.	
		Grant an additional +1 bonus when Assisting other characters (does not Stack).	
		Gain an additional +1 bonus when you are Assisted (does not Stack).	
Mind Haze	Psionic	+1 Resolve.	
	Secret Kn	Strong Hit: **Mind Haze** (Leadership, Sucess, not in Combat) Non Robot Target forgets the last hour.	
Negotiator		+1 Conversation and Resolve.	
		1 free Trade Goods Spare Time Roll per session.	
Recruiter		+1 Culture.	
		+1 Hit, Companion.	
		Drone & Companion Modification 'Multiply' only Costs 1 Resource (normally 2) for Companions.	
		A spacecraft with a Wealth, Leadership, Physical or Resolve Dedicated Workshop, that you have spent Influence on; gains +1 Crew (Maximum 5).	

Culture	Requirements	Benefits	Disadvantages
Archaeologist		+1 Planetoids.	
		+2 to all non-combat Rolls connected to History and Archaeology.	
		X'ion and Archon Tech Costs you 2 fewer Resources (minimum 5) if you pass a Spare Time Roll of 18t (does not Stack).	
Faction Trained		+2 Hit with all Weapons that match your Race or Build's Culture (see chart below).	–2 Hit with Weapons that do no match your Race or Build Culture.
Fashion Sense		+1 Conversation and Wealth OR +1 Leadership and Command (choose during Trait selection).	
		+1 Maximum Influence.	
Jack of all Trades		Reduce all Untrained Professional and Vehicle System Skill Roll penalties by 1.	
Laws and Customs		+1 Leadership.	
		+2 to know about, manipulate or escape from legal and cultural difficulties.	
		+2 Maximum Influence.	
Streetwise		Gain Minor Perk: Contact.	
		+2 to find information with a Culture Roll.	
		+2 to all Conversation and Culture Rolls to blend into crowds and societies.	

Cultural Weapons

Race / Build	Weapons
Corporation	Personal Weapons: Particle, Ion, Combat Computer, Drone.
	Spacecraft Weapons: Fighter.
Kaltoran	Personal Weapons: Irradiated, Self-Propelled, Dummy, Smoke, Electro-Gravity.
	Spacecraft Weapons: Battery.
Legion	Personal Weapons: Gauss, Rail, Kinetic, Shrapnel.
	Spacecraft Weapons: Warhead.
Nephilim	Personal Weapons: Bio Tech.
	Spacecraft Weapons: Bio Tech.
Palantor	Personal Weapons: Arc Fire, Self Guided, Combat Computer, Drone.
	Spacecraft Weapons: Fighter.
Remnant	Personal Weapons: Plasma, Laser, Psionic.
	Spacecraft Weapons: Burn.
Twi-Far	Personal Weapons: Energy.
	Spacecraft Weapons: Energy.
Zhou	Personal Weapons: Melee.
	Spacecraft Weapons: Boarding Party.

Physical	Requirements	Benefits	Disadvantages
Acrobatics	Min Ref 2	+1 Recovery.	
	Min Mov 2	+2 to all Rolls connected to gymnastics and physical stunts.	
		Take Cover Action does not make you Prone when you are Hit by an Attack with the Keyword: Slow. Instead you instantly gain a free Move.	
Capacity Training	Min Str 3	+1 Survival and Gunnery.	
		+4 Equipment Slots.	
Reaction Training	Min Ref 3	+1 Awareness and Gunnery.	
	Min Foc 3	+2 Defence.	
	Min Per 3		
Regular Work Out	Min Foc 3	+1 Survival and Gunnery.	−2 to all Spare Time Rolls.
		+10 Endurance.	
		+2 Recovery.	
Thief	Min Ref 3	+1 Awareness and Stealth.	
	Min Per 3	+2 to all Physical rolls connected to Sleight of Hand.	
		+1 Maximum Resources.	
Weapon Implant		Choose a non Drone or Companion Weapon to be mounted inside your body.	−1 Armour when at 0 Endurance.
		If this Weapon has the Keyword: Bio-Tech (or Energy if you are a Robot) gain Clips +1.	Must select at character creation or through Surgery.
		This Weapon requires 2 fewer Slots (minimum 1).	
		This Weapon gains the Keyword: Natural (is immune to Strong Hit: Disarm) and is a Gauntlet.	

Resolve	Requirements	Benefits	Disadvantages
Dedicated	Min Foc 3	+1 Psychology.	
		You may re-roll a failed Spare Time Roll once, with a −2 penalty.	
Faith		+1 Psychology.	Minor Complication: Obligated to follow religious code.
		+2 Fate.	
		+1 Maximum Influence.	−1 to all Spare Time Rolls.
			−1 Maximum Resources.
Fearless		+1 Recovery.	
		Immune to Strong Hit: Intimidate.	
		Ignore the first (non Legion Race) Suppression effect against you each Turn.	
Grav Reflection		Strong Hit: Grav Reflection (Block, Hit) Until your next Turn: If you are Equipped with a Electro-Gravity Weapon, Outfit or Utility Item and any character fails to Hit you with a non Analyse Attack: Make a Free Attack against them with their own Weapon (RoF 1, Cost 0 Ammo and Range is measured from you).	
Hatred		+1 Crit Dmg (+4 End Dmg if you are an NPC) vs Targets you are prejudiced against.	Gain prejudice against a race or group.
		Strong Hit: Fury (Attack, Hit) You and your Target take 5 or 10 Endurance Damage.	−2 Cover Steps vs Targets you are prejudiced against.
Loyalty		Choose a (non Drone) character (PC or NPC) to be loyal to.	Receive 5 Endurance Damage when the character you are Loyal to is Damaged.
		+1 Psychology.	
		+2 Defence and Hit when in the same Environmental Cover as the character you are Loyal to.	
Mind Worm	Psionic	+1 Psychology.	
		Strong Hit: Mind Worm (Attack, Hit, Psionic) Debuff non Robot Target: Their Next Action gains no Attribute bonus to their Attack Roll, Movement or Strong Hit Options.	
Relentless		+1 Psychology.	−15 Endurance (minimum 0).
		+5 Recovery.	
		+1 End Dmg, all Weapons.	

Awareness	Requirements	Benefits	Disadvantages
Alert	Min Foc 3 Min Per 3	+1 Survival. +1 Defence vs Stealth. +1 Defence vs Impair. Overwatch Action's Attack may be taken as a 'Free Action' during another character's Action (normally at the end of an Action), GM Discretion is given as to when this may happen.	
Deduction	Min Int 3	+1 Survival. +4 Hit, Analytical. Analyse Action also tells you information about an NPC's Attributes, Skills, Outfit, Weapons, Utility Items and current Health.	
Luminescent	Nephilim or Twi-Far	You can glow when you want to! Create Light: You can reduce all environmental Low Light Cover penalties within 6 of you by 1 Step. Strong Hit: Light Burst (Attack, Hit) You gain Limited Vision Heavy Cover (+4) until the start of your next Turn.	-2 Stealth. Enemies never have Low Light Cover Penalties when Attacking you.
Natural Sense		+1 Survival. +2 Hit, Natural. +2 to Combat Order. +2 Defence vs Impair.	
Perfect Aim		+1 Hit, all Weapons. Analyse grant a +2 Range Boost. Overwatch Attack has +2 Range.	
Smuggler		+1 Survival. +2 to all Awareness Rolls related to hiding and finding hidden objects. A single spacecraft that you have spent Influence on; gains +2 Secret Cargo. A spacecraft with a Survival Dedicated Workshop, that you have spent Influence on; gains +2 Secret Cargo space.	

Survival	Requirements	Benefits	Disadvantages
Chef		+1 Medicine and Planetoids. Food Supplies last twice as long for you and up to 5 Allies. A spacecraft with a Bio Tech, Medicine or Survival Dedicated Workshop, that you have spent Influence on; gains +2 Resupply.	
Makeshift		+1 End Dmg, Low Tech. +2 to all Skill Rolls connected to crafting non Weapons and Outfits. +2 to all (non Wealth) Untrained Skill Spare Time Rolls.	
Self-Reliant		+1 Physical, Awareness and Medicine. +2 to all Modification Spare Time Rolls. +1 Stealth.	Characters trying to Assist you have a −4 penalty to their Roll.
Tracker		+1 Awareness, Astronomy and Planetoids. +2 to all Skill Rolls to track Targets (including spacecraft). +2 Range, Analytical.	
Urban		+1 Physical and Awareness. +2 to Survival Skill Rolls in Urban environments. +1 to Trade Good Spare Time Rolls.	
Wilderness		+1 Physical, Awareness, Medicine and Planetoids. +2 to Survival Skill Rolls in Wilderness environments. +2 End Dmg, Melee.	

Professional Skill Traits

Mechanics	Requirements	Benefits
Aerospace		+2 to all Vehicle Repair Rolls.
		A spacecraft with a Mechanics Dedicated Workshop, that you have spent Influence on; gains +1 Hull (Maximum 5).
Armour Smith		+1 Engineering.
		Personalised Outfit Modification grants you an additional -1 Weight and +1 Slot.
		+2 to all Outfit Modification Spare Time Rolls.
Construction Theory		+1 Engineering and Programming.
		A spacecraft with a Mechanics Dedicated Workshop, that you have spent Influence on; gains +1 Hull (Maximum 5).
Maintenance		+1 Engineering and Programming.
		Jam (-1), all Weapons.
		May make 1 free spacecraft Maintenance Spare Time Roll per session.
Robotics		+1 Engineering and Programming.
		Drone & Companion Modification 'Multiply' only Costs 1 Resource (normally 2) for non Bio Tech Drones.
Tweak		+1 Engineering and Programming.
		Strong Hit: **Tweak** (Damage, Hit, Non Infinite Clips or Ammo) Gain +2 Endurance Damage on this Weapon for the remainder of the Combat (Stacks).

Electronics	Requirements	Benefits
Hardware		+1 Programming and Operations.
		+2 to all non-combat Skill Rolls connected to knowing about or working with computer hardware.
		+1 Range, Combat Computer and Drones.
Overcharge		+1 Programming and Operations.
		+2 End Dmg, Disruptor.
Power Flow		+1 Programming and Operations.
		+2 Hit, Non Low Tech.
		+1 End Dmg, Non Low Tech.
Reactor Control		+1 Programming and Operations.
		A spacecraft with a Electronics Dedicated Workshop, that you have spent Influence on; gains +1 Power (Maximum 5).
Shield Breaker		+1 Operations.
		Strong Hit: **Shield Breaker** (Damage, Hit, Energy) A Target with a Utility or Outfit item with Keyword: Shield is Suppressed.
		+1 Shield Dmg, Battery and Ordnance.
Weapon Smith		+1 Programming and Operations.
		+2 to all Weapon Modification Spare Time Rolls.

Programming	Requirements	Benefits
Calibrations		+1 Electronics and Operations.
		+1 Hit, Energy and Prototype.
		+1 Range, Drones.
Computer Science		+1 Mechanics, Electronics and Operations.
		+1 Hit and Range, Combat Computer.
Data Searcher		Programming Toolbox (Personal Computer) counts as a Toolbox (+1 bonus (does not Stack)) for all Trained Professional Skills.
		Programming Dedicated Workshop (Software Lab) counts as a Workshop for non Programming Research Spare Time Rolls.
		+1 to all Research Spare Time Rolls.
Hacker		+2 to all Rolls connected to electronic security systems (eg: hacking).
		+1 Hit, Combat Computer.
		Strong Hit: **Hack** (Combat Computer, Hit, only vs Robot) Choose the Target for the Target's next Attack (must be taken within 1 Turn), no self harm.
Software Engineer		+1 Electronics and Operations.
		A spacecraft with a Programming Dedicated Workshop, that you have spent Influence on: gains +1 CPU (Maximum 5).
Sync Fire System		+1 Mechanics and Operations.
		-1 Load, Drone.

Bio Tech	Requirements	Benefits	Disadvantages
Chemistry		+1 Medicine.	
		+2 to all non-combat Skill Rolls connected to knowing about or working with chemical components.	
		+1 Hit and End Dmg, Burn or Chemical.	
Flesh Herder		+1 Medicine.	
		+2 to all non-combat Rolls connected to Bio Tech Drones.	
		Drone & Companion Modification 'Multiply' only Costs 1 Resource (normally 2) for all Bio Tech Drones.	
Gene Manipulation		+1 Medicine.	
		You gain +1 to any Attribute (may go above Maximum if you have appropriate Secret Knowledge).	
Gene Weaver	Secret Kn	Gain +5 Endurance (up to +15) for each Implant and Splice Trait you have.	
		Ignore all Implant and Splice Trait Race Requirements.	
Nasty Toxins		+1 Medicine.	
		+1 End Dmg, Bio Tech and Chemical.	
		Strong Hit: **Toxin** (Damage, Hit, Bio Tech or Chemical) Target can not gain a Recovery until they receive First Aid.	
Psionic Splice	Max Foc 1	You are a Psionic.	Must select at character creation or through Surgery.
		Gain Language: Telepathy.	
		Mind gains Weapon Type: Psionic.	
		+4 Hit, Mind.	
		Strong Hit: **Psionic Scream** (Attack, Hit, Psionic) Target takes 4 End Dmg.	
Spontaneous Growth		+1 Medicine.	
		+1 Hit, Bio Tech.	
		Strong Hit: **Spontaneous Growth** (Attack, Hit, Bio Tech) This (Gun, Shell or Battery) Attack does not use any Ammunition (must have the required Ammunition to make this Attack).	

Medicine	Requirements	Benefits
Clinical Medicine		+1 Survival and Psychology.
		+2 to all Medicine Extended Care Healing Rolls.
		You may make 1 free Extended Care Healing Roll per session.
Pharmacist		+1 Survival and Bio Tech.
		You may make 1 free Spare Time Roll per session to acquire a Stim.
		You may spend 1 Fate Point to ignore the negative effects of a single Stim you have used on yourself or another character.
Surgeon		+1 Survival, Bio Tech and Psychology.
		+2 to Paramedics and Surgery Healing Rolls.
Field Medic		+1 Survival.
		Paramedics Heals an additional 1 (normally just 3) Point of Attributes Damage.
Nerve Strike		+1 Psychology and Bio Tech.
		Strong Hit: **Disrupt**: works vs Bio Tech Targets.
		+2 End Dmg, Natural.
Nutrition		+1 Survival, Bio Tech and Psychology.
		+5 Endurance.
		+1 Hit, Natural.

Psychology	Requirements	Benefits	Disadvantages
AI		+1 Conversation, Leadership and Bio Tech.	
		+2 to all non-combat Rolls connected to AI.	
		+1 Hit, Drones.	
Interrogation		+1 Leadership.	
		+2 to all Leadership Skill Rolls connected to forcing information out of NPCs.	
		+2 End Dmg, all Weapons.	
Linguistics		+1 Conversation, Culture, Leadership and Bio Tech.	
		Gain 2 Languages of your choice.	
		+2 to all non-combat Rolls connected to Languages.	
Memory Splice		Select two additional Primary Skills to be Trained in.	Gain two GM Defined Complications (eg: unwanted memories or personality traits).
			Must select at character creation or through Surgery.
Psi Master	Psionic	+1 Conversation, Leadership and Bio Tech.	
		+2 to all non-combat Rolls connected to Psionics.	
		+2 Hit, Psionic.	
Psionic Guard	Psionic	+2 Defence vs Psionics.	
		Strong Hit: **Psionic Guard** (Attack, Does not require Hit, Psionic) Remove 1 negative Effect or Debuff from any Target character within sight.	
		+1 Hit, Analytical.	
Read Motives		+1 Conversation and Leadership.	
		+2 to all Skill Rolls connected to reading NPC's motives and intentions.	
		+2 Combat Order.	

Astronomy	Requirements	Benefits
Astrometrics		+1 Engineering and Gunnery.
		+2 to all non-combat Rolls connected to astronomical phenomena.
		A spacecraft with a Awareness or Astronomy Workshop, that you have spent Influence on; gains +1 Sensors (Maximum 5).
Ionisation		+1 Engineering and Gunnery.
		Ion Weapons gain the Keyword: Disruptor.
		+2 Hit, Particle and Ion.
Particles & Light		+1 Engineering and Gunnery.
		Disruptors deal +2 End Dmg vs Targets for EACH 'Reduce all Limited Vision and Low Light penalties by' Step they are gaining from a non 'Create Light' source (you are exploiting their sensitive senses).
		+2 Hit, Gauss and Rail.
Radiation		+1 Hit and End Dmg, Irradiated.
		A spacecraft with a Mechanics or Planetoids Dedicated Workshop, that you have spent Influence on; gains +1 Engines (Maximum 5).
Rewind	Psionic	+1 Combat Order.
		Strong Hit: **Rewind** (Attack, Does not Hit, not Splash, Psionic) This (Gun, Shell or Battery) Attack does not use any Ammunition (must have the required Ammunition to make this Attack) and you gain a Free Overwatch Action.
Warp Time	Psionic	+1 Combat Order.
	Secret Kn	Strong Hit: **Warp Time** (Attack, Does not Require Hit) Take 5 End Dmg and gain an additional Action after this Action has completed (does not Stack), you may cause no Strong Hits during this additional Action.
Wayfarer		+1 Engineering and Command.
		+2 to all non-combat Rolls connected to Ley Lines.
		+50% non-combat spacecraft travel speed.

Planetoids	Requirements	Benefits	Disadvantages
Atmospherics		+1 Survival, Culture and Astronomy.	
		+2 to all non-combat Rolls connected to planet atmospheres.	
		You and your Allies' Oxygen tanks last twice as long.	
Flora and Fauna		+1 Survival and Astronomy.	
		+2 to all non-combat Rolls connected to Flora and Fauna.	
		+50% group non-combat Personal travel speed outside Urban environments.	
Geology		+1 Survival.	
		+2 to all non-combat Rolls connected to Geology and Minerals.	
		All non-Energy, non-Chemical Weapons with the Personalised Modification gain Pen 1 min 3.	
Gravitics		+1 Astronomy.	
		+1 Hit, Electro-Gravity and Self-Propelled.	
		Electro-Gravity equipment Cost 1 fewer Resources (minimum 2).	
Void Splice	Nephilim, Palantor or Zhou	+1 Survival.	-1 Armour when at 0 Endurance.
		Never requires 'Environmental Outfit or Equipment: Space' and one other Environment.	Must select at character creation or through Surgery.
Ley Vortex	Psionic	+1 Combat Order.	
		Strong Hit: **Ley Vortex** (Attack, Splash, Does not Require Hit) Take 5 End Dmg and create a Area of Limited Vision (Light Cover (+2)) until the start of your next Turn. Any character that moves into or starts their Turn inside this Area takes 1 Damage (no Armour) to a random (1d3+3) Attribute.	

Small Arms	Requirements	Benefits
Called Shot		May add up to +/- 1 to determine what Attribute is Damaged with RoF 1 Critical Hits (normally just 1d6).
Covering Fire		Strong Hit: **Covering Fire** (Damage, Does not Require Hit, RoF 2+) 1 Ally gains Heavy Cover (+4) or +1 Cover Step until your next Turn.
Crack Shot		Adjacent characters do not grant Cover to your Target.
		Ignore your Target's Front Cover (not Environmental or LImited Vision Cover).
Dirty Fighter	Kaltoran	Gain Strong Hit +1 vs Bleeding, Prone or Suppressed Targets. Or vs any Target during a Surprise Round.
Dual Draw		-1 Load, Dual Wield.
Fast Draw		+4 Hit, Surprise Round.
		All Weapons have -1 Draw time.
Ley Shot	Psionic	You may spend 1 Fate Point to make any of your non Psionic Weapons count as Psionic and gain +2 End Dmg until your next Turn.
Puncture Shot		+1 End Dmg, all Weapons.
		You may spend 1 Fate Point to apply the Bleeding Effect to a Target that you have caused Attribute Damage to this Turn.
Room Sweeper		+2 End Dmg, Shotgun.
		+1 Splash, Shotgun.
Sniper		+1 Range, RoF 1.
		Strong Hit: **Pinning** (Damage, Does not Require Hit) Non-Nemesis Target character in Entrenched Cover is Suppressed.
Split Shot		+1 End Dmg, RoF 2+.
		RoF 2+ Attacks may use 1d6 per 2 spaces when Spread Firing (normally 1d6 per 1 space).
Wild Shot		+1 Hit, Small.
		Snap Shot gains the Minor Effect: Hit +Extra RoF Dice.

Heavy Arms	Requirements	Benefits
Blast Zone		+1 Hit, Splash.
		Strong Hit: **Critical Hit**. Remove 'not Splash Damage' requirement (**Critical Hit** still only effects 1 Target within Splash area).
Bounce Shot		Thrown Weapons gain +1 Crit Dmg vs Prone Targets.
		Strong Hit: **Bounce** (Attack, Hit, Grenade) May move Splash location 3 in any direction (even around corners).
Cook Grenade		+2 End Dmg, Thrown.
		Grenades lose Keyword: Slow.
Coordinated Strike	Legion	Strong Hit: **Coordinated Strike** (Attack, Hit) A character or spacecraft Ally gains Strong Hit +1 vs your Target with their next Attack (must be taken within 1 Turn) (does not Stack).
Grav Force		Strong Hit: **Grav Wall** (Attack, Hit, Electro-Gravity) You and all character Allies within 3 of you gain +1 Armour vs Slow until your next Turn.
		Strong Hit: **Grav Blast** (Damage, Does not Require Hit, Shell or Electro-Gravity) Target character is pushed 3 spaces away from the source of this Attack.
Kill Zone		Strong Hit: **Kill Zone** (Damage, Does not Require Hit, RoF 3+) 'End Dmg +2, Shield Dmg +2 and Splash +1' OR 'Splash +2'.
Melt Armour		Strong Hit: **Melt** (Damage, Hit, Burn, First Range Increment or Direct Splash Hit) Reduce Target character or spacecraft's Armour by 1, until they have Downtime with a Workbench.
Pin Down		Strong Hit: **Pin Down** (Damage, Hit, End Dmg 6+) Non-Nemesis Target character is Suppressed if they receive 6 or more End Dmg from characters that are not you before your next Turn.
Plant Feet		Optional: If you Set Up 2 (and gain Pull Down 1) gain +2 Hit and Range on a non Melee Weapon.
Pulverise		Str Hit: **Pulverise** (Damage, Does not Require Hit, Crit Dmg 5+) Permanently reduce 2 sections of physical Environmental Cover within 1 of Target by 1 Step.
Set Alight		Strong Hit: **Set Alight** (Damage, Hit, Burn) Make a free Attack against Target character at the start of each of your Turns (at 0 range) until they gain First Aid (Set Alight Effects do not Stack multiple times) OR a Target spacecraft gains an On Fire Effect.
Shell Shock		Str Hit: **Shell Shock** (Damage, Hit, Crit Dmg 5+) Target character is Suppressed and gains a Move (can not move closer to you) as a Free Action.
Suppression Fire		Strong Hit: **Suppression Fire** (Damage, Does not Require Hit, RoF 3+, Crit Dmg 4+) Non-Nemesis Target character is Suppressed.
Tank Buster		Crit Dmg 5+ Weapons gain: Pen 2 min 4.

Tactical	Requirements	Benefits
Combat Stims		If you have a Medicine or Bio Tech Toolbox: Performing First Aid grants a character a Recovery and +2 Hit (does not Stack) with their next Attack Roll.
Disruptor Flash	Secret Kn	Your Disruptors gain +1 Critical Damage vs Henchmen.
		Strong Hit: Flash (Damage, Hit, Disruptor) Target character not in Entrenched Cover is Suppressed.
Fire Platform		+1 Slot, Drones.
		Once per Turn one of your Drones may Attack with 2 different Weapons (making two Attacks).
Grav Deflector	Armour 0-3	If you have a Active Electro-Gravity Weapon, Outfit or Utility Item: gain +1 Armour vs Slow.
Grav Master		+2 Range, Electro-Gravity.
Hug Cover	Armour 0-2	Gain +1 Armour (May exceed this Trait's Requirement) while in Environmental Cover.
Insignificant Target	Corporation	Strong Hit: Insignificant Target (Analyse, Hit) Gain +1 Cover Step until your next Turn.
Power Overload	Min Int 3	Strong Hit: Power Overload (Damage, Hit, Disruptor) Target character's Active non Low Tech or Bio Tech Weapon is Jammed.
Prepared		+2 Range, Overwatch.
		Overwatch gains the Minor Effect: +1 Cover Step.
Reposition	Min Move 3	Strong Hit: Reposition (Attack, Hit, Equipped Weapon is Weight 2 or under) Make a free Move and gain +1 Cover Step.
	Armour 0-3	
Running Dodge	Min Move 3	Full Move and Charge Actions grant you +1 Armour if you move at least 4 from your starting location.
	Armour 0-3	
Second Wind	Legion	You may spend 1 Fate Point to Heal 10 Endurance.
		+2 Recovery.
Sudden Strike		Strong Hit: Sudden Strike (Stealth, Hit) Boost next Attack: +1 Crit Dmg (must be taken within 1 Turn).
Swift Shadow		You may make 1 free Stealth Action per Turn if you start the Turn Stealthed.
Tactical Fall Back		Take Cover Action grants a Recovery if you don't move towards an enemy.
Tactical Care		You may Assist (Skill Roll of 10) a single character's Paramedics Healing Roll with a Tactical Skill Roll to Heal an additional 1 (normally just 3) Point of Attribute Damage (does not require you to have a Toolbox).
Target Painter		+2 End Dmg, Lock On.
		Strong Hit: Scramble (Combat Computer, Does not Require Hit) Remove a Locked On Effect from an character Ally.
Triangulation		All of your Drones gain Lock On +4.
		Strong Hit: Triangulation (Attack, Hit, Non Bio Tech Drone) Target character is Locked On.
Vicious	Nephilim	Strong Hit: Vicious (Damage, Does not Require Hit) You gain +2 Hit against this Target character or spacecraft for the remainder of the Combat.

Exotic	Requirements	Benefits
Brawler	Min Str 3	Pushed Targets are pushed +1 distance.
	Min Foc 3	Strong Hit: Stunning Blow (Damage, Hit, Blunt, Melee) Non-Nemesis Target character is suppressed.
Field Tested		-1 Load (minimum 1), Prototype.
		-1 Weight (minimum 1), Prototype.
Flesh Foreman	Corporation	+2 Movement, Combat Flesh.
Flesh Weaver	Nephilim	+1 Armour, Bio-Tech Drone.
Frenzy	Nephilim	Strong Hit: Frenzy (Damage, Hit, First Range Increment or Melee) +1 (non spacecraft) Armour and Combat Order until your next Turn.
Loyal Bond		A single Companion gains +1 Armour and End Dmg.
Lucky Edge	Kaltoran	Strong Hit: Lucky Edge (Attack, Hit) Ignore the next (non spacecraft) Strong Hit: Critical Hit against you, before your next Turn (does not Stack).
	Armour 0-3	
Martial Arts	Min Ref 3	+1 RoF, Melee.
	Secret Kn	Strong Hit: Disarm (Block or Impair, Hit) Target must spend a single Draw Action before they may use a currently Activated non Gauntlet Weapon.
Misdirect	Min Foc 3	Twice per Turn: if you take Endurance Damage from an Attack you may deal 3 Endurance Damage to an Adjacent (non Ally Drone or Companion) character as a Free Action and you take 3 less Endurance Damage from the Attack.
	Min Per 3	
No-One Falls		+2 Hit, Companion.
		If a Companion would die, you may spend 1 Fate Point to have them miraculously avoid Death.
Perfect Throw	Min Per 4	You may spend 1 Fate Point (before Attack Roll is made) to Boost a Thrown Attack: +1 End and Crit Dmg (does not Stack).
Push Forward		When you take a Take Cover Action, all of your Drones and Companions may make a free Move.
Requiem	Secret Kn	+2 Hit, Flesh.
		Recovery and Take Cover Actions resurrect a destroyed Combat Flesh Drone Body within 10 (it cannot Attack until your next Turn).
Special Ammo	Min Int 3	+1 Hit, Personalised.
		Strong Hit: Special Ammo (Damage, Hit, not spacecraft) Pick one: Target is knocked Prone OR Splash +1 OR Target isLocked On OR +2 End Dmg.
Special Shell	Min Int 3	You may spend 1 Fate Point to change the Variation (equal or lower Cost (ignore any Spare Time Roll Cost requirements)) of your Shell Weapon for a single Attack.

Vehicle System Skill Traits

Command	Requirements	Benefits	Disadvantages
Ace		Strong Hit: **K-Turn** (Manoeuvre, Success, Size 1-2) Rotate 90°.	
		Strong Hit: **Barrel Roll** (Command, Success, Size 1-3) Move sideways, 1 Space.	
Speed Freak		+1 Resolve.	You have -2 to all System Rolls while you are at Velocity 1 or 2.
		You gain +2 to all System Rolls while you are at Velocity 5 or 6.	
Tactician		+1 Leadership.	
		All Fighters Launched from your spacecraft gain +2 Hit and +1 Defence (does not Stack).	
Lots of Shouting		+1 Leadership.	
		Strong Hit: **Lots of Shouting** (Command, Does not Req Success) Your Velocity counts as 1 lower and your CPU counts as 1 higher to determine System Roll Order until the end of your next Command Phase (Stacks).	
Hold the Line		+1 Resolve and Leadership.	
		+2 Defence vs Boarding.	
		Strong Hit: **Hold the Line** (Command, Success) +1 Armour vs Boarding.	
Formation	Not Kaltoran	+1 Leadership.	
		Gain +1 Defence for each Ally spacecraft (not Ordnance) that are within 3 of you.	
		Gain +1 Hit for each Ally Fighter that is within 3 of you while you are Piloting a Fighter.	
Lone Wolf	Not Corporation	+1 Resolve.	
		All of your Weapons gain +2 Shield Dmg if you are Piloting a Fighter or are in a Size 1 or 2 spacecraft with no Ally spacecraft (including Fighters) within 4 spaces of you.	
Evasive Manoeuvre		+1 Resolve.	
		Strong Hit: **Evasive Manoeuvre** (Command, Success) Your spacecraft gains +1 Defence and all Weapons gain -1 Hit per your current Velocity until your next Turn (does not Stack).	
Brace for Impact	Min Foc 3	Strong Hit: **Brace for Impact** (Command, Success, Size 3+) Until the end of your Turn all of your spacecraft's System Rolls are at -2 and your spacecraft's Attributes may not take more than 1 Damage from any single source.	

Engineering	Requirements	Benefits	Disadvantages
It Never Ends	Min Int 3	+1 Mechanics and Electronics.	
		You may make a free Patch Job System Roll each Turn at -2.	
Jury Rig	Secret Kn	+1 Mechanics, Electronics and Medicine.	
		You may adjust the Attribute Location of any Damage dealt to your spacecraft by +/- 1 (calculated after all other adjustments, eg: Scan) (does not Stack).	
Pre-Prepped		+1 Mechanics and Electronics.	
		Your spacecraft gains +1 Regen.	
		Your spacecraft's Combat Jump System Roll requires 3 Successes (normally 4).	
Shields Up		+1 Electronics.	Your spacecraft has -1 Regen.
		Strong Hit: **Shields Up** (Engineering, Success) Regen Shields.	
Weak Circuits		If your Attack Deals Engine, Power or CPU Attribute Damage, deal 5 additional Shield Damage to your Target.	
Stealth Ship		+1 Electronics.	
		If your Size 1-3 spacecraft is the Aggressor in a Combat (started the fight), your opponents may not make any Attack Rolls against your spacecraft or make any Operations System Rolls, during their first Turn.	
Deck Hand		Strong Hit: **Get Back Out There!** (Engineering, Success) Rebuild one Fighter Body, this Fighter Body may be Launched instantly.	
Power Flow		+1 Electronics.	
		Divert Power System Rolls deal 1 less Shield Damage to your spacecraft (Stacks).	
		Strong Hit: **Power Flow** (Engineering, Success) Another character gains +2 to their next System Roll (must be taken this Turn).	
Organic Systems	Not Legion	+1 Mechanics, Electronics and Medicine.	
	Not Palantor	A single Nephilim spacecraft that you have spent Influence on; gains +2 Regen (does not Stack).	

Operations	Requirements	Benefits	Disadvantages
Spacecraft Hacker		+1 Programming. Strong Hit: **Hack Spacecraft** (Operations, Success) Increase or Decrease a Locked On Target's Velocity by 1 OR deal 3 Shield Dmg to them.	
Concussive Blast		If you fail an Attack Roll against a Target with a Warhead, you may Destroy that Warhead Body and push your Target 1 Space in any direction. +2 Shield Dmg, Warhead.	
Re-Route		You may spend 1 Fate Point to temporarily Heal all spacecraft Attribute Damage on your spacecraft for 1 Turn and grant +2 to all System Rolls until the end of the Turn.	
Efficient Supplies		+1 Psychology and Planetoids. Your spacecraft gains +2 Resupply. Your spacecraft gains +1 Regen. +1 Hit, Warheads.	
Ley Power Flow	Psionic Secret Kn	Strong Hit: **Ley Distortion Shield** (Operations, Success) All of your spacecraft's Fighters and Warheads gain +2 Armour until your next Turn (does not Stack). Strong Hit: **Ley Blast** (Operations, Success) You and any opponent take 5 Shield Dmg.	Your spacecraft requires +1 Combat Jump Success (normally 4).
Counter Measures		+1 Astronomy. Any Ordnance with the Locked On Effect on them have Strong Hit -1 vs your spacecraft (does not Stack).	
Hull Breach		+1 Engineering and Planetoids. Strong Hit: **Hull Breach** (Warhead, Hit, 1 use per RoF) Until your Target Successfully performs a Damage Control System Roll: They take 1 Crew Damage (no Armour), lose 1 On Fire Effect and lose 1 Boarded Effect at the start of each of their Turns.	
Navigator		+1 Programming, Astronomy and Planetoids. Your spacecraft may ignore the effects of any Environmental Object or Dust Cloud that it ends its movement in (but not those it passes through).	
Tweak Trajectory		+1 Programming and Astronomy. Strong Hit: **Tweak Trajectory** (Operations, Success) Move one of your spacecraft's Warheads or Fighter Bodies, 2 in any direction.	

Gunnery	Requirements	Benefits
Disruptor Pulse	Min Int 3	+1 Shield and End Dmg, Energy. Strong Hit: **Disruptor Shell** (Warhead or Battery, Hit, not Energy) Target loses all Locked On Effects it has applied to other spacecraft and it takes 2 Shield Dmg.
Careful Aim		Strong Hit: **Careful Aim** (Battery, Does not Require Hit) Gain +1 Hit with all Weapons for the remainder of this Combat (Stacks).
Blast Shot		+1 Shield Dmg, Battery. Strong Hit: **Blast Shot** (Battery, Hit) Reduce Size 1-3 Target's Velocity by 1 or Rotate them 45°.
Fresh Round		+1 Hit, Battery. Gain +2 Hit AND End or Shield Dmg on your next Attack (this Combat) after Reloading a (not Load 0) Weapon (does not Stack).
Munitions Logistics		+1 Physical. All Batteries (not Ammunition: 'RoF x1') on your spacecraft: gain additional Ammunition equal to its RoF.
Ship Defender		+1 Physical. Strong Hit: **Ship Defender** (Battery, Does not Require Hit) Make a free Attack with a Point Defence Weapon that has not Attacked this Turn.
Flak Wall		+1 Physical. +1 Crit Dmg vs Warheads, all Weapons. Strong Hit: **Flak Wall** (Battery, Does not Require Hit, Flak) Create 2 spaces of Dust Cloud 2 away from your Target.
Overload Shields		+1 Shield Dmg, Battery. Strong Hit: **Overload Shields** (Warhead or Battery, Hit) Reduce Target's Regen by 1 for the remainder of the Combat (Stacks).
Precise Shot		+1 Physical. +1 Shield Dmg, Battery. Strong Hit: **Precise Aim** (Operations or Battery, Success) Gain +2 Shield Dmg vs a Target with your next Attack (must be taken within 1 Turn).
Newtonian Gunner	Secret Kn	You can use Newtonian Physics to change the facing of your spacecraft without changing your flight direction! If your Size 1-4 spacecraft does not Rotate during your Turn, all characters may treat your spacecraft's Rear Arc as its Side Arc. Strong Hit: **Nose to Nose** (Manoeuvre, Success, Size 1-2) If your spacecraft does not Rotate this Turn, all characters may treat your spacecraft's Rear Arc as its Front Arc until your next Turn.

Weapons

Small Arms

Small Arms	Hit	End Dmg	Crit	Rng	Clips	Ammo	Load	RoF	Wgt	Weapon Type	Cost
Pistol	+1	3	3	4	4	RoF x6	1	1	1	Gun	1
Small											
Submachine Gun	+1	4	3	3	3	RoF x3	1	3 (+2d6)	1	Gun	2
Rifle		3	4	5	2	RoF x4	2	1*	2	Gun	2
*Strong Hit (5-6) with all RoF 1 Attack Rolls											
Assault Rifle	+2	4	4	4	3	RoF x4	2	2 (+1d6)	2	Gun	3
Jam (-1)											
Shotgun	+2	6	3	2*	5	RoF x1	1	2 (+1d6)	3	Gun or Shell (Pick One)	2
*Strong Hit (5-6) vs Targets within first Range Increment											

Heavy Arms

Heavy Arms	Hit	End Dmg	Crit	Rng	Clips	Ammo	Load	RoF	Wgt	Weapon Type	Cost
Grenade	-2	6	5	1	2	RoF x1	1	1	1	Shell, Thrown	1
Splash 2, Small, Slow, -2 to all Weapon Modification Spare Time Rolls.											
Disruptor Grenade	-2	8	3*	1	1	RoF x1	1	1	1	Thrown, Disruptor	1
Splash 1, Small, Slow, Energy, Blunt, Strong Hit (5-6) *+2 Crit Dmg vs Robots, -2 to all Weapon Modification Spare Time Rolls											
Strong Hit: Disrupt (Hit) Debuff ALL Damaged Targets Active Non Low Tech, Non Bio Tech Weapons: Lose Ammunition equal to RoF											
Satchel	-4	10	4	-2		RoF x1	2	1	2	Shell, Thrown	14t*
*1 Use: Splash 4, Slow, Pen 4 min 2, May make a Heavy Arms Skill Roll of 12 to place Satchel and time a delayed explosion											
Puncture Rifle		4	4	4	3	RoF x3	2	1	3	Gun	2
Slow, Pen 2 min 3, Maximum Range = Rng x5 (normally Rng x10)											
Cannon	-2	6	5	5	4	RoF x3	2	1	4	Gun or Shell (Pick One)	4*
Splash 1, Slow, Maximum Range = Rng x20 (normally Rng x10), *Cost Spare Time Roll 14t											
When fired at a spacecraft use: Hit +2, Shield Dmg 2, Crit 2 and Rng 2											
Auto Cannon	-4	6*	4	2*	3	RoF x5	2	4 (+3d6)	4	Gun	4**
Jam (1-3), *Optional: (Set Up 1, Pull Down 1, +2 Rng and +2 End Dmg), **Cost Spare Time Roll 14t											
Chemical Thrower		4	4	1	3	RoF x3	2	3 (+2d6)*	3	Chemical	4
Slow, Jam (1-5), Low Tech, All Targets have -1 Cover Step, *If you perform a Spread Fire with this Weapon: add +1d6 to each Attack Roll											

Tactical

Tactical	Hit	End Dmg	Crit	Rng	Clips	Ammo	Load	RoF	Wgt	Weapon Type	Cost
Mind	+Int	-	-	Foc	-	Inf	0	1	-	Analytical	Auto
Natural, No Variations or Modifications											
Targeting Laser	+Int -2	-	-	Foc +4	-	Inf	1	1	0	Combat Computer	14t
Small, Strong Hit (5-6)											
Strong Hit: Target Lock (Hit) Target is Locked On.											
Tactical Computer	+Int	-	-	Foc	Inf	10	2	1	1	Combat Computer	2
Lock On +2, Strong Hit (5-6)											
Strong Hit: Target Lock (Hit) Target is Locked On.											
Strong Hit: Weak Spot (Hit, Locked On) Until your next Turn, Boost all Attacks against Target: Endurance Damage +1.											
Strong Hit: Plot Trajectory (Hit, Locked On) Until your next Turn, Boost all Attacks against Target: Range +1.											
Strong Hit: Tactical Scan (Hit, Locked On) Until your next Turn, Debuff Target: -1 Cover Step (minimum Light Cover).											
Turret	-2		+1	+1				1 (+4)		Drone	0+
Defence: 8, Armour: 4, Movement: -, Slots: 4, Bodies: 1, Lock On +6, Set Up 2, Pull Down 1, Arc of Fire 180, Robot											
Crawler		2	2	3	-	Inf	0	2 (+1d6)	1 (+0)	Drone	1
Defence: 14, Armour: 2, Movement: 4, Slots: 0, Bodies: 1, Lock On +2, Energy, May be Set Up as a single Thrown Action (Rng = Str), Robot, No Variations.											
Swarm Drone		-1		-1				1 (+0)		Drone	2+
Defence: 18, Armour: 3, Movement: 6, Slots: 2, Bodies: 1, Lock On +4, May be Set Up as a single Thrown Action (Rng = Str), Robot											
Combat Drone	+1							2 (+4)		Drone	2+
Defence: 12, Armour: 4, Movement: 4, Slots: 3, Bodies: 1, Lock On +4, Robot											
Assault Drone	-2	+2		+1				2 (+14)		Drone	3+*
Defence: 8, Armour: 6, Movement: 2, Slots: 6, Bodies: 1, Lock On +4, characters can not move through Assault Drone, Robot, *Cost Spare Time Roll 12t											

	Hit	End Dmg	Crit	Rng	Clips	Ammo	Load	RoF	Wgt	Weapon Type	Cost
Assistant	+2							1 (+6)		Companion	1+*
Body Guard	+3			+1	+1			2 (+8)		Companion	4+*
Electro-Grav Gauntlet	+2	3	3	2	3	RoF x6	2	1	0	Melee, Impairment	3*
Disruptor Rifle	-2	5	2*	3	3	RoF x4	1	1	2	Disruptor	3

Assistant — Defence: 16, Armour: 2, Movement: 4, Slots: 2, Bodies: 1, *Cost Spare Time Roll 8t.
Controller may make Skill Rolls via this Companion at +0 (Companion can not Attack this Turn, Controller needs to take an Action with Minor Effect: Skill Roll).
Strong Hit: Helpful (Does not Req Hit) A single Ally gains Hit +2 on their next Attack (must be taken within 1 Turn).

Body Guard — Defence: 14, Armour: 4, Movement: 4, Slots: 5, Bodies: 1, *Cost Spare Time Roll 12t.
Controller may make Skill Rolls via this Companion at +0 (Companion can not Attack this Turn, Controller needs to take an Action with Minor Effect: Skill Roll).

Electro-Grav Gauntlet — Gauntlet, Electro-Gravity, Blunt, Armour vs Slow +1, No Variations. *Cost Spare Time Roll 14t.
Strong Hit: Float Target (Hit) Debuff Target: -1 Cover Step, reduce all Movement by 2 (minimum 0) and Push moves Target 1 additional space until your next Turn.

Disruptor Rifle — Lock On +6, Jam (1-5), Energy, Blunt, *+2 Crit Dmg vs Robots.
Strong Hit: Disrupt (Hit) Debuff Targets Active Non Low Tech, Non Bio Tech Weapons: Lose Ammunition equal to RoF.

Exotic	Hit	End Dmg	Crit	Rng	Clips	Ammo	Load	RoF	Wgt	Weapon Type	Cost
Limbs		Str -1	Str -1	–	–	–	0	2 (+1d6)	–	Melee, Impairment	Auto
Baton	+1*	4*	2	–	–	–	1	1	1	Melee	Free
Wrist Blade		3*	3	–	–	–	0	1	1	Melee	12t
Thrown Weapon	-2	3*	3	(1*)	– (3**)	– (6**)	1	2 (+1d6)*	1	Melee, *Thrown	12t
Balanced Weapon	*	4*	4	–	–	–	1	1	2**	Melee	1
Large Weapon	-2*	6*	5	–	–	–	2	1	5	Melee	2
Combat Bow	-2	3	3*	3*	10	1	1	1	3	Shell	1*
Combat Flesh			-1					1 (+8)		Drone	1+
Legion Hound	+2	4	3	–	–	–	1	2 (+8)		Companion, Melee	1*
Infestor Whip	+2	4*	3	1**	–	–	1	1	1	Melee, Impairment	2***
Field Prototype	+1	3	3	3			2	1	2	Gun	14t
Beta Prototype	-1	3	4	3			2	2 (+1d6)	3	Gun	3
Lab Prototype	-2	5	5	4			2	1	4	Gun	5
Nephilim Beast		5	4	–	–	–	1	2 (+10)		Companion, Melee	2*
Metal Chair	+1	4*	2	–	–	–	1	1	3	Melee	–
Plasma Torch (Mechanical Toolbox)	-4	2	4	–	–	–	2	1	2	Melee	–
Sedative (Medicine Toolbox)	-2	6	0	–	1	4	1	1	0	Melee	–
Exposed Wires	-2	5	4	–	–	Inf	1	1	1	Melee	–

Limbs — Natural, Small, Blunt, No Variations or Modifications.

Baton — Blunt, *If you have 4 or more Strength: you deal +1 End Dmg and have -2 Hit.

Wrist Blade — Small, Gauntlet, *If you have 4 or more Strength: +1 End Dmg.
Strong Hit: Stealth Strike (Hit) Attack does not break Stealth.

Thrown Weapon — Small, -2 to all Weapon Modification Spare Time Rolls, *If you have 4 or more Strength: +1 End Dmg, **Optional Weapon Type: Thrown (RoF 1).
Strong Hit: Stealth Strike (Hit) Attack does not break Stealth.

Balanced Weapon — *If you have 5 or more Strength: +2 End Dmg and -2 Hit, **Only ever requires 1 Hand (unless you have the Dual Wield Modification).

Large Weapon — Slow, *If you have 5 or more Strength you may have: +2 End Dmg and -1 Hit.
Strong Hit: Massive Bash (Hit, Target has less Strength than you) Target is knocked Prone and Pushed 1.

Combat Bow — Slow, *Analyse Action Grants +2 Damage and Range (Max +2), Maximum Range = Rng x5 (normally Rng x10), *Cost Spare Time Roll 14t.

Combat Flesh — Defence: 8, Armour: 4, Movement: 2, Slots: 2, Bodies: 1, Bio Tech.

Legion Hound — Defence: 16, Armour: 3, Movement: 12, Slots: 0, Bodies: 1, No Variations or Modifications. *Cost Spare Time Roll 10t.

Infestor Whip — Bio Tech, Strong Hit (5-6), No Variations, *If you have 4 or more Strength: +1 End Dmg. **Max range 5. ***Cost Spare Time Roll 14t.

Field Prototype — Prototype.

Beta Prototype — Prototype

Lab Prototype — Splash 1, Prototype, Slow, Set Up 1.

Nephilim Beast — Defence: 8, Armour: 5, Movement: 6, Slots: 0, Bodies: 1, Bio Tech.
*Cost Spare Time Roll 12t, You may spend 1 Fate Point to rebuild this destroyed Companion outside of combat without Downtime.

Metal Chair — Blunt, *If you have 5 or more Strength: +1 End Dmg.

Plasma Torch (Mechanical Toolbox) — Strong Hit: Melt Armour (Hit) Reduce Targets Armour by 1 (minimum 2).

Sedative (Medicine Toolbox) — Blunt

Exposed Wires — Strong Hit: System Shock (Hit) Target is Suppressed.

Gun Variations (May Select 1, Gun Only)

Variations	Hit	End Dmg	Crit	Rng	Clips	Ammo	Load	RoF	Wgt	Weapon Type	Cost
Burst Spores	-2		+1							Chemical	+1*
Bio Tech, Splash +1 OR +1 End Dmg (choose on Variation selection), *Cost Spare Time Roll 10t											
Gauss						+1 (+1d6)					+1
Jam (1-3)											
Ion					+2						+0
Energy											
Irradiated	-2	+1	+1				*				+1**
Low Tech, *Take 5 Endurance Damage every Action you spend Reloading or Un-Jamming this Weapon, **Cost Spare Time Roll 14t											
**May not be taken by characters without Endurance (Henchmen, Drones or Companions)											
Particle			-1		Inf	-1 xRoF					-1
Jam (1-5), Energy, Does not Work in Void											
Rail			+1	+1		-1 xRoF	+1				+1*
Lock On +2, Jam (1-5), *Cost Spare Time Roll 14t											
Self-Propelled			+1								+0
Low Tech, Works in Liquid											
Spine Launcher		+1	-1			-1 xRoF	-1	+2 (+2d6)			+1
Bio Tech											

Shell Variations (May Select 1, Shell Only)

Variations	Hit	End Dmg	Crit	Rng	Clips	Ammo	Load	RoF	Wgt	Weapon Type	Cost
Dispersion		-1	-1							Chemical	+0
Splash +1, Low Tech.											
Dummy		-3	-3								-1
Low Tech, Blunt.											
Strong Hit: **Fake Shock** (Hit) Target is Suppressed.											
Electro-Gravity		-2	-2		-1						14t
Electro-Gravity, Blunt.											
Strong Hit: **Float Targets** (Hit) Debuff All Targets: -1 Cover Step, reduce all Movement by 2 (minimum 0) and Push moves Targets 1 additional space until your next Turn											
Kinetic	+2										+0
Low Tech											
Shrapnel		+2	-1								+0
Splash +1, Low Tech.											
Smoke		-	-	+1	+1						-1
Splash +1, Low Tech, Creates an Area of Limited Vision (Light Cover (+2)) for 3 minutes, Does not Work in Void.											
Snare	+2*	-2	-2**	+1						Impairment**	+0
Low Tech, *Never add Str to your Hit, **any Escape vs Grab is done vs Defence 12+Crit Dmg, **you never count as Grabbing Target.											

Variations	Hit	End Dmg	Crit	Rng	Clips	Ammo	Load	RoF	Wgt	Weapon Type	Cost
Antimonic Acid	-2		+1								+1
										Burn	
Cryo-Gel	+1										10t
										Bio Tech	
	Strong Hit: **Freeze** (Hit) Debuff Target: Reduce all Movement by 1 (minimum 0) until they receive a First Aid Healing Roll.										
Napalm		+1									+0
										Burn, Does not Work in Void	
Neurotoxin		+1	-1*								+1**
	Bio Tech, *Critical Hit Attribute Damage Location 1d3+3 (normally 1d6). **Cost Spare Time Roll 14t										
	Strong Hit: **Neurotoxin** (Hit, 1 use per RoF) Non Robot Target takes 1 Attribute Damage (no Armour) to a random (1d3+3) Attribute.										
Synthetic Poison		*	-2*								+0
	Bio Tech, *+2 Damage vs Targets at 0 Endurance, Does not Work in Void										
	Strong Hit: **Synthetic Poison** (Hit) Non Robot Target takes 3 Endurance Damage at the Start of their Turn until they receive Paramedics or Extended Care (Synthetic Poison Effect can Stack up to 4 times).										

Variations	Hit	End Dmg	Crit	Rng	Clips	Ammo	Load	RoF	Wgt	Weapon Type	Cost
Body Mounted				-1			+1*				+1
	Gauntlet, **-2 Draw time, Immune to Strong Hit: **Disarm**										
Mounted Weapon	-1	-1	-1	-1			*		-**	***	-1
	Choose a Weapon of Weight 2 or more for this Weapon to be Attached to. Attached Weapon has -1 Hit and +1 Weight										
	*Drawn with Attached Weapon (0 Hands for this Weapon), *+1 Reload, **Weight 1-3 Weapons only,										
	***Not Thrown Weapon without Launcher Modification										
	Strong Hit: **Combo Strike** (Hit) Make a free Attack with Main Weapon at the same Target with Hit -2										
Tiny	-1	-1	-2	-1			-1		-1*		-1
	*If Weight is under 2 it is 'Small', +4 to hide Weapon										

Drone Variations (May Select 1, Drone Only)

Variations	Hit	End Dmg	Crit	Rng	Clips	Ammo	Load	RoF	Wgt	Weapon Type	Cost
Anti Grav	-2										14t
Armour: -1, Drone may Fly (may only Hover with a passenger if it has 4 or more Slots)											
Armoured				-1					+1 (+2)		+1
Defence: -2, Armour: +1, Movement: -1, Grants Heavy Cover (+4) to any adjacent characters behind it											
Holographic	-2	-2	-2		+2				(0*)		-1
Armour: +2, Energy, May be Set Up as a Prep Action (Rng = Int), *Requires 0 extra Equipment Slots to carry.											
Strong Hit: Distraction (Attack, Hit) Debuff Target: Strong Hit -1 on their next Attack if they do not Attack you or include you within a Splash area.											
Horror		+1		-1							+1
Defence: +2, Bio Tech, Lose Robot											
Security System	-4		+2	+2				-1			*
Lock On +8, Set Up +20, Pull Down +20, *Cost Influence not Resources, *Cost Spare Time Roll 14t											
Synth Steel									+1 (0*)		14t
Armour: -1, You may spend 1 Fate Point to rebuild all of this Drones destroyed bodies outside of combat without a Workbench or Downtime											
May be Set Up as a Thrown Action (Rng = Str -1), *Requires 0 extra Equipment Slots to carry.											
Utility	-2			-1							+0
Slots: -1, Counts as a Toolkit for all of your Trained Professional Skills, Equipped with all Toolboxes that its Controller has.											
Controller may make Skill Rolls via this Drone (Drone cannot Attack this Turn, Controller needs to take an Action with Minor Effect: Skill Roll).											

Melee Variations (May Select 1, Melee Only)

Variations	Hit	End Dmg	Crit	Rng	Clips	Ammo	Load	RoF	Wgt	Weapon Type	Cost
Arc Fire		+1									+1
Energy, Burn, Stealth -2, Pen 2 min 3											
Claw	-1	+1									+0
Composite	+1										+0
Hammer	+1		*	-1							+0
Blunt, *Deal +2 Endurance Damage vs Targets with Armour 4 or greater											
Injector	-2						+1	-1		Chemical*	+0
Slow, Gain Strong Hit +1 if you are behind your Target, *Chemical Variations that do not work in the Void can work in the Void											
Nano-Bone	-1	-1									14t
Bio Tech, Lose 'Blunt', Pen 1 min 3.											

Melee Shape Variations (May Select 1, Not Thrown, Melee Only)

Variations	Hit	End Dmg	Crit	Rng	Clips	Ammo	Load	RoF	Wgt	Weapon Type	Cost
Body Mounted	-2						-1				+1
Gauntlet, Immune to Strong Hit: Disarm											
Bayonet	-2	-1	-1				*		-**	***	-1
Choose a Weapon of Weight 2 or more for this Weapon to be Attached to, Attached Weapon has -1 Hit and +1 Weight											
*Drawn with Attached Weapon (0 Hands for this Weapon), **Weight 1-3 Weapons only, ***Not Thrown Weapon											
Long				2*			+1				+0
*Max range 2, +2 Hit with Overwatch											

Variation	Hit	End Dmg	Crit	Rng	Clips	Ammo	Load	RoF	Wgt	Weapon Type	Cost
Arc Beam	-2							+1 (+1d6)			+1

Requires: Secret Knowledge (Electronics: Fusion), Energy, Set Up 1.
If you perform a Spread Fire with this Weapon: add +2d6 to each Attack Roll.

| Archon Gene Shredder | -1 | +2 | -2 | -1 | -1 | | | +1 | | | +3 |

Requires: Secret Knowledge (Medicine: Archon Weaponry), *Deals no Damage to Robots, Burn, Pen 4 min 1

| Grav Render | | +1 | -1 | | | | | -RoF x1 | | | +0 |

Requires: Secret Knowledge (Programming: Electro-Gravity), Electro-Gravity, Set Up +1, All Successful Attack Rolls Push all Targets 1 or 2 spaces.

| Nephilim Borer Beetle | | | -1 | | | | | +1 | | | +1 |

Requires: Secret Knowledge (Bio Tech: X'ion Weaponry), Bio Tech, Slow,
Strong Hit: Bore (Hit) Target takes 1 Attribute Damage (no Armour) at the start of your Turn until they receive First Aid.

| Orbital Bombardment Array | -16 | +3* | +4* | +4 | | | | -RoF x1 | +2 | | -1 |

Requires: Secret Knowledge (Planetoids: Atmosphere), Lock On +10, Splash +3, Slow, Set Up +2, Limited inside use, *Attack Dmg delayed by 1d6 Turns.

| Psi Reaper | | -1 | +1 | | | | | -RoF x1 | +2 (+2d6) | -1 | Psionic | +2 |

Requires: Secret Knowledge (Psychology: Psionics), All Successful Attack Rolls Debuff Target: Strong Hit -1 on next Attack (within 1 Turn).

| Trash Launcher | +2 | +1 | -1 | -1 | +4* | | | | +2 | | -1 |

Requires: Secret Knowledge (Mechanics: Loading Systems), Slow, *You may loot Clips from any Weapon and use them with this Weapon.

| Void Cannon | -2 | +1 | * | | | | | | | Disruptor | +1 |

Requires: Secret Knowledge (Astronomy: Ley Lines), Slow, Splash +2. *+1 Crit Dmg vs (Robots, Psionics or Targets with the Shield Keyword).
Strong Hit: Disrupt (Hit) Debuff Targets Active Non Low Tech, Non Bio Tech Weapons: Lose Ammunition equal to RoF.

Prototype Gun Variations (Must Select 1 From Each Area, 'Gun Prototype' Only)

Barrel Variations	Hit	End Dmg	Crit	Rng	Clips	Ammo	Load	RoF	Wgt	Weapon Type	Cost
Cut Down	+2			-1					-1*		12t

*Small if Weight 1.

| Multi | -2 | +2 | | -1 | | -RoF x1 | | +1 (+1d6) | | | 14t |

Jam (1-5)

| Oversized | -4 | +2 | +1 | | | -RoF x1 | +1 | | | | 16t |

Jam (1-5).

| Well Made | | | +1 | | | | | | | | 10t |

Targeting Variations	Hit	End Dmg	Crit	Rng	Clips	Ammo	Load	RoF	Wgt	Weapon Type	Cost
Auto Targeter	-2										14t

Lock On +4, Lose Low Tech.

Gyro Stabiliser			+2						+1		16t
Iron Sight											10t
Spray		+2	-1	-1							12t

Splash 1.

Loader Variations	Hit	End Dmg	Crit	Rng	Clips	Ammo	Load	RoF	Wgt	Weapon Type	Cost
Backpacker Feeder	-2	+2		-1	6	RoF x3	-1*	+2 (+2d6)	+2		16t

Jam (1-5)., Set Up 1, *-1 Reload Time (Full Draw Time)

| Balanced Magazine | +1 | | | +1 | 2 | RoF x4 | | | | | 10t |
| Large Manual Feed | -2 | +1 | +1 | -2 | 6 | RoF x1 | | | +1 | * | 14t |

Slow, *May change Gun to Shell

| Small Rounds | | -2 | | | 4 | RoF x4 | | | | | 12t |

Weapon Modifications (May Select any Amount, Not Melee)

Modifications	Hit	End Dmg	Crit	Rng	Clips	Ammo	Load	RoF	Wgt	Weapon Type	Cost
Advanced Ammo	+1			+1						*	+1
*May be taken by Melee Weapons that can be Thrown											
Advanced Modification											+1
Add 1 of the following Keywords: Bio Tech, Blunt, Burn, Energy, Low Tech or the Weapon Type: Psionic.											
Archon Round				+1				*			18t
Optional, *For a single RoF 1 Attack, Strong Hit +1, Pen 1 min 4											
Archon Tech		-1		+1	-1						+5*
Archon Tech, Lose Low Tech, Strong Hit +1, *Requires Secret Knowledge to build if not found											
Dual Wield	-2	+2			-1		+1	+1 (+1d6)	+1*	**	+1
Optional, *1 Handed Weapons only (usually Weight 1), **If Gauntlet: takes 2 Gauntlet Slots, **Not Thrown											
Extended Barrel	-2			+1							10t
Extended Clip	-2				+RoF x1				*		12t
*Not Thrown Weapons											
Flash Light Attachment	-1										8t
Optional, Create Light: Reduce Low Light Cover penalties by 2 Steps in Splash 3 of your Target and against you.											
Laser Sight	+1										14t
Launcher	-1			+2	+2			+1	*		+1
*Thrown Only, *May use Snap Shot or Sighted Shot (Can not use Throw Action), *May have a single Gun Size Variation											
Low Quality	-2			-1							-1*
*Requires a Wealth Spare Time Roll 6t to regain Resources if you sell or trade this Weapon											
Modular	-1										+1
May Change Weapon Variations (paying any additional Cost) once per session during Downtime and don't lose spent Spare Time Points.											
+2 to all Weapon Modification Spare Time Rolls											
One Spare Clip					+1						14t
Optional, For one session only											
Personalised	+1*										12t
*Hit -4 when used by others											
Retractable	-1			-1					*		16t
Jam (1-5), +2 to hide Weapon, *Two less Equipment Slots (minimum 1)											
Shortened Clip	+2				+1	-RoF x1					+0
Spare Clip					+1				*		+1**
**May aquire multiple times. *+1 Slot for every 2 Spare Clips											
Suppressor System			*	-2				*			14t
Optional, *Attacks from this Weapon (Crit 4 or less and RoF 1) do not break Stealth.											
Strong Hit: **Suppressed Shot** (Attack, Does not Req Hit) This Attack cannot be seen by any character.											
Tactical Sight											12t
Analyse Action grants this Weapon +Int Hit Boost along with other benefits.											
Targeting Matrix											14t
Lock On +2, Lose Low Tech.											
Telescopic Lens									*		14t
*Not Thrown, Your Mind gains +4 Range while this Weapon is Drawn											
Temporary Advanced Ammo	+1			+1							14t
Optional, For one session only											
Tripod				*				+1	*		10t
*Not Thrown, Optional, Set Up 2, Pull Down 1, Arc of Fire 45, *Half Range Penalties while Prone with Sighted Shot Action											
X'ion Round	-4	+4	+1					*			18t
Optional, Bio Tech, Slow, *For a single RoF 1 Attack, Splash +2											
X'ion Tech	-2	+2	+2*	-1	-1				+1		+5**
X'ion Tech, Bio Tech, Slow, *Can only cause a Strong Hit: **Critical Hit** on a Target with 0 Endurance, **Requires Secret Knowledge to build if not found											

Melee Modifications (May Select any Amount, Melee Only)

Modifications	Hit	End Dmg	Crit	Rng	Clips	Ammo	Load	RoF	Wgt	Weapon Type	Cost
Advanced Modification											+1
Add 1 of the following Keywords: Bio Tech, Blunt, Burn, Energy, Low Tech or the Weapon Type: Psionic.
Aerodynamic Balance		-1		(0*)	(0*)	(1*)			*	Thrown*	16t
*Optional Weapon Type: Thrown (RoF 1, +1 Ammo if you have the Dual Wield Modification).
Archon Tech	+2	-1									+5*
Archon Tech, Strong Hit +1, *Requires Secret Knowledge to build if not found
Dedicated Maintenance	+2										14t
For one session only
Dual Wield	-2	+1					+1	+1 (+1d6)	+1*		+1
Optional, *1 Handed Weapons only (usually Weight 1)
Guards							+1				10t
Defence vs Impair +2
Low Quality	-2							+1			-1*
*Requires a Wealth Spare Time Roll 6t to regain Resources if you sell or trade this Weapon
Master Crafted			+1								22t*
*Cost +2 Resources for NPCs (and should rarely be taken on a Weapon that does not have the Keyword: Natural)
Personalised	+1*										12t**
*Hit -4 when used by others, **Can not be aquired with a Wealth Spare Time Roll
Retractable							-1		*		+1
+2 to hide Weapon, Disruptor Strong Hits Jam this Weapon, *Two less Equipment Slots (minimum 1)
Targeting Matrix											14t
Lock On +2, Lose Low Tech
X'ion Tech	-2	+2	+2*						+1		+5*
X'ion Tech, Slow, Bio Tech, *Can only cause a Strong Hit: **Critical Hit** on a Target with 0 Endurance, *Requires Secret Knowledge to build if not found

Drone & Companion Modifications (May Select any Amount, Drone or Companion Only)

Modifications	Hit	End Dmg	Crit	Rng	Clips	Ammo	Load	RoF	Wgt	Weapon Type	Cost
Defence System	-2										+1
Defence: -2, Your single Utility Item may be carried by this Drone/Companion (takes up 0 Slots, Cost must be paid)
Enhanced Mobility											+1
Defence: +2, Movement: +2
Fine Tune	+2										14t
This Modification is lost if Drone/Companion dies
Low Quality	-1	-1		-1							-1*
*Requires a Wealth Spare Time Roll 6t to regain Resources if you sell or trade this Drone/Companion.
Multiply		+1*						+1 (+1d6)*	(**)		+2***
Bodies: +1 *-1 End Dmg and RoF per destroyed or non Attacking Body, **+Weight is multiplied by Bodies, ***May purchase multiple times
Multispectral Sensors											+2
Defence: -2, Reduce ALL of YOUR Target's Limited Vision and Low Light Cover by 1 Step, YOUR Defence vs Stealth +1

Outfit (Max 1)

Outfit	Armour	Defence	Endurance	+ Cover	Front Cover	Slots	Weight	Cost
Clothing	0					8	0	Free
+1 Conversation								
Emergency Void Suit	1					4	3	10t
Able to function in Space environments.								
Combat Suit	1					8	1	1
Tactical Armour	2					10	2	2
Retractable	2					8	0	3
+1 Conversation, Not obvious that you are wearing Armour until it is Set Up, Set Up 1, Pull Down 1								
Assault Plates	3	–1				8	4	4*
Defence vs Impair +2, *Cost Spare Time Roll 14t								
Mech Suit	5	–2	+5	–1 Step	–1 Step	6	5*	6*
Defence vs Impair +6, Armour vs Slow –1, *May increase Cost by 2 to decrease Weight by 4, *Cost Spare Time Roll 14t, While not wearing this Mech Suit you may wear a Combat Suit (Armour 1, Slots 8, Weight 1, Cost 0).								

Outfit Variations (May Select 1, Outfit Only)

Variations	Armour	Defence	Endurance	+ Cover	Front Cover	Slots	Weight	Cost
Environmental Adaptation System						–2		+1*
Able to function in a specific** hostile environment, **You may spend 1 Fate Point to change this environment as a Free Action *Cost Spare Time Roll 14t								
Grav-Field								+1*
Shield, Electro-Gravity, Immune to non Direct Hit Damage from Attacks with the Keyword: Splash –1 Armour when at 0 Endurance, *Cost Spare Time Roll 14t								
Hardened Shell							+2	+1
Immune to Pen (Attacks against you never use the Keyword: Penetration)								
Haze Mesh				*				+1
*Cover grants you +2 additional Defence.								
Parasitic			–5					–1
Bio Tech, Removal of this Outfit requires a succesful Surgery Healing Roll								
Scram Suit						–2		+0
Shield, Remove any Locked On Effect on you at the start of your Turn								
Shield Nodes			+10					+1*
Shield, –1 Armour when at 0 Endurance, *Cost Spare Time Roll 14t								
Stealth Suit	–1	+1		+1 Step*			–1	+4**
Shield, *You always have Light Cover (+2) or +1 Cover Step, **Cost Spare Time Roll 14t Strong Hit: Invisible Strike (Attack, Does not Require Hit) At the end of your Turn make a Free Stealth Action.								
Symbiotic								+0
Bio Tech, +2 to all Outfit Modification Spare Time Rolls								
Synth Steel	+1*						–1	+0
*After you receive Strong Hit: Critical Hit you have –1 Armour (resolve Damage first) until you have Downtime and a Workbench, –2 to all Outfit Modification Spare Time Rolls								
Tactical Array Suit		+2				–2	+1	+2*
You and all Allies within 10 gain Lock On +2, *Cost Spare Time Roll 12t								
Technical Suit						–2	+1	+1*
Counts as a Toolbox (+1) for all Trained Professional Skills, *Cost Spare Time Roll 14t								
Tungsten Carbine							+1	+0
Armour vs Energy +1								

Outfit Modifications (May Select any Amount, Outfit Only)

Modifications	Armour	Defence	Endurance	+ Cover	Front Cover	Slots	Weight	Cost
Anti Grav Pack		+1				−2		+1
Take no falling Damage from 20 meters, may spend 1 Fate Point to land from any distance (eg: orbit)								
Archon Tech		+2		+1 Step		+2	−2	+6*
−1 Armour when at 0 Endurance, *Cost Spare Time Roll 16t								
Auto Med System						−1	+1	14t
May use 1 Stim during your Turn as a Free Action, +1 Recovery								
Body Mounted Light								8t
Optional, Reduce Low Light Cover penalties by 2 Steps in Splash 3 of any area and against you.								
Custom Fit						+2	−1	18t*
*Must be aquired by the character using this Outfit (Modification lost if looted from another character).								
Environmental System						−1		10t
Able to function in a specific hostile environment								
Jet Pack		−1				−2	+2	+2
You may spend 1 Fate Point to gain Movement +2 and fly for 1 Turn (or for 1 minute out of Combat).								
Low Quality		−1				−2		−1*
*Requires a Wealth Spare Time Roll 6t to regain Resources if you sell or trade this Weapon								
Pack Space						+2	+1	10t
Personalised						+2*	*	14t
*Slots −2 and Weight +2 when used by others								
Spikes								14t
−2 Conversation and Stealth								
Any adjacent character who is Grabbing you takes 5 Endurance Damage at the start of each of your Turns								
Tactical System						−1		8t
Short Range Comms								
X'ion Tech		+2	−2	−1 Step			+1	+6*
Bio Tech, +2 to all Outfit Modification Spare Time Rolls, *Cost Spare Time Roll 16t								

Utility Items (Max 1)

Utility Items	Armour	Defence	Endurance	+ Cover	Front Cover	Slots	Weight	Cost
Adjustable Camo Net							0	10t
Stealth +2								
Ammunition Pack						+2	3	1
All of your Weapons gain +1 Clip, You may spend 1 Fate Point at any time to grant you or an adjacent Ally +1 Clip								
Archon Tactical Array		+2					0	22t
Gauntlet, Shield, Defence vs Stealth +2, Short Range Comms								
Burst Shield				Light (+2)			0	1
Shield, Gauntlet, Take Cover Action grants you Immunity to Critical Hits while you have Endurance and are Gaining a Cover bonus								
Drone Control Module							2	12t
If you Control 1 Drone with 1 Body: that Drone Costs -1 Resource								
Large Combat Shield				Heavy (+4)		-2	4	12t
Gauntlet, you may not Move and Attack with a 2 Handed Weapon (Weight 2+) in the same Turn, -1 RoF with Limbs, grants Heavy Cover (+4) to adjacent characters that are behind you								
Legion Ghost Cloak				+1 Step*			1	1
Shield, Stealth +2, *Gain Light Cover (+2) or +1 Cover Step if you do not move for your Turn (you may Stealth)								
Med Spray							1	1
Gauntlet, Paramedics Heals an additional 1 (normally just 3) Point of Attributes Damage.								
Mobile Cover Field							0	2
Shield, Set Up 1*, Pull Down 1, *Creates Heavy Cover (+4) in two connecting adjacent spaces								
Mobile Stasis Wall							1	18t
1 use, Shield, Set Up 1.* *Creates up to 3 spaces of impassable and impenetrable Terrain in an adjacent space for 1 hour.								
Multispectral Visor							0	1
Reduce all of your Target's Limited Vision and Low Light Cover by 1 Step, Defence vs Stealth +2								
Omni Targeting Computer							0	14t
If you perform a Spread Fire Attack against a Target with the Lock On Effect on them: gain +1d6 to your Attack Roll								
Personalised Weapon Pack							2	16t
All of yours Weapons have -1 Draw (Full Reload and Un-Jam)								
Shield Emitter						-2	2	3
Gauntlet, Shield, Take Cover Action grants You or an Ally within 5: Heavy Cover (+4) or +1 Cover Step until your next Turn								
Stabiliser	*						0	1
Gauntlet, *Reduce penalties to your Armour while at 0 Endurance by 2 (to a minimum of -1)								
Tactical Headset		+1					0	14t
Short Range Comms, all of your Weapons gain Lock On +1								

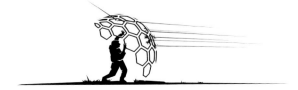

Misc Items and Services

Services:	Weight	Description	Cost
Access to Workshop	–	Gain access to a single Workshop for 1 session.	10t
Access to Dedicated Workshop	–	Gain access to a single Dedicated Workshop for 1 session.	16t
Access to Storage Space	–	Rent 4 Cargo space for up to 3 sessions.	10t
Enforcer Backup	–	Gain temporary aid of 1d3 Enforces for 1-2 sessions (GM discretion and controlled).	14t
Long Distance Spacecraft Travel	–	Up to 6 days travel for up to 5 character's.	14t

Medical and Spacecraft Repair	Weight	Description	Cost
Extended Care	–	Requires Toolkit, Heals 1 point of every Attribute and a Minor Condition (eg: poison).	2x 12t
Surgery	–	Requires Workshop, Heals 8 points of 1 Attribute and a Major Condition (eg: lost limb). May Retro to a Implant Trait.	2x 14t
Maintenance	–	Requires Toolkit, Repair 1 point of every Attribute and Minor Conditions (eg: virus).	2x 10t
Rebuild	–	Requires Workshop, Repair 8 points of 1 Attribute or Major Condition (eg: Replicator Drone infestation).	2x 14t
Change Out	–	Requires Workshop, Change 1 spacecraft Weapon / Trait / Attribute point, Influence Cost = Size.	14t

Environmental Equipment:	Weight	Description	Cost
Flash Light	1	Small, Load 1, Create Light: Reduce Low Light Cover penalties by 2 Steps in Splash 3 of any area and against you.	6t
2 Flares	1	2 uses Load 1, Thrown (Range 3), Reduce Low Light Cover penalties by 2 Steps in Splash 4 and by 1 Step in Splash 8.	8t
Specific Environmental Equipment	2	Able to function in a specific hostile environment (eg: Climbing gear, tent, cooking equipment, etc...).	12t
Survival Rations	1	Food and Water for 2 Days (1 week if you are Trained in Survival).	8t
Pallet of Supplies	1 Cargo	1 use, +6 Spacecraft Resupply, can be turned into 6 units of 'Food Supplies'.	8t
Food Supplies	4	7 days food and water (14 days if you are Trained in Survival).	10t

Computer Equipment:	Weight	Description	Cost
Head Set	1	Short Range Comms (100km).	12t
Satellite Backpack	3	Long Range Comms (400+km).	14t
Translator	1	Able to translate common languages. –2 to Conversation, Leadership and Culture skills when used.	18t
Non-Combat Drone	–	Drone, **Defence: 8, Armour: 2, Movement: 4, Weight 1 (+0), Slots: 0**	14t
GPS and Mapping Computer	1	Maps local area and tracks Allies.	12t

Tools:	Weight	Description	Cost
Toolkit	1	Small, Choose 1 Professional Skill, required for some Skill Rolls.	6t
Multi Tool	1	Small, Counts as Toolkit for 4 Professional Skills.	12t
Small Toolbox	0	Small, +1 to a single Trained Professional Skill (does not Stack), required for some Skill Rolls.	18t
Toolbox	2	+1 to a single Trained Primary Skill (does not Stack), required for some Skill Rolls.	14t
Omni Tool	1	Small, Counts as a Toolbox (+1, does not Stack) for all Trained Professional Skills.	20t

Workshops:	Cargo	Description	Cost
Workbench	0	Required for some skills.	10t
Workshop	1	Choose 1 Trained Primary Skill, also counts as Workbench, required for some skills.	14t
Dedicated Workshop	4	+2 to a single Trained Primary Skill (does not Stack), also counts as a Workbench and Workshop, required for some skills.	16t

Stims:	Weight	Description	Cost
Advanced Medical Supplies	1	1 use, Small, +4 to a single Medicine Healing Roll.	12t
Flesh Rejuvenator	0	1 use, Small, Paramedics Heals an additional 2 (5) Points of Attributes Damage (normally just 3).	14t
Stim Cocktail	0	1 use, Small, You or an adjacent Ally Heal 10 Endurance and can not Move next Turn.	8t
Clear Shot	0	1 use, Small, Take 5 Endurance Damage and Boost next Turn Attacks: Hit +4 (within 5 minutes) (does not Stack).	12t
Psi Stim	0	1 use, Small, Take 1 Focus Damage (not reduced by Armour) and Buff next Attack: Strong Hit +1 (within 1 Turn).	14t
Pack of Draz	2	1 use, you do not sleep for 1 night, gain 1 Spare Time Point	14t
Street Draz	0	1 use, Small, Armour +2 for 3 Turns and then take 1 Attribute Damage (Location 1d3+3, no Paramedics).	12t
Pure Draz	0	1 use, Small, Armour +2 for 1 combat and then take 2 Attribute Damage (Location 1d3+3, no Paramedics).	18t

Example Toolkit:	Weight	Description	Cost
Wrench	1	Required for some Mechanics Skill Rolls.	6t
Soldering Iron	1	Required for some Electronics Skill Rolls.	6t
Hand Computer	1	Required for some Programming Skill Rolls.	6t
Sample Jar	1	Required for some Bio Tech Skill Rolls.	6t
Bandages	1	Required for some Medicine Skill Rolls.	6t
Emotion Reader	1	Required for some Psychology Skill Rolls.	6t
Hand Telescope	1	Required for some Astronomy Skill Rolls.	6t
Prospectors Pick	1	Required for some Planetoids Skill Rolls.	6t

Example Toolbox:	Weight	Description	Cost
Bank Card	0	+1 to Wealth Skill Rolls (does not Stack), required for some Wealth Skill Rolls.	18t
Briefcase of Clothes	2	+1 to Conversation Skill Rolls (does not Stack), required for some Conversation Skill Rolls.	14t
Uniform with Insignia	0	+1 to Leadership Skill Rolls (does not Stack), required for some Leadership Skill Rolls.	18t
Digital Encyclopedia	2	+1 to Culture Skill Rolls (does not Stack), required for some Culture Skill Rolls.	14t
Sports Kit	2	+1 to Physical Skill Rolls (does not Stack), required for some Physical Skill Rolls.	14t
Psi Inhibitor	2	+1 to Resolve Skill Rolls (does not Stack), required for some Resolve Skill Rolls.	14t
Criminology Kit	2	+1 to Awareness Skill Rolls (does not Stack), required for some Awareness Skill Rolls.	14t
Cooking Set	2	+1 to Survival Skill Rolls (does not Stack), required for some Survival Skill Rolls.	14t
Mechanics Toolbox	2	+1 to Mechanics Skill Rolls (does not Stack), required for some Mechanics Skill Rolls.	14t
Electricians Tool Belt	2	+1 to Electronics Skill Rolls (does not Stack), required for some Electronics Skill Rolls.	14t
Portable Computer	2	+1 to Programming Skill Rolls (does not Stack), required for some Programming Skill Rolls.	14t
Chemistry Kit	2	+1 to Bio Tech Skill Rolls (does not Stack), required for some Bio Tech Skill Rolls.	14t
First Aid Kit	2	+1 to Medicine Skill Rolls (does not Stack), required for some Medicine Skill Rolls.	14t
Neural Probe	2	+1 to Psychology Skill Rolls (does not Stack), required for some Psychology Skill Rolls.	14t
Telescope	2	+1 to Astronomy Skill Rolls (does not Stack), required for some Astronomy Skill Rolls.	14t
Geology Kit	2	+1 to Planetoids Skill Rolls (does not Stack), required for some Planetoids Skill Rolls.	14t

Example Workshop:	Cargo	Description	Cost
Office Space	1	Required for some Wealth Skill Rolls.	14t
Voice Analysis System	1	Required for some Conversation Skill Rolls.	14t
Conference Room	1	Required for some Leadership Skill Rolls.	14t
Library	1	Required for some Culture Skill Rolls.	14t
Gym	1	Required for some Physical Skill Rolls.	14t
Sanctuary	1	Required for some Resolve Skill Rolls.	14t
Forensic Lab	1	Required for some Awareness Skill Rolls.	14t
Kitchen and Pantry	1	Required for some Survival Skill Rolls.	14t
Spacecraft Repair shop	1	Required for some Mechanics Skill Rolls.	14t
Repair Workspace	1	Required for some Electronics Skill Rolls.	14t
Software Lab	1	Required for some Programming Skill Rolls.	14t
Genetic Engineering Lab	1	Required for some Bio Tech Skill Rolls.	14t
Med Bay	1	Required for some Medicine Skill Rolls.	14t
Neural Analysis Lab	1	Required for some Psychology Skill Rolls.	14t
Observatory	1	Required for some Astronomy Skill Rolls.	14t
Surveyor's Lab	1	Required for some Planetoids Skill Rolls.	14t

Spacecraft Lists

Build (Must Select 1)

Build	Requirements	Benefits	Disadvantages
Extra Section	Min Size 3	You are an additional Section of another spacecraft (with your own seperate Attributes, Weapons, Stats and System Rolls) of at least Size 3. Each spacecraft Section occupies the same space and always moves together. You gain all Benefits and Disadvantages of the other Sections' Builds. No Section can be Destroyed unless two (or ALL if NPC) Sections have an Attribute reduced to –5 (–0 if NPC). All Sections' Attributes can never be reduced below –5 (–0 if NPC). At the start of a Combat, each character must decide what Section they are in. All Sections gain: Strong Hit: **To your Stations!** (System Roll, Success) Move a character to a different Section of your spacecraft. Only one Section has Resupply, all Sections use this Resupply.	Only one spacecraft Section may make Command System Rolls each Turn. All negative Effects applied to any Sections (eg: Locked On, On Fire or Boarded) are applied to all Sections (removal of an Effect, removes it from all Sections). If any Attribute is at –5 (–0 if NPC) or below, then no System Rolls can be made by that Section. All Sections have –1 Defence (Stacks).
Corporation		+4 Cargo. +1 Spacecraft Perk. +2 Defence vs Ordnance.	–1 Maximum all Attributes. –2 Quick Fix Repair Rolls.
Kaltoran		You may move through Liquids (your spacecraft is a submarine)! +1 Secret Cargo. Patch Job System Roll may be successfully rolled twice per Turn (normally once).	–2 Maximum Crew. On Fire Effect deals 2 Attribute Damage (normally 1) to 2 random Attributes (roll 2x 1d6).
Legion		If your spacecraft is at least Size 3: one Dedicated Workshop requires 2 less Cargo space (minimum 2). On Fire Effect deals Damage at the end of your Turn (normally at the start). One non Bio Tech Weapon gains +1 Hit and –1 Mount.	–2 Maximum CPU. –2 Cargo. –1 Spacecraft Perk (may remove an Automatic Perk).
Nephilim		Your spacecraft is partially Biological (eg: Bio Tech Workshops may be used for out of combat Repair Rolls). You may make 1 free System Roll each Turn at +0 (no Strong Hits). +4 Resupply. +2 Defence vs Boarding.	Your spacecraft has a GM defined personality. NPCs will easily remember your spacecraft. –2 Maximum Sensors. –2 Rebuild Repair Rolls.
Remnant		(data missing) ·	
Palantor		(data missing)	
Twi-Far		(data missing)	
Zhou		(data missing)	

NPC Build	Requirements	Benefits	Disadvantages
Mechonid	NPC	+5 Shields. +1 Armour vs Boarding Parties.	–3 Spacecraft Perks. –1 Maximum Hull, Engines and Crew.

Spacecraft Attribute Traits

Hull	Requirements	Benefits	Disadvantages
Hunk of Junk	Max Hull 3	+1 Secret Cargo.	NPCs like to mock your ship!
	Not NPC	-10 Influence Cost.	This Trait requires an additional Spare Time of 14t to Change Out.
			-1 (-2 if you are an NPC) Attribute Point.
			-2 Defence if you are an NPC.
Luxury	Not Kaltoran	All characters that have spent Influence on this spacecraft gain +2 Recovery.	+5 Influence Cost (in addition to this Trait's Cost).
		+2 Resupply.	-2 to all Repair Rolls (not including Patch Job).
		+2 Spacecraft Perks.	
Assault	Min Hull 2	+2 Regen.	
	Not Corporation	If you end your Turn in, or pass through the same space as another spacecraft that is not 2 Sizes bigger than you; deal 1 Attribute Damage (no Armour) to the other spacecraft and Move them 1 space in any direction (normally they move themselves).	
Military	Min Hull 3	-1 Mount, Batteries and Warheads.	
		+1 Defence.	
Hanger Bay	Min Hull 4	-2 Mount, Fighter.	
		+1 Bodies, Fighter.	

Engines	Requirements	Benefits	Disadvantages
No Jump Drive	Max Size 2	-10 Influence Cost.	Lose Jump Drive Spacecraft Perk.
			x10 travel time outside of Combat.
Stationary	Min Crew 2	Your Engine Attribute is immune to Damage.	You (and any connecting Sections) may never voluntarily increase Velocity (which starts at 0), but you may decrease it.
		+1 Armour.	You (and any connecting Sections) may never Rotate.
		+4 Cargo.	Lose Jump Drive Spacecraft Perk.
		+10 Resupply	-100% Non-Combat travel speed
		+2 Spacecraft Perks	
		+1 Weapon Slot	
Solar Sails	Max Eng 2	At the start of your Turn (before moving your current Velocity) and within a System with a Sun, you may gain a free 45° Rotation away from the Sun AND increase your Velocity by 1.	
	Not Legion		
	Not Twi-Far		
Thrust Vectoring		Strong Hit: **Thrust Vectoring** (Engineering, Min Velocity 2, Success) Make a free 45° Rotation and reduce your Velocity by 1.	
Ley Line Drive	Min Eng 3	+50% Non-Combat travel speed.	
	Secret Kn	Gain +1 Defence per Combat Jump Success (up to +4).	
Boosters	Min Eng 4	+2 Defence vs Ordnance.	
		Strong Hit: **Boost** (Engineering, Success) Increase your Velocity by 1 and immediately move forward 1 space.	
Displacement Drive	Min Pow 3	Under a flip-up shield is a large, round red button that takes a firm push to activate. The button itself can have a variety of labels, most commonly "Never Press this Button!"	
	Not Corporation		
	Secret Kn	All characters on a spacecraft may spend 1 Fate Point to instantly move your spacecraft 2d6 Jump Days Travel in a random Direction. If you have no Shields while doing this, take 2 Power Damage (no Armour).	

Crew	Requirements	Benefits	Disadvantages
Slave Crew	Min Size 3 Max Crew 3	At any time during your Turn you may take 1 Crew Damage (no Armour, and may be Repaired with Patch Job) and make a free System Roll at +2. –5 Influence Cost.	Your NPC crew may betray you!
Drone Crew		All characters that have spent Influence on this spacecraft gain +2 to all Drone Spare Time Rolls. Reduce all Crew Attribute Damage by 1 to a minimum of 1.	
Officer	Min Crew 2 Min Size 2	Your spacecraft gains a NPC officer. You may make 1 free System Roll each Turn at +2 (no Strong Hits).	+5 Influence Cost (in addition to this Trait's Cost).
Technical Crew	Min Crew 3	All characters that have spent Influence on this spacecraft gain +1 to all non Wealth Spare Time Rolls. +1 Crit Dmg, Boarding Party. +1 Engineering OR Operations (chosen on Trait selection).	–2 Hit, Boarding Party. +2 Influence Cost (in addition to this Trait's Cost).
Combat Crew	Min Crew 3	All characters that have spent Influence on this spacecraft gain +1 Hit to all Drones and Companions. +2 Hit, Boarding Party. +1 Command OR Gunnery (chosen on Trait selection).	
Veteran Crew	Min Crew 4 Secret Kn	All characters that have spent Influence on this spacecraft gain +1 Range to all Drones and Companions. +2 Hit, Boarding Party. +2 Defence vs Boarding Parties.	

Power	Requirements	Benefits	Disadvantages
No Shields		+1 Attribute Point per 2 Size (rounded up). +2 Defence.	You have no Shields (they can NEVER be increased). You will be Destroyed if you use the Jump Drive Spacecraft Perk.
Dispersion Shield		You may never take more than 5 Shield Damage from a single Attack. You may never take more than 5 Attribute Damage from a single Attack while you have Shields.	
Fractal Shields	Min Pow 2	Twice per session you may take no Attribute Damage from an Attack that reduces your Shields to 0.	+2 Influence Cost (in addition to this Trait's Cost).
Wrap Shield	Max Pow 3	+2 Defence.	
Directed Shields	Min CPU 4	Strong Hit: **Direct Shields** (Operations, Success) While you have Shields: gain +1 Armour vs the first Attack that Hits you before your next Turn (Stacks).	
Archon Shields	Min Pow 4 Min CPU 4 Secret Kn	+1 Armour +2 Regen	+10 Influence Cost (in addition to this Trait's Cost), +10 Influence Cost if you are an NPC.

CPU	Requirements	Benefits	Disadvantages
Manual Aim	Max CPU 2	+Per Hit, Warheads and Batteries.	-2 Hit, Warheads and Battery.
	Not NPC	+Foc Range, Batteries.	-3 Range, Battery.
		-5 Influence Cost.	May not perform the Calibrate, Seeker or Scan System Rolls.
			May not gain any benefits from the Locked On Effect.
Corporate Crap	Max CPU 1	Gain 1 extra Trait.	-2 Patch Job.
		-5 Influence Cost.	
Crack Targeter	Min CPU 2	Scan Boosts next Attack: +3 Shield Dmg.	
		+1 Shield Dmg, all Weapons.	
Auto Targeter	Min CPU 3	Calibrate may apply 2 Locked On Effects per Success (normally 1).	
	Min Sen 3	All Weapons gain Lock On +1.	
Dedicated Server	Min CPU 4	+1, all System and spacecraft Attack Rolls.	
		Workshops and Dedicated Workshops grant an additional +1 bonus to Skill Rolls.	
Decentralised Nodes	Min CPU 4	Reduce all Damage to your Power, CPU and Sensors by 2 to a minimum of 1.	

Sensors	Requirements	Benefits	Disadvantages
Combat Tuned		+1 Shield Dmg, all Weapons.	
Long Range Array	Min Sen 2	+2 Range, Batteries.	-2 Hit, Batteries
			-1 Shield Dmg, Batteries.
Jump Interdiction	Min Sen 2	At the End of your Turn, remove 1 Combat Jump Success from a spacecraft that	Illegal in many cultures!
	Min CPU 3	has the Locked On Effect applied to them.	
		Strong Hit: **Jam System** (Operations, Success) All Locked On Targets have -2 to their Operations Rolls until your next Turn.	
Sensor Probe	Min Sen 3	All Weapons gain Lock On +2.	
		Strong Hit: **Survey Probe** (Planetoids, Success) Gain a technical readout of a planetoid's atmosphere and material composition.	
		Strong Hit: **Deep Space Probe** (Astronomy, Success) If you spend 1 Fate Point you gain information on any spacecraft within 6 days jump travel of you (if on the Sector Map) or 1 days jump travel (if on a System Map).	
		Strong Hit: **Tracking Probe** (Operations, Success) You may track a Target spacecraft's location for 2d6 days (or GM defined duration).	
Supply Drop	Min Sen 4	If your spacecraft is appropriatly positioned (ie: in orbit of a planet) any characters that have spent Influence on this spacecraft may spend 1 Fate Point to call down a Supply Drop to a GM Defined location.	
	Min CPU 2	This Supply Drop may move one Cargo space of equipment from the spacecraft to the character's location and 2 Clips of Ammunition (another character may spend an additional Fate Point to increase the Clips by 4).	
		+1 Resupply.	

Size	Requirements	Benefits	Disadvantages
Heavy Fighter	Max Crew 2	Gain +1 Armour while you are moving at Velocity 4 or more.	Maximum of 2 characters on this spacecraft (normally unlimited).
		You may make 1 free Command System Roll each Turn.	-2 Size.
		+2 Defence.	-1 Armour.
		+1 Armour vs Boarding	
Small Frigate		+1 to all System Rolls.	Maximum of 4 characters on this spacecraft (normally unlimited).
		+1 Defence.	-1 Size.
Balanced	Not Legion	+1 Attribute Point.	
Hybrid Build	Secret Kn	You may select a second spacecraft Build.	+10 Influence Cost (in addition to this Trait's Cost).
Destroyer		+1 Size.	+5 Influence Cost (in addition to this Trait's Cost).
		+1 Shield Dmg, all Weapons.	
Dreadnought	Max Eng 2	+2 Size.	+10 Influence Cost (in addition to this Trait's Cost).
	Not Kaltoran	+1 Armour.	
		Reduce all Damage to Engines by 1.	
Freighter	Min Hull 4	+2 Size.	+1 Mount, all Weapons.
	Not Legion		-1 Weapon Slot.

Spacecraft Perks

Optional	Description
+5 Shields (Size 1-2)	(May not be taken by NPCs).
+1 Cargo	
+2 Resupply	
Deep Space SOS Beacon	Your spacecraft is equipped with several small, but valuable distress beacons.
Escape Pods (Size 3-5)	If you spacecraft is Destroyed, all player characters may take an Escape Pod to avoid Death.
Shuttle (Size 4-5)	Your spacecraft comes equipped with a small (less than Size 1) space worthy Shuttle. Able to ferry a small crew to and from a planetary surface.
Brig (Size 3-5)	Your spacecraft has a dedicated jail area, with multiple cells.
Armoury	A fully stocked Armoury allows your crew to regain all used Clips and Ammunition during their Downtime.
Additional Rooms (Size 3-5)	Your spacecraft has several more rooms than a spacecraft of its size would normally have.

Automatic	Description
Ejection Seats (Size 1-2)	If your spacecraft is Destroyed all player characters will be safely ejected and avoid Death as long as they have an Outfit suitable for the void of space.
Comm System	Your spacecraft is equipped with a Radio.
Life Support	Your spacecraft is equipped with air filtration, artificial gravity, waste disposal, temperature control and a myriad of other systems to allow life inside the safety of its hull.
Jump Drive	Your spacecraft is capable of opening a Jump Portal.
Docking Clamp (Size 2-5)	Your spacecraft is able to dock with other spacecraft.
Airlock (Size 2-5)	Your spacecraft has air cycle chambers that allow its crew to exit and enter from hostile environments.
Corridors (Size 3-5)	Your spacecraft is large enough to feature open chambers and corridors which its crew can use to walk around inside.
Small Rooms (Size 3-5)	Your spacecraft has several small rooms that can be used for a wide variety of purposes (eg: bedrooms).
Large Rooms (Size 5)	Your spacecraft has several very large rooms inside its considerable bulk.

Spacecraft Weapon Lists (May Select up to Your Weapons Slots)

Command	Hit	Shield Dmg	Crit	Rng	Clips	Ammo	Load	RoF	Mount	Weapon Type	Cost
Boarding Party	+Crew	-	1*	-	-	-	-	1	-	Boarding	Auto

No Variations or Modifications, *Treat Target as if it had no Shields or Armour

Bomber Squad	-2	Bodies	4	1	-	-	0	Bodies	4	Ordnance, Fighter	8

Defence: 14, Armour: 1, Movement: 2, Bodies: 2, Front and Side Arc, Lock On +2

Combat Squad		2+Bodies	2	1	-	-	0	Bodies	4	Ordnance, Fighter	8

Defence: 16, Armour: 1, Movement: 3, Bodies: 3, Front and Side Arc, Lock On +2, all Allies within 2 of a Combat Squad Body gain +2 Def vs Ord

Sentry	-4	3	3	Sensors	-	-	0	Bodies	2	Ordnance, Fighter	5

Defence: 12, Armour: 4, Movement: 0, Bodies: 1, Full Arc (normally Front and Side), Lock On +6

Operations	Hit	Shield Dmg	Crit	Rng	Clips	Ammo	Load	RoF	Mount	Weapon Type	Cost
Swarm		2	3	-	-	-	0	2 (+1d6)	1	Ordnance, Warhead	4

Defence: 12, Armour: 0, Movement: 3, Bodies: 15, Front and Side Arc, May Launch 3 Bodies at once (normally 1).
Launched Bodies must be placed in adjacent spaces to each other

Missile	-4	4	4	-	-	-	0	1	2	Ordnance, Warhead	5

Defence: 16, Armour: 1, Movement: 6, Bodies: 6, Front Arc (normally Front and Side), Strong Hit (5-6)

Rocket	-4	5	5	-	-	-	0	1	2	Ordnance, Warhead	6

Defence: 16, Armour: 1, Movement: 4, Bodies: 6, Front Arc (normally Front and Side), Strong Hit (5-6)

Torpedo	-4	10	5	-	-	-	0	1	3	Ordnance, Warhead	5

Defence: 12, Armour: 2, Movement: 2, Bodies: 4, Front Arc (normally Front and Side), Strong Hit (4-6)

Mines	-2*	5	5	-	-	-	0	1	3	Ordnance, Warhead	2

Defence: 12, Armour: 1, Movement: 0, Bodies: 10, Rear Arc (normally Front and Side), Strong Hit (5-6),
*You must immediately make 1 Free Attack (even mid movement) against any non Ally Target with the Locked On Effect that comes within 2.

Gunnery	Hit	Shield Dmg	Crit	Rng	Clips	Ammo	Load	RoF	Mount	Weapon Type	Cost
Point Defence	+1	1	2	1	-	Inf	0	2 (+1d6)	1	Battery	2

Full Arc (normally Front and Side), Lock On +2, +2 Defence vs Ordnance, The first Warhead each Turn that fails an Attack Roll against you is Destroyed

Blaster		3	4	Sensors	Inf	RoF x3	1	1	2	Battery	5

Front and Side Arc, Lock On +2, Strong Hit (5-6)

Burst	-2	4	4	Sensors	Inf	RoF x4	1	2 (+1d6)	2	Battery	5

Front and Side Arc, Lock On +2

Artillery	-4	5	4	Sen +2	Inf	RoF x1	1	1	3	Battery	5

Front and Side Arc, Lock On +4, Strong Hit (5-6), -1 Weapon Slot

Fighter Variations (May Select 1, Fighter Only)

Variations	Hit	Shield Dmg	Crit	Rng	Clips	Ammo	Load	RoF	Mount	Weapon Type	Cost
Manned Fighters	+2							**		***	+5

Defence: +2, Armour: +1, Bodies: −1, a player character may Pilot one of these Fighters, **+1 RoF per player character that is Piloting a Fighter.

***Piloting player character may spend 1 Fate Point to avoid Fighter Body Destruction (and their Death)

Nephilim Swarm	−2	−1									+0

Bio Tech, May Attack during the Turn they are Launched

Synth Steel Bots											+0

Bodies: +1, Energy

Warhead Variations (May Select 1, Warhead Only)

Variations	Hit	Shield Dmg	Crit	Rng	Clips	Ammo	Load	RoF	Mount	Weapon Type	Cost
Energy Charge		−1	−1								+0

Bodies: +6, Energy, after a failed Attack Roll: Destroy this Body.

Explosive	+1										+0
Infested	+2	*	−1								+2

*Bio Tech and Burn OR Robot and +1 Shield Dmg

Strong Hit: **Horrors** (Hit) Apply 1d3 (only 1 if Swarm Warhead) Boarded Effects to Target.

Micro		−2	−1						−1		+0*

Armour: −1, Defence: +2, Strong Hit −1, +1 Weapon Slot, *Size 1−2 spacecraft only.

Nuke	−2	−1	−2						+1		+5

Defence: −2, Low Tech, If you have unlaunched Bodies and take Hull Attribute Damage: then you take 1 random (1d6) Attribute Damage (no Armour)

Battery Variations (May Select 1, Battery Only)

Variations	Hit	Shield Dmg	Crit	Rng	Clips	Ammo	Load	RoF	Mount	Weapon Type	Cost
Bile	+2	+1		−1							+2

Bio Tech, Burn

Crack	+1										+0
Electromagnetic		+2		+1					+2		+5

Jam (1−5)

Flak											+2

Low Tech, +2 Defence vs Ordnance

Pulse Laser	+1	−1									+1

Energy, Burn

Living Weapon			−1						−1		+0

Bio Tech

Strong Hit: **Nephilim Horror** (Hit) Apply 1 Boarded Effect to Target.

Toxic			*						+1		+2

Low Tech, *When you deal Attribute Damage: Deal 1 additional Crew Attribute Damage (no Armour)

Battery Mount Variations (May Select 1, Battery Only)

Variations	Hit	Shield Dmg	Crit	Rng	Clips	Ammo	Load	RoF	Mount	Weapon Type	Cost
Broadside Mount				+2							+2
Side Fire Arcs only (normally Front and Side)											
Forward Mount				+1							+5
Front Fire Arc only (normally Front and Side)											
Omni Mount	-2			-1							+2
Full Arc (normally Front and Side)											

Fighter Modifications (May Select any Amount, Fighter Only)

Modifications	Hit	Shield Dmg	Crit	Rng	Clips	Ammo	Load	RoF	Mount	Weapon Type	Cost
Digital Targeting Array	-2										+2
Lock on +4											
Improved	+1										14t
Large Bay											+0*
Bodies: +2 -1 Weapon Slot, *May purchase multiple times											
Long Range Weaponry	-2	-1	-1	+1							+0
Lock On +2											
Seige			+2								+5
Defence: -2, Armour: +1, Bodies: -1, Movement: -1											

Warhead Modifications (May Select any Amount, Warhead Only)

Modifications	Hit	Shield Dmg	Crit	Rng	Clips	Ammo	Load	RoF	Mount	Weapon Type	Cost
Expanded Munitions								+1			14t
Bodies: +2											
Improved	+1										14t
Overloaded Warhead		+2									+2
Defence: -4											
Weapon Bank	-2	+1						+1 (+1d6)			+2*
Defence: +2, -1 Weapon Slot, *May purchase multiple times											
X'ion Tech	-2	+2	+2								+15*
X'ion Tech, Bio Tech, *Can only cause a Strong Hit: **Critical Hit** on a Target with 0 Shield, *Cost Spare Time Roll 16t											

Battery Modifications (May Select any Amount, Battery Only)

Modifications	Hit	Shield Dmg	Crit	Rng	Clips	Ammo	Load	RoF	Mount	Weapon Type	Cost
Archon Tech	-4	-2							+1		+15*
Archon Tech, Lose Low Tech, Lock on +6, Strong Hit +1, *Cost Spare Time Roll 16t											
Digital Targeting Array	-2										+2
Lose Low Tech, Lock on +4											
Improved	+1										14t
Weapon Bank	-2	+1						+1 (+1d6)			+2*
-1 Weapon Slot, *May purchase multiple times											

Index

Continued on next page >>

Acknowledgments

Created by
Wade Dyer (Design Ministries)

Writing
Jye Lambert (Setting)
Nicolas Logue (Setting)
Ryan Schoon (NPCs)
Simon Nolen (Flavour Text)
Stuart McNabb (Short Stories)

Additional Writing by
Adam Paciorek

Edited by
Joshua Yearsley

Artwork
Alexandrescu Paul
Clonerh Kimura (Cover)
Fyodor Ananiev
Niam Chou
Sarunas Macijauskas
Tan Ho Sim

Additional Artwork by
Eren Arik
Grzegorz Pedrycz
Jin Kim
Johnathan Chong
Kay Huang
Tyler Thull

Special Thanks
Chris Burch (Modiphius Entertainment)
Frank Mikes
Geordie Irvin
Logan Dyer
Mark Taylor
Timothy Roven (www.tabletopaudio.com)
www.kickstarter.com

Special Thanks to These Backers Who Have Given So Much More Than Just Their Money

Alister House
Brett Bond
Cameron Haggett
Chris Buckley & the Friday Night Imaginers
Christian Lasala
Christian Lasala
Christopher West
Dabney Bailey
David Beaudoin
Dylan Okeefe
Edwin KH Pau
Erica Pisani
Heather Avery
Ivlev Raul-Tiberiu
Jake Radcliffe
Jay Lapham
Joe Robinson
Joshua Ramsey
Ken Creelman
Lachlan Kingsford
Luke Pullar
Michael Buckley Jr
Mihai Bolda
Nicholas Price
Patrick "Bollywood" Sayet
Pawel Daruk
Ross Tuddin
Tom Killingbeck

Backers Who Contributed Their Ideas

Aaron Massung
Adrick Trotter
Alan Miles
Aljoscha Anolke
Andrew Gorman
Andrew Maak
Ben Meyer
Benjamin Berger
Brennan See
Bryan S
Chris Garland
Christoffer Sevaldsen
Conor Degroot
Dallas Scriven
Daniel Rhodes
Daniel Sweatman
David Williamson
Geordie Irvin
Grant Chapman
Ido Schwartz
Jacob Arthur
James Hodden
James K Mann
Jean-Christophe RANNOU
Jere Manninen
Jeremy Kear
John R. Smith
Jonathan McCulley
Joshua Bekker
Kami Saotori
Katelyn Gigante
Lachlan McDonald
Lorri Lambert
Luke Beard
Lyam Botting
Martin Lilja
Nathan Milfull
Nirmal Frankcombe
Patrick Venable
Pawel Daruk
Peter Liebert
Remi Fayomi
Robert D McCuaig
Romall Smith
Shea Shortridge
Stephen Lewis
Stuart Ellingson
Terry Standley & Winn Muller
Vegar Farsund
Victor Smith
Wei-Ying Ma
Wren Willis - Zairthos

Early Adopter Recognition

Adam Caverly
Adam Paciorek
Anders Stafberg
Andrew Cotgreave
Andrew Phillips
Bill Heron
Brooke Bennett
Carl Walter
Charles Crowe
Christian Nord
Cole Leadon
Darren Buckley
Dominik Dalek
Erich Lichnock & Rachel Jerilyn Teng
Felix Egner
Fredrik Oskarsson
Geoffrey Ford
Guillaume Gregoire
Hugh Ashman
Ingo Beyer
Jacob Wade
Jan Rosa
Jarrod McQueen
Johan Karlsson
John McNabb
John Murray
Jon Finn
Jonathan Hyde
Jose Manuel Romeo Cajal
Joseph Robles
Joshua Ramsey
José Manuel Palacios Rodrigo
Lars Holgaard
Leath Sheales
Maurice Strubel
Murrell Sippy
Myles Milner
Neil Mahoney
Nicholas Price
Olivier Darles
Oscar Simmons
Patrick Kraft
Phil Ward
Philip Rosberg
Pierre-Marie Coustumer
Ross Webb-Wagg
Rune Wandall-Holm
Ted Childers
Titus Lambert
Tobias Niemitz
Wade Geer
Yehuda Halfon

383

See:
www.fraggedempire.com

for a full list of Fragged Empire products,
free resources and tutorials.